The Complete Poems of
HUGH MacDIARMID

Hugh MacDiarmid was the pseudonym of Christopher Murray Grieve, who was born in 1892 in Langholm, Dumfriesshire. He attended school there where he was taught by the composer F. G. Scott, an important influence and later collaborator. He planned to become a teacher but abandoned this for journalism which gave him scope for the expression of his left-wing politics. During the First World War he served in the R.A.M.C. (1915–19), after which he worked as a journalist in Montrose and later in London and Liverpool. After a breakdown in health he retreated to a croft on Whalsay, in the Shetlands, where he lived in poverty. He worked as an engineer on the Clyde during the Second World War, afterwards settling at Biggar, Lanarkshire, where he and his second wife lived in a small cottage without indoor sanitation or electric light. In 1934 he joined the Scottish Communist Party but was expelled in 1938 because of his continued membership of the Scottish Nationalist Party, which he had helped to found in 1928. Awarded a Civil List Pension for his services to Scottish literature, he also received an honorary doctorate from Edinburgh University, the Fletcher of Saltoun Medal and the Foyle Poetry Prize.

Hugh MacDiarmid brought about a renaissance in Scottish culture and is now acknowledged as a great poet. During the twenties he began his attack on the existing cultural situation in Scotland, which he believed was provincial, out of touch with the mind of Europe and its own past. His aim was to resurrect the Scottish tradition that had petered out with Burns, and his early volumes, such as *Sangschaw*, contain some of the most vigorous poems written in Scottish. As the poet Tom Scott writes, 'It was clear at once that a poet of genius had arisen, using Scots with a new power, vitality, subtlety of thought, and grasp of diction and idiom.' However, MacDiarmid's dictum was 'Not precedent, but innovation' and he also sought to assimilate the distinctive attitudes and techniques of the Modern Movement into a truly contemporary Scots poetry. His output was prodigious but for many years his work was largely unavailable. *The Complete Poems of Hugh MacDiarmid* (published in two volumes) represents the definitive collection of his work.

Hugh MacDiarmid died in 1978.

THE COMPLETE POEMS OF
HUGH MacDIARMID

VOLUME I

Edited by
Michael Grieve and W. R. Aitken

Penguin Books

Penguin Books Ltd, Harmondsworth, Middlesex, England
Viking Penguin Inc., 40 West 23rd Street, New York, New York 10010, U.S.A.
Penguin Books Australia Ltd, Ringwood, Victoria, Australia
Penguin Books Canada Ltd, 2801 John Street, Markham, Ontario, Canada L3R 1B4
Penguin Books (N.Z.) Ltd, 182–190 Wairau Road, Auckland 10, New Zealand

First published by Martin Brian & O'Keeffe Ltd 1978
Published with corrections and an Appendix
in Penguin Books 1985

Made and printed in Singapore by
Richard Clay (S.E. Asia) Pte Ltd
Set in Bembo

AUTHOR'S NOTE

THESE volumes supersede my *Collected Poems*, first published in Britain and America in 1962 (and issued in a revised edition in America in 1967), and the later supplementary collections, *A Lap of Honour* (1967), *A Clyack-Sheaf* (1969) and *More Collected Poems* (1970). They reprint all the poems I have published in more than thirty books of poetry (or of prose and poetry) from my first book, *Annals of the Five Senses*, published in 1923, to the final publication of my *Direadh* poems in one volume, which appeared more than fifty years later in 1974. These books of poems (disregarding for this purpose most of the limited printings of a single poem or two) are reprinted in chronological order according to their year of publication, and in their entirety, and with their contents in the order in which they were printed within each book. However, a poem may not be printed here in its original context if it appears elsewhere in a different setting. From the *Collected Poems* of 1962 and its supplementary collections and from the later selections – *Selected Poems* (1970) and *The Hugh MacDiarmid Anthology* (1972) – only those poems are reprinted that were collected therein for the first time.

This arrangement means that my First and Second Hymns to Lenin are reprinted here at the dates of their first publication in 1931 and 1932, and not with the Third Hymn at the time of their republication as *Three Hymns to Lenin* in 1957; on the other hand, my three *Direadh* poems are reprinted under the date of their publication together in 1974, although the first was privately issued (in a very small edition) in 1938, and the second and third were printed in *Lucky Poet* in 1943.

The last section of these volumes reprints poems hitherto uncollected, and now gathered from more than forty different periodicals, many of them short-lived and not always available now in even the largest libraries; a few of the poems were published as contributions to books; some were broadcast. They are arranged here, year by year, according to the date of their first publication, from 1920 to the present year.

In the Prefatory Note to *A Lap of Honour* I wrote: 'I am now seventy-five, and cannot therefore promise that there will be any substantial further addition to the corpus of my poetry, except for my very long, unpublished, and still uncompleted "Impavidi Progrediamur".'

Nine years later the poem is still unpublished: I have simply abandoned the whole project. There is no proper sequence in which poems I attributed to *Impavidi Progrediamur* can be presented, but the interested reader will find in the Index of Titles a list of those poems that at one time or another I thought of including in that work. Other large-scale projects, such as 'Clann Albann' (with its parts 'The Muckle Toon' and 'Fier comme un Ecossais') and the complete 'Cornish Heroic Song for Valda Trevlyn', were either abandoned or subsumed in other works, and are not recorded here.

HUGH MacDIARMID

Biggar, Lanarkshire
September 1976

ACKNOWLEDGEMENTS

THE publisher acknowledges the financial assistance of the Scottish Arts Council in the publication of these volumes.

CONTENTS

Penny Wheep (1926)

CONTENTS

To Circumjack Cencrastus (1930)

First Hymn to Lenin and Other Poems (1931)

Second Hymn to Lenin (1932)

Scots Unbound and Other Poems (1932)

From Scottish Scene (1934)

Stony Limits and Other Poems (1934; 1956)

From *Scottish Eccentrics* (1936)

From *The Islands of Scotland* (1939)

From *The Golden Treasury of Scottish Poetry* (1940)

From *Lucky Poet* (1943)

From *Speaking for Scotland* (1946)

Poems of the East–West Synthesis (1946)

A Kist of Whistles (1947)

Poems to Paintings by William Johnstone 1933 (1963)

From The Company I've Kept (1966)

From A Lap of Honour (1967)

Early Lyrics (1968)

From *A Clyack-Sheaf* (1969)

From *More Collected Poems* (1970)

From *Selected Poems* (1970)

From *The Hugh MacDiarmid Anthology* (1972)

Dìreadh (1974)

Hitherto Uncollected Poems Contributed to Books and Periodicals (1920–1976)

Appendix

From
ANNALS OF THE FIVE SENSES
(1923)

A Moment in Eternity

TO GEORGE OGILVIE

THE great song ceased
– Aye, like a wind was gone,
And our hearts came to rest,
Singly as leaves do,
And every leaf a flame.

My shining passions stilled
Shone in the sudden peace
Like countless leaves
Tingling with the quick sap
Of Immortality.

I was a multitude of leaves
Receiving and reflecting light,
A burning bush
Blazing for ever unconsumed,
Nay, ceaselessly,
Multiplying in leaves and light
And instantly
Burgeoning in buds of brightness,
– Freeing like golden breaths
Upon the cordial air
A thousand new delights,
– Translucent leaves
Green with the goodness of Eternity,
Golden in the Heavenly light,
– The golden breaths
Of my eternal life,
Like happy memories multiplied,
Shining out instantly from me
And shining back for ever into me,
– Breaths given out

But still unlost,
For ever mine
In the infinite air,
The everlasting foliage of my soul
Visible awhile
Like steady and innumerable flames,
Blending into one blaze
Yet each distinct
With shining shadows of difference.

A sudden thought of God's
Came like a wind
Ever and again
Rippling them as waters over stars,
And swiftlier fanning them
And setting them a-dance,
Upflying, fluttering down,
Moving in orderly intricacies
Of colour and of light,
Delaying, hastening,
Blazing and serene,
Shaken and shining in the turning wind,
Lassoing cataracts of light
With rosy boughs,
Or clamouring in echoing unequalled heights,
Rhythmical sprays of many-coloured fire
And spires chimerical
Gleaming in fabulous airs,
And suddenly
Lapsing again
To incandescence and increase.

And again the wind came
Blowing me afar
In fair fantastic fires,
– Ivies and irises invading
The upland garths of ivory;
Queen daisies growing

In the tall red grass
By pools of perfect peace;
And bluebells tossing
In transparent fields;
And silver airs
Lifting the crystal sources in dim hills
And swinging them far out like bells of glass
Pealing pellucidly
And quivering in faery flights of chimes;
Shivers of wings bewildered
In alleys of virgin dream;
Floral dances and revels of radiance
Whirling in stainless sanctuaries;
And eyes of Seraphim,
Shining like sunbeams on eternal ice,
Lifted toward the unexplored
Summits of Paradise.

And the wind ceased.
Light dwelt in me,
Pavilioned there.
I was a crystal trunk,
Columnar in the glades of Paradise,
Bearing the luminous boughs
And foliaged with the flame
Of infinite and gracious growth,
– Meteors for roots,
And my topmost spires
Notes of enchanted light
Blind in the Godhead!
– White stars at noon!

I shone within my thoughts
As God within us shines.

And the wind came,
Multitudinous and light
I whirled in exultations inexpressible

– An unpicturable, clear,
Soaring and glorying,
Swift consciousness,
A cosmos turning like a song of spheres
On apices of praise,
A separate colour,
An essential element and conscious part
Of successive and stupendous dreams
In God's own heart!

And the wind ceased
And like a light I stood,
A flame of glorious and complex resolve,
Within God's heart.

I knew then that a new tree,
A new tree and a strange,
Stood beautifully in Heaven.
I knew that a new light
Stood in God's heart
And a light unlike
The Twice Ten Thousand lights
That stood there,
Shining equally with me,
And giving and receiving increase of light
Like the flame that I was
Perpetually.
And I knew that when the wind rose
This new tree would stand still
Multiplied in light but motionless,
And I knew that when God dreamt
And His creative impulses
Ran through us like a wind
And we flew like clear and coloured
Flames in His dreams,
(Adorations, Gratitudes, and Joys,
Plenary and boon and pure,
Crystal and burning-gold and scarlet

Competing and co-operating flames
Reflecting His desires,
Flashing like epical imaginings
And burning virgin steeps
With ceaseless swift apotheoses)
One light would stand unmoved.

And when on pinnacles of praise
All others whirled
Like a white light deeper in God's heart
This light would shine,
Pondering the imponderable,
Revealing ever clearlier
Patterns of endless revels,
Each gesture freed,
Each shining shadow of difference,
Each subtle phase evolved
In the magnificent and numberless
Revelations of ecstasy
Succeeding and excelling inexhaustibly,
—A white light like a silence
Accentuating the great songs!
—A shining silence wherein God
Might see as in a mirror
The miracles that He must next achieve!

Ah, Light,
That is God's inmost wish,
His knowledge of Himself,
Flame of creative judgment,
God's interrogation of infinity,
Searching the unsearchable,
—Silent and steadfast tree
Housing no birds of song,
Void to the wind,
But rooted in God's very self,
Growing ineffably,
Central in Paradise!

When the song ceased
And I stood still,
Breathing new leaves of life
Upon the eternal air,
Each leaf of all my leaves
Shone with a new delight
Murmuring Your name.

O Thou,
Who art the wisdom of the God
Whose ecstasies we are!

The Fool

HE said that he was God.
　'We are well met,' I cried,
'I've always hoped I should
　Meet God before I died.'

I slew him then and cast
　His corpse into a pool,
–But how I wish he had
　Indeed been God, the fool!

The Following Day

SCENT – *A remote Shooting Lodge beset with antlers of the wild red deer*

'MY house is crowned with horns
–Transpiercing horns of deer!
As were His brows with thorns.

Between two thieves He hung
Upon His Cross,
As here 'twixt earth and sky
Hang I.
A song a soldier sung
Jocundly in the dark
As now my heedless heart
—Oh, hark!
Defiant of its loss,
Jocundly in the dark,
My heart that crucified me here!

> "I nailed Him high
> 'Twixt earth and sky
> And Heaven shut
> Its flaming eye
> But
> Be nights as Hell
> I know full well
> My way to you, oblivious slut,
> Who all my roaring blood shall glut,
> Shall glut,
> Who all my roaring blood shall glut!

> "And when they loose Him from the tree
> At break of day
> I shall not care and shall not see
> —At break of day.
> My snoring head between your breasts
> Will snugly lie,
> Will snugly lie,
> My snoring head between your breasts
> Will snugly lie."

Every tine when morning came
Caught and held a flying flame,
But between her breasts he lay
Lost to day,
And between her spent breasts fell
Spent, to Hell!

'And I who have been crucified
Go light-foot in the morning-tide
—But hark!
The jocund notes like birds of prey
Go dark
Between me and the clarity of day!'

Spanish Girl [1]

Is then Aldebaran the star of hell
Lifting alone upon eternal night
One rose of light?
Ah! Fateful lamp
The blood of all mankind is oil for thee at last.
Upon the orgies of oblivion you cast
Your purple glooms.
My lost life quivers redly in your flame!

O Light that callest me by name,
Whom judgment's hoofs could not outstamp,
What deathless spell
Put you upon me still that I
In whose soul shrivelled all the sky
Should loose me from the detriments of dooms,
Shatter the shackles
Of incomputable debacles
And step incompetently free?

Can one light in a midnight single
One shadow from the rest,
One shadow when all shadows intermingle
—One passionate behest
Sever from night what day casts out,
Refuse to death what life repudiates?

[1] A recollection of Salonika.

O rose that will not let me rest
Espying me in the chaotic rout
What ghostly life now recreates
In shadow shape the man I was, and sets
Me with crepuscular passions quivering?
–Hell's parody of love in silhouette
Upon the stage of dissolution set!–
Can emptiness arise and sing?
Lethe my mouth of ashes wets
And puts a sung song in my heart.
My hollow loins acknowledge whom thou art.
My dusty veins are filled
With the red light that streams from thee.
I rise and come as thou hast willed,
O Light that makest me!
Nay, not Aldebaran but the rose you wear
Red in your cloudy hair!

Am I a disembodied memory
Embracing thee?
Your great breasts rise
In my imaginary hands.
I lie in endless impotence
Vague on your surging life,
Like lights in chaos are your eyes.
Me bodiless
Your arms constrain in ineffectual bands.
Dully I hear
What far distress,
What immemorial strife?

. . . Burn clearlier, Life, and penetrate
This partially-resurrected sense,
Half corpse, half ghost.
In this confusion dark and dense
But sounds are heard and meanings lost.

. . . Loosen the rose and put it to my ear!

Surely this urgent throbbing I have heard before
Knowing the whence and wherefore?

Burn more intense
Clasp me as in a vice.

. . . Ah no—
I am a void
Impossibly employed.
Vaguely I know and do not know.
So doth the sea
Receive infinity
Upon its whirling breasts.
I hear a multitudinous roar
And see within your eyes the flashing crests
Of tides that reach no shore.

. . . O weltering womanhood
On whose dispurposed mood
Flotsam
I am!

. . . O scarlet light of lust
Frenzying the disjunct dust!

. . . O thou who bearest me
Upon thy wildered courses timelessly
Hither and thither
And in the end no whither
When will the tyrannous rose wither
And let us lapse together
Vacant in space?

. . . O Whirlpool of Oblivion
Whereon my derelict life is spun
Cease your vain race
And let me like a shadow fall
To depths for ever held in nescience' thrall!

.   .   .   .   .   .

Morning
And quick winds scattering spice!
You let a ray of sunlight in.
Stand by the lattice – Sin
Bodied in living ivory
With dawn and darkness equal on your head
And one red rose
Flaming triumphantly
That down a white cheek throws
Impossible memories of the Night!
. . . Hark, the birds sing!
Throw wide the window to the light.
It shall not fall on flowers anywhere
Fair as your breasts are fair
Pulsing and glowing there.
It shall not hold
In momentary gold
Aught younger, aught more old.
The deft beams seek
With gestures sleek
Each nervous beauty in your conscious flesh.
. . . Sweet is the dawn and fresh
The dawn wind on the bed.

Why should I weary of my fate
Where sunlight is insatiate?
It is good to lie here
In endless mornings pale and clear
And see the roses trembling on the sill
And your breasts quivering still!
O thou whose unremitting lust
Constrains my dust!
And as the day declines
The red rose shines
Unspent,
Omnipotent!

Consummation

ABLAZE yet unconsumed I lay in thee
And instantly flame blended into flame,
As in a rising wind the light fires came.
Curve after curve climbed shining into me
I felt light flowing from your hands and feet,
I lay in incandescence 'twixt your thighs,
And saw the radiance mounting in your eyes
And heard your soaring heart's delirious beat.

Ablaze yet unconsumed I lie in thee.
Once lit such fires blaze to the end of time
To keener, clearer flaming still set free.
The spirit like a wind moves to and fro
Until in crystal heat, O Love Sublime,
One with eternity our bodies glow!

A Last Song

(Withered Wreaths)

THE heavens are lying like wreaths
Of dead flowers breaking to dust
Round the broken column of Time.

Like a fitful wind and a cold
That rustles the withered stars
And the wisps of space is my song,

Like a fitful wind and a cold
That whistles awhile and fails
Round the broken column of Time.

SANGSCHAW
(1925)

HABENT SUA FATA LIBELLI

The Bonnie Broukit Bairn

For Peggy

Mars is braw in crammasy,
Venus in a green silk goun,
The auld mune shak's her gowden feathers,
Their starry talk's a wheen o' blethers,
Nane for thee a thochtie sparin',
Earth, thou bonnie broukit bairn!
– But greet, an' in your tears ye'll droun
The haill clanjamfrie!

The Watergaw

Ae weet forenicht i' the yow-trummle
I saw yon antrin thing,
A watergaw wi' its chitterin' licht
Ayont the on-ding;
An' I thocht o' the last wild look ye gied
Afore ye deed!

There was nae reek i' the laverock's hoose
That nicht – an' nane i' mine;
But I hae thocht o' that foolish licht
Ever sin' syne;
An' I think that mebbe at last I ken
What your look meant then.

The Sauchs in the Reuch Heuch Hauch[1]

FOR GEORGE RESTON MALLOCH

THERE'S teuch sauchs growin' i' the Reuch Heuch
  Hauch.
Like the sauls o' the damned are they,
And ilk ane yoked in a whirligig
Is birlin' the lee-lang day.

O we come doon frae oor stormiest moods,
And licht like a bird i' the haun',
But the teuch sauchs there i' the Reuch Heuch
  Hauch
As the deil's ain hert are thrawn.

The winds 'ud pu' them up by the roots,
Tho' it broke the warl' asunder,
But they rin richt doon thro' the boddom o' Hell,
And nane kens hoo fer under!

There's no' a licht that the Heavens let loose
Can calm them a hanlawhile,
Nor frae their ancient amplefeyst
Sall God's ain sel' them wile.

I Heard Christ Sing

FOR H. J. C. GRIERSON

I HEARD Christ sing quhile roond him danced
The twal' disciples in a ring,
And here's the dance I saw them dance,
And the sang I heard Him sing.

[1] A field near Hawick.

Ane, twa, three, and their right feet heich,
Fower, five, six, and doon wi' them,
Seevin, aucht, nine, and up wi' the left,
Ten, eleevin, twal', and doon they came.

And Christ he stude i' the middle there,
And was the thirteenth man,
And sang the bonniest sang that e'er
Was sung sin' Time began.

And Christ he was the centrepiece,
Wi' three on ilka side.
My hert stude still, and the sun stude still,
But still the dancers plied.

O I wot it was a maypole,
As a man micht seek to see,
Wi' the twal' disciples dancin' roon',
While Christ sang like a lintie.

The twal' points o' the compass
Made jubilee roon' and roon',
And but for the click-click-clack o' the feet,
Christ's sang was the only soon'.

And there was nae time that could be tauld
Frae a clock wha's haun's stude still,
Quhile the figures a' gaed bizzin roon'
– I wot it was God's will.

> *Wersh is the vinegar,*
> *And the sword is sharp.*
> *Wi' the tremblin' sunbeams*
> *Again for my harp,*
> *I sing to Thee.*
>
> *The spirit of man*
> *Is a bird in a cage,*

That beats on the bars
Wi' a goodly rage,
And fain'ud be free.

Twice-caged it is,
In life and in death,
Yet it claps its wings
Wi' a restless faith,
And sings as it may.

Then fill my mouth
Wi' the needfu' words,
That sall turn its wings
Into whirlin' swords,
When it hears what I say.

Hearken my cry,
And let me speak,
That when it hears
It sall lift its beak,
And sing as it should.

Sweet is the song
That is lost in its throat,
And fain'ud I hear
Its openin' note,
As I hang on the rood.

And when I rise
Again from the dead,
Let me, I pray,
Be accompanied
By the spirit of man.

Yea, as I rise
From earth to Heaven,
Fain'ud I know
That Thou hast given
Consent to my plan–

Even as the stars
Sang here at my birth,
Let Heaven hear
The song of the earth
Then, for my sake.

The thorns are black,
And callous the nails.
As a bird its bars
My hand assails
Harpstrings . . . that break!

O I wot they'll lead the warl' a dance,
And I wot the sang sall be,
As a white sword loupin' at the hert
O' a' eternity.

Judas and Christ stude face to face,
And mair I couldna' see,
But I wot he did God's will wha made
Siccar o' Calvary.

Moonlight Among the Pines

THRAW oot your shaddaws
Owre the heich hillsides,
A' ye lang trees
Quhair the white mune rides.

My spirit 'ud darken
The sun in the East
For aye, gin my luve
Laid bare her white breist.

O shaddaw that derns
In my hert till a sicht
O' Luve sends it plungin'
A' else into nicht! . . .

'You Know Not Who I Am'

After the German of Stefan George

Ye kenna wha I am—but this is fac'.
I ha'ena yet by ony word or ac'
Made mysel' human . . . an' sune I maun tak'
Anither guise to ony I've yet ta'en.
I'll cheenge: an' yet my ain true sel' I'll hain,
Tine only what ye ken as me. I' vain
Ye'll seek to haud me, an' ye needna murn,
For to a form ye canna ken I'll turn
'Twixt ae braith an' the neist: an' whan I'm gane
Ye'll ha'e o' me what ye ha'e haen o' a'
My kindred since licht on the earth 'good da'—
The braith that gi'es ye courage, an' the fain
Wild kiss that aye into yer saul maun burn.

Overinzievar

The pigs shoot up their gruntles here,
The hens staund hullerie,
And a' the hinds glower roond aboot
Wi' unco dullery.

Wi' sook-the-bluids and switchables
The grund's fair crottled up,
And owre't the forkit lichtnin' flees
Like a cleisher o' a whup!

Ex vermibus

GAPE, gape, gorlin',
For I ha'e a worm
That'll gi'e ye a slee and sliggy sang
Wi' mony a whuram.

Syne i' the lift
Byous spatrils you'll mak',
For a gorlin' wi' worms like this in its wame
Nae airels sall lack.

But owre the tree-taps
Maun flee like a sperk,
Till it hes the haill o' the Heavens alunt
Frae dawin' to derk.

Au Clair de la Lune

FOR W. B.

> . . . *She's yellow*
> *An' yawps like a peany.*
> ANON.

> *They mix ye up wi' loony fowk,*
> *Wha are o' stars the mense,*
> *The madness that ye bring to me,*
> *I wadna change't for sense.*
> W. B.

I
Prelude to Moon Music

EARTH's littered wi' larochs o' Empires.
Muckle nations are dust.

Time'll meissle it awa', it seems,
An' smell nae must.

But wheest! – Whatna music is this,
While the win's haud their breath?
– *The Moon has a wunnerfu' finger*
For the back-lill o' Death!

II
Moonstruck

When the warl's couped soon' as a peerie
That licht-lookin' craw o' a body, the moon,
Sits on the fower cross-win's
Peerin' a' roon'.

She's seen me – she's seen me – an' straucht
Loupit clean on the quick o' my hert.
The quhither o' cauld gowd's fairly
Gi'en me a stert.

An' the roarin' o' oceans noo'
Is peerieweerie to me:
Thunner's a tinklin' bell: an' Time
Whuds like a flee.

III
The Man in the Moon

Oh lad, I fear that yon's the sea
Where they fished for you and me,
And there, from whence we both were ta'en,
You and I shall drown again.
　　　　　　　　　　　A. E. HOUSMAN

The moonbeams kelter i' the lift,
An' Earth, the bare auld stane,
Glitters beneath the seas o' Space,
White as a mammoth's bane.

An', lifted owre the gowden wave,
Peers a dumfoun'ered Thocht,
Wi' keethin' sicht o' a' there is,
An' bodily sicht o' nocht.

IV
The Huntress and Her Dogs

Her luchts o' yellow hair
Flee oot ayont the storm,
Wi' mony a bonny flaught
The colour o' Cairngorm.

Oot owre the thunner-wa'
She haiks her shinin' breists,
While th' oceans to her heels
Slink in like bidden beasts.

So sall Earth's howlin' mobs
Drap, lown, ahint the sang
That frae the chaos o' Thocht
In triumph braks or lang.

In the Hedge-Back

IT was a wild black nicht,
But i' the hert o't we
Drave back the darkness wi' a bleeze o' licht,
Ferrer than een could see.

It was a wild black nicht,
But o' the snell air we
Kept juist eneuch to hinder the heat
Meltin' us utterly.

It was a wild black nicht,
But o' the win's roar we
Kept juist eneuch to hear oor herts beat
Owre it triumphantly.

It was a wild black nicht,
But o' the Earth we
Kept juist eneuch underneath us to ken
That a warl' used to be.

Reid E'en

ILKA hert an' hind are met
'Neath Arcturus gleamin' bonnie,
Bien the nicht owre a' the warl'.
Hey, nonny, nonny!

But my hert sall meet nae maik
This reid-e'en or ony.
Luve an' a' are left behind.
– Hey, nonny, nonny!

Crowdieknowe

OH to be at Crowdieknowe
When the last trumpet blaws,
An' see the deid come loupin' owre
The auld grey wa's.

Muckle men wi' tousled beards,
I grat at as a bairn
'll scramble frae the croodit clay
Wi' feck o' swearin'.

An' glower at God an' a' his gang
O' angels i' the lift
–Thae trashy bleezin' French-like folk
Wha gar'd them shift!

Fain the weemun-folk'll seek
To mak' them haud their row
–Fegs, God's no blate gin he stirs up
The men o' Crowdieknowe!

The Eemis Stane

I' THE how–dumb–deid o' the cauld hairst nicht
The warl' like an eemis stane
Wags i' the lift;
An' my eerie memories fa'
Like a yowdendrift.

Like a yowdendrift so's I couldna read
The words cut oot i' the stane
Had the fug o' fame
An' history's hazelraw
No' yirdit thaim.

The Scarlet Woman

FOR ALEXANDER MCGILL

BLACK-BURNIN' shame is your garb, quo' they,
And syne gin you turn your face,
It lowes wi' a reid and laithly flame
That springs frae the evil place.

But noo I ha'e met you and seen for mysel'
Your face is the rare reid dawn,
And velvets o' nicht are the gouns you wear
To win the hert o' a man.

And a flame that springs frae the evil place,
And a flame that springs frae Heaven,
Are but as the thocht o' a man maun mak'
As his hert is richt or riven.

And glad I am that your face to me
Is the dawn, and no' dreadour,
Nor black affront but the bien nicht haps
Your bonnie form attour.

O burnin' rose o' the love o' God,
Pitch-darkness o' His will,
To Day and to Night, to Life and to Daith,
I gi'e me and fear nae ill.

The Frightened Bride

SEIL o' yer face! the send has come.
I ken, I ken, but awa' ye gan,
An' dinna fash, for what's i' yer hert
A' weemun ken an' nae man can.

Seil o' yer face! Ye needna seek
For comfort gin ye show yer plight.
To Gods an' men, coorse callants baith,
A fleggit bride's the seilfu' sicht.

The Last Trump

Suggested by the Russian of Dmitry Merezhkovsky

OWRE the haill warl' there's a whirrin'
An' a reishlin' an' a stirrin'
An' a muckle voice that cries:
'Let aal men rise!'

'Na, Na! Still the nicht is black.
I'll sleep on an' winna wauk.
Dinna reeze me. Dinna ca'.
Chapna' on my coffin-wa'.'

'Fegs, ye canna sleep, for noo
Gabriel mak's a hullaballoo.
Hark his trumpet's awfu' toot.
A' the deid maun up an' oot.'

Tootle-ootle-ootle-oo.
Tootle-oo.

'Gawa', gawa', an' let me lig,
Nae God 'ud awn me i' this rig
Or ha'e sic a rotten, stinkin'
Corpse as mine in's sunlicht blinkin'.

Gawa', gawa'.' 'Na, Na, my freen!
In yer grave ye're no' unseen.
Black affrontit tho' ye be
Up ye get – it's God's decree!

Up an' oot – an' say nae mair
Gleg or laith's no' here nor there.
Up – or God's begood to speir
Gin a'body's here!'

Cophetua

OH ! The King's gane gyte,
Puir auld man, puir auld man,
An' an ashypet lassie
Is Queen o' the lan'.

Wi' a scoogie o' silk
An' a bucket o' siller
She's showin' the haill Coort
The smeddum intil her!

Wheelrig

THERE'S a big black clood on the cantle o' Wheelrig,
And the waesome valley
'S fa'n like a dozened bird I'd fain tak' up i' my loof,
And ettle to rally.

Only a wee whiley-sin' it was fidgin' fu' fain
In its gowd and green –
Movin' i' the sun like a lassie,
Under her sweethert's een.

But the black clood grows on the cantle o' Wheelrig:
Wi' a cauld wund under't,
And the warld gaups at me like a saul frae its body,
Owre suddenly sundered!

Country Life

OOTSIDE!... Ootside!
There's dooks that try tae fly
An' bum-clocks bizzin' by,
A corn-skriech an' a cay
An' guissay i' the cray.

Inside!... Inside!
There's golochs on the wa',
A craidle on the ca',
A muckle bleeze o' cones
An' mither fochin' scones.

O Jesu Parvule

Followis ane sang of the birth of Christ, with the tune of
Baw lu la law.
                                    GODLY BALLATES

HIS mither sings to the bairnie Christ
Wi' the tune o' *Baw lu la law.*
The bonnie wee craturie lauchs in His crib
An' a' the starnies an' he are sib.
            Baw, baw, my loonikie, baw, balloo.

'Fa' owre, ma hinny, fa' owre, fa' owre,
A' body's sleepin' binna oorsels.'
She's drawn Him in tae the bool o' her breist
But the byspale's nae thocht o' sleep i' the least.
            Balloo, wee mannie, balloo, balloo.

The Innumerable Christ

Other stars may have their Bethlehem, and their
Calvary too.
                                    Professor J. Y. SIMPSON

W H A kens on whatna Bethlehems
Earth twinkles like a star the nicht,
An' whatna shepherds lift their heids
        In its unearthly licht?

'Yont a' the stars oor een can see
An' farther than their lichts can fly,
I' mony an unco warl' the nicht
        The fatefu' bairnies cry.

I' mony an unco warl' the nicht
The lift gaes black as pitch at noon,
An' sideways on their chests the heids
        O' endless Christs roll doon.

An' when the earth's as cauld's the mune
An' a' its folk are lang syne deid,
On coontless stars the Babe maun cry
        An' the Crucified maun bleed.

God Takes a Rest

From 'A Sea Suite'

As a man at nicht lets go o' life
And fa's into a sleep,
I cast me off frae the guid dry lan'
And turn yince owre to the deep.

I'll row the warl' like a plaid nae mair
For comfort roon' aboot me,
And the lives o' men sall be again
As they were lang, wi'oot me.

For I sall hie me back to the sea
Frae which I brocht life yince,
And lie i' the stound o' its whirlpools, free
Frae a' that's happened since.

In the Pantry

For N. M. Gunn

KNEDNEUCH land
And a loppert sea
And a lift like a blue-douped
Mawkin'-flee.

I'm famished, but fegs!
What's here for a man
But a wheen rubbish that's lain
Sin' Time began?

The sun has a goût
And the mune's hairy-mouldit,
And wha but auld Daith
Has a stummack to hold it?

I'll thraw the lot oot
And lippen to get fresh,
For the sicht o'ts eneuch
To turn my soul nesh!

Farmer's Death

FOR EDWIN MUIR

Ke-uk, ke-uk, ke-uk, ki-kwaik,
The broon hens keckle and bouk,
And syne wi' their yalla beaks
For the reid worms houk.

The muckle white pig at the tail
O' the midden slotters and slorps,
But the auld ferm hoose is lown
And wae as a corpse.

The hen's een glitter like gless
As the worms gang twirlin' in,
But there's never a move in by
And the windas are blin'.

Feathers turn fire i' the licht,
The pig's doup skinkles like siller,
But the auld ferm hoose is waugh
Wi' the daith intill her.

Hen's cries are a panash in Heaven,
And a pig has the warld at its feet;
But wae for the hoose whaur a buirdly man
Crines in a windin' sheet.

The Diseased Salmon

I'M gled it's no' my face,
But a fozie saumon turnin'

Deid-white i' the blae bracks o' the pool,
Hoverin' a wee and syne tint again i' the churnin'.

Mony's the face'll turn,
Like the fozie saumon I see;
But I hope that mine'll never be ane
And I can think o' naebody else's I'd like to be.

Whip-the-World

MOUNTAINS and seas
Birl under his wings
Till a' gaes in a kink
O' skimmerin' rings.

He lays on wi' his sang,
The wullie wee chap,
Till he gars earth bizz
Like a dozened tap.

Syne he hings sidelins
Watchin' hoo lang
It tak's till it staggers
Oot o' his sang.

Aye it tak's langer
And ane o' thae days
'I'll thraw't in a whirl
It'll bide in,' he says.

Ballad of the Five Senses

*To Sir Robert Bruce, President of the Burns Federation, in
appreciation of his efforts to foster a Scottish Literary Revival*

I

I WOT there was nae sicht nor scent,
Nae savour, substance, soon',
I didna see, smell, taste, or feel
Or hear as I ga'ed roon'.

As I ga'ed roon' the divers warl'
That ony man can ken
Wi' een and nose and ears and haun's
And mou' as I ga'ed then.

The warl' o' Earth and sea and sky,
And eke o' Heaven and Hell,
That separate seemed, as separate seemed
The warl' wi'in mysel'.

And time and space and change and daith
Were neist to nocht to me,
At will I'd bring the distant near
At will the deid I'd see. . . .

O I wist it is a bonny warl'
That lies forenenst a' men,
And that ony man wi' his senses five
As weel's the neist may ken.

II

I was as blithe to be alive
As ony man could be,
And felt as gin the haill braid warl'
Were made yince-yirn for me.

I wot I kept my senses keen,
I wot I used them weel.
As God felt whan he made the warl'
I aye socht to feel.

Times are yin sees things as they'd ne'er
Been seen afore ava',
As gin a' men had erst been blin',
Or the a'e First Day 'good da'.

Times are yin sees things as they'd ne'er
Been seen afore ava',
I wot I saw things fresh and full,
As few men ever saw.

O I wist it is a bonny warl'
That lies forenenst a' men,
But it's naething but a shaddaw-show
To the warl' that I saw then.

There was nae movement on the earth
But frae my hert it came,
'Let there be licht,' God said, and straucht
My een let oot the same.

Was it a tree? I couldna rest
Till 'neath my hert I kent
A pooer was pent gin it wan loose
Its boughs had heicher sent,

Had gi'en it bark 'gainst bolt and blast
Stranger than granite was,
And leaves sae green, a' ither greens
Were wan shaddaws.

I felt I could haud a' earth's trees
Dancin' upon my bluid,
As they were ba's that at a Fair
Stot in a loupin' flood. . . .

Yet sune I kent God or the warl'
Were no' for een to see,
Wi' body and saul I socht to staun'
As in Eternity.

Or bood I ha'e o' a' the warl'
But what my wits could mak',
And for the God made it and me
Nocht but my ain thochts tak'?

Oot o' the way, my senses five,
I ken a' you can tell,
Oot o' the way, my thochts, for noo'
I maun face God mysel'.

III

I cam' unto a place where there
Seemed nocht but naethingness,
Yet roon' and roon' me seemed to be
Things that were bodiless.

My senses there were nae mair use
Than gin I had had nane:
I felt their presence as they'd been
Thochts dernin' i' my brain,
Thochts no' like ony ither thochts
That ever I had ha'en.

They were like thochts for which a man
Can fin' nae words to tell,
Hoo' they compare wi' his ither thochts
E'en to his ain sel's sel.

And ilk ane differed frae the neist
As ilk ane did frae me:
And day and nicht, or life and daith
Mair like each ither be.

Water for stane micht weel be ta'en
Or Heaven and Hell seem yin,
A' differences men's minds can mak',
Maun end or ye begin. . . .

They were as blin' and deef and dumb,
They were as deid men be,
To a' that ony man alive
Can be or think or see.

And ilk ane differed frae the neist
As ilk ane did frae me:
And or ye 'good to coont them ye
Ga'ed 'yont infinity.

Yet weel I wot that life to each
Was bonny as to men,
Tho' I o' theirs as they o' mine
Could jot nor tittle ken.

Wae's me that thocht I kent the warl',
Wae's me that made a God,
My senses five and their millions mair
Were like banes beneath a sod.

For the warl' is like a flourishing tree,
And God is like the sun,
But they or I to either lie
Like deid folk i' the grun'.

IV

O gin ye tine your senses five,
And get ony o' theirs insteed,
Ye'll be as far frae what ye are
As the leevin' frae the deid.

And staun'in' as you're staun'in' noo,
And wi' things as they are

Ye'd be as gin ye stude upon
Anither kind o' star.

Leevin' quo' I and deid quo' I,
But daith may only be
A change o' senses so's a man
Anither warl' can see.

Or this warl' in anither way
For Heaven or Hell may be
But ither ways o' seein' the warl'
That ony man can see.

And God Himsel' sall only be
As far's a man can tell,
In this or ony ither life
A way o' lookin' at himsel'.

v

O I wist it is a bonny warl'
That lies forenenst a' men,
And that ony man wi' his senses five,
As weel's the neist may ken.

And I wist that that is a shaddaw show
To the warl's that can be seen
By men who seek as I ha' socht
And keep their senses keen.

But O I'm fain for a gowden sun,
And fain for a flourishing tree,
That neither men nor the Gods they'll ken
In earth or Heaven sall see!

In Glasgow

For F. G. Scott

How can I but be fearful,
Who know not what I do
More than did they whose labours
We owe this chaos to?

I'd rather cease from singing,
Than make by singing wrong
An ultimate Cowcaddens,
Or Gorbals of a song.

I'll call myself a poet,
And know that I am fit
When my eyes make glass of Glasgow,
And foresee the end of it!

La Fourmilière

For Denis Saurat

Tous ceux qui me parlent des génies ou des sots,
Peut-être des hautes affaires, peut-être des bagatelles,
Ne me semblent qu'une galerie des miroirs
Où tout ce qui passe est contourné pêle-mêle.

Ayant ni de concave ni de convexe,
Déchargés du sortilège vif-argent, voici
Dans le regard égal de la Vérité tous les gens,
Et leurs affaires, sont également fades et petits.

Hommage aux miroirs folâtres alors,
Aux âmes pleines de louange ou d'offense
Car, sans ceux, le monde ne me semblera comme
    il est, –
Rien qu'une fourmilière immense.

PENNY WHEEP
(1926)

Oor tree's no' daised wud yet
But's routh o' fruit to yield

Trompe l'oeil

As I gaed doon the hedgeback
Five blue eggs I saw,
It was as gin you'd looked at me
Wi' five een for twa.

Wheesht, Wheesht

Wheesht, wheesht, my foolish hert,
For weel ye ken
I widna ha'e ye stert
Auld ploys again.

It's guid to see her lie
Sae snod an' cool,
A' lust o' lovin' by–
Wheesht, wheesht, ye fule!

Ex ephemeride mare

I ha'e seen the Egypt herrings
Eelyin' in an emeraud sea,
And it's fain I could ha'e gane
In their skinklan' company.

Sae in deeps Thocht canna faddom
Dern the dreams that glint a wee
Through Time's shawls, and syne are tint
In dowf immensity.

Blind Man's Luck

HE juist sits oolin' owre the fire
And gin' a body speak t' him, fegs,
Turns up the whites o's een
Like twa oon eggs.

'I've riped the bike o' Heaven,' quo' he,
'And whaur ma sicht s'ud be I've stuck
The toom doups o' the sun
And mune, for luck!'

The Currant Bush

THERE'S no' a ressum to the fore
Whaur the hoose stood.
—Only a'e wild cur'n' buss wags
Tossils o' forfochen blood.

It's a lass that deed in childing,
Puir thowless cratur,
Wha alane o' a' her race
Is still at odds wi' natur'.

Cloudburst and Soaring Moon

CLOODBURST an' soarin' mune
And 'twixt the twa a taed
That loupit oot upon me
As doon the loan I gaed.

Noo I gang white an' lanely
But hoo I'm wishin', faith,
A clood aince mair cam' owre me
Wi' Jock the byreman's braith.

Feery·o'·the·Feet

'A DEID man's never
Feery o' the feet,
Jock, five years buried
Maun be far frae fleet,
Sae, lad ye needna worry,
He'll no' hae's in a hurry.'

Aye, lass! but Resurrection's
The danger that dings a',
We maun up braw an' early
Gin we're to win awa',
Else sune's the trumpet's blared
There'll be twa daiths in oor kirkyaird.

Somersault

I LO'E the stishie
O' Earth in space
Breengin' by
At a haliket pace.

A wecht o' hills
Gangs wallopin' owre,
Syne a whummlin' sea
Wi' a gallus glower.

The West whuds doon
Like the pigs at Gadara,
But the East's aye there
Like a sow at the farrow.

Song

THERE's an unco tune
That ony wund wafts
Frae a piper playin'
Wantin' the chafts.

And an unboorn man
Withooten a shape
Whiles sings a sang
You canna escape.

Tak' note o' the tune,
Gi'e words to the sang,
Or you'll ha'e nae peace
Whaurever you gang.

Sea-Serpent

From 'A Sea Suite'

The soul grows clotted by contagion,
Imbodies, and imbrutes till she quite lose
The divine property of her first being.

MILTON

IT fits the universe man can ken
As a man's soul fits his body;

And the spirit o' God gaed dirlin' through't
In stound upon stound o' pride
Draughtin' his thick–comin' notions o' life
As fast as they flashed in owre'm
When there was sea and licht and little beside.

His joy in his wark gied it lint–white lines
Brichter than lichtnin's there.
Like starry keethins its fer–aff coils
Quhile the nearer rings
Ran like a raw o' siller girds
On the wan–shoggin' tap o' the waters
And soupled awa' like wings.

Round the cantles o' space Leviathan flickered
Like Borealis in flicht
Or eelied thro' the poorin' deeps o' the sea
Like a ca' o' whales and was tint to sicht,
But aye in its endless ups–and–doons
As it dwined to gleids or walloped in rings
God like a Jonah whirled in its kite
But blithe as a loon in the swings.

Syne it gethered in on itsel' again
And lowed like the plans o' Heaven,
A michty puzzle o' flames that mirrored
The ends o' the thocht
– For aince He had hit upon Life itsel'
Hoo c'u'd the mere mak'in o' lives
Keep gien'm the thrills He socht?

And the serpent's turned like a wud sin' syne
That canna be seen for the trees
Or's tint as the mid–day sun is tint
In the glory o' its rays,
And God has forgotten, it seems,
In the moniplied maze o' the forms
The a'efauld form o' the maze.

Whiles a blindin' movement tak's in my life
As a quick tide swallows a sea.
I feel like a star on a starry nicht,
A'e note in a symphony,
And ken that the serpent is movin' still,
A movement that a' thing shares,
Yet it seems as tho' it twines in a nicht
When God neither kens nor cares.

But mebbe yet the hert o' a man
When it feels the twist in its quick
O' the link that binds it to ilka life,
A'e stab in the nerves o' the stars,
'll raise a cry that'll fetch God back
To the hert o' His wark again?
– Though Nature and Man ha'e cried in vain
Rent in unendin' wars!

Or does the serpent dern wi' a mortal wound
Unseen in its unseen side,
And are the surges that still come owre us
Like the thraws o' a stricken man
– Wi' the pooer to inform undeemis lives
Wi' the single movement o' life nae mair
But ebbin' fast – and ebbin' for aye –
Tho' we skinkle ahint like pools in the san'?

O Thou that we'd fain be ane wi' again
Frae the weary lapses o' self set free,
Be to oor lives as life is to Daith,
And lift and licht us eternally.
Frae the howe o' the sea to the heich o' the lift,
To the licht as licht to the darkness is,
Spring fresh and fair frae the spirit o' God
Like the a'e first thocht that He kent was His.

Loup again in His brain, O Nerve,
Like a trumpet-stang,

Lichtnin–clear as when first owre Chaos
Your shape you flang
– And swee his mind till the mapamound,
And meanin' o' ilka man,
Brenn as then wi' the instant pooer
O' an only plan!

Locked

THE folk a' yammer that they've never seen
A corpse thraw owt like thine;
But e'en alive ye were byordinar thrawn
As we ken fine.

They've wide-flung ilka door and ilka drawer
But syne ye thraw like mad.
Nowt's lockit i' the hoose abies my hert.
– *Thraw on, my lad!*

Thunderstorm

I'SE warran' ye're rawn for the yirdin'
An' no' muckle wunner,
When the lift's like a revelled hesp
I' the han's o' the thunner.

God's banes! when the haill warl' dirls
An' jows like a bell
An' the lichtnin's fleerin' atour
I'm waesome mysel'.

Hungry Waters

FOR A LITTLE BOY AT LINLITHGOW

THE auld men o' the sea
Wi' their daberlack hair
Ha'e dackered the coasts
O' the country fell sair.

They gobble owre cas'les,
Chow mountains to san';
Or lang they'll eat up
The haill o' the lan'.

Lickin' their white lips
An' yowlin' for mair,
The auld men o' the sea
Wi' their daberlack hair.

Tam

EEN that were blue as corncockles
'll twinkle nae mair,
Nor a lauch like the simmer lichtnin'
Jouk i' the air.

A face that was reid as a cock's kaim
Is grey as a stane,
And a man for the weemun is lyin'
Himsel' – alane.

Focherty

DUNCAN Gibb o' Focherty's
A giant to the likes o' me,
His face is like a roarin' fire
For love o' the barley-bree.

He gangs through this and the neebrin' shire
Like a muckle rootless tree
–And here's a caber for Daith to toss
That'll gi'e his spauld a swee!

His gain was aye a wee'r man's loss
And he took my lass frae me,
And wi' mony a quean besides
He's ta'en his liberty.

I've had nae chance wi' the likes o' him
And he's tramped me underfit.
–Blaefaced afore the throne o' God
He'll get his fairin' yet.

He'll be like a bull in the sale-ring there,
And I'll lauch lood to see,
Till he looks up and canna mak' oot
Whether it's God – or me!

Sabine

A LASS cam' to oor gairden-yett
An' ringle-e'ed was she,
And sair she spiered me for a leaf,
A leaf o' savin'-tree.

An' white as a loan soup was she,
The lass wha'd tint her snood,
But oot my gudewife cam' an' straucht
To rate the slut begood.

The lassie looked at her an' leuch,
'Och, plaise yersel',' said she,
'Ye'd better gi'e me what I seek
Than learn what I've to gi'e.'

Parley of Beasts

AULD Noah was at hame wi' them a',
The lion and the lamb,
Pair by pair they entered the Ark
And he took them as they cam'.

If twa o' ilka beist there is
Into this room sud come,
Wad I cud welcome them like him,
And no' staun' gowpin' dumb!

Be chief wi' them and they wi' me
And a' wi' ane anither
As Noah and his couples were
There in the Ark thegither.

It's fain I'd mell wi' tiger and tit,
Wi' elephant and eel,
But noo-a-days e'en wi' ain's sel
At hame it's hard to feel.

The Love-sick Lass

As white's the blossom on the rise
The wee lass was
That 'bune the green risp i' the fu' mune
Cannily blaws.

Sweet as the cushie's croud she sang
Wi' 'r wee reid mou' –
Wha sauch-like i' the lowe o' luve
Lies sabbin' noo!

Wild Roses

Wi' sae mony wild roses
Dancin' and daffin',
It looks as tho' a'
The countryside's laffin'.

But I maun ca' canny
Gin I'm no' to cumber
Sic a lichtsome warld
Wi' my hert's auld lumber.

Hoo I mind noo your face
When I spiered for a kiss
'Ud gae joukin' a' airts
And colourin' like this!

The Widower

AULD wife, on a nicht like this
Pitmirk and snell
It's hard for a man like me
To believe in himsel'.

A wheen nerves that hotch in the void,
And a drappie bluid,
And a buik that craves for the doonfa'
Like a guisand cude.

For Guid's sake, Jean, wauken up!
A word frae your mou'
Has knit my gantin' timbers
Thegither or noo.

The Long Black Night

THE nicht gangs stilpin' thwart the mune
A' stoichert up wi' starnies there.
Whaur are ye gan', O braw black nicht,
Wi' yer strawn o' beads sae fair?

'I dinna ken,' says the lang black nicht,
Thringin' the starns on's shouders there.
'I maun gang stilpin' thwart the mune,
But I kenna whaur – nor care.'

To One Who Urges More Ambitious Flights

DINNA come tae bauld my glead,
It'll be a bear-meal-raik.
Wee bit sangs are a' I need,
Wee bit sangs for auld times' sake!
Here are ferlies nae yin sees
In a bensil o' a bleeze.

The Dead Liebknecht

After the German of Rudolf Leonhardt

HIS corpse owre a' the city lies
In ilka square and ilka street
His spilt bluid floods the vera skies
And nae hoose but is darkened wi't.

The factory horns begin to blaw
Thro' a' the city, blare on blare,
The lowsin' time o' workers a',
Like emmits skailin' everywhere.

And wi' his white teeth shinin' yet
The corpse lies smilin' underfit.

In Mysie's Bed

THEY ha'e laid the black ram i' Mysie's bed,
And keepit it frae baain'
Wi' a gude fotherin' o' kail-blades and a cloot
Soaken i' milk.

Quo' Mysie, lauchin', 'Gin I s'ud wed
He may be ca'd a man
But I'll haud him as dumb, ye maun ha'e nae doot,
As owt o' this ilk.'

Guid Conceit

FEAR not, my hert, and what can ail ye?
Be you ever free and prood
As yon bonnie capercailyie
Wingin' owre the winter clood!

Morning

THE Day loups up (for she kens richt weel
Owre lang wi' the Nicht she mauna lig)
And plunks the sun i' the lift aince mair
Like a paddle-doo i' the raim-pig.

Under the Greenwood Tree

After the Cretan

A SODGER laddie's socht a hoose,
A hoose and toon to bide in.
He's fund a road but never a hoose
Or toon the haill warld wide in.

And syne he's come to an auld green tree
– Then wae for a sodger loon
Wha's tint his way frae the battlefield
And here maun lay him doon.

There's brainches here for his graith o' war,
A root to tether his horse,
And a shaddaw for a windin' sheet
To row aboot his corse.

The Three Fishes

After the Cretan

I AM a fisher lad and nane
Can better wield a gad than me,
And a'e day to the burn I've gane
And got me fishes three.

I've gi'en them to my minnie syne
And in the pan they're loupin',
When straucht they cheenge to lassies fine
And send my mither gowpin'.

O three braw queans, I see them plain
And a' as different as can be,
But noo they're ane, my mither's gane,
And Love's alane wi' me.

The Robber

After the Cretan

A ROBBER cam' to my hoose
And theft was a' his ploy,
Nor gowd nor siller could he find
And sae he stow my joy.

He stow the kisses frae my mou'
And mony a lauch and tear,
And syne begood upon my bluid
And toomed it vera near.

I gied him a' he wanted
And mebbe a wee thing mair,
I dinna ken what a' he took
But that's no' here nor there.

For aye he gied for a' he took,
And better gied than took,
And I've a bonnie laddie noo
And breists for him to sook.

Bombinations of a Chimaera

I

GIN I resisted ill
I'd haud it in me still
Dernin' aneth my will
– *Resist not ill!*

Till nicht sall fa' nae mair,
Thunder nor lichtnin' there,
But a' thing grown fu' fair
And nae Daith there.

The fox has its hole
And in my soul
Room shall I gi'e
A' God let's be.

And sall resist nae ill
While ocht is made to kill
And ocht defenceless still
In token o' His will.

Gin Murder like a clood
Whiles comes owre my bluid
I'se warrant it is food
That's needfu' to my guid.

And Poverty and Daith
I need them as Earth needs
The winter's bitter braith
To lowse the simmer's seeds.

Sin' God has cherished us
Wi' carefu' cruelty
Let us wi' nae mair fuss
Follow his husbandry.

II

But wha 'ud follow God
Maun tak' a flegsome road!
It's time to try God's way
When we've his poo'er tae.

For we can kill, but wha
Can fetch to life ana'?
We mauna follow God
Afore we ken the road.

III

Christ descendit into Hell
And for a' that we can tell
A' that's guid on Earth may be
Gaen' like Him through devilry.

But he didna bide in Hell,
Didna turn a Deil Himsel',
And gin we'd wun through it tae
We maun try to find His way.

IV

O the Earth may be in Hell,
I may be a Deil mysel',
Mebbe Christ gaed through it but
Ithers in't foraye are shut.

A' that's guid on Earth may be
Gaen' like Christ through devilry?
– Then the devilry ser's God tae
Only in anither way?

Wha can say which is the better?
Wisna Christ the Devil's debtor?

V

Christ was sent to save mankind.
That's eneuch for us, you'll find
God Himsel'
May gang to Hell
To save the Deil
In time as weel.

That's no' for us – we're nocht but men,
The ways o' God we canna ken,
So let's
Leave'm alane
To square His debts
And mind oor ain.

VI

The sun pits oot a fire
And the flames o' Hell turn wan
As through the ugsome place
Passes the Son o' Man.

He looks aboot him syne,
Hell isna to be seen,
But ceases to exist
As it had never been.

VII

When foxes ettle
Hoose-dogs to be,
And eagles settle
In the hen-ree,

The meek may inherit
The Earth, but till then
We maun ha'e spirit
Gin we're to be men.

VIII

Earth's sma'-bookit
Under a clood
That gars't shine bricht
As ony star could.

O little I thocht
It could seem sae fair
Till my black mood
Kindled it there!

IX

Bonnie, Earth shines frae the heich o' the lift
But eagles rise frae't to begin wi'
And syne are nocht but dust o' its dust
When their wings are din' wi.

I rise and fa' in my restless way
And Earth seems big syne or sma'
But it'll be the same at the end as tho'
I'd never flown ava!

x

As the stane frae the sepulchre's
Mooth fell doon
I sall be shot
O' the warld's wecht soon.

The wecht o' my body,
The wecht o' my soul,
Like the stane frae the mooth
O' the sepulchre roll.

This is the tune
Fu' o' elation
That'll wauken the giants
In the cave o' creation.

Scunner

YOUR body derns
In its graces again
As dreich grun' does
In the gowden grain,
And oot o' the daith
O' pride you rise
Wi' beauty yet
For a hauf-disguise.

The skinklan' stars
Are but distant dirt.
Tho' fer owre near
You are still – whiles – girt

Wi' the bonnie licht
You bood ha'e tint
– And I lo'e Love
Wi' a scunner in't.

Servant Girl's Bed

THE talla spales
And the licht loups oot,
Fegs, it's your ain creesh
Lassie, I doot,
And the licht that reeled
Loose on't a wee
Was the bonny lowe
O' Eternity.

Jimsy: an Idiot

WHEN Jimsy lauchs there's naething
But his lauchter to be seen,
As gin he'd flyped himsel'
Afore your vera een.

He tak's the licht o' Heaven
As a gargle for his mooth
And a'e movement o' his chafts
Mells the North and Sooth.

He owre's the Earth as a snake
Swallows an egg, and but
A glisk o' the lift's to be seen
Like a holin' rabbit's scut.

And afore God kens whaur He is
He's under the pap o' his hass
And his teeth are closin' ahint Him
And His pass is Jonah's pass.

Empty Vessel

I MET ayont the cairney
A lass wi' tousie hair
Singin' till a bairnie
That was nae langer there.

Wunds wi' warlds to swing
Dinna sing sae sweet,
The licht that bends owre a' thing
Is less ta'en up wi't.

The Fairmer's Lass

THE fairmer's lass has kilted her coats
An's muckin' oot the byre,
Her hair is a' aboot her een
An' her braid face is fire.

'*The worms ha'e a' come oot o' the earth
An' streek their lengths a' airts.
Their reid nebs eisen i' the sun
But wae's me for oor herts!*

'*The aidle-pool is a glory o' gowd
– My hert is black inside,
The worms may streek to their herts' content
But they ha'e nocht to hide.*'

The Bonnie Lowe

ABOUN the snaw-white channel
The bluid-reid roosies bleeze
– *Ai, lassie, but I'd liefer hae*
The mou' ye winna gie's.

Like greeshuckle the petals lie
O' roosies tashed to bits
– *But a'e wee cheep for evermair*
In flame has rowed my wits.

Sunny Gale

THE trees were like bubblyjocks
In the wild gowd wind,
The way that they fattened
And the way that they thinned
And the stramash they made.

Noo wi' taps streekit oot,
Eisenin' into the sun,
Their leafs scrauchin'; and syne
Swallin' back on the grun'
And tint in the shade.

But aye they raxed oot
Whustlin' heich in the lift
And aye loutit back
Wi' orra leafs left adrift
In their shaddaws' black whirlpools

Round my lugs the a'e meenit
In squabbles o' green
And the neist in a wan doze
Fer awa' they'd be seen
Or half-smoored i' the mools.

On the Threshold

Suggested by the French of Gustave Kahn

GUISERS I ken
Your fause faces under
Hidena' the face
That has thrilled me wi' wunder.

Ye ships that rock
A' the seev'n seas owre
Through nane o' your keels
Need my een fash to glower.

By land nor water
Nor lift sall I find
The love I can never
Get oot o' my mind.

The warld canna haud
The quean that I seek
Yet nocht sall the door
That leads to her steek. . . .

Life keeks in the winda,
Daith tirls at the pin
– But she loups to the threshold
To welcome me in.

Krang

SIDEWAYS hurled
The krang o' a warld
The sun has flensed
Is lyin' forenenst.

'Whirlwind, whirlwind
Cwa' and look sharp
And gi'e me a tune
On this white harp.

'And I sall sing
The kind o' sang
That roond the krang
O' a world s'ud ring.'

Supper to God

S'UD ye ha'e to gi'e
His supper to God
What like fare
'Ud ye set on the brod?

Lint-white linen
And siller-ware
And a tassie o' floo'ers
In the centre there?

Pot-luck 'ud be best,
I need ha'e nae fear
Gin God s'ud come
To's supper here.

Deal scrubbed like snaw
And blue-and-white delf
And let ilk ane
Rax oot for hisself.

A' that I'd ask
Is no' to ken whan,
Or gin it's Him
Or a trev'lin man.

Wi' powsoudie or drummock,
Lapper-milk kebbuck and farle,
We can aye wecht the wame
O' anither puir carle.

From 'Songs for Christine'

Aetat a year and a half

I
Fairy Tales

ITHER folks' fairy tales
'll no' dae for you.
You maun ha'e your ain
As new as you're new.

In the licht o' the mune
We'll gang oot wi' a girn
And see if we canna
Catch them yince-yirn.

Fairy tales are aye best
When they're catched on the hop,
– There's naething worth ha'en
To be hed frae a shop.

II
The Bubblyjock

It's hauf like a bird and hauf like a bogle
And juist stands in the sun there and bouks.
It's a wunder its heid disna burst
The way it's aye raxin' its chouks.

Syne it twists its neck like a serpent
But canna get oot a richt note
For the bubblyjock swallowed the bagpipes
And the blether stuck in its throat.

The Quest

I
I canna see you, lass,
For your face and your hair.
Are you mair than them
For they're ill to spare?

There's something I'd hear
Wert no' for your voice
Wert better worth hearin'
– But wow for the choice!

II
C'wa' into the darkness
– Whatever's to ken
Aiblins your flesh
'll no' hide frae me then!

But if need be I'll tak' ye
Through Daith to fin' oot
And be haud'n nae mair
Wi' a shaddaw o' doot.

And och! for your beauty
And och! for your braith
Gin you're the wumman I want
On the yon side o' Daith!

Gairmscoile

AULDER than mammoth or than mastodon
Deep i' the herts o' a' men lurk scaut-heid
Skrymmorie monsters few daur look upon.
Brides sometimes catch their wild een, scansin' reid,
Beekin' abune the herts they thocht to lo'e
And horror-stricken ken that i' themselves
A like beast stan's, and lookin' love thro' and thro'
Meets the reid een wi' een like seevun hells.
... Nearer the twa beasts draw, and, couplin', brak
The bubbles o' twa sauls and the haill warld gangs black.

Yet wha has heard the beasts' wild matin'-call
To ither music syne can gi'e nae ear.
The nameless lo'enotes haud him in a thrall.
Forgot are guid and ill, and joy and fear.
... My bluid sall thraw a dark hood owre my een
And I sall venture deep into the hills
Whaur, scaddows on the skyline, can be seen
– Twinin' the sun's brent broo wi' plaited horns
As gin they crooned it wi' a croon o' thorns –
The beasts in wha's wild cries a' Scotland's destiny thrills.

The lo'es o' single herts are strays; but there
The herds that draw the generations are,
And whasae hears them roarin', evermair
Is yin wi' a' that gangs to mak' or mar
The spirit o' the race, and leads it still
Whither it can be led, 'yont a' desire and will.

I

Wergeland, I mind o' thee – for thy bluid tae
Kent the rouch dirl o' an auld Scots strain,
– A dour dark burn that has its ain wild say
Thro' a' the thrang bricht babble o' Earth's flood.
Behold, thwart my ramballiach life again,
What thrawn and roothewn dreams, royat and rude,
Reek forth – a foray dowless herts condemn –
While chance wi' rungs o' sang or silence renshels them.

(A foray frae the past – and future tae
Sin Time's a blindness we'll thraw aff some day!)
. . . On the rumgunshoch sides o' hills forgotten
Life hears beasts rowtin' that it deemed extinct,
And, sudden, on the hapless cities linked
In canny civilisation's canty dance
Poor herds o' heich-skeich monsters, misbegotten,
. . . Streets clear afore the scarmoch advance:
Frae every winnock skimmerin' een keek oot
To see what sic camsteerie cast-offs are aboot.

Cast-offs? – But wha mak's life a means to ony end?
This sterves and that stuff's fu', scraps this and succours that?
The best survive there's nane but fules contend.
Na! Ilka daith is but a santit need.
. . . Lo! what bricht flames o' beauty are lit at
The unco' een o' lives that Life thocht deid
Till winnock efter winnock kindles wi' a sense
O' gain and glee – as gin a mair intense
Starn nor the sun had risen in wha's licht
Mankind and beasts anew, wi' gusto, see their plicht.

Mony's the auld hauf-human cry I ken
Fa's like a revelation on the herts o' men
As tho' the graves were split and the first man
Grippit the latest wi' a freendly han'

... And there's forgotten shibboleths o' the Scots
Ha'e keys to senses lockit to us yet
– Coorse words that shamble thro' oor minds like stots,
Syne turn on's muckle een wi' doonsin' emerauds lit.

I hear nae 'hee-haw' but I mind the day
A'e donkey strunted doon a palm-strewn way
As Chesterton has sung; nae wee click-clack
O' hoofs but to my hert at aince comes back
Jammes' Prayer to Gang to Heaven wi' the Asses;
And shambles-ward nae cattle-beast e'er passes
But I mind hoo the saft een o' the kine
Lichted Christ's craidle wi' their canny shine.

Hee-Haw! Click-Clack! And Cock-a-doodle-doo!
– Wull Gabriel in Esperanto cry
Or a' the warld's undeemis jargons try?
It's soon', no' sense, that faddoms the herts o' men,
And by my sangs the rouch auld Scots I ken
E'en herts that ha'e nae Scots 'll dirl richt thro'
As nocht else could – for here's a language rings
Wi' datchie sesames, and names for nameless things.

II

Wergeland, my warld as thine 'ca' canny' cries,
And daurna lippen to auld Scotland's virr.
Ah, weel ye kent – as Carlyle quo' likewise –
Maist folk are thowless fules wha downa stir,
Crouse sumphs that hate nane 'bies wha'd wauken them.
To them my Pegasus tae's a crocodile.
Whummelt I tak' a bobquaw for the lift.
Insteed o' sangs my mou' drites eerned phlegm.
... Natheless like thee I stalk on mile by mile,
Howk'n up deid stumps o' thocht, and saw'in my eident gift.

Ablachs, and scrats, and dorbels o' a' kinds
Aye'd drob me wi' their puir eel-droonin' minds,
Wee drochlin' craturs drutling their bit thochts

The dorty bodies! Feech! Nae Sassunuch drings
'll daunton me. – Tak' ye sic things for poets?
Cock-lairds and drotes depert Parnassus noo.
A'e flash o' wit the lot to drodlich dings.
Rae, Martin, Sutherland – the dowless crew,
I'll twine the dow'd sheaves o' their toom-ear'd corn,
Bind them wi' pity and dally them wi' scorn.

Lang ha'e they posed as men o' letters here,
Dounhaddin' the Doric and keepin't i' the draiks,
Drivellin' and druntin', wi' mony a datchie sneer
. . . But soon we'll end the haill eggtaggle, fegs!
. . . The auld volcanoes rummle 'neath their feet,
And a' their shoddy lives 'll soon be drush,
Danders o' Hell! They feel th' unwelcome heat,
The deltit craturs, and their sauls are slush,
For we ha'e faith in Scotland's hidden poo'ers,
The present's theirs, but a' the past and future's oors.

A Herd of Does

Gildermorie

THERE is no doe in all the herd
Whose heart is not her heart,
O Earth, with all their glimmering eyes
She sees thee as thou art.

Like them in shapes of fleeting fire
She mingles with the light
Till whoso saw her sees her not
And doubts his former sight.

They come and go and none can say
Who sees them subtly run
If they indeed are forms of life
Or figments of the sun.

So is she one with Heaven here,
Confounding mortal eyes,
As do the holy dead who move
Innumerous in the skies.

But now and then a wandering man
May glimpse as on he goes
A golden movement of her dreams
As 'twere a herd of does.

'U Samago Moria'

To Anna Akhmatova

O LOVELY life that swimming in the sea
Awaitest still the coming of the Prince,
Unknown, unseen, but in thy heart long since
Clear-imaged – golden Immortality!
Fair as Aphrodite, in infinite space,
Thou dost arise, and trembling like a star,
But sound of oars not glint of gold afar
Reward the lonely passion of thy face.

He comes at last upon the witless tide,
Bobbing to shore. Behold thy Bridegroom now,
The promised one for whom thy heart has cried,
As suddenly toward thee he is spun,
Lifting above the waves his salt-white brow
And leprous nosehole snoring to the sun!

Your Immortal Memory, Burns!

THOUGHT may demit
Its functions fit
While still to thee, O Burns,
The punctual stomach of thy people turns.

Most folks agree
That poetry
Is of no earthly use
Save thine – which yields at least this Annual Excuse!

Other cults die:
But who'll deny
That you your mob in thrall
Will keep, O Poet Intestinal?

From wame to wame
Wags on your fame,
Once more through all the world
On fronts of proud abdomena unfurled.

These be thy train,
No-Soul and No-Brain,
And Humour-Far-From-It,
Bunkum and Bung, Swallow-All and Vomit.

Palate and Paunch,
Enthusiasts staunch,
Gladly aver again,
'Behold one poet did not live in vain!'

'But us no Buts!'
Cry Gullet and Guts
Whose parrots of souls
Resemble a clever ventriloquist's dolls.

Be of good cheer
Since once a year
Poetry is not too pure
A savoury for shopkeepers to endure!

And, dined and wined,
Solicitors find
Their platitudes assume
The guise of intuitions that illume

The hidden heart
Of Human Art
And strike in ignorance
On wonders of unpredicated chance.

A boozy haze
Enchants your lays
And Gluttony for a change
Finds Genius within accosting range,

And cottons on!
– Thy power alone
The spectacle attests
Of drunken bourgeois on the Muses' breasts!

Only thy star
Falls from afar
To swim into the ken
Of countless masses of befuddled men,

In their hearts' skies
Like barmaids' eyes
Glabrous to glitter till
Their minds like rockets shoot away and spill

These vivid clots
Of idiot thoughts
Wherewith our Scottish life
Is once a year incomparably rife!

·   ·   ·   ·

Belly will praise
Thee all its days
And spread to all nations
Thy fame in belchings and regurgitations,

While mean minds soar
And hiccoughs adore
And butcher-meat faces
Triumphant, transfigured, example thy graces!

A DRUNK MAN LOOKS AT THE THISTLE
(1926)

Vast imbecile mentality of those
Who cannot tell a thistle from a rose.
This is for others....
SACHEVERELL SITWELL

To F. G. Scott

CAN ratt-rime and ragments o' quenry
And recoll o' Gillha' requite
Your faburdoun, figuration, and gemmell,
And prick-sangs' delight?

Tho' you've cappilowed me in the reapin'
– And yours was a bursten kirn tae ! –
Yet you share your advantage wi' me
In the end o' the day.

And my flytin' and sclatrie sall be
Wi' your fantice and mocage entwined
As the bauch Earth is wi' the lift
Or fate wi' mankind !

A Drunk Man Looks at the Thistle

I AMNA fou' sae muckle as tired – deid dune.
It's gey and hard wark coupin' gless for gless
Wi' Cruivie and Gilsanquhar and the like,
And I'm no' juist as bauld as aince I wes.

The elbuck fankles in the coorse o' time,
The sheckle's no' sae souple, and the thrapple
Grows deef and dour: nae langer up and doun
Gleg as a squirrel speils the Adam's apple.

Forbye, the stuffie's no' the real Mackay.
The sun's sel' aince, as sune as ye began it,
Riz in your vera saul: but what keeks in
Noo is in truth the vilest 'saxpenny planet'.

And as the worth's gane doun the cost has risen.
Yin canna throw the cockles o' yin's hert
Wi' oot ha'en' cauld feet noo, jalousin' what
The wife'll say (I dinna blame her fur't).

It's robbin' Peter to pey Paul at least. . . .
And a' that's Scotch aboot it is the name,
Like a' thing else ca'd Scottish nooadays
– A' destitute o' speerit juist the same.

(To prove my saul is Scots I maun begin
Wi' what's still deemed Scots and the folk expect,
And spire up syne by visible degrees
To heichts whereo' the fules ha'e never recked.

But aince I get them there I'll whummle them
And souse the craturs in the nether deeps,
– For it's nae choice, and ony man s'ud wish
To dree the goat's weird tae as weel's the sheep's!)

Heifetz in tartan, and Sir Harry Lauder!
Whaur's Isadora Duncan dancin' noo?
Is Mary Garden in Chicago still
And Duncan Grant in Paris – and me fou'?

Sic transit gloria Scotiae – a' the floo'ers
O' the Forest are wede awa'. (A blin' bird's nest
Is aiblins biggin' in the thistle tho'? . . .
And better blin' if'ts brood is like the rest!)

You canna gang to a Burns supper even
Wi' oot some wizened scrunt o' a knock-knee
Chinee turns roon to say, 'Him Haggis – velly goot!'
And ten to wan the piper is a Cockney.

No' wan in fifty kens a wurd Burns wrote
But misapplied is a'body's property,
And gin there was his like alive the day
They'd be the last a kennin' haund to gi'e –

Croose London Scotties wi' their braw shirt fronts
And a' their fancy freen's, rejoicin'
That similah gatherings in Timbuctoo,
Bagdad – and Hell, nae doot – are voicin'

Burns' sentiments o' universal love,
In pidgin English or in wild-fowl Scots,
And toastin' ane wha's nocht to them but an
Excuse for faitherin' Genius wi' *their* thochts.

A' *they*'ve to say was aften said afore
A lad was born in Kyle to blaw aboot.
What unco fate mak's *him* the dumpin'-grun'
For a' the sloppy rubbish they jaw oot?

Mair nonsense has been uttered in his name
Than in ony's barrin' liberty and Christ.
If this keeps spreedin' as the drink declines,
Syne turns to tea, wae's me for the *Zeitgeist!*

Rabbie, wad'st thou wert here – the warld hath need,
And Scotland mair sae, o' the likes o' thee!
The whisky that aince moved your lyre's become
A laxative for a' loquacity.

O gin they'd stegh their guts and haud their wheesht
I'd thole it, for 'a man's a man' I ken,
But though the feck ha'e plenty o' the 'a' that',
They're nocht but zoologically men.

I'm haverin', Rabbie, but ye understaun'
It gets my dander up to see your star
A bauble in Babel, banged like a saxpence
'Twixt Burbank's Baedeker and Bleistein's cigar.

There's nane sae ignorant but think they can
Expatiate on *you*, if on nae ither.
The sumphs ha'e ta'en you at your wurd, and, fegs!
The foziest o' them claims to be a – Brither!

Syne 'Here's the cheenge' – the star of Rabbie Burns.
Sma' cheenge, 'Twinkle, Twinkle.' The memory slips
As G. K. Chesterton heaves up to gi'e
'The Immortal Memory' in a huge eclipse,

Or somebody else as famous if less fat.
You left the like in Embro in a scunner
To booze wi' thieveless cronies sic as me.
I'se warrant you'd shy clear o' a' the hunner

Odd Burns Clubs tae, or ninety-nine o' them,
And haud your birthday in a different kip
Whaur your name isna ta'en in vain – as Christ
Gied a' Jerusalem's Pharisees the slip

– Christ wha'd ha'e been Chief Rabbi gin he'd lik't! –
Wi' publicans and sinners to forgether,
But, losh! the publicans noo are Pharisees,
And I'm no' shair o' maist the sinners either.

But that's aside the point! I've got fair waun'ert.
It's no' that I'm sae fou' as juist deid dune,
And dinna ken as muckle's whaur I am
Or hoo I've come to sprawl here 'neth the mune.

That's it! It isna me that's fou' at a',
But the fu' mune, the doited jade, that's led
Me fer agley, or 'mogrified the warld.
– For a' I ken I'm safe in my ain bed.

Jean! Jean! Gin *she's* no' here it's no' *oor* bed,
Or else I'm dreamin' deep and canna wauken,
But it's a fell queer dream if this is no'
A real hillside – and thae things thistles and bracken!

It's hard wark haud'n' by a thocht worth ha'en'
And harder speakin't, and no' for ilka man;
Maist Thocht's like whisky – a thoosan' under proof,
And a sair price is pitten on't even than.

As Kirks wi' Christianity ha'e dune,
Burns Clubs wi' Burns – wi' a'thing it's the same,
The core o' ocht is only for the few,
Scorned by the mony, thrang wi'ts empty name.

And a' the names in History mean nocht
To maist folk but 'ideas o' their ain',
The vera opposite o' onything
The Deid 'ud awn gin they cam' back again.

A greater Christ, a greater Burns, may come.
The maist they'll dae is to gi'e bigger pegs
To folly and conceit to hank their rubbish on.
They'll cheenge folks' talk but no' their natures, fegs!

I maun feed frae the common trough ana'
Whaur a' the lees o' hope are jumbled up;
While centuries like pigs are slorpin' owre't
Sall my wee 'oor be cryin': 'Let pass this cup'?

In wi' your gruntle then, puir wheengin' saul,
Lap up the ugsome aidle wi' the lave,
What gin it's your ain vomit that you swill
And frae Life's gantin' and unfaddomed grave?

I doot I'm geylies mixed, like Life itsel',
But I was never ane that thocht to pit
An ocean in a mutchkin. As the haill's
Mair than the pairt sae I than reason yet.

I dinna haud the warld's end in my heid
As maist folk think they dae; nor filter truth
In fishy gills through which its tides may poor
For ony *animalculae* forsooth.

I lauch to see my crazy little brain
– And ither folks' – tak'n' itsel' seriously,
And in a sudden lowe o' fun my saul
Blinks dozent as the owl I ken't to be.

I'll ha'e nae hauf-way hoose, but aye be whaur
Extremes meet – it's the only way I ken
To dodge the curst conceit o' bein' richt
That damns the vast majority o' men.

I'll bury nae heid like an ostrich's,
Nor yet believe my een and naething else.
My senses may advise me, but I'll be
Mysel' nae maitter what they tell's. . . .

I ha'e nae doot some foreign philosopher
Has wrocht a system oot to justify
A' this: but I'm a Scot wha blin'ly follows
Auld Scottish instincts, and I winna try.

For I've nae faith in ocht I can explain,
And stert whaur the philosophers leave aff,
Content to glimpse its loops I dinna ettle
To land the sea serpent's sel' wi' ony gaff.

Like staundin' water in a pocket o'
Impervious clay I pray I'll never be,
Cut aff and self-sufficient, but let reenge
Heichts o' the lift and benmaist deeps o' sea.

Water! Water! There was owre muckle o't
In yonder whisky, sae I'm in deep water
(And gin I could wun hame I'd be in het,
For even Jean maun natter, natter, natter). . . .

And in the toon that I belang tae
– What tho'ts Montrose or Nazareth? –
Helplessly the folk continue
To lead their livin' death! . . .

    [1]*At darknin' hings abune the howff*
    A weet and wild and eisenin' air.
    Spring's spirit wi' its waesome sough
    Rules owre the drucken stramash there.

    And heich abune the vennel's pokiness,
    Whaur a' the white-weshed cottons lie,
    The Inn's sign blinters in the mochiness,
    And lood and shrill the bairnies cry.

    The hauflins' yont the burgh boonds
    Gang ilka nicht, and a' the same,
    Their bonnets cocked; their bluid that stounds
    Is playin' at a fine auld game.

    And on the lochan there, hauf-herted
    Wee screams and creakin' oar-locks soon',
    And in the lift, heich, hauf-averted,
    The mune looks owre the yirdly roon'.

    And ilka evenin', derf and serious
    (Jean ettles nocht o' this, puir lass),
    In liquor, raw yet still mysterious,
    A'e freend's aye mirrored in my glass.

    [1] From the Russian of Alexander Blok.

Ahint the sheenin' coonter gruff
Thrang barmen ding the tumblers doun;
'In vino veritas' cry rough
And reid-een'd fules that in it droon.

But ilka evenin' fey and fremt
(Is it a dream nae wauk'nin' proves?)
As to a trystin'-place undreamt,
A silken leddy darkly moves.

Slow gangs she by the drunken anes,
And lanely by the winnock sits;
Frae'r robes, atour the sunken anes,
A rooky dwamin' perfume flits.

Her gleamin' silks, the taperin'
O' her ringed fingers, and her feathers
Move dimly like a dream wi'in,
While endless faith aboot them gethers.

I seek, in this captivity,
To pierce the veils that darklin' fa'
– See white clints slidin' to the sea,
And hear the horns o' Elfland blaw.

I ha'e dark secrets' turns and twists,
A sun is gi'en to me to haud,
The whisky in my bluid insists,
And spiers my benmaist history, lad.

And owre my brain the flitterin'
O' the dim feathers gangs aince mair,
And, faddomless, the dark blue glitterin'
O' twa een in the ocean there.

My soul stores up this wealth unspent,
The key is safe and nane's but mine.
You're richt, auld drunk impenitent,
I ken it tae – the truth's in wine!

The munelicht's like a lookin'-glass,
The thistle's like mysel',
But whaur ye've gane, my bonnie lass,
Is mair than I can tell.

Were you a vision o' mysel',
Transmuted by the mellow liquor?
Neist time I glisk you in a glass,
I'se warrant I'll mak' siccar.

A man's a clean contrairy sicht
Turned this way in-ootside,
And, fegs, I feel like Dr. Jekyll
Tak'n' guid tent o' Mr. Hyde. . . .

Gurly thistle – hic – you canna
Daunton me wi' your shaggy mien,
I'm sair – hic – needin' a shave,
That's plainly to be seen.

But what aboot it – hic – aboot it?
Mony a man's been that afore.
It's no' a fact that in his lugs
A wund like this need roar! . . .

> [1]*I ha'e forekent ye! O I ha'e forekent.*
> *The years forecast your face afore they went.*
> *A licht I canna thole is in the lift.*
> *I bide in silence your slow-comin' pace.*
> *The ends o' space are bricht: at last – oh swift!*
> *While terror clings to me – an unkent face!*

> *Ill-faith stirs in me as she comes at last,*
> *The features lang forekent . . . are unforecast.*
> *O it gangs hard wi' me, I am forspent.*
> *Deid dreams ha'e beaten me and a face unkent*

[1] Freely adapted from the Russian of Alexander Blok.

And generations that I thocht unborn
Hail the strange Goddess frae my hert's-hert torn! . . .

Or dost thou mak' a thistle o' me, wumman? But for thee
I were as happy as the munelicht, withoot care,
But thocht o' thee – o' thy contempt and ire –
Turns hauf the warld into the youky thistle there,

Feedin' on the munelicht and transformin' it
To this wanrestfu' growth that winna let me be.
The munelicht is the freedom that I'd ha'e
But for this cursèd Conscience thou hast set in me.

It is morality, the knowledge o' Guid and Ill,
Fear, shame, pity, like a will and wilyart growth,
That kills a' else wi'in its reach and craves
Nae less at last than a' the warld to gi'e it scouth.

The need to wark, the need to think, the need to be,
And a' thing that twists Life into a certain shape
And interferes wi' perfect liberty –
These feed this Frankenstein that nae man can escape.

For ilka thing a man can be or think or dae
Aye leaves a million mair unbeen, unthocht, undune,
Till his puir warped performance is,
To a' that micht ha' been, a thistle to the mune.

It is Mortality itsel' – the mortal coil,
Mockin' Perfection, Man afore the Throne o' God
He yet has bigged himsel', Man torn in twa
And glorious in the lift and grisly on the sod! . . .

There's nocht sae sober as a man blin' drunk.
I maun ha'e got an unco bellyfu'
To jaw like this – and yet what I am sayin'
Is a' the apter, aiblins, to be true.

This munelicht's fell like whisky noo I see't.
– Am I a thingum mebbe that is kept
Preserved in spirits in a muckle bottle
Lang centuries efter sin' wi' Jean I slept?

– Mounted on a hillside, wi' the thistles
And bracken for verisimilitude,
Like a stuffed bird on metal like a brainch,
Or a seal on a stump o' rock-like wood?

Or am I juist a figure in a scene
O' Scottish life A.D. one-nine-two-five?
The haill thing kelters like a theatre claith
Till I micht fancy that I was alive!

I dinna ken and nae man ever can.
I micht be in my ain bed efter a'.
The haill damned thing's a dream for ocht we ken,
– The Warld and Life and Daith, Heaven, Hell ana'.

We maun juist tak' things as we find them then,
And mak' a kirk or mill o' them as we can,
– And yet I feel this muckle thistle's staun'in'
Atween me and the mune as pairt o' a Plan.

It isna there – nor me – by accident.
We're brocht thegither for a certain reason,
Ev'n gin it's naething mair than juist to gi'e
My jaded soul a necessary *frisson*.

I never saw afore a thistle quite
Sae intimately, or at sic an 'oor.
There's something in the fickle licht that gi'es
A different life to't and an unco poo'er.

> [1]*Rootit on gressless peaks, whaur its erect
> And jaggy leafs, austerely cauld and dumb,*

[1] From the Belgian poet, George Ramaekers.

> *Haud the slow scaly serpent in respect,*
> *The Gothic thistle, whaur the insect's hum*
> *Soon's fer aff, lifts abune the rock it scorns*
> *Its rigid virtue for the Heavens to see.*
> *The too'ering boulders gaird it. And the bee*
> *Mak's honey frae the roses on its thorns.'*

But that's a Belgian refugee, of coorse.
This Freudian complex has somehoo slunken
Frae Scotland's soul – the Scots aboulia –
Whilst a' its *terra nullius* is *betrunken.*

And a' the country roon' aboot it noo
Lies clapt and shrunken syne like somebody wha
Has lang o' seven devils been possessed;
Then when he turns a corner tines them a'.

Or like a body that has tint its soul,
Perched like a monkey on its heedless kist,
Or like a sea that peacefu' fa's again
When frae its deeps an octopus is fished.

I canna feel it has to dae wi' me
Mair than a composite diagram o'
Cross-sections o' my forbears' organs
– And mine – 'ud bring a kind o' freen'ly glow.

And yet like bindweed through my clay it's run,
And a' my folks' – it's queer to see't unroll.
My ain soul looks me in the face, as 'twere,
And mair than my ain soul – my nation's soul!

And sall a Belgian pit it into words
And sing a sang to't syne, and no' a Scot?
Oors is a wilder thistle, and Ramaekers
Canna bear aff the gree – avaunt the thocht!

To meddle wi' the thistle and to pluck
The figs frae't is *my* metier, I think.

Awak', my muse, and gin you're in puir fettle,
We aye can blame it on th' inferior drink.

T. S. Eliot – it's a Scottish name –
Afore he wrote 'The Waste Land' s'ud ha'e come
To Scotland here. He wad ha'e written
A better poem syne – like this, by gum!

Type o' the Wissenschaftsfeindlichkeit,
Begriffsmüdigkeit that has gar't
Men try Morphologies der Weltgeschichte,
And mad Expressionismus syne in Art.

> [1]*A shameless thing, for ilka vileness able,*
> *It is deid grey as dust, the dust o' a man.*
> *I perish o' a nearness I canna win awa' frae,*
> *Its deidly coils aboot my buik are thrawn.*
>
> *A shaggy poulp, embracin' me and stingin',*
> *And as a serpent cauld agen' my hert,*
> *Its scales are poisoned shafts that jag me to the quick*
> *– And waur than them's my scunner's feerfu' smert!*
>
> *O that its prickles were a knife indeed,*
> *But it is thowless, flabby, dowf, and numb.*
> *Sae sluggishly it drains my benmaist life*
> *A dozent dragon, dreidfu', deef, and dumb.*
>
> *In mum obscurity it twines its obstinate rings*
> *And hings caressin'ly, its purpose whole;*
> *And this deid thing, whale-white obscenity,*
> *This horror that I writhe in – is my soul!*

Is it the munelicht or a leprosy
That spreids aboot me; and a thistle
Or my ain skeleton through wha's bare banes
A fiendish wund's begood to whistle?

---

[1] Adapted from the Russian of Zinaida Hippius.

The devil's lauchter has a *hwll* like this.
My face has flown open like a lid
– And gibberin' on the hillside there
Is a' humanity sae lang has hid ! . . .

My harns are seaweed – when the tide is in
They swall like blethers and in comfort float,
But when the tide is oot they lie like gealed
And runkled auld bluid-vessels in a knot !

The munelicht ebbs and flows and wi't my thocht,
Noo movin' mellow and noo lourd and rough.
I ken what I am like in Life and Daith,
But Life and Daith for nae man are enough. . . .

And O ! to think that there are members o'
St. Andrew's Societies sleepin' soon',
Wha to the papers wrote afore they bedded
On regimental buttons or buckled shoon,

Or use o' England whaur the U.K.'s meent,
Or this or that anent the Blue Saltire,
Recruitin', pedigrees, and Gude kens what,
Filled wi' a proper patriotic fire !

Wad I were them – they've chosen a better pairt,
The couthie craturs, than the ane I've ta'en,
Tyauvin' wi' this root-hewn Scottis soul;
A fer, fer better pairt – except for men.

Nae doot they're sober, as a Scot ne'er was,
Each tethered to a punctual-snorin' missus,
Whilst I, puir fule, owre continents unkent
And wine-dark oceans waunder like Ulysses. . . .

> [1] *The Mune sits on my bed the nicht unsocht,*
>   *And mak's my soul obedient to her will;*

[1] Suggested by the German of Else Lasker-Schüler.

And in the dumb-deid, still as dreams are still,
Her pupils narraw to bricht threids that thrill
Aboot the sensuous windin's o' her thocht.

But ilka windin' has its coonter-pairt
– The opposite 'thoot which it couldna be –
In some wild kink or queer perversity
O' this great thistle, green wi' jealousy,
That breenges 'twixt the munelicht and my hert. . . .

Plant, what are you then? Your leafs
Mind me o' the pipes' lood drone
– And a' your purple tops
Are the pirly-wirly notes
That gang staggerin' owre them as they groan.

Or your leafs are alligators
That ha'e gobbled owre a haill
Company o' Heilant sodgers,
And left naethin' but the toories
O' their Balmoral bonnets to tell the tale.

Or a muckle bellows blawin'
Wi' the sperks a' whizzin' oot;
Or green tides sweeshin'
'Neth heich-skeich stars,
Or centuries fleein' doun a water-chute.

Grinnin' gargoyle by a saint,
Mephistopheles in Heaven,
Skeleton at a tea-meetin',
Missin' link – or creakin'
Hinge atween the deid and livin'. . . .

(I kent a Terrier in a sham fecht aince,
Wha louped a dyke and landed on a thistle.
He'd naething on ava aneth his kilt.
Schönberg has nae notation for his whistle.) . . .

(Gin you're surprised a village drunk
Foreign references s'ud fool in,
You ha'ena the respect you s'ud
For oor guid Scottish schoolin'.

For we've the maist unlikely folk
Aye braggin' o' oor lear,
And, tho' I'm drunk, for Scotland's sake
I tak' my barrowsteel here!

Yet Europe's faur eneuch for me,
Puir fule, when bairns ken mair
O' th' ither warld than I o' this
– But that's no' here nor there!) . . .

Guid sakes, I'm in a dreidfu' state.
I'll ha'e nae inklin' sune
Gin I'm the drinker or the drink,
The thistle or the mune.

I'm geylies feart I couldna tell
Gin I su'd lay me doon
The difference betwixt the warld
And my ain heid gaen' roon'! . . .

Drums in the Walligate, pipes in the air,
Come and hear the cryin' o' the Fair.

A' as it used to be, when I was a loon
On Common-Ridin' Day in the Muckle Toon.

The bearer twirls the Bannock-and-Saut-Herrin',
The Croon o' Roses through the lift is farin',

The aucht-fit thistle wallops on hie;
In heather besoms a' the hills gang by.

But noo it's a' the fish o' the sea
Nailed on the roond o' the Earth to me.

Beauty and Love that are bobbin' there;
Syne the breengin' growth that alane I bear;

And Scotland followin' on ahint
For threepenny bits spleet-new frae the mint.

Drums in the Walligate, pipes in the air,
The wallopin' thistle is ill to bear.

But I'll dance the nicht wi' the stars o' Heaven
In the Mairket Place as shair's I'm livin'.

Easy to cairry roses or herrin',
And the lave may weel their threepenny bits earn.

Devil the star! It's Jean I'll ha'e
Again as she was on her weddin' day. . . .

Nerves in stounds o' delight,
Muscles in pride o' power,
Bluid as wi' roses dight
Life's toppin' pinnacles owre,
The thistle yet'll unite
Man and the Infinite!

Swippert and swith wi' virr
In the howes o' man's hert
Forever its muckle roots stir
Like a Leviathan astert,
Till'ts coils like a thistle's leafs
Sweep space wi' levin sheafs.

Frae laichest deeps o' the ocean
It rises in flight upon flight,
And 'yont its uttermaist motion
Can still set roses alight,
As else unreachable height
Fa's under its triumphin' sight.

Here is the root that feeds
The shank wi' the blindin' wings
Dwinin' abuneheid to gleids
Like stars in their keethin' rings,
And blooms in sunrise and sunset
Inowre Eternity's yett.

Lay haud o' my hert and feel
Fountains ootloupin' the starns
Or see the Universe reel
Set gaen' by my eident harns,
Or test the strength o' my spauld
The wecht o' a' thing to hauld!

– The howes o' Man's hert are bare,
The Dragon's left them for good,
There's nocht but naethingness there,
The hole whaur the Thistle stood,
That rootless and radiant flies
A Phoenix in Paradise! . . .

Masoch and Sade
Turned into ane
Havoc ha'e made
O' my a'e brain.

Weel, gin it's Sade
Let it be said
They've made me mad
– That'll da'e instead.

But it's no' instead
In Scots, but insteed.
– The life they've led
In my puir heid.

But aince I've seen
In the thistle here
A' that they've been
I'll aiblins wun clear.

> *Thistleless fule,*
> *You'll ha'e nocht left*
> *But the hole frae which*
> *Life's struggle is reft!* . . .

Reason ser's nae end but pleasure,
Truth's no' an end but a means
To a wider knowledge o' life
And a keener interest in't.

We wha are poets and artists
Move frae inklin' to inklin',
And live for oor antrin lichtnin's
In the haingles atweenwhiles,

Laich as the feck o' mankind
Whence we breenge in unkennable shapes
> – *Crockats up, hair kaimed to the lift,*
> *And no' to cree legs wi'!* . . .

We're ootward boond frae Scotland.
Guid-bye, fare-ye-weel; guid-bye, fare-ye-weel.
– A' the Scots that ever wur
Gang ootward in a creel.

We're ootward boond frae Scotland.
Guid-bye, fare-ye-weel; guid-bye, fare-ye-weel.
The cross-tap is a monkey-tree
That nane o' us can spiel.

We've never seen the Captain,
But the first mate is a Jew.
We've shipped aboord Eternity.
Adieu, kind freends, adieu! . . .

In the creel or on the gell
O' oor coutribat and ganien,
What gin ithers see or hear
Naething but a gowkstorm?

Gin you stop the galliard
To teach them hoo to dance,
There comes in Corbaudie
And turns their gammons up ! . . .

You vegetable cat's melody !
Your *Concert Miaulant* is
A triumph o' discord shairly,
And suits my fancy fairly
– I'm shair that Scott'll agree
He canna vie wi' this. . . .

Said my body to my mind,
'I've been startled whiles to find,
When Jean has been in bed wi' me,
A kind o' Christianity !'

To my body said my mind,
'But your benmaist thocht you'll find
Was "Bother what I think I feel
– Jean kens the set o' my bluid owre weel,
And lauchs to see me in the creel
O' my courage-bag confined." ' . . .

I wish I kent the physical basis
O' a' life's seemin' airs and graces.

It's queer the thochts a kittled cull
Can lowse or splairgin' glit annul.

Man's spreit is wi' his ingangs twined
In ways that he can ne'er unwind.

A wumman whiles a bawaw gi'es
That clean abaws him gin he sees.

Or wi' a movement o' a leg
Shows'm his mind is juist a geg.

I'se warrant Jean 'ud no' be lang
In findin' whence this thistle sprang.

Mebbe it's juist because I'm no'
Beddit wi' her that gars it grow! ...

A luvin' wumman is a licht[1]
That shows a man his waefu' plicht,
Bleezin' steady on ilka bane,
Wrigglin' sinnen an' twinin' vein,
Or fleerin' quick an' gane again,
And the mair scunnersome the sicht
The mair for love and licht he's fain
Till clear and chitterin' and nesh
Move a' the miseries o' his flesh. ...

O lass, wha see'est me
As I daur hardly see,
I marvel that your bonny een
Are as they hadna seen.

Through a' my self-respect
They see the truth abject
        – *Gin you could pierce their blindin' licht*
        You'd see a fouler sicht! ...

O wha's the bride that cairries the bunch
O' thistles blinterin' white?
Her cuckold bridegroom little dreids
What he sall ken this nicht.

For closer than gudeman can come
And closer to'r than hersel',
Wha didna need her maidenheid
Has wrocht his purpose fell.

[1] Suggested by the French of Edmond Rocher.

O wha's been here afore me, lass,
And hoo did he get in?
    – A man that deed or I was born
    This evil thing has din.

And left, as it were on a corpse,
Your maidenheid to me?
    – Nae lass, gudeman, sin' Time began
    'S hed ony mair to gi'e.

    But I can gi'e ye kindness, lad,
    And a pair o' willin' hands,
    And you sall ha'e my breists like stars,
    My limbs like willow wands,

    And on my lips ye'll heed nae mair,
    And in my hair forget,
    The seed o' a' the men that in
    My virgin womb ha'e met. . . .

Millions o' wimmen bring forth in pain
Millions o' bairns that are no' worth ha'en'.

Wull ever a wumman be big again
Wi's muckle's a Christ? Yech, there's nae sayin'.

Gin that's the best that you ha'e comin',
Fegs but I'm sorry for you, wumman!

Yet a'e thing's certain – Your faith is great.
Whatever happens, you'll no' be blate! . . .

Mary lay in jizzen
As it were claith o' gowd,
But it's in orra duds
Ilka ither bairntime's row'd.

Christ had never toothick,
Christ was never seeck,
But Man's a fiky bairn
Wi' bellythraw, ripples, and worm-i'-the-cheek! . . .

Dae what ye wull ye canna parry
This skeleton-at-the-feast that through the starry
Maze o' the warld's intoxicatin' soiree
Claughts ye, as micht at an affrontit quean
A bastard wean!

Prood mune, ye needna thring your shouder there,
And at your puir get like a snawstorm stare,
It's yours – there's nae denyin't – and I'm shair
You'd no' enjoy the evenin' much the less
Gin you'd but openly confess!

Dod! It's an eaten and a spewed-like thing,
Fell like a little-bodies' changeling,
And it's nae credit t'ye that you s'ud bring
The like to life – yet, gi'en a mither's love,
– Hee, hee! – wha kens hoo't micht improve? . . .

Or is this Heaven, this yalla licht,
And I the aft'rins o' the Earth,
Or sic's in this wanchancy time
May weel fin' sudden birth?

The roots that wi' the worms compete
Hauf-publish me upon the air.
The struggle that divides me still
Is seen fu' plainly there.

The thistle's shank scarce holes the grun',
My grave'll spare nae mair I doot
– *The crack's fu' wide; the shank's fu' strang;*
A' that I was is oot.

My knots o' nerves that struggled sair
Are weel reflected in the herb;
My crookit instincts were like this,
As sterile and acerb.

My self-tormented spirit took
The shape repeated in the thistle;
Sma' beauty jouked my rawny banes
And maze o' gristle.

I seek nae peety, Paraclete,
And, fegs, I think the joke is rich
– Pairt soul, pairt skeleton's come up;
They kentna which was which! . . .

Thou Daith in which my life
Sae vain a thing can seem,
Frae whatna source d'ye borrow
Your devastatin' gleam?

Nae doot that hidden sun
'Ud look fu' wae ana',
Gin I could see it in the licht
That frae the Earth you draw! . . .

Shudderin' thistle, gi'e owre, gi'e owre!
A'body's gi'en in to the facts o' life;
The impossible truth'll triumph at last,
And mock your strife.

Your sallow leafs can never thraw,
Wi' a' their oorie shakin',
Ae doot into the hert o' life
That it may be mistak'n. . . .

O Scotland is
THE barren fig.
Up, carles, up
And roond it jig.

Aula Moses took
A dry stick and
Instantly it
Floo'ered in his hand.

Pu' Scotland up,
And wha can say
It winna bud
And blossom tae.

A miracle's
Oor only chance.
Up, carles, up
And let us dance!

Puir Burns, wha's bouquet like a shot kail blaws
– Will this rouch sicht no' gi'e the orchids pause?
The Gairdens o' the Muses may be braw,
But nane like oors can breenge and eat ana'!

And owre the kailyaird-wa' Dunbar they've flung,
And a' their countrymen that e'er ha'e sung
For ither than ploomen's lugs or to enrichen
Plots on Parnassus set apairt for kitchen.

Ploomen and ploomen's wives – shades o' the Manse
May weel be at the heid o' sic a dance,
As through the polish't ha's o' Europe leads
The rout o' bagpipes, haggis, and sheep's heids!

The vandal Scot! Frae Brankstone's deidly barrow
I struggle yet to free a'e winsome marrow,
To show what Scotland micht ha'e hed instead
O' this preposterous Presbyterian breed.

(Gin Glesca folk are tired o' Hengler,
And still need breid and circuses, there's Spengler,
Or gin ye s'ud need mair than ane to teach ye,
Then learn frae Dostoevski and frae Nietzsche.

And let the lesson be – to be yersel's,
Ye needna fash gin it's to be ocht else.
To be yersel's – and to mak' that worth bein'.
Nae harder job to mortals has been gi'en.

To save your souls fu' mony o' ye are fain,
But deil a dizzen to mak' it worth the daein'.
I widna gi'e five meenits wi' Dunbar
For a' the millions o' ye as ye are.)

I micht ha'e been contentit wi' the Rose
Gin I'd had ony reason to suppose
That what the English dae can e'er mak' guid
For what Scots dinna – and first and foremaist should.

I micht ha'e been contentit – gin the feck
O' my ain folk had grovelled wi' less respec',
But their obsequious devotion
Made it for me a criminal emotion.

I micht ha'e been contentit – ere I saw
That there were fields on which it couldna draw,
(While strang-er roots ran under't) and a'e threid
O't drew frae Scotland a' that it could need,

And left the maist o' Scotland fallow
(Save for the patch on which the kail-blades wallow),
And saw hoo ither countries' genius drew
Elements like mine that in a rose ne'er grew. . . .

Gin the threid haud'n us to the rose were snapt,
There's no' a'e petal o't that 'ud be clapt.
A' Scotland gi'es gangs but to jags or stalk,
The bloom is English – and 'ud ken nae lack ! . . .

O drumlie clood o' crudity and cant,
Obliteratin' as the Easter rouk
That rows up frae the howes and droons the heichs,
And turns the country to a faceless spook,

Like blurry shapes o' landmarks in the haar
The bonny idiosyncratic place-names loom,
Clues to the vieve and maikless life that's lain
Happit for centuries in an alien gloom. . . .

Eneuch! For noo I'm in the mood,
Scotland, responsive to my thoughts,
Lichts mile by mile, as my ain nerves,
Frae Maidenkirk to John o' Groats!

What are prophets and priests and kings,
What's ocht to the people o' Scotland?
Speak – and Cruivie'll goam at you,
Gilsanquhar jalouse you're dottlin!

And Edinburgh and Glasgow
Are like ploomen in a pub.
They want to hear o' naething
But their ain foul hubbub. . . .

The fules are richt; an extra thocht
Is neither here nor there.
Oor lives may differ as they like
– The self-same fate we share.

And whiles I wish I'd nae mair sense
Than Cruivie and Gilsanquhar,
And envy their rude health and curse
My gnawin' canker.

Guid sakes, ye dinna need to pass
Ony exam. to dee
– Daith canna tell a common flech
Frae a performin' flea! . . .

It sets you weel to slaver
To let sic gaadies fa'
– *The mune's the muckle white whale*
I seek in vain to kaa!

The Earth's my mastless samyn,
The thistle my ruined sail.
– Le'e go as you maun in the end,
And droon in your plumm o' ale ! . . .

Clear keltie aff an' fill again
Withoot corneigh bein' cryit,
The drink's aye best that follows a drink.
Clear keltie aff and try it.

Be't whisky gill or penny wheep,
Or ony ither lotion,
We 'bood to ha'e a thimblefu' first,
And syne we'll toom an ocean ! . . .

'To Luna at the Craidle-and-Coffin
To sof'n her hert if owt can sof'n : –

Auld bag o' tricks, ye needna come
And think to stap me in your womb.

You needna fash to rax and strain.
Carline, I'll *no'* be born again

In ony brat you can produce.
Carline, gi'e owre – O what's the use?

You pay nae heed but plop me in,
Syne shove me oot, and winna be din

– Owre and owre, the same auld trick,
Cratur withoot climacteric ! . . .

'Noo Cutty Sark's tint that ana',
And dances in her skin – Ha ! Ha !

I canna ride awa' like Tam,
But e'en maun bide juist whaur I am.

I canna ride – and gin I could,
I'd sune be sorry I hedna stude,

For less than a' there is to see
'll never be owre muckle for me.

Cutty, gin you've mair to strip,
Aff wi't, lass – and let it rip!'...

Ilka pleesure I can ha'e
Ends like a dram ta'en yesterday.

And tho' to ha'e it I am lorn
– What better 'ud I be the morn?...

My belly on the gantrees there,
The spigot frae my cullage,
And wow but how the fizzin' yill
In spilth increased the ullage!

I was an anxious barrel, lad,
When first they tapped my bung.
They whistled me up, yet thro' the lift
My freaths like rainbows swung.

Waesucks, a pride for ony bar,
The boast o' barleyhood,
Like Noah's Ark abune the faem
Maun float, a gantin' cude,

For I was thrawn fu' cock owre sune,
And wi' a single jaw
I made the pub a blindin' swelth,
And how'd the warld awa'!...

What forest worn to the back-hauf's this,
What Eden brocht doon to a bean-swaup?
The thistle's to earth as the man
In the mune's to the mune, puir chap.

The haill warld's barkin' and fleein',
And this is its echo and aiker,
A soond that arrears in my lug,
Herrin'-banein' back to its maker,

A swaw like a flaw in a jewel
Or *nadryv*[1] jaloused in a man,
Or Creation unbiggit again
To the draucht wi' which it began. . . .

Abordage o' this toom houk's nae mowse.
It munks and's ill to lay haud o',
As gin a man ettled to ride
On the shouders o' his ain shadow.

I canna biel't; tho' steekin' an e'e,
Tither's munkie wi' munebeam for knool in't,
For there's nae sta'-tree and the brute's awa'
Wi' me kinkin' like foudrie ahint. . . .

Sae Eternity'll buff nor stye
For Time, and shies at a touch, man;
Yet aye in a belth o' Thocht
Comes alist like the Fleein' Dutchman. . . .

As the worms'll breed in my corpse until
It's like a rice-puddin', the thistle
Has made an eel-ark o' the lift
Whaur elvers like skirl-in-the-pan sizzle,

Like a thunder-plump on the sunlicht,
Or the slounge o' daith on my dreams,
Or as to a fair forfochen man
A breedin' wife's beddiness seems,

[1] Tragical crack (Dostoevski's term).

Saragossa Sea, St. Vitus' Dance,
A *cafard* in a brain's despite,
Or lunacy that thinks a' else
Is loony – and is dootless richt ! . . .

Gin my thochts that circle like hobby-horses
'Udna loosen to nightmares I'd sleep;
For nocht but a chowed core's left whaur Jerusalem lay
Like aipples in a heap ! . . .

It's a queer thing to tryst wi' a wumman
When the boss o' her body's gane,
And her banes in the wund as she comes
Dirl like a raff o' rain.

It's a queer thing to tryst wi' a wumman
When her ghaist frae abuneheid keeks,
And you see in the licht o't that a'
You ha'e o'r's the cleiks. . . .

What forest worn to the backhauf's this,
What Eden brocht doon to a bean-swaup?
– A' the ferlies o' natur' spring frae the earth,
And into't again maun drap.

Animals, vegetables, what are they a'
But as thochts that a man has ha'en?
And Earth sall be like a toom skull syne.
– Whaur'll its thochts be then? . . .

The munelicht is my knowledge o' mysel',
Mysel' the thistle in the munelicht seen,
And hauf my shape has fund itsel' in thee
And hauf my knowledge in your piercin' een.

E'en as the munelicht's borrowed frae the sun
I ha'e my knowledge o' mysel' frae thee,
And much that nane but thee can e'er mak' clear,
Save my licht's frae the source, is dark to me.

Your acid tongue, vieve lauchter, and hawk's een,
And bluid that drobs like hail to quicken me,
Can turn the mid-day black or midnicht bricht,
Lowse me frae licht or eke frae darkness free.

Bite into me forever mair and lift
Me clear o' chaos in a great relief
Till, like this thistle in the munelicht growin',
I brak in roses owre a hedge o' grief. . . .

I am like Burns, and ony wench
Can ser' me for a time.
Licht's in them a' – in some a sun,
In some the merest skime.

I'm no' like Burns, and weel I ken,
Tho' ony wench can ser',
It's no' through mony but through yin
That ony man wuns fer. . . .

I weddit thee frae fause love, lass,
To free thee and to free mysel';
But man and wumman tied for life
True can be and truth can tell.

Pit ony couple in a knot
They canna lowse and needna try,
And mair o' love at last they'll ken
– If ocht ! – than joy'll alane descry.

For them as for the beasts, my wife,
A's fer frae dune when pleesure's owre,
And coontless difficulties gar
Ilk hert discover a' its power.

I dinna say that bairns alane
Are true love's task – a sairer task
Is aiblins to create oorsels
As we can be – it's that I ask.

Create oorsels, syne bairns, syne race.
Sae on the cod I see't in you
Wi' Maidenkirk to John o' Groats
The bosom that you draw me to.

And nae Scot wi' a wumman lies,
But I am he and ken, as 'twere
A stage I've passed as he maun pass't,
Gin he grows up, his way wi' her! . . .

A'thing wi' which a man
Can intromit's a wumman,
And can, and s'ud, become
As intimate and human.

And Jean's nae mair my wife
Than whisky is at times,
Or munelicht or a thistle
Or kittle thochts or rhymes.

He's no a man ava',
And lacks a proper pride,
Gin less than a' the warld
Can ser' him for a bride! . . .

Use, then, my lust for whisky and for thee,
Your function but to be and let me be
And see and let me see.

If in a lesser licht I grope my way,
Or use't for ends that need your different ray
Whelm't in superior day.

Then aye increase and ne'er withdraw your licht.
– Gin it shows either o's in hideous plicht,
What gain to turn't to nicht?

Whisky mak's Heaven or Hell and whiles mells baith,
Disease is but the privy torch o' Daith,
– But sex reveals life, faith!

I need them a' and maun be aye at strife.
Daith and ayont are nocht but pairts o' life.
– Then be life's licht, my wife! . . .

Love often wuns free
In lust to be strangled,
Or love, o' lust free,
In law's sairly tangled.

And it's ill to tell whether
Law or lust is to blame
When love's chokit up
– It comes a' to the same.

In this sorry growth
Whatna beauty is tint
That freed o't micht find
A waur fate than is in't? . . .

Yank oot your orra boughs, my hert!

God gied man speech and speech created thocht,
He gied man speech but to the Scots gied nocht
Barrin' this clytach that they've never brocht
To onything but sic a Blottie O
As some bairn's copybook micht show,

A spook o' soond that frae the unkent grave
In which oor nation lies loups up to wave
Sic leprous chuns as tatties have
That cellar-boond send spindles gropin'
Towards ony hole that's open,

Like waesome fingers in the dark that think
They still may widen the ane and only chink
That e'er has gi'en mankind a blink
O' Hope – tho' ev'n in that puir licht
They s'ud ha'e seen their hopeless plicht.

This puir relation o' my topplin' mood,
This country cousin, streak o' churl-bluid,
This hopeless airgh 'twixt a' we can and should,
This Past that like Astarte's sting I feel,
This arrow in Achilles' heel.

Yank oot your orra boughs, my hert!

Mebbe we're in a vicious circle cast,
Mebbe there's limits we can ne'er get past,
Mebbe we're sentrices that at the last
Are flung aside, and no' the pillars and props
O' Heaven foraye as in oor hopes.

Oor growth at least nae steady progress shows,
Genius in mankind like an antrin rose
Abune a jungly waste o' effort grows,
But to Man's purpose it mak's little odds.
And seems irrelevant to God's. . . .

Eneuch? Then here you are. Here's the haill story.
Life's connached shapes too'er up in croons o' glory,
Perpetuatin', natheless, in their gory
Colour the endless sacrifice and pain
That to their makin's gane.

The roses like the saints in Heaven treid
Triumphant owre the agonies o' their breed.
And wag fu' mony a celestial heid
Abune the thorter-ills o' leaf and prick
In which they ken the feck maun stick.

Yank oot your orra boughs, my hert!

A mongrel growth, jumble o' disproportions,
Whirlin' in its incredible contortions,
Or wad-be client that an auld whore shuns,
Wardin' her wizened orange o' a bosom
Frae importunities sae gruesome.

Or new diversion o' the hormones
Mair fond o' procreation than the Mormons,
And fetchin' like a devastatin' storm on's
A' the uncouth dilemmas o' oor natur'
Objectified in vegetable maitter.

Yank oot your orra boughs, my hert!

And heed nae mair the foolish cries that beg
You slice nae mair to aff or pu' to leg,
You skitin' duffer that gars a'body fleg
– What tho' you ding the haill warld oot o' joint
Wi' a skier to cover-point!

Yank oot your orra boughs, my hert!

There *was* a danger – and it's weel I see't –
Had brocht ye like Mallarmé to defeat: –
'Mon doute, amas de nuit ancienne, s'achève
En maint rameau subtil, qui, demeuré les vrais
Bois mêmes, prouve, hélas! que bien seul je m'offrais
Pour triomphe la faute idéale de roses.'[1]

Yank oot your orra boughs, my hert!

I love to muse upon the skill that gangs
To mak' the simplest thing that Earth displays,
The eident life that ilka atom thrangs,
And uses it in the appointit ways,
And a' the endless brain that nocht escapes
That myriad moves them to inimitable shapes.

[1] The line which precedes these in Mallarmé's poem is 'Aimai-je un rêve?' and Wilfrid Thorley translates the passage thus:

> 'Loved I Love's counterfeit?
> My doubts, begotten of the long night's heat,
> Dislimn the woodland till my triumph shows
> As the flawed shadow of a frustrate rose.'

Nor to their customed form nor ony ither
New to Creation, by man's cleverest mind,
A' needfu' particles first brocht thegither,
Could they wi' timeless labour be combined.
There's nocht that Science yet's begood to see
In hauf its deemless detail or its destiny.

Oor een gi'e answers based on pairt-seen facts
That beg a' questions, to ebb minds' content,
But hoo a'e feature or the neist attracts,
Wi' millions mair unseen, wha kens what's meant
By human brains and to what ends may tell
– For naething's seen or kent that's near a thing itsel'!

Let whasae vaunts his knowledge then and syne
Sets up a God and kens *His* purpose tae
Tell me what's gart a'e strain o' maitter twine
In sic an extraordinary way,
And what God's purpose wi' the Thistle is
– I'll aiblins ken what he and his God's worth by this.

I've watched it lang and hard until I ha'e
A certain symp'thy wi' its orra ways
And pride in its success, as weel I may,
In growin' exactly as its instinct says,
Save in sae fer as thwarts o' weather or grun'
Or man or ither foes ha'e'ts aims perchance fordone.

But I can form nae notion o' the spirit
That gars it tak' the difficult shape it does,
Nor judge the merit yet or the demerit
O' this detail or that sae fer as it goes
T' advance the cause that gied it sic a guise
As maun ha'e pleased its Maker wi' a gey surprise.

The craft that hit upon the reishlin' stalk,
Wi'ts gausty leafs and a' its datchie jags,

And spired it syne in seely floo'ers to brak
Like sudden lauchter owre its fousome rags
Jouks me, sardonic lover, in the routh
O' contrairies that jostle in this dumfoondrin' growth.

What strength 't'ud need to pit its roses oot,
Or double them in number or in size,
He canna tell wha canna plumb the root,
And learn what's gar't its present state arise,
And what the limits are that ha'e been put
To change in thistles, and why – and what a change 'ud boot. . . .

I saw a rose come loupin' oot[1]
Frae a camsteerie plant.
O wha'd ha'e thocht yon puir stock had
Sic an inhabitant?

For centuries it ran to waste,
Wi' pin-heid floo'ers at times.
O'ts hidden hert o' beauty they
Were but the merest skimes.

Yet while it ran to wud and thorns,
The feckless growth was seekin'
Some airt to cheenge its life until
A' in a rose was beekin'.

'Is there nae way in which my life
Can mair to floo'erin' come,
And bring its waste on shank and jags
Doon to a minimum?

It's hard to struggle as I maun
For scrunts o' blooms like mine,
While blossom covers ither plants
As by a knack divine.

[1] The General Strike (May 1926).

'What hinders me unless I lack
Some needfu' discipline?
– I wis I'll bring my orra life
To beauty or I'm din !'

Sae ran the thocht that hid ahint
The thistle's ugsome guise,
'I'll brak' the habit o' my life
A worthier to devise.

'My nobler instincts sall nae mair
This contrair shape be gi'en.
I sall nae mair consent to live
A life no' fit to be seen.'

Sae ran the thocht that hid ahint
The thistle's ugsome guise,
Till a' at aince a rose loupt oot
– I watched it wi' surprise.

A rose loupt oot and grew, until
It was ten times the size
O' ony rose the thistle afore
Hed heistit to the skies.

And still it grew till a' the buss
Was hidden in its flame.
I never saw sae braw a floo'er
As yon thrawn stock became.

And still it grew until it seemed
The haill braid earth had turned
A reid reid rose that in the lift
Like a ball o' fire burned.

The waefu' clay was fire aince mair,
As Earth had been resumed
Into God's mind, frae which sae lang
To grugous state 'twas doomed.

Syne the rose shrivelled suddenly
As a balloon is burst;
The thistle was a ghaistly stick,
As gin it had been curst.

Was it the ancient vicious sway
Imposed itsel' again,
Or nerve owre weak for new emprise
That made the effort vain,

A coward strain in that lorn growth
That wrocht the sorry trick?
– The thistle like a rocket soared
And cam' doon like the stick.

Like grieshuckle the roses glint,
The leafs like farles hing,
As roond a hopeless sacrifice
Earth draws its barren ring.

The dream o' beauty's dernin' yet
Ahint the ugsome shape.
– Vain dream that in a pinheid here
And there can e'er escape!

The vices that defeat the dream
Are in the plant itsel',
And till they're purged its virtues maun
In pain and misery dwell.

Let Deils rejoice to see the waste,
The fond hope brocht to nocht.
The thistle in their een is as
A favourite lust they've wrocht.

The orderin' o' the thistle means
Nae richtin' o't to them.
Its loss they ca' a law, its thorns
A fule's fit diadem.

And still the idiot nails itsel'
To its ain crucifix,
While here a rose and there a rose
Jaups oot abune the pricks.

Like connoisseurs the Deils gang roond
And praise its attitude,
Till on the Cross the silly Christ
To fidge fu' fain's begood!

Like connoisseurs the Deils gang roond
Wi' ready platitude.
It's no' sae dear as vinegar,
And every bit as good!

The bitter taste is on my tongue,
I chowl my chafts, and pray
'Let God forsake me noo and no'
Staund connoisseur-like tae!' ...

The language that but sparely floo'ers
And maistly gangs to weed;
The thocht o' Christ and Calvary
Aye liddenin' in my heid;
And a' the dour provincial thocht
That merks the Scottish breed
– These are the thistle's characters,
To argie there's nae need.
Hoo weel my verse embodies
The thistle you can read!
– But will a Scotsman never
Frae this vile growth be freed? ...

O ilka man alive is like
A quart that's squeezed into a pint
(A maist unScottish-like affair!)
Or like the little maid that showed
Me into a still sma'er room.

What use to let a sunrise fade
To ha'e anither like't the morn,
Or let a generation pass
That ane nae better may succeed,
Or wi' a' Time's machinery
Keep naething new aneth the sun,
Or change things oot o' kennin' that
They may be a' the mair the same?

The thistle in the wund dissolves
In lichtnin's as shook foil gi'es way
In sudden splendours, or the flesh
As Daith lets slip the infinite soul;
And syne it's like a sunrise tint
In grey o' day, or love and life
That in a cloody blash o' sperm
Undae the warld to big't again,
Or like a pickled foetus that
Nae man feels ocht in common wi'
– But micht as easily ha' been!
Or like a corpse a soul set free
Scunners to think it tenanted
– And little recks that but for it
It never micht ha' been at a',
Like love frae lust and God frae man!

The wasted seam that dries like stairch
And pooders aff, that micht ha' been
A warld o' men and syne o' Gods;
The grey that haunts the vievest green;
The wrang side o' the noblest scene
We ne'er can whummle to oor een,
As 'twere the hinderpairts o' God,
His face aye turned the opposite road,
Or's neth the floo'ers the drumlie clods
Frae which they come at sicna odds,
As a' Earth's magic frae a spirt,
In shame and secrecy, o' dirt!

Then shak' nae mair in silly life,
Nor stand impossible as Daith,
Incredible as a'thing is
Inside or oot owre closely scanned.
As mithers aften think the warld
O' bairns that ha'e nae end or object,
Or lovers think their sweethearts made
Yince-yirn – wha ha'ena waled the lave,
Maikless – when they are naebody,
Or men o' ilka sort and kind
Are prood o' thochts they ca' their ain,
That nameless millions had afore
And nameless millions yet'll ha'e,
And that were never worth the ha'en',
Or Cruivie's 'latest' story or
Gilsanquhar's vows to sign the pledge,
Or's if I thocht maist whisky *was*,
Or failed to coont the cheenge I got,
Sae wad I be gin I rejoiced,
Or didna ken my place, in thee.

O stranglin' rictus, sterile spasm,
Thou stricture in the groins o' licht,
Thou ootrie gangrel frae the wilds
O' chaos fenced frae Eden yet
By the unsplinterable wa'
O' munebeams like a bleeze o' swords!

Nae chance lunge cuts the Gordian knot,
Nor sall the belly find relief
In wha's entangled moniplies
Creation like a stoppage jams,
Or in whose loins the mapamound
Runkles in strawns o' bubos whaur
The generations gravel.
The soond o' water winnin' free,
The sicht o' licht that braks the rouk,

The thocht o' every thwart owrecome
Are in my ears and een and brain,
In whom the bluid is spilt in stour,
In whom a' licht in darkness fails,
In whom the mystery o' life
Is to a wretched weed bewrayed.

But let my soul increase in me,
God dwarfed to enter my puir thocht
Expand to his true size again,
And protoplasm's look befit
The nature o' its destiny,
And seed and sequence be nae mair
Incongruous to ane anither,
And liquor packed impossibly
Mak' pint-pot an eternal well,
And art be relevant to life,
And poets mair than dominies yet,
And ends nae langer tint in means,
Nor forests hidden by their trees,
Nor men be sacrificed alive
In foonds o' fates designed for them,
Nor mansions o' the soul stand toom
Their owners in their cellars trapped,
Nor a' a people's genius be
A rumple-fyke in Heaven's doup,
While Calvinism uses her
To breed a minister or twa!

A black leaf owre a white leaf twirls,
A grey leaf flauchters in atween,
Sae ply my thochts aboot the stem
O' loppert slime frae which they spring.
The thistle like a snawstorm drives,
Or like a flicht o' swallows lifts,
Or like a swarm o' midges hings,
A plague o' moths, a starry sky,

But's naething but a thistle yet,
And still the puzzle stands unsolved.
Beauty and ugliness alike,
And life and daith and God and man,
Are aspects o't but nane can tell
The secret that I'd fain find oot
O' this bricht hive, this sorry weed,
The tree that fills the universe,
Or like a reistit herrin' crines.

Gin I was sober I micht think
It was like something drunk men see!

The necromancy in my bluid
Through a' the gamut cheenges me
O' dwarf and giant, foul and fair,
But winna let me be mysel'
– My mither's womb that reins me still
Until I tae can prick the witch
And 'Wumman' cry wi' Christ at last,
'Then what hast thou to do wi' me?'

The tug-o'-war is in me still,
The dog-hank o' the flesh and soul –
Faither in Heaven, what gar'd ye tak'
A village slut to mither me,
Your mongrel o' the fire and clay?
The trollop and the Deity share
My writhen form as tho' I were
A picture o' the time they had
When Licht rejoiced to file itsel'
And Earth upshuddered like a star.

A drucken hizzie gane to bed
Wi' three-in-ane and ane-in-three.

O fain I'd drink until I saw
Scotland a ferlie o' delicht,

And fain bide drunk nor ha'e't recede
Into a shrivelled thistle syne,
As when a sperklin' tide rins oot,
And leaves a wreath o' rubbish there!

Wull a' the seas gang dry at last
(As dry as I am gettin' noo),
Or wull they aye come back again,
Seilfu' as my neist drink to me,
Or as the sunlicht to the mune,
Or as the bonny sangs o' men,
Wha're but puir craturs in themsels,
And save when genius mak's them drunk,
As donnert as their audiences,
– As dreams that mak' a tramp a king,
A madman sane to his ain mind,
Or what a Scotsman thinks himsel',
Tho' naethin' but a thistle kyths.

The mair I drink the thirstier yet,
And whiles when I'm alowe wi' booze,
I'm like God's sel' and clad in fire,
And ha'e a Pentecost like this.
O wad that I could aye be fou',
And no' come back as aye I maun
To naething but a fule that nane
'Ud credit wi' sic thochts as thae,
A fule that kens they're empty dreams!

Yet but fer drink and drink's effects,
The yeast o' God that barms in us,
We micht as weel no' be alive.
It maitters not what drink is ta'en,
The barley bree, ambition, love,
Or Guid or Evil workin' in's,
Sae lang's we feel like souls set free
Frae mortal coils and speak in tongues
We dinna ken and never wull,

And find a merit in oorsels,
In Cruivies and Gilsanquhars tae,
And see the thistle as ocht but that!

For wha o's ha'e the thistle's poo'er
To see we're worthless and believe 't:

A'thing that ony man can be's
A mockery o' his soul at last.
The mair it shows't the better, and
I'd suner be a tramp than king,
Lest in the pride o' place and poo'er
I e'er forgot my waesomeness.
Sae to debauchery and dirt,
And to disease and daith I turn,
Sin' otherwise my seemin' worth
'Ud block my view o' what is what,
And blin' me to the irony
O' bein a grocer 'neth the sun,
A lawyer gin Justice ope'd her een,
A pedant like an ant promoted,
A parson buttonholin' God,
Or ony cratur o' the Earth
Sma'-bookt to John Smith, High Street, Perth,
Or sic like vulgar gaffe o' life
Sub specie aeternitatis –
Nae void can fleg me hauf as much
As bein' mysel', whate'er I am,
Or, waur, bein' onybody else.

The nervous thistle's shiverin' like
A horse's skin aneth a cleg,
Or Northern Lichts or lustres o'
A soul that Daith has fastened on,
Or mornin' efter the nicht afore.

Shudderin' thistle, gi'e owre, gi'e owre....

Grey sand is churnin' in my lugs
The munelicht flets, and gantin' there
The grave o' a' mankind's laid bare
– On Hell itsel' the drawback rugs!

Nae man can ken his hert until
The tide o' life uncovers it,
And horror-struck he sees a pit
Returnin' life can never fill! . . .

Thou art the facts in ilka airt
That breenge into infinity,
Criss-crossed wi' coontless ither facts
Nae man can follow, and o' which
He is himsel' a helpless pairt,
Held in their tangle as he were
A stick-nest in Ygdrasil!

The less man sees the mair he is
Content wi't, but the mair he sees
The mair he kens hoo little o'
A' that there is he'll ever see,
And hoo it mak's confusion aye
The waur confoondit till at last
His brain inside his heid is like
Ariadne wi' an empty pirn,
Or like a birlin' reel frae which
A whale has rived the line awa'.

What better's a forhooied nest
Than shasloch scattered owre the grun'?

O hard it is for man to ken
He's no creation's goal nor yet
A benefitter by't at last –
A means to ends he'll never ken,
And as to michtier elements
The slaughtered brutes he eats to him
Or forms o' life owre sma' to see
Wi' which his heedless body swarms,

And a' man's thocht nae mair to them
Than ony moosewob to a man,
His Heaven to them the blinterin' o'
A snail-trail on their closet wa'!

For what's an atom o' a twig
That tak's a billion to an inch
To a' the routh o' shoots that mak'
The bygrowth o' the Earth aboot
The michty trunk o' Space that spreids
Ramel o' licht that ha'e nae end,
– The trunk wi' centuries for rings,
Comets for fruit, November shoo'ers
For leafs that in its Autumns fa'
– And Man at maist o' sic a twig
Ane o' the coontless atoms is!

My sinnens and my veins are but
As muckle o' a single shoot
Wha's fibre I can ne'er unwaft
O' my wife's flesh and mither's flesh
And a' the flesh o' humankind,
And revelled thrums o' beasts and plants
As gangs to mak' twixt birth and daith
A'e sliver for a microscope;
And a' the life o' Earth to be
Can never lift frae underneath
The shank o' which oor destiny's pairt
As heich's to stand forenenst the trunk
Stupendous as a windlestrae!

I'm under nae delusions, fegs!
The whuppin' sooker at wha's tip
Oor little point o' view appears,
A midget coom o' continents
Wi' blebs o' oceans set, sends up
The braith o' daith as weel as life,
And we maun braird anither tip

Oot owre us ere we wither tae,
And join the sentrice skeleton
As coral insects big their reefs.

What is the tree? As fer as Man's
Concerned it disna maitter
Gin but a giant thistle 'tis
That spreids eternal mischief there,
As I'm inclined to think.
Ruthless it sends its solid growth
Through mair than he can e'er conceive,
And braks his warlds abreid and rives
His Heavens to tatters on its horns.

The nature or the purpose o't
He needna fash to spier, for he
Is destined to be sune owre grown
And hidden wi' the parent wud
The spreidin' boughs in darkness hap,
And a' its future life'll be
Ootwith'm as he's ootwith his banes.

Juist as man's skeleton has left
Its ancient ape-like shape ahint,
Sae states o' mind in turn gi'e way
To different states, and quickly seem
Impossible to later men,
And Man's mind in its final shape,
Or lang'll seem a monkey's spook,
And, strewth, to me the vera thocht
O' Thocht already's fell like that!
Yet still the cracklin' thorns persist
In fitba' match and peepy show,
To antic hay a dog-fecht's mair
Than Jacob *v.* the Angel,
And through a cylinder o' wombs,
A star reflected in a dub,
I see as 'twere my ain wild harns
The ripple o' Eve's moniplies.

And faith ! yestreen in Cruivie's een
Life rocked at midnicht in a tree,
And in Gilsanquhar's glower I saw
The taps o' waves 'neth which the warld
Ga'ed rowin' like a jeelyfish,
And whiles I canna look at Jean
For fear I'd seen the sunlicht turn
Worm-like into the glaur again !

A black leaf owre a white leaf twirls,
My liver's shadow on my soul,
And clots o' bluid loup oot frae stems
That back into the jungle rin,
Or in the waters underneath
Kelter like seaweed, while I hear
Abune the thunder o' the flood,
The voice that aince commanded licht
Sing 'Scots Wha Ha'e' and hyne awa'
Like Cruivie up a different glen,
And leave me like a mixture o'
A wee Scotch nicht and Judgment Day,
The bile, the Bible, and the *Scotsman*,
Poetry and pigs – Infernal Thistle,
Damnition haggis I've spewed up,
And syne return to like twa dogs !
Blin' Proteus wi' leafs or hands
Or flippers ditherin' in the lift
– Thou Samson in a warld that has
Nae pillars but your cheengin' shapes
That dung doon, rise in ither airts
Like windblawn reek frae smoo'drin' ess !
– Hoo lang maun I gi'e aff your forms
O' plants and beasts and men and Gods
And like a doited Atlas bear
This steeple o' fish, this eemis warld,
Or, maniac heid wi' snakes for hair,
A Maenad, ape Aphrodite,
And scunner the Eternal sea?

Man needna fash and even noo
The cells that mak' a'e silver wi'm,
The threidy knit he's woven wi',
'Ud fain destroy what sicht he has
O' this puir transitory stage,
Yet tho' he kens the fragment is
O' little worth he e'er can view,
Jalousin' it's a cheatrie weed,
He tyauves wi' a' his micht and main
To keep his sicht despite his kind
Conspirin' as their nature is
'Gainst ocht wi' better sicht than theirs.

What gars him strive? He canna tell –
It may be nocht but cussedness.
– At best he hopes for little mair
Than his suspicions to confirm,
To mock the sicht he hains sae weel
At last wi' a' he sees wi' it,
Yet, thistle or no', whate'er its end,
Aiblins the force that mak's it grow
And lets him see a kennin' mair
Than ither folk and fend his sicht
Agen their jealous plots awhile,
'll use the poo'ers it seems to waste,
This purpose ser'd, in ither ways,
That may be better worth the bein'
– Or sae he dreams, syne mocks his dream
Till Life grows sheer awa' frae him,
And bratts o' darkness plug his een.

It may be nocht but cussedness,
But I'm content gin a' my thocht
Can dae nae mair than let me see,
Free frae desire o' happiness,
The foolish faiths o' ither men
In breedin', industry, and War,
Religion, Science, or ocht else

Gang smash – when I ha'e nane mysel',
Or better gin I share them tae,
Or mind at least a time I did!

Aye, this is Calvary – to bear
Your Cross wi'in you frae the seed,
And feel it grow by slow degrees
Until it rends your flesh apairt,
And turn, and see your fellow-men
In similar case but sufferin' less
Thro' bein' mair wudden frae the stert! . . .

I'm fu' o' a stickit God.
THAT'S what's the maitter wi' me,
Jean has stuck sic a fork in the wa'
That I row in agonie.

Mary never let dab.
SHE was a canny wumman.
She hedna a gaw in Joseph at a'
But, wow, this seecund comin'! . . .

Narodbogonosets[1] are my folk tae,
But in a sma' way nooadays –
A faitherly God wi' a lang white beard,
Or painted Jesus in a haze
O' blue and gowd, a gird aboot his heid
Or some sic thing. It's been a sair come-doon,
And the trade's nocht to what it was.
Unnatural practices are the cause.
Baith bairns and God'll be obsolete soon
(The twaesome gang thegither), and forsooth
Scotland turn Eliot's waste – the Land o' Drouth.

But even as the stane the builders rejec'
Becomes the corner-stane, the time may be
When Scotland sall find oot its destiny,
And yield the *vse-chelovek*[2]

---

[1] God-bearers.   [2] The All-Man or Pan-Human.

– At a' events, owre Europe flaught atween,
My whim (and mair than whim) it pleases
To seek the haund o' Russia as a freen'
In workin' oot mankind's great synthesis. . . .

Melville[1] (a Scot) kent weel hoo Christ's
Corrupted into creeds malign,
Begotten strife's pernicious brood
That claims for patron Him Divine.
(The Kirk in Scotland still I cry
Crooks whaur it canna crucify!)

Christ, bleedin' like the thistle's roses,
He saw – as I in similar case –
Maistly, in beauty and in fear,
'Ud 'paralyse the nobler race,
Smite or suspend, perplex, deter,
And, tortured, prove the torturer.'

And never mair a Scot sall tryst,
Abies on Calvary, wi' Christ,
Unless, mebbe, a poem like this'll
Exteriorise things in a thistle,
And gi'e him in this form forlorn
What Melville socht in vain frae Hawthorne. . . .

Spirit o' strife, destroy in turn
Syne this fule's Paradise, syne that;
In thee's in Calvaries that owrecome
Daith efter Daith let me be caught,

Or in the human form that hauds
Us in its ignominious thrall,
While on brute needs oor souls attend
Until disease and daith end all

[1] Herman Melville.

Or in the grey deluded brain,
Reflectin' in anither field
The torments o' its parent flesh
In thocht-preventin' thocht concealed,

Or still in curst impossible mould,
Last thistle-shape men think to tak',
The soul, frae flesh and thocht set free,
On Heaven's strait if unseen rack.

There may be heicher forms in which
We can nae mair oor plicht define,
Because the agonies involved
'll bring us their ain anodyne.

Yet still we suffer and still sall,
Altho', puir fules, we mayna ken 't
As lang as like the thistle we
In coil and in recoil are pent.

And ferrer than mankind can look
Ghast shapes that free but to transfix
Twine rose-crooned in their agonies,
And strive agen the endless pricks.

The dooble play that bigs and braks
In endless victory and defeat
Is in your spikes and roses shown,
And a' my soul is haggar'd wi't. . . .

Be like the thistle, O my soul,
Heedless o' praise and quick to tak' affront,
And growin' like a mockery o' a'
Maist life can want or thole,
And manifest forevermair
Contempt o' ilka goal.

O' ilka goal – save ane alane;
To be yoursel', whatever that may be.
And as contemptuous o' that,
Kennin' nocht's worth the ha'en',
But certainty that nocht can be,
And hoo that certainty to gain.

For this you still maun grow and grope
In the abyss wi' ever-deepenin' roots
That croon your scunner wi' the grue
O' hopeless hope
– And gin the abyss is bottomless,
Your growth'll never stop! . . .

What earthquake chitters oot
In the Thistle's oorie shape,
What gleids o' central fire
In its reid heids escape,
And whatna coonter forces
In growth and ingrowth graip
In an eternal clinch
In this ootcuissen form
That winna be outcast,
But triumphs at the last
(Owre a' abies itsel'
As fer as we can tell,
Sin' frae the Eden o' the world
Ilka man in turn is hurled,
And ilka gairden rins to waste
That was ever to his taste)?

O keep the Thistle 'yont the wa'
Owre which your skeletons you'll thraw.

I, in the Thistle's land,
As you[1] in Russia where
Struggle in giant form
Proceeds for evermair,

[1] Dostoevski.

In my sma' measure 'bood
Address a similar task,
And for a share o' your
Appallin' genius ask.

Wha built in revelations
What maist men in reserves
(And only men confound!)
A better gift deserves
Frae ane wha like hissel
(As ant-heap unto mountain)
Needs big his life upon
The everloupin' fountain
That frae the Dark ascends
Whaur Life begins, Thocht ends
– A better gift deserves
Than thae wheen yatterin' nerves!

For mine's the clearest insicht
O' man's facility
For constant self-deception,
And hoo his mind can be
But as a floatin' iceberg
That hides aneth the sea
Its bulk: and hoo frae depths
O' an unfaddomed flood
Tensions o' nerves arise
And humours o' the blood
– Keethin's nane can trace
To their original place.

Hoo mony men to mak' a man
It tak's he kens wha kens Life's plan.

But there are flegsome deeps
Whaur the soul o' Scotland sleeps
That I to bottom need
To wauk Guid kens what deid,

Play at stertle-a-stobie,
Wi' nation's dust for hobby,
Or wi' God's sel' commerce
For the makin' o' a verse.

'Melville, sea-compelling man,
Before whose wand Leviathan
Rose hoary-white upon the Deep,'[1]
What thou hast sown I fain 'ud reap
O' knowledge 'yont the human mind
In keepin' wi' oor Scottish kind,
And, thanks to thee, may aiblins reach
To what this Russian has to teach,
Closer than ony ither Scot,
Closer to me than my ain thocht,
Closer than my ain braith to me,
As close as to the Deity
Approachable in whom appears
This Christ o' the neist thoosand years.

As frae your baggit wife
You turned whenever able,
And often when you werena,
Unto the gamin' table,
And opened wide to ruin
Your benmaist hert, aye brewin'
A horror o' whatever
Seemed likely to deliver
You frae the senseless strife
In which alane is life,
– As Burns in Edinburgh
Breenged arse-owre-heid thoro'
A' *it* could be the spur o'
To pleuch his sauted furrow,
And turned frae a' men honour
To what could only scunner

[1] Quoted from Robert Buchanan.

Wha thinks that common-sense
Can e'er be but a fence
To keep a soul worth ha'en'
Frae what it s'ud be daein'
– Sae I in turn maun gi'e
My soul to misery,
Daidle disease
Upon my knees,
And welcome madness
Wi' exceedin' gladness
– Aye, open wide my hert
To a' the thistle's smert.

And a' the hopes o' men
Sall be like wiles then
To gar my soul betray
Its only richtfu' way,
Or as a couthie wife
That seeks nae mair frae life
Than domesticity
E'en wi' the likes o' me –
As gin I could be carin'
For her or for her bairn
When on my road I'm farin'
– O I can spend a nicht
In ony man's Delicht
Or wi' ony wumman born
– But aye be aff the morn!

In a' the inklin's cryptic,
Then, o' an epileptic,
I ha'e been stood in you
And droukit in their grue
Till I can see richt through
Ilk weakness o' my frame
And ilka dernin' shame,
And can employ the same
To jouk the curse o' fame,

Lowsed frae the dominion
O' popular opinion,
And risen at last abune
The thistle like a mune
That looks serenely doon
On what queer things there are
In an inferior star
That couldna be, or see,
Themsel's, except in me.

Wi' burnt-oot hert and poxy face
I sall illumine a' the place,
And there is ne'er a fount o' grace
That isna in a similar case.

Let a' the thistle's growth
Be as a process, then,
My spirit's gane richt through,
And needna threid again,
Tho' in it sall be haud'n
For aye the feck o' men
Wha's queer contortions there
As memories I ken,
As memories o' my ain
O' mony an ancient pain.
But sin' wha'll e'er wun free
Maun tak' like coorse to me,
A fillip I wad gi'e
Their eccentricity,
And leave the lave to dree
Their weirdless destiny.

It's no' withoot regret
That I maun follow yet
The road that led me past
Humanity sae fast,
Yet scarce can gi'e a fate
That is at last mair fit

To them wha tak' that gait
Than theirs wha winna ha'e't,
Seein' that nae man can get
By ony airt or wile,
A destiny quite worth while
As fer as he can tell
– Or even you yoursel'!

And O! I canna thole
Aye yabblin' o' my soul,
And fain I wad be free
O' my eternal me,
Nor fare mysel' alane
– Withoot that tae be gane,
And this, I ha'e nae doot,
This road'll bring aboot.

The munelicht that owre clear defines
The thistle's shrill cantankerous lines
E'en noo whiles insubstantialises
Its grisly form and 'stead devises
A maze o' licht, a siller-frame,
As 'twere God's dream frae which it came,
Ne'er into bein' coorsened yet,
The essence lowin' pure in it,
As tho' the fire owrecam' the clay,
And left its wraith in endless day.

These are the moments when a' sense
Like mist is vanished and intense,
Magic emerges frae the dense
Body o' bein' and beeks immense
As, like a ghinn oot o' a bottle,
Daith rises frae's when oor lives crottle.

These are the moments when my sang
Clears its white feet frae oot amang
My broken thocht, and moves as free
As souls frae bodies when they dee.

There's naething left o' me ava'
Save a' I'd hoped micht whiles befa'.

Sic sang to men is little worth.
It has nae message for the earth.
Men see their warld turned tapsalteerie,
Drookit in a licht owre eerie,
Or sent birlin' like a peerie –
Syne it turns a' they've kent till then
To shapes they can nae langer ken.

Men canna look on nakit licht.
It flings them back wi' darkened sicht,
And een that canna look at it,
Maun draw earth closer roond them yet
Or, their sicht tint, find nocht insteed
That answers to their waefu' need.

And yet this essence frae the clay
In dooble form aye braks away,
For, in addition to the licht,
There is an e'er-increasin' nicht,
A nicht that is the bigger and
Gangs roond licht like an airn band
That noo and then mair tichtly grips,
And snuffs it in a black eclipse,
But rings it maistly as a brough
The mune, till it's juist bricht enough –
O wull I never lowse a licht
I canna dowse again in spite,
Or dull to haud within my sicht?

The thistle canna vanish quite.
Inside a' licht its shape maun glint,
A spirit wi' a skeleton in't.

The world, the flesh, 'll bide in us
As in the fire the unburnt buss,
Or as frae sire to son we gang
And coontless corpses in us thrang.

And e'en the glory that descends
I kenna whence on *me* depends,
And shapes itsel' to what is left
Whaur I o' me ha'e me bereft,
And still the form is mine, altho'
A force to which I ne'er could grow
Is movin' in't as 'twere a sea
That lang syne drooned the last o' me
– That drooned afore the warld began
A' that could ever come frae Man.

And as at sicna times am I,
I wad ha'e Scotland to my eye
Until I saw a timeless flame
Tak' Auchtermuchty for a name,
And kent that Ecclefechan stood
As pairt o' an eternal mood.

Ahint the glory comes the nicht
As Maori to London's ruins,
And I'm amused to see the plicht
O' Licht as't in the black tide droons,
Yet even in the brain o' Chaos
For Scotland I wad hain a place,
And let Tighnabruaich still
Be pairt and paircel o' its will,
And Culloden, black as Hell,
A knowledge it has o' itsel'.

Thou, Dostoevski, understood,
Wha had your ain land in your bluid,
And into it as in a mould
The passion o' your bein' rolled,
Inherited in turn frae Heaven
Or sources fer abune it even.

Sae God retracts in endless stage
Through angel, devil, age on age,

Until at last his infinite natur'
Walks on earth a human cratur
(Or less than human as to my een
The people are in Aiberdeen);
Sae man returns in endless growth
Till God in him again has scouth.

For sic a loup towards widsom's croon
Hoo fer a man maun base him doon,
Hoo plunge aboot in Chaos ere
He finds his needfu' fittin' there,
The matrix oot o' which sublime
Serenity sall soar in time!

Ha'e I the cruelty I need,
Contempt and syne contempt o' that,
And still contempt in endless meed
That I may never yet be caught
In ony satisfaction, or
Bird-lime that winna let me soar?

Is Scotland big enough to be
A symbol o' that force in me,
In wha's divine inebriety
A sicht abune contempt I'll see?

For a' that's Scottish is in me,
As a' things Russian were in thee,
And I in turn 'ud be an action
To pit in a concrete abstraction
My country's contrair qualities,
And mak' a unity o' these
Till my love owre its history dwells,
As owretone to a peal o' bells.

And in this heicher stratosphere
As bairn at giant at thee I peer. . . .

O Jean, in whom my spirit sees,
Clearer than through whisky or disease,
Its dernin' nature, wad the searchin' licht
Oor union raises poor'd owre me the nicht.

I'm faced wi' aspects o' mysel'
At last wha's portent nocht can tell,
Save that sheer licht o' life that when we're joint
Loups through me like a fire a' else t' aroint.

Clear my lourd flesh, and let me move
In the peculiar licht o' love,
As aiblins in Eternity men may
When their swack souls nae mair are clogged wi' clay.

Be thou the licht in which I stand
Entire, in thistle-shape, as planned,
And no' hauf-hidden and hauf-seen as here
In munelicht, whisky, and in fleshly fear,

In fear to look owre closely at
The grisly form in which I'm caught,
In sic a reelin' and imperfect licht
Sprung frae incongruous elements the nicht!

But wer't by thou they were shone on,
Then wad I ha'e nae dreid to con
The ugsome problems shapin' in my soul,
Or gin I hed – certes, nae fear you'd thole!

Be in this fibre like an eye,
And ilka turn and twist descry,
Hoo here a leaf, a spine, a rose – or as
The purpose o' the poo'er that brings 't to pass.

Syne liberate me frae this tree,
As wha had there imprisoned me,
The end achieved – or show me at the least
Mair meanin' in't, and hope o' bein' released.

I tae ha'e heard Eternity drip water
(Aye water, water!), drap by drap
On the a'e nerve, like lichtnin', I've become,
And heard God passin' wi' a bobby's feet
Ootby in the lang coffin o' the street
– Seen stang by chitterin' knottit stang loup oot
Uncrushed by th' echoes o' the thunderin' boot,
Till a' the dizzy lint-white lines o' torture made
A monstrous thistle in the space aboot me,
A symbol o' the puzzle o' man's soul
– And in my agony been pridefu' I could still
Tine nae least quiver or twist, watch ilka point
Like a white-het bodkin ripe my inmaist hert,
And aye wi' clearer pain that brocht nae anodyne,
But rose for ever to a fer crescendo
Like eagles that ootsoar wi' skinklan' wings
The thieveless sun they blin'
          – And pridefu' still
That 'yont the sherp wings o' the eagles fleein'
Aboot the dowless pole o' Space,
Like leafs aboot a thistle-shank, my bluid
Could still thraw roses up
          – And up!

O rootless thistle through the warld that's pairt o' you,
Gin you'd withstand the agonies still to come,
You maun send roots doon to the deeps unkent,
Fer deeper than it's possible for ocht to gang,
Savin' the human soul,
Deeper than God himsel' has knowledge o',
Whaur lichtnin's canna probe that cleave the warld,
Whaur only in the entire dark there's founts o' strength
Eternity's poisoned draps can never file,
And muckle roots thicken, deef to bobbies' feet.

A mony-brainchin' candelabra fills
The lift and's lowin' wi' the stars;
The Octopus Creation is wallopin'
In coontless faddoms o' a nameless sea.

I am the candelabra, and burn
My endless candles to an Unkent God.
I am the mind and meanin' o' the octopus
That thraws its empty airms through a' th' Inane.

And a' the bizzin' suns ha'e bigged
Their kaims upon the surface o' the sea.
My lips may feast for ever, but my guts
Ken naething o' the Food o' Gods.

'Let there be Licht,' said God, and there was
A little: but He lacked the poo'er
To licht up mair than pairt o' space at aince,
And there is lots o' darkness that's the same
As gin He'd never spoken
                    – Mair darkness than there's licht,
And dwarfin't to a candle-flame,
A spalin' candle that'll sune gang oot.
– Darkness comes closer to us than the licht,
And is oor natural element. We peer oot frae't
Like cat's een bleezin' in a goustrous nicht
(Whaur there is nocht to find but stars
That look like ither cats' een),
Like cat's een, and there is nocht to find
Savin' we turn them in upon oorsels;
Cats canna.
                    Darkness is wi' us a' the time, and Licht
But veesits pairt o' us, the wee-est pairt
Frae time to time on a short day atween twa nichts.
Nae licht is thrawn on *them* by ony licht.
Licht thraws nae licht upon itsel';
But in the darkness them wha's een
Nae fleetin' lichts ha'e dazzled and deceived
Find qualities o' licht, keener than ony licht,
Keen and abidin',
That show the nicht unto itsel',
And syne the licht,
That queer extension o' the dark,

That seems a separate and a different thing,
And, seemin' sae, has lang confused the dark,
And set it at cross-purposes wi' itsel'.

O little Life
In which Daith guises and deceives itsel',
Joy that mak's Grief a Janus,
Hope that is Despair's fause-face,
And Guid and Ill that are the same,
Save as the chance licht fa's!

And yet the licht is there,
Whether frae within or frae withoot.
The conscious Dark can use it, dazzled nor deceived.
The licht is there, and th' instinct for it,
Pairt o' the Dark and o' the need to guise,
To deceive and be deceived,
But let us then be undeceived
When we deceive,
When we deceive oorsels.
Let us enjoy deceit, this instinct in us.
Licht cheenges naething,
And gin there is a God wha made the licht
We are adapted to receive,
He cheenged naething,
And hesna kythed Hissel!
Save in this licht that fa's whaur the Auld Nicht was,
Showin' naething that the Darkness didna hide,
And gin it shows a pairt o' that
Confoondin' mair than it confides
Ev'n in that.

The epileptic thistle twitches
(A trick o' wund or mune or een – or whisky).
A brain laid bare,
A nervous system,
The skeleton wi' which men labour

And bring to life in Daith
– I, risen frae the deid, ha'e seen
My deid man's eunuch offspring.
– The licht frae bare banes whitening evermair,
Frae twitchin' nerves thrawn aff,
Frae nakit thocht,
Works in the Darkness like a fell disease,
A hungry acid and a cancer,
Disease o' Daith-in-Life and Life-in-Daith.

O for a root in some untroubled soil,
Some cauld soil 'yont this fevered warld,
That 'ud draw darkness frae a virgin source,
And send it slow and easefu' through my veins,
Release the tension o' my grisly leafs,
Withdraw my endless spikes,
Move coonter to the force in me that hauds
Me raxed and rigid and ridiculous
            – And let my roses drap
Like punctured ba's that at a Fair
Fa' frae the loupin' jet!
            – Water again! . . .

Omsk and the Calton turn again to dust,
The suns and stars fizz out with little fuss,
The bobby booms away and seems to bust,
And leaves the world to darkness and to us.

The circles of our hungry thought
Swing savagely from pole to pole.
Death and the Raven drift above
The graves of Sweeney's body and soul.

My name is Norval. On the Grampian Hills
It is forgotten, and deserves to be.
So are the Grampian Hills and all the people
Who ever heard of either them or me.

What's in a name? From pole to pole
Our interlinked mentality spins.
I know that you are Deosil, and suppose
That therefore I am Widdershins.

Do you reverse? Shall us? Then let's.
Cyclone and Anti? – how absurd!
She should know better at her age.
Auntie's an ass, upon my word.

This is the sort of thing they teach
The Scottish children in the school.
Poetry, patriotism, manners –
No wonder I am such a fool. . . .

Hoo can I graipple wi' the thistle syne,
Be intricate as it and up to a' its moves?
A' airts its sheenin' points are loupin' 'yont me,
Quhile still the firmament it proves.

And syne it's like a wab in which the warld
Squats like a spider, quhile the mune and me
Are taigled in an endless corner o't
Tyauvin' fecklessly. . . .

The wan leafs shak' atour us like the snaw.
Here is the cavaburd in which Earth's tint.
There's naebody but Oblivion and us,
Puir gangrel buddies, waunderin' hameless in't.

The stars are larochs o' auld cottages,
And a' Time's glen is fu' o' blinnin' stew.
Nae freen'ly lozen skimmers: and the wund
Rises and separates even me and you.[1]

I ken nae Russian and you ken nae Scots.
We canna tell oor voices frae the wund.

[1] Dostoevski.

The snaw is seekin' everywhere: oor herts
At last like roofless ingles it has f'und,

And gethers there in drift on endless drift,
Oor broken herts that it can never fill;
And still – its leafs like snaw, its growth like wund –
The thistle rises and forever will! . . .

The thistle rises and forever will,
Getherin' the generations under't.
This is the monument o' a' they were,
And a' they hoped and wondered.

The barren tree, dry leafs and cracklin' thorns,
This is the mind o' a' humanity,
– The empty intellect that left to grow
'll let nocht ither be.

Lo! It has choked the sunlicht's gowden grain,
And strangled syne the white hairst o' the mune.
Thocht that mak's a' the food o' nocht but Thocht
Is reishlin' grey abune. . . .

O fitly frae oor cancerous soil
May this heraldic horror rise!
The Presbyterian thistle flourishes,
And its ain roses crucifies. . . .

No' Edinburgh Castle or the fields
O' Bannockburn or Flodden
Are dernin' wi' the miskent soul
Scotland sae lang has hod'n.

It hauds nae pew in ony kirk,
The soul Christ cam' to save;
Nae R.S.A.'s ha'e pentit it,
F.S.A.'s fund its grave.

Is it alive or deid? I show
My hert – wha will can see.
The secret clyre in Scotland's life
Has brust and reams through me,

A whummlin' sea in which is heard
The clunk o' nameless banes;
A grisly thistle dirlin' shrill
Abune the broken stanes.

Westminster Abbey nor the Fleet,
Nor England's Constitution, but
In a' the michty city there,
You mind a'e fleggit slut,

As Tolstoi o' Lucerne alane
Minded a'e beggar minstrel seen!
The woundit side draws a' the warld.
Barbarians ha'e lizards' een.

Glesca's a gless whaur Magadalene's
Discovered in a million crimes.
Christ comes again – wheesht, whatna bairn
In backlands cries betimes?

Hard faces prate o' their success,
And pickle-makers awn the hills.
There is nae life in a' the land
But this infernal Thistle kills. . . .

  Nae mair I see
  As aince I saw
  Mysel' in the thistle
  Harth and haw!

Nel suo profondo vidi che s'interna,
Legato con amore in un volume,
(Or else by Hate, fu' aft the better Love)
Ciò che per l'universo si squaderna;

Sustanzia ed accidenti, e lor costume,
Quasi conflati insieme per tal modo,
(The michty thistle in wha's boonds I rove)
Che ciò ch'io dico è un semplice lume.[1]

And kent and was creation
In a' its coontless forms,
Or glitterin' in raw sunlicht,
Or dark wi' hurrying storms.

But what's the voice
That sings in me noo?
– A'e hauf o' me tellin'
The tither it's fou!

It's the voice o' the Sooth
That's held owre lang
My Viking North
Wi' its siren sang. . . .

Fier comme un Ecossais.

If a' that I can be's nae mair
Than what mankind's been yet, I'll no'
Begink the instincts thistlewise
That dern – and canna show.

Damned threids and thrums and skinny shapes
O' a' that micht, and su'd, ha' been
– Life onyhow at ony price! –
In sic I'll no' be seen!

Fier comme un Ecossais.

[1] Wicksteed's translation of Dante's Italian (Paradiso, canto xxxiii, 85–90) is as follows: 'Within its depths I saw ingathered, bound by love in one volume, the scattered leaves of all the universe; substance and accidents and their relations, as though together fused, after such fashion that what I tell of is one simple flame.'

The wee reliefs we ha'e in booze,
Or wun at times in carnal states,
May hide frae us but canna cheenge
The silly horrors o' oor fates.

Fier – comme un Ecossais!

There's muckle in the root,
That never can wun oot,
Or't owre what is 'ud sweep
Like a thunderstorm owre sheep.

But shadows whiles upcreep,
And heavy tremors leap . . .
C'wa', Daith, again, sned Life's vain shoot,
And your ain coonsel keep! . . .

Time like a bien wife,
Truth like a dog's gane –
The bien wife's gane to the aumrie
To get the puir dog a bane.

Opens the aumrie door,
And lo! the skeleton's there,
And the gude dog, Truth, has gotten
Banes for evermair. . . .

Maun I tae perish in the keel o' Heaven,
And is this fratt upon the air the ply
O' cross-brath'd cordage that in gloffs and gowls
Brak's up the vision o' the warld's bricht gy?

Ship's tackle and an eemis cairn o' fraucht
Darker than clamourin' veins are roond me yet,
A plait o' shadows thicker than the flesh,
A fank o' tows that binds me hand and fit.

What gin the gorded fullyery on hie
And a' the fanerels o' the michty ship
Gi'e back mair licht than fa's upon them ev'n
Gin sic black ingangs haud us in their grip?

Grugous thistle, to my een
Your widdifow ramel evince,
Sibness to snakes wha's coils
Rin coonter airts at yince,
And fain I'd follow each
Gin you the trick'll teach.

Blin' root to bleezin' rose,
Through a' the whirligig
O' shanks and leafs and jags
What sends ye sic a rig?
Bramble yokin' earth and heaven,
Till they're baith stramulyert driven!

Roses to lure the lift
And roots to wile the clay
And wuppit brainches syne
To claught them 'midyards tae
Till you've the precious pair
Like hang'd men dancin' there,

Wi' mony a seely prickle
You'll fleg a sunburst oot,
Or kittle earthquakes up
Wi' an amusin' root,
While, kilted in your tippet,
They still can mak' their rippit....

And let me pit in guid set terms
My quarrel wi' th' owre sonsy rose,
That roond aboot its devotees
A fair fat cast o' aureole throws
That blinds them, in its mirlygoes,
To the necessity o' foes.

Upon their King and System I
Glower as on things that whiles in pairt
I may admire (at least for them),
But wi' nae claim upon my hert,
While a' their pleasure and their pride
Ootside me lies – and there maun bide.

Ootside me lies – and mair than that,
For I stand still for forces which
Were subjugated to mak' way
For England's poo'er, and to enrich
The kinds o' English, and o' Scots,
The least congenial to my thoughts.

Hauf his soul a Scot maun use
Indulgin' in illusions,
And hauf in gettin rid o' them
And comin' to conclusions
Wi' the demoralisin' dearth
O' onything worth while on Earth. . . .

I'm weary o' the rose as o' my brain,
And for a deeper knowledge I am fain
Than frae this noddin' object I can gain.

Beauty is a'e thing, but it tines anither
(For, fegs, they never can be f'und thegither),
And 'twixt the twa it's no' for me to swither.

As frae the grun' sae thocht frae men springs oot,
A ferlie that tells little o' its source, I doot,
And has nae vera fundamental root.

And cauld agen my hert are laid
The words o' Plato when he said,
'God o' geometry is made.'

Frae my ain mind I fa' away,
That never yet was feared to say
What turned the souls o' men to clay,

Nor cared gin truth frae me ootsprung
In ne'er a leed o' ony tongue
That ever in a heid was hung.

I ken hoo much oor life is fated
Aince its first cell is animated,
The fount frae which the flesh is jetted.

I ken hoo lourd the body lies
Upon the spirit when it flies
And fain abune its stars 'ud rise.

And see I noo a great wheel move,
And a' the notions that I love
Drap into stented groove and groove?

It maitters not my mind the day,
Nocht maitters that I strive to dae,
– For the wheel moves on in its ain way.

I sall be moved as it decides
To look at Life frae ither sides;
Rejoice, rebel, its turn abides.

And as I see the great wheel spin
There flees a licht frae't lang and thin
That Earth is like a snaw-ba' in.

(To the uncanny thocht I clutch
– The nature o' man's soul is such
That it can ne'er wi' life tine touch.

Man's mind is in God's image made,
And in its wildest dreams arrayed
In pairt o' Truth is still displayed.)

Then suddenly I see as weel
As me spun roon' within the wheel,
The helpless forms o' God and Deil.

And on a birlin' edge I see
Wee Scotland squattin' like a flea,
And dizzy wi' the speed, and me!

I've often thrawn the warld frae me,
Into the Pool o' Space, to see
The Circles o' Infinity.

Or like a flat stone gar'd it skite,
A Morse code message writ in licht
That yet I couldna read aricht

The skippin' sparks, the ripples, rit
Like skritches o' a grain o' grit
'Neth Juggernaut in which I sit.

Twenty-six thoosand years it tak's
Afore a'e single roond it mak's,
And syne it melts as it were wax.

The Phœnix guise 't'll rise in syne
Is mair than Euclid or Einstein
Can dream o' or's in dreams o' mine.

Upon the huge circumference are
As neebor points the Heavenly War
That dung doun Lucifer sae far,

And that upheaval in which I
Sodgered 'neth the Grecian sky
And in Italy and Marseilles,

And there isna room for men
Wha the haill o' history ken
To pit a pin twixt then and then.

Whaur are Bannockburn and Flodden?
– O' a'e grain like facets hod'n,
Little wars (twixt that which God in

Focht and won, and that which He
Took baith sides in hopelessly),
Less than God or I can see.

By whatna cry o' mine oot-topped
Sall be a' men ha'e sung and hoped
When to a'e note they're telescoped?

And Jesus and a nameless ape
Collide and share the selfsame shape
That nocht terrestrial can escape?

But less than this nae man need try.
He'd better be content to eye
The wheel in silence whirlin' by.

Nae verse is worth a ha'et until
It can join issue wi' the Will
That raised the Wheel and spins it still,

But a' the music that mankind
'S made yet is to the Earth confined,
Poo'erless to reach the general mind,

Poo'erless to reach the neist star e'en,
That as a pairt o'ts sel' is seen,
And only men can tell between.

Yet I exult oor sang has yet
To grow wings that'll cairry it
Ayont its native speck o' grit,

And I exult to find in me
The thocht that this can ever be,
A hope still for humanity.

For gin the sun and mune at last
Are as a neebor's lintel passed,
The wheel'll tine its stature fast,

And birl in time inside oor heids
Till we can thraw oot conscious gleids
That draw an answer to oor needs,

Or if nae answer still we find
Brichten till a' thing is defined
In the huge licht-beams o' oor kind,

And if we still can find nae trace
Ahint the Wheel o' ony Face,
There'll be a glory in the place,

And we may aiblins swing content
Upon the wheel in which we're pent
In adequate enlightenment.

Nae ither thocht can mitigate
The horror o' the endless Fate
A'thing 's whirled in predestinate.

O whiles I'd fain be blin' to it,
As men wha through the ages sit,
And never move frae aff the bit,

Wha hear a Burns or Shakespeare sing,
Yet still their ain bit jingles string,
As they were worth the fashioning.

Whatever Scotland is to me,
Be it aye pairt o' a' men see
O' Earth and o' Eternity

Wha winna hide their heids in't till
It seems the haill o' Space to fill,
As t'were an unsurmounted hill.

He canna Scotland see wha yet
Canna see the Infinite,
And Scotland in true scale to it.

Nor blame I muckle, wham atour
Earth's countries blaw, a pickle stour,
To sort wha's grains they ha'e nae poo'er.

E'en stars are seen thegither in
A'e skime o' licht as grey as tin
Flyin' on the wheel as 'twere a pin.

Syne ither systems ray on ray
Skinkle past in quick array
While it is still the self-same day,

A'e day o' a' the million days
Through which the soul o' man can gaze
Upon the wheel's incessant blaze,

Upon the wheel's incessant blaze
As it were on a single place
That twinklin' filled the howe o' space.

A'e point is a' that it can be,
I wis nae man 'll ever see
The rest o' the rotundity.

Impersonality sall blaw
Through me as 'twere a bluffert o' snaw
To scour me o' my sense o' awe,

A bluffert o' snaw, the licht that flees
Within the Wheel, and Freedom gi'es
Frae Dust and Daith and a' Disease,

– The drumlie doom that only weighs
On them wha ha'ena seen their place
Yet in creation's lichtnin' race,

In the movement that includes
As a tide's resistless floods
A' their movements and their moods –

Until disinterested we,
O' a' oor auld delusions free,
Lowe in the wheel's serenity

As conscious items in the licht,
And keen to keep it clear and bricht
In which the haill machine is dight,

The licht nae man has ever seen
Till he has felt that he's been gi'en
The stars themsels insteed o' een,

And often wi' the sun has glowered
At the white mune until it cowered,
As when by new thocht auld's o'erpowered.

Oor universe is like an e'e
Turned in, man's benmaist hert to see,
And swamped in subjectivity.

But whether it can use its sicht
To bring what lies withoot to licht
To answer's still ayont my micht.

But when that inturned look has brocht
To licht what still in vain it's socht
Ootward maun be the bent o' thocht.

And organs may develop syne
Responsive to the need divine
O' single-minded humankin'.

The function, as it seems to me,
O' Poetry is to bring to be
At lang, lang last that unity. . . .

But wa'es me on the weary wheel!
Higgledy-piggledy in't we reel,
And little it cares hoo we may feel.

Twenty-six thoosand years 't'll tak'
For it to threid the Zodiac
– A single roond o' the wheel to mak'!

Lately it turned – I saw mysel'
In sic a company doomed to mell,
I micht ha'e been in Dante's Hell.

It shows hoo little the best o' men
E'en o' themsels at times can ken,
– I sune saw *that* when I gaed ben.

The lesser wheel within the big
That moves as merry as a grig,
Wi' mankind in its whirligig,

And hasna turned a'e circle yet
Tho' as it turns we slide in it,
And needs maun tak' the place we get,

I felt it turn, and syne I saw
John Knox and Clavers in my raw,
And Mary Queen o' Scots ana',

And Rabbie Burns and Weelum Wallace,
And Carlyle lookin' unco gallus,
And Harry Lauder (to enthrall us).

And as I looked I saw them a',
A' the Scots baith big and sma',
That e'er the braith o' life did draw.

'Mercy o' Gode, I canna thole
Wi' sic an orra mob to roll.'
– '*Wheesht! It's for the guid o' your soul.*'

'But what's the meanin', what's the sense?'
– '*Men shift but by experience.*
'*Twixt Scots there is nae difference.*

They canna learn, sae canna move,
But stick for aye to their auld groove
– *The only race in History who've*

Bidden in the same category
Frae stert to present o' their story,
And deem their ignorance their glory.

The mair they differ, mair the same.
The wheel can whummle a' but them,
– *They ca' their obstinacy "Hame",*

And "Puir Auld Scotland" bleat wi' pride,
And wi' their minds made up to bide
A thorn in a' the wide world's side.

There ha'e been Scots what ha'e ha'en thochts,
They're strewn through maist o' the various lots
– *Sic traitors are nae langer Scots!*

'But in this huge ineducable
Heterogeneous hotch and rabble,
Why am *I* condemned to squabble?'

'*A Scottish poet maun assume*
The burden o' his people's doom,
And dee to brak' their livin' tomb.

Mony ha'e tried, but a' ha'e failed.
Their sacrifice has nocht availed.
Upon the thistle they're impaled.

You maun choose but gin ye'd see
Anither category ye
Maun tine your nationality.'

And I look at a' the random
Band the wheel leaves whaur it fand 'em.
                              'Auch, to Hell,
I'll tak' it to avizandum.' . . .

O wae's me on the weary wheel,
And fain I'd understand them!

And blessin' on the weary wheel
Whaurever it may land them! . . .

But aince Jean kens what I've been through
The nicht, I dinna doot it,
She'll ope her airms in welcome true,
And clack nae mair aboot it. . . .

                .   .   .   .

The stars like thistle's roses floo'er
The sterile growth o' Space ootour,
That clad in bitter blasts spreids oot
Frae me, the sustenance o' its root.

O fain I'd keep my hert entire,
Fain hain the licht o' my desire,
But ech! the shinin' streams ascend,
And leave me empty at the end.

For aince it's toomed my hert and brain,
The thistle needs maun fa' again.
– But a' its growth 'll never fill
The hole it's turned my life intill! . . .

Yet ha'e I Silence left, the croon o' a'.

No' her, wha on the hills langsyne I saw
Liftin' a foreheid o' perpetual snaw.

No' her, wha in the how-dumb-deid o' nicht
Kyths, like Eternity in Time's despite.

No' her, withooten shape, wha's name is Daith,
No' Him, unkennable abies to faith

– God whom, gin e'er He saw a man, 'ud be
E'en mair dumfooner'd at the sicht than he

– But Him, whom nocht in man or Deity,
Or Daith or Dreid or Laneliness can touch,
Wha's deed owre often and has seen owre much.

O I ha'e Silence left,

                 – 'And weel ye micht,'
Sae Jean'll say, 'efter sic a nicht!'

THE LUCKY BAG
(1927)

The Glog-Hole

I KEN a glog-hole
    That looks at the sky
As much as to say
    I'm as deep as you're high!

At the Window

GAE whussle on your thoom, lad,
    Gae whussle on your thoom,
You'd sook the laverocks oot o' the lift
    Till a' the lift is toom!

Syne wheeple on the bane, laddie,
    Wheeple on the bane.
You needna blaw on onything else;
    I'll pay nae heed till then.

Ulysses' Bow

BETTER violer never screeded on a silken coord
    Or kittled a cat's tripes wi's finger-en's,
But the lift is yəlla as biest milk,
    And the eagle roosts wi' the hens,
And the licht o' life is lourd,
    And the voices nocht but men's.

My hert-strings werena broken – then why's he gane
　　And left them when he canna fin' their marrow
– A clarsach made for his playin',
　　A warld to mak' a star o' ! –
To the feckless fingers o' sunlicht
　　Or the lichtnin's random arrow?

The Morning Gift

'O WHAT can be my mornin' gift
　　Noo a' we hae we hae in common?'
– To wauk and see you're still the man
　　I thocht you were yestreen or gloamin' !

And ken that what gaed on owre nicht
　　Has left the warld as erst it was
Sin', wauknin', in your een I see
　　Daylicht, no' bluid, as in a glass !

'O what can be my mornin' gift
　　Noo a' we hae we hae in common?'
– To wauk and in your een to see
　　My ain face like a happy omen !

The Old Laird

MOOTHLIE as snails when they come snowkin'
　　Oot owre the drookit swaird
　　Cam' she in by to the drucken laird,
Whaur he sat happy bowkin'.

'I'm no' fou eneuch for you,' quo' he,
    Syne bawled for the room to catch it,
     'Awa' and mird wi' your maiks, ye smatchet,
And mint nae mair wi' me!'

The Baukie Bird

O LOVE is like the baukie bird,
    I canna follow its flicht.
Wi' mony a killywimple
    It glints and's tint to sicht.

And Work is like the ivy-tod
    It derns in through the day
Till guid meat toddles in the pot
    And supper's on the way.

But wow! the restless shadow syne
    Athwart the weather-glim.
'It's Sandy to the worm,' I cry,
    And I maun follow him.

Prometheus

O WHY maun I lie
    On this cauld, black gridle
As gin a' the poo'er
    Had gane frae my middle?

Swee the black Earth
    Owre the sun's face again.
– Aiblins I'll dance
    Fu' merrily then!

Mind's End

THERE's nocht but whiles presents itsel'
  To me as tho' my mind
Had been, in its development,
  A stage left fer behind.

And as things roond upon my brain
  And look as famous men
May look on mean wee hames aince mair
  I see my ain sel' then.

And waur than that – for mean wee hames
  Fu' famous men hae bred;
The michty things that kyth in me
  Were born in me nor fed.

But, as they look me through, I ken
  The time comes slow but shair
When Earth'll ootgrow the human mind
  As it had ne'er been there.

Lost Soul

IT was on a cauld gull day
The puir auld cratur flew away.
I'm gled it wisna me Daith shoo'd
Sae suddenly oot o' flesh and bluid.

And they say she tined her way?
I widna wonder, a gate sae grey –
Her that aye hoped the self-same hole
'Ud haud her body and her soul!

Jenny Rintherout

SHE daes naething but lauch and greet
    The haill o' the lee-lang day,
The skirl at the tail o' the guffa,
    And syne the opposite way.

The sabbin' is like to brek her hert,
    The lauchin' to split her heid.
– Then let them ding her in blauds atween them!
    She'll no' be richt till she's deid.

Hide-and-Seek

'Té hé,' quoth Jenny, 'keik, keik, I see you
    And noo it's my turn to hide.'
But she never hid vera faur awa'
    Afore she was my bride.

'Té hé,' cries Jenny, 'keik, keik, d'ye see me?'
    It's no' that she's owre weel hid,
Yet I canna find her – for wha wad look
    Under a coffin lid?

Death and the Hen-Wife

O LEESE me on the eagle
    And leese me on the smew,
But wae's me for a' the hens
    Wha's couthie necks I drew!

Leese me on the white sun,
  Leese me on the mune,
But wae's me for my twa een
  Noo a' their seein's dune.

Derelict

THE toom houk dirls
  Wi' the jow o' the tide
And there's nowt but banes
  For a crew inside.

Wi' the jow o' the tide
  The toom houk dirls
And the lady Mune lookin'
  Scunners and girles.

Consummation

SUNBURST on a heather hill
  Minds me o' the gallus day
I first 'bood to tak' my will
  Tho' I howd the warld away.

I've been nearer mony anither
  Wumman's hert than I was then,
But I'd gie them a' thegither
  For yon first reid glisk again.

At the Sign of the Thistle

THE greatest poets
　　Never wrote a word.
Their sang is a' where,
　　Like a buneheid bird;
　　　　And but for it
　　　　Nane could be writ.

The greatest thinkers
　　Passed on nae thocht.
Alane, unkent,
　　Like Titans they focht;
　　　　Withoot their strife
　　　　There 'ud be nae life.

Tho' to the feck
　　A' sang is vain
And they've nae thocht
　　That's worth the ha'ein',
　　　　By sang and thocht
　　　　A' Fate is wrocht.

Easy pluck roses
　　To sing o' or think,
E'en tho' they grow
　　On Hell's black brink,
　　　　But wha'll risk hissel'
　　　　There for a thistle?

Easy to heed
　　Nocht for the mob
And trauchle on
　　Wi' a pickthank job
　　　　When ye ken what it is
　　　　– But the like o' this?

It disna seem worth't,
    Yet 'yont kennin' I ken
That the best I can dae
    For mysel' and a' men
        Is to tyauve wi' the thistle
        Till Gabriel's whistle.

Unthinkable Thocht,
    Unsingable Sang,
To thee for aye
    My hert sall belang,
        Type o' His poo'ers
        Wha's ways are no' oors!

Dandelion

I SAW my brain as the sun micht see
    A dandelion ba'
And think it was its ain
    Pale image that it saw.

I saw my brain as the sun micht see
    A dandelion ba'
– And noo like a starry sky
    My thochts owre a'thing blaw.

TO CIRCUMJACK CENCRASTUS
or THE CURLY SNAKE
(1930)

Is cam's is direach an lagh.
(Crooked and Straight is the law.)
ANCIENT GAELIC PROVERB

To the consternation of the Seminaries, the last number of the review God
reproduced photographs of God by Man Ray, side by side with fetishes from
Upper Oubanghi.

PAUL MORAND

A gulf divides the exaltations of the mystics from the tachypraxia of the
micro-splanchnic hyperthyroidics or the ideo-affective dissociations of the
schizothymes.

DE SANCTIS

To Circumjack Cencrastus

THERE is nae movement in the warld like yours.
You are as different frae a'thing else
As water frae a book, fear frae the stars . . .
The licht that History sheds on onything
Is naething to the licht you shed on it.
Time's dourest riddles to solution slide
Like Lautréamont's cormorant: and Man
Shudders to see you slippin' into place . . .
The simple explanations that you gi'e
O' age-lang mysteries are little liked
Even by them wha best appreciate
The soond advice you gied to Mither Eve,
                              Or think they dae.

The beneficiaries o' incredible change
Are naturally conservative, even as
Resetters o' ancestral loot are aye
Strang on the Law. The horror maist folk feel
On seein' you is natural eneuch.
There is nae movement in the warld like yours
Save faith's, that can move mountains, gin it shak's
The grund 'neath its ain feet for practice whiles
And there's nae sayin' what'll happen neist.
Man sees the changin' warld and feels changed tae
Like ane wha sittin' in a standin' train
Sees anither pass, and thinks it's his that's gaen'
                              – And fegs it is !

Poets in throes o' composition whiles
See you as fishermen in favourite pools
May see a muckle fish they canna catch
Clood-like beneath the glitterin' fry they can,
Contra nando incrementum, lyin'
Under the roarin' cataracts o' Life,

Like the catalysis that underlies
A' the illusions o' romantic love.
Poets! – to whom a yellow primrose is
A yellow primrose, and nae mair, or less!
– Can you be in their harns and no' the pool
Yet wi' a sudden bowspring on the air
                Ootshine the sun?

The dooble tongue has spoken and been heard.
What poet has repeated ocht it said?
There is nae movement in the warld like yours.
Vain is the image o' Leviathan
And vain the image o' reflectit throes,
For you rin coonter to the rhythms o' thocht,
Wrenched oot o' recognition a' words fail
To haud you, alien to the human mind,
Yet in your ain guid time you suddenly slip,
Nae man kens hoo, into the simplest phrase,
While a' the diction'ry rejoices like
The hen that saw its ugly ducklin' come
                Safe to the shore again.

Come let us face the facts. We ken that there's
Nae invocation that's no' fause but this.
Christ saw you when he said that 'wha believe
In me shall dae like me – *and greater things.*'
He is nae Christian that's fa'n short o' this,
But och Christ tint you in the seein' tae.
Come let us face the facts. He should ha' socht
Faith in themsel's like his – no' faith in him.
His words condemned his followers, and himsel',
(Dostoevski ev'n, preferrin' Christ to truth)
And we ha'e seen through twenty centuries syne
Nocht but the lang withdrawal o' the licht
That kythed in him, as 'twere an ebbin' sea
That leaves ahint a waste o' mudflats till
                It come again.

A sorry metaphor, for ony sea
Covers or uncovers the same bed o' glaur
Even as the ebb and flow o' life and art
Leaves the dreich mob unchanged – gin you're no' there.
There is nae movement in the warld like yours
Save sic divergences as dinna leave
Things a' the mair the same the mair they change
But alter them forever in a way
Unheralded and unbelievable
As gin the tide-toucht mud becam' a tune,
A sky, a problem in psychology,
Or something unimaginable as them
                              Gin they'd no' been

A'thing on earth repeats itsel' but you
And a'thing langs to pit an end to change.
The praise o' you is no' for ony man
Wha seeks to big Jerusalem onywhaur
And be at ease, for he's nae suner there
Than roond its wa's your fatal music dirls
And doon they coup like Jericho's again.
Vain sorrow hides your enigmatic gleam
Cleavin' through ilka confidence owrethrawn,
Through ilka difference and decay and daith,
Streight as an arrow on its endless way
Or like a fire that spreids in secret till
                              Its haud's complete.

And mairtyrs to their ain stupidity
You set Earth's generations a' alowe
And the neist victim lauchs or grues to see
His predecessor in the acid licht.
The residue o' gowd is unco sma'
And centuries gang to mak' a single grain
While a' the dross o' pomp and circumstance
Burns clear awa' as it had never been.
The hopes and fears o' a' but twa-three men
At best are foolish first, syne null and void.

– O Holy Office, be mair rigorous still
And shrivel up the sameness still to be
                          Afore it's born!

As Shelley in the Hoose o' Commons shrieked
In horror at the bestial shapes seen there
Perpetuatin' needless poverty
And mindlessness and fraud and curst conceit
Sae a' the warld is manifest in you
– Religion, Art, Commerce and Industry,
Social and Sexual Relationships,
A' to be lauched at wi' contempt or lang,
Like Queen Victoria or Locarno noo
Or mercifully forgotten – yet your flame
Riddles but canna ridicule Shelley
And Buddha's still a solid darkness in't
                          And Christ a live controversy.

Buddha, no' India! Christ and no' the Kirk!
Yet they maun baith be sune forgotten tae
And a' the Past be juist a wisp o strae
Thrawn on the bonfire that the thocht o' ye lichts.
There is nae mystery in Life or Daith
Save as man mak's it by his ignorance
(Which sers its purpose to your hidden growth),
Your coils are no' at variance tho' they seem
And a'thing fa's into its place at last
Wit turns to ignorance, laughter to the joke.
You mak' a concertina o' the sun
                          And cut a' airts at aince.

A' airts at aince – but life is faur owre slow,
And freedom inconceivable to man.
Licht moves a thoosand times faster than his nerves,
His een are neist to blin', his ears to deef.
It tak's a Dostoevksi to believe
And disbelieve a thing at aince, and that's
A puir beginnin' to *your* cantrips, fegs,

Tho' snails may dream that they'll be eagles yet,
Men Gods and that the unkent future's set
Plain as a pikestaff tho' they canna see't
(And no' – Heaven help us – undecided yet!)
As life is to a bairn afore it kens
                    Whether it's Broon's or Smith's . . .

I blink at Yeats as micht a man whom some
Foul sorcery had changed into a pig,
At Yeats, my kingly cousin, and mind hoo
He prophesied that Eire 'ud hae nae Burns
(Tho' it has tried to mair than aince) but haud
Its genius heich and lanely – and think o' Burns,
That Langfellow in a' but leid, and hoo
Scots since has tint his maikless vir but hains
His cheap emotions, puir ideas, and
Imperfect sense o' beauty, till my race
Lack ev'n the foetus' luck o' Smith or Broon
(A Hobson's choice to burst nae pigskin owre)
                    Bein' a' Jock Tamson's bairns.

But weary o' recrimination sune
And in slant licht some movement o' you thraws
See a' the warld become an amber haze,
A sunny flood in which humanity lies
Troot-like, wi' motionin' fins and beckonin' tail,
And wan inscrutable ensnarin' een,
As I've seen often in the Esk or Ewes;
Yet as I look its gantin' mou' becomes,
Clearer than Whistle Binkie bards could draw,
Tho' this was a' the ettle o' their clan,
The waefu' gape o' a wee bairn's smile,
Semihiante labello o' Catullus, there.
                    – O my wee troot!

Freedom is *inconceivable*. The word
Betrays the cause – a habit o' the mind,
Thinkin' continually in a certain way,

Generation after generation, till it seems
This is Thocht's fixed unalterable mode;
And here's the reason at aince why human Thocht
Is few men's business and sae scant and shawl,
And men hate poems dry and hard and needs
Maun hae them fozy wi' infinity.
'The way a woman walkin' in the street
Kicks oot her skirt ahint her is the thing,
Mair than her soul, gin the exact word's found,
                              To gar the Heavens open.'

Then fix the babby in a guid Scots word,
That language no' o' Pan but Peter Pan,
(Christ leuch wi' toom gans aince, the Lord Buddha
Was in a crawl o' bairns aboot the doors)
The dowf and daft-like babby and the way
Its murgeons munk oor manhood and gaup up
Sillier than ever on the face o' Daith.
Mankind ends as it sterted, mappiemou'd,
And never bites aff mair than it can – sook,
And fain, gin Blake was wrang and fools got there,
'Ud mak' an antirrhinum in Heaven at last
                              For ither bairns than oors or us.

The poet's hame is in the serpent's mooth,
No' in his ain, or ither man's, or flooer's.
Nae wumman ever had a tongue like this,
No' even the twinklin' aphrodisiac tip
O' Helen's slidin' through her roondit lips
Or Saint Sophia's whisperin' in God's lug
Or subtler members in the warld the day
I aiblins ken owre muckle o', or wull,
Or wad! – subtler, tho' as inferior still
To this as birds' sangs (sae-ca'd) are to men's,
Or fancy stuff that's tint its *caoin* is
To Gaelic music that like Whisky's best
                              Ta'en *mar a tha e*

There's ane amang the birds that's perfect, ane
Amang the fish, men say – I kenna which;
My verse bein' fallible's no' poetry yet
And that is a' that I'm concerned aboot.
The consciousness that maitter has entrapped
In minerals, plants and beasts is strugglin' yet
In men's minds only, seekin' to win free,
As poets' ideas, in the fecht wi' words,
Forced back upon themsel's and made mair clear,
Owrecome a' thwarts whiles, miracles at last.
Shairly the process should be clear to Scots.
What ither country has a vantage point
                    Like Faire na h-Abha?

Few are the Scots that ever heard o't tho'!
Wha stands there sees the gleams (like Cythna's signs,
Clear elemental shapes wha's sma'est change
A subtler language wi'in language mak's
That learners wi' owre muckle *blas na beurl*',
A' tangled up in their *o-hill-i-ha's*,
Can never seize on!) o' a caulder stream
Than in Avranches' park at peep o' day
Barefut Valéry, writin' *Pythia*, found,
Kennin' how nigh impossible it is
To dae ocht worth the daen' and hoo ill
To keep frae wastin' time on ither things,
                    And gaed hame drunk wi' will.

It has a look as o' the pooer that's made
The haill warld, whiles, and instantly that's dune
Turn't to anither and faur harder task,
As micht a poet frae the wark that keeps
His hoosehold bein and lets him turn secure
(Gin only yon *was* easier and left scouth)
                    To his true job.

        Ignore the silly figure, you that play
        Like Artur Schnabel, to nae gallery,

In programmes, free frae 'fireworks' (as he said
To ane complainin' 'nocht but Schubert!' aince,
'To gi'e folk nae chance to prefer the waur')
Unlike a' ither virtuosos', bein',
(Like you – in anither sense tae, relentless judge)
              'Borin' a' through.'

Here is the task to which it conjures us –

  'When man to man the haill warld owre
  Sall brithers be for a' that?'
      (I've a sneaky feelin' roond my hert
      That I'm gaen' to settle doon . . .)
  Napoleon near-haund had the poo'er
  To solve the problem Man's workin' at.

  I needs maun think, gin the chance I stake
  O' Gaeldom regained, hoo a' mankind
  Writhes like the cut-up pairts o' a snake
  To jine aince mair – as he'd fain ha'e jined.

  Comparin' wi' his the silly hopes –
  Ex nihil, nihil – sae mony Scots
  Cherish the day, Napoleon's phrase drops
  'Che coglione!' balm on my thoughts!

  'What is Cencrastus but the wriggle
  O' Man's divided vertebrae?'
  – Gin that were a' I wadna jiggle
  For my pairt wi't anither day,

  For human unity needna mean
  Ocht to the problems I'm concerned wi',
  Nae anaconda but a green
  Kailworm is a' that seems to me.

  Messieurs les Anglais, wha preferred
  Lenin to Napoleon, see
  As sma' again wi' that compared
  Crawls ev'n your perfidy!

To think nae thocht that's e'er been thocht afore
And nane, that's no' worth mair than a' that ha'e;
And no' be like the Christian folk wha cry
'Religious Truth's been found – a' men can dae's
To feebly reproduce some fragments o't.'
Germans in music – in religion Jews,
Nationality in Algebra even,
Guid kens what savages in nearer things
Cramp and exhaust us in their several spheres,

> *Hunters were oot on a Scottish hill*
> *A'e day[1] when the sun stude suddenly still*
> *At noon and turned the colour o' port*
> *A perfect nuisance, spoilin' their sport.*
> *Syne it gaed pitch black a' thegither.*
> *Isn't that juist like oor Scottish weather!*

If we tak' mair than we in turn can gie,
And fail, beneath their natures and oor ain,
And the haill Warld's, to keep the glintin' streams
                    O' Unnatural Thocht at work.

> *Ev'n as in writing this, I fear*
> *That aiblins I'm nae mair than thrang*
> *Echoin' some puir German sang*
> *(That was the fashion o' yester-year,*
> *Haringer, Heym, or Zech or Benn,*
> *The Sturz and Schrei that younger men*
> *In their gehackten Satzen shed*
> *– But can a Scot be weel-eneuch read,*
> *Alive to Kasack, Loerke, Mell,*
> *Billinger and mair than I need tell*
> *Or by his ain nose yet be led*
> *To end, or no' bide ony langer,*
> *Endlich offen und Empfänger,*
> *Or better still anticipate*
> *The neist sae-ever transient state*

[1] The day of Christ's crucifixion.

And scrawl a phrase frae Scotland yet
On the palimpsest o' th' Infinite?)
Or doot that my cauld current flows
Only frae Husserl, say, and shows
That motion needs maun be explained
Eidetically, or hoo Thocht strained
Through mair and mair ἐποχαί gies
The a priori o' a' ideas,
While ithers think yon crystal wa'
Merks Heaven . . . or America! . . .

There is nae movement in the warld like yours,
Save his, wha, ere he writes, kens he'll no' fail
To recognise his dear ev'n tho' her hair
(A'e threid o' which, pu'd through his nails, 'ud frizz
In coontless kinks, like Scotland's craziest burn
– Aye, yon bright water even wi' the sky
That if, when we were bairns, we threw corks on't
We panted to keep up wi' them in vain)
Whiles loosened owre him like the sun at noon
That insubstantialises a' the warld
Is syne bound, coil on coil in sma'er space
                To show the smoothness o' her brow;
    I saw her in the lily-beds,
    I saw her in the snaw,
    I saw her in the white sun
    That burned the warld awa'
Nor sings o' Barra wha has never seen,
Phaedria and Acrasia . . . slipshod wark.

Shaddows that feed on the licht for aye
Hauntin' the waters that canna win free,
The wild burn loups but you haud it fast
As the hands o' the past haud me.

A burn may dream o' a warld aince mair
O' water and licht and nocht beside,
But has aye as faur to gang as it's gane,
And a burn in the dark roots' clutch 'll bide

Tint in a windhaw or siller swirl
Bigger and blacker the roots strike back,
As whiles through a high-falutin' o' love
I hear my body mockin' my talk. . . .

Yet wae for the poet wi' nocht but his bluid
  For a bardic goon.
Like the last dark reid crawberries under the firs
  His life'll be sune.
      Bodach cleòcain deirg.

For he that's aince lain in the Yellow Stag's Couch
  – Leabaidh an Daimh Bhuidhe –
'll never sing frae the Ruigh Bristidh Cridhe[1]
  The sangs he s'ud to ye.
      Bodach cleòcain deirg. . . .

The Mavis of Pabal

I am the mavis o' Pabal
  Back on the tap o' the hill,
My voice and wings still wantin'
  A wee thing in strength and skill.
I am the mavis o' Pabal, lang
I've lain wi' my heid on my breist
In a day that was dark, my sang
Forgotten like licht in the East,
  But the dawn is breakin' at last
  And I'm back on the tap o' the hill
  And I'll sing as I sang in the past
  – If singin' depends upon will!

I am the mavis o' Pabal,
  A pool cut aff frae the sea,
A tree withoot roots that stands
  On the ground unsteadily.

[1] The Sheiling of the Broken Heart

I should ha'e stayed wi' the rest
Doon in Coille Ghruamach still
And no' ettled to be on the crest
O' this bricht impossible hill,
 For poetry's no' made in a lifetime
 And I lack a livin' past;
 I stand on the tap o' the hill
 – But the miracle canna last!

Maun I flee the Atlantic tae
 Whaur ten thoosand o' the clan
Host whaur the first ane landit
 – I'd leifer ha'e seen nae dawn.
Can I sing them back hame again?
The nicht has lasted owre lang,
And I doot if American clansmen
Are worth the orts o' a sang.
 – O it's fine to be back in the sun
 And the shoots are tender and green
 But I'm lanely, and flute as I will,
 There's nae sign o' a mate to be seen!

The Parrot Cry

Tell me the auld, auld story
O' hoo the Union brocht
Puir Scotland into being
As a country worth a thocht.
England, frae whom a' blessings flow
What could we dae withoot ye?
Then dinna threip it doon oor throats
As gin we e'er could doot ye!
 My feelings lang wi' gratitude
 Ha'e been sae sairly harrowed
 That dod! I think it's time
 The claith was owre the parrot!

Tell me o' Scottish enterprise
And canniness and thrift,
And hoo we're baith less Scots and mair
Than ever under George the Fifth,
And hoo to 'wider interests'
Oor ain we sacrifice
And yet tine naething by it
As aye the parrot cries.
    Syne gie's a chance to think it oot
    Aince we're a' weel awaur o't,
    For, losh, I think it's time
    The claith was owre the parrot!

Tell me o' love o' country
Content to see't decay,
And ony ither paradox
Ye think o' by the way.
I doot it needs a Hegel
Sic opposites to fuse;
Oor education's failin'
And canna gie's the views
    That were peculiar to us
    Afore oor vision narrowed
    And gar'd us think it time
    The claith was owre the parrot!

A parrot's weel eneuch at times
But whiles we'd liefer hear
A blackbird or a mavis
Singin' fu' blythe and clear.
Fetch ony native Scottish bird
Frae the eagle to the wren,
And faith! you'd hear a different sang
Frae this painted foreigner's then.
    The marine that brocht it owre
    Believed its every word
    – But we're a' deeved to daith
    Wi' his infernal bird.

It's possible that Scotland yet
May hear its ain voice speak
If only we can silence
This endless-yatterin' beak.
The blessing wi' the black
Selvedge is the clout!
It's silenced Scotland lang eneuch,
Gi'e England turn aboot,
 For the puir bird needs its rest –
 Wha else 'll be the waur o't?
 And it's lang past the time
 The claith was owre the parrot!

And gin that disna dae, lads,
We e'en maun draw its neck
And heist its body on a stick
A' ither pests to check.
I'd raither keep't alive, and whiles
Let bairns keek in and hear
What the Balliol accent used to be
Frae the Predominant Pairtner here!
 – But save to please the bairns
 I'd absolutely bar it
 For fegs, it's aye high time
 The claith was owre the parrot! . . .

Like ony theologian busy wi'
The Formgeschichte o' the Haly Writ
I turn and glower at Scotland, conscious o'
The haill Entwicklung des Naturgefühls
– And Nature's ain revolt at ilka point.
Nae soond except a mugwort's rustlin' whiles,
The chill that like a blanch o' lichtnin' fa's
Frae the sun's sel' upon the amplest scene,
A mavis seen in twenty ways at aince,
And yon cauld stream like the auld bards wha kept
Their bodies still, their minds alert and clear,
And tholed nae intermingledons between

Objects o' sense and images o' mind,
                    Eternity and Eriskay.

From the Scots Anthology

I

We're a'e clan here; I micht as weel
Ha'e been a Campbell as a MacNeill.

II

Alas that life is past
Noo I'm a laird at last.

III

I'm deid, no' daft, and dinna need
A folly o' flooers aboot my heid.

IV

Here lie MacDonalds glad to tine
A' that's become o' Scotland syne.

V

Croon me wi' blackthorn noo; in life
Droighneach[1] resisted a' my strife.

VI

Nae man that wants to ha'e ideas
Aboot life efter daith sud wait till he dees.

VII

The warld has fadit frae view
As Benbecula used to
And nae seagull follows my curragh noo.

VIII

My grave's no' bad; they've put intill't
Twa o' the Sassenachs I kill't.
I'll kill them again as sune as the horn
Toots on the Resurrection Morn.

[1] A metre called 'blackthorny' because of its intricacy.

IX

You've taen frae me the man that I loved.
Hoo do you think that in Heaven I'll ken
Him noo that you've made him ane o' your saints?
Keep.him; I'd leifer no' see him again.

X

I'm deid. That's a' that's aboot it.
If you werena livin' you wadna doot it.

XI

Here in this forhooied nest
To a cauld egg I pit my breast,
And may Eternity dae the rest.
                              I canna mair.

Tho' I'm still eerie whiles upon the hills
Withoot the English sodgers in pursuit,
I ha'e seen a' the coffin-stanes o' Time
Wha aince o' verses like the serpent work
On Innis Draoinich's crosses dreamt and ken
Art canna gang back to ignorance o' itsel',
Tine ocht that consciousness has won for it,
Or find new equilibrium except
By mair and mair self-knowledge. Men like me
Are traitors to't if we dae ocht but help
To big the Third Convention, lang delayed,
. . . 'Strength beyond hope and despair
Climbing the third stair.'[1] . . .
(Where men can think without first haen to feel)
Aiblins owre lang, since lack o't drags us back
                    Like ghaists to an inferior life.

[1] T. S. Eliot's 'Ash Wednesday'.

A fool sings 'O it's braw to see
The mortal coil come adder-like
Oot o' the heather at yin's feet
And owre the glintin' water strike
In corkscrew style and instant glide
Frae sicht again on yonder side.

'Wad that the Zeitgeist, progress, a'
The warld's perplexities thegither
Micht as sma-bookit slide across
Oor vision in the sunny weather,
And leave the gowden warld ahint
Withoot a single crinkle in't.' . . .

I have been frequently astonished, letting go[1]
My dead at last, to see them so at home
In death, so unexpectedly at rights,
So in their element that in a trice
'Twas ill to fathom they had ever lived. . . .
You only, you come back, and seem to try
To come in touch with something that will ring
Out suddenly, and show that you are here. . . .
O rob me not of what I've hardly learnt,
For I am right and you are wrong if still
You covet anything of so-called life.
We change all this, and see there's nothing here
In the clear light of our perfected selves.

I had more faith in you, and it confounds
All my ideas to find you here again,
You who changed most abysmally of all.
Not that your death is still incredible
(Although the manner of it tore apart
All we had been from aught we since could be
And made it difficult for us to find
Ourselves again). The trouble is that you
Were terrified to die, and keep your fear

---

[1] Adapted from the German of Rainer Maria Rilke.

Where fear is out of question, and so lose
A bit of your eternity, and lapse
Back here where nothing is as yet itself
– That broken, merged for the first time in the All,
You cannot see as even here you could
Life's upward irreversible way, and fall
By the dead weight of grievance from the spheres
To which you now belong to this poor past.
– *That* wakes me often like a thief at night.

Would I could think that you came sportively,
Because you are too certain of yourself,
O'erspilling your abundance, like a child
Going careless where grown folks must needs have care.
But ah! You ask for something. In my bones
That fact goes back and forward like a saw.
You ask for something. Though you were a dream
Tormenting me, pursuing me at nights,
When I retreat into my lungs and bowels
And the last poorest chamber of my heart,
E'en that were easier borne. . . . What do you ask?

What can I do for you? Is something, left
Behind you inadvertently, crying
Incessantly to find where you have gone
And vainly craving to be after you?
Where is it? Must I seek it in some part
Of life you never knew you had at all –
And failed to reckon with before you died?
Then I'll go there at once, and watch the ways
Of women about the doors and with their young,
Converse with all and sundry, and secure
An audience of the King, suborn the priests
To let me enter their holy places – yea,
And above all I will, when I've learned much,
Look simply at the animals until
An essence from them imperceptibly
Glides into me – stand in their eyes awhile

And witness how they put me out again
Gently, incuriously, and unjudged.

I'll get the gardeners to name their flowers
That in what I remember I may bring
Some faint suggestions of their myriad scents;
And fruits – I'll buy fruits till that country's like
Our old idea of what Heaven would be.

Full fruits! Ah, these you understood, set them
On plates before you, counterbalancing
Their weights with colours; and like fruits you saw
Women and children driven hither from within
Into their lives, and naked bore yourself
Fruit-like at last before the mirror here
Looking at yourself till like a pool your look
Closed over you, insubstantialised
(And no more saying: 'This am I, no that is')
In those pure depths from which it had no wish
That you should ever re-emerge. Blessed!

Thus had I kept you, as you steeped yourself
Deep in the mirror. Why come differently?
What to recant? To tell me what? Is there
A sacrificial weight in amber beads
A visual recollection fails to show?
My memory cannot tell the purport now
Of looks so urgent and discharactered,
Or why your body's graces all appear
Like lines of destiny on an outheld palm.

Come to the candle. I don't fear the dead.
If they are to be seen my eyes will see
Them naturally enough. Come hither then.
See this cut rose. The light's as shy of it
As 'tis of you. It, too, need not be here,
But if 't had stayed outside, unmixed with me,
It would have kept on growing and ere this

Have fallen apart – whereas it lingers here;
And yet – what is my consciousness to it?

Do not be frightened if I understand,
(Ah, there! It comes to me) for I must know
Even though the knowledge kills. I know you're here.
Even as a blind man fumbles round a thing
I feel your plight and have no name for it.
Let us lament together – the broken mirror
And you found naked in your hiding place.

Can you still weep? You cannot. All your tears
Contributed to ripen you and sent
The saps within you mounting in a life
That climbed and circled – to that height from which
Your fate reclaimed you, taking bit by bit
And daily more, till nothing but the core
Was left, full of the green seeds of your death;
And these you tasted in your hunger too
And found an after-sweetness in your mouth.

From this self-sacrifice your life returned
All trembling and mistrustful to its tasks.
How strange your most familiar organs seemed
(All save that one, exigent and estranged)
To your blood refluent from that secret source
Whether you had to drive it, make it eat,
Again and yet again, the while it looked,
The ingrate thing, as though you poisoned it.
You forced it finally – and lo! it ran
Too fast, too fast, it ran. You sought to cry:
'Whoa there! You're far enough. Too far for me
To herd you back' – but suddenly you knew
'Twas gone too far indeed, beyond recall.
The time to drive it back would come no more
Like a recurrent illness. You were free.

How short your life was, put against the hours
You sat surrendering all you might have been
To that blind germ of destiny again.
O tragic task! O task beyond all power!
How day by day you undid all you'd grown,
Made yourself down to other ends and still
Had courage to be proud of doing it well,
And then you looked for your reward at last
As children do when they take medicine
But you'd to do your own rewarding too
You were too far away from us even then.
No one could think of anything to please.
You knew it, and sat up in childbed there
And from the mirror that was you received
Your own self back, eager as a woman is
Dressing for visitors and doing her hair.

And so you died, as other women died
Before you in that cosy home, the death
Of women lying-in, who'd close themselves
Again, and only be themselves, but ah!
Cannot because the darkness enters in
And will not be denied – the darkness that
Women give birth to with – the outer dark.

Surely the keening women should have keened
In truth – women who weep for pay and whine
The whole night through, if they are paid enough,
When there's no other sound. Customs, hither.
We need more customs. Let us show our grief.
We acquiesce too readily – and so
You, dead, come back that you and I may mourn
Your death more adequately. Hear me then.
Fain would I throw my voice as 'twere a cloth
Over your remains, and have all I am
Torn into rags for ever, were mourning all.
Beyond all lamentation I accuse –
Not him who drew you back out of yourself

(I do not know him – he is all mankind)
But I impeach the world in him the Man.

If my life holds a state of having been
A child I can't recall – the purest state
Of being a child my earliest childhood knew,
I do not want to know it – I want to make
An angel of it without seeing it
And send it into the very front rank
Of shouting angels who remember God.
The agony has lasted far too long.
It is beyond us – this anachronism
Of false love spawning out of habit,
And claiming as its rights the wrongs it does.
Where is the man who has the right to own
What only snatches itself up at nights
Blissfully as a child might snatch a ball?

Are you still here, unseen? You knew as much
Of all this and might have had so much,
Open for everything, like a dawning day.
Women can suffer. To love's to be alone.
Poets know love's a readiness to change.
You were both woman and poet, and both form part
Of what our memories distort as you.
You grew so homely, taking in your looks
Like flags the morning after a fête – and all
You wanted was a long day's work, but ah!
The work was never done – is not done yet!

If you're still here – if in this darkness there's
A place in which your spirit hovers still
About the tired sounds of my lonely voice
Hear me, help me, for see we disappear,
Not knowing when, into anything beyond our thought
Even as a landsman's eyesight fails to hold
The Deity on the shoulders of a ship,
When its own lightness lifts it suddenly
Up and away into the bright sea wind. . . .

Gin I sud cry 'aince Scotland led the warld
In education but didna lead itsel'.'

    Oor four Universities
    Are Scots but in name;
    They wadna be here
    If ither folk did the same
    – Paid heed tae a' lear
    Exceptin' their ain,
    For they'd cancel oot syne
    And leave us wi' nane.

    I summoned the students
    And spiered them to tell
    Where Trenmor triumphed
    Or Oscar fell.
    'Dammit,' I cried,
    'But here is a mystery –
    That nane o' ye ken
    The first word in history!'

    I tested them neist
    In geography and there
    Their ignorance was such
    As gar'd me despair.
    Innis Fada and Rosnat
    Made them look green as
    I'd spoken o' places
    On the faur side o' Venus!

    But, och, when I cam'
    To Arts and Letters,
    The gomerils gapit
    And shamed their begetters!
    – Even Muireadhach Albannach,
    Lachlan Mor of his stem,
    And Finlay Macnab
    Meant naething to them!

> *The professors were waur*
> *Than the students were even,*
> *And yattered in Sanskrit*
> *Or Czech – wi' a leaven*
> *O' some kind o' English,*
> *A leid o' their ain;*
> *God grant I may never*
> *Hear the like o't again!*
>
> *'I'm beggin' your pardon*
> *A mistake has been made.*
> *It was SCOTS Universities*
> *I was seekin',' I said.*
> *'To condemn your ignorance*
> *'Ud indeed be to wrang you*
> *When in Hell here there isna*
> *A Scotsman amang you!'*

'And history has nae ither example o'
Sicna blin' leadership o' the less blin'
– A country wi' nae culture o' its ain,
Nae religion, that's contributed nocht
To human thocht: and hates and fears
Ideas as nae ither country does
        For centuries on end.
There's apathy elsewhaur, no' this ill-will.'

> *Lourd on my hert as winter lies*
> *The state that Scotland's in the day.*
> *Spring to the North has aye come slow*
> *But noo dour winter's like to stay*
>   *For guid,*
>   *And no' for guid!*
>
> *O wae's me on the weary days*
> *When it is scarce grey licht at noon;*
> *It maun be a' the stupid folk*
> *Diffusin' their dullness roon and roon*
>   *Like soot,*
>   *That keeps the sunlicht oot.*

Nae wonder if I think I see
A lichter shadow than the neist
I'm fain to cry: 'The dawn, the dawn!
I see it brakin' in the East.'
> *But ah*
> *– It's juist mair snaw!*

Strauchtway I see this fear and hatred is
The measure o' the task that Destiny's put
Upon the Scottish people, and their vain
> Ettle to jouk the kittle role.
The coontervailin' force'll yet win free
> – And's 'good to kyth in me!

Is this the meanin' o' the stream that flows
Roond the warld yont the sea's horizon then?
> *Denn wo Natur im reinen Kreise waltet,*
> *Ergreifen alle Welten sich . . .*
Man here into his ain circumference fa's
But whatna consolation's this to ane
Wha kens that Buddhist seers can often reach
The sun's corona and hoo Swedenborg
Whiles gaed to ither planets, and visited
A heavenly body aince that lay ootside
The solar system a' thegither?

> *'O frati,' dissi, 'che per cento milia*
> *perigli siete giunti all' occidente,*
> *a questa tanto picciola vigilia*
> *de' vostri sensi, ch'è del rimanente*
> *non vogliate negar l'esperienza,*
> *di retro al sol, del mondo senza gente.*
> *Considerate la vostra semenza:*
> *fatti non foste a viver come bruti,*
> *ma per seguir virtute e conoscenza.'*

I ken the stars that seem sae faur awa'
Ha'e that appearance juist because my thocht

Canna yet bridge the spiritual gulf atween's
And the time when it will still seems remote
                    As interstellar space itsel'
Yet no' sae faur as 'gainst my will I am
Frae nearly a'body else in Scotland here.
But a less distance than I'll drive betwixt
                    England and Scotland yet
(Wrang–heidit? Mm. *But heidit! That's the thing.*)

> *I ken what gars the feck o' folk*
> *Accept the rule o' Fate*
> *And till last year*
> *Used whiles to fear*
> *A' men, at least in Scotland here,*
> *'Ud gang that thowless gait.*
>
> *But I ha'e found co-workers syne*
> *In whom I see the licht*
> *O' wills like mine*
> *Increasin' shine*
> *– In a'e shape to unite.*
>
> *Nae doot in ithers I dinna ken,*
> *Gin I could only see,*
> *The spirit's at work*
> *– And it may lurk*
> *Unkent in neist to a'body,*
> *Unkent to a' eternity.*
>
> *For I've nae hope o' maist folk . . . yet.*
> *The few in whom it shines*
> *'ll aiblins multiply*
> *Till by and by*
> *The haill shape, big or sma', defines,*
>
> *The shape o' Scotland's purpose,*
> *Its profitable will,*
> *– Or imitation o't*
> *Due to oor faulty thought,*
> *But wi' its ain pooer still.*

(Scotland's purpose to the warld's
A comparison to me
As 'twere a bonny dear
To the serpent at her ear
Movin' like the Fir-chlisne
                    There.)

Sae we maun sing as we were richt
And canna be mista'en,
Nor doot by sicna sang
No' Fate but Destiny plain
'll kyth amang's or lang,
And Error set Reason ga'en.

As lanely in the croodit streets
We gang, yet here and there
There beeks in Scottish een
A licht owre lang unseen,
But what it yet may mean
To Scotland, and to mair
Than Scotland, we're no' shair
And in the meantime needna care
But act as tho' we were. . . .

The Muse to whom his hert is given,
Historia Abscondita,
's already workin' like a leaven
To manifest her law.

The Gaelic sun swings up again
And to itself doth draw
A' kindlin' things, while a' the lave
Like rook is blawn awa' . . .

'Come tell me more of Scotland[1]
– I know its many poets,

---

[1] These verses were published as a separate poem in the *Irish Statesman* under the title of 'The Irish in Scotland (to a visitor from France).'

Byron, Lermontov and Wergeland,
And how Kant and Satie show its
Blood in their diverse ways;
And how Jean Rictus lived
In Edinburgh – Chopin too;
And what Stendhal says
              Of Scottish airs,
And now I'd fain hear you. . . .

I asked him if he'd heard
Of Burns or Sir Walter Scott,
Of Carlyle or R. L. S.
He said that he had not.
' Some people think that these
Are representative . . . I don't.
At least, you've little to forget,
And should assimilate with ease,
              From that false Scotland free,
All that's worth knowing yet.'

I took him to the islands
Where the wells are undefiled
And folk sing as their fathers sang
Before Christ was a child,
Then by gask and laggan and coul
To Aigas in Strathglass
Where he heard a port on the golden chanter
That can never be heard by a fool,
              And lastly to Lochan na Mna
That will respond, I believe,
To me, if I want her
As Lake Saima couldn't to Soloviev.

'Ón áird tuaidh tig in chabhair'
I said as we turned south,
And quoted 'A theachtaire thig ón Róimh,'
With blessings on the honey mouth
That loved the forests of Alba,

Cut down now, that may grow again
Thanks to the branch of Ireland
Growing among us with might and main
And 'Dia libh, a laochraidh Ghaoidheal'
            And 'curse the Sassenachs'
And left him, twenty miles from Carlisle,
            On his way back to France. . . .

Wad that I held Staoiligary
        And the four pennies o' Drimisdale,
And had never seen a news-sheet,
        No' even 'The Daily Mail',
The fifteen generations afore me
        Could lippen me no' to fail
Into the darkness o' alien time,
        To carry my sang and sgeul
As the duck when she hears the thunder
        Dances to her ain Port a' Beul! . . .

At dawn at the heid o' Clais Linneach
            A mile frae Fuaran Dhé
I saw a wee clood that awa doon
            In Glen Guisachan lay.
It grew as the sun's strength grew
Till it filled ilka glen and corrie
And covered a' but the heichmaist taps
O' the Cairngorms billowin' hoary.

The sun's licht on the clood reflected
            As on the waves o' a sea,
And as frae the Ark on Ararat
            The warld then was to me;
Syne fifty miles owre the mist-ocean
Wha but Alasdair MacMhaighstir stude?
Pricked oot in the blue and gowd there
In his maist idiosyncratic mood!

Faurer awa', steeply, oot o' the sun-bathed
               Distant Atlantic's waters
The great poets o' Gaelic Ireland
               Soared up frae the rags and tatters
O' the muckle grey mist o' Englishry –
Phoenix-flight frae the ashes upbeatin' –
Raifteri, Ó Rathaille, Ó Súilleabháin,
Feiriter, Haicéad, and Céitinn!

No' muckle's been tint in the Deluge
               Suppose it subsides nae mair.
I'm brawly content wi' what's left,
               And the ignorance flowin' doon there
Emphasises by way o' contrast
The glorious music abune
– Great poems manifestin' at aince
Ilka phase o' the sun and mune! . . .

Sall moudiewarps like eagles thrill
               Wi' a' the warld at view?
Blether o' Burns and Tannahill
               Wha kenna you[1]
And roost their mice wha never saw
               The Lion ava'?

Puir Rimbaud in his Bateau Ivre
               Gaed skitin' roond a dub;
O' Earth and no' juist Hell un livre
               The puir bit cub
Had aiblins made, gin he'd survived,
               Whaur your boat thrived.

Jaupin' the stars, or thrawin' lang strings
               O' duileasg owre the sun
Till like a jeelyfish it swings
               In deeps rewon,
And in your brain as in God's ain
               A'thing's ane again!

[1] Alasdair MacMhaighstir Alasdair.

Auld Noah in his sea–barn was
      Your canny prototype;
Moses juist halved a burn, whereas
      You'd seas to flype,
And Melville sailed to jouk the world
      Through which you hurled,

As in his lines Valéry tries
      To keep but their ain life,
Whereas in yours sea, earth, and sky's
      A' hotchin' rife,
Your genius copes wi' a' that is
      In endless ecstasies.

The blythe broon wren and viein' linnet
      Tune up their pipes in you,
The blackcock craws, the reid hen's in it,
      Swan and cuckoo;
Fishes' and bees' and friskin' calves'
      Acutes and graves! . . .

O time eneuch for Heaven or Hell
      Efter a man is deid,
But while we're here it's life itsel',
      And meikle o't we need,
And, certes, coupin' up the Earth,
      You f'und nae dearth!

Praisin' Morag or dispraisin',
      What does a poet care?
Sugar Brook's tune, sea's diapason,
      A's grist that's there.
Sodger, sailor, and poet chiel
      – And man as weel!

Wad that in thae thrang modern times
      I micht inherit,
And manifest in a' my rhymes,
      Your dowless spirit,

That balks at nought – aye competent
          To be – and ken't!

Like Leontiev and you I'd keep
          A' Earth's variety,
And to the endless challenge leap
          O' God's nimiety
– Aiblins, like Him and you, great Gael
          Whiles see Life haill,

As in yon michty passage in
          The Bhagavad-Gîta where
A' Nature casts its ooter skin
          And kyths afore us, bare,
Compliqué, nombreux, . . . et chinois!
          The airmy o' the Law!

Is there nae man amang them that has worn
The violet or the scarlet goon, and been
In Rome or in Valladolid or Louvain,
Or kens his country in its Latin poets
As weel as in its English versifiers,
And Dunbar's debt to Catholic liturgy
That gars me read him, and syne Burns, and feel
As if I'd waukened up in Heaven to find
That efter a' the Plymouth Brethren were richt? . . .
Is there nae man amang them that has seen
In yon unsullied stream the symbol o'
The unity frae which a' movement springs,
Centrifugal force reflectin' the spirit's vision,
As Isadora, oor countrywoman, did,
Or consciousness o' ilk hypostasis
– Empiric, ethic, rational – cleared in turn,
The abstract disciplines we sairly need.
Till '*l'art de penser juste*' is freed again
          Frae *la trahison des clercs?*

I was a bard in Alba and Eire
    Two hundred years ago.
Michael Comyn was one of my friends
Who was two men, you know,
A Protestant buck outside
And a Jacobite at heart,
And I wish I had half his skill
In the poet's art,
Yet I tread the way that he trod
And play a similar part,
Still filling a friendless page
In a different indifferent age,
But oh – *na h-éachta do chuaidh.*

I visited Reformation Scotland
With Fearghal long before that
And saw all that would come to pass
To the land in that foul trap caught,
And what have I found since then
But centuries' additional cause
To deplore the scholarship lost
And the ancient laws,
Everyman a priompallán now?
At every Cross in Scotland I pause,
Crying (in Scots) like O'Heffernan
Ceist cia chinneochadh dán?
Or – *Ionmolta malairt bhisigh!*

Or if I go up on a wing
And scan over Europe again
I feel like 'The Wandering Hawk,'
No Phœnix, that's plain,
But as I hang there I hear
Fearfeasa's and Laoiseach's lament
Echoed by Russian poets
In their winter of discontent,
Tyutchev's double existence
And Foeth to the mob unkent

Right down to Byely's intense
Quest for an exit at last
From the desert of nonsense
In the teeth of the Bolshevik blast.

What wonder if I crave too
'Heaven – let me be beautiful
And fall from sublime heights to earth,
Benign, like the golden sun's rule,
And all-embracing as it.'
Fain I'd alight again
Weary of infinite strife
On a monumental world all lit up
With intelligent love of life.
A salt wind off a heaving sea
Is not what Scotland needs,
But my song cannot change and cry
For a while to him that reads
The world is passing as bloom from branch,
Or even lie like an Autumn sky over
A rich country of fruits . . . and seeds.
                    All comes in due season.
                    Fuar lem in oidhche-se d'Aodh.

O I hae tint you and maun quick rin owre
A' I hae said – and left unsaid to say it –
Since last I saw you mak' the warld a farl,
                '*Truth isna seized; it dawns,*'
But in the middle o' the nicht what guarantee
Has ony man, tho' day's lang followed nicht,
It'll dae't again, or Truth keep growing clearer
To human consciousness? Clearer? Or's ever kythed
                To ony man's mind at a'?

Thocht's aiblins no' the e'e to see it wi'
And has anither purpose, tho' it may keep
Men frae some *vision extra-retinière*
Beasts ha'e and plants and bairns, and maist folk still,

But if Thocht's no' the e'e to see it wi'
What Thocht sees is mair important still
And if Truth's shown to bairns and stupidity
Taps deeps that pit a' brains beside the mark
And I maun choose 'twixt Thocht and Truth chaps me
                    Thocht a' the time.

But you're no' Truth in ony case, but Error,
The endless Error, puir Shelley sae misca'd,
                    Es irrt der Mensch, so lang er strebt
The glorious snake that flourishes and feeds
                    On a' the rays o' Licht,
Slidin' sae smoothly that it mak's
Cacophony o' Valéry's esses even
And Tagore's Vasuki juist a belly-thraw.
(I maun look up the mediæval reference again
            To Christ as the worm,
For we're no' used to snakes in Scotland here
And h'ae suffered frae Knox on the heid sae lang
That we micht tak' a blindworm, or at best
                    An adder, for Cencrastus!)

I think on a' Humanity and mind
Koltzov's great figure o' a lass wha's breists
Heaved in a passion, but didna cast up
                    Her foundation o' sand,
And foresee the time when maist folk *wull*,
But hope that I'm owre canny a Scot for that!

I was a bard in Alba and Eire, but the Muse
That I'm concerned wi' noo has heard o' neither,
And it wad tak' a life as lang's Methuselah's
For ony Scot or Irishman to big
Machineries o' expression like the English, French or German
                    – That haena circumjacked you yet;
But shairly we metaphysical Scots can play
A pairt in this great enterprise still,

Scotland's cauld and grey, you say,
But it's no' ill to prove
Oor dourest hills are only
Rainbows at a'e remove

We Aiberdeen Doctors be Subtler Doctors yet
And no' keep yatterin' aboot dogs and daisies
And debatin' whether Marykirk or Milngavie,
Jessie o' Dunblane or Hieland Mary's bonniest,
And playin' the Mairch o' the Yammerin' Men.
Plato was a son o' Athens, no' Apollo,
And I – belang the Muckle Toon, of coorse,
Yet ken the plight the hird in the *Noctes* kent
– The frenzy o' the immaterial soul in maitter droonin'
And warslin' wi' unkent poo'ers to get a fithaud yet
                    On the greensward o' genius!

Gowdfinches were rife on the Borders
Till the eighteen-forties but syne
Disappeared and didna come back
Till the new century started,
But wherever there's thistles and hardheids
There's charms o' them noo.
Wad the Borders could mak' good a'
            Their losses like this!

A cock siskin sings in a spruce,
Crossbills are thrang wi' the rowans,
And a big crap o' beechmast has brocht
Mair bramblings aboot than ever,
I'll hear them breezin' afore
They leave for the North again,
And aiblins I'll follow them there
            And aiblins I'll no'.

A'e winter thirteen waxwings, hungry
Wi' their crossin' frae Europe, stript
Yon brier o' its hips in a hurry,
And I aince saw a yellow-browed warbler

Near by; and four grey shrikes in the Dale;
And there's nae sayin' what I'll no' see
In the neighbourhood yet, nae maitter
                    Hoo lanely and quiet it looks. . . .

(Yet it'll gie me mair joy to see
Ocht natural tho' rare
– A honey-buzzard, or peregrine –
Than a Roc or Moa there. . . .)

I hear a fool (Plotinus he is ca'd)
Say, 'Intelligence was a Unity, but alas
                    Didna bide as it was,
But unkent to itsel' turned mony-fa'd,
Grew pregnant . . . Wae for its posterity!
Better there ne'er had been a Secondary!'
And turn to Thocht as wha to a trauchled wife,
Mindit in sair times o' blithe coortin' days
                    Turns to'r and says:
'Your fond dream little recked o' sic a life.
Yon were the happy days. Wad ye no' lief
Ha'e a' sin syne undune, wi'ts want and grief?'
And hears her say: 'You think I little kent?
I kent a'richt – and yet was willin',
                    And that's the mood I'm still in.'
And little tho' the cratur's life has meant
– Hers and her man's and bairns' a' meanly spent –
I ken that she is richt and a' her pain
And seemin' waste o' effort better than nane
                    Tho' I'd fain
Ha'e had her tyauvin' on a different plane
Few folk ha'e ever gained or 'll ever gain,
A number that'd no' be sair increased if a'
The need for ither effort was ta'en awa'
                    – As it'll yet be ta'en!

You say it isna lawfu'
To speir frae whence it springs,

As 'twere to place and motion
Subject like ither things
For it neither comes here
Nor yet can gang awa'
Tho' whiles we see't and whiles
It canna be seen at a'.

You say that we maun wait
As men wait for the dawn,
But the sun's way by nicht
Is plain to Everyman,
And tho' we mauna seek
This secret source, you say,
Some o's'll find it yet
– At least in the same way.

When Wordsworth saw Lucy row'd
In Earth's diurnal course
Wi' rocks and stanes and trees
He saw by science perforce,
And contrair to human sense;
We gang mair contrair still
Wi' ideas we canna express
Except by a miracle.

The trouble is that words
Are a' but useless noo
To span the gulf atween
The human and 'highbrow' view
– Victims at ilka point
O' optical illusions,
Brute Nature's limitations,
And inherited confusions.

Silence is the only way,
Speech squares aye less wi' fact.

Silence – like Chaos ere the Word
That gar'd the Play enact
That sune to conscious thocht
Maun seem a foolish dream.
Nae Word has yet been said,
Nae Licht's begun to gleam.

Tyutchev was richt and men maun gang
Awa' frae life to find
Haill worlds o' magic thochts
Day's licht can only blind, –
Thochts that they ne'er can share
Sin' each man's faurer are
Frae ony ither man's
Than star frae wide-set star
And faurer frae his usual sel'
Than Heaven is frae Hell.

But a' the stream o' consciousness
In maitter as in a tunnel lost
'll yet win free and jaw
Owre the warld's edge tost
Like a gowden waterfall
Naething can backward turn,
Nor spin in a vicious roond
Like yon apodeictic burn.

O wad that men could think
No' rationalise insteed
Mere preconceptions till
Nae real thocht's in their heid
And wad that they kent hauf
As muckle o' themsels
And things that maitter mair
As Science o' chemicals.

I'm gratefu' for the stream
That rids us o' vain dreams

And thraws us back upon
Oorsels' wi' its clear gleams,
And yet we mauna be
Objective like the Greeks
Blind o' a'e e'e – and no' the ane
That humour steeks!

As Wordsworth shair o' his ain mind
The precipice whiles socht
Whaur a' else fa's awa'
And vanishes into thocht
Sae I repudiate here
As treachery to mankind
Contentment wi' the graces men
Like beasts or floo'ers may find.

And look to see the fountain
That loups to a certain height
And fa's again and rises,
As tho' were the sun's delight
To brak' its shaft and glitter
Frae abune on its scattered sparks,
Flee oot, autonomous as art,
Through a' the Heaven's arcs.

But that's no yet and tho' I'm flegt
When there's nae gleam to see
I ken fu' weel that Chaos still
Freedom and pooer maun gie
To organisin' Reason that else
'Ud lack a' life and beauty,
And that Ignorance, Pain and Daith
Are needit – yet a wee.

Man's curse has never been
His disregard o' the past
But the way in which he's let
It haud his spirit fast,

And next to the Past the Present
Binds him hand and fit,
And but for his surrender
He could ha' been heicher yet
Frae ocht that ony man is
Than men frae the brutes, I wis.

The way that maist men think
And feel's beneath contempt
And frae a' that seems established
We canna be owre quick exempt –
Tho' the theory o' 'Historic patience'
Applies to a'thing as to nations
And I maun gie a special section
To Scotland's case in this connection!

The day is comin' when ilka stane
'll hae as guid as a human brain
And frae what they are noo men
Develop in proportion then
        (At least it's hoped they will
            And no' be owretaen still)
While sex and ither hauf way stages
Perish wi' the barbarous Ages,
Tho' maist folk then as noo nae doot
'll hae 'the misfortune no' t' exist,'
And the feck o' the rest 'll lead a life
That to ocht worth while 'ud never be missed.

For the eternal evil's no'
Tragedy, but the absence o't,
No senseless extremes but the sordid mean,
No pooer but a pooerless lot,
No' the sharp and deep, but the dull and flat,
No' Hell but no' ha'en even that,
And the triviality o' a'
But the haill o' human thocht.

O the Devil is naething strange.
His face is the crood's or oor ain
When we cease to be oorsel's
And become 'like abody' again –
When we cease to be oorsels
And try to be English insteed
And o' oor distinctive Scots
Tradition see but a gleid
– Tho' I see a' its morse code whiles
In the Anglophile night
As compared wi' Cencrastus
Gin' that's glintin' bright
As Blake at times descried
The showery form o' Enion
At the loved Terror's side. . . .

Shairly we metaphysical Scots can play
A pairt in this great enterprise even yet
– A pairt that aiblins 'll mak' up and mair
In twa-three years for a' we've left undune
For centuries

Even as a Scot that few Scots ken
Ballantyne, did awa'
Wi' the hellish agony men
Accepted as the law
O' Childbirth until then
– Tho' gin it took us a'
That time in sic a maitter
Nae wonder we're sae faur ahint
In things o' a kittler natur'!

                    If we turn to Europe and see
Hoo the emergence o' the Russian Idea's
Broken the balance o' the North and Sooth
And needs a coonter that can only be
                    The Gaelic Idea
To mak' a parallelogram o' forces,
         Complete the Defence o' the West,

And end the English betrayal o' Europe.
(Time eneuch then to seek the Omnific Word
                    In Jamieson yet.
Or the new Dictionary in the makin' noo,
                    Or coin it oorsels!)

A sideless, bottomless, endless sea
             Is no' for me,
A waesome jobble, nae skyline seen,
Nae land, 'loved mansionry, jutty or frieze,
Or coign o' vantage' that comfort's yin's een
Or a 'procreant cradle' to man's mind gies.
Still less can I thole the silly emotion
That conjures up, confrontin' the ocean,
A Land Under Waves or some sic freak
Like the 'bune-sky Heaven Christians seek.

Folk wi' the sea, wha nae mair ha'e hoped,
             Ha'e never coped.
Their sangs are the sangs o' gulls no' men.
Their Hebrides are like Coleridge's talk
Gien' glisks o' intelligibility, then
The foggy curtain again draps back.
– Wad it had lifted and left bare
The meanin' o' the islands there
While owre the restless gulf folk saw
No' Tir nan Og, but America!

Unguardit frontier facin' a West
             No' o' the Blest!
It's no Missus Kennedy Fraser's sangs,
A' verra weel for Sasunnachs and seals,
That'll voice the feelin's movin' amang's
To whom the sicht as to men appeals.
Let's hear nae mair o' Tir nan Og
Or the British Empire! See the fog
Is liftin' at last, and Scotland's gien,
Nae bletherin' banshee's, but Europe's een. . . .

I often think that it may be
In Scotland yet as in Germany.

That ill altho' things are the day
We may ha'e an Aufklarung tae.

And rise frae a Lohenstein's bombast
To a Goethe or Schiller juist as fast

And as the Germans did wi' Klopstock
Sae Burns become to Scottish folk

Wi' a' the annual orgy gane
Like the ongauns o' the Hain

Tho' Grobianism and Eulenspiegel's
Made bubblyjocks o' a' oor eagles. . . .

Aodhagán ÓRathaille sang this sang
That I maun sing again;
For I've met the Brightness o' Brightness
Like him in a lanely glen,
And seen the hair that's plaited
Like the generations o' men.

'Wha'e'er she is, I daurna look,
Eidolon o' a fallen race,
Wi' lifted e'en, as fain I wad,
Upon her noonday face
– Tholin' my ancestors' assize
For centuries in a minute's space!

And yet as tho' she didna see
The hopeless boor I was
She's taen me to her white breists there,
Her bricht hair owre us fa's.
She canna blame me gin I fail
To speir my fortune's cause.'

O wad at least my yokel words
Some Gaelic strain had kept
As in Othello's sobs the oaths
O' Thames, no' Venice, leapt,
And aye in puir Doll Tearsheet's shift
The Queen o' Egypt stept.[1]

The modest daisy like the Rose
O' a' the Warld repetalled
– Fain through Burns' clay MacMhaighstir's fire
To glint within me ettled.
It stirred, alas, but couldna kyth,.
Prood, elegant and mettled.

Nor owre my life's accursed acre
Dunvegan threw a bough,
To look as it had flourished there,
Nane seekin' to speir how.
Nae borrowed grace in this puir place
The particular Fates allow.

Illustrious, cardinal, aulic, curial
– Can e'er my tongue be these?
I ken fu' weel I ha'e nae words
To match Divine Philosophy's
Yet aiblins, tho' they canna last,
She needs her misalliances!

And yet . . . and yet . . . it isna richt
To waste hersel on me;
Fu' mony a belted earl 'ud fain
Ha'e sic fair company.
I doot that when I ope my mooth
In horror yet she'll flee.

[1] With acknowledgments to Georges Lafourcade.

And yet . . . and yet . . . nae doot she kens
Better than me her need,
And gin I aped the gentry's tongue
'Ud flee wi' greater speed,
– Or is't a freak o' humour gars
Her dally wi' my leid?

And will she lauch ahint her haund
At my uncouth demeanour,
Comparin' my orra love wi' that
Some popinjay has gien her?
– At least by tryin' to seem refined
It's clear I'd juist chagrin her.

Chagrin her – and chagrin mysel,
For, certes, I'm alowe
Whether she loves me, guid kens why,
Or needs rouch hoose, I trow,
Or thocht to tease and jink me syne,
Maitters fell little – now!

Aodhagán ÓRathaille sang this sang
That aince mair I sing here.
It's oh my dear, and oh my dear,
And oh my dear, my dear.
The time to love is short, is short.
We'll love – afore we speir.

. . . But tho' I'm blinded in her licht
The hardy doot's still rife
That aiblins I am sair beginked
Thro' sma' experience o' life,
And favoured here wi' nae King's dochter,
But juist . . . a minister's rinawa wife. . . .

Scots folk are feared to educate their bairns
Owre weel in case, ootgrown, they're syne despised,
And gin they catch them readin' poems, forsooth

Hale them back to their lessons fast or else
Gar them rin messages or play fitba' even,
And abune a' they'd ha'e them be as like
Themsels as possible – but 'better aff' –

Wheesht, my wee man, wheesht.
Folk winna come rinnin'
    And pointin'
    And cryin'
'Look at him, look at him!
    He disna ken
Longinus or Rimbaud
    And never will.'
              No' them.
              Nae fear.
Then wheesht, my wee man, wheesht.

As if they werena handicapped eneuch
In bluid and settin' at the stert, puir souls,
Nae wonder that for centuries nae Scot
        Mackenzie, Marr, the best o' Scots
        Are frae their donnart country hid
        Like him wha's sunk mair Spanish gowd
        Off Scotland than th' Armada did.[1]
Has glimpsed the possibilities o' Art
Content to tak' a' (little as that's been)
Frae ither nations and gi'e nocht in turn,
Aye, use what's ta'en against the spirit even
        Frae which it comes.

Struldberg, Orlando, Wandering Jew,
Scots History lives in me anew.
As King by King comes to my mind
A dish o' orts is a' I find.

El Rey de Escocia no es nada.

         [1] R. B. Cunninghame Graham.

For nane was king o' ocht but pairts,
And Bruce, a hero in certain airts,
Was Norman first and Scotsman second
And aye o' self, no' Scotland, reckoned.

El Rey de Escocia no es nada.

And Chairlie o' the gowden heid
Won little support till he was deid
And maist that's left's frae folks wha'd tak'
The ither side gin' he cam' back.

El Rey de Escocia no es nada.

And Rosebery, 'oor uncrooned King'
His fiky wits could never bring
To bother lang wi' the race o' Scots.
The Derby oftener claimed his thochts.

El Rey de Escocia no es nada.

And as for ony Wettin or Windsor
– But oh, losh me if I begin, sir!
They're juist as like bein' Scottish Kings
As Scotland's Scottish in ither things.

El Rey de Escocia no es nada.

Imagine Burns, Scott, Carlyle, Lauder
Kings – Could onything be madder?
God micht ha' dune, gin he'd been livin'
But he played safe, preferrin' Heaven!

El Rey de Escocia no es nada.

I'm oot for shorter oors and higher pay
And better conditions for a' workin' folk
But ken the hellish state in which they live's
Due maistly to their ain mob cowardice.

Yet tho' a' men were millionaires the morn
              As they could easily be
They'd be nae better than maist rich folk noo
And nocht that maitters much 'ud be improved
              And micht be waur.

> '*A*' *complain o*' *want o*' *siller,*
> *Nane complain o*' *want o*' *wit.*'

It's waesome that millions s'ud be cut off
Frae Art, like the Neanderthal brutes at large
When Plato raised his een to Socrates
And heard his haly virtuosities.
But what's to dae? We micht as weel grieve owre
Beasts no' bein' able to read, and seek to teach,
As waste the energies that can address
Their mental betters on the mass o' men.
Aye, lower oor standards a fraction o' an inch
To reach a' men insteed o' ane – or nane!

> *No!*
> *I dinna prefer whippets*
> *Or a Rotary Club*
> *Or Kirk Work*
> *Or* '*the Picters*'
> *Or onything at a*'
> *To what you ca*'
> '*Arid intellectual exercises.*'
> *Au contraire!*
> *Richtly we try to stop*
> *Ony man we find*
> *Spreidin*' *a foul disease*
> *O*' *the body – no*' *the mind,*
> *But we wadna be sae sairly curst,*
> *Wi*' *either if we put the latter first!*

Let them maist conscious o' haen betrayed
Their country, for 'narrow nationalism' condemn

Ideas like mine, as wha care and ken least
O' poetry mak' the maist o' Burns's claims,
And syne denounce my internationalism tae
Gin I cite Russian, German, and Irish names
Instead o' stickin' to the *Golden Treasury*,
And brag o' pigmies like Bruce or Hume or Caird
Or Scotch Theology or Thrift or onything Scotch
As wha micht roost a dub and ha'e nae een
                        For the Seven Seas.

I ha'e nae sympathy for ophthalmic ills
Save whiles clear-sighted folks' wearied wi'
                Owre muckle o' the unforeseen,
                Or sceptics' desperately bent
                On penetratin' the unkent,
Yet mind when I'd a puirer view o' you
Than ony I've had syne (and see it still
Clearer in memory than it was in fact
And clearer faur than a' I've had since then,
Tho' each in turn was clearer than the lave,
And's tint the mair the clearer it was).

Frae Anither Window in Thrums

Here in the hauf licht waitin' till the clock
Chops: while the winnock
Hauds me as a serpent hauds a rabbit
Afore it's time to grab it
– A serpent faded to a shadow
In the stelled een its een ha'e haud o'

Here in the daurk, while like a frozen
Scurl on Life's plumm the lozen
Skimmers – or goams in upon me
Wan as Dostoevski
Glowered through a wudden dream to find
Stavrogin in the corners o' his mind,

– Or I haud it, a 'prentice snake, and gar
Heaven dwine to a haunfu' haar
Or am like cheengeless deeps aneth
Tho' ice or sunshine, life or death,
Chequer the tap; or like Stavrogin
Joukin' his author wi' a still subtler grin. . . .

And yet I canna for the life o' me see
That I'd write better poetry
If like the feck o' Scots insteed
I read the books they read
And drew my thochts o' God and Man
Frae Neil Munro and Annie Swan!

Fu' weel I ken I would mak' verses which
'Ud notably enrich
'Oor Scots tradition' – in the minds
O' ministers and hinds;
And fain I'd keep as faur frae that
As Proust frae Johnnie Gibb – that's flat!

– Can I get faurer frae't than here
Whaur a' life's fictions disappear
And I'm left face to face wi' nocht
But sicna drab splash as brocht
My like to be, to mak' wi't what I can,
Back at the stert whaur a' began? –

Seed in my womb, I ken nae mair
Than ony wife what bairn I'll bear
– Christ or a village idiot there
A thronèd king, or corpse i' the air? . . .

Nature to Art is still a witch
Confinin't by waefu' metamorphosis
To Life, a memory mindin' which
It bairnlies itsel' again like this. . . .

For if it's no' by thocht that Poetry's wrocht
It's no' by want o' thocht
The verse that flatters ignorance maun seem
To ignorant folk supreme
Sin' nane can read the verse that disna
The damned thing bides as if it isna!

Maun I tae sing a useless sang
                'La chanson grise
Où l'Indécis au Précis se joint.'
Naebody else can listen to
– Like shades o' music missin' to
A' but ane in a listenin' thrang,

And perfect it forever mair
Like Proust wha thocht he couldna sleep
Sae lang that, sleepin', he'd still a deep
Unsleepin' sense o' sleeplessness there,

And borrowed frae that in turn the thocht
That he'd been soond asleep frae the stert;
And syne – but och! the sang in my hert
Coonts ilka shadow frae nicht to nocht!

– Like Proust, or the Glesca man wha deed
And said to Charon: 'It's unco queer;
I dreamt I was deid, and no' juist here
At hame on a Sawbath day insteed!' . . .

Enclosed in silence, Earth's sang, unhurriet
Dwines through the endless stages it needs
As 'twere the kind o' life Daith leads
In the deid aince they are buriet. . . . .

That's the condition o't or near
Grey glumshin' o' the winda here,
– As fit a subject for immortal sang
As ocht wi' which men's minds are thrang . . .

Here at the heicht o' her dance
Athikte's off in a dwam
– Gane in a kink
And no' able to think
By what mischance
She's tint her 'I am,'
Or hoo to win back
Her knowledge and knack.

As ane that wauks in the nicht
Oot o' a croodit dream
 Openin' blin' een
 On a toom black scene
 Till life in a fricht
 Like Daith 'bood seem
 Gantin' at her
 A fish oot o' water,

Athikte withoot avail,
Drooned, 'ud dance on the plain
 O' the oorie sea
 But the nimbleness she
 Had in feet in a tail
 Is no' to capture again,
And even the art o' M'Diarmid
Leaves her a connached mermaid.

And ane in which Truth, Nature, Wimmen
– A' threidbare themes – gang timely dim in.

Tho' few hae's muckle's Dostoevski's een
To see wi' – or be seen;
– God and themsel's but things they read
In penny novelettes instead –
The difference 'twixt the few and mony
In this puir licht seems sma' if ony.

And tho' I summon up Gods, priests and seers,
Warriors and saints, ilk ane peers
– A' the great names in history –
Wi' the same airgh: a mystery;
Man pits into the lift nae face
That isna equally oot o' place.

Here in the hauf licht hoo I've grown!
Seconds but centuries hae flown
Sin I was a reporter here
Chroniclin' the toon's sma' beer
Tinin' the maist o' life to get
The means to hain the least wee bit.

> *I wha aince in Heaven's height*
> *Gethered to me a' the licht*
> *Can nae mair reply to fire,*
> *'Neth deid leafs buriet in the mire.*

> *Sib to dewdrop, rainbow, ocean,*
> *No' for me their hues and motion.*
> *This foul clay has filed me till*
> *It's no' to ken I'm water still.*

Pars aboot meetins, weddins, sermons, a'
The crude events o' life-in-the-raw
Vanish like snowflakes on this river . . .
Dans le flot sans honneur de quelque noir mélange . . .
On wha's black bank I stand and shiver;
Nakit! – What gin the boss, as weel he micht,
Comes in and switches on the licht?

The Twentieth Century at Eternity
Gapes – and the clock strikes: Tea!
And sombrous I arise
Under his silly eyes
And doon the stairs, the devil at my back.
I doot the morn I'll get the sack!

'What was I dae'n sittin' in the dark?'
'Huntin' like Moses for the vital spark,
– A human mole
Wi' a hole for a soul?'
'I sud think o' my wife and faimly'
I listen to him tamely.

'Cut oot this poetry stuff, my lad. Get on
Wi' advts. and puffs, and eident con
The proofs; it's in you gin you care
To dae't and earn (your maister) mair.
    Furth Fortune fill the fetters!
Apply yersel' to what's worth while
And I'll reward ye: that's my style.'

'Yessir, I'm sorry. It'll no'
Heppen again. The clock was slow
And I was slower still, I'm sorry
In gettin' back again afore ye
To sicna state as fits the job
O' ane wha's brains you lout to rob.'

Curse on the system that can gie
A coof like this control o' me
– No' that he's in the least bit waur,
Or better, than ither bosses are –
And on the fate that gars a poet
Toady to find a way to show it!

Curse his new hoose, his business, his cigar,
His wireless set, and motor car
Alsatian, gauntlet gloves, plus fours and wife,
– A'thing included in his life;
And, abune a', his herty laughter,
And – if he has yin – his hereafter.

Owre savage? Deil the bit! That's nocht
To what men like the Boss deserve;
Maist men that is – anon I'll gie
Them a' their paiks, wi' muckle verve.

He has an angry birthmark on his cheek,
>   ... *Le roy Scotiste*
>   *Qui demy face ot, ce dit-on,*
>   *Vermeille comme une amatiste*
>   *Depuys le front jusq'au menton. ...*
A purple pig's fit – a' his skin
Sud lowe forever in black burnin' shame
To mak' his ootside like his in.

I'd send it owre him like a flypin knife
Till like a carcase in a butcher's shop
He fronts the world – affrontin' it;
A rinnin' wound that nocht'll stop.

For sae the will to ignorance o' his kind,
Their line o' least resistance ruins life
As wha maun tine through foul disease
The heich ideas wi' which he's rife. ...

Curse a'thing that gars me pretend or feel
That life as maist folk hae't is real
Or waste my time on their ideas
Or silly sociabilities,
Service, meanin' or ocht that'll tak'
My mind off ony verse it'll mak'.

>   *I'm no' the kind o' poet*
>   *That opens sales o' work. ...*

Curse on my dooble life and dooble tongue,
– Guid Scots wi' English a' hamstrung –

>   *Speakin' o' Scotland in English words*
>   *As it were Beethoven chirpt by birds;*
>   *Or as if a Board school teacher*
>   *Tried to teach Rimbaud and Nietzsche.*

And on this curst infirmity o' will
That hauds me bletherin' this way still
On things that like a midge-swarm pass
Sub specie aeternitatis.

    Athikte I hae sung
    Wi' a loose and gallus tongue,
    Made a clamour better-suited,
    To the Trollop, Life, I doot it,
    Than to ane wha's never set fit
    In a vulgar spirit yet.

    Dulcinea aye turns oot to be
    Aldonsa to a man like me
    Yirdit in this plight alive
    A' in vain I shout and strive
    – And, gin I gied owre, my hert's beat
    Faurer still 'ud fleg your feet.

Gin but the oor 'ud chop and set me free
Frae this accursed drudgery
Aiblins – aince I had had my tea –
I could address mysel' to poetry,
Sufferin' nae mair th' embarrassment o' riches
Wi' which desire brute circumstance bewitches
Till my brain reels and canna faddom which is,
'Mid endless cues, the ane for which it itches,

    Thrang o' ideas that like fairy gowd
    'll leave me the 'Review' reporter still
    Waukenin' to my clung-kite faimly on a hill
    O' useless croftin' whaur naething's growed
    But Daith, sin Christ for an idea died
    On a gey similar but less heich hillside.
    Ech, weel for Christ: for he was never wed
    And had nae weans clamourin' to be fed!

As 'tis I ken that ilka instant gies,
If I could haud it lang eneuch to seize
Them, coontless opportunities
For reams o' verse in as many different keys,
– And that's damned nonsense for they canna a'
Lead t'owt worth while – gin owt's worth while ava'.

　　(*Hell tak this improvisin'*
　　That leads a' airts and nane;
　　A kind o' anti-poetry
　　That is true poetry's bane!)

Athikte I dreamt that you were here
Lyin' by me like a wumman in the daurk.
I heard the breathin' o' the seven seas
Faint as the matins o' a licht-lost lark,
– Or was it my ain happy hert that passed
My hearin', and was tint in sleep at last . . .
Athikte, I thocht I kent I didna ken
Which o's was you and which me, then.
The haill warld pillowed on my shouder, licht,
As gin I'd been the sun by nicht.

Athikte I dreamt that you were here
But I am as a man wha's love is deid.
She comes in a' her beauty to his bed
But when he wauks, the toom nicht's there insteed
Sae a' the poet's moods I hae
Look in the cruel licht o' day
As silly as an effort to
Cuddle a ghaist my airms gang through.
And ilka sang is like a moon
That hings, a bonny aught, at noon. . . .

I'm weary o' the shapes mere chance can thraw
In this technique and that; and seek that law
To pit the maitter on a proper basis
My faith in which a feature o' the case is

I canna deal wi' here, but efter tea
Will – if the wife and bairns – we'll wait and see . . .
A' this is juist provisional and 'll hae
A tea-change into something rich and Scots
When I wha needs use English a' the day
Win back to the true language o' my thochts.

Stars are equal in wecht
Tho' they differ in size:
Betelgeuse, tight as the sun,
'ud draw in the skies
As Earth recovers a stane
Thrawn up frae the lift again.

Space 'ud fauld up and leave
Us ootside it (i.e.
Naewhaur) – as, whiles, I feel
A thocht o' Dunbar in me
Grow heavy until it has brocht
A' Shakespeare's sequence to nocht.

Scots letters, Dunbar, are juist names
For the effects o' a star
O' Finality deep in my mind
Pu'in' things asklent frae afar
– Fegs! English 'll look a gey fool
If this bias seizes the bool!

'Scots is a thing o' the Past'
Maist folk say: and 'There's nae
Pittin' back the hands o' the clock'
And 'History nane can undae.'
– Can they no? In the darkness here
My coorse, either way, is fell clear.

And a' the day lang as I wark
In the office here
I feel the drag on my mind

O' a star that ettles to veer
The way o' life – till at nicht
I sit blin' in its licht! . . .

O Knowledge, wha can say
What benefit it is
To think o' China in Milngavie?
Felis demulcta mitis.

A man rakes through the ages
But kens his stature yet is
Nae cubit mair than erst it was.
Felis demulcta mitis.

And a' he comprehends
O' life and love and ditties
Is – ony cat 'll purr if stroked;
Felis demulcta mitis.

A' men can ken and think
Depends on what their wit is;
Procrustes plays at Proteus;
Felis demulcta mitis.

O Knowledge, wha can tell
That o' ye ilka bit is
No' juist a dodge to hide faur mair?
Felis demulcta mitis. . . .

'There's owre mony yads in the fire,'
Cries my Muse, and her taengs hae taen
A'thing but Godheid and Scottishness
Oot o' my sang again!

Whaur is the fool that hasna wished
That he'd been God and no' anither,
And ev'n in daen't thocht o' a'
Frae sicna role micht gar him swither

And kent God even better by that
Yet ev'n in feelin' he kent Him better
Kent that nae man can think o' God
In terms ayont his ain puir natur'
And syne, in kennin that, kent God
As something he could never ken
And felt his ain life soarin' up
To hidden heichts, like some great Ben?

On sicna heichts I'll big my nest
Soar thence and sing, licht doon and rest,
And whiles see a' the warld as yince
An airman fleein' through the mist
Saw in a rift wi' startled een
A promontory sheep and wist
Hoo dangerously laigh he'd been.
– *Aye! That's what's ca'd a nose-dive, Prince!*

I wha wad sing as never Scotsman sang afore
(And could owre easily, but in anither sense!)
And yet as naebody but a Scotsman ever will
The tables for my unkent God's communion fence
– Queerly eneuch (tho' a' my braidclaith's nakedness)
Feelin' like ony ordinar' elder, mair or less.

Cette antique union du Poète et du Prêtre . . .

Sheep's face be gane. My spirit canna be mair
Than a distortit memory o' the U.P. Kirk
As lang as you're aboot. Aye, tho' I ordain,
Wi' layin' on o' hands, and covert smirk,
The whore o' Babylon – or ony ither whore –
To join the Session, it'll be a tethered splore,

Haud'n to the common God like a bird in a cage;
E'en Clootie winna ser' me for he's naething but
God's ain sel' flyped, and apt to richt himsel'
At disconcertin' times – as a silly gut
Whiles hides in a dirl o' music tae
Its intention to brak' in the usual way.

And aye the veil is rent and a' I see
In horror-stricken blasphemy is mysel'
As in a mirror, and owre my shoulder, Daith,
And 'yont Daith Life again – an endless swell
O' mountain efter mountain, a faithfu' flock
Each wi' a bawbee for the collection poke!

I'm the original
Plasm o' the ocean.
Feebly amused
At God's last notion

He ettles to use me
Like a conjurer's hat
And gar me evolve
He disna ken what –

Countries wi' their flora
And fauna – but lor!
He forgets hoo often
He's dune it afore.

I couldna thole
The process again
If he didna aye think
It has juist dawned on his brain,

If he didna aye wonder
Hoo faur he could cairry it
– Losh me when he canna
As muckle as vary it!

I'm the original
Plasm o' the ocean;
Humour accoonts
For my ditherin' motion.

There is nae limit to the modes in which
The minds o' men the Universe construe
Save that they're only men's – o' a'e wee star
A'e kind o' its life, and o' that kind as few
Men hae't, the product – Prima Facie, then
Scant is the value o' the minds o' men.

My memory is the warld's: a bearded king.
A lovely wumman, and the rest's a dust
O' nations that gaed through me to their daith
What o' the life that's gane that I su'd trust
The life to come? The Future like the Past
'll leave a puckle fragments at the last.

A wanton wumman and a shaggy king
Why sud their memory survive the years?
Wimmen as fair and men wi' langer beards
Are as they'd never been. Fact disappears
And leaves a silly fable in its place,
A whirl o' chariots or a whippet race.

Progress? There is nae progress; nor sall be,
The cleverest men aye find oot again
For foolish mobs that follow to forget,
As in the Past, the knowledge men ha'e haen
At stented periods frae the dawn o' Time:
And Sisyphus anew begins his climb.

The cleverest men? Or are there cleverer still?
Those nameless wha by ither standards judge
Than knowledge, beauty, length o' beard or aucht
That history uses, and wha winna budge
To humour fame or sense – and are they no'
The mighty masses that we ken nocht o'?

Or cleverer still, the beasts, the plants, the dirt
Frae which a' comes and back to it returns.
Man's destiny is inseparable frae the clods

And a' Life's divers shapes Earth inly spurns
As ane wha sees that a' men's thochts are but
Disguises for the a'e reality o' rut. . . .

>   The God I speak o's him wha made
>   The warld and ither warlds that are
>   As different frae't as Nicht frae Day
>   Or Life frae Death
>   – The God in whom religions centre,
>   No' Him that lifts unkennable ayont
>   Creation and Creator baith!

Wha by Divine can think o' nocht but life
Raised to the heichest poo'er, to mair
Than genius is to common-sense,
Mid-day to mirk,
Ettlin' to turn into angels syne
As caterpillars into moths,
May grub in a kirk.

The Gowden Eagle disna stegh itsel'
On sic cocoons; the betterment o' man,
And a' that life is or sall become
Are nocht to *that* God,
But wha' for a' Creation cares nae mair,
Nor less, than for a whigmaleerie, tak's a'e step
Alang his endless road.

God the Creator still maun ser'
The mindless fools wha canna . . .
But to see ev'n him as weel as ony man
Can gin he tries
They maun unbig the warld they're pairt o'
And brak' the foond whaur the serpent
As a sacrifice lies,

The immortal serpent wa'd up in life
As God in the thochts o' men.

– Open the grave o' the universe
And it'll loup oot again;
And your een sall be like the Bible syne
Gin its middle was tint
And Genesis and Revelation
Alane left in't

Suddenly my verse 'll gie men
Glisks o' the serpent wallopin'
Wi' a' that they are gien' way afore it
As a nichtmare rides;
Wi' a' that they are turnin' to pairt o't
Like silly shapes that thow in a dream,
Like Athikte here, or the bumbaized warld
The Flood row'd in its tides.

This, at best, is the God that men
Can humanly ken; and the serpent's
The clearest sense o' the nature o' life
To which they can win
– God whirlin' in Juggernaut while under its wheels
The generations are drawn and vanish
Like rouk in the sun! . . .

Nil nisi divinum stabile est; caetera fumus . . .

> *Sall Jewry breed a Christ*
> *Gaeldom canna equal,*
> *Or India wi' a Buddha*
> *Prevein anither sequel? . . .*

He'll ca' nocht else a Heaven if he'd fain
Hae's fit insteed upon the heathery miles
Or wi' the lobster-fishers sail again
To Fladda Chuain and the Ascrib Isles.

If there's a Heaven it maun vie
Wi' this auld land o' his wha's hillsides lirk
Like elephant skins as he gangs by
Aince mair 'twixt John o' Groats and Maidenkirk. . . .

The Jews wha aince set oot to big
A new Jerusalem by the Forth
Stopt – Auld Reekie ser'd their turn;
They kent to come nae faurer North.

Sae faur their Asian madness blauds.
It canna file this gowden realm,
Nor Brocken-like can Calvary
Oor mountains in its mole-hill whelm! ...

A wee kirk squats aneth the hills
Wi' Latin windas reid and blue;
It's naething but its ain inside
That's whiles begairied wi' their hue.

Ootlandish colours canna shine
Oot owre the hills that stand aboot,
And gin the congregation's dyed
They're still like Scots folk comin' oot,

And see again a michty warld
Frae silly whigmaleeries free,
And a' the skyline wipit clean
O' ony trumpery Trinity! ...

Noo in synoptic lines
A Scot becomes a God
– A God in Murray tartan
To whom nae star's abroad.

Wha's idle fit owreturns
This stane and that to show
Asia's hotchin millions,
A mune wi' nocht below.

He looks wi' equal een
On a'thing deid and livin'
His bauchles in the Zeitgeist,
His bonnet cocked in Heaven! ...

There's naething that a man can be
That's mair than imbecile to me
In the licht o' totality.

Nae man worth ca'n a man can thole
To be haud'n doon to ony role.
— Fegs! I'm no' browdened on the whole.

Hoo can I sing lest I begink
Mysel' wi' a sang less mine than I think
Or some short-circuit o' a kink?

And what but that is this a'e doot
Still glimmerin' in a warld o' soot?
What else'd I ha'e gin *that* gaed oot? . . .

He looks at me and I looks at him
Dod, says I, but you're lookin' dim.
What has happened to dowse your glim,
        Auld snake? says I.
You canna be in your usual trim.
Ha'e a drap o' this. It'll buck you up.
Dinna be feart. Juist the tiniest sup
        — It's the real Mackay.

Wad you believe 't? He swallowed the lot,
And didna alter a tittle or jot.
I envy your cheek, and mair sae your throat,
        Auld snake, says I.
The haill o' the warld by the time you've got
To a deoch an doris 'll be dry, by gum
— Except for the fact that that'll be *rum*
        The haill o' the warld'll be dry! . . .

(*Can I get deeper doon than this*
Amang the warld's inanities?
Oh, fegs, there's deeper faur to gang.
This wadna keep life gaen lang.

Lee go your brain and try again
It's no' sae easy as it's payin'
To be a fule like Lauder. Dod!
It's less by tryin' than gift o' God.

Gift o' God! The only road
To Paradise! Nae doot my load
O' thochts awaits a better joke
For easement tae, as stupider folk
Are eased, by puirer jokes, o' theirs,
And in the end a' Man's affairs,
Like settin' a thief to catch a thief
'll find their ain absurd relief.

Nae doot! But Man's resource o' Wit
Is faur eneuch frae that as yet.
We're a' o's pent in some belief
Or hope that lacks the right relief
To look as silly as it should
And does to minds a thocht less crude
But gin Life in the lang rin's a'
A joke – is that a joke ava'?

I canna see't; but that's no' odd –
Owre nice for Lauder and for God,
I'm feart lest in the end I'll be
Bored to daith in Eternity,
That muckle Hippodrome Hereafter
Whaur a'thing's swallowed up in laughter,
Wi' Lauder's kilt and Chaplin's feet
Supernumerary to the Paraclete.

Let's try again . . .)

The problems o' the Scottish soul
Are nocht to Harry Lauder;
I met a lassie in Maybole,
Athikitty, they ca'd her.

I thocht I'd woo her, but aye at the squeak
O' my muckle buits she was aff like a streak
Sae I tried it syne in my stockin' soles
And dootless I'd ha'e fund her
But I lost my way – nae wonder,
For they were fu' o' holes.

Then fare you weel Athikitty,
I'll try nae mair, says I
It's haurdly for the likes o' me
To plague a wench sae shy.
There's ither pebbles on the beach
But I'll admit – you are a peach.
I could ha'e had you a' the same
But it'd ha' been a darned shame
– For to gang barefit, d'ye no' see,
'Ud ha' been owre barefaced for me!

(Is this Scots humour? Like a poet wha's
No' in the mood and finds ideas and words
Fell lourd and dour that else were licht as birds
My memory in puir, fushionless outlines draws,
Offsettin' Lauder's, and my ain *that* breeds,
A' kinds o't frae Dunbar richt doon to Burns
Till I'm fair hotchin' wi' its coontless turns
– A routh o' entertainment dowed, that only needs
Yokin' again to Scots, to loup to life;
But still twixt it and me, a smeekit glass,
Hings this hauf-English, winna let me pass,
And mak's my harns wi' reelin' shadows rife,
Faur ayont which, unkent, lie kinds o' fun
That kent 'ud mak' a' ither humours dun.
– O lauchter that in turn becomes the joke
Lead thou me on – alternate fire and smoke!

Lead thou me on – to still mair leadin' on;
There is nae goal, for ony goal 'ud be
A lauch to last for a' Eternity
Wi' nocht ootwith itsel' on which to hone

The keener sense that ser's for aye to pit
The stage afore it in a form absurd
Thus feedin' the crescendo still unheard
When utmaist wit's like idiocy void o' wit.
This is the inevitable end – there is nae joke
That mak's the warld or ony aspect o't
A thing to lauch at but itsel' has got
An airgh o' humour like a nickerin' moke;
Lauchter's nae lauchin' maitter – fegs,
The time 'll come, as shair as eggs is eggs
When I myself 'll be as firmly stuck
In some auld rut o' humour as the ruck.

Certes the time 'll come, but no' juist yet!
Is this Scots humour – (This is it! . . .)

(Can I no' think o' Lauder as Beethoven thocht
O' General Abercrombie in Eroica No. 3?
Pince-sans-rire, I doot I'm thinkin'
Less o' Beethoven than o' Satie.

Embryons desseches; the ghaist o' the cuttin' machine.
'll ser' me for anither Holothurie
Or for ocht else the trouble wi' me bein'
As I've just said, that I'm aneth the sea,

And canna rise. Fu' mony a doonsin' gem
The dark, unfathomed caves o' ocean bear,
And true appreciation o' Lauder's ane,
Ineffably amusin' – awa' doon there!)

There's owre mony killywimples in your singin'
It minds me o' my een
When they seek to spae the weather by the sun
And there's nocht but rainbows to be seen.

The lintie sang coonterpoint when the ouzel yelpit
But your sang's faurer frae me
Than the sun frae the earth when its rays in the grey lift
Blinter like honesty.

If a'e man brocht an Empire into bein'
At the tea-table on blottin' paper wi' reluctant ink
Aiblins I'm nearer, even in sic half-formed dreams,
To re-creatin' Scotland than I think.

'Three centuries syne the Wittelsbachs and Bismarcks
Had an alliance – can it no' be renewed?'
– Three centuries syne, and thirty, o my hert,
Wi' what auld friendships are you no' endued?

Three centuries hence, and thirty, o my hert!
What unborn giants loup within your womb!
– What tho' to that new Empery past you noo,
Scotland, ignorin' you, gangs, girt in gloom? . . .

(What 'ud you hae? Gin Lauder and
Your boss and a' Mankind turn't suddenly
To study your immortal works what better
'Ud you be then? What better 'ud *they* be?

Look what they've made o' God. Thank God
Your mind is no' a puzzle for ither folk like His.
Let them abee – for each o's lives
Fishlike, accordin' to his lichts, I wis.

And gin you ferlie maist folk still
Gainst a' the Past are pigmies, yet content,
Hoo big d'ye think's the ambition to be ither
That in a puckle heids like yours is pent?)

Even my wife whiles fails to see
– And wha can blame her? Fegs no' me! –
What ails me that I canna win
Wi' a' my brains the comfortin'
Security that maist folk hae
(*Folk in oor station, that's to say*)
But aye on ruin's brink maun sway,
And risk her and the bairns tae
– It's no' as if I could be shair
My verse at last'll be worth mair. . . .

Oot in ilka brainstorm
Withoot an umbrella
Whaever saw the like
O' sic a foolish fella! ...

Up to the een in debt I stand
My haill life built on shiftin' sand
And feel the filthy grit gang grindin'
Into my brain's maist delicate windin'.
And gin a' Thocht at sicna time
Is present to me what's the use?
It's bad eneuch to droon in slime
And no' rive a' Eternity loose
And pu' it doon alang wi' me
Into the foul diurnal sea,
To mak' a bonny pair at last
Wi' starfish, bottles and corks upcast. ....

He has nae treasure in his pooch
– Except a quid pro quo;
And mony a bricht Saint Andrew
That nane but he can show!

It isna fair to my wife and weans
It isna fair to mysel',
To persist in poverty-stricken courses
And never ring Fortune's bell.
Thoosands o' writers wi' nae mair brains
In their heids than I've in my pinkie
Are rowin' in wealth while I toil for a dole,
– Hoo's that accoontit for, thinkee?

Oh, it's easy, easy accoontit for, fegs.
I canna gie the folk hokum.
I can poke 'em and shock 'em and mock 'em,
But the a'e thing needfu' is hokum!
It pits a' thing else on its legs.

Losh! They'd ha' put me a brass plate up
In Langholm Academy,
And asked me to tak' the chair
At mony a London Scots spree.
They'd a' gien me my portrait in oils
By Henry Kerr, and the LL.D.,
And my wife and weans 'ud been as weel aff
As gin I'd been a dominie,

> If I'd only had hokum, hokum,
> Juist a wee thing common hokum!

A seat on the Bank o' Scotland buird,
And a public for my poetry, . . .

> If I'd only had hokum, hokum,
> A modicum o' hokum!

It maitters little what line ye tak'
If you hae hokum wi't;
Butter or snash, it's a' alike,
Gar them laugh or greet.
There's naething the public winna stand
And pay for through the nose,
Barrin' the medicine that's ser'd up neat,
Whether it's bitter or whether it's sweet,
Wi' nae hokum to the dose.

> But what I canna accoont for's no'
> Bein' able to gie folk hokum.
> I can joke 'em and sock 'em and choke 'em
> But the a'e thing needfu' is hokum.
> – I wish I was Neil Munro.

It isna fair to my wife and weans,
It isna fair to mysel'.
The day's lang by when Gaels gaed oot
To battle and aye fell.

I wish I was Harry Lauder,
Will Fyffe or J. J. Bell,
– Or Lauchlan Maclean Watt
For the maitter o' that!
– Dae I Hell!

Oh, it's hokum, hokum, hokum,
And this is as near't as I'll get.
The nearest I've got yet,
Losh, but it's unco like *it*,
        – That sine-qua-non,
            A soupçon
        O' precious hokum-pokum!

Here in the hauf licht waitin' till the clock
Chops: while the winnock
Hauds me, as a serpent hauds a rabbit
Afore it's time to grab it
– A serpent faded to a shadow
In the stelled een its een hae haud o'. . . .

O I hae tint you. Quick. I'm wastin' time
Gettin' nae fithaud on yon greensward yet,
Inspexi lucem, subito quae erepta est mihi.
The brilliance o' form nae langer shines
Upon the subject-maitter o' my poem
I've let owre muckle in't no' needfu' to
The licht that su'd ha'e been my a'e concern,
Dulled and debauched my work, forgotten ev'n
Hoo my hert louped when I beheld
A crab-like dooble canon aince
And saw hoo frae the tenth bar a'
The music ran backward to the stert[1]
And felt as gin Squire's poem had passed
And let me see the Mune again.
O I hae tint you (*gin e'er I saw*)
                You that can ne'er be tint.

[1] Schönberg's 'The Moonspot.'

Ca' into question, foolish brain, the way
By as muckle as mentionin' them I share
The antics o' the antirrhinumists.
And, gin' the feck o' folk mean little, why
I aye look back to less – to plants and beasts,

> *It's no the purpose o' poetry to sing*
> *The beauty o' the dirt frae which we spring*
> *But to cairry us as faur as ever it can*
> *'Yont nature and the Common Man.*

Like some puir spook that's no content in Heaven
(A figure that's a variant o' the fau't)
But needs maun haunt Earth still; and swear I've made
My verses sic' a Noah's Ark – o' troot,
Cormorants, ducklings, serpents, and losh kens what
I might please W. H. Hamilton yet
Wi' a sang to a Hairy Oubit or Green Serene,
Secondary sex characters in Asparagus Officinalis,
Or buck-eye poisonin' o' the Honey Bee,
Or Fungicidal Dusts for the Control o' Bunt,
To fill the gaps in *Holyrood*.

'Owre muckle in't.' Hoo keen folk are to keep
Poetry 'in its place'! But you're on better lines
When you point out my leid is scarcely Scots
Tho' gin I used the full canon o't
I'd still be anomalous like Wordsworth wha
Changed diction but no' metre; and syne speir,
Gin a'thing maun be lauched at and burnt up,
What Scottish Nationalism or Poetry maitter?
The answer's easy. It's eneuch to say
'Let's mak' a better joke in politics and art
Than the English yet – and damn consistency!'
('Let's mak' a better joke *addressed to Scots*
                         Is nearly it!)
I'm back to my original stanza noo
It's no' juist arbitrary like the Warld
But is a different if no' a better joke
A joke o' my ain, tho' I've ended it

Wi' a bare vestige o' the auld bob-wheel
To show that there is corn in Egypt yet.
And if it hauds a troot it's no' because
I share the anglin'-mania o' maist Scots
Mair than their anglo-mania tho' I guddled aince
In the Water o' Milk: But just because
They're equally fishy, and the World's
No' faur eneuch oot o' the sea frae which it cam'
                              To suit me yet.

I ha'ena seen you haill, Cencrastus, and never may
But ken fu' weel the way you're movin',
Coil upon coil frae ooter dark to licht
And ev'n what's clear changes its appearance
Frae minute to minute as the noise o' horns
Twixt Eliot's Waste Land and Day's Parlement o' Bees.

No' in appearance only but in fact
Deeper than ony man, or Time can faddom.
For ae thocht differs sae muckle frae the neist
(Machinery's effect on life's a minor case)
A' ither differences – hedgehogs frae lilies –
Are nocht to it's. Yet centuries o' sic thochts
Through life and a' the arts and sciences strewn
Whiles kyth aefauld in you.

– A noise o' horns – or as Mary Macleod
Wi' a wheen sangs frae her careless hert owreturned
The traditions o' thoosands o' years
And altered twa literatures – aye gied her mode
Sae strang a haud that a' that gaed afore
Was blotted oot as it had never been
Folks' natures and notions changed until
It seemed impossible they'd been ocht else
Ev'n in the deepest things – the way they loved
And saw the coloured warld wi' their ain een.
A' men are changelings owre and owre again
And their last state is maistly a' they ken
                              Or think there is.

Gae tell a banker or onybody else
A change o' stress on vowels or consonants
'll change the haill o' life in twa-three years
– That ony system gies equally good results
But different as apples frae oranges
And ask him if he wants a warld confined
To a strict diet on a single fruit
And isna fear't o' universal scurvy syne
For it's a form o' that that blights a' life
Belief in ocht, no' a' its opposites tae,
And there's nae health except where this complex
Bright action thrills through ilka stagnancy
And clears the way – for still mair o't!

Auld Mary Macleod in her tartan tonnag
Has drunk her whisky and snuffed her snuff,
And the Lord has put a new sang in her mooth,
Hallelujah that's the stuff!

It alters the haill complexion o' life
And mak's a deid language o' a' we've kent
The music the bards for thoosands o' years
Missed is hers by an accident.

When folk say 'God made the world' and think
It took Him a' His time
And canna imagine – a' they canna imagine
Let them mind Mary's rhyme.

When folk say 'God . . . ,' but juist as the bards
Were whummelt, the thocht o' God
Sae lang unchallenged in maist folk's heids
Maun gang the same road.

For freedom means that a lad or lass
In Cupar or elsewhaur yet
May alter the haill o' human thocht
Mair than Christ's altered it.

Aye dae, the morn, for the haill o' creation
                    Mair than Mary for Gaelic sang
– Or dizzens o' them in different airts
                    At aince be thrang.

I never set een on a lad or a lass
                    But I wonder gin he or she
Wi' a word or deed 'll suddenly dae
                    An impossibility.

                    A'e thing's certain: Christ's Second Comin'
                    'll no' be to Scotland whaurever it is.

Auld Mary Macleod in her tartan tonnag
Has finished her bottle and toomed her mull
And the sang the Lord put new in her mooth
Has turned unspeakably dull.

But no' as dull as in maist ither airts
The mind o' Scotland's aye been,
And I hope it'll be in them a' at aince
That the neist miracle's seen. . . .

Then dern nae mair 'neath yon twa-neukit mune
Nor whaur the sunlicht fills the lift wi' gool
– Puir poems concerned wi' incomplete ideas!
Barra, Acrasia – Dr Moreau's Islands!
I see the beast surge up in ilka face.
There is nae man or wumman, reasonable soul,
Frae instinct free and slaves to nae brute law.
A' forms grotesque or comely, gross lines and fine
Athikte wi' a glance reduces still
To the auld balance and bauch interplay.
Orgasms o' common crises – hate, lust, love,
Marriage, parenthood, etcetera.
Men praisin' Nature, and rejoicin' that
They keep their youthfu' spirit to the last,
                    Bourbons and baboons!

I canna be in the Antipodes quick eneuch
At ony minute to keep pace wi' you,
And gin I see you it is aye like some
Lateen that comes alang at dusk as though
Impelled by naething but th' advancin' nicht
What is there that lifts up a man's hert mair
Than seein' sic a ship come bowlin', alang
Breist-high towards him, careerin' owre the sea?
It seems to ha' borrowed something o' the air
Something o' the water, and unites them baith,
Their offspring and their bond; but syne I hear
Its sailors like a sparrow's scaldachan
And ken it's in Australia at maist
           They'll see the *tràigh adhairt*.[1]

Cheepin' and squeakin' like a puckle mice
Aneth a firlot! There's a deeper joke
Ahint the *gàir nan tonn* than they jalouse.
They micht as weel bide in the Islands whaur
To 'strains o' little meanin'' folk wi' less
Reap corn, or deer come doon to graze wi' sheep,
And fishermen can ha'e the undeemis stars
Like scorlins roond their thowl-pins ilka nicht
Or ony gudge look through his window-bole
Past nettles, dockens, apple-ringie, heather reenge
And think they're on his rizzar bushes there,
And sae they are as weel as onywhaur else!
The sea gies up its deid. It's a' it gies.
Its deid, or livin' – the apprentice deid!

Even as youth's blindness hauds the body dear
And only slowly, slowly, year by year,
The dark thins and the een o' love grow clear,
My hert'll stiffen and rejoice nae mair
In the lost lilac and the lost sea-voices,
Whaup's cry or goose's gansel o' mankind

---

[1] Used here in the literal sense, 'the coming forward of the beach.'

Nor set toom forms atween the ivory yetts
Nor curtain them wi' *siantan dubha*, tears,
Or Iolaire's, or angels', wings; but haud
The warld a photo o' me as a loon
I canna mind o' haen been at a'
A state I put awa' wi' spung-taed pranks
                    Wi' nae precociousness.

A state removed, as 'Little Goodie'[1] yet
Nae doot'll dae awa' wi' a' the stars.
For Nature's like grown men and wimmen thrang
Wi' hi-spy, smuggle the geg, crawflee, and tig,
Merry-my-tanzie, and beds o' Edinburgh.
And politics, religion, and a' men's ploys
Are nocht but new names for the same auld games
What use for Christ to cry to sic-like folk
To leave a' else ahint and follow him?
I'm no' a Christian but I canna say
That Christianity's failed – it's no' been tried,
Yet it's the warst romanticism o' a'
That ettles to be 'classical' again
                    Sae lang since Calvary.

There is nae Kirk; we've only poetry left,
Poetry – or golf, or gairdening, or the like!

Weel then! Tak' back the gowpenfu' o' dirt[2]
That took on life a wee while neath your hand
Shatter, unnatural Nature, heedlessly,
Needlessly, anither Design for a Man.

When you see ither – laicher – forms o' life
Oot o' this waesome corpse poorin' in croods
Are you complacent, findin' them at least
Obedient, mair obedient, to your moods?

[1] Sun-spurge – infallible against warts.
[2] Adapted from the French of Madame Ackermann.

Or d'you still dream that this chimera, hope,
Man, and 'yont man – 'll be some fine morn's morn?
You'd be a mither? You've conceived sic things?
To wark, then, wumman! Let the bairn be born!

Mak' a reality o' your fondest dream.
Alas, the distance is owre faur, the gap
Owre deep, for you to cross, nae maitter
Hoo keen you are, between your thocht and lap.

Daith is the only fruit you'll manage
In a' your future struggles to reach and pu'.
Aye mair failures, aye coontless creations
To bear – and bury too.

For graves and cradles multiply themsels',
Age follows age upon your road in vain.
The idea flees you, the ideal that draws you
Infinitely – only to withdraw again! . . .

The relation o' John Davidson's thocht
To Nietzsche's is mair important
Than a' the drivel aboot 'Hame, Sweet Hame'
Fower million cretins mant.

And gin we canna thraw aff the warld
Let's hear o' nae 'Auld grey Mither' ava,
But o' Middle Torridonian Arkose
                Wi' local breccias,
Or the pillow lavas at Loch Awe. . . .

Noo let me turn aside
And truly classical
Sing sangs at last of all
Things of true Scottish pride
– Sing twenty sangs at last
In mair than diamond cast.

They winna be the things
Maist Scots 'll recognise
– Deceits, delusions, lies,
Ocht that a poet sings
Wha wins a mob's applause
Or furthers ony cause.

They winna be the things
The English 'll admit
Wha's poets hae always writ
Great English verse that springs
No' frae true poetry's source
Nor wi' its final force.

They winna be the things
The French 'll readily praise
Fast in their narrow ways
Nae maitter what prood wings
They wag in Germany's eyes
But seldom in the skies. . . .

I

The MacSwiney Pipers

This happened in Glasgow yesterday.
The dark buildin's made a sober frame
For the bricht colours o' the movin' picture
As, on the bugle-ca', the sections gaed
Flame upon flame into place,
The bairns o' thirty parishes,
In gowd, green, lilac, siller and blue,
A' the warld's colours collected at aince,
(By a new and greater Glasgow School)
                In yon drab square.

Ahint the weans cam' thoosands
O' queans in the Sodality o' Mary
Wi' bouquets o' lily o' the valley
And ither white flooers; the Italians

Brocht a fresh glory to the show
Their hauflins cairryin' a life-size
Statue, carved in wud, o' the Virgin and Child,
Its gilt frame wi' swingin' gowd bells
Makin' sunlicht whaur there had never
(In the memory o' the auldest inhabitant)
                    Been ony afore.

They'd a tableau o' Calvary tae
Wi' the supplicant Magdalene bent
Amang the irises and ferns
At the fit o' the Cross; and in the Polish group
A laddie in claith o' gowd heidit
St Casimir's banner, and a reid-mantled lass
Cairried wheatears and grapes on a cushion
While a' St Brigid's lassies gaed by
Wi' leaves o' the vine in their hair
And bunches o' clear green grapes
                    At the sides o' their heids.

The Poles moved to a version o' 'Ora Pro Nobis'
Timed for slow mairchin'; ither bands
Played hymns or 'Killarney'
But I'm a Scot and my hert loupt up
When the MacSwiney Pipers
Made martial music o' 'Annie Laurie,'
Leadin' the waves o' colour
Agin the greyness o' Glasgow.
– It was worth bein' born a Scot
O' Presbyterian stock to enjoy
The MacSwiney Pipers at last
                    As muckle as that! . . .

II
The Weapon

Scots steel tempered wi' Irish fire
Is the weapon that I desire.

III
The Two Bruces

There were twa Robert Bruces.
Ane edited 'The Glasgow Herald.'
The ither focht for Scotland
When it was *less* imperilled.

IV
The Mortician

What do you think o' Roberton (Hugh)
And the glorious movement in music he's makin'?
He'd better ha'e stuck, gie the Devil his due,
To a different kind o' *undertakin'!*

V
Strangers

Strangers are in my true love's hame
Strangers wha hardly ken her name
And tho' the country looks the same
    It canna be.

Strangers are in my true love's hame.
She had to leave it when they came,
And oh! the strangers are no' to blame
    – And neither's she!

VI
Landscape

O weel I ken a hill, a road,
  Can whiles a picture make
As profound as the face o' God
  – In a sketch by Blake!

VII
The Head of Clanranald

Nae man can clim'
A' Earth's mountains.
I ha'e gane faur
In Gandhi and Lenin
And in Dostoevski seen
When the summit seemed reached
Aye anither ayont it
And turned and come back.

Christ in the springtime
And Buddha in autumn,
Nietzsche for practice
And Hegel for fun. . . .
Tabard o' Russia
And ghast Himalayas,
The stance frae which Pascal
Was fleggt at the stars,
And the whummelled summits
Dante climbed doon,
Wha frae the pash
O' Caledon craves?

Here frae the heid
O' Clanranald I see
Things in due measure
Sin I'm in my ain;
And whiles in the sun
The Earth frae my feet
Seems to vanish – and syne
I ken it entire! . . .

VIII
Better a'e gowden lyric
Than a social problem solved

Tho' maist folk never see
The beauty that's evolved
And think a million times mair
O' their ain waugh welfare.

Better a'e gowden lyric
That nane but the poets see
Than a Messiah's praise in a day
The mob in its vain moods gies
In turn to a Prince or jockey,
A Tancy, or Jennie, Lee.

Better a'e gowden lyric
The mob'll never ken
For this in the last resort
Mak's them less apes, mair men,
And leads their leaders albeit
They're owre blin' to see it.

Better a'e gowden lyric
Than Insurance, Bankin', and Law,
Better a'e gowden lyric
Than the Castle's soarin' wa';
Better a'e gowden lyric
Than onything else ava!

    If you should say my poem has won
    Freedom for fules in faur Cathay
    Then aiblins wi' a better poem,
    I micht hae freed them frae folly tae!
    And if you say my poem has been
    A blessin' to wimmen in Tibet
    You may be richt, but as for me
    I never can forget
    I hadna them in mind at the time
    But yon thrawn fit and kittle rhyme!

IX

Treason

I've socht ye in and oot o' season.
Noo it's time that I learnt reason.
I'll nae langer vainly eisen
   While my youth and vigour pass.
Aiblins I'll be less displeasin'
   To some no' displeasin' lass.

Tho' you've ripened it's nae reason
Why my hert should hing to wizen
In a wind that grows mair freezin',
   And fa' rotten to the grass.
If for true love's wine I'm guisan'
   I maun try a weaker glass.

Oh there's teasin' and there's teasin'
But your cruelty shows nae easin'
And in fact it's aye increasin'
   And has come to sic a pass
That I'm contemplatin' treason
   – Equally in vain alas ! . . .

The only road is endless. Few ha'e ta'en't.
Sma' as a bawbee is the sphere o' Man.
Gin' the diameter o' ilka coin that's e'er
Been minted's taen and added up and made
The radius o' human life 't'ud be nae odds.
A' but an odd man here and there 'ud bide
Sae close to the centre o't it micht as weel
Be juist a bawbee still or threepenny bit,
As thick as flies upon a plat o' shairn
In simmer – and nane thinks to try the sun.
Gang near them and they'll row your heid in crape,
A black and stinkin' clood that's Hell itsel'.
Leave them to their Aiberdeen and Twal' Mile Roond!

The only road is silence, for nae sang
Has yet been sung and aiblins ne'er will be
That isna haud'n like a fly as weel
To the same plat o' shairn. The only road
Is dark withoot a whistle. There's nae road
Unless we mak' it – gin it can be made,
For nocht's been thocht oot yet and nocht's been planned
And a' humanity has dune's to crood
The puslock in the season and syne breed
Their like to cover it mair blackly yet
Neist season, and the neist, and there's nae end
To the numbers it'll haud at last
                    Like angels on a needle's point.

A' fell content, shair o' their common-sense,
Agreein' that Intelligence is the warld's licht
And man's chief glory (in sma' doses taen)
But dreidin' its indifference to 'established views'
And what they ca' 'the wisdom o' the ages.'
Intelligence – in natural science aye,
But never brocht to bear on human life.
Men's notions o' the warld in which they live
Ha'e changed but no' their notions o' themsels.
A' the ideas o' the best and wisest men
Doon to three hundred years syne and faur less
Ha'e gane owreboard but in regaird to themsels
                    Maist men are prehistoric still!

Therefore it's a queer man that disna think
He has a mind o' his ain and's fit to judge
His mental betters and to deprecate
Owre muckle intellectuality,
But tho' he kens fu' weel that Science has brocht
As everyday necessities to us a'
A host o' things that no' a century syne
Were luxuries beyond the dreams o' kings
He winna see that similar methods micht
Enrich folks' mental lives as muckle tae

And fegs they need that mair. Nae beggar's pooch
Ever compared as puirly wi' a King's
           As maist folks' 'minds' wi' Minds!

X
The Wild Beast Show

Bostock and Wombwell's Menagerie
          That used to come roon'
          When I was a loon
Is off the roads and a' thing else
          'll follow it soon.

The macaws that smelt o' reid ink
          The leopards like eau de cologne
          I could tell by the nose alone
And the lions and tigers by . . . well,
          I'm glad it's gone.

The rumblin' vans are doon the road
          And'll come this way nae mair.
          At forty odd it's here nor there
Tho' a' the animal and vegetable worlds
          Hine in thin air. . . .

XI
North of the Tweed

Cauld licht and tumblin' cloods. It's queer
There's never been a poet here. . . .

Shades o' the Sun-King no' yet risen
Are sleepin' in a corner on the straw.
Despair seems to touch bottom time and again
But aye Earth opens and reveals fresh depths.

The pale-wa'd warld is fu' o' licht and life
Like a glass in which water faintly stirs.
Gie owre a' this tomfoolery, and sing
The movin' spirit that nae metaphor drawn
Frae water or frae licht can dim suggest.
Leid in nae mere Longinian hypsos come
But in inhuman splendours, triumphin' wi'
'A dazzlin' disregard o' the soul.'
                              Nocht else 'll dae.

Water nor licht nor yet the barley field
That shak's in silken sheets at ilka braith,
Its lang nap thrawin' the quick licht aboot
In sic a maze that tak's and gies at aince
As fair oot-tops the coontless ripplin' sea.
There's nae chameleon like the July fields;
Their different colours change frae day to day
While they shift instantly neath the shiftin' licht
Yet they're owre dull for this, stagnant and dull;
And even your een, beloved, and your hair
Are like the barley and the sea and Heaven
That flaw and fail and are defeated by
                              The blind turns o' chance.

Thinkna' that I'm ungratefu', wi' nae mind
O' Deirdre and the fauld o' sunbeams[1] yet,
Or canna find on bracken slopes abune the bog
The orchis smellin' like cherry-pie;
Or that the sun's blade cuttin' straightly through
A cloudy sea fails wi' my cloudy hert,
Releasin' it frae self-disgust until I tine
A' sense o' livin' under set conditions
And live in an unconditioned space o' time
Perfect in ilka pulse and impulse, and aince mair
A seven-whistler in Kintyre, or yon broon hill
That's barren save for fower pale violets on
                              A South-leanin' bank.

[1] 'Fold of sunbeams' – Glendaruel.

I've sat amang the crimson buds o' thrift
Abune the sea whaur Buachaille herds the waves;
And seen the primrose nightglow to the North
Owre Moray and the flat sea while the West
Still held a twinkle o' the morning-star,
(For in the Cairngorms simmer nicht and dawn
Come close, but canna thraw the larks' hours oot);
And hoo should I forget the Langfall
On mornings when the hines were ripe but een
Ahint the glintin' leafs were brichter still
Than sunned dew on them, lips reider than the fruit,
And I filled baith my basket and my hert
                              Mony and mony a time?

And yet you mind, dear, on the bridal hill
Hoo yon laich loch ootshone my een in yours,
Nor wi' the heather could oor bluid compete,
Nor could the ring I gi'ed you when your hand
Lay on the crucifers compare wi' them
Save for a second when the sun seized on't.
Hair of the purple of Strathendrick Hill,
Slant e'en wi' pupils like blue-stane washed wi' rain
And the whites owre white and the hunted look
Here tak' your bairn; I've cairried it lang eneuch,
Langer than maist men wad, as weel you ken.
Noo I'll pipe insteed – what tune'll you hae? –
                              On Rudha nam Marbh.[1]

XII

Cares the nightingale
Who hears it sing? Many another bird
By day or night, on mountain or in vale
Sings and is heard.
You cannot sing until your flight
Leaves you no audience but the light. . . .

[1] 'The Point of the Dead.'

XIII

The fire of your flight in the height of the heavens
  Surprises my eyes like a sight of your song. . . .

XIV

Your song is much the same as theirs
Who sing for love or love of song
The other forms of life among
Nor care what else their passion shares
  So be it that their mates reply
Or their ingenuous lives o'erspill
In miracles of music still;
  But if 'tis love why should you fly
Beyond response into the sky
And if 'tis art why soar to show
No better than abounds below? . . .

XV

Think you, fond bird, to you 'tis given
To live at once in Earth and Heaven
When every height your wings attain
  Is but the depth they fall again,
And even your song is but such breath
As Life might draw, surviving Death,
If Immortality's vain grace
Emparadised the commonplace? . . .

XVI

Many a lovelier bird than you
Flaunts on earth a vivid hue
While you sit obscurely by
Cherishing the secret might
That can put it out of sight.
Man and beast are left behind
In a turning of the wind.
  Tell me, have you never seen
On your pinnacle serene

Upstarts of the human race
Void of meaning as of grace
In a sudden great machine?
Did the engine's dreadful roar
Quench awhile your glorious voice?
Did you start your song again
With the old assurance then?

XVII

Earth may dwindle 'neath your flight.
    Till it is seen no more.
Fly on, fly on, you've far to fly
    Before your flight is o'er
If in the sun's clear pool you'd see
Your body like a memory.
    Despite your distance from the earth
    The sun no nearer seems
    But in the endless sands of light
    A phantom water gleams
    – And yet once more you start to sing
    As tho' you glimpsed your mirrored wing! . . .

XVIII
Separatism

If there's a sword-like sang
That can cut Scotland clear
O' a' the warld beside
Rax me the hilt o't here,

For there's nae jewel till
Frae the rest o' earth it's free,
Wi' the starry separateness
I'd fain to Scotland gie. . . .

XIX
Bonnie Prince Charlie

A' isna gowd that glitters
And weel I mind ane came
And kindled in oor lyart hills
What look't like livin' flame.

Tho' a's no' gowd that glitters
He keeps his meed o' fame.
It's easier to lo'e Prince Chairlie
Than Scotland – mair's the shame! . . .

XX
The Lion Rampant

O the lion is aff the flag again
And reengin' the countryside.
Mony a hird in his hirsel sees
The glint o' a gowden hide.
Only the day afore yesterday, strewth,
It kythed in Sauchiehall Street
Wi' Sir Robert Horne in its mooth,
Lum hat and spats a' complete.
I'm wonderin', aince it digests him,
If insteed o' its usual roar,
It'll prate aboot Empire and Tariff Reform,
Or actually silence the bore.

O the lion is oot o' the flag again
And whasae leases a moor
'll aiblins get mair than he bargains for
Gin he disna ken the spoor.

My hert is merry, merry
At the thocht o' the squashed remains
O' sportsmen suddenly – very ! –
Findin' mair than deer for their pains.
O the lion is oot o' the flag again
And whiles I feel't in my hert –
Ramsay Macdonald claimed to be Scots
And I crunched him for a stert !

Damn a country whaur turnin' a corner
You could lippen on nocht but a sheep !
Thank God for a lion on Greenock quay
Its vigil aince mair to keep,
And when the American clansmen land
No' bash them wi' a paw
But by the gangway tak' its stand
And gently aff them draw
As they come trippin' doon't,
Their imitation kilts and gar
The blighters look for a' the warld
Precisely as they are ! . . .

A' that's eternal fears fulfilment. Whiles
I look at Scotland and dumfounded see't
A muckle clod split off frae ither life,
Shapeless, uncanny, unendurable clod
Held in an endless nightmare (like a foetus
Catcht up in a clood) while a voice
Yowls in my lug : 'You'll find nae way oot.
Its spell is no' to brak,' and syne I see
My fellow countrymen as gin they were
The Thing that loups at noon frae nature whiles,
Unshaped but visible, horrible and august,
Blastin' the sicht like a' thing seen at aince,
The Black Mass o' the Scottish people,
                    Like Werfel's Bocksgesang.

It's little I care for mysel' or my freens.
My concern's wi' humanity, waefully imperfect

And in peril o' destruction. *That* gars me seek
In the secret pairts o' my spirit and like Dante
Cry oot on the heedless and laggard.
In the shock o' despair, the hopelessness,
The ὀργασμός o' liberated hate and lust,
A new element comes into bein' – wider
And stranger than ocht that the clay can ken,
The mysterious meetin' place, where for a flash
Earthly touches divine and wins new strength,
Courage to face past and present that promise
That frae their base frenzies may come even yet
            Something worth while.

A Moment in Eternity

The great song ceased
– Aye, like a wind was gone,
And our hearts came to rest,
Singly as leaves do,
And every leaf a flame.

My shining passions stilled
Shone in the sudden peace
Like countless leaves
Tingling with the quick sap
Of immortality.

I was a multitude of leaves
Receiving and reflecting light,
A burning bush
Blazing for ever unconsumed,
Nay, ceaselessly,
Multiplying in leaves and light
And instantly
Burgeoning in buds of brightness,

– Freeing like golden breaths
Upon the cordial air
A thousand new delights,
– Translucent leaves
Green with the goodness of Eternity,
Golden in the Heavenly light
– The golden breaths
Of my eternal life,
Like happy memories multiplied,
Shining out instantly from me
And shining back for ever into me,
– Breaths given out
But still unlost,
For ever mine,
In the infinite air,
The everlasting foliage of my soul
Visible awhile
Like steady and innumerable flames,
Blending into one blaze
Yet each distinct
With shining shadows of difference.

A sudden thought of God's
Came like a wind
Ever and again
Rippling them as waters over stars,
And swiftlier fanning them
And setting them a-dance,
Upflying, fluttering down,
Moving in orderly intricacies
Of colour and of light,
Delaying, hastening,
Blazing and serene,
Shaken and shining in the turning wind,
Lassoing cataracts of light
With rosy boughs,
Or clamouring in echoing unequalled heights,

Rhythmical sprays of many-coloured fire
And spires chimerical
Gleaming in fabulous airs,
And suddenly
Lapsing again
To incandescence and increase.

And again the wind came
Blowing me afar
In fair fantastic fires,
– Ivies and irises invading
The upland garths of ivory;
Queen daisies growing
In the tall red grass
By pools of perfect peace;
And bluebells tossing
In transparent fields;
And silver airs
Lifting the crystal sources in dim hills
And swinging them far out like bells of glass
Pealing pellucidly
And quivering in faery flights of chimes;
Shivers of wings bewildered
In alleys of virgin dream;
Floral dances and revels of radiance
Whirling in stainless sanctuaries;
And eyes of Seraphim,
Shining like sunbeams on eternal ice,
Lifted towards the unexplored
Summits of Paradise.

And the wind ceased.
Light dwelt in me,
Pavilioned there.
I was a crystal trunk,
Columnar in the glades of Paradise,
Bearing the luminous boughs
And foliaged with the flame
Of infinite and gracious growth,

– Meteors for roots,
And my topmost spires
Notes of enchanted light
Blind in the Godhead!
– White stars at noon!

I shone within my thoughts
As God within us shines.

And the wind came,
Multitudinous and light
I whirled in exultations inexpressible
– An unpicturable, clear,
Soaring and glorying,
Swift consciousness,
A cosmos turning like a song of spheres
On apices of praise,
A separate colour,
An essential element and conscious part
Of successive and stupendous dreams
In God's own heart!

And the wind ceased
And like a light I stood
A flame of glorious and complex resolve,
Within God's heart.

I knew then that a new tree,
A new tree and a strange,
Stood beautifully in Heaven.
I knew that a new light
Stood in God's heart
And a light unlike
The Twice Ten Thousand lights
That stood there,
Shining equally with me,
And giving and receiving increase of light
Like the flame that I was
Perpetually.

And I knew that when the wind rose
This new tree would stand still
Multiplied in light but motionless,
And I knew that when God dreamt
And His creative impulses
Ran through us like a wind
And we flew like clear and coloured
Flames in His dreams,
(Adorations, Gratitudes and Joys,
Plenary and boon and pure,
Crystal and burning-gold and scarlet
Competing and co-operating flames
Reflecting His desires,
Flashing like epical imaginings
And burning virgin steeps
With ceaseless swift apotheoses)
One light would stand unmoved.

And when on pinnacles of praise
All others whirled
Like a white light deeper in God's heart
This light would shine
Pondering the imponderable.
Revealing ever clearlier
Patterns of endless revels,
Each gesture freed,
Each shining shadow of difference,
Each subtle phase evolved
In the magnificent and numberless
Revelations of ecstasy
Succeeding and excelling inexhaustibly,
– A white light like a silence
Accentuating the great songs!
– A shining silence wherein God
Might see as in a mirror
The miracles that He must next achieve!

Ah Light
That is God's inmost wish
His knowledge of Himself,
Flame of creative judgment,
God's interrogation of infinity,
Searching the unsearchable,
– Silent and steadfast tree
Housing no birds of song,
Void to the wind,
But rooted in God's very self,
Growing ineffably,
Central in Paradise!

When the song ceased
And I stood still,
Breathing new leaves of life
Upon the eternal air,
Each leaf of all my leaves
Shone with a new delight
Murmuring Your name.

O Thou,
Who art the wisdom of the God
Whose ecstasies we are! . . .

O human thocht that maun aye owre thraw.
A' that it touches, create but to destroy,
Amid the desolation language rises
And towers abune the ruins and music wi't.
Poetry's the movement that the mind invents
For its expression, even as the stars,
And wins to a miraculously calm, assured,
Awareness o' the hidden motives o' man's mind
                          Nocht else daur seek.

To hell wi' happiness!
I sing the terrifying discipline
O' the free mind that gars a man
Mak' his joys kill his joys,

The weakest by the strongest,
The temporal by the fundamental
(Or hope o' the fundamental)
And prolong wi' in himself
Threids o' thocht sae fragile
It needs the help and contrivance
O' a' his vital poo'er
To haud them frae brakin'
As he pu's them owre the gulfs.
Oor humanity canna follow us
To lichts sae faur removed.
A man ceases to be himsel'
Under sicna constraint.
Will he find life or daith
At the end o' his will,
At Thocht's deepest depth,
Or some frichtfu' sensation o' seein'
Nocht but the ghastly glimmer
O' his ain puir maitter?
                    What does it maitter?
                    It's the only road.
The beaten track is *beaten* frae the stert.

Man's the reality that mak's
A'things possible, even himsel'.
Energy's his miracle
But hoo little he's dune wi't yet,
Denyin't at ilka turn.
Ilka change has Eternity's mandate.
But hoo little we've changed since Adam,
Frightened to open oor minds,
Frightened to move.
To the foolish a' comes and gangs lichtly
But what can we dae wha's spirits
Unceasingly strew dark on oor days
And pride themsel's on't, makin' life harsh
In oor herts, since a' that's Eternal
                    Fears fulfilment.

But maist poets even follow ane anither
Like sheep through a gap in a dyke
Drawin' 'their' ideas frae a fringe
O' the Kabbala, withoot kennin'
Whaur they come frae or what they mean
And no' fashin' to gang back
To the sources themsels to see
Gin there's no' better anes there untouched
Than the wheen that ha' aye been taen
– No' stoppin' to speir if they wadna
Be better to think for themsels
At this time o' day, no' refurbish
          Notions o' slaverin' savages,
On which they're borne as I've seen in a spate
Tree-trunks, sheep, bee skeps and the like
          On the bible-black Esk.

Ah, double nature, distinct yet ane,
Like Life and Thocht. For Nature is
A moment and a product o' the Mind,
And no' a Mind that stands abune the warld
Or yet rins through it like a knotless threid
But coincides wi't, ane and diverse at aince;
An eternal solution and eternal problem.
A' things substitute themsel's, ane for the ither.
And everything joins on to everything else,
A tissue o' multiple meanings? Oor myriad symbols
Are the masks o' the Cosmos; and Man's job's
To mak' myriads mair, a new *Imitation*.
Confrontin' the impassive eternal universe
Wi' the states o' his restless hert?
Then what I'll turn to noo, like a loon
Clingin' at Manhood still to a Noah's Ark
Or cairdboard ferm? Ocht I can ha'e – a'thing –
Is nae mair use to me noo than my mither's womb,
And I've tint my amusement at maitter,
The quick-change artist,
Ashamed o' ha'en a'e form instead o' anither,

And hastenin' to cheenge it – the haste that is
Its a'e reality – and canna find ocht
Wha's unavoidable annoyance ony langer
May be taen as Apollinaire took
                    The War – wi' irony!

The wecht o' water in the ocean and
The immeasurable distances o' the stars
Nae mair annihilate or affect my thocht;
And I can counterbalance mony anither
Blind force o' Nature wi' byordinar ease,
And yet it's still a multitudinous melee o' forms,
A thrang stream in which beauty is tint
As sune as it kyths; and even as a few men's thocht,
Their fringe o' consciousness and will, is thrawn up
Oot o' the dark and void, perishable and fine
As a hair, wi' its fate still ungaurdit,
– Aye, even as Man roamin' the Earth
For a thoosand centuries at last gied birth
To a wheen men learnin' to be prudent and think
Wha's learnin' seemed juist to reverse
The motions that led them to 't
Cryin' sympathy, tenderness and the law o' luve,
But the words were nae suner spoken
Than the lips that spoke them were whelmed in the spate
And the braith that made them broke like a bubble
– Sae I, pinnin' my faith to Thocht, ken weel
Its accidental character, weakness, and limits,
And that a' but a few men trust naethin' sae little
As this poo'er that alane divides – can divide –
Them frae the beasts that perish; frae bees and ants
Wi' their wonderfu' organisations. What has man dune
That I should prefer his arts and ideas
To the hives o' bees or colonies o' ants
                    Or think God does?

Santayana and Bruce frae a spider
Learnt different lessons, and there's ithers to learn.

Man's in the makin' but henceforth maun mak' himsel'.
Nature has led him sae faur, up frae the slime
Gi'en him body and brain – and noo it's for him
To mak' or mar this maikless torso.
Let him look to Nature nae mair;
For her will's to create ane wi' the poo'er
To create himsel' – if he fails, she fails
And the metal gangs back to the pot,
     And the process
Begins a' owre. If he wins he wins alane.
     It lies wi' himsel.

Up frae the slime, that a' but a handfu' o' men
Are grey wi' still. There's nae trace o't in you.
Clear withoot sediment. Day withoot nicht.
A' men's institutions and maist men's thochts
Are tryin' for aye to bring to an end
The insatiable thocht, the beautiful violent will,
The restless spirit of Man, the theme o' my sang
Or to the theme o't what Man's spirit and thocht
Micht be if men were as muckle concerned
Wi' them as they are wi' fitba' or wimmen,
Poets' words as the neist door neighbours'
And if they werena aye at the mercy
O' the foul mob when they kyth in an antrin man
A property snake to the snake that blends and twists,
Flashing, wise, sinuous, dangerous creature,
Offspring of mystery and the world without end
    That rises and spreids its hood
    And leans and listens
    In ecstasy swaying
Even whaur by the Feshie the sandpipers twitter
And the reid and white foxgloves wag in the wind
Or wha's coils eely awa' like water through sand
Or are like the stags in the Forest o' Gaick
You maun strike on the flanks to wauken
When they'll up and owre the hill-taps
    Like flashes o' lichtnin'.

Earth's rinnin' doon like a clock;
A' its changes mak' for the final
State o' No Change? In the mighty field
Owre which the tide is fleetin'
To leave bare a' meanin' at last
Will some coonter-force suddenly appear?
There's nae sign o't yet, and what if it does
Tellin' a similar story
In anither language and style?
I see your coils twined to a point
Faur ayont Ophiuchus (as on Monadh nan Eun
And by mony a green bealach I see
The tragic struggle betwixt
Demoniacal pooers o' beauty
On the a'e hand and on the ither
Truths, quiet and salutary,
Shinin' frae afaur); and a'thing else
A grey skin you've cast, Cencrastus,
Loupin' there oot o' hule; and cry 'Thocht'
Tho' I ken that nae thocht 'll survive
– Nocht at last but a quality o' mind
Committed to nae belief;
No' Thocht, but a poo'er to think,
And 'ud fain stake *that* in a Scottish form
                    In the endless hazard.
A poo'er to think, no' to be led astray,
Eident and lintwhite and caulder than ice
Takin' a' that you can frae the sun
And gi'en nocht in return, your coils are no'
Mair numerous than the plies o' my brain.
Your scepticism gangs nae deeper.
A single movement shows that Licht
Flows frae nae central source in Heaven
But is a product o' ilka star itsel'.
Syne in a single lirk you haud
Mair darkness than midnicht or men's herts.
Hoo can my mind be ane wi' you
To whom Man's fate or Earth's is o' sma' concern?

Hoo can my mind be ane wi' you
Understandin' a' that is and is to be
As weel as men think they ken
Some period o' history and can seize
On the aefauld principle that lay under
A' its divers facts (tho' they canna)?
Yet, if I dinna, I'm a bairn wha thinks
           The Mune's made o' green cheese!

Unconscious goal of history, dimly seen
In Genius whiles that kens the problem o' its age
And works at it; the mass o' men pursue
Their puir blind purposes unaware o' you,
And yet frae them emerges tae your keen
Clear consequences nae man can gauge
Save in relation to some ancient stage;
Sae History mak's the ambitions o' great men
Means to ends greater than themsels could ken,
– Greater and ither – and mass ignorance yields,
Like corruption o' vegetation in fallow fields,
The conditions o' richer increase; – at last
The confusion's owre, the time comes fast
When men wauk to the possibility
O' workin' oot and makin' their destiny
In fu' consciousness and cease to muddle through
Wi' nae idea o' their goal – and nae mair grue!

Let nane cry that the right men arena here
– That urgent tasks await that nane can dae.
Times oft mistak' their problems in that way.
At the richt time the richt men aye appear.
If Scotland fills us wi' despair we may
Be proposin' a goal that disna lie
Onywhaur in history's plan the noo; we sigh
In vain – because we canna think in vain
And oor desire'll hae its due effect
In the lang run altho' oor age rejects.
But a'e thing's certain – nae genius'll come,

Nae maitter hoo he's shouted for, to recreate
The life and fabric o' a decadent State
That's dune its work, gien its Idea to the world,
The problem is to find in Scotland some
Bricht coil o' you that hasna yet uncurled,
And, hoosoever petty I may be, the fact
That I think Scotland isna dune yet proves
There's something in it that fulfilment's lacked
And my vague hope through a' creation moves.

The Unconscious Ideas that impel a race
Spring frae an ineffable sense o' hoo to be
A certain kind o' human being – Let's face
This fact in Scotland and we'll see
The fantasy o' an unconquerable soul
Neath nations' rivalries, persecutions, wars,
The golden casket o' their Covenant, their goal,
Shrined in a dwelling that ootshines the stars,
A dwelling o' delight no' made wi' hands,
For wha's sake till the gaen oot o' the Sun
They'll hew the Sassenach, the Amalekite, the Hun
Nor sacrifice the least fraction o' their will
To independence while they've a tittle still
O' their Unconscious Idea unrealised.
Is Scotland roupit that I su'd gie owre
My quest for onything, hooso'er disguised,
That wi' a new vitality may endower
My thieveless country: and mak' it mair
Intelligently allied to your hidden purpose there
Sae that my people frae their living graves
May loup and play a pairt in History yet
Wi' sufferin's mair like a Genius's than a slave's,
Vieve strands in your endless glories knit?
By thocht a man mak's his idea a force
Or fact in History's drama: he canna foresee
The transformations and uses o' the course
The dialectics o' human action and interaction 'll gie
The contribution he mak's – it'll a' depend

On his sincerity and clearness in the end
And his integrity – his unity with you;
Strivin' to gie birth to that idea through
Him wha o' makin' his meanin' clear
May weel despair when you disappear – or appear.
Stir me, Cencrastus. If the faintest gleam
O' you kyths in my work fu' weel I ken
That your neist movement may lowse a supreme
Glory – tho' I'm extinguished then!

If there is ocht in Scotland that's worth ha'en
There is nae distance to which it's unattached
– Nae height, nae depth, nae breadth, and I am fain
To see it frae the hamely and the earthly snatched
And precipitated to what it will be in the end
A' that's ephemeral shorn awa' and rhyme nae mair
Mere politics, personalities, and mundane things,
Nor mistak' ony philosophy's elaborate and subtle form
That canna fit the changed conditions, for your trend
Drawin' a' life's threids thegither there
Nor losin' on the roonaboots, nor gainin' on the swings
But like the hairst that needs baith sun and storm,
Simmer and winter, Life and Daith . . . A' roads are closed;
North, South, East, West nae mair opposed.
Withoot a leg to stand on, like a snake
Wi' impossible lustres I shake.
Earth contracts to a single point of licht
As men, deceived by their een, see stars at nicht,
And the religious attitude has found
In Scotland yet a balancin' ground. . . .

An image o' the sea lies underneath
A' men's imaginations – the sea in which
A' life was born and that cradled us until
We cam' to birth's maturity. Its waves bewitch
Us still or wi' their lure o' peacefu' gleamin'
Or hungrily in storm and darkness streamin'.

The imagination has anither poo'er – the snake,
He who beats up the waters into storm
Wha's touch electrifies us into action;
In th' abyss o' their origin, their basic form,
A' oor imaginations partake
O' ane or th' ither – the sea or the snake.

The twasome control a' the drama o' life.
Gin we talk o' love and freedom, and tell
Oor dreams o' order and peace, equality and joy
We are under the blissfu' waters' spell
And oor een and oor voices betray
Oor inspiration in the bricht sea's sway.

Gin we speak o' Imperial Poo'er, Aristocracy,
Authority, Privilege, Control o' the world
The music changes – on a rattle o' drums
We rise to heights o' glory and death: we've unfurled
An oriflamme; in the glitter o' the latest ideas
The auld serpent is a' yin sees.

The words and ideas change: but under them still
The serpent stirs or the sea allures.
We're deceived nae mair: 'neath a certain plane
Science, art, a's but the ravings
O' th' poo'ers o' th' abyss; men the instrument
O' the water or the serpent.

They strive forever to master the minds o' men
And rule them wi' strange rhythms. Few ken them.
Maist folk gang through life and never see
The marionettes they are – what forces pen them
Subservient to the serpent's magic or
The charmin' o' the sea that has nae shore.

But there are aye a wheen minds in whom
The surgings and writhings cease.
They dismay anger wi' their smile
And o' diverse notions mak' harmonies

Wi' freendly understandin's flashin' speech
Or unexpected tranquilisin' wit.

My love is to the light of lights
As a gold fawn to the sun
And men, wha love ocht else, to her
Their ways ha' scarce begun.

For God their God's a jealous God
And keeps her frae their sight
He hasna had her lang eneuch
Himsel' to share his delight

And kens gin he'd been worth his saut
He'd ha' made her first, no' last,
Since but a'e glimpse, a'e thocht, o' her
Discredits a' the Past.

(A'e glimpse, a'e thocht, and men might cease
To honour his tardy pooers;
And he's no' shair she winna prove
To be no' his – but oors!)

Yet praise the Past sin' but for it
We never might ha' seen her
– And still to oor een maun temper wi't
The glory that's been gi'en her.

My love she is the hardest thocht
That ony brain can ha'e,
And there is nocht worth ha'en in life
That doesna lead her way.

My love is to a' else that is
As meaning's meaning, or the sun
Men see ahint the sunlight whiles
Like lint-white water run. . . .

For them there's nae mair sea; the snake
Is chained in the depths o' a bottomless pit
The serene fury o' ha'en seen th' ineffable's theirs
They are absolved frae a' worship and gang
In the strength o' their ain souls – it is they
Wha recreate man's thocht and change his state;
By what are they ken't – for whom nocht prepares?
Only their like 'll no' guess wrang
But twa features they hae – whatever they say
Is something that few can believe; and yet
Never the opposite to general belief.
They never come except in due season
And croon a' controversies wi' a reason
Never heard o' before – yont ilka faction
– AND AYE A REASON FOR ACTION!

Is cam's is dìreach an lagh.

Si l'orvet voyait,
Si le sourd entendait,
Pas un homme ne vivrait.

NOTES

I do not consider any explication of my references to Valéry, Husserl, Leontiev, Tyutchev, and many others necessary here, but the following notes on a few of my more obscure allusions may be useful to certain readers: –

p. 194.   *The blessing wi' the black selvedge*, the Union of the Parliaments.

p. 196.   *The Three Conventions* – material, moral, metaphysical – refers to Professor Denis Saurat's great book of that name. and to the philosophy it expounds.

p. 208.   *Ón dird tuaidh tig in chabhair* (help comes from the northern airt), from a poem by Teig Og, Teig Mor's son, the most eminent Irish bard of the fifteenth century.

p. 208.   *A theachtaire thig ón Róimh*, a noble poem in defence of the art of poetry, arguing that if poetry be a fiction it is yet more lasting than that fiction which is human life, attributed by Miss Knott (vide *Irish Syllabic Poetry*) to the famous Gilbride Albanach MacNamee (Giolla-Brighde Albanach MacConmidhe) (?) 1180–(?) 1260.

p. 209.   *Dia libh, a laochraidh Ghaoidheal* (God be with the Irish host), Aonghus Mac Daighre Ó Dálaigh's poem, well known in Sir Samuel Ferguson's translation.

p. 209.   *Twenty miles from Carlisle* refers to Langholm in Dumfriesshire, the author's birthplace, as does *The Muckle Toon* on p. 216.

p. 210.   Alasdair MacMhaighstir Alasdair (Alexander Macdonald) the greatest of the Scots Gaelic poets. *The Birlinn of Clanranald, Sugar Brook, In Praise of Morag*, and *In Dispraise of Morag* are the titles of some of his principal poems. The reference at the end (sarcastic, as is the detachment by ellipsis of the epithet 'et chinois,' to indicate Macdonald's rebel vein) is to George Meredith's sonnet, *Lucifer in Starlight*.

p. 213.   *Na h-éachta do chuaidh* (the good that is gone), from Aodh Buidhe MacCruitín's (†1755) poem which exhibits the same spirit as *The Parliament of Clan Thomas* which voices contempt of the bardic caste for the native upstarts who profited out of the nation's decay.

p. 213.   *Priompallán*, dung-beetle.

p. 213.   *Ceist cia chinneochadh dán?* (who would desire a poem?) – Mahon O'Heffernan's cry, lamenting the decay of bardic art.

p. 213.   *Ionmolta malairt bhisigh* (A change for the better deserves praise) – Eochy O'Hosey's satire on the simpler poetry in time of bardic decay. He has abandoned, he affirms, intricate carven ornament and adopted 'a common sort of easy art that will bring him more praise.' Of old composition almost broke his heart, but this new verse is 'a great cause of health!'

p. 213.   *The Wandering Hawk* (An Seabhac Siubhail), by Muiris Ó Gríofa (Maurice Griffin), *c.* 1778 – a Jacobite poem memorable for its odd Apocalyptic air as the poet looks out on Europe.

p. 214.   Eochaidh Ó Heoghusa's (Eochy O'Hosey or O'Hussey) (*c.* 1600) poem, *Fuar lem in oidhche-se d'Aodh*, best known through Mangan's vigorous, if free translation, 'Cold for Hugh I deem this night.'

p. 224.   Aodhagán Ó Rathaille (Egan O'Rahilly), 1670–1726, in his splendid aisling *Gile na gile* ('The Brightness of Brightness'), 'sees, in the image of an Irish maiden, that idea of which Plato dreamed; and this strange pulchritude also is Eire herself – the secret Ireland of the Gael.'

p. 227.   *El Rey de Escocia no es nada*, the comment of one of the survivors of the Spanish Armada on his experiences in Scotland, to which he crossed from Ireland.

p. 229.   *As they could easily be*, an espousal of the Social Credit Proposals of Major C. H. Douglas.

FIRST HYMN TO LENIN
AND OTHER POEMS
(1931)

First Hymn to Lenin

To Prince D. S. Mirsky

FEW even o' the criminals, cravens, and fools
Wha's voices vilify a man they ken
They've cause to fear and are unfit to judge
As they're to stem his influence again
But in the hollows where their herts should be
    Foresee your victory.

Churchills, Locker-Lampsons, Beaverbrooks'll be
In history's perspective less to you
(And them!) than the Centurions to Christ
Of whom, as you, at least this muckle's true
– 'Tho' pairtly wrang he cam' to richt amang's
    Faur greater wrangs.'

Christ's cited no' by chance or juist because
You mark the greatest turnin'-point since him
But that your main redress has lain where he's
Least use – fulfillin' his sayin' lang kept dim
That whasae followed him things o' like natur'
    'Ud dae – and greater!

Certes nae ither, if no' you's dune this.
It maitters little. What you've dune's the thing,
No' hoo't compares, corrects, or complements
The work of Christ that's taen owre lang to bring
Sic a successor to keep the reference back
    Natural to mak'.

Great things ha'e aye ta'en great men in the past
In some proportion to the work they did,
But you alane to what you've dune are nocht
Even as the poo'ers to greater ends are hid
In what's ca'd God, or in the common man,
    Withoot your plan.

Descendant o' the unkent Bards wha made
Sangs peerless through a' post-anonymous days
I glimpse again in you that mightier poo'er
Than fashes wi' the laurels and the bays
But kens that it is shared by ilka man
    Since time began.

Great things, great men – but at faur greater's cost!
If first things first had had their richtfu' sway
Life and Thocht's misused poo'er might ha' been ane
For a' men's benefit – as still they may
Noo that through you this mair than elemental force
    Has f'und a clearer course.

Christ said: 'Save ye become as bairns again.'
Bairnly eneuch the feck o' us ha' been!
Your work needs men; and its worst foes are juist
The traitors wha through a' history ha' gi'en
The dope that's gar'd the mass o' folk pay heed
    And bide bairns indeed.

As necessary, and insignificant, as death
Wi' a' its agonies in the cosmos still
The Cheka's horrors are in their degree;
And'll end suner! What maitters 't wha we kill
To lessen that foulest murder that deprives
    Maist men o' real lives?

For now in the flower and iron of the truth
To you we turn; and turn in vain nae mair,
Ilka fool has folly eneuch for sadness
But at last we are wise and wi' laughter tear
The veil of being, and are face to face
    Wi' the human race.

Here lies your secret, O Lenin, – yours and oors,
No' in the majority will that accepts the result

But in the real will that bides its time and kens
The benmaist resolve is the poo'er in which we exult
Since naebody's willingly deprived o' the good;
    And, least o' a', the crood!

At My Father's Grave

The sunlicht still on me, you row'd in clood,
We look upon each ither noo like hills
Across a valley. I'm nae mair your son.
It is my mind, nae son o' yours, that looks,
And the great darkness o' your death comes up
And equals it across the way.
A livin' man upon a deid man thinks
And ony sma'er thocht's impossible.

Prayer for a Second Flood

There'd ha'e to be nae warnin'. Times ha'e changed
And Noahs are owre numerous nooadays,
(And them the vera folk to benefit maist!)
Knock the feet frae under them, O Lord, wha praise
Your unsearchable ways sae muckle and yet hope
    To keep within knowledgeable scope!

Ding a' their trumpery show to blauds again.
Their measure is the thimblefu' o' Esk in spate.
Like whisky the tittlin' craturs mete oot your poo'ers
Aince a week for bawbees in the kirk-door plate,
– And pit their umbrellas up when they come oot
    If mair than a pulpitfu' o' You's aboot!

O arselins wi' them! Whummle them again!
Coup them heels-owre-gowdy in a storm sae gundy
That mony a lang fog-theekit face I ken
'll be sooked richt doon under through a cundy
In the High Street, afore you get weel-sterted
    And are still hauf-herted!

Then flush the world in earnest. Let yoursel' gang,
Scour't to the bones, and mak' its marrow holes
Toom as a whistle as they used to be
In days I mind o' ere men fidged wi' souls,
But naething had forgotten you as yet,
    Nor you forgotten it.

Up then and at them, ye Gairds o' Heaven.
The Divine Retreat is owre. Like a tidal bore
Boil in among them; let the lang lugs nourished
On the milk o' the word at last hear the roar
O' human shingle; and replenish the salt o' the earth
    In the place o' their birth.

Museum Piece

I WAS born o' a woman – ane o' the last
    O' that famous race
Afore it was ta'en back into man
    Its original place.

The difference was at bay in her,
    And, kennin' its doom,
Made me a poet; the woman in me kens
    Poetry bears mair than the womb.

Nature never abandoned a fairer
    Aince-mair-promisin' field.
(It'll be leavin' man next.) Failure micht almost ha' been left
    To flourish there and bide concealed.

Poetry's incomprehensible stuff? You'd rather
    The white breist and tenty hand?
But Nature kens what it's da'en – even women in their day
    Were whiles ill to understand.

Charisma and My Relatives

To William McElroy

No' here the beloved group; I've gane sae faur
(Like Christ) yont faither, mither, brither, kin
I micht as weel try dogs or cats as seek
In sic relationships again to fin'
The epopteia I maun ha'e – and feel
    (Frae elsewhere) owre me steal.

But naewhere has the love-religion had
A harder struggle than in Scotland here
Which means we've been untrue as fechters even
To oor essential genius – Scots, yet sweer
To fecht in, or owre blin' to see where lay,
    The hert o' the fray.

We've focht in a' the sham fechts o' the world.
But I'm a Borderer and at last in me
The spirit o' my people's no' content
Wi' ony but the greatest enemy,
And nae mair plays at sodgers but has won
    To a live battle-grun'.

A fiercer struggle than joukin it's involved.
Oorsels oor greatest foes. Yet, even yet,
I haud to 'I' and 'Scot' and 'Borderer'
And fence the wondrous fire that in me's lit
Wi' sicna barriers roond as hide frae'ts licht
  Near a'body's sicht.

And cry 'as weel try dogs or cats as seek
In sic relationships again to fin'
The epopteia' that, yet f'und, like rain
'Ud quickly to the roots o' a' thing rin
Even as the circles frae a stane that's hurled
  In water ring the world.

Sae to my bosom yet a' beasts maun come,
Or I to theirs, – baudrons, wi' sides like harps,
Lookin' like the feel o' olives in the mooth,
Yon scabby cur at whom the gutter carps,
Nose-double o' the taste o' beer-and-gin,
  And a' my kin.

And yet – there's some folk lice'll no' live on,
I'm ane o' them I doot. But what a thocht!
What speculations maun a man sae shunned
No' ha'e until at last the reason's brocht
To view acceptable, as the fact may be
  On different grun's to them and me.

Pedigree[1]

IF I'd to wale for ancestors, I'd ha'e
(Ahint my faither wi' his cheeks like hines
And my mither wi' her 'sad fish' lines)
Auld Ringan Oliver and the Caird o' Barullion;
And on my wife's side – as clear as day
Still in that woman in a million,
Keepin' me alert while savourin' wi' joy
Her infernal depths – John Forbes o' Tavoy,
For I never see her kaimin' her hair
But I mind o' his beard in Driminor there.

The Burning Passion

TO CARMEL HADEN GUEST

'From Homer and Polygnotus I every day learn more clearly that in our life here
above ground we have, properly speaking, to enact Hell.' (*Briefwechsel zwischen
Schiller und Goethe* VI 230).

WAD that the burnin' passion aince attained
Whether by lichtnin' flash or creepin' dawn
Nae langer came and gaed but held for aye,
Wi'ts growth, gin Change is needfu' still to Man,
Ha'ein' as in, no' o', perfection
Its haill direction.

---

[1] *For account of Oliver see pp.* 136–140 *A. and J. Lang's* Highways and Byways in
the Border. *Billy Marshall the Caird of Barullion, King of the Gypsies of the Western
Lowlands, died* 1792, *aged* 120. *He had been seventeen times lawfully married and was,
after his* 100th *year, the avowed father of four children by 'less legitimate affections'. See
note in Scott's* Guy Mannering *and Mr. James Murray MacCulloch of Ardwall's
letter,* Blackwood's Magazine, August, 1817. *For Forbes see the story of this sequel
to the burning of Congarf in Picken's* Traditional Stories of Old Families.

But oh! the apathy that fixes on
Men wha accordin' to the spirit live
– The constant problem o' recapturin'
At ony cost, and haudin', the fugitive
Grace that alane can fetch, oor glisks o't teach,
     Genius within reach.

Afore each sovereign feat the swimmer maun
Gang under, and hoo mony times, and oft
The source o' inspiration's ill to trace.
Still, still, we see it, infinitely aloft,
And struggle on – but gin oor poo'ers gi'e oot
     What will ha'en struggled boot?

A line, a word, – and emptiness again!
The impotent desire to ken aince mair
The shinin' presence, and the bitter sense
O' bein' unjustly treated, wi' despair
Cryin' 'better to see and tine, no' see ava'
     Like maist men' – ah!

This thocht o' a' wha haena had a glisk
And canna understand oor torments syne
Gi'es courage to us – and the lust to bring
Like cruelties to them, tho' we ken fine
The veritable vision withdrawn alane
     Can gi'e (no justify) the pain.

No' justify, tho' we maun think it does
Or be indifferent to its effects,
Or wi' oor peers, or but oorsels, concerned,
Yet ken hoo genius a' oor themes rejects,
Syne gars the heavens open apropos
     'God' or the sea or Uncle Joe.

A'thing is equal here, and only here,
And ony o' my relatives may be
Occasions for genius. Let me look again.

A'thing is equal here – sae faur's we see –
Yet genius fa's unequally, here and there,
    And nane kens when nor where.

Juist as frae ony couple genius springs,
There is nae tellin' save wi' folk owre auld
Or impotent. The stupidest pair on earth
Are still as likely to strike in the blin'fauld
Maze o' manseed upon the vital spark
    As folk o' merit, means, or mark.

Wanted a technique for genius! Or, at least,
A means whereby a' genius yet has done
'll be the stertin' point o' a' men's lives,
No' zero, as if life had scarce begun,
But to owrecome this death sae faur ben in
    Maist folk needs the full[1] floo'er o' Lenin.

Be this the measure o' oor will to bring
Like cruelty to a' men – nocht else'll dae;
The source o' inspiration drooned in bluid
If need be, owre and owre, until its ray
Strengthens in a' forever or's hailly gane
    As noo save in an antrin brain.

Beyond Exile

PRAISE God that still my feet can find
    In distant lands the old hill-road,
And tread always no alien clay
    But their familiar sod.

[1] Pronounced to rhyme with English 'gull'.

And all the ocean's broad estate
     Be but a gleaming band to me
That slips between the bending fields
     To find no foreign sea.

No stranger's roof-tree covers me,
     Albeit I travel far and wide,
And sundering leagues but closer bind
     Me to my darling's side.

And if I pass the utmost bourne
     Why, then, I shall be home again –
The quick step at the quiet door,
     The gay eyes at the pane!

Salonika, 1916

The Liquid Light

THE pairts o' Langholm the Esk reflects
Seem like maist women, better than they are,
Just as, a wee bit flown and *dilutior*,
I'm better than when sober by faur.

Country Folk

COUNTRY folk, bein' wice, are content
To view the eagle's flight
Frae faur below, and no' gang near
Its eyrie's ugsome sicht.

Religion and Love

'FRAE the mysteries o' religion seldom
And never frae the mysteries o' love
Should the veil be torn' – the auld cant
Fits your cowardice still like a glove.
The veil's roond your een – naewhere else.
They are naked and unashamed
And the only mystery aboot them
Is the way they're denied and defamed
By ignorance ca'in itsel' awe
    And folly guisin' as law.

The Prostitute

LET sweethearts, wives, and mithers
    Be what they can.
Nature ootrins oor tidy thochts
    And in its plan
Your place is greater than theirs
    – Servin' nae man, but Man.
Their life to Life may steek its doors;
    Keep open yours.

The Church of My Fathers

THIS is the kirk o' my faithers
And I ken the meanin' at last
O' its pea-green wa's and chocolate pillars
And am stricken aghast

For here, ready for the road,
Religion was biddin' goodbye.
Her hoose was toom and she'd turned
Wi' hopeless een sullen and dry
For a last look roond when a blast
O' lichtnin' tore frae the sky
And struck her deid where she stood.
In the dismantled room
Hauf-lifelike still she stands
Decomposin' in the gloom.
To the faithfu' seein' nae difference
She's in her usual still
And the hoose is fitly furnished
In keepin' wi' God's will.
I ha'e nae doot they're richt,
But, feech, it's a waesome sicht!

The Hole in the Wall

No' the love o' women, and nae concern
Wi' my personal interests, gi'es
This look to my een, this curve to my mooth,
But a deeper cause than these.

I share them wi' mony wi' whom
I share little else – they come frae the haill
Past o' mankind wha lived and loved
Like us, wi' nae ither avail.

'Wha's the bairn like? Faither or mither.'
'I'd hair like honey at his age tae.'
'Juist look at this photo o' Uncle Sam.
It's no' ill to ken whaur his nose comes frae.'

It means that nature's still seekin'
In ilka man born a way oot
Experimentin' again and maist o' us ken
Failin' again withoot doot.

You're a fechter tae? The best o' news.
The fecht sae faur frae owre
Has haurdly begun, and'll wax foraye
In proportion to oor power.

For a' my een are as different frae yours
As twa chestnuts are frae a horse's,
And to oor mooths the wind and the wave
Are mair like identical forces,

Even my poetry yet may hint
The imperious curve or the quiet look
Through which the haill o' the world'll find
The ootlet it has sae lang sook.

Individual glory is little.
We're sodgers. Let each
Dae his duty, not care wha makes
– Sae lang as it's made – the breach.

As in mony a poem the emphasis
O' the poet's expression we tine
Through no' understandin' the metrical structure
Sae wi' lives like yours and mine.

Like when Uncle Dick wi' his pinkie crookt
    Made yon gesture o' his,
A raither slow line, half-blocked, half-reprovin',
    And suddenly Liz
    – Dirty Dick! Liz-Quiz! –
In a slightly buoyant anapaestic tone
    Threw the dog a bone,
And a wealth o' new rhythms was syne let loose
To mither's dismay, a' through the hoose.

Another Turn of the Screw

'I TRY to mind a'body I ken
But tine coont and am face to face
Wi' a host o' shapes and voices flegsome
As the eternal silences o' space.'

'And fu' o' the tragedy springin'
Frae sic mooths and een o' men,
As their soonds and looks gi'e way
To the void again.'

'Ah, if they werena sae fine and clear,
Wrocht in sic rare detail,
Fraught wi' sic delicate shades o' meanin'
– A' to nae avail!'

Fear? What's fear to a Border man?
Can a poet be cowed by fear
Wha's incomprehensible images suddenly
Are understood, and seem aye t'been clear?

'But what is poetry but anither
Less-easily-vanquished-nae-doot
Voice-shape that in turn fa's abreid
And lets the same silence up through't?'

The void only seems that to us
In sic temporary shapes oorsels.
What gars us speak o' appearances
Is an appearance tae, and nocht else.

The Seamless Garment

Whene'er the mist which stands 'twixt God and thee
Defecates to a pure transparency
                                    COLERIDGE

You are a cousin of mine
      Here in the mill.
It's queer that born in the Langholm
      It's no' until
Juist noo I see what it means
To work in the mill like my freen's.

I was tryin' to say something
      In a recent poem
Aboot Lenin. You've read a guid lot
      In the news – but ken the less o'm?
Look, Wullie, here is his secret noo
In a way I can share it wi' you.

His secret and the secret o' a'
      That's worth ocht.
The shuttles fleein' owre quick for my een
      Prompt the thocht,
And the coordination atween
            Weaver and machine.

The haill shop's dumfoonderin'
      To a stranger like me.
Second nature to you; you're perfectly able
      To think, speak and see
Apairt frae the looms, tho' to some
That doesna sae easily come.

Lenin was like that wi' workin' class life,
    At hame wi't a'.
His fause movements couldna been fewer,
    The best weaver Earth ever saw.
A' he'd to dae wi' moved intact
      Clean, clear, and exact.

A poet like Rilke did the same
    In a different sphere,
Made a single reality – a' a'e 'oo' –
    O' his love and pity and fear;
A seamless garment o' music and thought
But you're owre thrang wi' puirer to tak' tent o't.

What's life or God or what you may ca't
    But something at ane like this?
Can you divide yoursel' frae your breath
    Or – if you say yes –
Frae your mind that as in the case
O' the loom keeps that in its place?

Empty vessels mak' the maist noise
    As weel you ken.
Still waters rin deep, owre fu' for soond.
    It's the same wi' men.
Belts fleein', wheels birlin' – a river in flood,
Fu' flow and tension o' poo'er and blood.

Are you equal to life as to the loom?
    Turnin' oot shoddy or what?
Claith better than man? D'ye live to the full,
    Your poo'er's a' deliverly taught?
Or scamp a'thing else? Border claith's famous.
Shall things o' mair consequence shame us?

Lenin and Rilke baith gied still mair skill,
    Coopers o' Stobo, to a greater concern
Than you devote to claith in the mill.
    Wad it be ill to learn

To keep a bit eye on their looms as weel
And no' be hailly ta'en up wi' your 'tweel'?

The womenfolk ken what I mean.
   Things maun fit like a glove,
Come clean off the spoon – and syne
   There's time for life and love.
The mair we mak' natural as breathin' the mair
Energy for ither things we'll can spare,
   But as lang as we bide like this
Neist to naething we ha'e, or miss.

Want to gang back to the handloom days?
   Nae fear!
Or paintin' oor hides? Hoo d'ye think we've got
   Frae there to here?
We'd get a million times faurer still
If maist folk change profits didna leav't till
A wheen here and there to bring it aboot
– Aye, and hindered no' helped to boot.

Are you helpin'? Machinery's improved, but folk?
   Is't no' high time
We were tryin' to come into line a' roon?
   (I canna think o' a rhyme.)
Machinery in a week mak's greater advances
Than Man's nature twixt Adam and this.

Hundreds to the inch the threids lie in,
   Like the men in a communist cell.
There's a play o' licht frae the factory windas.
   Could you no' mak' mair yoursel'?
Mony a loom mair alive than the weaver seems
For the sun's still nearer than Rilke's dreams.

Ailie Bally's tongue's keepin' time
   To the vibration a' richt.
Clear through the maze your een signal to Jean
   What's for naebody else's sicht

Short skirts, silk stockin's – fegs, hoo the auld
Emmle–deugs o' the past are curjute and devauld!

And as for me in my fricative work
  I ken fu' weel
Sic an integrity's what I maun ha'e,
  Indivisible, real,
Woven owre close for the point o' a pin
   Onywhere to win in.

Water of Life

WHA looks on water and's no' affected yet
By memories o' the Flood, and, faurer back,
O' that first flux in which a' life began,
And won sae slowly oot that ony lack
O' poo'er's a shrewd reminder o' the time
  We ploutered in the slime?

It's seldom in my active senses tho'
That water brings sic auld sensations as that
(Gin it's no' mixed wi' something even yet
A wee taet stronger); but in lookin' at
A woman at ony time I mind oor source
  And possible return of course.

Happy wha feels there's solid ground beneath
His feet at ony time – if ony does.
Happy? That's aiblins ga'en a bit owre faur.
I only mean he differs frae me thus
Tho' I'm whiles glad when a less shoogly sea
  Than ithers cradles me.

And if I'm no' aye glad o't it's because
I was sae used to waters as a loon
That I'm amphibious still. A perfect maze
O' waters is aboot the Muckle Toon,

Apairt frae't often seemin' through the weather
    That sea and sky swap places a'thegither.

Ah, vivid recollection o' trudgin' that
Crab-like again upon the ocean-flair ! –
Juist as in lyin' wi' a woman still
I feel a sudden cant and sweesh aince mair
Frae Sodom or Gomorrah wi' yon Eastern whore
    T'oor watery grave o' yore.

She clung to me mair tightly at the end
Than ane expects or wants in sic a case,
Whether frae love or no' I needna say,
A waste o' guid material – her face
Fastened on mine as on a flag a sooker
    And naething shook her.

Although my passion was sair diluted then
I mind the cratur' still frae tip to tae
Better than ony that I've troked si' syne
– The gowden pendants frae her lugs, her skin
Sae clear that in her cheeks the glints 'ud play
As whiles wi' bits o' looking-glass as loons
    We'd gar the sun loup roon's.

Nae doot the sudden predicament we shared
Has fixed her in my mind abune the lave,
A kind o' compensation for the way
She was sae tashed and lightlied by the wave
Oot o' my recognition and slarried by
    The infernal sly.

A man never faced wi' death kens nocht o' life.
But a' men are? But micht as weel no' be !
The ancient memory is alive to few
And fewer when it is ken what they see,
But them that dae fear neither life nor death,
    Mindin' them baith.

Nae man can jouk and let the jaw gang by.
To seem to's often to dodge a silly squirt
While bein' whummled in an unseen spate
Lodgin' us securely in faur deeper dirt
Or carryin' us to heichts we canna see
    For th'earth in oor e'e.

Nae gulfs that open 'neath oor feet'll find
Us hailly at a loss if we juist keep
The perspective the deluge should ha' gien's
And if we dinna, or if they're mair deep
Than even that is muckle guidance in,
    It's there altho' we're blin'.

Whatever is to be, what's been has been;
Even if it's hailly undune that deed'll bear
A sense o' sequence forever in itsel',
Implyin', and dependent on, what erst was there,
Tho' it's no' conscious o't – less conscious o't
    Than men o' their historic lot.

Hoo I got oot o' yon I dinna ken,
But I am ready noo at ony time
To be hurled back or forrit to ony stage
O' ocht we've ever been twixt sun and slime
Or can become, trustin' what's brocht aboot
    A' th'ither sequels to the water-shute.

Shall wellspring and shower, ebb-tide and neap,
Refuse their separate pairts cryin' let's be ane,
In function as natur', appearance as fact?
Foul here, fair there, to sea and sky again
The river keeps its course and ranges
    Unchanged through a' its changes.

Wha speak o' vice and innocence, peace and war,
Culture and ignorance, humility and pride,
Describe the Fairy Loup, the thunder-plump,
The moss-boil on the moor, the white-topped tide;

And the ane as sune as the tither'll be
    Brocht doon to uniformity.

Ah, weel I ken that ony ane o' them,
Nae maitter hoo vividly I ca't to mind,
Kennin' the world to men's as light to water,
Has endless beauties to which my een are blind,
My ears deaf – aye, and ilka drap a world
    Bigger than a' Mankind has yet unfurled.

Excelsior

Sae worked the instinct in the seas
And jungles we were born in
But sicna cares are useless noo
Tho' aiblins no' for scornin'.

Sae worked the kindnesses we got
Frae shadows gane ayont recall.
Sae work whatever relationships
May haud us still in thrall.

Still on we fare and tine oor need
O' modern mither's as monkey's care,
Syne wives, bairns, freens, and in the end
Oorsels we weel can spare.

And aye the force that's brocht life up
Frae chaos to the present stage
Creates new states as ill for us
As oors for eels to gauge.

The promise that there'll be nae second Flood
I tak' wi' a' the salt I've saved since then.
Extinction? What's that but to return
To juist anither Muckle Toon again?
– A salutary process bringin' values oot
    Ocht less 'ud leave in doot.

It teach't me mony lessons I've ne'er forgot –
That it's no' easy to thraw cauld water on life;
The changes a man can safely undergang
And bide essentially unchanged; the strife
To tak' new forms and in it no' forget
    We've never managed yet.

The Factory Gullets and the Skipper's Pool
Are different as Dr. Jekyll and Mr. Hyde
But the quick changes o' the Esk that joins
These twa afore it meets the Solway Tide
'Ud faur ootrin the divers thochts o' Man
    Sin' Time began.

And yet, tho' hospitable to them a',
The Esk is drawn on like a knotless threid
Juist owre lang for's to see the end o't yet,
Tho' noo and then I tak' it in my heid
That the pirn in the hills it's birlin' frae
    Maun near ha' ser'd its day.

Or else I feel like payin' oot line
Forever to an unimaginable take,
And ken that in the Buck and Croon Hotels
They'd lauch my tale to scorn, altho' gudesake,
They credit mony hardly less faur-fetched.
    Heaven kens if mine is stretched!

The Buck and Croon Hotels – guid judges baith
O' credibility I've cause to ken;
A wee hauf wi' the emphasis on the wee,
And day and daily d'they no' see again
A miracle clean-flypit, in the maitter
    O' wine turn't back to water?

Weel the Waterside folk kent what I mean;
They were like figures seen on fountains whiles.
The river made sae free wi' them – poored in and oot
O' their een and ears (no' mooths) in a' its styles,

Till it clean scooped the insides o' their skulls
    O' a' but a wheen thochts like gulls.

Their queer stane faces and hoo green they got!
Juist like Rebecca in her shawl o' sly.
I'd never faur to gang to see doon there
A wreathèd Triton blaw his horn or try,
While at his feet a clump o' mimulus shone
    Like a dog's een wi' a' the world a bone.

SECOND HYMN TO LENIN
(1932)

Second Hymn to Lenin

TO MY FRIENDS NAOMI MITCHISON AND HENRY CARR

AH, Lenin, you were richt. But I'm a poet
(And you c'ud mak allowances for that!)
Aimin' at mair than you aimed at
Tho' yours comes first, I know it.

An unexamined life is no' worth ha'in'.
Yet Burke was richt; owre muckle concern
Wi' Life's foundations is a sure
Sign o' decay; tho' Joyce in turn

Is richt, and the principal question
Aboot a work o' art is frae hoo deep
A life it springs – and syne hoo faur
Up frae't it has the poo'er to leap

And hoo muckle it lifts up wi' it
Into the sunlicht like a saumon there,
Universal Spring! for Morand's richt –
It s'ud be like licht in the air –

> Are my poems spoken in the factories and fields,
>   In the streets o' the toon?
> Gin they're no', then I'm failin' to dae
>   What I ocht to ha' dune.

> Gin I canna win through to the man in the street,
>   The wife by the hearth,
> A' the cleverness on earth 'll no' mak' up
>   For the damnable dearth.

> 'Haud on, haud on; what poet's dune that?
>   Is Shakespeare read,
> Or Dante or Milton or Goethe or Burns?'
>   – You heard what I said.

– A means o' world locomotion,
The maist perfected and aerial o' a'.
Lenin's name's gane owre the haill earth,
But the names o' the ithers? – Ha !

What hidie-hole o' the vineyard d'they scart
Wi' minds like the look on a hen's face,
Morand, Joyce, Burke, and the rest
That e'er wrote; me noo in like case?

Great poets hardly onybody kens o'?
Geniuses like a man talkin' t'm sel'?
Nonsense ! They're nocht o' the sort
Their character's easy to tell.

They're nocht but romantic rebels
Strikin' dilletante poses;
Trotsky – Christ, no' wi' a croon o' thorns
But a wreath o' paper roses.

A' that's great is free and expansive.
What ha' they expanded tae?
They've affected nocht but a fringe
O' mankind in ony way.

Barbarian saviour o' civilization
Hoo weel ye kent (we're owre dull witted)
Naething is dune save as we ha'e
Means to en's transparently fitted.

Poetry like politics maun cut
The cackle and pursue real ends,
Unerringly as Lenin, and to that
Its nature better tends.

Wi' Lenin's vision equal poet's gift
And what unparalleled force was there !
Nocht in a' literature wi' that
Begins to compare.

Nae simple rhymes for silly folk
But the haill art, as Lenin gied
Nae Marx-without-tears to workin' men
But the fu' course insteed.

Organic constructional work,
Practicality, and work by degrees;
First things first; and poetry in turn
'll be built by these.

You saw it faur off when you thocht
O' mass-education yet.
Hoo lang till they rise to Pushkin?
And that's but a fit!

    Oh, it's nonsense, nonsense, nonsense,
    Nonsense at this time o' day
    That breid-and-butter problems
    S'ud be in ony man's way.

    They s'ud be like the tails we tint
    On leavin' the monkey stage;
    A' maist folk fash aboot's alike
    Primaeval to oor age.

    We're grown-up folk that haena yet
    Put bairnly things aside
    – A' that's material and moral –
    And oor new state descried.

    Sport, love, and parentage,
    Trade, politics, and law
    S'ud be nae mair to us than braith
    We hardly ken we draw.

    Freein' oor poo'ers for greater things,
    And fegs there's plenty o' them,
    Tho' wha's still trammelt in alow
    Canna be tenty o' them –

In the meantime Montéhus' sangs –
But as you were ready to tine
The Russian Revolution to the German
Gin that ser'd better syne,

Or foresaw that Russia maun lead
The workers' cause, and then
Pass the lead elsewhere, and aiblins
Fa' faur backward again,

Sae here, twixt poetry and politics,
There's nae doot in the en'.
Poetry includes that and s'ud be
The greatest poo'er amang men.

– It's the greatest, *in posse* at least,
That men ha'e discovered yet
Tho' nae doot they're unconscious still
O' ithers faur greater than it.

You confined yoursel' to your work
– A step at a time;
But, as the loon is in the man,
That'll be ta'en up i' the rhyme,

Ta'en up like a pool in the sands
Aince the tide rows in,
When life opens its hert and sings
Withoot scruple or sin.

Your knowledge in your ain sphere
Was exact and complete
But your sphere's elementary and sune by
As a poet maun see't.

For a poet maun see in a'thing,
Ev'n what looks trumpery or horrid,
A subject equal to ony
– A star for the forehead!

A poet has nae choice left
Betwixt Beaverbrook, say, and God,
Jimmy Thomas or you,
A cat, carnation, or clod.

He daurna turn awa' frae ocht
For a single act o' neglect
And straucht he may fa' frae grace
And be void o' effect.

Disinterestedness,
Oor profoundest word yet,
But hoo faur yont even that
The sense o' onything's set!

The inward necessity yont
Ony laws o' cause
The intellect conceives
That a' thing has!

Freend, foe; past, present, future;
Success, failure; joy, fear;
Life, Death; and a' thing else,
For us, are equal here.

Male, female; quick or deid,
Let us fike nae mair;
The deep line o' cleavage
Disna lie there.

Black in the pit the miner is,
The shepherd reid on the hill,
And I'm wi' them baith until
The end of mankind, I wis.

Whatever their jobs a' men are ane
In life, and syne in daith
(Tho' it's sma' patience I can ha'e
Wi' life's ideas o' that by the way)
And he's nae poet but kens it, faith,
And ony job but the hardest's ta'en.

The sailor gangs owre the curve o' the sea,
The hoosewife's thrang in the wash-tub,
And whatna rhyme can I find but hub,
And what else can poetry be?

The core o' a' activity,
Changin't in accordance wi'
Its inward necessity
And mede o' integrity.

Unremittin', relentless,
Organized to the last degree,
Ah, Lenin, politics is bairns' play
To what this maun be!

SCOTS UNBOUND
AND OTHER POEMS
(1932)

The light will again come out of the North.
                    Balzac's Séraphita.

Do threasgair an saol is do shéid an ghaoth mar smál
Alastram, Caesar is an mhéid do bhi 'na bpáirt;
Tá an Teamhair 'na féar, is féach an Traoi mar tá,
'S na Sasanaigh féin, dob fhéidir go bhfaighdís bás.[1]

---

[1] A translation of this Irish Gaelic verse is:

> Life conquereth still; as dust the whirlwinds blow –
> Alexander, Caesar, and all their power and due!
> Tara is grass, and Troy itself lieth low –
> It may be that death will reach the English too.

The Back o' Beyond

BEND doon, the sunsmite oot o' your een,
To this lanely pool and see
A'e shadow gantin' 'mang shadows there
And mind aince mair wi' me
Hoo months afore they were born
Mony a fine simmer's day
'S come doon through their mither's joy
To where men lay.

Stand up; and at midday yet
What a glunsh we get!

Milk-Wort and Bog-Cotton

TO SEUMAS O'SULLIVAN

CWA' een like milk-wort and bog-cotton hair!
I love you, earth, in this mood best o' a'
When the shy spirit like a laich wind moves
And frae the lift nae shadow can fa'
Since there's nocht left to thraw a shadow there
Owre een like milk-wort and milk-white cotton hair.

Wad that nae leaf upon anither wheeled
A shadow either and nae root need dern
In sacrifice to let sic beauty be!
But deep surroondin' darkness I discern
Is aye the price o' licht. Wad licht revealed
Naething but you, and nicht nocht else concealed.

Lynch-Pin

To 'AE'

HERE where I sit assembling in the sun
The salient features o' my structure o' banes
I feel that somewhere there's a missing one
That mak's a dish o' whummle o' my pains.
Sma' but the clue to a' the rest, and no'
In ony woman hidden nor on this earth,
And if there's ony ither world, hoo it's got there,
If 't has, I ken nae mair than hoo I ken my dearth
That yet fills my haill life wi' the effort
To embody a' creation – and find this ort.

An Apprentice Angel

To L. M. W.

1

TRY on your wings; I ken vera weel
It wadna look seemly if ony ane saw
A Glasgow Divine ga'en flutherin' aboot
In his study like a drunk craw.

But it 'ud look waur if you'd to bide
In an awkward squad for a month or mair
Learnin' to flee afore you could join
Heaven's air gymkhana aince you get there

Try on your wings, and gi'e a bit flap,
Pot belly and a', what does it maitter?
Seriously prepare for your future state
– Tho' that's never been in your natur'!

II

As the dragonfly's hideous larva creeps
Oot o' the ditch whaur it was spawned
And straight is turned to the splendid fly,
Nae doot by Death's belated hand
You'll be changed in a similar way,
But as frae that livin' flash o' licht
The cruel features and crawlin' legs
O' its former state never vanish quite
I fancy your Presbyterian Heaven
'll be haunted tae wi' a hellish leaven.

Water Music

To William and Flora Johnstone

Wheesht, wheesht, Joyce, and let me hear
Nae Anna Livvy's lilt,
But Wauchope, Esk, and Ewes again,
Each wi' its ain rhythms till't.

I

Archin' here and arrachin there,
Allevolie or allemand,
Whiles appliable, whiles areird,
The polysemous poem's planned.

Lively, louch, atweesh, atween,
Auchimuty or aspate,
Threidin' through the averins
Or bightsom in the aftergait.

Or barmybrained or barritchfu',
Or rinnin' like an attercap,
Or shinin' like an Atchison,
Wi' a blare or wi' a blawp.

They ken a' that opens and steeks,
  Frae Fiddleton Bar to Callister Ha',
And roon aboot for twenty miles,
  They bead and bell and swaw.

Brent on or boutgate or beshacht
  Bellwaverin' or borne-heid,
They mimp and primp, or bick and birr,
  Dilly-dally or show speed.

Brade-up or sclafferin', rouchled, sleek,
  Abstraklous or austerne,
In belths below the brae-hags
  And bebbles in the fern.

Bracken, blaeberries, and heather
  Ken their amplefeysts and toves,
Here gangs ane wi' aiglets jinglin',
  Through a gowl anither goves.

Lint in the bell whiles hardly vies
  Wi' ane the wind amows,
While blithely doon abradit linns
  Wi' gowd begane anither jows.

Cougher, blocher, boich and croichle,
  Fraise in ane anither's witters,
Wi' backthraws, births, by-rinnin's,
  Beggar's-broon or blae – the critters!

Or burnet, holine, watchet, chauve,
  Or wi' a' the colours dyed
O' the lift abune and plants and trees
  That grow on either side.

Or coinyelled wi' the midges,
  Or swallows a' aboot,
The shadow o' an eagle,
  The aiker o' a troot.

Toukin' ootrageous face
    The turn-gree o' your mood,
I've climmed until I'm lost
    Like the sun ahint a clood.

But a tow-gun frae the boon-tree,
A whistle frae the elm,
A spout-gun frae the hemlock,
And, back in this auld realm,
Dry leafs o' dishielogie
To smoke in a 'partan's tae'!

And you've me in your creel again,
    Brim or shallow, bauch or bricht,
Singin' in the mornin',
    Corrieneuchin' a' the nicht.

II

Lappin' on the shirrel,
    Or breengin' doon the cleuch,
Slide-thrift for stars and shadows,
    Or sun-'couped owre the heuch'.

Wi' the slughorn o' a folk,
    Sightsmen for a thoosand years,
In fluther or at shire
    O' the Border burns' careers,

Let them popple, let them pirl,
    Plish-plash and plunk and plop and ploot,
In quakin' quaw or fish-currie
    I ken a' they're aboot.

And 'twixt the pavvy o' the Wauchope,
    And the paspey o' the Ewes,
And the pavane o' Esk itsel',
    It's no' for me to choose.

Be they querty, be they quiet,
    Flow like railya or lamoo,
Only turn a rashmill or
    Gar a' the country tew,

As it's froggin' in the hills,
    Or poors pipestapples and auld wives,
Sae Waich Water glents and scrows,
    Reels and ratches and rives.

Some day they say the Bigly Burn
    'll loup oot frae its scrabs and thistles,
And ding the bonnie birken shaw
    A' to pigs and whistles.

And there's yon beck – I winna name't –
    That hauds the fish that aince was hookit
A century syne – the fisher saw't,
    And flew, and a' his graith forsookit.

And as for Unthank Water,
    That seeps through miles o' reeds and seggs,
It's aye at pilliewinkie syne
    Wi' the gowdnie's eggs.

Nae mair than you could stroan yoursel'
    The biggest o' them you may say,
Yet lood and still I see them stoan
    To oceans and the heaven's sway.

Fleetin' owre the meadows,
    Or cleitchin' in the glaur,
The haill world answers to them,
    And they rein the faurest star.

Humboldt, Howard, Maury,
    Hildebrandsson, Hann, and Symons,
A digest o' a' their work's
    In these dour draps or diamonds.

And weel I ken the air's wild rush
    As it comes owre the seas,
Clims up and whistles 'twixt the hills,
    Wi' a' the weather gi'es

O' snaw and rain and thunder,
    Is a single circle spun
By the sun's bricht heat and guided by
    Earth's spin and the shapes o' the grun'.

Lappin' on the shirrel,
    Or breengin' doon the cleuch,
I can listen to the waters
    Lang – and no' lang – eneuch.

Wheesht, wheesht, Joyce, and let me hear
    No' Anna Livvy's lilt,
But Wauchope, Esk, and Ewes again,
    Each wi' its ain rhythms till't.

Tarras

I

This Bolshevik bog! Suits me doon to the grun'!
For by fike and finnick the world's no' run.
Let fools set store by a simperin' face,
Ithers seek to keep the purale in place
Or grue at vermin – but by heck
The purpose o' life needs them – if us.
Little the bog and the masses reck
O' some dainty-davie or fike-ma-fuss.
Ho for the mother of usk and adder
Spelderin' here in her coal and madder
Faur frae Society's bells and bladder.

The fog-wa' splits and a gair is set
O' corbie oats and corcolet
And drulie water like sheepeik seeps
Through the duffie peats, and cranglin' creeps,
Crowdles like a crab, syne cowds awa',
Couthless eneuch, yet cuttedly tae,
Tho' here and there in a sudden swaw
Corky-heidit as if in a playsome way,
But its lichtest kinks are a cowzie sport,
That nocht can cuddum – nocht can sort
For't, endless torsion, riddlin' port.

Ah, woman-fondlin'! What is that to this?
Saft hair to birssy heather, warm kiss
              To cauld black waters' suction.
              Nae ardent breists' erection
But the stark hills'! In what dry-gair-flow
Can I pillow my lowin' cheek here
Wi' nae paps' howe below?
What laithsome parodies appear
O' my body's secrets in this oorie growth
Wi' its peerieweeries a' radgie for scouth
And the haill ratch and rive o' a world uncouth?

Her cautelles! On cods o' crammasy sundew
Or wi' antrin sprigs o' butterwort blue,
Here in a punk-hole, there in a burn,
She gecks to storm and shine in turn,
Trysts wi' this wind and neist wi' that,
Now wi' thunder and syne wi' snaw,
Bare to the banes or wi' birds in her hat,
              – And has bairns by them a',
                            – Bairns!

Bycomes o' bogs and gets o' cairns,
Ultimate flow of her flosh and ferns . . .
The doup of the world is under you here
And, fast in her shochles, she'll find ye,

When you're drawn to where wind and water shear,
Shuttles o' glaur, and shot-heuch, to wind ye,
Till you peughle and hoast in the shug-bog there,
While she lies jirblin' wide to the air
And now and then lets a scannachin flare.

Come pledge her in a horse-punckin then!
Loons to a byssim, pock-shakin's o' men,
Needna come vauntin' their poustures to her.
Their paramuddle is whey to her heather.
To gang through her mill they maun pay
Ootsucken multure to the auld vulture,
Nor wi' their flauchter-spades ettle to play,
Withoot thick paikies to gaird their cul-ture!
What's ony schaftmon to this shud moss?
Or pooky-hair to her matted boss?
– Pledge her wha's mou' can relish her floss!

II

Why I Became a Scots Nationalist

GI'E me Scots-room in life and love
And set me then my smeddum to prove
In scenes like these. Like Pushkin I
My time for flichty conquests by,
Valuing nae mair some quick-fire cratur'
Wha hurries up the ways o' natur',
Am happy, when after lang and sair
Pursuit you yield yoursel' to me,
But wi' nae rapture, cauldly there,
Open but glowerin' callously,
Yet slow but surely heat until
You catch my flame against your will
And the mureburn tak's the hill.

Scots Unbound

Divertissement Philologique

To Robin and Margaret Black

Cwa; think o' nocht but the colours then
 And catch me in the trebuck, lad.
English words are wide o' the mark
 In a viese like this, b'Gad,
O' hasart bennels and falow breckan
 – Juist ettle through yon far wuds
The divers degrees and shades to reckon
O' umbrate, thester, and mark, to the cluds
 At last they wallow in,
Or in the pyrnit fields that to ozmilt dwine
 Or in the waters that rin,
Sae lang submerged but on the skyline
 Kyth wips o' orpine afore they're din;
 Syne let's begin
If we're to dae richt by this auld leid
 And by Scotland's kittle hues
To distinguish nicely 'twixt sparked and brocked,
Blywest and chauve, brandit and brinked,
And a' the dwaffil terms we'll need
 To ken and featly use,
Sparrow-drift o' description, the ganandest gait,
Glaggwuba, ἀκριβῶς, to dae as we ocht,
Bring oot a' the backward tints that are linked
Frae purpie to wan in this couthless scene
 – You see what I mean!
English is owre cauld-casten-to
For the thochts that Scotland should gar us brew.

 Warth skura windis mikila,
 Withondans haubida seina.

    Trudan ufaro waurme.
    Krimi, carmine and crimson;
    κόκκος, cochineal, vermis, vermilion.
    Bestail, grains, vins, fruictz.[1]
    Haithi, timrjan, thaurnus, blowans,
    Fani, hugs. Hwaiwa us siggis?[2]
        Silence, come oot o' him![3]
        Keep oot, che vor' ye![4]

Be a' that's jonet, sarrigold, orenze,
Rudede, moriane, katmogit,
Emeraud, endorrede, and electre,
Blae and mouskit, resplaid in oor verses yet,

Wi' blunket, blanchard, sorrit, reve,
Bassynt ga'en ghaist in the sun-fire,
And lattoun, lech as greenstane or trapp,
– Ilk macklike, landrien, shire.

But colour in Scotland's owre thrawn and obscure
    For the een to ha'e the chief say?
Let's try smell then, and the sense o' taste
    Sae often bound up wi't tae.
Can you name as you turn your nose to a wind
    Or look in the opposite airt
This odour and that that's blended wi't
    And hoo each plays its separate pairt?
Some through the nosetirls alane and some
    Mair through the nerves o' the mou',
– Hoo a bricht licht's nim while a flann or youm
    Affects the throat like lamoo,
    Or the air like butter whiles has a gout,
Or a black soss hotterin' in the sun,
Ugg iper, gars you grue or tant?

[1] Rabelais.
[2] The Wufilic Gospel.
[3] Christ in the synagogue at Nazareth to the unclean spirit in the poor man.
[4] Shakespeare: *King Lear*.

Fegs, you're on dour and attrie grun'
(Dour, ordure, oh! durus amor!)
And you'll chowl wi' mony a snirkam here
As you catch this snoak or the ither;
    And the words you want,
Oorie and nesh eneuch, I fear,
'll tak' an unco gettin' thegither
As you get a youk frae some broc-faced place
Or the world gangs a' knedeuch in your face;
And, certes, it's only in Scots you'll find,
Tho' few can use them, words o' the kind.

Blaw ye south! man, for forsooth,
Here your tongue's awak in your mouth.
– 'Ill-thief, blaw the beggar south,
And never drink be near his drouth'[1]
Mak' nae mistalk. Properlies similar to these
Ha'e different effects in Eire a' thegither
Whaur 'nae wits harden in the misty rushes,
Broon bogs, hills o' granite, magenta heather.'[2]

Mony a natkin to kittle your muns;
And, withoot ony weasel-blawin',
A knaggim here and a yowther there
Has you hwindle-faced or gruntle-thrawn!

Mony a thocht the result o' a cens
A body's nose is owre deef to tell?
Mony a sairing, muff and foost
That words can gi'e nae magdum o'?
Haud on! We'll mak' them morigerate yet
And mair than sic nek-herring show,
Or naked neked, that's a' maist folk ken
– Wi' serpent-tongues in oor salers again.

---

[1] Adapted from Burns.
[2] See Bernard Shaw's *John Bull's Other Island.*

You see or ken nocht withoot sensations o' touch,
    Or the subtlest effects upon you o' shape.
Even aboot things you've never touched,
    Forms that a' nameable forms escape?
There's mair in the feel o' things than's kent by the hands,
    Mair in their look than een can see,
        That neist to naebody understands
        Or due wecht to them can gi'e.
          For want o' a' jedgry.
Hence a' oor kittle Scots words, hair splittin',
Nice shades o' meanin', aye closer fittin'
Ganand, in rayndoun, 'mair slink in the turn',
And the way wi' a landscape we see oorsels in it,
        Ken it in terms o' oor mombles faur mair
        Than we're often, if ever, aware.
        The vivisection o' the word made flesh
        Is eneuch to mak' ony man nesh.
No' the Esk that rins like a ribbon there
But gi'es and tak's wi' the cluds in the air
And ootwith its stent boonds lies at the root
O' the plants and trees for miles roondaboot,
And gethers its tributaries, yet pulse-beats back
Up through them and a' that mak's it helps mak'
Sae I wad that Scotland's shape 'ud appear
As clear through a' its sub-shapes here
As whiles through my separate works I see
        Their underlyin' unity;
Even as a workman automatically sees
A' that belangs to his craft in a scene,
A' done – to do – possibilities,
Be it forestry, drainage, or fermin', gi'en,
Or a man versed in history anither lacks
An atmosphere o' associations mak's,
A special climate transformin' it a',
Oor nature's unconscious goal, oor bias,
Advances this and recedes the ither,
And sae their influences upon us fa',
Feed us or fail us, and in a' ways try us,

And country and consciousness mell thegither.
                    Misk, and misgar, wi' nebawae life,
                    And nig-ma-nies o' floo'ers,
                    It tak's nae ogertfow poet to sing
                    Sic a wowf and wurl-like land as oors;
                    – But nae 'Northman's thing made South-folk's
                        place'
                        Is worth a curse in ony case!

Sae my mind hawk-steadies owre the moor
'Mang the glorifluikins and gloffs o' a lift
Owre big ne gnede. But what obiuse
Atour me gars the universe shift,
What gylooms range its glents and glooms,
Investigabill tows o' the rack o' cluds
Upcastin' here and thorter there,
That in cat's hair streams or pack-merchans scuds
        I ken nae mair than a wag-string here.
        A feckless raipfu' as ever you saw,
A conjunct-feftment o' earth and air,
Tho' my oralog has nae moyne ava',
Nor houpitas for the stars or sun
Or the frape and frawartschip o' the grun'
                    Wi' its gads o' ice and helms o' weet,
                    Fires o' stanes and battles o' straw,
                    Bands o' whins, and, tring by tring,
                    A' its pry withoot jedgry there.
Noblay and nooslan in turn I tak
But baith determined ahint my back,
Couped frae a hule nae man can see
Whether earth-fast or howyn like me,
Tho', unlike maist, my muse gars't seem
That time itsel' has me hemilled roond,
Kennable and changin', no' borrell, space,
And that I hing in a livin' lift
Aye renewed and reshaped wi'in itsel;
And dedicate to the deemless scheme
O' the transformations o' a soul, hecht

The soul of extension, that has nae boond,
Sheer plenitude wi' its prevert face,
A quenchless flame that fills the haill place,
    In nae perpetua clad
    Through schene and swaar
   But on fedren faw, like a watergaw,
     Wi' a' the colours there are
   – Or struggle syne, in a backthraw
  Owre a world gane harth and haw.

Cwa; think o' nocht but the subtlest skills
Gubert in folk like you and me,
Kennin' hoo language, a tortoise competin'
Wi' licht's velocity, compares wi' sicht,
Tho' we canna imagine life withoot it,
Weird world-in-the-world, and seldom think richt
    O' the limitations no' lettin't gi'e
In libraries as muckle's in the turn o' an e'e,
Till whiles it seems there isna a taet
In a' creation it couldna state
But the neist instant we ken hoo sma'
A pairt o' life can be voiced ava',
– Nae words for the simplest experiences even,
Sae that, set doon in oor best freen's mind,
A *terra incognita* we'd find
      Yont a' believin'
Wi' here and there some feature we kent
But baffled whichever airt we went
Wi' unexpected groupin's, proportions, shapes,
Mismarrows through which a' sense escapes.
Kennin' my slughorn and a' my strynds
The language side o' sic gulfs lures me maist
Wi' words inouth, nane speaks or minds
Withoot muckle keach, afore me raised
In shapes that excite or dow me mair
     Than ocht in the world ootby there.
A' horns to the lift; cat's horns upmaist!
    But muckle that faceless lurks

In yon subdominal scene is no' to be faced?
   Your spirit the fell task shirks?

Cwa; think o' nocht but the colours then.
    It's the easiest way.
   Nigro-ruber, nigro-coeruleus,
   Dacklie, gule, blue day,
Sheep's lichtnin', dim-top brilliants, stopango gems,
– Nae mair o' your uchhas, imphms, and hems;
We'll tak' the country on oor backs,
   Green breese and crammasy cow,
   Richt through to black-be-lickit,
And whummle ony luppen rainbow I trow
  In the bowl o' oor occipitit;
And back again. Licht lifts the world's fax.
   The lucken-browed bront
   O' Scotland's on't.
Cwa; think o' nocht but a'thing then
And catch me in a trebuck, lad,
English words are wide o' the mark
  In a viese like this, b'Gad!

Depth and the Chthonian Image

On looking at a ruined mill and thinking of the greatest

TO JOHN MACNAIR REID

Absolvitur ab instantia is decreed
In every case against you men array.
Yours is the only nature stiflin' nocht,
Meetin' a' the experiences there are to ha'e
And never meetin' ane o' them raw-edged.
Ripe, reconcilin' mind, sublimely gauged,

Serene receptiveness, nae tongue can speak
Your fair fey form felicitously enow,
Nae subtle mind seek your benmaist howe
And gar your deepest implications beek.
The mills o' God grind sma', but they
In you maun crumble imperceptibly tae.
Nor shadowed nor lit up by ony thocht,
Nae perfect shinin' o' a simmer's day
Vies wi' your ark's assopat speed
In its pure task engaged.
Time and Eternity are no' at odds
In you as in a' that's Man's – and God's,
For nane can look through you as through the sun and see
Some auld adhantare wi' neuked bonnet there,
Urphanömen – o' what? Ah, no, alluterlie
You deal afflufe wi' a' that's fordel and nae gair
In your allryn activity lets kyth
        The faur-side o' your sneith.

As life to death, as man to God, sae stands
This ruined mill to your great aumrie then,
This ruined mill – and every rinnin' mill?
The awte or bait o' everything you ken
And tak' it quicker than a barber's knife
Wi' nocht aclite. There is nae chance o' strife.
Micht a' the canny your abandon see!
Nor ony din they mak' let them forget
Their generations tae and creeds'll yet
Crine to a sic-like laroch while the lets-a-be
O' a' your pairts as eidently agree.
Nocht needs your wa's mair audience to gi'e.
Forever ample baith in scouth and skill,
Watchin' your aws by nicht it seems to me
The stars adreigh mimic their drops and 'mang hands
There is nae nearer image gi'en to life
O' that conclusive power by which you rin
Even on, drawin' a' the universe in,
Than this loose simile o' the heavenly hosts

Vainly prefigurin' the unseen jaups
Roond your vast wheel – or mair waesome ghosts
O' that reality man's pairt o' and yet caps
Wi' Gods in his ain likeness drawn
          – Puir travesties o' your plan.

To picture the invisible via the stars
Is the least boutgate that man's speech can gang,
As for your speed the analogy o' sleep,
Your speed and your boon millin' – no' even the lang
Processes o' metamorphosis in rock
Can fetch that ben to him like the shadowy flock
O' atoms in himsel' precariously seen,
Queer dirlin' o' his cells at sic an 'oor,
He whiles can note wha hasna else the poo'er,
Laichest Brownian movements swarmin' to his een
As neath a microscope – a deemless thrang,
To catch their changin' time, and get the hang
O' a' their swift diminishments doon the steep
Chutes o' dissolution, as he lay amang
The mools already, and watched the maggots' wars
Upon his flesh, and sune its finitude mock
Their midgeswarm jaws until their numbers fa'
To a'e toom mou', the fremit last o' a'
The reelin' corruption, its vain mudgeons there
Wi' motions that nae measure can seize on
As micht the sun to earth's last look appear
Like yon cart-wheel that raxes to a cone
Afore the spider lets its anchorage slip,
          An insect in its grip.

Nae knowledge its ain offices here
Can seek to magnify and ithers suppress.
An arbiter frae corruption free hauds sway
Unlike man's mind that canna ken unless
It decks its data wi' interpretation
To try to mak' a rational creation.
Hence a' men see contains faur mair than's seen,

Remembrance o' the past, fancy o' the future.
To memory and imagination you stand neuter
As 'twere a scientist confrontin' the gi'en
That nae logical, *a priori*, or ither reasons confess
And yet are carriers o' value that redress
His rational world frae bein' senseless tae,
Tho' here, as in sma'er things, nae inspired guess,
Teleological reasonin' or rapport sheer,
Gi'es minds like his sic valuable dilation.
You're no' its meanin' but the world itsel'.
Yet let nae man think he can see you better
By concentratin' on your aneness either.
He pits his mind into a double fetter
Wha hauds this airt or that, no' baith thegither.
You are at aince the road a' croods ha' gane
        And alane wi' the alane.

Alane wi' the alane, yet let us no' forget
Theistic faith's but, extrapolate, plottin' on
The curve o' sae-ca'd knowledge science has made
– Science and theism ha'e their roots in common
(Tho' few can credit sic a teachin' noo!) –
And needs the same redress as sciences do
To say the least. Alane wi' the alane remains
A relative conception as self-betrayed
As heidstrang science dispensin' wi' sic aid
As frae the world's allogic, kept in mind, it gains.
Nae mutual justice, undue claims foregone,
Sympathy wi' divers ootlooks and endeavours shown,
Union o' knowledge's kingdoms piously prayed,
Is less a movement leadin' awa' frae you
Than ony in the opposite airt to it,
Nor can a poet as I am cease to con,
Heedless o' baith, your prime significance
To lead his muse a needle-angel's dance
By hailin' truth a mathematical point
Wi' nae relation to the ooter world,
Whether the times are in or oot o' joint

O' scant concern since a'thing earthly's hurled
– You tae – indifferent, *adiaphora*, faur alow
      Ocht this tak's heed o'.

Aye balk and burral lie the fields o' life.
It fails to acresce a kennin' frae the past,
In a' its fancied contacts wi' what's meant
When it seems shairest in worst backspangs cast;
Its heritage but a bairn's pairt o' gear,
A puir balapat at hairst its fingers speir
And often mairket a toom barley-box;
Aye in bad breid despite their constant toil,
As bairns in their bairnliness, a cursed coil
Hauds men content wi' casual sweetie-pokes
O' a' creation's gear; and little is amassed
Maist folk can life-rent – nocht hain at last.
Yet o' the way-drawn profit wha tak's tent?
The feast is spread yet helplessly they fast,
Aye win an Irishman's rise wi' unco strife,
Cast oot frae a' their dues by the silly fear
That hauds them in habits o' poortith still,
While by them brim the torrents to your mill,
The vast way-drawing that denies mankind
Or pairt or parcel in science or in art
Till bare as worms the feck o' them we find.
Each generation at zero still maun start
And's doomed to end there, wi' a' that they forgaed
      Caught in the suction o' your lade.

Or pairt or parcel in science or in art.
– Or even in life! Hoo few men ever live
And what wee local lives at best they ha'e.
Sirse, science and art might weel rin through the sieve,
Or jow like backfa's when the mill is set.
If maist folk through nae elf-bores dribbled yet
But in some measure lived to a' life is.
Wad that their latent poo'ers 'ud loup alist,
Kyth suddenly a' their wasted past has missed,

And nae mair leave their lives like languages,
– Mere leaks frae streamin' consciousness as if
Thocht roon' itsel' raised wa's prohibitive
O' a' but a fraction o' its possible sway –
But rax in freedom, nocht inhibitive,
In fearless flourishin' amidwart,
Fed by the haill wide world and feedin' it,
Universal life, like an autonomous tongue
In which some vision o' you micht be sung,
Let us remove a' lets and hindrances then
Even as the principle o' limitation, God,
Packed wi' posterity, silent like the deid,
And aye respondin' to a lesser need,
Has vanished like a clood that weighed on men
Owre lang – till your pure radiance glowed.

Ein Mann aus dem Volke – weel I ken
Nae man or movement's worth a damn unless
The movement 'ud gang on withoot him if
He de'ed the morn. Wherefore in you I bless
My sense o' the greatest man can typify
And universalise himsel' maist fully by.
Nocht ta'en at second-hand and nocht let drift,
Nae bull owre big to tackle by the horns,
Nae chance owre sma' for freedom's sake he scorns,
But a' creation through himsel' maun sift
Even as you, nor possible defeat confess,
Forever poised and apt in his address;
Save at this pitch nae man can truly live.
Hence to these ruins I maun needs regress
– As to the facts o' death and a' the past again,
Beast life, plant life, minerals, water, sky,
A' that has been, is, is to be – frae you
Clear seen, still clearer sicht to pursue.
Similia similibus rotantur, a' facts amang
I seek the *Ereigniswerden*'s essence then
That shows a' that seems kent in it wrang
And gars a' else point back to it again,

Their worth to guide wha can use them hence
    To your fulfillin' experience.

Elschaddai. Emelachan.[1] We only want
The world to live and feel its life in us?
But the world lives whether we dae or no',
A's vice that abates life or can blin' us
To your final epopteia – contents us with
The hearin' o' the ear, no' the vision swith,
The life o' shadows, mere tautology,
Ony curious fig-leaf o' the mind whereby
Humanity has socht to hide its sin,
Portentous prison-hooses o' fause thocht we see
'Science' big heicher daily – a' that can pin us
To the spectral frae the live world, come atween us
And the terrible crystal, the ineffable glow.
Diseases o' the will that needs maun fin' us
Less potent to act, and a' the clichés and cant,
Limitations o' personality, pap for pith,
Robotisation, feminism, youth movements,
A' the super-economic programme's intents
Set grey, a hellish parody (oot there
Forenenst your blazin' energy), and its
Perpetual fause alarms, shams o' seemin' fair,
Fixed fallacies auld as man, sheer waste o' wits
– Oh, you are no' the glory mankind desires
    Yet naething else inspires!

The recurrent vividness o' licht and water
Through every earthly change o' mood or scene
Puirly prefigures you – a' Nature's dreamt,
And no' dune, thrang wi' ither plans, has been
A fog twixt you and us. It's nocht to ken
Something has happened – save only when

---

[1] *Elschaddai*, the Self-Sufficient One.
  Emelachan means: 'Your spirit is tranquil and silent, your soul is delicate, your flesh and blood are strong, both easily roar like the waves of the sea, then gentleness speaks in you: come and be calm.'

'Mang mony alternatives sic choice was ta'en.
You aye exclude a' ither possibilities.
A'e voice may cry alood: 'Wha ever sees
You to hairy goon and mossy cell has gane.'
Anither proclaim the vital vision gi'en
'Ud move to deeds frae care o' consequence clean.
But baith are wrang – the reckless and the fremt.
And in your radiant licht man's first truth's seen
– Tho' still the last and least to matter
In a' their fond affairs to the mass o' men –
The love o' economics is the mainspring
O' a' the virtues. Eternity like a ring,
Virile, masculine, abandoned at nae·turn
To enervatin' luxury
Aboot me here shall ever clearer burn,
And in its licht perchance at last men'll see
Wi' the best works o' art, as wi' you tae,
          Chance can ha'e nocht to dae!

Cheville

FOR KAIKHOSRU SORABJI

WHO remembers the Great Flood? The scope
Of the waters and their deafening din
Towering like God over the spirits of men,
Flocks, forests, and villages cast to the deep,
Who can sustain the menace of Nature
And praise forces to which life is straw
– Or glimpse them without seeming to outgrow
His mortality in huge recognition?
Tiger-cub torrent, shall I watch you and try
To think of all water is to the world? –
Seeing, and sorry for, all drowned things, sorry
Yet with, *cheville*, a sense of God's glory.

Dytiscus

THE problem in the pool is plain.
Must men to higher things ascend
For air like the Dytiscus there,
Breathe through their spiracles, and turn
To diving bells and seek their share
Of sustenance in the slime again
Till they clear life, as he his pool
To starve in purity, the fool,
Their finished faculties mirrored, fegs,
Foiled-fierce as his three pairs of legs?
Praise be Dytiscus-men are rare.
Life's pool still foul and full of fare.
Long till to suicidal success attain
We water-beetles of the brain!

The Oon Olympian

COME a' nit-wits, knaves and fools,
Conventional folk, and celebrate
Goethe's centenary, and cry again
Hoo noble he was, serene, and great.

You're likely judges to pronounce
On sicna qualities nane can doot
And least o' a' yoursel's, wha ha'e
The big battalions to boot.

Is there a humble soul who lacks
A' lear, yet's no' a specialist
On the beautifu', and good, and true
And o' creation feels the gist?

Things hidden frae the wise are yours,
The brain-prood err this way and that,
Thank God the general mind o' Man,
Securely ignorant, stands pat.

Great Goethe represented this;
Your ain kind *in excelsis* he,
And a successfu' business man
Even Faust, at last, we see.

Yet no' because he's ane o' you
Owre you fork his colossal legs,
– Or aiblins gang up parallel;
Wi' sic a giant it's ill to tell.
Maist o' you dinna ken or care
That or ocht else aboot him, fegs,
– Tak'n his genius juist forgrantit,
As he took a' thing else he wantit.

The haill thing's sham – evasion o' thocht
By hook or crook; and empty fame.
As Goethe in his time was blin'
To a' worth while, sae in his name,

To creative force you turn blin' een,
Dodgin like him a' mental strife,
Intent to win by cowardice
And life-denial Eternal Life.

Order? – o' weaklin's wha require
Safe-gairdit lives and daurna trust
Their inner sel's; and Form? – that fears
Further developments o' Dust.

Ersatz antiquity that turns
Poetry to nocht but a preserve
For educatit folk, wha find
The present owre muckle for their nerve.

A moderate literature that tak's
Ready-made conventions o' the real,
Misses a Hölderlin, and hates
A Jean Paul like the deil,

Ignores brute facts and a' the deep
Fissures o' life and pays nae heed
To dialectic logic workin' at aince
In coontless coonter ways insteed

O' the cosh continuity
A stabilisation fool
Like Goethe, false to his ain age,
Mak's his privy dookin' pool.

Owre nice to look Daith in the face,
Or tak' cognisance o' decay
Nae man worth ca'in a man can thole
Sic thowless things as you the day.

Lang while a sheer anachronism
A life devoted to the muse?
– Oor impotence as poets in this
We'll aiblins plausibly excuse.

Or cry that you reflectit weel
The coorse that history 'bood tak'
– And ca' it genius to be swept
On willy-nilly wi' the pack?

But a' the wisdom o' the past,
A' the glozin', trimmin', truth,
Since beauty against beauty wars,
Life'll aye thraw off wi' little ruth.

Consciousness springs frae unplumbed deeps
And maist o' men mak' haste
To kep odd draps in shallow thoughts

And let the rest rin waste.
Quickly forgettin' ocht they catch
    Depends upon the kittle coorse
O' a wilder fount than they daur watch
Free-springin' in its native force
Against the darkness o' its source.

Wha fear the cataract and like
    Some spigot's drip insteed,
Wha prate o' laws and turn blin' een,
    On the anarchy that's gied,
Owreshadowed wi' its chaos still,
Even sic puir arbitrary forms
May weel haud to – they need them ill –
Thoughts faur frae elementary storms
Tricklin' through thin domestic pipes
To their wee ta'en-forgrantit types.

Auld Goethe never wet his feet
    But had the water laid on
Baith H. and C., nor kent nor cared
    The deeps his pipes made raid on,
A michty expert on H_2O
Almaist hailly in terms o' taps
Plus a shoo'er o' rain, a river's flow,
Even a keek at the sea perhaps
– But Oh! that the Heavens had opened and let
A second Flood on this plumber's pet!

Hoist them like ba's, ye fountains, yet
    Upon your loupin' jets,
O' wha's irregular ups and doons
    Nae metronome the measure gets,
The fools wha think that they can pose
    As authorities on thought
Yet daurna look whence it arose
Nor faddom the conditionin' o't
– And let the bobbin' craturs think
It's them that gars you rise and sink!

Poet wha *ootgrew* Poetry
Weel may Philistia approve
Your cute prolepsis and the sheer
Opportunism o' your move,

Deny a' human values and applaud
Man's vegetative side, pleased wi'
Your *Gelegenheitsgedicht*, like Keats'
Poetry that comes like leafs to a tree.

This isna poetry? Sing
Some simple silly sang
O' willows or o' mimulus
A river's banks alang.

Aboot the metamorphosis
O' plant and beast a poet may
Sing but o' the struggle for't
In man and cosmos – nay!

The intricacies o' the mind
For poetry arena suited.
Be like a daisy and you'll be
A poet – wha can doot it?

Keep clear communication lines
Whatever else you keep,
For poets 'bood to follow
Each ither aye like sheep.

Nor speir hoo faur you paved the way
For Poetry's relegation or
Juist kent what public you could ha'e
'Ud gang that airt – and ran before.

Nae ivory too'er! Poets mauna seek
To jouk the common needfu' jobs
And general interest o' mankind.
That o' a' use their verses robs.

Goethe was richt; the 'Farbenlehre'
Was his best work; and he did richt
In turnin' Faust to drainage schemes
And fashin' nae mair wi' verbal sleight.

And I am richt in ga'en back
In like wise to the Muckle Toon;
And dungarees are better wear
For a man than a scarlet goon.

Nae poet can be nocht but that;
But man, freend, citizen, as weel.
Let him tak' tent he disna tine
Sicht o' a' that in poet's zeal.

Nae ivory too'er! Goethe was richt
In thus growin' oot o' poesy
– Wad Christ'd ootgrown religion tae
And gane back to the carpentry!

Auld banes be oors! Let poets dee young
Sic foolishness is no' for us
While a 'Times Literary Supplement'
Promotes oor donnart hobbies thus.

Wha fund in Poetry a *cul-de-sac*
Wi' poetic justice to anither
Blin' alley turned, and witless missed
The times' trend a'thegither,

And drag on noo i' the least alive
To the vital in life and letters.
Your fifty years' funeral in Weimar
Still the 'rinnin' concern' o' your debtors.

Hach! Bein' nae bourgeois perquisite
The *Fortwirkende* in mankind
Has ta'en a coorse restrictin' you
To a meaner role than you divined.

Pragmatic test? What do you think
You mean to the world's *workers* noo?
'Continually operative' – no' in them
If still in a dispensable few.

If still in a dispensable few
A whilie langer – and then
Life's saltatory way'll mak' them
Deid ends, as you to me or apes to men.

Ridiculous optimist, maintain
Your proofless unity o' the real.
There's pluralisms abroad at last
Ha'e a' sic follies in a creel.

The quantum theory's dung to blauds
The classic picture o' the world.
Nae shameless syncretism ser's
Sic humpty-dumpties aince doonhurled

A' the King's horses, a' his men
Can never cock them up again
– But there's eneuch Aunt Sallies left
To shy at still, nae mind what's gane.

Ah! weel micht Goethe cry that Daith
Is Nature's plan for life t' abound.
For Life *and Daith!* And the same need
For supersession in culture's found.

It's time you had it. There can be
Nae revolutions worth the name
Wha's leaders till in spiritual things
Uphaud auld fetishes o' Fame.

Let Lunatscharskies blether on
O' 'divine monuments o' ancient thought'
The psyche's the richt to revolution tae
– And canna ha'e owre muckle o't.

Ideas by the company they keep
Are kent, and henceforth nane worth ha'en
– And or lang nane ava' – 'll be seen
Wi' ony o' yours, oon Olympian.

Come a' you nitwits, knaves and fools
O' the educatit classes,
The name o' Goethe isna kent
– And never will be – to the masses.

The Scott Centenary

THEN we've Sir Walter Scott's as weel,
They say he tae was great
– But this'll dae; it matches fine
A' Scotland did to merk the date!

Antenora

THE stream is frozen hard. Going by
This wintry spectacle I descry
How even Edinburgh folk may be
In Scotland, not Antenora, yet,
Not traitors to their land, condemned
To a frore fate in Cocytus' pit,
But seasonably Scottish in their way,
And thaw, though hellish slow, some day!

Of John Davidson

I REMEMBER one death in my boyhood
That next to my father's, and darker, endures;
Not Queen Victoria's, but Davidson, yours,
And something in me has always stood
Since then looking down the sandslope
On your small black shape by the edge of the sea,
– A bullet-hole through a great scene's beauty,
God through the wrong end of a telescope.

From
SCOTTISH SCENE
or THE INTELLIGENT MAN'S GUIDE TO ALBYN
(1934)

Scotland

I

JUST think how terrible it would be
If the people who name
The Housing Scheme streets and bungalows
Could play the same game
With the things in Scotland that really matter
– Its peerless glories of land and water!

We would waken up some morning to find
That by way of a change
The Grampians had been re-christened
The Amy Mollison Range;
And of course, Killiecrankie by then
Would be Princess Margaret Rose Glen.

With Barriesque whimsicality
Ben Nevis, one fears
Might become Sky-View Summit,
And the Tay Churchill's Tears,
And Glasgow be modernized still
As Maxtontown or Horneville.

Arthur's *Seat* on account
Of the vulgar dubiety
Would be better transformed
To King's *Head* most folks would agree,
And instead of the Forth that marine gorge
Should be dubbed the Fifth in honour of George.

Enough? thank God our place-names
Antedated our Anglicization,
But in other and far more vital
Respects, alas, our nation
Is ruined by equivalents of calling
Briareach the Pines, or Bellevue for Schiehallion.

II

Canty, Ethie, Usan, Catterline,
Pennan, Crovie, Embo, Forse,
Clyth, Sarclet, Staxigoe, Keiss
– We know our Scotland well, of course.

The names of all the Shetland Isles
We rattle off like lightning thus,
The Orkneys then, the Hebrides,
Like coloured balls in an abacus.

And Cunningham and Lennox
And all our ancient provinces
– No fool among us but in his mind
Better than an ordnance survey sees!

And *Scotia Irredenta*
That down into England goes
As far as the Humber-Mersey Line
– O every true Scotsman knows!

For our educational system
Is so good that instantly
If Scotland's mentioned every place
Within its bounds at once we see,

See, and know all about it,
Past, present, future – all
Its history and its interests
Our synoptic wits recall.

And all our nation's matchless types,
Haaf-fishers, Berwickshire bondagers,
And scores of others fill our thoughts,
And the minutiae of their affairs.

Local speech variants – every true Scot
Has all these cunning shibboleths pat;
Intranational differences of every kind
Are a hobby he's an expert at.

Nor is the whole lost in the parts,
All Scotland seen save Scotland yet;
He sees his land as a unity too,
And Creation in terms of it.

The future concerns him even more
Than the past or the present do;
He boasts of his proleptic power
– And is entitled to!

O every Scot knows the Loch of the Lowes,
Cappercleuch, Langhaugh, and Eddleston,
And Capplegill and Shortwoodend,
Like the knobs on his own backbone.

Invergarry, Tomdoun, and Clunie Inn,
Dornie, Strome Ferry, and Achnasheen,
And Kinlochewe and Loch Maree
Like the lines on his hands are seen.

'Suilven, Canisp, Ben More Assynt'
Our infants chant on their mothers' knees;
And often even – the little rogues –
A long while before they first reach these!

And sometimes a Scot on entering Heaven
Has to cry: 'It's queer – but I quite forget
This clachan's name – unless it's a new scheme
Of the Scottish Board of Health's – Aye, that'll be it!'

.   .   .   .   .

What? You claim you're a Scotsman too?
Come, let us test you then, my friend.
Where is Quothquhan Law? And where
Does the Molendinar begin and end?

Where are Fladda Chuain and the Ascrib Isles?
Where's Handa Island? And how can you tell
A Hawick man from a Langholm man?
And where's Padanaram? You're doing well.

Now for your futurist faculty then!
When will Scots people begin to know
As much about Scotland as ghosts in a fog
And not care far less? – I thought so!

Tam o' the Wilds and the Many-Faced Mystery

To William Soutar

TAM was a common workin' man,
Or, raither, an uncommon ane;
An eident worker a' his days,
In his scanty leisure a roamin' ane.
He never wasted a penny piece
– Troth, he never had ane to waste! –
He never wasted a meenut either,
But o' ilk ane made the maist.

Early and late he did his darg
And in the wee sma' 'oors atween
Tyauved twice as hard at kittler work.
It seemed he seldom steckit his een.
Early and late he did his darg.
His nose was aye on the grindstane
He couldna been puirer; his hame was yet
In happiness faur frae the hindest ane.

For idle convenin' wi' ither folk
He never had an instant to spare;
He never saw the inside o' a pub,
Or hung aboot bletherin' in the Square,

But lang efter a'body else was in bed
And syne lang afore they waukened again
Tireless he roved alang the seashore
Or inland owre field and forest and ben.

Thinkna' he was ony unsocial chiel
– The test o' that was his wife and weans;
Their happy faces settled a' doots,
Puirest o' the puir yet rich 'yont a' means.
Tam never had a stroke o' wardly luck
But a desperate fecht frae beginnin' to end,
Yet his wife and weans were brawly content
– Their joy ony hand in his ploys to lend.

It was a' the help that he ever got.
For the feck o' folk couldna faddom at a'
A workin' man wi' a purpose in life
'Yont his work and a dram and fitba',
Or mebbies the Kirk, but what could he want
Wi' this passion for nature and science?
It was sheer presumption in a man o' his class
– Settin' human nature, in fact, at defiance!

Set him up wi' his bottles and pill-boxes,
Sea-traps and nets and a' his gear
As if he was an educated man,
When a'body kent he'd neist to nae lear!
It wasna canny that the likes o' him
Should be pokin' his neb night in night oot
Into things that teachers and ministers even
No' to speak o' the gentry kent naething aboot.

Kent naething aboot and, fegs, cared less!
– A' the ugsome vermin o' the laigh creation,
Worms, lice, and the like. Certes, the man
Had shairly nae sense o' his proper station.
As for his wife she was if onything waur
Gien' hoose-room to hotchin' rubbish like yon.
Her hoose was a weavin' zoo that gar'd
Ony decent wumman grue to think on.

What man in his sober senses 'ud set
Cases o' preserved spiders and pickled snails
Roond his cottage wa's instead o' a picter
O' His Royal Highness the Prince o' Wales?
It shouldna be allowed. That's a' that's aboot it.
Let him think instead o' the Wrath To Come.
He'd better spend his time on his bendit knees
Lookin' to see if there's ony 'white in the lum'!

The Health Authorities should pit a stop
To sicna ongauns or there 'ud be a plague.
Let the Police act! It fleggit the lieges
To ken that while they slept sic a vaig
Was reengin' aboot, whiles bidin' a' night
Like a beast in a hole in the grun' even.
What was he really da'en? Douce folk
A' thocht it was some sly poachin' or thievin'!

But the years ga'ed by and Tam keepit on
A mystery to a'body aboot'm – Nay,
A greater mystery for noo it was clear
Whatever his object it didna pay.
He wasna a penny the better for't a',
And wha'd tak' an interest in folly like that?
Naebody gie'd him credit for knowledge even
– Nae honour to the place; a human bat!

Mony an ill gruize he got lyin' oot
A' nicht in snell winds or on water-logged grun',
Gane gyte a'thegither owre his crabs and bandies,
His powets and paddocks, but wadna be done;
Aye thrang wi' black doctors that fulped in a pool
Or wasps' bikes like ba's o' paper hung to a tree
– He'd been a bonny nickem frae his earliest days
And aye got the waur the aulder he'd be!

Yet strugglin' on bawbee by bawbee
His hame was bein 'yont the lave o' his kind

And his bairns like onybody else's bairns,
Weel-fed, weel-pit-on, and didna mind
The sorry esteem their faither was held in
Or the dark suspicions that clung to him still
But in a' their spare time and holidays helped
Mair boxes and bottles wi' bugs to fill.

Whiles a workmate tackled him bluntly and speired
'What's the use o't a'? – what dy'e hope to get?'
But Tam answered: 'Naithing, except the joy o't,
And mair knowledge o' wheen things than ony man yet.'
Syne his disadvantages were pointed oot
– Shairly it stood to reason rich and colleged men
Wi' books and apparatus galore kent mair
To stert wi' that he could ever hope to ken?

'Na', faith!' said Tam, 'tho' I'm handicapped
Wi' sair lack o' siller and lear nae doot
It's naething that's in ony book yet
Or money can buy I'm maist fashed aboot.
I've strength and patience and a pair o' gleg een,
And it isna education, riches, or good birth
Advances science maist – else lang syne
A'd ha'e been learnt that's to learn on earth.'

'But what pit it into your heid ava'
To trauchle wi' this?' anither speired.
Tam shook his heid: 'That's no' easy kent
Aiblins the best that I can come near't
Is just wi' a proper reverence to say
The Maker o' a' things made me like this
– And muckle that maist folk think faur beneath
Their notice, certes, isna beneath His!

'If ony man has seen onything yet
O' the beauties o' nature in land, sea, or sky,
That's only the merest minimum
O' the glories that await the open eye.

Wherever we turn the haill warld is rife
Wi' glories o' hue and design that nae man
Has ever seen mair than the least fraction o'
And nae science has noted, or ever can.'

O few kent better than Tam himsel'
Hoo muckle o' a' God's bothered to mak'
Is beneath the notice and ootwith the ken
O' maist folk and hoo little trouble they tak'
To jalouse and enjoy the riches o' Nature
– He lived in a different warld frae theirs;
The warld God made, and mak's ilka day,
– Completely ootweighin' ony human affairs.

It'd be a meagre and mean creation
Limited to the general interests o' men;
Tho' botany, ichthyology, and a' the rest
Are no' for the workin' man we ken,
And for few o' the upper classes even
Except a wheen faddists o' little accoont
– God forbid owre mony like Tam should think
The usual run o' life stupid and soar abune't!

Yet maist folk bogged in clish-ma-claver,
Or, accordin' to their different degrees,
On a solid basis o' dull conventions,
In things o' kirk and State and maitters like these
Miss a million times mair o' the wonders o' life
Than Tam missed gi'en average routine the bye
Night after night up a tree wi' the birds
Or in a badger's hole or eagle's nest to lie.

Every wave o' the sea, every inch o' the land
Was fu' o' a thousand ferlies to him
That no' a'e man in a million ever sees.
Custom mak's creation sae scant and dim

To the feck o' folk, used juist to this or that
And esteemin't accordingly till they canna believe
That a' in and aboot them teems an unseen world
Stranger and bonnier than ocht but God could conceive.

Tam shrank frae nocht born in fear or disgust.
Whaur maist folk scunnered he thrilled wi' delight.
Mere size he kent was naething to gang by.
God spent nae less skill on the obscurest mite
And the man that 'ud follow in the steps o' God
Maun open his hert to the haill wide world
– No' be cut off frae't in ony human rut
Till a' its glories are in vain unfurled.

'Waste your lives, fools, in needless sleep.
Nature at least is never at rest!'
And sae he kent, when to its mossy bed
The skylark flew and the swallow to its nest
And the mellow thrush its requiem ended
And the wood-pigeon settled doon for the night,
The nightjar got thrang wi' its spinnin'-wheel
And the moths flew oot for his delight.

The Oak-Egger Moth, the Green Silver-Line,
The lovely China Moth a' were his;
And his helminthology cairried him deep
Into the benmaist dens o' the forests I wis.
Weather was nae bar and mony a wild night
O' lightning and rain and wind he spent
In an auld dyke back or cup in the hills
On the wonders o' nature still intent.

The landrail craiks the haill night through
And a whilie etter sunrise still;
The coot and the waterhen get noisy whiles
In the wee sma' 'oors; a thoosand cries fill
The howe o' darkness – the boom o' the snipe,
The birbeck o' the muirfowl, the plover's wail,

And doon by the sea the ring-dotterel's pipe
And the plech-plech o' the oyster-catcher never fail.

And mony a polecat, stoat, and weasel
Blew on him or hizzed as he suddenly appeared,
And whiles when he dozed in the sea-caves or woods
He was waukened – never in the least bit feart –
By something pit-pattin' against his legs
And f'und a rat or a foumart there
Or even a badger as curious as he
To study what this could be in its lair.

Wha kent ocht o' fish alang that grey coast[1]
Save herrin' and haddock and cod and a wheen mair
That folk could eat – the only test applied?
Tam saw and studied day efter day there
The Sandsucker and the Blue-striped Wrasse,
Six kinds o' Gobies, the Saury Pike,
Yarrell's Bleny, and the Silvery Gade
(Lang lost to science), and scores o' the like.

The Bonito, the Tunny, the Sea-Perch and the Ruffe,
The Armed Bullhead, the Wolf-fish, and the Scad,
The Power Cod and the Whiting Pout,
The Twaite Shad and the Alice Shad,
The Great Forked Beard, the Torsk, the Brill,
The Glutinous Hag, the Starry Ray,
Muller's Topknot and the Unctuous Sucker,
– These, and deemless ithers cam' his way.

A cod's stomach for the smaller fry
Was aye his happiest huntin' grund
For testaceous and crustaceous rarieties
– Mony new to Scotland, or even science, he fund –
Fish lice, sea mice, Deid Men's Paps, actinias,
And algae and zoophytes yont number
Were rescued thence and ta'en in triumph
His humble wee but-and-ben to cumber.

[1] Morayshire.

And lang by his ain fireside he'd sit
Studyin' an Equoreal Needle-Fish
Ane o' his lassies fund; or watchin'
An anceus or ensirus in a dish
Wi' a care that took in ilka move,
Detail, and habit o' these peerie things,
Soomin' wi' quick motions o' their ciliate fins,
While he coonted and measured spines, rays, and rings.

He heard the corn-buntin' cry 'Guid-night'
And the lark 'Guid-mornin',' and kent by sight
And call-note the Osprey and the Erne,
The Blue-Hawk and the Merlin and the Kite,
The Honey Buzzard and the Snowy Owl,
The Ring Ouzel, the Black Cap, the Wood Wren,
The Mealy Redpole, the Purple Heron, the Avocet,
The Gadwell, the Shoveller, and the Raven.

He loved the haill o' the countryside
And kent it as nae ither man ever kent
The coast rocks wi' the wild seas lashin' their feet,
And the myriads o' seabirds that cam' and went,
Kittywake, guillemot, razor-bill, puffin,
Whiles darkenin' the air wi' their multitudes,
Wheelin' in endless and varyin' airts
– He kent them singly in a' their moods.

Fishin'-boats shoot oot frae the rocky clefts
In which the harbours are formed – below
The Gardenstown boats and Crovie's to the right,
The fleets frae Fraserburgh eastward show,
Westward the boats frae Macduff and Banff,
Whitehills, Portsoy, Findochtie, the Buckies
– He wishes he was aboard each at aince
Kaimin' their nets to see that his luck is!

Far owre the Moray firth the Caithness mountains
Are clearly picked oot 'gainst the evenin' sky.

The hills o' Morven and the Maiden's Pap
A' stand within the scope o' his eye,
And every slope o' hard grauwacke he kens,
The Reid Hill o' Penman, the Bin Hill o' Cullen,
The Dens o' Aberdour, Auchmeddie, and Troup
– Shairly a land nae man can be dull in!

Here's the beach where he catched the Little Stint
Efter lang pursuit, wi' excitement shakin'
Like a cock's tail on a windy day.
Here's the Balloch Hills wi' forkt lightnin' straikin'
Where he fund the rare mosses and ferns he socht
And here's Tarlair and the muckle rocks
He fell owre to get at a wheen martens aince
– He'd to thole mony fa's and unco sair knocks.

He kent the pretty snappin'-like noise
O' the Death's Heid Moth in its caterpillar state;
Like electric sparks the chrysalis squeaks,
Mair especially aboot its changin' date,
And as for the perfect insect itsel'
He kent a' the range o' its mournfu' tongue
While its muckle bricht een were believed to reflect
The Flames o' Hell frae which it had sprung.

He saw a falcon haudin' a paitrik
In its talons and calmly awaitin' its death,
– Nae expandin' o' a wing to keep balance there,
Nae laceratin' the victim while still it had breath,
Tho' the bird's last struggle gar'd it quiver a wee,
Syne, motionless a meenut mair to be quite
Shair life was extinct, it off wi' the heid
And skinned and carved the rest as a surgeon might.

A heron stared at him wi' its bright yellow e'e
Fu' in the face as if askin' what right
He had in solitudes where the human form
Is sae seldom seen, syne slowly in his sight

Its lang neck doobled quietly doon on its breist,
Its dark and lengthened plumes shook, and it rose
Wi' a wild shreik that gliffed ilka bird and beast.

The Sandpiper screamed; the Pigeon cooed;
The Pipit cam' fleein' aboot him; frae the heather
The Moor-cock sprang on its whirring wing,
Curlews and Plovers and a' thegither
Were sairly stirred up, but Tam never moved
Till the inmates o' the glen and mountain aince mair
Disappeared whence they'd come and naething
But solemn stillness resumed its sway there

Tam was a Scotsman o' a splendid type
O' which our puir country is near bereft.
We're a' owre weel-educated noo I doot
To ha'e ony real knowledge – or love o't – left
And as for love o' auld Scotland itself
And knowledge o't, fegs, Tam's pinkie kent
Faur mair than the fower and a hauf millions o's
Livin' the day in oor heids ha'e pent!

He kent the Crenard-star, supposed to ha' been
The maist numerous o' Ocean's inhabitants.
Noo there's only a'e kind in the Scottish seas
And that's rarely seen; and frequented the haunts
O' the Leptochinum – that green Ascidian –
And Drummond's Echiodon, and often longed
To traverse the untrodden caverns o' the deep
For the inconceivable things wi' which they thronged.

He spoke o' each cratur as if ane fell like it
Yet no' the same 'ud be washed up next tide
Or come roon the next corner. His descriptions are final.
He had the seein' eye frae which naething could hide
And nocht that cam' under his een was forgotten.
Fluently and vividly he could aye efter describe
The forms, and habits o' a' the immense
Maingie o' animals he saw – an incredible tribe!

A Scot aince as common and noo as rare
As the Crenard-star itsel' in Time's drumlie tide,
First-hand knowledge was what he aye prized
And personal observation was his constant pride,
But oor lives are sae arranged instead
That little o' the life o' the country comes
In to us noo, and even that maun recede
And leave oor haill world nocht but suburbs and slums.

A'e thing is certain – then as noo
Save wi' his ain sel' nae man should fash
Muckle wi' men at a'. Man's proper study
Is onything but Man and Tam kent weel
When folk talked o' noxious and dangerous beasts
Nane answered that description in the haill o' nature
Better than maist men – worthless and vicious
To their ain kind and to ilka ither cratur.

                    .   .

I had written this and I suddenly thocht
O' ane withdrawn frae the common life o' men
Shut awa' frae the warld in a sick-room for aye,
Yet livin' in what a wonderfu' world even then
– The pure world o' the spirit; less kent
To nearly a'body than Tam's interests even,
And I saw in his sangs the variety o' creation
Promise in a new airt mair than a' he was leavin'.

A Scotsman o' a faur rarer type
Than Tam o' the Wilds, and still mair needit,
Tho' still less likely than Tam's kind even
By the feck o' oor folk to be prized or heedit,
– Shair to be scorned, if heard o', for a fool
By the mindless hordes that are fitba' mad,
Or certain that better entertainment than ocht
In nature or spirit in the cinema's had!

God save me frae hasty judgment tho'
When I see infinities in twa sic opposite ways,
For there's nae kennin' what ony man in the mob
May ha'e, in his hert if in nae ither place,
Or deeper than thocht or conscious feelin'
In his sensuous nature and mere animal life
– Laigh or heich in the scale, however we rate it,
There's nae point less than anither wi' God's sel' rife.

O Thou inscrutable, Maker o' a' these,
Wha dealt oot endless hardship to honest Tam
And gar'd him sell his prized collections and brought him
In ruin to the grave, while ithers – no' worth a damn
I micht ha' said; at least they'd naething to show! –
Prospered aboot him; and condemns this ither to lie
Cut off frae life while morons multiply
– In what unreached world yet is your meaning to know?

One Thing Sure

No matter how science develops, my dear,
    One thing is perfectly sure.
Most joy will still come from forgetting it all,
    Sweet nothings will always endure.

Let wisdom increase a million fold;
    Lads and lassies will still, it is clear,
Make fools of themselves as we do and know
    It's only then that they don't, my dear.

The cleverer I am, the wider my view,
    Of Past, Present, and Future, the more
I'll rejoice to give it the slip and be
    All in all with you as of yore.

The Prime Mover

Go map the currents of the seas,
The courses of the stars, my friend,
But I know movements that have thrilled
Mankind from the first and will to the end.

No mazy evolutions these,
Though but for them we'd know of none;
The most entrancing sight on Earth
– The first toddlings of a little one.

They matter most; the rest depend
On them for value and for being.
Who, blind to them, sees anything else
Has no conception of what he's seeing.

Fly Down, Eagle . . .

Come doon, eagle; come doon, sun!
Licht upon my sheckle bane.
Tell me hoo to gar the black
Shadows frae my sang begane!

Flee back, eagle; flee back, sun.
There's naething you can tell.
A' my woes are human anes
That I maun solve mysel'!

And ithers blacker still maun come
Nae suner that is done
Tho' each in turn may syne ootsoar
The eagle and ootshine the sun.

Envoi: On Coming Home

SCOTTISH Jews comin' doon frae the mountains
Wi' the laws on their stany herts;
Minor prophets livin' i' the Factory Close
Or ahint the gasworks – fresh sterts?

Folk frae the Auld Testament are talkin'
O' Christ but I'm no' deceived.
Bearded men, cloakt wimmen, and in gloom
The gift o' Heaven's received.

Scottish Jews comin' doon frae the mountains,
Minor prophets frae vennel and wynd,
In weather as black as the Bible
I return again to my kind . . .

> The Sauria in their ain way
> Had nuckle to commend them.
> Fell fearsome craturs, it's a shame
> That Nature had to end them.
>
> And faith! few men aboot the day
> But hae guid cause to speir
> Why sicna auld impressive forms
> Had to dee for them t'appear:
>
> Sae aiblins wi' traditional Scots,
> Covenanters and the lave,
> Wha's grand auld gurly qualities
> Deserve a better stave.
>
> But they hung on – and still hing on –
> Survivals frae an age lang dune.
> Gin they'd deed a century syne
> They'd whiles shine oot . . . like the mune! . . .

Away, away, to the mune and the devil
Wi' these muddlers, ditherers, ancient disputants,
Auld Lichts, Wee Frees, Burnsians, London Scots!
Let them awa' like shadows at noon to their haunts!

To their clubs in Pall Mall wi' Elliot and Horne,
Skelton and Gilmour and Montrose and the lave
And a' the ither bats and ugsome affairs
That hae made Scotland sae lang a Gothic grave!

Peter Pan nae langer oor deity'll be
And oor boast an endless infantilism.
Away, wi' the auld superstitions. Let the sun up at last
And hurl a' sic spooks into their proper abysm.

STONY LIMITS AND OTHER POEMS
(1934; 1956)

I dedicate this book
to
VALDA AND JAMES MICHAEL

I had the fortune to live as a boy
In a world a' columbe and colour-de-roy
As gin I'd had Mars for the land o' my birth
Instead o' the earth.

Nae maitter hoo faur I've travelled sinsyne
The cast o' Dumfriesshire's aye in me like wine;
And my sangs are gleids o' the candent spirit
Its sons inherit.

Ho, My Little Sparrow

Ho, my little sparrow! For well I know
The profound and subtle soft lights in your eyes
Mean no more than two grains of wheat
In a basin full of water. And so
    I call you my little sparrow,
    For so a sparrow's wings go.

Ho, my little sparrow! Sparrows are common
Yet who can describe their thousand and one changes
Of colour as they quiver in the sun
Like thoughts of old rainbows? But what omen
    Is this? – All the live arc at home in
    Your look again, woman!

Iolaire

As an eagle stirs up her nest,
    Flutters over her young,
Urges them into the void, swoops underneath,
And rests a struggler on her back for a space
    Would the songs I sung
    Might be to my race.

Alba, mother eagle, support me.
    He who sings
Struggles and cannot yet float upwards
From the high valleys among the Cairngorms like those
    Of your true brood; on the wings
    Whose movement is repose.

The Monument[1]

FEW ken to whom this muckle monument stands,
Some general or admiral I've nae doot,
On the hill-top whaur weather lang syne
Has blotted its inscribed palaver oot.
Yet it's a worthy landmark faur and near
Juist as, in a' the affairs o' men,
Nonentities – kings, bankers, and the like –
Wha's vera names they briefly or never ken
Control the thowless mobs wha care faur less
For a' earth's poets and philosophers
Or onybody else o' lastin' worth
Than for sic figureheids as this stane ser's
Fitly to memorise in keepin' wi'
His rank and emptiness baith, for a' to see.

The Skeleton of the Future

At Lenin's Tomb

RED granite and black diorite, with the blue
Of the labradorite crystals gleaming like precious stones
In the light reflected from the snow; and behind them
The eternal lightning of Lenin's bones.

A Moorlander Looks Forward to a Bride

TO GORDON BOTTOMLEY

A WOMAN'S een where licht's as scarce as here?
Her nails in sic a place like stars'll glow!
Truth, it's nae vilipendin' she's to fear.

[1] On Whita Hill, Langholm.

I'm used to makin' the maist o' sma' affairs.
Blither wi' a wheen heather cowes and spirts o' grass
Than ither folk wi' Earth's maist prodigal show
I mak' a world I'd swap for nane o' theirs
And twist by twist ken a' its wankishin'.
What will I no' then wi' a haill live lass?
Treasure the canna and misprize her skin?
Ken the wra moors but no' her benmaist thocht?
Wreath on my clew a' the threids that mak'
This manufacture till it looks if you please
At sun-up like a whey-drap in a cheese,
And leave sic braw material unwrocht?
– The bottle o' port that's a' the cheese can lack!

In the Foggy Twilight

I LAY in the foggy twilight
In a hollow o' the hills and saw
Moisture getherin' slowly on the heather cowes
In drops no' quite heavy eneuch to fa'.

And I kent I was still like that
Wi' the spirit o' God, alas!;
Lyin' in wait in vain for a single grey drop
To quicken into perfect quidditas.

The Point of Honour

On watching the Esk again

I WOULD that once more I could blend her
    With my own self as I did then
Vivid and impulsive in crystalline splendour
    Cold and seething champagne.

(Cut water. Perfection of craft concealed
In effects of pure improvisation.
Delights of dazzle and dare revealed
In instant inscapes of fresh variation.

Exhilarating, effortless, divinely light,
In apparent freedom yet reined by unseen
And ubiquitous disciplines; darting, lint-white,
Fertile in impulse, in control – keen.

Pride of play in a flourish of eddies,
Bravura of blowballs, and silver digressions,
Ringing and glittering she swirls and steadies,
And moulds each ripple with secret suppressions.)

Once, with my boy's body little I knew
But her furious thresh on my flesh;
But now I can know her through and through
And, light like, her tide enmesh.

Then come, come, come, let her spend her
Quivering momentum where I lie here,
Wedding words to her waves, and able to tend her
Every swirl and sound with eye and ear.

No more of mere sound, the least part!
I know how it acts, connecting words, implying
A rate of movement, onomatopoeic art,
Or making a reader start trying
To interpret the mouth's actual movement
As a gesture; or acting directly
Like a tune – a mode that is different
From the rest as darkness from light to me,
These intelligible, this a mystery.
Is not consciousness of a sound an act
Of belief in it; are not movements of muscles
Transferred, apprehended, as rhythms, or fact
Of nature some other sense claims, like the tussles

You arouse of thought, hearing, touch and sight,
Variety of experience, a baffling medley
Till one wins, and I cease to know you aright
Yet dare not embezzle the dramatic insights,
The generative questionableness, knowing well
The greater risk of taking no risks,
Creating no ecstasies, changing the mights
Of old safe ecstasies to counters, discs,
Transports reduced to play-level,
The problematic, the murderous element
Of all art eschewed; no mad leap taken
Into the symbol, driving like your stream
Through all mere images, all that may seem
Its very character; the engagement
Twixt man and being forsaken.
All stale, unprofitable, flat and thin,
No restless eager poem that speaking in
A thousand moods achieves a unity,
No wracking indispensable energy,
Only emotions forgotten in tranquillity.
Seductive solutions, genteel clarities,
What have I or you to do with these?
Am I too old to spring like a salmon
And confined to Goethean gammon?
– And yet in the summer-time you
Sometimes come down to that too.

Nay the boy's spirit its lessoning got;
Dissympathy with nature, sheer sensual force,
Lust of light and colour, the frequent note
Of free enthusiasm in its course.

What troubling flavour in this heady wine?
It hides not Dionysos' but Astarte's sting?
Mid the elemental enemies – cold, ravening brine –
The intellectual flame's survival I sing.

Malicious and unaccountable twinkle, free
Beyond human freedom from the laws of causation?
Nay, gaily, daily, over abysses more ghastly
Men cast spider-webs of creation.

(Nay, the last issue I have all but joined,
But my muse still lacks – and so has missed all –
The right temper, like yours, which goes to the point
Of the terrible; the terrible crystal.

Some day I cry – and may cry my life through –
Serene and modest in self-confidence like you
I will capture the world-free illusion two
Of naught, and they one, like me and the sun's rays.

For in you and in me moves a thought
So passionate and live like a plant or beast
It has its own architecture and has brought
A new thing to Nature – mine vague, yours exprest.

If I find yours I will find my own.
What lack of integrity prevents me?
Where is the reach-point (it exists I've known long
Waiting for me) of this integrity?

Found I shall know it like a turned lock's click
But I fumble and juggle again and again.
Your every least move does the trick
But I watch your quick tumblers in vain.)

But one sweep of motion in the world to-day,
The unwearying flood of the river,
Inexplicable, alien! Water, whither away
In a flight that passes and stays forever?

Full from the rains, but the flood sediment gone;
Under the brace of the glancing current
Each pebble shines as with a life of its own,
Electric, autonomous, world-shaking-divergent.

Or comes the disturbing influence with which I tingle
Only from the shoals of fishes that seem
As though they'd be stranded there on the shingle
From the swaying waters they teem?

A wagtail flits but noiseless – by knowledge awed
Of some great unseen presence? or food its gob in? –
Then suddenly, with expanding sweetness, a glad
Clear note rings out: Revelation! ; Robin?

Stranded. I with them! Would I wish to bend her
    To me as she veers on her way again
Vivid and impulsive in crystalline splendour
    Cold and seething champagne?

No. So life leaves us. Already gleam
In the eyes of the young the flicker, the change,
The free enthusiasm that carries the stream
Suddenly out of my range.

In the Caledonian Forest

I

THE geo-selenic gimbal that moving makes
A gerbe now of this tree now of that
Or glomerates the whole earth in a galanty-show
    Against the full moon caught
Suddenly threw a fuscous halation round a druxy dryad
    Lying among the fumet in this dwale wood
As brooding on Scotland's indecrassifiable race
    I wandered again in a hemicranic mood.

She did not change her epirhizous posture
But looked at me steadily with Hammochrysos eyes
While I wondered what dulia might be her due
And from what her curious enanthesis might arise,
And then I knew against that frampold background
This freaked and forlorn creature was indeed
With her great shadowed gastrocnemius and desipient face
The symbol of the flawed genius of our exheredated breed.

As in Antichthon there among the apoproegmena
A quatr' occhi for a long time we stood
While like a kind of springhalt or chorea
The moonshine flickered in the silent wood,
Or like my own aporia externalised,
For her too slight kenosis made it impossible for me to woo
This outcast Muse, or urge the long-lost cause we might
            advance even yet,
Conjunctis viribus, or seek to serve her, save thus ek parergou.

II

They are not endless these variations of form
Though it is perhaps impossible to see them all.
It is certainly impossible to conceive one that doesn't exist.
But I still keep trying to do both of these
And though it is a long time now since I saw a new one
I am by no means weary yet of my concentration
On phyllotaxis here in preference to all else,
All else – but my sense of sny.

The gold edging of a bough at sunset, its pantile way
Forming a double curve, tegula and imbrex in one,
Seems at times a movement on which I might be borne
Happily to infinity; but again I am glad
When it suddenly ceases and I find myself
Pursuing no longer a rhythm of duramen
But bouncing on the diploe in a clearing between earth and air
Or headlong in dewy dallops or a moon-spairged fernshaw
Or caught in a dark dumosity or even
In open country again watching an aching spargosis of stars.

Ephphatha

ONLY a sheep's fodder bush and a screw pine
And a dark sea going by at a piaffer
And a little palæocrystic light keeping watch
Through the phengites of this panopticon
On mankind in the last stages of pellagra.

Now the light, the paxwax of infinity,
Becomes rigid as a bar of iron.
No phosphene or photopsia any longer
Can supplement or supplant it, and in vain
A voice still cries 'Ephphatha' which means nothing
In the poor pasilaly of all other sound
Which is no more than a rattle of broken bones
On the invisible pamphract of God.

First Objectives

TO JOHN HENRY MACKAY

HERE let us swear that we shall know
No kind, no thought, of compromise
Till all false values we destroy
        That true ones may arise.

Not boasts of better blood alone,
Not titles bought nor vain degrees
Of masonic mediocrity;
        These, and far more than these.

Not murderers in soldiering's name,
Not thieves of licensed usury,
But with them all who in judgment sit
        Our mortal foes shall be.

All profiteers, monopolists,
And all who claim to own the earth,
These with the others we'll remove.
          Mankind will know no dearth.

All who have power to withhold or give
Or mete life's means to other men,
Or any coercive power at all
          We'll ban from human ken.

All censors, police, and teachers who
Instead of just opening out impose;
And parents who fix their children's lives
          – War to the life on those!

And above all the Church must go
– True values may not be ours to make
Strive as we will, but this is sure
          – The false are ours to break!

The Belly-Grip

COME let us put an end to one thing
          Now that science gives us the power,
And make it impossible for any men
          To exercise for another hour
Any influence on other men that depends
On economic pressure to gain its ends.

Come let us finish the whole damned farce
          Of law and order on murder based,
On the power to coerce and starve and kill,
          With all its hypocrisy, cruelty, and waste;
And safe from all human interference give
Every man at least ample means to live.

Come let us transfer all moral issues
  And social relations to a higher plane
Where men may agree, but if they don't
  Can never be forced to submit again
To the will of others by hunger and want.
It's time to end the sadistic cant.

Come let us put a premium then
  On pure example and persuasive force,
Not that they're likely to carry far
  In maintaining present conventions, of course,
Since these all depend on the belly-grip
And will change completely when that's let slip.

For no religion, no form of government,
  Has ever had any sanction except
Brute needs ruthlessly taken advantage of,
  And these science has now triumphantly o'erleapt.
The fools who say men must still bear any yoke
Have no gifts, save cruelty, more than most other folk.

Nor has any other man in politics to-day
  Nor in industry, commerce, or the money swindle,
Nor will any man in the future, thank God.
  Our kings and statesmen in a few years will all dwindle
To nothing, big though they may loom to-day,
– Only apprentice nothings upon mankind prey.

There have been men in the course of history
  Giants compared to the mass of their fellows,
But they took no part in the fraud of ruling.
  How big compared to the average, tell us,
Let alone to any the centuries treasure
Are Mosley and Lloyd? – Not a cheese-mite's measure!

Let us believe in the intelligence and decency
  Of the majority of men if properly treated
And their power when a great opportunity
  Is frankly presented to rise and meet it,

And abjure the impious nonentities who still,
As hitherto, would fain impersonate God's will.

All that humanity through the ages has won
        Owes nothing to them or any of their kind,
If our life lost any real asset none
        Of these could attempt to regain it you'd find
– Only a MacDonald, a Baldwin, a Thomas
Are the God-like creatures science threatens to take from us!

We'll survive the loss! The kindly common men
        Upstarts like these deem unfit for freedom
Will not have the slightest difficulty
        Once such blind leaders cease to mislead 'em
In establishing a right good fellowship
Forever free of the belly-grip.

Song of the New Economics

I HEAR in an audience of countless millions
A sanctimonious voice giving thanks
To a God that the tone of the speaker
As one made in his own, and most men's, image ranks
For old age pensioners' pennies and widows' mites
And threepenny bits from children's banks,
Men's belts tighter and mothers' breasts drier
And foodstuffs destroyed and machines set idle
        To save the mightiest empire
        The world has ever seen,
And the face is the face of the Cheshire cat
But the tail is the tail of the Manx,
For here and there is an unstopped ear
Like a trench that arrests a prairie fire
And the voice it hears is a still small voice
That utters the one word: 'Liar!'

'History repeats itself,' I hear a man jabber,
'And the anti-Douglasite arguments
Remind me of the Simian speeches
Against the human developments.
I remember many of the grandfather apes
Used precisely the same phrases as to-day
The orthodox economists are using,
And if they had got their way
Man's incredible variation
Would have been nipped in the bud
And we'd all have been monkeys still
And – Oh! It's all very well to scoff!
But who even now can say
We wouldn't have been better off?

Pray let us at least think twice
And not just abandon the old idea
Of earning a living by the sweat of our brow
As our rash progenitors gave up
Prehensile tails and the primaeval
Forest economy of nuts that I trow
Was certainly a better mode of life
Than millions of men have now.'

'Or,' says a second, 'are likely to have
Unless – one crime to another leading –
We follow up that initial break
With the fine old arboreal breeding
By this new departure whose advocates
Douglas, Orage, and a few
Others of that highbrow crew! –
Are further already from most men
Than average humans from monkeys got
For many a long æon.
Personally I think the time has come
To move in the opposite direction
And not keep outgrowing ourselves like this
At the call of a modernist section,
Peradventure we haven't gone too far yet,

Let us revert. We well may find
That Tarzan of the Apes is in truth
The Hitler of All Mankind!'

But it's 'Oh! for one glance from Jehovah's eye
To make our vile misgivings fly,'
And 'Oh! for one cheer like that which broke
From English hearts when Jesus spoke,'
But the fools befouled in their prayer don't see
    The greater miracle happening here,
For the Niagara of Cant has been shot again
And one by one intrepid swimmers appear
And their voices over the whole hullabaloo
Ring out and their eyes shine clear
For the God of Hosts has been beaten before
By a Greater whom 'nobody understood'
And men must come singly to manhood still
While the monkeys stay in the wood

            For Manhood will out
            Without a doubt
            Whatever may happen
            To the mindless rout.

But a new voice cries: 'Does MacStatesman think
The whole world must go blind because he has?'
And suddenly pointing straight at the Zany
MacStatesman's turns into a cannon's mouth
Without altering his appearance any,
And his piety dissolves in the stink
Of wave upon wave of poison gas,
For MacStatesman was never the man to shrink
From the operation of the Iron Laws,
        And no pity will make him pause,
        Degradation, disease, and death must increase
        Till the hole of mankind is so accustomed to these
        That it sees – or almost! – as clearly as he sees
            With his own worm-eaten sight
        That they are unchangeably natural and right.

(*Singing*):

We aren't murderers of course
    For we keep within the Law,
And make it too! So you can't catch us
    Do what you will. Ha, ha! Ha, ha!

Infant mortality, suicide,
    And crime, insanity, and disease
May all tell the self same story
    But we pay no heed to these.

Securely based on ignorance
    And cruelty and fear we know
Nobody else can possibly be right
    Even if we're wrong – *for we've told God so!*

There is no appeal beyond us
    And, though by every fact belied,
Our insane sense of fitness to rule
    Lets us listen to naught beside,

Educated chimps who yet know at heart
    We're less fit to guide men now
Than any baboon when the human mind
    First broke away from the parent bough!

But Mankind has been through all this before
For far less, MacStatesman, and we defy you.
Though ninety-nine per cent of the world's population
Are behind you history will yet belie you
And destroy all these false values you deem
In the unalterable nature of things
That true values may at last emerge
When needless toil no longer enrings
Nor exploitation debases the soul of man,
And the freedom of the world is his and his only task
To realise his manhood as well as he can,

For the Problem of Quantity is solved.
There is abundance for all,
But the Problem of Quality now
Confronts us with an insistent call,
And who can blame the countless host
Who would fain dodge that at any cost?
And who but MacStatesman and Co. will lose most?

On to the New World! On a stone in the old
Let this simple tale of the past be told:

          Here lies MacStatesman
               – As he always did!
          The grimmest thing the merciful
               Earth ever hid!

          It took him in
               – As he never took it
          With his libel that it hadn't
               Enough for all yet!

          But all Earth has given
               Wouldn't be any lack
          Against its service
               In taking him back!

          For the eggs of the Future aren't all laid
               In Montagu Norman's beard
          Though that holds a collection Edward Lear
               Would find sufficiently weird;
And the desperate efforts of the earliest men
To keep and extend their dawning humanity,
(For the horrors of War, and Peace, to-day are less
Than the perils that beset their spirits, I guess;
Pioneers who precariously transmitted the flame
That now keeps the world safe for hypocrisy)
Are reflected in a kindred spirit again
Which will triumph like theirs – but, if to the same

End, though as many centuries hence,
As this dying civilisation's immense
Stupidity and bestiality,
With equivalents again of MacStatesman and Co.,
Then God deny us this victory
And end the world now at a blow!

Genethliacon for the New World Order

To Ann Orage, a Few Days Old

The world is thrilling from pole to pole
　　With joy to-day
For the time is at hand from the glorious
Building of Man to knock away
The scaffolding all bestuck with names
　　That has always seemed
The uglier every time that a glimpse
　　Of the work behind it has streamed
Through a chink of the framework and advts.
　　None of the builders now,
Least of all Jesus, can point
To his share in the finished structure, I trow,
　　For every individual contribution
　　　　Is lost in the whole.
They all built better far than they knew
　　And none foresaw the goal,
For the contribution of the nameless people
　　Was the main thing after all.
Who could foresee an unknown flower
Having seen the leaves, the stem, and the root
– Let alone the glory of the approaching hour
Now all human history rounds to its fruit?
Hence the blinding star-like surprise of the work
　　When the scaffolding shall fall.

The whole world is thrilling from pole to pole
    With the first clear ray
Of the starry life of the Earth that at last
    Transfigures its clay.

All is deepening darkness. I see no shred
Of light at all. I hear no sound
But cries of horror and distress in the night.
No comfort or hope is anywhere to be found.
The end of the world is at hand.
Chaos reclaims it. Creation has failed,
And in a last glance back like a drowning man's
Over all that has been the end must be hailed
For nothing has appeared that had any chance
Or deserved or birth or continuance.

It is always darkest just before the dawn.
Lo! the day comes that Christ foreran
    As the antedawn the true day;
The antedawn true too in its way
    Howsoever fitful and grey,
And not cast out but caught up, confirmed, and completed.
    So all that has been born deserved birth
        And lives, transfigured, forever,
           And the whole earth
Is now like the broad daylight in which all
The divisions that seemed when the light was small
    From the true vision like a scaffolding fall.
Let all men rejoice, rejoice, rejoice,
    For every human hope is redeemed
And the planetary noonday of Man confirms and completes
    Every tentative light that has ever gleamed.

But why can I catch no glimpse
Of this glory you speak of then?
Surely my eyes are open too,
I am just as anxious to find it as you
– But I seek like all but all men
For a single gleam but in vain!

Who can see the unborn child
Whose look is not turned inside?
The mother is too busy bringing to life
To flash at random her eyes of pride;
Only chance gleams from them have been caught
In art, religion, and moods like that.
Even the mother cannot foresee
The lineaments of the child to be
Nor tell the sex or character.
Nor is that needfu at all to her.
But she knows the child when it is born.
So will mankind, though now so forlorn.
For the time is at hand – it is always
Darkest just before the dawn – and as
A woman's labour, life's most terrible pain,
Suddenly into joy must pass
When she sees the new-born child so here
All the awful agonies of mankind,
All the difficulty and darkness, in a moment
Will be transformed into joy you'll find.

> *But where is this child you speak of,*
> *The heir and fulfilment of all the hopes of mankind?*
> *I hear no chorus of angels, I see no star,*
> *By which this second Bethlehem to find.*

The glory of man is where it has always been
– In the goodness and simplicity and patience
Of the vast majority of the people
One and the same in all the nations
Just as genius is always the same,
Simple and for all; that is why
The names disappear – you need not seek
In fame but in anonymity,
In anyone else but in yourself.
Everyman is the meaning and desire
Of the world – if he looks at himself
And not to the ends of the earth, to Gods and Kings

And all to whom the curse of the slaver clings,
He will flash with the immortal fire.

Life and that far more abundantly
Than in these twenty centuries all
The Christians put together in their wildest dreams
Have dreamt possible is now within Everyman's call,
If Everyman has the courage at last to be
What he is, and has been through all history,
And lets his common practice and principle guide
All the world henceforth – and naught beside.

Shall the evolution of mankind be stayed,
As the sun was once stayed in the skies,
By a banking system that from its lying books
Refuses to lift its eyes?
Shall a few dullards pent in vicious circles
Impose a like closed order on all;
Shall the creative spirit that launched life's process
Let it end and under the fiat fall
Of a Montagu Norman, a Ramsay MacDonald,
And they and like figures, incredibly small
Set against Man, and set against God,
Hold us all in a Jericho with an unbreakable wall?
These impious pigmies have no existence
Save as figments of Everyman's self-betrayal.

All the movements in religion and culture,
All wars, have only been
Surface commotions that left
The depths unchanged and serene.
– The great simplicities of life,
Being alive, and love, and parentage,
And having leisure for contemplation and fun
When material tasks no longer engage –
The majority of people everywhere have always
Had these and no more.
All so-called history has left them untouched
Like an endless store

Of deep-hidden wine that has matured
In silence and obscurity against the hour
Of the birth of Man's plenary power,
His sovereign purpose and ineffable dower.

What cobwebs still seek to hide
This peerless elixir?
What shadows now the sun is here
Would fain refuse to stir?
Who cries that mankind yet
Must be ruled over – by whom?
And denied the fruits of their labour,
Made abjure the fruits of their womb,
And refused the right to rejoice
In the birth of the heir of all hopes?
– The vanity of all these would-be rulers
Is a feather-whisk that with the flood-tide copes.
All reputations scurry away like shadows
In the commonsense of the masses of men.
They are lost in brotherly love
And shall never be seen again.

Can we not trust ourselves,
The kindly peaceable masses of men
Who have gained nothing by anything else
And can never have aught to gain?
Can we not trust ourselves when anyone else
We trust instead must needs trust in us
And is nothing apart from that?
Can we not trust ourselves
As these vain voices declare;
Will they tempt us still to Right or Left
When all we need is to stand foursquare,
When all we need is here in ourselves,
Not there or there or elsewhere?
A plague on all their parties then!
– The time is past for all that.

Without us there can be no war or want,
And there will be none, for we stand pat
By the kindliness, peace, and good will
Unaffected by colour or creed
Of the common people all the world over
And trust that alone to lead.

Who shall stick a name on the mystery
        Of a new-born spirit – who dares
Seize on the millionth part that is all they can see
        And claim any child as theirs?
All the life of men must go free of rule
        As the unpredictable children it bears,
And as easily as to these unknowable, with love,
        Life is fitted for freedom in all its affairs.
It is unnecessary to know anything
        – Enough that the child should be.
Love cares not what it may think or do.
Can the womb refuse to deliver the child,
        Or life deny life's liberty?

It is a poor thing indeed
For cowardly voices to cry: 'Beware,
Restrain yourselves. Safety first. Have a care,'
When genius is at the top of its form
And the growth of the ages at last
Apprehends the nature of its maturity,
And the good all things have worked together for
Is in widest commonalty cast.
Come, broach the good wine laid up
Against this day since time began!
Behold how it shines in the light that breaks
From the whole earth seen as a star again
        In the general life of man!

        O this is the time for all mankind
                To rejoice without a doubt
        – And break the neck of the bottle
                If the cork will not come out!

Etika Preobrazhennavo Erosa

IT is easy to cry
I am one with the working classes
But no task in the world surpasses
In difficulty his who would try,
Must try since he is not, succeed or die.
Miseducated and more articulate,
Sensitised by what numbs their fate
And raised up by what keeps them down,
Only by the severest intellectual discipline
Can one of the bourgeois intelligentsia win
Up to the level of the proletariat
On this side of the grave or that
– The only goal worth aiming at.
     O remorseless spirit that guides me
       The way seems infinite;
    What endless distance divides me
       From the people yet!

It is next to impossible still
For me to bear any other man close – for deep
Differences surge up like a blast from Hell,
Yet I know full well
All the distinctions that divide
Man from man must be swept aside,
Sweep each other aside, cancel out,
All sources of individual pride
Are like straws on a whirling tide
Or like trees which have dried up but still sway
    In the breeze with the others
Or like men feeding on hopes drier than hay
Not knowing what they eat but always eating.
The War put an end to individuals.
They are no longer of interest – even to themselves.

A question of getting down to it, but how? Long days
I've spent in film studios considering the ways
Producers have tried to get under the skin
And far enough in but couldn't win.
Die freudlose Gasse, a simplistic city
Swimming in petty-bourgeois self-pity;
All the double tendency of the Teuton *Lichtspiel*
Towards the real and away from the real;
The concoction instead of the experience;
A sketchy intellectual landscape, not the search for the truth;
Routines of literary closets, *Abwege*, ricochettings
Into vortices of pseudo-psychologisings;
Not profound relationships but only exhibits,
Chic, treacherous, effete – O it's clearer yet
The only way to get is just to get,
For Christ's sake let us cease being subtile,
Abandon every specious wile.
   Fear of the maximum? Oh, ho!
    You are no way near it.
   It won't serve to take the human mind
    Just as far as it can go.
    You must take the spirit
     Further . . .
  It is necessary to go all the way at least
   And there are no fellow-travellers.

The artist of keen nerve-ends
Can no longer yield to his periphery;
To a topography that gives neither the lie of the land
Nor its consistency, where figures of speech
Go stalking as men and women, skins drawn
Over hollow bodies, ephemera, momentarily illusive.
He must break through that aura – he must give
Intensive character-convergence, make outstand
Character-relations that do not merely spread
Like valiant steam into an ominous but compelling world,
And stop being just a bloody showman

Of guilt or innocence stuffed with straw.
Not *Lulu* but *Kameradschaft* points the way
    To something far more drastic than the law
    – Not of life or art! but theirs too – allows to-day.

That is the way – one step in a *Kino*
Sluggish amid jingo lost-glory and *Bockbier* films,
Set to goosestep measures and ¾ *Takt*;
One step at least on grounds of mass-reference,
Outside the land of proletarian rule at that!;
All the difference between Pabst and Pommer;
Between an artist and the ingenious composers
Of sophisticated *Kino*-doggerel. Yet what
Is this and every such artistic fact
No matter how 'sincere' the creative act
But a sop to Cerberus? the 'cultural compulsives'
At work on 'our fellow-travellers'? Rather nods from Homer
Than such kitsch. Who are Pabst
And Pommer when the *exegi monumentum aere perennius*
Is rattling on the scrap-iron heap? Let me hence,
Better luck elsewhere may cheer the roamer.
This wisdom after the event is not the life or art
    That's whitening every bourgeois heart,
        There's no time to be arch
        On the revolutionary march.

Let us look elsewhere – not to the chief turnbuckles
Holding and regulating us in the machine
Of an apparently more purposeful existence.
That's all clinkers we know though a few
Bewildered folk are still poking in the ash;
Nor where after prolonged aching priapism now
A pathological flabbiness is left pointing nowhere;
Least of all where fools are still trying to play
Each of the stops on the old-fashioned flute,
(As well read novels, or newspapers even, or Hansard;
Take Ramsay MacDonald seriously, or go to church)

          – Bunches of hams and shysters,
          With all the fat thumb business
          And a *Yiddishkeit* crutch –
In *Jew Süss, Stempanyov, Uncle Moses*
Sweetishly seductive, the poky bedroom, the symbolical red light,
Till when the curtain drops we shudder, seeing,
As if staring unblinkingly
At a 'mystic photo' painted on the proscenium,
On the walls, on the faces of the audience,
          The poor lamb being tupped.
– But to Russia for a breath of fresh air!

Let us climb to where the people can be found
          Ranged in their millions
As history is climbing to world unity
– As who, when he gains a great summit
Finds he has no need to look below
To know his altitude – his eyes, his mind
Have no concern with the faithful aspect of the place,
The structure of the rocks and mountains,
Nor any tendency to exploit the scene,
To turn it to a fine 'effect';
Since the world is removed from the world here.
The terror and glory of alp and glacier veil themselves.
What is communicated is feeling, but feeling of a rare kind,
The infinitely remote, the impalpable, a mingling
Of cloud and snow, a suspension of motion
Attract the surrendered spirit.
O beata solitudo! O sola beatitudo!
– All else is only the temporary wish
Of the half-wakened proletariat
          To become bourgeois themselves.

This is the music of humanity,
Here 'where everything is forgiven,
And it would be impossible not to forgive';
Justification of all life in the balance of obliteration,
Mercy and stability in the ultimate release

Of the individual soul, forgiveness
In the knowledge that no individual deed
Eventually matters individually;
All the seeming divisions of life
Merely the glow upon glow in still more lucid glow
Of this outwelling of light
– A shape having no beginning or end,
    Moving upwards within itself,
    Turning backwards upon itself,
    Passing through itself, and continuing
        The process forever;
    The beat of the universal pulse
    And magic of the great *Bescherung*.
    ... But who knows this summit, this peak moment,
        As Lenin kept his beat in Russia,
    Or as one who in the circle of *tabla taranga*
    Finds the time between two precipitating notes
    To arrange a drum that has got off key by a hair's breadth?

Thalamus

I

BUSY as any man in those centres of the brain
Where consciousness flourishes I yet cherish more
The older, darker, less studied regions
Of cranial anatomy through which, momently, pour
Myriads of sensations, hundreds fleetingly combined
    into feelings, and now and then
Amongst them a species of thought more profound
Than any other that is known to man.

The younger organs have not superseded
These older ones which have a different mental life.
I am aware at times between them
Of co-operation and at times of strife,

But these dark places intimate now and again
A kind of knowledge the younger seldom recognise
    as such, but revealing
As superior a permanence to the other sort as that
    does
To what men call feeling.

Let fools think science has supplanted poetry;
Rationalism, religion. Even physically
The older parts are more than holding their own;
The fools are liars to their own anatomy.

II

The incapacity and distrust of most folk
For mere reason is well founded
If they only knew the reason for it
In their true nature and destiny grounded,
    When reason has its full due
    That will have it too.

Meanwhile reason, used or misused,
Usurps man's consciousness;
Life's other and greater tide flows unseen
And its presence men hardly guess,
    Or the subtle ubiquitous ways
    It shapes and limits all reason says.

Men are held to a fraction of their lives,
And reason discounts for the most part
All stray overflowings of life's deeper flood,
Instincts, intuitions, religion, art,
    And tho' a small part of the whole
    Would fain have entire control.

But who reason well know all too well
That that unseen tide now and again
Lifts into consciousness far greater truths
Than reason itself can attain
    Truths to thoughts I wis
    As thought to feeling is.

The truths that all greater thinkers have seen
At the height of their genius – and then
Spent most of their days denying
Or trying to scale down to mere reason's ken
    – The height to which all life must tend
    And securely hold at the end.

But proud of their cortex few
Have glimpsed the medial nuclei yet
Of their thalamus – that Everest in themselves
Reason should have explored before it
    As the corpora geniculata before any star
    To know what and why men are.

O misguided science pursuing
All tasks but the greatest of all
While away beyond this life's scant scope
In a glorious unseen waterfall
    Pours all but all of life's best,
    We turn our poor mills with the rest.

These mills of Satan; these hellish hives
In which men sink to the status of slaves,
Treadmills of rationalising,
Tho' his spirit each man still privily laves
    In the live waters he yet misesteems
    As naught but vain dreams.

The Sense of Smell

SMELL they say is a decaying sense
    In civilised man,
And literature that pays much attention to it
    As decadent comes under the ban.

So they say who not knowing even themselves
    Think to know all else.
It's a different story of smell altogether
    That modern science tells.

Its monopoly of direct access to the cortex demands
    From disparagers of this sense
Who yet rely on cortical knowledge good grounds
    For their different preference.

Scandal to have no fit vocabulary even
    For this mighty power,
– Empyreumatic, alliaceous, hircine;
    Blind windows in a magic tower!

But reason unconcerned with what is of such
    Overwhelming concern to the mind
Is only a false face the nature of consciousness
    Continues to hide behind.

In Memoriam: Liam Mac'Ille Iosa

WHERE is the cock to the bonnet, the swing to the kilt,
The skirl of the pipes in Scotland now;
The range of the tartans outrainbowing the rainbow,
The hooching in reels that like flood-tides lilt?
Mar a tha e as the good whisky is
Everything in Scotland should be, I trow;
Aye, like the big music that within itself varies
Subtly as only a MacCrimmon knows how,
Or those shades of difference in sound that Gaelic
– Shibboleths of infinity – alone possesses
That no man of spirit can be less quick,
Less expert in, than another,
Even as there cannot be any growth
Of perfection but only growth in it.

For what mess of pottage, what Southern filth,
What lack of intricacy, fineness, impossible achievement,
Have we bartered this birthright, for what hurdy-gurdy
Exchanged this incomparable instrument?
O come, come, come, let us turn to God
And get rid of this degrading and damnable load,
So set we can give our spirits free play
And rise to the height of our form. There is no going astray,
More than there is for the rose shining full-blown,
Full to perfection with itself alone.
Come, let us obey the creative word.
God will make us flash like the blade of a sword.
Only that which aspires to a *caoin*, an edge like it,
Like a melody tends to the infinite.

I am a poet; our fools ask me for logic not life.
Scotland has too much logic; but whither are all the clouds going
With which like Scotland our spirits are rife,
Before Eternity like a great wind blowing,
The race of the piled clouds after a gale
Across the world, over its cliffed edge, over the vale
Of Death till they dapple another country
As if crowding softly, softly, O God, into Thee?
O Liam, Liam, sheer white-top speeding full sail,
Lost world of Gaeldom, further and further away from me,
How can I follow, Albannach, how reachieve
The unsearchable masterpiece? You leave
No more than a swallow when the passage of its flight
So dwells in the eye one can half-believe
Its lines remain, a tracery on the light.

Am I a nightingale to remember too
What the swallow forgets – our Itys', our Alba's, death?
     While still beyond the Hebrides there in the west
     Heaven itself shines like that pheasant's breast!
Or content myself with the flight patterns you have flown through?
Meaning as an end of desire is value.
But an end of desire for Scotland? By what miracle of faith

Shall I carry that supreme song through?
Does it come to me like those forms and landscapes
Which seem to spring from a floating point of light
Our closed eyes behold just before we sleep
With endless fertility in inevitable shapes
Like Creation complete in God's sight?
    To no less a height
    My note must leap.
Ah! Thou art gone forever and have forgotten, Liam,
With the forgetfulness that one with the remembering I must know
If I, the poet, am to hold the scheme
Of both these worlds, this vast twin-theme,
    In one note – so!
    For I cannot fail
    Thinking of you so far away
To go as into the next valley and to a remote distance, yea,
To the end of the world, goes the voice of the nightingale.

Ad te Domine appello; so even as Pascal against Rome
No matter what all other men think, desire, and feel
For Scotland to-day we irreconcilables carry our appeal
Completely over their heads and straight to God home.
Let them do likewise and we may meet them there
(For a moment!) – but not elsewhere.

Vestigia Nulla Retrorsum

In Memoriam: Rainer Maria Rilke 1875–1926

HALOPHILOUS living by these far northern seas
How shall our sweetgales or Iceland poppies show
Their sympathy with your cleistogamic flowers,
    Or this baragouin of ours
Save as a tawny frogmouth cry
    Simultaneous with your nightingale?

Yet our abreption from the abderian accidie
Of most men brings us near you; we too go
Where no way save Alsirat can avail.

We too drank beer once in the common world
But not without acorus in it ever;
Knew women in maidenhead, maternity, and menopause,
     But know them better where none has
Entered since Time began or ever can
Save in our gynandromorphic moods. But soon
Our chalones parted us from that life of Man
Till crag-and-tail we stood with towering cliffs that sever
Us from Earth but elsewhere turn low green slopes and boon.

We set your image upon a naked stone
At our lectisternium here, with immarcescible flowers,
Since they are fashioned solely from the darkness and the light,
In such wise as is pleasing in the sight
Of our not-inexpert laevorotatory muse;
In such wise as – at other angles to the sun –
In paying homage you were wont to use;
And note its subtle changes through the moving hours
Yet save for the most obvious have scarce begun.

A naked stone that from the castle wall
Of Duino itself riven might be brought here to serve!
And yet no different from many another stone
Of this small island incredibly grey and lone.
Valéry did not know how you could bear to live
In that old stronghold of silence visible.
We do, who know the response our own bare stones can give,
Each turning in the sunlight to a naked nerve,
A brief boustrophedon of Heaven and Hell.

No more is interposed between God and us
But the last difference between human and divine,
And yet we have not chosen between Heaven and Hell,
Too alive to both. When but the last films of flesh fell,

When we were in the world and yet not in it,
And the spirit seemed to waver its eyas wings
Into the divine obscurity, it could not win it.
We would not, if we could, the difference resign
Between God and us – the God of our imaginings.

In shades of lastery and filemot and gridelin,
Stammel and perse, our chesil and turbary lie
Far from Scotland, that land of liripoops we left
        On these sterile stones, all else bereft,
To watch the lacertine gleams, the lightning hummers, still.
Nature with her excessive being no more could come
Over us here, we thought, as prophecy over Paul;
Lagophthalmic as God himself we yet descry
Overwhelming nimiety in this minimum!
What logodaedaly shall we practise then?
What loxodromics to get behind the light?
Glistening with exoskeletal stars we turn in vain
This way and that and but changing perigraphs gain,
Parablepsies, calentures, every cursèd paranthelion
Of this theandric force Pepper's-ghosting God.
There is an accidie in all acceptance shown.
Is this God cheating too? Yet we will not. The fight
Continues under next to nothing's still more hopeless load.

We cannot read this quipu of the air,
This ogham on the stones, even as geologists fail
To tell from the striae which of two opposite ways
The ice went; and all upon which we can gaze
Is as obvious as the effects of the Flood and yet
Its waters did not penetrate very deep
Nor disturb Earth's strata much; nor will thought deeper get.
Even as rustics deplore an early spring – yet hail,
So we all hope of God repudiate – and keep.

But ah! there is an accidie in the fight as well.
The edge of the sword becomes serene in our hands.
This is no less an acceptance; and we know
A kindred peace in the heart of the conflict glow;

The cyclone's centre is a core of peace.
We too have fallen in the sink of swords,
Stricken suddenly with love of our enemies,
The stupid end no human ingenuity withstands
Alike to deeds and words and lack of deeds and words.

We would not if we could, but must we when we can?
Is this the sorry end of all our subtleties,
Unconscious compromise, natural yielding, brute collapse?
Our lost origin our acropetal striving saps.
Or human consciousness seems to us
Like thunder through successive banks of fog to go
Bubbling up between them furious
And muffled again; and among these mysteries
We poets sit ceraunic as a chalumeau.

Nor twissel-tongued can we penelopise;
Shut our eyes despite their madarosis of the sun.
Any island's too small for more than life and death.
And in the darkest night with bated breath
To grope our way over familiar stones made foreign
By any parapsis in a petty Ragnarök
Will not avail us. Such paraplegias we have borne
While over us Heaven's last lauwines seemed to run
– Only the scaphism of the stars anew to brook!

Stony Limits

In Memoriam: Charles Doughty, 1843–1926

UNDER no hanging heaven-rooted tree,
Though full of mammuks' nests,
Bone of old Britain we bury thee
But heeding your unspoken hests
Naught not coeval with the Earth
And indispensable till its end

With what whom you despised may deem the dearth
Of your last resting-place dare blend.
Where nature is content with little so are you
So be it the little to which all else is due.

Nor in vain mimicry of the powers
That lifted up the mountains shall we raise
A stone less of nature's shaping than of ours
        To mark the unfrequented place.
You were not filial to all else
Save to the Dust, the mother of all men,
And where you lie no other sign needs tells
(Unless a gaunt shape resembles you again
In some momentary effect of light on rock)
But your family likeness to all her stock.

Flowers may be strewn upon the grave
        Of easy come easy go.
Fitly only some earthquake or tidal wave
O'er you its red rose or its white may throw
But naught else smaller than darkness and light
– Both here, though of no man's bringing! –
And as any past time had been in your sight
Were you now from your bed upspringing,
Now or a billion years hence, you would see
Scant difference, eyed like eternity.

How should we have anything to give you
        In death who had nothing in life,
Attempting in our sand-riddles to sieve you
Who were with nothing, but the sheer elements rife?
Anchor of truth, facile as granite you lie,
A plug suspended in England's false dreams.
Your worth will be seen by and by,
Like God's purpose in what men deem their schemes,
Nothing ephemeral can seek what lies in this ground
Since nothing can be sought but the found.

The poem that would praise you must be
Like the glass of some rock, sleek brown, crowded
With dark incipient crystal growths, we see;
Or a glimpse of Petavius may have endowed it
With the tubular and dumb-bell-shaped inclusions surrounded
 By the broad reaction rims it needs.
I have seen it in dreams and know how it abounded
– Ah! would I could find in me like seeds! –
As the north-easterly garden in the lunation grows,
A spectacle not one man in ten millions knows.

I belong to a different country than yours
And none of my travels have been in the same lands
Save where Arzachel or Langrenus allures
Such spirits as ours, and the Straight Wall stands,
But crossing shear planes extruded in long lines of ridges,
Torsion cylinders, crater rings, and circular seas
And ultra-basic xenoliths that make men look midges
Belong to my quarter as well, and with ease
I too can work in bright green and all the curious interference
Colours that under crossed nicols have a mottled appearance.

Let my first offering be these few pyroxenes twinned
On the orthopinacoid and hour-glass scheme,
Fine striae, microline cross-hatchings, and this wind
Blowing plumes of vapour forever it would seem
From cone after cone diminishing sterile and grey
In the distance; dun sands in ever-changing squalls;
Crush breccias and overthrusts; and such little array
Of Geology's favourite fal-de-lals
And demolitions and entrenchments of weather
As any turn of my eyes brings together.

I know how on turning to noble hills
And stark deserts happily still preserved
For men whom no gregariousness fills
With the loneliness for which they are nerved
– The lonely at-one-ment with all worth while –

I can feel as if the landscape and I
Became each other and see my smile
In the corners of the vastest contours lie
And share the gladness and peace you knew,
– The supreme human serenity that was you!

I have seen Silence lift his head
And Song, like his double, lift yours,
And know, while nearly all that seems living is dead,
You were always consubstantial with all that endures.
Would it were on Earth! Not since Ezekiel has that faw sun ringed
A worthier head; red as Adam you stood
In the desert, the horizon with vultures black-winged,
And sang and died in this still greater solitude
Where I sit by your skull whose emptiness is worth
The sum of almost all the full heads now on Earth
– By your roomy skull where most men might well spend
Longer than you did in Arabia, friend!

On a Raised Beach

To James H. Whyte

ALL is lithogenesis – or lochia,
Carpolite fruit of the forbidden tree,
Stones blacker than any in the Caaba,
Cream-coloured caen-stone, chatoyant pieces,
Celadon and corbeau, bistre and beige,
Glaucous, hoar, enfouldered, cyathiform,
Making mere faculae of the sun and moon
I study you glout and gloss, but have
No cadrans to adjust you with, and turn again
From optik to haptik and like a blind man run
My fingers over you, arris by arris, burr by burr,
Slickensides, truité, rugas, foveoles,

Bringing my aesthesis in vain to bear,
An angle-titch to all your corrugations and coigns,
Hatched foraminous cavo-rilievo of the world,
Deictic, fiducial stones. Chiliad by chiliad
What bricole piled you here, stupendous cairn?
What artist poses the Earth écorché thus,
Pillar of creation engouled in me?
What eburnation augments you with men's bones,
Every energumen an Endymion yet?
All the other stones are in this haecceity it seems,
But where is the Christophanic rock that moved?
What Cabirian song from this catasta comes?

Deep conviction or preference can seldom
Find direct terms in which to express itself.
Today on this shingle shelf
I understand this pensive reluctance so well,
This not discommendable obstinacy,
These contrivances of an inexpressive critical feeling,
These stones with their resolve that Creation shall not be
Injured by iconoclasts and quacks. Nothing has stirred
Since I lay down this morning an eternity ago
But one bird. The widest open door is the least liable to intrusion,
Ubiquitous as the sunlight, unfrequented as the sun.
The inward gates of a bird are always open.
It does not know how to shut them.
That is the secret of its song,
But whether any man's are ajar is doubtful.
I look at these stones and know little about them,
But I know their gates are open too,
Always open, far longer open, than any bird's can be,
That every one of them has had its gates wide open far longer
Than all birds put together, let alone humanity,
Though through them no man can see,
No man nor anything more recently born than themselves
And that is everything else on the Earth.
I too lying here have dismissed all else.
Bread from stones is my sole and desperate dearth,

From stones, which are to the Earth as to the sunlight
Is the naked sun which is for no man's sight.
I would scorn to cry to any easier audience
Or, having cried, to lack patience to await the response.
I am no more indifferent or ill-disposed to life than death is;
I would fain accept it all completely as the soil does;
Already I feel all that can perish perishing in me
As so much has perished and all will yet perish in these stones.
I must begin with these stones as the world began.

Shall I come to a bird quicker than the world's course ran?
  To a bird, and to myself, a man?
  And what if I do, and further?
I shall only have gone a little way to go back again
And be like a fleeting deceit of development,
Iconoclasts, quacks. So these stones have dismissed
All but all of evolution, unmoved by it,
(Is there anything to come they will not likewise dismiss?)
As the essential life of mankind in the mass
Is the same as their earliest ancestors yet.

Actual physical conflict or psychological warfare
  Incidental to love or food
Brings out animal life's bolder and more brilliant patterns
  Concealed as a rule in habitude.
  There is a sudden revelation of colour,
  The protrusion of a crest,
  The expansion of an ornament,
– But no general principle can be guessed
From these flashing fragments we are seeing,
These foam-bells on the hidden currents of being.
The bodies of animals are visible substances
And must therefore have colour and shape, in the first place
Depending on chemical composition, physical structure, mode of
   growth,
Physiological rhythms and other factors in the case,
But their purposive function is another question.
Brilliant-hued animals hide away in the ocean deeps;
The mole has a rich sexual colouring in due season

Under the ground; nearly every beast keeps
Brighter colours inside it than outside.
What the seen shows is never anything to what it's designed to hide,
The red blood which makes the beauty of a maiden's cheek
Is as red under a gorilla's pigmented and hairy face.
Varied forms and functions though life may seem to have shown
They all come back to the likeness of stone,
So to the intervening stages we can best find a clue
In what we all came from and return to.
There are no twirly bits in this ground bass.

We must be humble. We are so easily baffled by appearances
And do not realise that these stones are one with the stars.
It makes no difference to them whether they are high or low,
Mountain peak or ocean floor, palace, or pigsty.
There are plenty of ruined buildings in the world but no ruined stones.
No visitor comes from the stars
But is the same as they are.
– Nay, it is easy to find a spontaneity here,
An adjustment to life, an ability
To ride it easily, akin to 'the buoyant
Prelapsarian naturalness of a country girl
Laughing in the sun, not passion-rent,
But sensing in the bound of her breasts vigours to come
Powered to make her one with the stream of earthlife round her,'
But not yet as my Muse is, with this ampler scope,
This more divine rhythm, wholly at one
With the earth, riding the Heavens with it, as the stones do
And all soon must.
But it is wrong to indulge in these illustrations
Instead of just accepting the stones.
It is a paltry business to try to drag down
The arduus furor of the stones to the futile imaginings of men,
To all that fears to grow roots into the common earth,
As it soon must, lest it be chilled to the core,
As it will be – and none the worse for that.
Impatience is a poor qualification for immortality.

Hot blood is of no use in dealing with eternity.
It is seldom that promises or even realisations
Can sustain a clear and searching gaze.
But an emotion chilled is an emotion controlled;
This is the road leading to certainty,
Reasoned planning for the time when reason can no longer avail.
It is essential to know the chill of all the objections
That come creeping into the mind, the battle between opposing ideas
Which gives the victory to the strongest and most universal
Over all others, and to wage it to the end
With increasing freedom, precision, and detachment
A detachment that shocks our instincts and ridicules our desires.
All else in the world cancels out, equal, capable
Of being replaced by other things (even as all the ideas
That madden men now must lose their potency in a few years
And be replaced by others – even as all the religions,
All the material sacrifices and moral restraints,
That in twenty thousand years have brought us no nearer to God
Are irrelevant to the ordered adjustments
Out of reach of perceptive understanding
Forever taking place on the Earth and in the unthinkable regions
            around it;
This cat's cradle of life; this reality volatile yet determined;
This instense vibration in the stones
That makes them seem immobile to us)
But the world cannot dispense with the stones.
They alone are not redundant. Nothing can replace them
Except a new creation of God.

I must get into this stone world now.
Ratchel, striae, relationships of tesserae,
    Innumerable shades of grey,
    Innumerable shapes,
And beneath them all a stupendous unity,
Infinite movement visibly defending itself
Against all the assaults of weather and water,
Simultaneously mobilised at full strength
At every point of the universal front,

Always at the pitch of its powers,
The foundation and end of all life.
I try them with the old Norn words – hraun
Duss, rønis, queedaruns, kollyarum;
They hvarf from me in all directions
Over the hurdifell – klett, millya hellya, hellyina bretta,
Hellyina wheeda, hellyina grø, bakka, ayre, –
And lay my world in kolgref.

This is no heap of broken images.
Let men find the faith that builds mountains
Before they seek the faith that moves them. Men cannot hope
To survive the fall of the mountains
Which they will no more see than they saw their rise
Unless they are more concentrated and determined,
Truer to themselves and with more to be true to,
Than these stones, and as inerrable as they are.
Their sole concern is that what can be shaken
Shall be shaken and disappear
And only the unshakable be left.
What hardihood in any man has part or parcel in the latter?
It is necessary to make a stand and maintain it forever.
These stones go through Man, straight to God, if there is one.
What have they not gone through already?
Empires, civilisations, aeons. Only in them
If in anything, can His creation confront Him.
They came so far out of the water and halted forever.
That larking dallier, the sun, has only been able to play
With superficial by-products since;
The moon moves the waters backwards and forwards,
But the stones cannot be lured an inch farther
Either on this side of eternity or the other.
Who thinks God is easier to know than they are?
Trying to reach men any more, any otherwise, than they are?
These stones will reach us long before we reach them.
Cold, undistracted, eternal and sublime.
They will stem all the torrents of vicissitude forever
With a more than Roman peace.

P

Death is a physical horror to me no more.
I am prepared with everything else to share
Sunshine and darkness and wind and rain
And life and death bare as these rocks though it be
In whatever order nature may decree,
But, not indifferent to the struggle yet
Nor to the ataraxia I might get
By fatalism, a deeper issue see
Than these, or suicide, here confronting me.
It is reality that is at stake.
Being and non-being with equal weapons here
Confront each other for it, non-being unseen
But always on the point, it seems, of showing clear,
Though its reserved contagion may breed
This fancy too in my still susceptible head
And then by its own hidden movement lead
Me as by aesthetic vision to the supposed
Point where by death's logic everything is recomposed,
Object and image one, from their severance freed,
As I sometimes, still wrongly, feel 'twixt this storm beach and me.
What happens to us
Is irrelevant to the world's geology
But what happens to the world's geology
Is not irrelevant to us.
We must reconcile ourselves to the stones,
Not the stones to us.
Here a man must shed the encumbrances that muffle
Contact with elemental things, the subtleties
That seem inseparable from a humane life, and go apart
Into a simple and sterner, more beautiful and more oppressive world,
Austerely intoxicating; the first draught is overpowering;
Few survive it. It fills me with a sense of perfect form,
The end seen from the beginning, as in a song.
It is no song that conveys the feeling
That there is no reason why it should ever stop,
But the kindred form I am conscious of here
Is the beginning and end of the world,
The unsearchable masterpiece, the music of the spheres,

Alpha and Omega, the Omnific Word.
These stones have the silence of supreme creative power,
The direct and undisturbed way of working
Which alone leads to greatness.
What experience has any man crystallised,
What weight of conviction accumulated,
What depth of life suddenly seen entire
In some nigh supernatural moment
And made a symbol and lived up to
With such resolution, such Spartan impassivity?
It is a frenzied and chaotic age,
Like a growth of weeds on the site of a demolished building.
How shall we set ourselves against it,
Imperturbable, inscrutable, in the world and yet not in it,
   Silent under the torments it inflicts upon us,
     With a constant centre,
With a single inspiration, foundations firm and invariable;
     By what immense exercise of will,
Inconceivable discipline, courage, and endurance,
     Self-purification and anti-humanity,
       Be ourselves without interruption,
         Adamantine and inexorable?
It will be ever increasingly necessary to find
In the interests of all mankind
Men capable of rejecting all that all other men
    Think, as a stone remains
Essential to the world, inseparable from it,
    And rejects all other life yet.
Great work cannot be combined with surrender to the crowd.
   – Nay, the truth we seek is as free
From all yet thought as a stone from humanity.
Here where there is neither haze nor hesitation
Something at least of the necessary power has entered into me.
I have still to see any manifestation of the human spirit
That is worthy of a moment's longer exemption than it gets
From petrifaction again – to get out if it can.
All is lithogenesis – or lochia;
And I can desire nothing better,

An immense familiarity with other men's imaginings
Convinces me that they cannot either
(If they could, it would instantly be granted
– The present order must continue till then)
Though, of course, I still keep an open mind,
A mind as open as the grave.
You may say that the truth cannot be crushed out,
That the weight of the whole world may be tumbled on it,
And yet, in puny, distorted, phantasmal shapes albeit,
It will braird again; it will force its way up
Through unexpectable fissures? look over this beach.
What ruderal and rupestrine growth is here?
What crop confirming any credulities?
Conjure a fescue to teach me with from this
And I will listen to you, but until then
Listen to me – Truth is not crushed;
It crushes, gorgonises all else into itself.
The trouble is to know it when you see it?
You will have no trouble with it when you do.
Do not argue with me. Argue with these stones.
Truth has no trouble in knowing itself.
This is it. The hard fact. The inoppugnable reality,
Here is something for you to digest.
Eat this and we'll see what appetite you have left
For a world hereafter.
I pledge you in the first and last crusta,
The rocks rattling in the bead-proof seas.

O we of little faith,
As romanticists viewed the philistinism of their days
As final and were prone to set over against it
Infinite longing rather than manly will –
Nay, as all thinkers and writers find
The indifference of the masses of mankind, –
So are most men with any stone yet,
Even those who juggle with lapidary's, mason's, geologist's words
        And all their knowledge of stones in vain,

Tho' these stones have far more differences in colour, shape and size
    Than most men to my eyes –
Even those who develop precise conceptions to immense distances
    Out of these bleak surfaces.
All human culture is a Goliath to fall
To the least of these pebbles withal.
A certain weight will be added yet
To the arguments of even the most foolish
And all who speak glibly may rest assured
That to better their oratory they will have the whole earth
For a Demosthenean pebble to roll in their mouths.

I am enamoured of the desert at last,
The abode of supreme serenity is necessarily a desert.
My disposition is towards spiritual issues
Made inhumanly clear; I will have nothing interposed
Between my sensitiveness and the barren but beautiful reality;
The deadly clarity of this 'seeing of a hungry man'
Only traces of a fever passing over my vision
Will vary, troubling it indeed, but troubling it only
In such a way that it becomes for a moment
Superhumanly, menacingly clear – the reflection
Of a brightness through a burning crystal.
A culture demands leisure and leisure presupposes
A self-determined rhythm of life; the capacity for solitude
Is its test; by that the desert knows us.
It is not a question of escaping from life
But the reverse – a question of acquiring the power
To exercise the loneliness, the independence, of stones,
And that only comes from knowing that our function remains
However isolated we seem fundamental to life as theirs.
    We have lost the grounds of our being,
    We have not built on rock.
Thinking of all the higher zones
Confronting the spirit of man I know they are bare
Of all so-called culture as any stone here;
Not so much of all literature survives
As any wisp of scriota that thrives

On a rock – (interesting though it may seem to be
As de Bary's and Schwendener's discovery
Of the dual nature of lichens, the partnership,
Symbiosis, of a particular fungus and particular alga).
These bare stones bring me straight back to reality.
    I grasp one of them and I have in my grip
The beginning and the end of the world,
My own self, and as before I never saw
The empty hand of my brother man,
The humanity no culture has reached, the mob.
Intelligentsia, our impossible and imperative job!

'Ah!' you say, 'if only one of these stones would move
– Were it only an inch – of its own accord.
    This is the resurrection we await,
– The stone rolled away from the tomb of the Lord.
    I know there is no weight in infinite space,
        No impermeability in infinite time,
But it is as difficult to understand and have patience here
        As to know that the sublime
Is theirs no less than ours, no less confined
To men than men's to a few men, the stars of their kind.'
    (The masses too have begged bread from stones,
        From human stones, including themselves,
    And only got it, not from their fellow-men,
        But from stones such as these here – if then.)
Detached intellectuals, not one stone will move,
Not the least of them, not a fraction of an inch. It is not
    The reality of life that is hard to know.
It is nearest of all and easiest to grasp,
But you must participate in it to proclaim it.
– I lift a stone; it is the meaning of life I clasp
Which is death, for that is the meaning of death;
How else does any man yet participate
    In the life of a stone,
How else can any man yet become
Sufficiently at one with creation, sufficiently alone,
Till as the stone that covers him he lies dumb

And the stone at the mouth of his grave is not overthrown?
– Each of these stones on this raised beach,
    Every stone in the world,
Covers infinite death, beyond the reach
Of the dead it hides; and cannot be hurled
Aside yet to let any of them come forth, as love
    Once made a stone move
  (Though I do not depend on that
    My case to prove).
So let us beware of death; the stones will have
Their revenge; we have lost all approach to them,
But soon we shall become as those we have betrayed,
And they will seal us fast in our graves
As our indifference and ignorance seals them;
    But let us not be afraid to die.
No heavier and colder and quieter then,
No more motionless, do stones lie
    In death than in life to all men.
It is not more difficult in death than here
– Though slow as the stones the powers develop
To rise from the grave – to get a life worth having;
And in death – unlike life – we lose nothing that is truly ours.

Diallage of the world's debate, end of the long auxesis,
Although no ébrillade of Pegasus can here avail,
I prefer your enchorial characters – the futhorc of the future –
To the hieroglyphics of all the other forms of Nature.
Song, your apprentice encrinite, seems to sweep
The Heavens with a last entrochal movement;
And, with the same word that began it, closes
Earth's vast epanadiplosis.

Placenta Previa; or, The Case of Glasgow

IT'LL be no easy matter to keep the dirt in its place
And get the Future out alive in *this* case!

To R.M.B.

From the Island of Bruse Holm

NAE man, nae spiritual force, can live
In Scotland lang. For God's sake leave it tae
Mak' a warld o' your ain like me, and if
'Idiot' or 'lunatic' the Scots folk say
At least you'll ken – owre weel to argue back
You'd be better that than lackin' a' they lack!

First Love

I HAVE been in this garden of unripe fruit
    All the long day,
Where cold and clear from the hard green apples
    The light fell away.

I was wandering here with my own true love,
    But as I bent o'er,
She dwindled back to her childhood again
    And I saw her no more.

A wind sprang up and a hail of buds
    About me rolled,
Then this fog I knew before I was born
    But now – cold, cold!

The Pot Hat; or, Ballad of the Holy Grail

HE's broken the ceremonial pot
    O, it's broken forever.
Into a thousand orts
    He's gane and gar'd it shiver.

It sat at the feet o' the witches
    Mair lurid than the nails on the toes
O' yon nether maimers squat in their mess
    When he dirled it frae under their nose.

Gloomy under the skinklan' gauds,
    Grumblin' wi' their skins still awash
Wi' the ale, they lout on the hearth-stane
    Beaten, lamentin' the smash.

Huddlin' like thunder cloods they heard him
    Like the lichtnin' laugh
– 'Sorrow on the day we've seen
    This bright blinkin' calf.'

The meet wishin'-bowl o' the carlines
    Is shingle to his wud tide;
The auld mind-can is broken and strewn
    In shards on ilka side.

Frae the beginnin' o' time that moody kettle,
    That roomy-brewin' ewer, was the deep o' rest,
Feasted they did wha got to that lucky well,
    Wham the wily wimmen had as their guest.

Fu' o' hugs they had been for him tae
    And cried him to sit under the ewer
But he hugged ill-will and felt feedin' in him
    The bowl-brakin' poo'er.

Warder o' the seed-spell abode, he'd come hame
    Frae the far hunt when the day was din
Joggin' into the cellar gloomy and icy
    Amang the shaggy kin o' the Inn.

The huggin' Goths were thrang inside
    And the cry gaed up:
'The son o' man has come into the cellar,
    Beware for the magic cup.'

But ane o' the wimmen replied
    In the throes o' her spite and malice:
'Rammin' strong men tho' you are
    Even you canna brak oor chalice.

'There's nane to match it; the mightiest o' Kings
    Canna get its marrow onywhere;
The wale o' truce-cups; the essence
    O' a' Easter's foresight is there.'

Then he seized the broth-stane *glari*[1]
    And slogged it against a pillar,
But it was borne back haill yont her skirts
    And lood was the jeer intill'r.

Syne a voice frae naewhere kennin' the harlot,
    The Eden-seether, the wisdom o' the adder,
Cried: 'Clour it on her heid – for that's harder
    Than ony cauldron on Earth.' Sae he had her.

Risin' frae the knees he brocht the dish doon
    Wi' the haill o' his wecht on the heid
O' yon churlish enchantress and at aince
    The muckle beaker was dung abreid.

'Ochone, my treasure is gane frae me,
    There's nae mendin' this a'e thing sae choice,
Oot through my ain fury gangs the ale-keel o' my hoose.'
    In endless lamentation she's lifted her voice.

---

[1] *Glari*, Icelandic for glass or glazed ware.

He's taen nae notice; stridin' owre the flair
He's lifted the entire ring o' the hull
O' yon ewer o' the Earth-ruiner and worn it
As a holy trophy enringin' his skull.

Damned Colonials

DON'T let us be like damned colonials howlin'
Against God's body-line bowlin'!

Shetland Lyrics:

To 'A. T. CUNNINGHAME'

I

With the Herring Fishers

'I SEE herrin'.' – I hear the glad cry
And 'gainst the moon see ilka blue jowl
In turn as the fishermen haul on the nets
And sing: 'Come, shove in your heids and growl.'

'Soom on, bonnie herrin', soom on,' they shout,
Or 'Come in, O come in, and see me,'
'Come gie the auld man something to dae.
It'll be a braw change frae the sea.'

O it's ane o' the bonniest sichts in the warld
To watch the herrin' come walkin' on board
In the wee sma' 'oors o' a simmer's mornin'
As if o' their ain accord.

For this is the way that God sees life,
The haill jing-bang o's appearin'
Up owre frae the edge o' naethingness
– It's his happy cries I'm hearin'.

'Left, right – O come in and see me,'
Reid and yellow and black and white
Toddlin' up into Heaven thegither
At peep o' day frae the endless night.

'I see herrin',' I hear his glad cry,
And 'gainst the moon see his muckle blue jowl,
As he handles buoy-tow and bush-raip
Singin': 'Come, shove in your heids and growl!'

2
Deep-Sea Fishing

I SUDDENLY saw I was wrang when I felt
That the gapin' mooths and gogglin' een
O' the fish were no' what we should expect
Frae a sea sae infinite and serene.

I kent I'd be equally wrang if I wished
My nice concern wi' its beauty to be
Shared by the fishermen wha's coarser lives
Seemed proof to a' that appealed to me.

Aye, and I kent their animal forms
And primitive minds, like fish frae the sea,
Cam' faur mair naturally oot o' the bland
Omnipotence o' God than a fribble like me.

3
Colla Firth in Winter

NAE mair wi' a bricht kerchief rowed roon her heid
Bonnie lass by bonnie lass eidently bends
Owre the lang row o' farlins doon the quayside
Wi' piles o' glitterin' herrin' at her quick finger ends.

There's a press o' craft roond the pierheid nae mair,
Sailin' boats, motor boats, drifters and a'
Wi' cran baskets swingin' and trollies kept ga'en
A' the 'oors o' the mornin' as hard's they can ca'.

I dodge oot and in o' the shadowy voes
Wi' nae fishermen to crack wi', nae lassies to tease.
There's naething to hear and naething to see
Save whiles a ferlie my ain spirit gi'es.

Why am *I* still here while a' else is awa'?
Why has time ta'en the lave and spared naething but me?
Is it freendship or juist the whim o' a foe?
Naething else can I miss wi' this riddle to ree!

4
A Daughter of the Sea

A WUMMAN cam' up frae the blae deeps o' the sea
And 'I'm Jeannie MacQueen,' she said, lauchin', to me.

But it's 'Gi way wi' your oyster-shine, lassie, gi way'
– For she'd a different colour in the nail o' each tae.

5
Gruney

YOU say there's naething here
        But a bank o' snaw?
But the sun whiles shows in't
        Gleg een ana'.

I'll be like these white birds
        Sittin' facin' the ocean
Wi' here and there in their stillness
        Vigil's pin–point motion.

6
The Bonxie[1]

I'LL be the Bonxie, that noble scua,
That infects a' ither birds wi' its qualms.
In its presence even the eagle
Forbears to pounce on the lambs.

For it fechts wi' nocht less than itsel'
And prefers to encoonter great odds.
Guid-bye to mankind. Henceforth I'll engage
Only angels, archangels, devils and gods.

7
To a Sea Eagle

I USED to walk on solid gr'und
Till it fell awa' frae my feet
And, left in the void, I'd instantly
To get accustomed wi't.

Watchin' your prood flight noo I feel
As a man may dae wi' a bairn,
For withoot ony show at a'
In deeper abysses I'm farin'.

Aye, withoot ony show at a',
Save whiles a sang I may sing
Gets in resonance wi' the sun
And ootshines't like a turnin' wing.

8
De Profundis

I DELIGHT in this naethingness
Mair than ever I did
In the creation it yielded
And has aince mair hid.

[1] The Great Scua.

Sae an ardent spirit
Should submerge a' it's learned
And enjoy to the full
Whatna leisure it's earned.

For what is the end
O' a' labour but this?
– Earth's fruits to the flesh;
To the soul the Abyss.

9
Shags' Nests

SHAGS build their slatternly nests
On a ledge o' a slot
In the rocky coast, where they're easily found
Frae below by a man in a boat.

But they canna be seen frae abune
– And in that remind me
Aince mair o' the death-bound spirits o' men
That, climbin', I've left behind me.

10
Mirror Fugue

WHILES I've seen a wheen gulls
Seem to equal the croods
O' the white waves by joinin'
Hands wi' the cloods,
Till atween them they've made
A complete and clear
Heavenly facsimile
O' the hydrosphere
– Till the shapes in the lift
And the seas' wild smother
Seemed baith to mak'
And to mirror each other.

But my thochts that gang questin'
    Abune the haill earth
Whiles fly where there's naething
    To eke oot their dearth.
They are to the laigh then
Like the stars or the sun
Where ony reflection's
Confined to the one
        – They are to the Earth
        Like licht, or its lack,
        Earth maun tak' as it gets
        And no' answer back.

And they are to the heich
    – Wha can tell what they are?
Or chart the diplomacy
    O' star upon star?
For the Earth is a star
As weel as the neist
Tho' few are alive
To the fact in the least
        – And for a' I can ken
        My fremt notions may be
        Hand in glove wi' a' else
        In ways kittle to see.

Ostentatiously tho' the gulls
Wi' the cloods dado up
I'm content to establish
A mair gingerly grup.
As wi' flash upon flash
O' sheet-lichtnin' in space
The relation atween them
Is whiles ill to trace.
        Sae wi' thocht upon thocht
        There's a structure nae doot,
        But I'm blithe in the meantime
        Juist to hae them glint oot.

Aye, wi' thocht upon thocht,
Like the wild-fire playin'
My richt hand needna ken
What my left hand's da'en.
Tho' the seas' wud marble
In a mackerel lift's glassed
Through the hollow globe flaughts
Frae ootside it are cast
  Flames fickler to partner
  Than the gulls and the cirrus.
  But the cutchack can wait
  While the gleids still bewhirr us.

For the queerest sensation
Intriguin' the air
A' agog for the former
Is there – and no' there.
The queerest sensation
Intriguin' the air
Kyths kir as a rabbit.
And whuds through a gair.

Glory on the water and grace in the welkin
But how sall I follow this flicker away,
Why follow, how fail, this fey flicker there,
  This faint flicker where,
Wi' my wingbeats biddin' good-bye to the gulls,
To the sea, and the sun, and a' the laigh?

Ex-Parte Statement on the Project of Cancer

*It is certain that all bodies whatsoever, though they have no sense, yet have perception . . .
and whether the body be alterant or altered, evermore a perception precedeth operation;
for else all bodies would be alike one to another. . . .*

                                        FRANCIS BACON: *Natural History*.

            YOU say cancer's increasin'
            – No' juist in me –
            And wonder what the reason
                For that can be.
            Aiblins I can tell you
            If you'll listen a wee.

If I canna juist claim to speak
'Frae the inside' yet
I ken something o' the maitter frae 'the growin' end'
        And keep learnin' bit by bit,
And as there's whiles a green light in the sky that looks
Frae an alien and enemy world a'thegither,
Tho' it's juist as natural as ony ither,
Believe you me there's a light whiles comes
Frae the thing itsel' in yin's thingumyums
That brings a third apparatus o' sight
(Neither the ane we use in daylight
Nor look at a reid light in darkness wi')
Into use automatic'ly
– A provision we wadna ken we had ava',
Ony mair than maist folk ken they've even twa',
        If the need for't didna arise
        And ca' on oor eyes
To cope wi' cases makin' the difference atween
Say a bird's eye view and a worm's eye view
Juist tweedledum and tweedledee, if you ken what I mean.
        – Cancer's no' sae easy to see through.
        (I'm no' concerned here to deal
        Wi' the kind o' sight in a' we feel

Or the poo'er o' things like cancer to reveal
Oor nature to us in unco ways
That are only for oor privy gaze,
And I needna refer to the way
We cancerous ken each ither – almost as 'homo's' dae)
But science has advanced a lot lately
    As a'body kens – or thinks he kens –
And, put bluntly, to my mind it's nae
        Mere coincidence
That cancer's increasin' pari passu.

But afore I leave the question o' sight
– Or insight in t'it as you might say –
It was anither poet, if I mind right,
      Wha ettled to display
    The fact that no' juist the eyes
    But ilka pairt o' the body
    Can see, should occasion arise.
The vision extra-retinière
He ca'd it, and fegs he didna err,
But the apparatus involved and what they see
Varies of course indescribably
And isna juist on a par at a'
Wi' Sir John Parsons' twa
– The arrangement o' achromatic scotopic vision
In a hauf-light wi' its primitive rod apparatus,
As compared wi' chromatic photopic vision
In sunlight by means o' the cone mechanism.
– That juist tak's us
    To the fringe o' the schism!

The point to seize on is this
If we're to plumb the abyss.
Sir John was right in findin'
A parallel atween that dual vision
And the protopathic-epicritic opposition
In sensation – but he ended where I begin,
He was nearer my mark in sayin'

The mechanism o' the eyes and muscular movements
O' the eyeballs and eyebrows, and o' hand and body
    To the eyes through the pulvinar,
Mak' a system o' massed co-ordinated
Parallel-performances that ha'e nae maik
In the human frame *or indeed elsewhere*
– Mark these last three words! But is cancer not
Anither apparatus – yieldin' the greatest vision o' the lot?

Rilke was wrang when he said that the world
Is aye tryin' to become invisible in the minds o' men.
Au contraire, it's tryin' to become visible, baith in life
And, syne, differently adjusted, in daith again;
        And I think it's beginnin' to succeed
        At last – at least in an antrin heid.

But it's mair than the duality o' oor sensory system
That'll ha'e to be conclusively unfurled
– Millions o' poo'ers that ha'e similarly missed them –
Afore men comprehend the world!
Yet they've made progress in the last few years.
Got windows in mony o' their cerebral recesses
Tho' still geyly darkened wi' ignorance and fears
        And cursèd anthropocentricism
        – That worst astigmatism.
The nuclei o' the thalamus provoke new guesses,
The lobby o' the latticed layer[1]
Is treated wi' contempt nae mair,
Aye, they ken the pulvinar's nae cushion where
Fancy can rest idly, the thalamus nae retreat,
Nae chamber o' seclusion, as the Greeks were wont to ca' it,
    But gaird a region o' unceasin'
    Originatin' activity. I've a reason
    For stressin' that second adjective
    Connected wi' the way I live
    And sune maun cease to live
    (Yach! Dinna let that give you sic a frisson.
    Cancer breeds as you'd expect

---

[1] The 'intercalated cell.'

A humour sib to the subject.[1]
Yin maun give and take. The way
Cancer mak's maist folk grue
Is naething to the way
Non-cancerous life mak's cancer grue.
You talk aboot the soul, where I'm
Ta'en up wi' chorionic villi a' the time.
The natural subjects o' my talk
Are things like apogamy and yelk-stalk;
And if you'll permit anither joke
– Altho' I've nae desire to shock –
Cancer's trophoblastic character
Chimes wi' my puritan instincts, sir!)
In the limited sense that you'll
Hear the word 'life' used as a rule
– As if cancer tae wasna a livin' thing,
Mair livin' than the rest o' me, by jing!,
Aye, and a' the processes that run
Frae oor corpses in the grun'.

But to gang back. I said: 'Wi' nae maik
In the human frame or indeed elsewhere.'
Mind this, and it'll put you on the right track.
'*It tak's a man o' brains to be a paranoiac.*'
(I'm no' juist thinkin' o' the way defeated Germany
After vain struggles is seekin' refuge at last
By livin' in the darkest aspects o' itsel',
Gives the future an anal kiss, finds its hope in Hell,
As the likeliest way, the sooner the better,
O' throwin' off the intolerable strains
Oor present system imposes on man,
Altho' the rest o' us may stand aghast
And deliberate whether we should let her
We may come to it oorsel's afore lang tae,
Tho' the fatal, the self-destructive, urge o' humanity

[1] Scotland's been sayin' for mony a year:
'Noo look here, MacDiarmid. Get this clear.
We want nane o' your monousious humour here!'

Towards civilisation is no' sae easily
To be jouked, I doot. Ah, weel, we'll see,
But what it really seems impossible to dae
–Except for the Nietzsches and Baudelaires, and me –
Is to live in baith worlds at aince; and Cancer
And ither diseases, and daith, provide little answer
    To that problem either, for they
    A' strive for a monopoly,
    They're a' fu' o' Diesseitigkeit,
    Destitute o' Moralität, averse to Sittlichkeit.)
    But there's nae reason kent to science why
    Ony psychological impulse a man comes by
    Shouldna pursue *an independent course*
    Forever 'yont a' regaird for its original source,
    – And organised life has aye a kittle time indeed
    To keep its components frae fleein' abreid.

You see what I'm drivin' at. My inside knowledge tells
Me Cancer comes frae vagrant primary germ-cells
Which, instead o' formin' a mair or less complete
Embryo or embryoma juist delete
That customary gesture to normal life, skip it, and give rise
(Cancer, by crikey, kens nae compromise!)
To a larva or phorozoon o' *indefinite*
Unrestricted poo'ers o' growth! You get
My meanin' noo? Cast back your mind's eyes
Owre the five phrases I've had to italicise
And you'll see the connection that amang them lies.
– Ech! Germany hasna gane nearly far enough,
I doot – the 'verirrte Keime' are the stuff.
    Aye – it'll pay you to recollect it –
    'The stane that the builders rejected.'
    Life in daith – this is the thought sublime;
    Das Werden in das Vergehen all the time!

Remember what I said aboot sight, and, list!
– I stress anither adjective to keep my implication terse –
Than trypsin and amylopsin there probably exist
Nae mair powerfu' substances in the *visible* universe.

Visible to whom, I ask – and wait the answer.
They werena strong enough to stare oot my cancer.

There's been nae advance in the human intellect for the past
Twa thoosand years at least, and if Nature at last
Has given up hope, found that a cul-de-sac,
The increase o' cancer may mean she's harkit back
(Changed her gait to gang – if you nab
My seely punnin' – sidelins like a crab)
To an alternative she's aye had up her sleeve.
I'm a prejudiced pairty nae doot, but sae are you
Upon the ither side, and tho' it's true
I've mebbies aye been predisposed this way
– Through a lang alternation o' generations tae –
You'll admit at least I've a fair inklin'
Into your kind o' life, while you've nae wrinklin'
O' first-hand knowledge o' mine – I can see them baith
In pairt at least, and lookin' at the world the day
And thinkin' o' maist men and their prospects I can say
Wi' a' moderation: 'There's mony waur things than Cancer, faith!'

And if I translated the sense o' cancer directly
Into words — O they exist, in Scots — they would be
To almost a 'body else like those Berlioz invented
For his *Chorus o' Shades*[1] and syne repented;
But drunk wi' implacable will and mordacity.

On The Oxford Book of Victorian Verse

MOST poets to a muse that is stone-deaf cry.
This English poetry that they vaunt so high,
What is it except for two or three men
Whose best work is beyond all but a few men's ken?

[1]For 'this language of the dead, incomprehensible to the living,' Berlioz wrote
a pure gibberish – of which the censor demanded a translation – but subsequently
substituted French in this composition, saving his unknown tongue for the
Damnation de Faust.

Stupidity will not accept the fact, and so
Cheek by jowl with Shakespeare and Milton must go
Even in famous anthologies the incredibly small,
A Domett, Toke Lynch, and Wathen Mark Call.

A horde no man is the better for reading,
A horde no man is the worse for not heeding,
Create with these the notion that poetry's less rare
Than it is; that there's something for most men there.

Something – but what? Poetry's not written for men
And lies always beyond all but all men's ken
– Only fools – countless fools – are deceived by the claims
Of a Menella Bute Smedley and most other names.

So when this book is revised for reissue
Let us have you included lest somebody should miss you.
Here with your peers – Squire, Church, and Strong,
Masefield, Noyes, de la Mare. *Oh Lord! how long?*[1]

Towards a New Scotland

I

IN these lane voes whaur the airms o' bare land
Lie on the grey waters like shadows oor boat
Seems to haud a' the life that there is – there's nae need
To rin a line oot; there's nae fish to be got
        – Yet aye there's a cry, 'I see white in the lum'
        And up on the line coontless ferlies come.

[1] The names at the end were objected to and in the first edition the last two lines
were printed as:
        Here with your peers – Spoof, Dubb, and Blong,
        Smiffkins, Pimple, and Jingle. *Oh Lord! how long?*

Toom tho' the waters may look, useless oor quest,
We find on ilka hook a yield 'yont a' hope
– A scallop, a hoo, a sea-sponge, and syne
A halibut big as a table-top
    – Never say die; tho' auld Scotland seems bare
    Oot wi' your line; there's prodigies there.

II

As the hills o' Morven were hills afore
The Himalayas or Alps were born
And established through a' geological time,
Can look at sic muckle ephemera wi' scorn

Sayin': 'We saw you come and we'll see you gang
Nae maitter hoo you may too'er the day,'
Sae a' the giantisms o' England and Empire
Auld Scotland can dismiss in the self-same way.

III

Was it for little Belgium's sake
Sae mony thoosand Scotsmen dee'd?
And never ane for Scotland fegs
Wi' twenty thoosand times mair need!

IV

I wad dae onything for you, Scotland, save
– Even tho' your true line should be wi' such –
Become like ninety per cent o' Scots;
That 'ud be askin' faur owre much!

V

Ah, Scotland, you ken best. Why should I complain
That my poo'ers tae canna redound to you,
But micht hae been jewels elsewhere if I'd foreseen
    An' been to you a kennin' mair untrue?

Why should I complain when for centuries back
You've cast sae muckle aside that maist men deem
The best you bred – maist fit to serve and honour you,
    And elsewhere these worthless glories gleam?

Why I should complain wha least o' a' men rate
What you rejected as foreigners and renegades rate,
But at whatever cost approve your barrenness
    Faur abune a' their meretricious state?

The time isna ripe yet and in vain I hae tried
To separate the base elements you ne'er could accept
Frae sic faint forerinners o' your comin' dawn
    As whiles I thocht within me leapt.

Ah, Scotland, you ken best. I've been hailly wrang,
Mista'en bog-fires for your true licht at last.
Yet gladly I rejected ither literatures for yours,
    Nor covet them noo you've ootcast!

And sae my failure suddenly reveals itsel'
A pairt – a strengthenin' – o' your reserved intent;
Harder the task, greater the triumph; I'm prood to be
    Failin' the latter wi' the former blent.

Ah, Scotland, you ken best. Why should I complain
That my poo'ers tae canna redound to you;
They couldna been jewels elsewhere; I couldna been
    To you ony mair – or less – untrue!

VI

My dreams for you, Scotland, no' till I heard
Them repeated on ither folks' lips did I ken
Their utter inadequacy to your need
And rejoice in your steadfast sterility again.

My dreams for you, Scotland, they flamed in me
To a monstrous height while I dreamed them alane;
I kent they were better than ocht that opposed
Save you – and you hadna spoken to me then.

My dreams for you, Scotland, as soon as I heard
Ithers cry I was right and repeat what I'd said
I kent I was hopelessly wrang and was glad
O' the light sic fools inadvertently shed!

VII

Let nae man think he can serve you, Scotland,
Withoot muckle trial and trouble to himsel'.
The slightest service to you compares
Wi' fetchin' a bit o' Heaven doon into Hell.

Let wha wad serve you reflect for a minute
On a' the thoosands that seemed to and failed to
– Ony service demands heich qualities then
These coontless thoosands ne'er scaled to.

And even at the best hoo mony folk coont
O' the least consequence to you since Time began.
Lightly to fancy he's o' the favoured few
Nearly aye disposes o' the claims o' a man.

Nay, fegs, it's wi' you as wi' a lion-cub
A man may fetch hame and can play wi' at first,
But if he has it lang, it grows up and syne
– Suddenly his fool's paradise is burst!

VIII

Surely the weediest of all the sons of Mars,
    The final shakings of his poke,
A pimply-faced Cockney soldier in Edinburgh Castle
    I saw, and thus he spoke.

Looking down upon the heaving city there
    As o'er the precipice he spat:
'Gor-blimey, we've made Scotland wot she is;
    Wot would she be wivaht?'

From 'The War with England'

THE social scene could be little
    But confusion and loss to me,
And, Scotland, better than all your towns
    Was a bed of moss to me.
I had to lie on the hills and watch
The founts that to keep their tryst
Had found their way through the wards of the rock
Slower than the second coming of Christ
    To know how my task was priced.

I was better with the sounds of the sea
    Than with the voices of men
And in desolate and desert places
    I found myself again.
For the whole of the world came from these
And he who returns to the source
May gauge the worth of the outcome
And approve and perhaps reinforce
Or disapprove and perhaps change its course.

Now I deal with the hills at their roots
    And the streams at their springs
And am to the land that I love
    As he who brings
His bride home, and they know each other
Not as erst, like their friends, they have done,
But carnally, causally, knowing that only
By life nigh undone can life be begun,
    And accept and are one.
– *When was anything born in Scotland last,*
    Risks taken and triumphs won?

Hymn to Sophia: The Wisdom of God

(See *La Russie et l'Eglise Universelle*, by Vladimir Solovyov)

OUR broken cries of shame dispute
 Death's pitiless and impious law
As the whole Earth with straining hearts
 Towards thee we draw.

Conscious that still in sexes split
 And generations without end,
We cannot to the emprise yet
 A due strength bend.

And the rose knows us not and wastes
 Its precious power; and in the stone
Obliviously sleeps a strength
 Beyond our own.

Yet will creation turn to thee
 When, love being perfect, naught can die,
And clod and plant and animal
 And star and sky,

Thy form immortal and complete,
 Matter and spirit one, acquire,
– *Ceaseless till then, O Sacred Shame,*
 Our wills inspire!

The Progress of Poetry

A FEW moments ago I would fain have thought
Of the movements that from age to age produced
The great crustal arches and downfolds and thus wrought
Vast changes of land and sea.

Now I am loosed.
There seems a vaster change in me.
Unthinkable for a moment as if they were not
Those fragments of which I had hoped to think
In Skye and the Ord of Caithness, with all my beloved lot
Of cornbrash, and coral rag, and forest marble sink
Below my speculative power – yet not from my spirit's sight
But each as when a film unexpectedly stops running
And dynamic significance is lost and one sees instead
A sharp static beauty and feels after all it is sometimes grand
To look long and intently at one thing at a time,
So, dissociated from my stream of consciousness, these
Familiar objects of my thought are separated
From all their usual aspects and stand
In a strangeness fools might deem sublime
Like that appearance of a new earth and heaven
　　　To an airman given
When he first sees a cloud's upper surface below
Him carved dazzlingly like a field of mountainous snow.
This has been a test perhaps to see if I
Would even yet to mere fancy fall
Or be, as beneath a Mediterranean sky
Content to turn subject into object withal,
To that outwardness of which the limestone relief in that clear light
Is both encouragement and model – though the power
Of concentrating on the object of passionate thought until
It seems to come to life and exist of its own right
Has not tempted me in this trying hour
As fully as it might perhaps – I have not felt the awe,
I have not seen in these bright stationary forms
That flow begin which is the law
Of all creative work, until they rise
To the full height of the imaginative act
That wins to the reality in the fact,
And child of our incalculable Scottish storms
Suddenly I see with ecstasy
(My life resuming its normal course
And all my beloved stones

And other old interests – and none as if by force –
Taking their place in it as easily
As in that clear still scene, but with very different tones,
Colours and appearances – now dark, tumultuous, and to my heart)
Elpeodigra eard, and know I must go there,
Not in a swift ship over the blue Aegean sea,
Or fishing boat leaping to the flash
Of red oars in the early sunlight
In Phaleron Bay, but over cold knotted hacking waters where
Nap nihtscua, and no presentness, greets art.
Far, far, and nigh impossible is this journey
Abandoned by almost all men else, and rash
Would any man be of mere whim to venture so,
But the *gana* rises in me and I go
(Walking off with Villon who found out for himself
What all subsequent French poetry consists of forgetting,
And on that ever darker and more difficult course,
The progress of poetry to the present day,
That leads from the proud adventures of the Theban eagle
'With a voice for the intelligent,' full of shafts
From the current politics of Athens, Thebes, Aegina, and the gossip
Of the Court of Heiro and the famous fancy
Of the shrill whetstone on the tongue which drew him on
Gratifying the superior senses, to Meredith's
'Death is the word of a bovine day'
And all his acrobatic figurations, and so
To the marvellous obscurity of Rilke
Where what begin as metaphors all turn
To autonomous imaginative realities all pursuing
Their infinitely complicated ways on ampler pinions
Than sailed yon azure deep. Poetry has suffered no decline
In leaving gold shining like a blazing fire at night
Above all other lordly wealth to come thus far
To 'the crooked trouble-laden Embryo
That holds, as though it feared some frightfulness,
Its hands before its half-completed eyes
And on whose high domed forehead sits the fear
Of all those things which it has never suffered' . . .)

And already, see, in the dark forms as never in the clear,
The vague cavernous shade in which the common people move,
The spirit rises, and all my friends are here,
Every myrionous human Calvary of modern life,
And I bid farewell to the melancholy, the disillusion,
The ideal heavenly virgins, the moon, the hate of our kind,
Vanished youth, and all juvenile enthusiasms, . . .
Hail, Gogol, we are of like mind!
I seek to plumb no deeper yet awhile,
My engine's taken up the depth I dropped again
Through the great overfall and's in the famous plume,
Prodigious jet of rushing winds that fling
A barrage of ice for miles to leeward of the peak
Over whose summit now I find the slip-stream
Strangely bereft of its accustomed force.

Balefire Loch[1]

O NEVER heed the earnin'-grass,
        The foolstanes and the carmele,
Be edgie if you're to come wi' me.
        The artation's wi' yersel'.

It's a cauld coal to blaw at,
        Ilka step'll be to your clift
Owre cobblie grun' for switchbells even
        To the middle o' the lift.

[1] It seems advisable to gloss a few words in this poem (which, like passages in my 'Water Music' and 'Scots Unbound,' is primarily an exercise of delight in the Scots sense of colour), viz: earnin'-grass, butterwort; foolstanes, orchis morio, and mascula (Linnaeus); carmele, heath-peas (Gaelic, cairmeal); clift, crotch; duchas (guttural), ancestral home or hereditary provenance; cheliderect, a kind of serpent; cheirotherium, labyrinthodont; green-sloke, oyster-green; blehand, a brownish colour inclining to purple or violet; cannel, cinnamon; bawd's bree, (the colour of) hare soup; baudequin, tissue de fil d'or; arress, stone-edge; bedene, in sequence; on grufe, lie flat on your belly; bank, ruff or roll.

To the bezel, collet, cabochon
    O' the ring that hauds the jewel,
The chine o' the bottomless barrel o' Hell,
    The hob o' the quenchless fuel.

Up, up, into the dullyeart heights
    O' this duchas o' my dreams!
The swallow bigs in the cot-hoose wa';
    The phoenix there it seems.

Nae fish can live but the cardui there,
    The bonniest o' them a',
Wi' its dark olive back and bright reid belly,
    And underfins crimson and snaw.

And nocht else save whiles a cheliderect
    'Neath the butter-docks shoots green-sloke,
Or a cheirotherium still lays a hand
    On a dour unprintable rock.

Haul yersel' up by the blasted birns
    And lower on the doudlar syne
Till you turn an arress whaur the sun
    Inalow you seems to shine.

On grufe, and stop your groozin' syne,
    Like a top the waters spin.
Blehand and cannel their colours flee,
    Bawd's-bree to baudequin.

As if to twice its erstwhile size,
    Deil's addle at its root,
Fusin' a' darkness and a' light
    The sun had floo'ered oot.

Pitmirk and noon in ane combined,
    But stained wi' richer dyes
Than either had that blout by blout
    These deeps bedene devise.

While owre us muckle lintwhite cloods
  Like the bare doups o' pious Jews,
Gang up on catsteps as it were
  Frae this sacred pool they use.

The bandless gas beats mony a bank
  Amang yon glairy alga yet,
Bide whaur ye are! There's time eneuch
  To plumb and scale the infinite.

Scotland's Pride

LET us have no more talk of the service they gave,
Tell us no more as you have told us so long
That these were noble or clever or brave,
And deserve their place your great sons among;
Take a hundred years and let the facts decide.
Put all the conventional tributes aside,
And who's done aught for you, Scotland? Who's tried?

Have we fewer starving, fewer in want
In Scotland during the period in review?
Have we fewer slums despite all the cant,
Or thousands of homes yet that would make swine spew?
Is there less land under cultivation or more?
Aren't we worse off on every score?
Then what the Hell are they famous for?

All your nobility can be stroked off first,
Titles they may have – but none to respect.
No country in the world has ever been cursed
With such a gang of hyaenas as have somehow annexed
All your dukedoms and earldoms and historic estates,
No man of them heeds save in as much as he gets
Wealth to waste in London who would else starve on his wits.

Your divines come next. They may have served God,
But they have certainly rendered no service to man;
The prestige you give them is undoubtedly odd,
Since great though they be not even you can
Once they are dead say who the Devil they were,
But in ninety-nine cases in a hundred prefer
To forget them completely and in that do not err.

As for your politicians, not a man of them's been
Other than a servant of your deadliest foe.
Look round the whole country to-day and it's seen
Not one of them has aught to his credit to show.
Notable statesmen no doubt – but for whose good but their own?
Come, let any use they've accomplished be shown,
Your affairs all to rack and to ruin have gone.

You've had your usual supply of so-called great sons
In the period in question, but their filial regard
Wouldn't do credit, it seems, to a skunk's ones,
And if you still think that this verdict's too hard,
To problems a damned sight harder you're tied,
And the only men who have really tried
To solve them are a few on the rebel side,
Despised, rejected, hounded down and decried
By the fools on whom like a fool you've relied.

The Little White Rose

To John Gawsworth

THE rose of all the world is not for me.
I want for my part
Only the little white rose of Scotland
That smells sharp and sweet – and breaks the heart.

Cattle Show

I SHALL go among red faces and virile voices,
See stylish sheep, with fine heads and well-wooled,
And great bulls mellow to the touch,
Brood mares of marvellous approach, and geldings
With sharp and flinty bones and silken hair.

And through th' enclosure draped in red and gold
I shall pass on to spheres more vivid yet
Where countesses' coque feathers gleam and glow
And, swathed in silks, the painted ladies are
Whose laughter plays like summer lightning there.

In a Neglected Graveyard

HERE lies Walter Elliot
Under a stone to tell you that
You needn't restrict
        Agricultural supplies
Any longer – now he's here
        To help them to rise;
In his right place at last,
Making up for his past.

Lament for the Great Music

FOLD of value in the world west from Greece
Over whom it has been our duty to keep guard
Have we slept on our watch; have death and dishonour

Reached you through our neglect and left you in lasting sleep?
That we see you no longer and are as body without soul,
Nidh inmheadhonach idir bheith ann agus gan bheith ann![1]

Vain as Christ's cry upon the cross the sense
Of God's desertion or that endless exile
To which God does not matter since it springs
From the incommensurableness of men's desires and goods,
Each man, like the angels of St. Thomas, a separate species
Tending to a unique perfection so that even God
Cannot redeem the exile. Vain as Christ's cry
If that indeed were vain, as in vain we ask!
To remember the great music and to look
At Scotland and the world to-day is to hear
An Barr Buadh[2] again where there are none to answer
And to feel like *Oisín d' éis na Féine*[3] or like Christ
          In that least homoousian hour.

Vain as Christ's cry in Scotland to-day,
Vain as the early Christians' superstitious expectation
(As when the cumulus clouds proper to thunder
In addition to their own conjunction of high light and deep shadow
Take on the wildly prophetic colours of snow)
Which those who call themselves Christians now
(Reconciled to an indefinite postponement of the blessed occasion)
Say was happily mistaken, since from that disappointment
– One of the first great purifications of the Christian faith –
The Christianity which they have inherited has grown,
– 'Yellow with God'![4] *Ionmolta malairt bhisigh,*[5]
So doubtless we are truer Scots, truer men,
Despite mere appearances than you old masters of the *Ceol Mor*.

[1] 'A somewhat in a state between existence and non-existence.'
[2] The horn with which Fionn summoned his battalions; also the name Padraic Pearse gave it when he founded a little Gaelic paper wherewith to arouse national idealism.
[3] A withered babbling old man, 'Oisín after the Fiana' (i.e. when his love for Ireland made him return to it from Tír na n-Óg), in that immortal phrase which has in it more than Virgilian tears.
[4] One of Séan Ó Neachtain's comical instances of the blunders of would-be speakers of English, as when the clown says 'yellow with God' for *buidhe le Dia*.
[5] Eochy O'Hosey's pungent, 'A Change for the Better Deserves Praise!'

And, besides, as *The Scotsman* says, it is likely enough
The great music has had a real if imponderable influence
On subsequent piping after all – like Christ on the Kirk!
     – My God, can you not read history and see
     They have never had what you are fain to save?

Who would wish to undo nineteen hundred years
Of world-history and Christian experience, let alone
Scotland's vast progress in the last century or so?
There's no knowing what greater purifications are to come.
I feel them in my bones. Even we, we Christians and Scots
Will soon seem as primitive and impure – *as na cianaibh*[1] –
As the earliest Christians or you do to us.

Are we, looking at all the accumulated wealth
Of Scotland to-day, to be as foolish as Fearghal
And for the sake of a few pibroch – for *Scarcity of Fish*,
Lament for the Children, and *The Pretty Dirk*[2] –
Cry like him: 'In that bright land of shining fields
I received not the Lord's Body . . . I was deceived . . .
Though I owned all Alba, better were one mass!'
Or prize a *cruit*[3] of Irish wood above all our forests?

Is it any argument to say that the Pope of Rome
And England's Primate and Scotland's Moderator
And their countless underlings would not recognise
Christ if he appeared among them, or at least
Not immediately, especially if he appeared
(Not privily to one of them, when the rest
Would all the more disbelieve – but to all)
In a Byzantine guise – in the unfamiliar,
Somewhat familiarly unfamiliar, guise not of the Canon
But of the uncanonical writings and made them feel

[1] From strange lands.
[2] 'Scarcity of Fish,' 'Lament for the Children,' 'The Pretty Dirk' – names of great pibroch.
[3] Hand-harp; a famous story in bardic history when Gilbride came to Scotland to recover Donough's *cruit* and received the answer that its own possessor prized it above all Scotland's forests, although it was only a bit of an Irish tree.

A sense of spiritual reversion? Surely it would be
Against the spirit of the religion whose fundamental charter
Is that 'God so loved the world,' for a figure
So mysterious, and tremendous, and above all forbidding
As would denounce all the practical necessities of life
And know nothing of the growth of Immanentism,
The revelation of unity in the widest differences,
And the steady elimination from religion
Of the sheer arbitrariness that during its history
Friend and foe alike so often attributed to it
(And not even speak in the *beurla*[1] at that
But in an uncouth jargon almost as bad as Scots)
To emerge at this juncture – like a bull in a china shop?

> *Cibé eaglais leanas siad*
> *ní tháinig riamh rompa féin*
> *má sí sin an eaglais fhíor*
> *cionnas shaorfaid Críost ar bhréig.*[2]

It is equally absurd to say that most of those
Keenest on pipe-music only know its degenerate forms,
And that these are the foes of the great music
Not knowing the difference between studying you and knowing you.
It is equally absurd to say that lovers of music
The world over have neglected you to their loss,
That you showed the way to far greater heights
Than all the other courses music has followed.
Is the whole of modern music to be dismissed
With derision and scorn as when Gráinne
Having lost a romantic husband decided to settle down
With a rich and important one, and married Fionn,
And Oisin cried, while she bowed her head with shame,
'*Dar linne, a Fhinn, coimheudfair féin Gráinne go maith as so suas!*'[3]
But if there be any in the world susceptible

---

[1] The English language.
[2] 'Whatsoever Church they *follow* it never was in being *before* themselves; if that then be the true Church how will they exonerate Christ from lying?' (Giolla Brighde Ó Heoghusa, died 1614).
[3] 'It is likely, Fionn, that you will take good care of Grainne henceforward!'

Of loyalty to the great music yet, such words of mine
Will be no *Ard-fostadha-na-féinne.*[1]
No matter how contemptuously I dismiss the plea
That an intelligence other than human, even if capable
Of understanding our concepts, would probably see no reason
For interpreting the universe as we must, your music
As I hear it is not as you did and may well be
Unrecognisable to you. You were good Catholics
– Watching me narrowly now from the *dachaidh bhuan*[2] –
And your attitude to the course of history
And to your contemporary duties was similar to theirs
And indeed you islanders knew and I cannot deny
That the shells of molluscs generally have a dextral screw
Since a right-twisted shell lies apt for the waves
Breaking upon it to press it more closely to the rock;
And there are ingenious ways of accounting
For occasional left-twisted shells! All this
Only shows how far from the great music I am.
Gabhlánach an rud an scéaluidheacht.[3]
If I cannot reach any satisfactory solution
Of the problem of God's relation to time
Your art is more inexplicable in terms of your beliefs
Than men's lack of it to-day in terms of theirs.
Meaning regarded as an end of desire is value
And unifies succession in time. Like Christianity
Your art is *sui generis* and since it refuses
Any explanation in terms of the ordinary forces
Laws and standards of the world, we must seek
An interpretation of these in terms of it
Or find something analogous to the fact that the God
Of Christianity may appear adequate
If not as an explanation at least as a solution
Of the world we know; and quarrel no more

[1] The Height of the arrestation of the Fiana, where under the influence of a cozening fairy-woman's mischief Fionn lost his head and hurled venomous reproaches at his chieftains till they all deserted him, but Caoilte ran after them and prevailed on them to return.
[2] The everlasting home.
[3] 'Romances are involved in affairs.'

With the cry that history had to happen
    And is its own justification.

These things will pass. 'The world will come to an end
But love and music will last for ever.'
Sumeria is buried in the desert sands,
Atlantis in the ocean waves – happier these
Than Scotland, for all is gone, no travesty
Of their ancient glories lives
On the lips of degenerate sons as here.
That is what is hard to bear; the decivilised have every grace
As the antecedent of their vulgarities,
Every distinction as the precedent of their mediocrities,
No silly tune but has the excuse
That the feint was suggested, made easy,
By some once living sweetness.
Pride they have bartered for a lowly mind.
Some forgetfulness has befallen these sons of Scotland
If they suppose it suffices to claim Scotland
In virtue of shooting the grouse or as the price
Of drinking whisky – a vulgar doggerel
Concocted plainly, without excess of involution,
Prospers best now! Praise no man nor any satirise!
    An mhaith do bhí ná bí dhi
    An mhaith atá, tar tairse . . .[1]

We wear our laurels with a difference,
Seeing a regiment leaving for the front
A light of destiny used to play about them.
Nothing would ever be the same again. Already
We caught a glimpse of the glory of history,
The halo of honour. But now we go our ways
With no such illumination round our heads
And no sense of inferiority to those
Who had it. We too are playing our parts
In greater battles that have no romance;
Glory and genius belong to the past

[1] 'The good that hath been, meddle not with; the good that now is dwell on
that' (writ sarcastic).

When people still thought in terms of individuals.
Now only weaklings do, seeking for strength
In lives more tangled and desperate than their own.
We who are strong think only in terms
Of classes and masses, in terms of mankind.
We have no use for the great music.
All we need is a few good-going tunes.

Behind these voices there are others crying
The entire race is on the wrong track. It is impossible
To continue this search for unattainable ends.
It is a matter of finding one's way
From romantic dreams to honest recognition of truth,
To substitute reality for ideas, and find the harmony
Between desire, ability, and will in man.

It is in vain to cry to either of these
'In the individual Scot as in his country
All fineness of living, all vitality, all art
Is necessarily lost. There is nothing but ruins;
        Ground for the unconscionable alien,'
Or to murmer in hopeful explanation
        'God must still be creating – still sinking himself
Irrecognisably in lower and lower forms of life.'

Others will tell you that men of the Isles charged
At Bannockburn to the skirl of the pipes,
That the sound of the pibroch rose loud and shrill
Where the fire was hottest at Waterloo;
At Alma its notes made the blood
Surge in the veins of the Forty-Second;
To the fainting men and women in the residency at Lucknow
The far-off strains heralded miraculous deliverance.
At Dargai the pibroch sent the Gordons
Storming up the heights – and so the story goes on.
And they will tell you how when Scotland brought home
The greatest of her heroes dead – the routineer Haig,
Whose lack of imagination carried him through;
But at what loss! – it was only when the piper came down the nave

Pouring forth the lament which enshrines the heroes of Flodden
And all the dead in all the Floddens of History
Only then did the eyes grow dim with tears,
The sob rise in the throat, and sorrow for him
Who called the nation to put their backs to the wall
Find fit expression – for the world can change beyond expression
But the heart of man changes not
(Like the God each side invokes in every war)
And yesterday, and to-day, and forever
The bagpipes commit to the winds of Heaven
The deepest emotions of the Scotsman's heart
In joy and sorrow, in war and peace.
What is a mere question of the relative merit
Of pibrochs in one period as against another
In comparison with that? Are the heights of Dargai
Not more important than the heights of art?
What does it matter what we are fighting for
So long as the good fight goes on and the same excuses serve?
A living dog is better than a dead lion
And to pretend that they are the self-same beast
    Does no harm to the latter!
Cha till, cha till, cha till mi tuille' ...[1]
    I do not wonder at it.

Your occasions were trumpery as theirs and far from my liking,
Welcomes to Royalty, Salutes to Chiefs; and I marvel
At the music that towered into Eternity from them
– From the kiss of a king's hand[2] I would have given nothing for
And the like. But so it is in the world of the spirit.
The difference not only of degree but of kind

[1] The lament composed by Donald Ban MacCrimmon on the eve of setting out with his chief in 1745; Sir Walter Scott's translation reads:
    'Return, return, return shall I never
    Though MacLeod should return, not alive shall MacCrimmon,
    In war nor in peace, ne'er return will MacCrimmon.'
[2] 'I gave a kiss to the King's hand' – this tune was played extempore by Patrick Mor MacCrimmon when, in May 1657, the King's army was lying before Stirling and there was a competition among the pipers (eighty of whom were present); the King (King Charles the Second) noticing that Patrick Mor MacCrimmon received special respect from the others called him to his side and gave him his hand to kiss.

Between the germinal idea and its consummation
Can beggar description. So the humble endeavour
To convince mankind of invincible ignorance
Led to Platonic intellectualism, and Spinoza's quest
For the good life for man reached final expression
In the starkest affirmations of the metaphysical categories
With which the armoury of thought is equipped.

– A fig for most of your pretexts! But my soul for the results
– A little later when it is mine to give! Only one occasion
Would I have loved to witness – after Inverurie[1]
When Lord Louis Gordon's pipers kept silence
Since Duncan Ban MacCrimmon was his prisoner.
No Scottish Army or English, no army in the world,
Would do that to-day – nor ever again –
For they do not know and there is no means of telling them
That Kings and Generals are only shadows of time
But time has no dominion over genius.

Yet the waves will not wash the feet
Of MacLeod's Maidens[2] for ever, and all modern Science
May vanish from human memory as the great days
Of Assyria and Egypt and Rome when they seemed
Indestructible as Europe and America now
In their triumphs of aeroplanes, wireless, and submarines.
The State has its root in time. It will culminate in time.
Greater things than this will fall. All Religion will fall.
Neither moral principles nor artistic forms
Have any eternity ahead of them. How much
Are we at bottom obliged to hold fast to?
Who can guarantee that two and two
        Are not five on Jupiter?

Thou language where language ends; thou time
Standing upright for ever on the path of vanishing hearts;

---

[1] At the battle of Inverurie, 1745; 'the silent bagpipes of Lord Louis Gordon on the morning after the battle of Inverurie was the greatest tribute ever paid to genius.'

[2] MacLeod's Maidens – the rocks that stand sentinel in the Minch.

Thou feeling to whom, Oh thou change of feeling into what?
Heartspace growing out of us; innermost part of us rising over us,
Surging out in holy farewell! Thou Inner standing round us
As experienced distance, as the other side of air,
Pure, towering, uninhabitable – once inhabited here!

You remind me now of a sunset by the Urr and the Peaks of Screel
When the tide-forsaken river was a winding ribbon of ebony
Faintly washed with silver. With the passing of the splendour from the
       heights
The middle distance and foreground were suddenly lit up
With a light (like that in which shingle lies under the sea-tide's forefoot)
Bursting from some hidden spring of the afterglow. All else
Was darker save the quickened feeling – like the sense of a man
Who returns from foreign scenes to the country of his blood and birth.
The light melted from the water: mist curtained the hills,
But, breaking from the mist, the peaks again took shape.
Dark and mysterious, yet clear and vivid, under the kindling
          constellations.
Even as you look to me away beyond Scotland now
In the night of our national degradation.
The line of the river was lost but out of the distance pressed
The swelling murmur of the hunting tide of the Solway.
The estuary would soon be a sea and a mirror for the stars.

Is not the rich fruit of the Arbor Vitae
Which is all antiquity and no decay
Rejected because of its rough concealing rind
By the forest pigs, though it contains meat
Of heart-succouring savour and drink of brain-renewing power?
Beside it, Tartar-like, sits the times' civility
And eats its dead dog off a golden dish.
The abomination of desolation is always in the holy places.

Is Scotland not that small unsightly root,
That leaf darkest and with prickles on it
That in another country bears a peerless flower
But not in this soil? Or did it bloom here once

And can it bloom no more? Or is the secret
Of Uamh an Òir¹ still spiritually accessible
To such of the sons of men as worthily undertake the search?
Or are we seeming people but the disfigured fairies in Glen Brittle,
The dead leaves necessary to the coming flowering?
After having found the supreme and wonderfully retarded
Flower of culture man grieves at not being able
To make the general public understand it. He is ready
To renounce the pride of never being satisfied
In favour of that other pride
Of being intelligible to all – In vain!
But I know the root I am gripping in the darkness here
Is the unstruck note that vies all the others scope,
That deepest root from which even Freedom can unfold.
I too who have never become eingebürgert elsewhere
Feel changed in Scotland, grown strange to myself,
And waken to its realities as baffled Samson woke
Shorn and tethered. My native land should be to me
As a root to a tree. If a man's labour fills no want there
His deeds are doomed and his music mute.
This Scotland is not Scotland. How can I think of you
In these cities you never saw, a different world altogether,
Swollen huge with thoughts not thought that should have been
          thought,
Watchwords not proclaimed, songs not sung,
Tears unshed for ever and deeds undone beyond achievement now?
These denationalised Scots have killed the soul
Which is universally human; they are men without souls;
All the more heavily the judgment falls upon them
Since it is a universal law of life they have sinned against.
To try to relate your art to this is like insisting
That the man in the moon come to terms with the man in the street.
If I were on one of the islands on a sunny day
Reverse of the Brocken spectre, every flash I saw
Of wing or wave, look of an eye, curve of a lip,
Swing of a kilt, would surely magnify itself
Into the land of light you inhabit. Nay, I feel

¹ A legend of the island of Barra.

I know your music best when as it were an island pool
Away here I hold a glass of water between me and the sun
And can only tell the one from the other by the lint-white quiver,
The trembling life of the water – like a man bending his head
As from outside, as a man can, to look at his whole mind
As if it did not belong to him though he knows
It is yet that by which he knows all that he knows.
It is that marvel of all marvels, the perfect knowledge
Of knowing that what is known is perfect
Yet distinct and vital from the perfection with which that is known.
– The *peripeteia* that not only follows but forepoints and forelays
The course of the spirit which blows where it lists.
It is the realisation of the light upon which
Not only life but the very existence of the universe depends;
Not only animal life but earth, water, air.
If it faded it would mean the end of 'everything.'
It does not fade. Our spirit is of a being indestructible.
Its activity continues from eternity to eternity.
It is like the sun which seems to set to our earthly eyes
But in reality shines on unceasingly.
It is the movement which the mind invents
For its own expression not otherwise than the stars.

As every faculty, with every minutest organ of our nature,
Owes its whole reality and comprehensibility
To an existence incomprehensible and groundless
Because the ground of all comprehension, not without the union
Of all that is essential in all the functions of our spirit,
Not without an emotion tranquil from its very intensity,
Shall we worthily contemplate in the magnitude
And integrity of the world that life-ebullient stream.

It is not lawful to inquire from whence it springs,
As if it were a thing subject to space and time.
It neither approaches hither nor again departs from hence elsewhere.
But it either appears to us or it does not appear.
So we ought not to pursue it with a view to detecting
Its secret source, but watch in quiet till it suddenly shines upon us;

Preparing ourselves for the blessed spectacle as the eye
Waits patiently for the rising sun. The mind creates only to destroy;
Amid the desolation language rises, and towers
Above the ruins; and with language, music;
Its apprehension an activity of concentrated repose
So still that in it time and space cease to be
And its relations are with itself, not with anything external.

It is the supreme reality (not the Deity of personal theism)
Standing free of all historical events in past or future,
Knowable – but visible to the mind alone;
Wherefore the Church for its own purposes borrowed
The method you carried to perfection, and in plain-song
Found the musical voice of a dividuality
Which has no communal link with mankind
Though, having the mystic association of primitive music,
It still has the power to work on human superstition.
Yet the neuma, the song which hangs on to the end of a word
Without a word – *uaill-ghuth an Aoibhnis*[1] –
Avails it little now – the parrot-like contrivance
Of the jubilant sound signifying that the heart conceives
What it is unable to express. It is not in the Church
That men now find, when they must, some similar means
Of indicating a rapt and mysterious
Communion with the spiritual world.
But the Ceol Mor is only yours in your own perfect form.
(The gracing that brings the notes of the melody from the flat to the
          round
Are only melisma between notes in India and Araby,
To smooth the transitions between the notes like the movements
Of the dancers who do not disclose the physical means
Of their passing from pose to pose.)
It is world-wide, ageless. It is the Sufi *Nida* and *Saut;*
It is the Indian *Ragas*, and melodies of the old *slokas* and *ghazals*,
Deliberately cast in a non-rhythmic mould because the composers knew
That rhythm is an animal function, whereas poetry and music,
Involving no bodily activity of the artist in their making,

---

[1] 'The exultant note of joy', the title of O'Heffernan's passionate song.

Can exist in a purely psychological relation to society
And would be equally 'true' in a world of disembodied spirits;
And, as Plato knew, it is futile for artists
To discuss subtle distinctions, nuances of the scale,
And listen as though they sought to discover secrets,
While all of them in the practice of their art neglect
The theories of the mind and follow nothing but the law of their own
       ears.
The supreme reality is visible to the mind alone.
Let these impious imitators and charlatans all go then
As Alasdair Mac Mhaighstir Alasdair would have sent every red-coat
Ad bhileach dhubh a's cocàd innt'
    Sgoiltear i mar chàl mu 'n cluais![1]

Seeing your music so, I am filled with lightness and exaltation
As though by some miracle exempt from the rule of life,
From time, consequence, and price – an illusion
Proceeding from within me as music from an instrument,
– But no sooner do I begin to recognise
This aerial independence of circumstance
As the illusion of love itself and to whisper: This is love,
Than the illusion is dissipated, fleeing as Eros fled
Before Psyche's lamp and I see that I am naked
And am ashamed and glad when the shadows cover me.
– Do lights cast shadows? Have all the lights that streamed
From wings and waves and eyes and lips into your radiance
Made me their antipodes: or grey and bare
And well-nigh lifeless as your islands actually are.
Ah, it is necessary to see the islands to know you,
As one only half-understands Homer till one has seen
The Greek islands really dancing in chorus
From the high blue shoulder of a toppling wave,
But no longer in the Hebrides is there only
Water and fire as of yore; the grey rocks
Are gaining ground and the seas are black with their shadows.

I am as lonely and unfrequented as your music is.
I have had to get rid of all my friends,

   [1] 'His black hat, bordered and cockaded, split like a cabbage round his ears.'

All those to whom I had to accommodate myself.
If one's capital consists in a calling
And a mission in life one cannot afford to keep friends.
I could not stand undivided and true amongst them.
Only in the solitude of my thought can I be myself
Or remember you clearly. It is like hearing a dipper's song.
Most of our songbirds are heard without accompaniment
But the dipper seldom except among rushing waters
Which obscure the music, diminish its volume, and rob it
Of much of its sweetness. I heard one once by a stream run low
After a long drought and took him for a mavis at first.
No doubt a large flat rock behind him was a sounding-board
Enhancing the beauty and volume of the melody;
Even so it was wonderfully rich. We allow too little
As a rule for the babbling stream or the cascade's roar.

Ah, happy they who no less lonely
Are companioned by a future – who foresee
The struggle of a nation into consciousness of being,
The significance of that being, and the necessity
Of the forms taken by the struggle towards it
And sing accordingly
– Subtle, intangible, a distant music
Heard only in the lull of the gusty wind;
They are animated and restrained in the soul
Not by that instinctive love of a native land
To which all can respond but by a mystical sense
Of the high destiny of a nation – swallowed up
Neither in the delights of living nor in the torment
Of the problem of individual existence.
But I am companioned by an irrecoverable past,
By a mystical sense of such a destiny foregone . . .
Time out of mind . . . Oh, Alba, my son, my son!

And yet this darkness is related to your light.
Only such a light could make one see
So great a darkness. So those who have had to dwell
In solitude, at the furthest remove from their fellows,

Serve the community too. Their loneliness
Is only because they belong to a wider community
Than that of their immediate environment,
Not to one country or race, but to humanity,
Not to this age but to all time,
As your pibrochs reached to Eternity
– Your pibrochs that are like the glimpses
Of reality transcending all reason
Every supreme thinker has, and spends the rest of his life
Trying to express in terms of reason;
Your pibrochs that in the grey life of these islands
Are like the metaphysic of light in the style of Plotinus,
The great one-word metaphors of the Enneads,
Gleaming Godlike in the dry and formal diction,
The light that *has* been on sea and land;
Or as I have seen before the East had begun to brighten
On a hill at the point where the fir forests give way
To moorland while below me was tumbled scree
– At which hour and altitude the silence is absolute;
No sound of bird or beast, no breath of wind,
A stillness so oppressive that one caught one's ears
Straining in vain for any small sound to rise from the glen –
Suddenly from the stillness and the shadows of the night
The day came, a thing created, a great majestic presence
Taking possession from sky to range and range to sea
And instantly the silence was broken by a shower
Of silvery notes floating down across the morning
And looking up I saw a skurry of jackdaws
Diving headlong for the screes – as they fell
They caught the first sunbeams and twinkled like stars.
But it was their sharp clear notes, softened by the distance,
Which arrested the senses as a greeting to the day,
Like a peal of bells which glittered as they rang,
But the shadows of the hillside closed upon the salute,
The silence came again, and in a minute or two the dawn was gone.

I am horrified by the triviality of life, by its corruption and
        helplessness,

No prospect of eternal life, no fullness of existence, no love without
        betrayal,
No passion without satiety. Yet life could be beautiful even now.
But all is soiled under philistine rule. What untouched spiritual
        powers
Are hidden in the dark and cold, under the suffocating atmosphere
Of philistine life, waiting for a better time when the first ray of light
And breath of fresh air will call them to life and let them unfold?
Civilisation has hitherto consisted in the diffusion and dilution
Of habits arising in privileged centres. It has not sprung from the
        people.
It has arisen in their midst by a variation from them
And it has afterwards imposed itself on them from above.
A state composed exclusively of such workers and peasants
As make up most modern nations would be utterly barbarous.
Every liberal tradition would perish in it. The national and historic
Essence of patriotism itself would be lost, though the emotion no doubt
Would endure, for it is not generosity that the people lack.
They possess every impulse; it is experience they cannot gather
For in gathering it they would be constituting the higher organs
That make up an aristocratic society. Day, the surrounding world,
        the life of men
Is entangled and meaningless; society is the endless human triviality;
The judgment of the world pulls at the roots of the best plants of life.
Man himself, aside from historic aggregations, is only
The shadow of a passing cloud, his very existence hardly more than
        an illusion.
His thought resembles the ray of a fountain; it rises, sparkles,
Reaches a certain height and falls and begins the process again.
– Would it were even beginning again in Scotland to-day!
There is no tyranny so hateful as a vulgar anonymous tyranny like ours.
It is all permeating, all thwarting; it blasts every budding novelty
And sprig of genius with its omnipresent and fierce stupidity.

Yet there is no great problem in the world to-day
Except disease and death men cannot end
If no man tries to dominate another.
The struggle for material existence is over. It has been won.

The need for repressions and disciplines has passed.
The struggle for truth and that indescribable necessity,
Beauty, begins now, hampered by none of the lower needs.
No one now need live less or be less than his utmost.
And in the slow and devious development that has brought men to
        this stage
Scottish genius has played a foremost role. Yet I turn to you,
For unselfish intellect rises like a perfume
Above the faults and follies of the world of will.
But for the excellence of the typical swift life no nation
Deserves to be remembered more than the sands of the sea.

I am only that Job in feathers, a heron, myself,
Gaunt and unsubstantial – yet immune to the vicissitudes
Other birds accept as a matter of course; impervious to the effects
Of even the wildest weather, no mean consideration in a country
        like this;
And my appetite is not restricted to any particular fare.
Hence I am encountered in places far removed from one another
And widely different in an intimately topographical sense
– Spearing a rat at the mouth of a culvert at midnight
And bolting an eel on the seashore in the half light of dawn –
Communal dweller yet lone hunter, lumbering yet swift and
        sustained flier,
The usual steely expression of my eyes does not flatter me;
Few birds perhaps have so successfully solved
The problem of existence as my grey lar.ky self
That in light or darkness, wet or shine, subsists
By a combination of alertness, patience, and passivity.
A kind of Caoilte Mac Rónáin[1] too; but it takes
        All my wits in Scotland to-day.

This is the darkness where you have been; and have left
I think forever. It is the darkness from which nothing is cast out,

[1] 'The grey spare swift runner, he who saved Fionn once by that wonderful feat of gathering couples of all the wild beasts and birds of Ireland (a ram and a crimson sheep from Inis, two water-birds from the Erne, two cormorants from the Cliath, two foxes from Slieve Gullion, and the rest).'

No loss, no wanton pain, no disease, no insanity,
None of the unripe intelligence of so-called dead nature,
Abortive attempts of nature to reflect itself.
All the unintelligible burden that alone leads to the height
Where it seems that extremes meet and I could reach you
i bh-fogus do dhul ar neamh-nidh,[1] with a *léim éanamhail*.[2]

In this depth that I dare not leave
I who am no dilettante of chaos and find
No bitter gratification in the contemplation of ultimate Incoherence
Know that the world is at any given moment anything it may be called
And ever more difficult to group round any central character,
Yet it is out of this aimless dispersion, all these zig-zagging efforts,
All this disorderly growth, that the ideal of an epoch ends
By disentangling itself. Myriads of human activities
Are scattered in all directions by the indifferent forces
Of self-interest, passion, crime, madness – but out of their number
Some few of these activities are endowed with a little constancy
By the pure in heart, for reasons which seem to respond
To the most elementary designs of the spirit.
Civilisation, culture, all the good in the world
Depends ultimately on the existence of a few men of good will.
The perspective will converge upon them yet.
I dare not leave this dark and distracted scene.
I believe in the necessary and unavoidable responsibility of man
And in the ineluctable certainty of the resurrection
And know that the mind of man creates no ideas
Though it is ideas alone that create.
Mind is the organ through which the Universe reaches
Such consciousness of itself as is possible now, and I must not brood
On the intermittence of genius, the way consciousness varies
Or declines, as in Scotland here, till it seems
Heaven itself may be only the best that is feasible
For most people, but a sad declension from music like yours.
Yes, I am prepared to see the Heavens open
And find the celestial music poor by comparison.
Yet my duty is here. It is now the duty of the Scottish genius

[1] 'On the confines of vanishing.'   [2] 'Bird-like leap.'

Which has provided the economic freedom for it
To lead in the abandonment of creeds and moral compromises
Of every sort and to commence to express the unity of life
By confounding the curse of short-circuited thought,
Circumscribing consciousness, for that is the thought
Of compromise, the medium of the time-server.
This must be done to lead men to cosmic consciousness
And as it cannot be quick, except on occasion
And that the creative instant, the moment of divine realisation,
When the self is lit up by its own inner light
Caused in the self by its intensity of thought
Possibly over a long period, it must be thought of as a craft
In which the consummation of the idea, not in analysis but in synthesis,
Must be the subject of the object – life.
Wherefore I cannot take the bird-like leap to you
Though well I know that: 'He that can endure
To follow with allegiance a fallen lord
Does conquer him that did his master conquer.'

I dare not leap to you now. But after all since I cannot believe
You will ever be really for everyone or even for many
And are likely to pursue in the hereafter
A separate destiny from theirs – or simply because
I long to hear the great pipers play their great music themselves.
And they all dead (save one) centuries before I was born,
And have one glimpse of my beloved Scotland yet
As the land I have dreamt of where the supreme values
Which the people recognise are states of mind
Their ruling passion the attainment of higher consciousness,
And their actual rulers those in whom they find,
Or think they do, the requisite knowledge for such attainments
And where one is not required to believe anything
But even warned of the dangers of doing so
Except with infinite qualifications and care,
My duty done, I will try to follow you on the last day of the world,
And pray I may see you all standing shoulder to shoulder
With Patrick Mor MacCrimmon and Duncan Ban MacCrimmon
          in the centre

In the hollow[1] at Boreraig or in front of Dunvegan Castle
Or on the lip of the broken graves in Kilmuir Kirkyard,[2]
While, the living stricken ghastly in the eternal light
And the rest of the dead all risen blue-faced from their graves
(Though, the pipes to your hand, you will be once more
Perfectly at ease, and as you were in your prime)
All ever born crowd the islands and the West Coast of Scotland
Which has standing room for them all, and the air curdled with angels,
And everywhere that feeling seldom felt on the earth before
Save in the hearts of parents or in youth untouched by tragedy
That in its very search for personal experience often found
A like impersonality and self-forgetfulness,
And you playing: 'Farewell to Scotland, and the rest of the Earth,'
The only fit music there can be for that day
– And I will leap then and hide behind one of you,
A's caismeachd phìob-mòra bras-shròiceadh am puirt.[3]

Look! Is that only the setting sun again?
Or a piper coming from far away?

Skald's Death

> I HAVE known all the storms that roll.
> I have been a singer after the fashion
> Of my people – a poet of passion.
>   All that is past.
> Quiet has come into my soul.
>   Life's tempest is done.
>   I lie at last
> A bird cliff under the midnight sun.

[1] i.e. the pipers' hollow where the students at the college of the MacCrimmons (1500–1800) practised. Ten generations of MacCrimmons were the hereditary pipers of MacLeod of MacLeod, whose seat is at Dunvegan Castle in the Isle of Skye. Boreraig was where the MacCrimmons lived.

[2] Near Dunvegan.

[3] 'While the notes of the great pipes shrilly sound out their cries' (from Alasdair Mac Mhaighstir Alasdair).

POEMS EXCISED FROM THE FIRST EDITION

Edinburgh Toun[1]

O EDINBURGH toun, Edinburgh toun,
Police are setting steel-boxes roun
To shoot the workin'-classes doun
Under a Chief Constable – Whoa, horsie, steady! –
Juist the spit-image o' 'Peacemaker' Neddy.

A Judge Commits Suicide[2]

A JUDGE has sentenced himself to a suicide's grave?
– The nearest to a just sentence any judge ever gave.

Harry Semen[3]

I KEN these islands each inhabited
Forever by a single man
Livin' in his separate world as only
In dreams yet maist folk can.

[1] Deleted and 'First Love' substituted in the first edition.
[2] Deleted from the first edition and not included in the second.
[3] Deleted and 'The Progress of Poetry' substituted in the first edition.

Mine's like the moonwhite belly o' a hoo
Seen in the water as a fisher draws in his line.
I canna land it nor can it ever brak awa'.
It never moves, yet seems a' movement in the brine;
A movin' picture o' the spasm frae which I was born,
It writhes again, and back to it I'm willy-nilly torn.
A' men are similarly fixt; and the difference 'twixt
  The sae-ca'd sane and insane
Is that the latter whiles ha'e glimpses o't
  And the former nane.

Particle frae particle'll brak asunder,
Ilk ane o' them mair livid than the neist.
A separate life? – incredible war o' equal lichts,
Nane o' them wi' ocht in common in the least.
Nae threid o' a' the fabric o' my thocht
Is left alangside anither; a pack
O' leprous scuts o' weasels riddlin' a plaid
  Sic thrums could never mak'.
Hoo mony shades o' white gaed curvin' owre
To yon blae centre o' her belly's flower?
Milk-white, and dove-grey, wi' harebell veins.
Ae scar in fair hair like the sun in sunlicht lay,
And pelvic experience in a thin shadow line;
Thocht canna mairry thocht as sic saft shadows dae.

Grey ghastly commentaries on my puir life,
A' the sperm that's gane for naething rises up to damn
In sick-white onanism the single seed
Frae which in sheer irrelevance I cam.
What were the odds against me? Let me coont.
What worth am I to a' that micht ha'e been?
To a' the wasted slime I'm capable o'
Appeals this lurid emission, whirlin' lint-white and green.
Am I alane richt, solidified to life,
Disjoined frae a' this searin' like a white-het knife,
And vauntin' my alien accretions here,
Boastin' sanctions, purpose, sense the endless tide

I cam frae lacks – the tide I still sae often feed?
O bitter glitter; wet sheet and flowin' sea – and what beside?

Sae the bealin' continents lie upon the seas,
    Sprawlin' in shapeless shapes a' airts,
Like ony splash that ony man can mak'
    Frae his nose or throat or ither pairts,
Fantastic as ink through blottin'-paper rins.
But this is white, white like a flooerin' gean,
Passin' frae white to purer shades o' white,
Ivory, crystal, diamond, till nae difference is seen
Between its fairest blossoms and the stars.
Or the clear sun they melt into,
And the wind mixes them amang each ither
Forever, hue upon still mair dazzlin' hue.

Sae Joseph may ha'e pondered; sae a snawstorm
Comes whirlin' in grey sheets frae the shadowy sky
And only in a sma' circle are the separate flakes seen.
White, whiter, they cross and recross as capricious they fly,
Mak' patterns on the grund and weave into wreaths,
Load the bare boughs, and find lodgements in corners frae
The scourin' wind that sends a snawstorm up frae the earth
To meet that frae the sky, till which is which nae man can say.
They melt in the waters. They fill the valleys. They scale the peaks.
There's a tinkle o' icicles. The topmaist summit shines oot.
Sae Joseph may ha'e pondered on the coiled fire in his seed,
The transformation in Mary, and seen Jesus tak' root.

John Maclean (1879-1923)[1]

ALL the buildings in Glasgow are grey
With cruelty and meanness of spirit,
But once in a while one greyer than the rest
    A song shall merit

[1] Deleted and 'The Little White Rose' and 'Cattle Show' substituted in the first edition.

Since a miracle of true courage is seen
For a moment its walls between.

Look at it, you fools, with unseeing eyes
And deny it with lying lips!
But your craven bowels well know what it is
    And hasten to eclipse
In a cell, as black as the shut boards of the Book
You lie by, the light no coward can brook.

It is not the blue of heaven that colours
The blue jowls of your thugs of police,
And 'justice' may well do its filthy work
    Behind walls as filthy as these
And congratulate itself blindly and never know
The prisoner takes the light with him as he goes below.

Stand close, stand close, and block out the light
As long as you can, you ministers and lawyers,
Hulking brutes of police, fat bourgeoisie,
Sleek derma for congested guts – its fires
Will leap through yet; already it is clear
Of all Maclean's foes not one was his peer.

As Pilate and the Roman soldiers to Christ
Were Law and Order to the finest Scot of his day,
One of the few true men in our sordid breed,
A flash of sun in a country all prison-grey.
Speak to others of Christian charity; I cry again
For vengeance on the murderers of John Maclean.
Let the light of truth in on the base pretence
Of Justice that sentenced him behind these grey walls.
All law is the contemptible fraud he declared it.
Like a lightning-bolt at last the workers' wrath falls
On all such castles of cowards whether they be
Uniformed in ermine, or blue, or khaki.

Royal honours for murderers and fools! The 'fount of honour'
Is poisoned and spreads its corruption all through,
But Scotland will think yet of the broken body
And unbreakable spirit, Maclean, of you,
And know you were indeed the true tower of its strength,
As your prison of its foul stupidity, at length.

Ode to All Rebels[1]

*In his appearance not overdazzling; so that you might without difficulty recognise him
as belonging to that class of men of letters who are continuously hated by the Rich.*
                                        PETRONIUS, *Satiricon* lxxxiii.

Wherefore are all they happy that deal very treacherously?
                                        JEREMIAH, XII. I (Vulgate).

I MIND when my first wife died.
        I was a young fella then,
Strang, and ta'en up wi' life, and she'd come
        By a sudden and terrible en',
My haill warld gane – but I was livin' on
        Tho' hoo I could hardly ken.
Yet even in the middle o' kistin' her
In the hour o' my grief I felt the stir
        O' auld feelin's again.
Feelin's I had when I courted her first,
No' syne, and hated noo and cursed.
Hoo could I trust love again if a'
The tender ties twixt us twa
Like this could be wantonly snapt,
While afore her corpse was decently hapt
I was kindlin' aince mair in a different airt,
My rude bluid warnin' my woe for its pairt
It 'bood ha'e anither wife, and sune?

[1] Deleted and 'Lament for the Great Music' substituted in the first edition.

Nay, I felt the cratur juist hoverin' roon.
At ony meenut her face 'ud kyth.
– Ahint my dule and self-scunner already,
    My Second, you were skinklan' blithe.
Or I kent gin you'd be virgin or widdy,
    A thocht I mind ha'en
Even as frae lowerin' the coffin I raze
Conscious o' my nature in a wud amaze
And strauchtened up my muckle animal frame
That kent what it wanted and kent nae shame
    And stood in a burst o' sun
    Glowerin' at the bit broken grun'.

I aince kent a man wi' one eye
    Sae his body was fu'
    O' licht a' through. . . .
Kate's eyes were sea-green. She was ane o' the last
    To ha'e them that hue
    Tho' in the distant past
It was common eneuch, that's true.
    While Jean's were sky-blue.
    And sae I could cry
I'd mairriet the sea and syne the sky
    And seen the ane gang dry
      And the ither
        Curl up and wither
        Like a floo'er and die.
Sea-green were Kate's! What's that you say?
    Impossible? A lie?
No. It's nae mistake. They werena juist grey
    But the oculi caesii
    Tacitus refers to,
The 'eagle hath not so green,
So quick, so fair an eye'
O' Shakespeare – Plautus's oculi herbei,
And the great eyes wi' a green circle
Bacon thocht promised lang life;
And ha'e you no' even read Villa Real's

Great treatise in praise o' green eyes?
*   – Then you ken naething aboot them,*
*   You and silly surprise!*
*   Kate's were sea-green, I tell you.*
*   Shairly I kent my ain first wife!*

When the second cam' in due course I felt
    I'd seen her afore tho' I hadna
Her actual appearance only confirmed

(ὑπεροχῇ τῆς ἑαυτῶν κεφαλῆς
                                – PLOTINUS)

*   Scotland, when it is given to me*
*   As it will be*
*   To sing the immortal song*
*   The crown of all my long*
*   Travail with thee*
*   I know in that high hour*
*   I'll have, and use, the power*
*   Sublime contempt to blend*
*   With its ecstatic end,*
*   As who, in love's embrace,*
*   Forgetfully may frame*
*   Above the poor slut' face*
*   Another woman's name.*

A' I'd jaloused but up to then wadna
Permit to appear ony clearer.
I dinna ken if a thocht she badna
Gied her a like foreknowledge o' me
– Faceless, formless, yet me to a t –
But I fancy it did; we're no' ca'd to
Ken muckle about weemun in sic maitters
And for the maitter o' that wi oor ain naturs
No' only keep mair to the tap than we need
But the possible's shallow eneuch indeed.
Oh, we were happy a' richt – it seemed

My previous marriage was juist something I'd dreamed
Or heard concernin' anither man.
I couldna fit the twa into ony plan.
And let me be perfectly honest – I'd had
Anither quean or twa afore I first wed
And after the second a side-slip whiles
And bein' the kind o' fella I am
Comparin' my sweetherts' various styles
  The conclusion to which I cam'
Was that ony o' mony a thoosand
Forbye the cratur I actually got
'Ud ha'e seemed as convincin' and fore-thought
And wi' a' their differences the life I'd ha'e led
Wi' ony ane o' them I micht ha'e wed
  'Ud ha'e been fell near the same
  As wi' yon particular dame.

 O Love it is a lovely thing,
   Two healthy lads respond.
 But little, little can foresee
   Of what must lie beyond.

 For love leads in two opposite ways
   And they've no chance of knowing
 From same-seeming eyes and lips and hair
   Which of the two they're going.

 They turn to meet their natural need,
   One finds domestic bliss;
 The other a lock hospital
   To rot with syphilis.

 Which seems to be no concern of God's
 Though to them, of course, it makes all the odds;
 Or so one thinks, knowing but one of the roads. . . .

 Or two lads love; one takes his lass
   Into the meadow where the grass-tops wag o'er her
 And teaches her the animal pleasures there
   And gives her the great gift of horror.

The other pursues identical methods,
  He too takes his lass where the grass-tops jig above
And teaches her the self-same lesson,
  And only fills her with love. . . .

'The Colonel's too gallant, too romantic, too old,'
  She sadly admitted, 'it's true
To appreciate the Great Discovery of the Age
  – That women like It too!' . . .

The functions of the gonadal and the peptic glands
  Are of like importance and no more or less
And while their operation's normal
  No more disturb us or obsess.

To make sex out ethereal and inspiring
  Hides the belief that it's ugly and obscene
In all such sublimation of it only
  A variant of the Christian vilification's seen.

In male or female the normal operation
  Does not interfere in any way at all
With any further function, interest, or occupation,
  Spiritual, intellectual, emotional, or physical.

Knowing this, let us sit back awhile and laugh
  Watching the 'cultural compulsives' at work
On bourgeois scientists to-day – and foreknowing the cupboards
  In which all the remaining puritan skeletons lurk. . . .

  I ha'ena seen the bairns
  Since Jean divorced me
– Mona and Fergus and wee Peter –
  And never mair may see,
  – Save whiles in memory.
Yet I lo'ed them as dearly as ony man
  Can lo'e his spawn
– Tho' I hated to see repetitions

In them o' her and me,
Juist 'cauld kail het again'
As in maist ither folk I see,
Till as wi' second marriage that tae
Wi' my taste began to agree,
That, and even the measure they had
        O' common humanity,
They're developin' differently nae doot
        Than if I'd still been aboot
But whether for better or waur
        Or neither wha can say?
I'd hae hated like Hell I ken
        To influence them ony way.
Yet my absence may ha'e dune that tae.
        I wadna ken the bairns
        Even if I saw them again.
What I mind o' them canna correspond
        Wi' what they've grown, that's plain,
And the faitherly instinct isna sae deep
        As to tell me they're my ain.
We need propinquity and habit then
        Oor bairns to ken
And reason and feelin' are o' nae avail
        When these handrails fail,
And it's only for a wee while we can recognise
        – If ever – what nearest to us lies.

It's no' the thing itsel' that taks nae accoont
O' the personality o' the folk concerned,
The common denominator cancels oot.
It's for the variations mankind's aye yearned,
It was queer at first when in what we did
My previous experiences were whiles discerned
– A' the auld endearments and tricks o' the game;
It was nocht but the wumman that wasna the same –
Uncanny, disturbin', but sune they gi'ed
An extra relish to oor relations I learned.
Refinements o' sensibility, like this,

Are the way that's led us up frae the brute,
Tho' it took us a wee while to savour them a'
We contributed to progress withoot ony doot.
In the middle o' oor life thegither
  And the bairns arrivin'
I kent if they a' suddenly vanished
  It 'ud tak' nae strivin'
For me to forget them as hailly
And sune as the first. Life'd still be drivin'
Me awa' frae a' faithfu' standards.
   The auld lusts 'ud be rivin'
The clod o' my loss wi' new growth.
For mony years at least I had ample scouth
  – And kent it, wi' nae connivin' –
For forgettin' the wife o' my bosom
And my bairns, s'ud I suddenly lose 'm,
Almaist as easily as I'd forgotten puir Kate
And the unborn bairns we'd anticipate
And tho' I ne'er said a word o't to Jean
Aye mair and mair clearly I saw
Sexual relations arena personal at a'
But the least intimate things in the world,
And can be passionately wanted and enjoyed by twa
Wi' nocht else in common, and livin' thegither
Is mainly a means o' hidin' frae each ither
– And oorsel's – ahint the silly impermanent
Ties that gin a' their oots and ins were kent
'Ud tell us naething o' sex life even,
Let alane ocht else. I've had a' I want o't
Lang syne, and noo if I visit the haunt o't
   I ken a' action is nocht
   But the habit and haven
   O' the puir or poo'erless in thocht
   – The stranghauld o' the callous and craven.

Thank God for laundries. It used to be terrible
  To think o' the things weemun saw.

A man felt indecently exposed
    While they never kythed ava'.
He never kent hoo muckle they kent
    As they washed his claes.
A' he did unbeknown, in the dark,
    Was open to their gaze
While ahint their couthy ways lay
    A life he missed a'thegither.
Thank God we can live at last
    Equally ignorant o' ane anither.
The mair that develops in ilka direction
    The better we a' sall be,
The goal o' the process we're followin' oot
    Is to live unconsciously
– 'As for livin' oor machines 'll dae that
    For us in the guid times comin'.
Wherever you gang in the world the day
You hear their premonitory bummin'
Tho' you may think it's only a parson
    Or a politician on the B.B.C.' –
(There's naething ony man ever can think
    Humanity canna accept and hide
As weemun the ways o' their sex
    And as douce and canty bide,
We rebels maun think the unthinkable then
And nocht else and get clean ootside
Owre faur to hear onybody wheedlin' again
'It looks cauld ootside frae inside.
Come in by – come in owre the fire'
And syne the auld question what mair
Ony sane man can desire.)
And already the difference o' the sexes
Has practically ceased to exist
Tho' humanity still grows in its bland omnitude
Like a eunuch wi' a teratoma cyst.

    I used to write sic bonny sangs
    A'body wi' pleasure and profit could read,

Even yet a bit discipline's a' that I need
To mak' mysel' ane o' the greatest poets
Puir Scotland's ever managed to breed.
Why dae I turn my back on a' that
And write this horrible rubbish instead?
– Sustain me, spirit o' God, that I pay
These seductive voices nae heed!

Here at the heicht o' passion
    As lovers dae
I can only speak brokenly
    O' trifles tae.
Idiot incoherence
    I ken fu' weel
Is the only language
    That wi' God can deal.

And as o' my weemun and oor bairns
    I feel aboot a'
Accepted standards, the framework o' life,
    Ilka sae-ca'd law
Man-made or 'divine'. Into the pit then
    You say a life maun fa'?
Precisely. A'thing. There's naething left.
    Ane maun choose 'twixt the twa;
The painfu' convulsions o' dubious reveille
O' which I'm a still mair dubious ally
And the grey torpidity o' certain sleep
In which maist a'body else is rowed sae deep.
Mind, its no' juist leavin' reality ahint
And enterin' a state in which a'thing's tint
At first, but at second and third and fourth as weel
And ilka subsequent state, and tho' one may feel
Boondless joy ane can never win free
Frae unspeakable horror – a state that minds me
O' hoo Kate a'e day afore we were mairried,
And students still, aince turned her bit heid
    (Her hair that shone in the sun
    As sae mony weemun's has done)

And watched me wi' quizzical een
As I cam' on her heels up to the obscene
   Case spread oot for the class. I returned her look
Wi' ane strictly accordin' to the book,
As I fingered the vagina lyin' afore me
   – Carcinoma o' the uterus – while o'er me
   Swept the thocht: 'Darlin' the neist may be you'
   – I saw deep eneuch then, and saw true,
      And yet lo'ed her, I confess,
      Gin nane the mair certes nane the less.

O she was fu' o' lovin' fuss
When I cut my hand and the bluid gushed oot
And cleverly she dressed the wound
And row'd it in a clout.

O tenderly she tended me
But deep in her een I saw
The secret joy that men are whiles
Obliged to bleed ana'.

I thanked her kindly and never let on,
Seein' she couldna understand,
That she wished me a wound faur waur to staunch
– And no' i' the hand!

Nay, that's a puir preliminary
   Notion o' the feelin'
– The general intelligence
   Is quite debarred frae dealin'
Wi' even the thocht o' sic a state,
   The simplest glisk sends 't squealin'
For shelter to religion, law, or 'love'
   As tho' the haill warld's reelin'.
Yet the case I've cited didna lead
To Chaos, but to oor weddin' instead,
And the like happens wi' maist 'darin'' ideas.
But I've gane in the opposite airt frae these.

I tae ha'e been ta'en up the mountain heich
And invited a' Earth's kingdoms to see
(Sae faur as that's permitted, for it's wrapt
In mists gey often or at least clood–capt
And tho' a man may see them a' frae its cantle
It's no' a' at aince his een tak' in a hantle
– Or a hantle him!), yet I've bent nae knee to Reason
– Except in mockery – for mony a season
And syne, for there's nae arguin' against Reason,
Only, as your mood determines, teasin',
Gibin', invective, or simple No,
– Tho' to keep to the last's damned hard I'll show –
Risen, said: 'Excuse me, but noo I'm awa',
Your show's no' what it used to be at a'.
I'll transfer my custom to that hussy
Adrasteia, if she's no' owre busy
    And no' bother to come back
    – Unless to gi'e you twice the sack!'

I saw mysel' in the mirror ga'en oot.
    My een had the pitch-black
Look o' amaurosis and the irises
    Didna dilate or contract
On the sudden application or withdrawin' o' the sun,
    A' strength my body seemed to lack.
I was naked and kent I'd been born
    Deaf and blind in fact.
But I heard a scientist declare:
'I question if complete fatuity's there.
His touch seems perfect and we maun suppose
Individuality, number, position, a' those
Ither perceptions are his that in the normal case
Gang wi't, o' objects as they coexist in space
Or are continuous in point o' time.
He prefers certain kinds o' food and I'm
Certain we could trace in him maist
O' the original objects o' desire, puir baist
– If we'd the time and patience to waste.

I speired his mither what he likes to handle best
And she said: 'Ocht he can alter the shape o'.'
Then I sloped back my brow a wee thing faurer
For weel I kent that that 'ud gar her
And Reason couped into the mirror and be it confest,
– Merrily I leuch at the jape O! –
(Save it was Ramsay MacDonald or Caesar
Or Plato or some ither great geyser,
And in fact there's nae human bein'
No' at least twice juist what I was seein')
– It was only her word against mine
And that's nae evidence as we ken fine –
  Losh me, but I couldna tell
  Which was her and which mysel'!
The angelic state to which I've attained
Disna lust for bluid and a bowler hat again
Or for onything else that men can ha'e.
I ken I canna be seen by men.
Maist things in the warld are like that they ken,
And maist folk fancy that they'll win tae
  To a similar state to mine noo
– Tho' they're no' in ony great hurry to,
And hing on for a' they are worth
To the empty things o' the earth.
They believe in ither things they canna see
Then why should they no' believe in me
But presume to pick and choose atween
The things they themsel's ca' the unseen?
Nonsense? But dae they get as muckle fun
Frae my antics as frae theirs I've whiles won,
– Tho' angels lack humour and it's no' sae easy
To divert me noo as it used to be.
The haill warld's vanished like Kate and Jean
   As it had never been.
  I tell you it never existed
   And even if it had
I could never ha'e filed mysel' as I did
Wi' filthy life, and will again – no' me

But yon imbecile facsimile.
I want naething – naething.
Oot o' the mirror wi' that chowlin' face
Or I'll smash 't wi' my invisible wing!
Wha? God? Farcie in that face! I've seen
Mony brawer men hingin' on the Gallows-green
– But angels dinna behave that way?
Hoo d'ye ken? Are you an angel tae?

'Blasphemiae . . . aliquanto sonant gratiores in aure Dei
Quam ipsum Alleluja vel quaecumque laudis jubilatio
Quanto enim horribilior et foedior est blasphemia
Tanto est Deo gratior.'

Sae nae doot you're pleasin' him
        Still better than me
    Wi' your horrible wisdom
        And integrity;
    (If you only meant them, certes, they'd be
        The nonpareil o' blasphemy)
    While, tryin' to be sly,
    I only curry favour, a spy
    Double-crossin' mysel',
    A 'cheated cheat' o' the Maist High,
    Evadin' the maist cruel war
        God can wage wi' me,
    That o' leavin' me withoot
        The War He cam' to gie.

Come test my een. I tell you there's nocht,
There's naebody alive or can be, on this plane.
Measure my een. They're as guid as yours.
Average een and fell like your ain.
No' sea-green een, but a common colour
Yet they can see naething you say you see.
I dinna believe it exists ava',
And I'm shair you canna prove it to me.
The self-same een, but a different world
And you canna imagine what my een see.

If I tried to tell, it would seem to you
– I'm content that it should – sheer idiocy,
While, if I believed a' you believe in was,
And you tried to describe it I'd feel still mair
Something I was time oot o' mind mowed
As 'twere my ain foetus hauntin' me there,
Blether nae mair aboot justice and crime,
Guid and ill, life and daith, man and wumman,
         God and man.
My een are as guid as yours and see nocht
O' ony o' these – fegs, shairly you can
Credit your ain een withoot needin' me
To see the same things in order to see.
Besides, you've the rest o' humanity.
Needin' me to a' that's puir testimony.
I tell you my een are the marrows of yours
But mine canna see the truth and yours can
– Or is't the ither way roond? – and that's juist
The essence o' a' that can be ca'd God's plan.
Wi' nae fairness or reason as you will agree.
Wha sae wanton as that but God can be?
There's only a'e thing that you maun see
And that's – that there's nae necessity,
     And that the essence o' a' law
     Is that there is nae law ava'.
Twirp, think what you like, but let me be.

I'd be better deid? Nae doot! Wha wadna?
     A' the Christians think they will
     Or think or say they dae
     But, in a sort o' way,
Maist o' them keep on livin' still.
But I've deed a wheen times noo and ken
It'll no help maitters to dae't again.
Besides there's nae ither way
O' deein' than the ways they ha'e.
If I could think o' a completely new kind
O' daith, to try't aince I michtna mind.

Puir Judas – wrangly – thocht it worth a hang.
Frae a *nouveau riche* what mair could you hope?
But, in this alien form, to keep livin' amang
Self-styled life gi'es my funny gifts mair scope.
Why d'ye no' kill me? You canna. That's why,
Aye roond the neist corner in wait I lie.
For my quarrel is endless and winna dee.
        My quarrel is endless and no' wi' you
        Or wi' onybody or ocht else noo,
        Or that ever can be, in view,
And nocht can dae ocht wi' a man like me.
My interests are foreign to history,
        And still mair foreign to hope.

        Are the livin' sae muckle use
        That we need to mourn the deid?
        Or wad it yield better results
        To reverse their rôles insteed?
        The millions slain in the War
        – Untimely, the best o' oor seed? –
        Wad the warld be ony the better
        If they were still livin' indeed?
        The achievements o' sic as are
        To the notion lend nae support;
        The haill history o' life and daith
        Yields nae scrap o' evidence for't.
        – Keep ga'en to your wars, you fools, as o' yore;
        I'm the civilisation you're fechtin' for.

For oot o' naething what beauty arises
We poets ken – if we dinna ken hoo –
Wha only the impossible pursue
(A' else comes to us owre easily
Needin' nae pursuit – oor job's to keep free)
Till naething suddenly surprises
– Seize the vision, my spirit, seize it, mak' haste! –
Wi' τὸ τιμιώτατον, wi' 'what maitters maist,'
What else unmisnamed can you stand for, rebels?

(Leave a' that to MacDonald; he'll manage the lot.
I'm certain o' that – I was aince a Scot.)
And why, oh why, on onything else waste
A quiver o' the precious strength that alane
Can live in the void that by that's whiles graced?
The revolutionary spirit's ane wi' spirit itsel'!
    Let a' thing else gang to Hell.
          Responsibility's a fearsome load
              Nae man can bear.
              Rebels, try nae mair
          Be as irresponsible as God.
(The Baccarat scandal was bad eneuch
But to see the King o' King's cheatin' – wheuch!)
The advice I gi'e you is simply this:
Keep oot o' a' else except the abyss.
Rive Joy oot o' Terror's clenched nieve
Gie't a'e look, syne back again heave.
You'll no' see it twice. The Beauty that's won
Frae Terror's aye something new under the sun.

   O weel may timid and graspin' folk
   Rejoice that aince as the Scriptures state
   An innocent man was tortured to Daith
   For their benefit: and be pleased – noo they hae't.

     I tell you it's a' ane to me
Whether a man's a murderer or the Pope o' Rome
Or the King o' England or Robbie Burns.
    I'd as sune be the ane as the ither
        Or them a' by turns
    There's naething yon idiot grues to touch mair,
    For he still shares the peculiarity o' kennin' things,
    Than the ootside o' a kettle coated wi' soot,
    Which accoonts for my fancy for Rilke and Blok,
       – That hardly needs pointin' oot.
     But trace the connections
        In a' directions
And you'll aiblins ken what I'm aboot.

Think not that I forget a single pang
          O' a' that folk ha'e tholed,
Agonies and abominations 'yont a' tellin'
          Sights to daunt the maist bold.

There are buildings in ilka toon where daily
          Unthinkable horrors tak' place.
I am the woman in cancer's toils,
          The man withoot a face.

I am a' cruelty and lust and filth,
          Corruption and law-made crime,
– The helpless prisoners badgered in their cells
          In every land and clime.

A' 'gallant sodgers' murderin' for pay,
          (Plus 'little Belgium' or like affairs)
– And heroic airmen prood to gi'e
          Puir tribes hell frae the air.

And a' the hidden but nae less hideous deeds
          Soond citizens are aye privily at
– Only the mean natures and vicious looks
          O' their bairns, themsel's, or their underlings caught.

O there's as muckle o't in Britain here
          As in Sing-Sing or in Cayenne
– Differently disguised, of course, and dernin'
          In the maist 'decent and God-fearin'' men.

There is nae horror history's ever kent
          Mob passion or greedy fear wadna soon
Mak' them dae owre again – slovens and cowards
          Movin' pig-eened in their daily roon'.

They face nocht – their haill lives depend
          On ignorance and base contempt
For a' that's worth-while in the poo'ers o' Man
          – Frae ony share in't exempt.

In the midst o' plenty in poverty,
To Art nae better than apes
– Thinkna that I'm unaware
O' ane o' their ugsome shapes. . . .

You may thank God for good health
And be proud to be pure
In body and mind – unlike some.
I am not so sure.

You may feel certain that God
Is on the side of the sane
And prefers your condition to syphilis.
I am not so sure.

Congratulate yourselves you're spared
The ghastly ills others endure.
God's with the majority surely.
I am not so sure. . . .

Leviathans that mimic the expression of God's will
Ha'e men in thrall – 'laws' they daurna owrespill,
Hydraulic poo'er to Money's and Industry's mill
　　　Under the illusion o' progress they tine
Their birthright for livin' daith, and a' their skill
　　　Mak's mindless machines o' Mankind.

Victim o' nae dialectic system, o' nae
Intricate web o' human beliefs to gainsay
Ocht that but for it I'd naturally think, feel, or dae,
Lookin' back on a' that – a' that ither men
Are and dae and think – I feel just as when
A clean man amang ither men first comes to ken
　　　Some o' them ha'e venereal disease,
Vague, terrible phenomenon o' a warld no' his ain;
　　　And the diseased men's callousness sees. . . .

Blindin' licht is waur than the dark.
Cataclysm in the mirror. What's that I see?

I heard reason shriek and saw her flee
    Through the weiks o' my e'e
    And kent it was me.
(It was bound to be. The fact can be proved
For the simple reason that I hadna moved.)
She was richt! It is. But I ken vera weel
Nae man can believe that anither can don
Sic impossible lustres as yon.
I am poured oot like water and a' my banes are oot o' joint.

My hert is like wax; it's melted in the midst o' my bowels.
Yon boat, the sun, I aince burnt ahint me
Had never a lowe like this ava';
But as the lourd earth is the same alow
Tho' insubstantialised in the sunshine
I see the slack mooth and gogglin' een
Ahint this glory and ken them for mine
Nor if I could wad I tine for a meenut
Divine in human or human in divine.
O dooble vision fechtin' in the glass!
Noo licht blots oot sic last distinctions o' class.
    O magical change. O miracle.
    I am suddenly beyond mysel'.
        Reid, white, and square,
    Tearin' the soul to rags.

Folk recognise – wi' regret it may be –
Man's kinship wi' the maist laithsome brute
Jogglin' his protrudin' sternum there
And lettin' his animal noises oot.
    A' they can ha'e patience wi',
    A' they can pity,
A' they can hide in their madhouses,
    In their gaols and hospital wards,
Fat herts, lourd lugs, shut een,
A' that's badly, malformed, obscene,
    Mankind accepts and guards;
But when an angel kyths, a man
Infinitely superior to man, as here,

Frae a man nae better than ither men,
An idiot like them, they howl wi' fear,
Or perjure their sicht, and gibe and jeer
And deny that the like can ever appear,
        Let alane be ane wi' the ither.

'L'extrême esprit est accusé de folie
        Comme l'extrême défaut;
Rien que la médiocrité n'est bon.
        C'est sortir de l'humanité
        Que de sortir du milieu.'

'Und wir, die an *steigendes* Glück
denken, empfänden die Rührung,
die uns beinah bestürzt,
wenn ein Glückliches *fällt*.'

It's against a' sense and what's the use
O' decency, worship, a shepherded soul,
If a cratur like this can suddenly emerge?
– Regairdless o' a' that maist men can thole,
Yet visibly dowered wi' the licht o' lichts
The glory o' God he shows yet denies,
When even if they tried like vices themsel's
Insteed o' the wisdom and virtues they prize
Nane o' them, no' even the maist reverend and upright,
'Ud ever be transfigured in similar wise.
God s'ud consult wi' the King or the Kirk
Or get the Medical Profession to advise,
No' act in sic an irrational way
In decidin' on wha he glorifies,
And no' – as owre often – let scallywags,
Topers and lechers, win sic a prize.
Wi' a' due respect we'll no' follow his lead.
Mankind at least maun aye keep its heid.
The wise are confounded; calculations upset,
Law set at naught, and order contemned.
– O the Angel o' Daith is covered wi' een
But I stand in a guise still mair terribly gemmed.

– I think you are richt.
Culture's leadin' to the extinction o' Man.
    What? Stop the culture?
        That's no' my plan.
    I am Ishmael, the only man,
        Wha's the freend o' a' men.
    (And wha has ever been certain o' ocht
        Here recognises certainty's voice again.)
        I tell you a' else is vain.
    Eden's wide-open, unchanged; and nocht shuts us frae 't
        But impious delusions o' oor ain.

– Ilka man that blethers o' honest toil,
And believes in rewards and punishments,
In a God like Public Opinion,
And the sanctity o' the financial system,
A' that appeal to the Past or the Future,
Or think that twa and twa mak' fower,
Or that they can judge twixt virtue and vice,
Health and disease, sanity and insanity,
Or that thocht can be its ain judge;
Wha canna believe in something for naething,
(No' stoppin' to speir whence their vera lives come);
Ilka man that is feart o' leisure,
Ilka man that wi' needless darg shuts oot
The free, abundant, intolerable licht;
A' the men o' science, the enemies o' truth;
A' imposers and accepters o' ony taboos;
A' taskmasters and performers o' tasks;
Ilka man that says we maun haud thegither,
Dependent on each ither – no' juist on God;
That we are members o' ane anither,
And canna stand alane – no' hailly alane –
Or escape frae the auld apron strings and cry
'Wumman, what ha'e you to dae wi' me?'
A' that are feart o' becomin' owre clever
And prefer a decent stupidity.
A' that cry 'Haud – that's ga'en owre faur.

We dinna ken where – if at a' – it'll stop.'
A' that believe we should be o' a'e mind
Or at least agreed upon certain things,
Obey the same laws, honour the same God,
Subscribe to some 'common humanity,'
Deny that the wind aye blaws where it lists
And's no' in the habit o' answerin' prayer,
Say that God prefers the just to the unjust,
A' that trust external authority,
A' short circuiters o' consciousness,
Believers in ony State or system or creed.
A' that expect clear explanations,
Fixed standards and reasonable methods.
A' the rulers and a' the ruled
                    And a'body else.
These are the devils, the impious ideas,
Rebels, a' cries o' 'Haud – Ha'e a care,'
          Tell us where oor enemies are.
Oor task is to destroy them a' and return
Victorious to the spirit that in us should burn,
Oor sole concern, a' but a' men spurn,
And that spurns a' men – a' men, even us;
And can mak' nocht o' the word victorious.

Then quietly, quietly, quietly
Wi' nae excitement or noise.
     It's rarely a rebel
          Raises his voice.

There's nae necessity.

We are like somebody wha hears
A wonderfu' language and mak's up his mind
To write poetry in it – but ah!
It's impossible to learn it, we find,
Tho' we'll never ha'e ony use again
For ither languages o' ony kind.

The only song for which I care
Is one other men may hear
But cannot understand
Save as a man may 'share'
But cannot really bear
        Another's pain.

It's neither here nor there
Whether or not men listen.
What they thinks of no account,
That is their own affair,
For which who sings can spare
        No time or thought.

It's such a song as all men sing
Tho' few ever hear themselves
Or could believe it if they did;
As utterly unreasonable a thing
As would be some constant mourning
        That couldn't get used to death.

As one dog barking may set
Another off till all the dogs
Are howling together at the moon
Is what may happen to mankind yet
If such a song should ever get
        Free tongue – as I desire.

But, of course, that cannot be,
Most men are naturally unable
To hear a song like that at all
And those who can at once agree
That it's some sweeter melody
        And at once it is – to them.

And soon there's nobody left, you see,
To hear it as it really is,
For reason with good reason

Must always pack its jury
And none can question its decree
    In the nature of the case.

All men die, and, of course, men say
We must accept the fact
Whether we like it or not.
There's no use carrying on that way,
What can we hope to gain by it, pray?
    – My song's like that.

It's such a song that if another
Is heard to sing it raises
The very devil in all men's hearts
And makes them quick to smother
Such a source of endless bother
    – Lest they're heard at it too!

Many a voice they've buried alive
In conspiracies of silence,
Many a voice still sings unheard
Behind thick walls no sound can drive
A way through, nay, might easier rive
    The gaolers' hearts.

Just so who hears the nightingale
Cries: 'Beautiful must be
The land you learned your song in,'
And hears without avail
The lying bird reply: 'Words fail
    To tell its ugliness.'

So reason grounds itself on groundlessness.

And do I seek to speak again
Even in such a form as this
The impossible words? – Of course I don't,
I only say – and say in vain –
There's nothing else for which I'm fain
    Or care a damn about.

Let all men laugh as at a child
Crying broken-hearted for the moon
– Fit cause for manly laughter!
God himself would needs have smiled
If he had ever heard such wild
  Nonsense from Nazareth – if not Calvary!

The child is right and must not be
Consoled until the world ends
Nor eat nor sleep but night and day
Cry on unceasingly.
In any other child I see
  A monstrous brat of death, not Life.

As far as mankind is concerned
Plotinus, Pascal, and the rest
Who said them never really said
Such things; all men long since discerned
They cannot be said and so they've learned
  To treat them as unspoken.

Yet the infamous alliance
Of Aristotle and Plato
With the murderers of Socrates
Is nothing to the reliance
To meet any such defiance
  Most men have in each other.

For, of course, they punish us too
– Tho' the crime we're guilty of
Is impossible and undone –
As viciously as they can do;
And all wise men to the godless crew
  Play Anytus and Meletus
– All wise men condemn the true
  As Pontius Pilate did.

Your song, O God, that none dare hear
Save the insane and such as I
Apostates from humanity
Sings out in me with no more fear
Than one who thinks he has the world's ear
  From his padded cell
— Insane enough, with you so near,
   To want, like you, the world as well!

THE BIRLINN OF CLANRANALD
(BIRLINN CHLANN–RAGHNAILL)

Translated from the Scots Gaelic of Alasdair MacMhaighstir Alasdair

(1935)

The Birlinn of Clanranald

Being a ship-blessing, together with a sea-incitement made for the crew of the Birlinn of the Lord of Clanranald.

GOD bless the craft of Clanranald
When brangled first with the brine,
Himself and his heroes hurling;[1]
The pick of the human line!

The blessing of holy Triune
On the fury of the air;
The sea's ruggedness smoothed away
Ease us to our haven there!

Father who fashioned the ocean
And winds that from all points roll,
Bless our lean ship and her heroes,
Keep her and her whole crew whole!

Your grace, O Son, on our anchor,
Our rudder, sails, and all graith
And tackle to her masts attached,
And guard us as we have faith!

Bless our mast-hoops and our sail-yards
And our masts and all our ropes,
Preserve our stays and our halyards,
And confirm us in our hopes!

Holy Ghost, be you our helmsman
To steer the course that is right.
You know every port under Heaven.
We cast ourselves on your sleight!

[1] Himself, i.e. The Chief.

The Blessing of the Arms

God's blessing be on our claymores
And flexible grey toledos
And heavy coats of mail-harness
Through which no dull blade can bleed us!

Bless our shoulder-belts and gorgets
And our well-made bossy targes,
Bless each and all of our weapons,
And the man who with it charges.

Bless our gleaming bows of yew-wood
Good to bend in battle-mêlée,
And birchen arrows, not to splinter
In the surly badger's belly.

Bless every dirk, every pistol,
Every kilt of noble pleating,
Every martial apparatus
With us under this ship's sheeting.

Lack no knowledge then or mettle
To do brave deeds with hardihood
While still four planks of her remain
Or pair of overlaps holds good.

With her drowned boards yet for footstools
Or a thole-pin above water
Let ocean not numb your resource,
Your hearts inchoate horror shatter.

Keep up a herculean struggle.
If the sea detects no weakness,
Her pride at last will be o'ercome
And reward your prowess with meekness.

As your foe in a land battle
Seeing your strength is left untouched
Is more apt to weaken in onslaught
Than be in fiercer furies clutched,

So with the sea; if you maintain
Set resolve and dauntless spirits
She will at length, as God's ordained,
Humble herself to your merits.

Incitement for Rowing to Sailing-Place

To put the black well-fashioned yewship
    To the sailing-place
Thrust you out flexible oarbanks
    Dressed to sheer grace;
Oars smooth-shafted and shapely,
    Grateful for gripping,
Made for lusty resolute rowing,
    Palm-fast, foam-whipping;
Knocking sparks out of the water
    Towards Heaven
Like the fire-flush from a smithy
    Updriven,
Under the great measured onstrokes
    Of the oar-lunges
That confound the indrawn billows
    With their plunges,
While the shrewd blades of the white woods
    Go cleaving
The tops of the valleyed blue-hills
    Shaggily heaving.
O stretch you, pull you, and bend you
    Between the thole-pins,
Your knuckles snow with hard plying
    The pinewood fins;

All the big muscular fellows
    Along her lying
With their hairy and sinewy
    Arms keep her flying,
Raising and lowering together
    With a single motion
Their evenly dressed poles of pinewood
    Mastering the ocean.

A Herculean planked on the fore-oar
    Roaring: 'Up, on with her!'
Makes all the thick shoulder muscles
    Glide better together,
Thrusting the birlinn with snorting
    Through each chill sea-glen;
The hard curved prow through the tide-lumps
    Drives inveighing,
On all hands sending up mountains
    Round her insistence.
Hùgan, the sea says, like Stentor;
    Héig, say the thole-pins.
Rasping now, on the timbers,
    Of the shirred surges!
The oars jib; blood-blistering
    Slowly emerges
On each hard hand of the rowers
    In berserk fettle
Hurling on the trembling oakplanks,
    Caulking, and metal,
Though nailheads spring with the thunder
    Thumping her thigh.
A crew to make a right rocking
    The deeps to defy,
Working the lean ship like an auger
    Through walls of water,
The bristling wrath of blue-þlack billows
    No daunting matter.

They are the choice set of fellows
　　To hold an oarage
Outmanœuvring the dark swirlings
　　With skill and courage,
Without a point lost or tiring,
　　Timely throughout,
Despite all the dire devilment
　　Of the waterspout!

Then after the sixteen men had sat at the oars to row her against the wind to a sailing-place, Calum Garbh, son of Ranald of the Seas, who was on the fore-oar, recited an iorram (or rowing song) for her, as follows:

And now since you're selected
– No doubt true choice effected! –
Let rowing be directed
　　　　　　Bold and set.

Give a rocking pointedly,
Without lapse or lack of netteté,
So all sea-problems set yet be
　　　　　　More than met.

A well-gripped stubborn rocking
From bones and sinews yoking,
The steps from her oarbank knocking
　　　　　　Foam to fire.

Incite each other along
And a good so-go-all song
From the fore man's mouth fall strong
　　　　　　To inspire.

Oar's sawdust on the rowlocks,
Hands run with sores like golochs,
Waves' armpits like any mollusc
　　　　　　Screw the oars.

Cheeks be lit all blazing red,
Palms of skin all casing shed,
While sweat off every face and head
                  Thumping pours.

Stretch you, pull you, and bend you
The blades the pine-trees lend you,
Ascend, descend, and wend you
                  Through the sea.

Banks of oars on either side
Set your labour to her tide
And spray on ocean's thorter-pride
                  Throw freely.

Row as one, cleanly, clearly;
Through flesh-thick waves cut sheerly;
A job that's not done wearily
                  Nor snail-wise.

Strike her evenly without fluther.
Often glance at one another
So in your thews still further
                  Vim may rise.

Let her oak go skelping through
Big-bellied troughs of swingeing blue;
In their two thighs pounding too
                  Each spasm down.

Though the hoary heaving ocean
Swell with even more commotion,
Toppling waves with drowning notion
                  Roar and frown,

And incessant wash pour in
O'er her shoulders and the din
Groan all round and sob to win
                  Through her keel,

Stretch you, pull you, and bend you.
The red-backed sleek shafts tend you.
With the pith strong arms lend you
        Victory feel.

Put that headland past your prow
Where you strain with sweat-drenched brow
And lift the sails upon her now
        From Uist of the sheldrakes!

*Then they rowed to a sailing-place. They took in the sixteen oars which were swiftly
pruned down against her thigh to avoid sheet-ropes. Clanranald ordered his gentlemen to
see to the disposition in the places for which they were qualified of men who would not be
daunted by any spectre from the deep nor any chaos in which the ocean might involve them.
After the selection every man was ordered to take up his appointed place, and accordingly
the steersman was summoned to sit at the rudder in these words:*

Set at the rudder a brawny
    Grand fellow,
Top nor trough of sea can unhorse,
    Coarse skelp nor bellow;
Broad-beamed, well-set, full of vigour,
    Wary withal;
Who hearing the shaggy surges
    Come roaring
Her prow expertly to the rollers
    Keeps shoring;
Who will even keep her going
    As if unshaken,
Adjusting sheet and tack – glances
    Windward taken;
Yielding no thumb-long deviation
    Of her true course
Despite the bounding wave-summits'
    Opposing force;
Who will go windward so stoutly
    With her when needed,
Though nailhead nor rib in her oak
    But shrieks – unheeded;

Whom no spectre sprung from the abyss
    Could shift or dismay,
Or grey sea to his ears upswoln
    E'er tear away
From his set place while yet alive
    Helm under armpit!
Under his charge whatever's been placed
    Nothing has harmed it.
A match for old ocean rough-glenned
    With inclemency!
Who no rope strains tackwindwarding
    But easily
Lets run and tacks under full canvas
    None so meetly
And her tacking on each wavetop
    Binds so featly,
Straight harbourwards under spray-showers
    Running so sweetly!

There was appointed a shrouds-man.

Set another stalwart fellow
    For shrouds-grasping;
With finger-vices, great hand-span,
    For such clasping;
Sage, quick; to help with the yard's end
    When that's needed,
With masts and gear, leave no neighbour
    Task unheeded;
Wind-wise, and aptly adjusting
    With shrouds-manning
The sheet's-man's slackings – and t'assist
    In all ways scanning.

A sheet's-man was set apart.

Set too on the thwart a sheet's-man
    With great arms ending
In horny compulsive fingers
    For the sheet-tending;

Pull in, let out, as is wanted,
    With strength of grabbing;
Draw in when beating to windward,[1]
    The blast crabbing;
And release when the gust again
    Ceases rending.

There was ordered out a tacksman.

Dispose another sturdy sailor,
    Masterfully
To keep the tack to her windward,[1]
    And deal duly;
The tack to each cleat his changing
    Up and down bringing,
As a fair breeze may favour
    Or ill come swinging;
And if he sees tempest threaten
    Against the shock
Let him shear the tack without mercy
    Down to the stock.

There was ordered to the prow a pilot.[2]

A pilot in the prow be standing.
    Let him afford
Us ever reliable knowledge
    Of what's toward
And keep confirming the steersman
    In our right going,
For he is the veritable Pole Star
    We must have showing;
Suresightedly taking a landmark
    With the trained vision
That is the God of all weathers
    On such a mission.

[1] The tack (Gaelic: *cluas*, ear) is the the lower foremost corner of a sail.
[2] *Màirnealach* (the Gaelic designation here) is a pilot chiefly for observing the weather from the look of the skies.

There was set apart a halyard-man.

Take place at the main halyard
    A clear-headed
Athletic fellow, with vigour
    And care wedded,
An able fellow without flurry,
    Grim and alert,
To take from her and give to her
    Just and expert,
To lie with hand of due power
    There on the halyard,
The weight of his grasp decisive
    Rive oakwoodward;
Not tie the halyard about the cleat
    Tight beyond use
But fix it firmly, cunningly,
    With running noose;
Thus over the pin squirting, humming,
    Now as it's roped,
Yet should perchance the prop be sundered
    It may be stopped!

There was set apart a teller-of-the-waters, since the sea was becoming too rough, and the
steersman said to him:

I'll have at my ear a teller
    Of the waters;
Let him keep close watch windward
    On these matters;
A man somewhat timid, cautious,
    Not altogether
A coward however! – Keeping
    Stock of the weather,
Whether in his fore or stern quarter
    The fair breeze is,
Blurting out without hesitation
    Aught he sees is

Peril-spelling to his notion;
    Or, should he spy
The likeness of a drowning sea
    Roaring down, cry
To put our stem swiftly to it.
    Insistently
Clamorous at the least threat of danger
    This man must be,
And not fear to give the steersman
    Any hint of hazard.
– But let him be the one teller
    Of the waters heard,
And not the whole of you bawling
    Advices mixed,
A distraught steersman not knowing
    Who to heed next!

There was ordered out a baler, since the sea was rushing over them fore and aft:

Let attend on the baling space
    A hardy hero
Not to be cramped or benumbed
    By cold at zero,
Raw brine or stinging hail dashing
    In thrashing showers
Round his chest and neck, – but armoured
    In dogged powers,
A thick round wooden baling-can
    In his swarthy hands,
Throwing out the sea forever
    As soon as it lands;
Never straightening his lithe backbone
    Till his task's o'er,
Not one drop left in her bottom
    – Or keelson-floor!
Were her planks holed till for a riddle
    She well might pass
He'd keep her all dry as a bottle's
    Outside glass!

Two men were appointed for hauling the peak-downhauls, since it appeared that the sails would be torn from them by the exceeding boisterousness of the weather:

> Put a pair of hefty fellows
>> Thick-boned, strong-thewed,
> To take charge of her peak-downhauls
>> With force and aptitude;
> With the power of great fore-arms
>> In till of need
> To haul them in or let them run,
>> But always lead
> When wayward back to the middle;
>> For this two men
> Of the Canna men, Donnchadh Mac Chomaig
>> And Iain Mac Iain,
> Were chosen – deft and definite fellows
>> In brawn and brain.·

Six men were chosen to man the ship's floor as a precaution against the failing of any of those mentioned, or lest the raging of the sea might pluck one overboard, one of these six might take his place:

> Let's have six men, quick and clever
>> To give a hand,
> Going through the ship in all directions,
>> A nimble band,
> Each like a hare on a mountain top
>> And dogs copping him,
> Dodging this way and that, and having
>> Nothing stopping him;
> Handy men, quick in the uptake,
>> Spry and observant,
> To fill any breach as needed
>> Are who we want;
> Men who can climb the hard smooth ropes
>> Of the slender hemp
> As in May trees of a thick-wood
>> Only squirrels can attempt;

Gleg fellows, shrewd to take from her
  As desired
Or give respite meet and restful;
  Keen, untired.
Such the six the ship of MacDonald
  Has now acquired.

Now that every convenience pertaining to sailing had been put in good order and every brave dependable fellow had taken up the duty assigned to him, they hoisted the sails about sunrise on St. Bride's Day, beginning their course from the mouth of Loch Ainort in South Uist.

The Voyage

The sun bursting golden-yellow
  Out of his husk,
The sky grew wild and hot-breathing,
  Unsheathing a fell tusk,
Then turned wave-blue, thick, dun-bellied,
  Fierce and forbidding,
Every hue that would be in a plaid
  In it kneading;
A 'dog's tooth' in the Western quarter[1]
  Snorters prophesied;
The swift clouds under a shower-breeze[2]
  Multiplied.
Now they hoisted the speckled sails
  Peaked and close-wrought,
And stretched out the stubborn shrouds
  Tough and taut
To the long resin-red shafts
  Of the mast.
With adroit and firm-drawn knotting
  These were made fast
Through the eyes of the hooks and rings;
  Swiftly and expertly

[1] 'Dog's tooth' – broken bit of rainbow.
[2] *Fuaradh-froise* – the breeze that precedes a shower.

Each rope put right of the rigging;
    And orderly
The men took up their set stations
    And were ready.
Then opened the windows of the sky
    Pied, grey-blue,
To the lowering wind's blowing,
    A morose brew,
The sea pulled on his grim rugging
    Slashed with sore rents,
That rough-napped mantle, a weaving
    Of loathsome torrents.
The shape-ever-changing surges
    Swelled up in hills
And roared down into valleys
    In appalling spills.
The water yawned in great craters,
    Slavering mouths agape
Snatching and snarling at each other
    In rabid shape.
It were a man's deed to confront
    The demented scene,
Each mountain of them breaking
    Into flamy lumps.
Each fore-wave towering grey-fanged
    Mordantly grumps
While a routing comes from the back-waves
    With their raving rumps.
When we would rise on these rollers
    Soundly, compactly,
It was imperative to shorten sail
    Swiftly, exactly.
When we would fall with one swallowing
    Down into the glens
Every topsail she had would be off.
    – No light task the men's!
The great hooked big-buttocked ones
    Long before

They came at all near us were heard
 Loudly aroar
Scourging all the lesser waves level
 As on they tore.
It was no joke to steer in that sea
 When the high tops to miss
Seemed almost to hear her keel scrape
 The shelly abyss!
The sea churning and lashing itself
 In maniacal states,
Seals and other great beasts were even
 In direr straits,
The wild swelth and the pounding waves
 And the ship's nose
Scattering their white brains callous
 Through the billows
They shouted to us loudly, dreadfully,
 The piteous word: –
'Save us or we perish. We are subjects.
 Take us aboard.'
Small fish that were in the waters,
 Murderously churned,
Floated on the top without number
 White bellies upturned.
The stones and shells of the floor even
 Came to the top
Torn up by the all-grabbing motion
 That would not stop.
The whole sea was a foul porridge
 Full of red scum
With the blood and ordure of the beasts,
 Ruddy, glum,
While screaming with their gill-less mouths,
 Their jaws agape,
Even the air's abyss was full of fiends
 That had no shape.
With the paws and tails of great monsters
 Gruesome to hear

Were the screeching towerers. They would strike
    Fifty warriors with fear.
The crew's ears lost all appetite
    For hearing in that din,
Rabble of mad sky-demons,
    And their watery kin
Making a baying so unearthly,
    Deeper than the sea-floor,
Great notes lower than human hearing
    Ever heard before.
What then with the ocean's turmoil
    Pounding the ship,
The clamour of the prow flenching whales
    With slime-foiled grip,
And the wind from the Western quarter
    Restarting her windward blast,
Through every possible ordeal
    It seemed we passed.
We were blinded by the sea-spray
    Ever going over us;
With, beyond that, like another ocean,
    Thunders and lightnings to cover us,
The thunderbolts sometimes singeing
    Our rigging till the smoke
And stench of the reefs smouldering
    Made us utterly choke.
Between the upper and lower torments
    Thus were we braised,
Water, fire, and wind simultaneously
    Against us raised.
– But when it was beyond the sea's power
    To make us yield
She took pity with a faint smile
    And truce was sealed,
Though by that time no mast was unbent,
    No sail untorn,
Yard unsevered, mast-ring unflawed,
    Oar not shag-shorn,

No stay unstarted, halyard or shroud unbroken.
    Fise. Faise.[1]
Thwart and gunwale made confession
    In similar wise.
Every mast-rigging and tackle
    The worse of wear;
Not a beam-knee or rib of her
    Unloosened there;
Her gunwale and bottom-boards
    Were confounded;
Not a helm left unsplit,
    A rudder unwounded.
Every timber creaked, moaned, and warped.
    Not a tree-nail
Was unpulled, no plank had failed
    To give in the gale.
Not a part that pertained to her
    But had suffered
And from its first state and purpose
    Sadly differed.
The sea proclaimed peace with us
    At the fork of Islay Sound
And the hostile barking wind
    Was ordered off the ground.
It went to the upper places of the air
    And become a quiet
Glossy-white surface to us there
    After all its riot,
And to God we made thinksgiving
    That good Clanranald
Was spared the brutal death for which
    The elements had wrangled.
Then we pulled down the speckled canvas
    And lowered
The sleek red masts and along her bottom
    Safely stored,

---

[1] Sounds of tearing.

And put out the slender well-wrought oars
    Coloured, and smooth to the hand,
Made of the pine cut by Mac Bharais
    In Finnan's Island,
And set up the right-royal, rocking, rowing,
    Deft and timeous,
And made good harbour there at the top
    Of Carrick-Fergus.
We threw out anchors peacefully
    In that roadstead.
We took food and drink unstinting
    And there we stayed.

From
SECOND HYMN TO LENIN AND OTHER POEMS
(1935)

On the Ocean Floor

Now more and more on my concern with the lifted
　　waves of genius gaining
I am aware of the lightless depths that beneath them lie;
And as one who hears their tiny shells incessantly raining
On the ocean floor as the foraminifera die.

Wagner

It's easy to manipulate the great regions
Of the human soul and sometimes I see
The whole articulation as if
I'd outgrown it – mere child's play to me.

All I want is a pig's life personally;
Plenty of women and wine – though of course
I'm vastly amused at the thought of being
Incidentally an historical force.

A Dog's Life[1]

'Tell me,' I asked a cripple who goes on all fours
Like a dog, pads on his hands, 'Don't poor souls like you
Feel the need to believe in something beyond this world
Far more than we others do?'

'No. Not with a life like mine,' he replied.
'It's not we who need God. He could tell us no more
If he does exist than we understand already
And are thankful for.'

[1] With acknowledgments to Pär Lagerkvist.

Killing No Murder[1]

GREETINGS from the grave to you, my murderers!
I bear you no grudge for killing me.
Each one seeks to promote what he thinks the right,
And doubtless you think you did rightly.

You believe in your ancestors' teaching,
'I am the master and you the serf,'
And you regard being master as an honour,
A special privilege you inherit and deserve.

But I took my stand with the lowly
And passionately appealed to them too
To reply to your ancestors' descendants,
'We are no servants, no masters you.'

Thus I injured you in your pride
And shook the people in their mad belief
That you are made of superior stuff,
Born to be rulers, with the world in fief.

I hurt your pride and you took your revenge.
We were both convinced we were right,
Serving the just cause as every man must
According to his light.

Then may my spilt blood help to decide
If your right or mine shall prevail;
Your injured pride or the people's suffering
At last in world-judgment turn the scale.

[1] *A striking example of literary prophecy, this poem is a free translation of the remark-able poem, 'Die Stimme des Gemordeten,' from his volume, Brennende Erde (Burning Earth), Munich, 1920, in which the manner of his death fourteen years later was forecast by Erich Mühsam, the Socialist writer, officially stated to have committed suicide in the Oranienburg Concentration Camp, but actually murdered by the Nazis. May the ultimate issue it predicts come as true as the author's forecast of how he would die!*

If the people's liberation fell
Overboard with the ballast of my poor life
Then your killing me matters little
And in vain from the start was my strife.

But if from my blood springs up
The seed which you did not will
Then exultingly I'll praise the moment
When fear of me compelled you to kill.

For so murder's arm would become
An instrument in Freedom's great task
And in death even more than in life
I'd advance it – what more could I ask?

My murder would herald your end then,
My spirit live in your overthrow
And when the goal I sought is achieved
In the hearts of all free men glow.

So I leave it to time to show
Which of us shall triumph at last,
– Community, or Money-and-Arms,
The glorious future or brutish past.

Enough! The death I have suffered
Has steeled my comrades anew to the fight,
Greetings from the grave to you, murderers!
The battle goes on. And who wins is right!

After the Siege

THE world to-day is like a city
That's been long besieged but now
When the siege is raised the mass of the people
No chance of relief allow.

They wouldn't know what to do, poor dears,
Without their dire accustomed straits,
So they keep to a Spartan diet of rats
While Plenty waits at the gates.

At the Cenotaph

ARE the living so much use
That we need to mourn the dead?
Or would it yield better results
To reverse their roles instead?
The millions slain in the War –
Untimely, the best of our seed? –
Would the world be any the better
If they were still living indeed?
The achievements of such as are
To the notion lend no support;
The whole history of life and death
Yields no scrap of evidence for't. –
Keep going to your wars, you fools, as of yore;
I'm the civilisation you're fighting for.

One of the Principal Causes of War

O SHE was full of loving fuss
When I cut my hand and the blood gushed out
And cleverly she dressed the wound
And wrapt it in a clout.

O tenderly she tended me
Though deep in her eyes I could tell
The secret joy that men are whiles
Obliged to bleed as well.

I thanked her kindly and never let on,
Seeing she could not understand,
That she wished me a wound far worse to staunch –
And not in the hand!

O Ease My Spirit

And as for their appearances, they four had one likeness, as if a wheel had been in the midst of a wheel.

EZEKIEL

O EASE my spirit increasingly of the load
Of my personal limitations and the riddling differences
Between man and man with a more constant insight
Into the fundamental similarity of all activities.

And quicken me to the gloriously and terribly illuminating
Integration of the physical and the spiritual till I feel how easily
I could put my hand gently on the whole round world
As on my sweetheart's head and draw it to me.

Knowledge of God

TO AN OXFORD GROUPER

I KNOW all you can say and understand too well
Your determination to credit Christ too
With the sort of mysticism, that's sufficed so many
From Paul, who began it, down to you.

But hold! In future with me just remember
That Christ at any rate had the sense,
With probably as close personal knowledge of God,
Never to speak of His religious experience.

Birth of a Genius Among Men

THE night folded itself about me like a woman's hair.
Thousands of dispersed forces drawn as by a magnet
Streamed through the open windows – millions of stars poured through;
What destiny were they seeking in us, what outlet?

An immense vigour awoke in my body.
My breast expanded and overflowed into the night.
I was one with Scotland out there and with all the world
And thoughts of your beauty shone in me like starlight.

You were all female, ripe as a rose for the plucking,
I was all male and no longer resisted my need.
The earth obeyed the rhythm of our panting.
The mountains sighed with us. Infinity was emptied.

To both of us it seemed as if we had never loved before.
A miracle was abroad and I knew that not merely I
Had accomplished the act of love but the whole universe through me,
A great design was fulfilled, another genius nigh.

Yet I lay awake and as the daylight broke
I heard the faint voices of the Ideas discuss
The way in which they could only express themselves yet
In fragmentary and fallacious forms through us.

As Lovers Do

HERE at the height of passion
        As lovers do
I can only speak brokenly
        Of trifles too.

Idiot incoherence
I know full well
Is the only language
That with God can deal.

At the Graveside

THERE is no stupid soul who neither knows
The rudiments of human history
Nor seeks to solve the problems of this life
But still must give his witless testimony
On huge conundrums. – Faithless in small things,
Let all such cease their fond imaginings.
The eyes of fools are on the ends of God.
I postpone all such thoughts beneath this sod.

Light and Shadow

Like memories of what cannot be
Within the reign of memory . . .
That shake our mortal frames to dust.
SHELLEY

ON every thought I have the countless shadows fall
Of other thoughts as valid that I cannot have;
Cross-lights of errors, too, impossible to me,
Yet somehow truer than all these thoughts, being with
      more power aglow.

May I never lose these shadowy glimpses of unknown
      thoughts
That modify and minify my own, and never fail
To keep some shining sense of the way all thoughts at last
Before life's dawning meaning like the stars at sunrise pale.

Behind the Symbols

LET the hearts of my people be lifted up
Once more with the daily sight
Of an eagle wheeling on majestic vans
    That is our Scottish birthright.

Fill their lives again with the noblest form
    At liberty in Europe still –
The red stag pausing with lifted hoof
    On the sun-assailing hill.

For these are among Earth's glorious symbols
    To souls of men needing symbols yet
And a man must be well nourished on these
    To embrace the Infinite.

But the supreme spirit enters into all
    As an otter into its watery home
As if without dividing its flow
    And making no ripple, bubble, or foam.

Even so in the course of time I hope
My people will open their hearts until
They are like the lochs the hill-streams feed
    Forever – but cannot overspill.

Folly

THEY called him a wastrel. It was perfectly clear
Half the energy and ability he threw away
On his frivollings and vices, on puss and on booze,
Could have beaten the foremost men of his day
In any decent line he might have cared to choose.

Yet there he was. The fool chose just to *live*,
Gratifying follies with powers that would have sufficed
To carry him high in commerce, church or state – giving
Himself to high jinks instead – a barbarous choice that surprised
All who spend their lives wasting the reasons for living.

From an 'Ode to All Rebels'

Deluded men despise me when I have taken human form.
BHAGAVAD-GITA, IX. II. Cf. JOHN I. 10.

As the heavy earth is the same below
Though insubstantialised in the sunshine
I see a man's slack mouth and goggling eyes
Behind this glory and know them for mine
Nor if I could would I lose for a moment
Divine in human or human in divine.
O double vision fighting in the glass!
Now light blots out this last distinction of class.
 O magical change, O miracle
 I am suddenly beyond myself.
  Red, white, and square,
 Tearing the soul to rags!

Folk recognise – with regret it may be –
Man's kinship with the most loathsome brute
Joggling his protruding sternum there
And letting his animal noises out,
 All they can have patience with,
 All they can pity,
All they can hide in their madhouses,
 In their gaols and hospital wards,
All that's diseased, misshapen, obscene,
 Mankind accepts and guards;

But when an angel appears, a man
Infinitely superior to man, as here,
From a man no better than other men,
An idiot like them, they howl with fear,
Or perjure their sight, and gibe and jeer
And deny that the like can ever appear,
　　Let alone be one with the other.

　　　'*L'extrême esprit est accusé de folie*
　　　　　Comme l'extrême défaut;
　　　Rien que la médiocrité n'est bon.
　　　　　C'est sortir de l'humanité
　　　　　Que de sortir du milieu.'

　　　'*Und wir, die an steigendes Glück*
　　　denken, empfänden die Rührung,
　　　die uns beinah bestürzt,
　　　wenn ein Glückliches fällt.'

It's against all sense and what's the use
Of decency, worship, a shepherded soul,
If a creature like this can suddenly emerge –
Regardless of all most men can thole,
Yet visibly dowered with the light of lights,
The glory of God he shows yet denies,
When even if they tried like vices themselves,
Instead of the wisdom and virtues they prize,
None of them, not even the most reverend and upright,
Would ever be transfigured in similar wise?
God should consult with the Government or Church
Or get the medical profession to advise,
Not act in such an irrational way
In deciding on who He glorifies,
And not – as too often – let scallywags,
Lechers and topers, win such a prize.
With due respect we'll not follow His lead.
Mankind at least must always keep its head.
The wise are confounded, calculations upset,

Law set at naught, and order contemned –
O the Angel of Death is covered with eyes
But I stand in a guise still more terrible gemmed. –
  I think you are right.
  Culture's leading to the extinction of Man.
  What? Stop the culture?
    That's not my plan.
I am Ishmael, the only man
Who's the friend of all men.
(And who has ever known certitude
Must here recognise its voice again!)
  I tell you all else is vain.

– Every man who havers about honest toil
And believes in rewards and punishments,
In a God like Public Opinion
Or conformable to human reason,
And the sanctity of the financial system,
All that appeal to the Past or the Future,
Or think that two and two make four,
Or that they can judge 'twixt virtue and vice,
Health and disease, sanity and insanity,
Or that thought can be its own judge;
Who cannot believe in something for nothing
(Not stopping to ask whence their lives come);
Every man who is afraid of leisure,
Every man who with needless toil shuts out
The free, abundant, intolerable light;
All the men of science, the enemies of truth;
All imposers and accepters of any taboos;
All taskmasters and their bondagers,
Every man who says we must hold together,
Dependent on each other – not just on God;
That we are members of one another
And cannot stand alone – not wholly alone –
Or escape from the old apron-strings and cry
'Woman, what have you to do with me?'
All who are afraid of becoming too clever

And prefer a decent stupidity;
All who cry: 'Hold – that's going too far.
We don't know where – if at all – it'll stop';
All who believe we should be of one mind
Or at least agreed upon certain things,
Obey the same laws, honour the same God,
Subscribe to some 'common humanity';
Deny that the wind always blows where it lists
And isn't in the habit of answering prayer;
Say that God prefers the just to the unjust,
That differences are only evolved to be
Resumed into undifferentiated oneness again;
All who trust any external authority,
All short circuiters of consciousness,
Believers in any State or system or creed,
All who expect clear explanations,
Fixed standards, and reasonable methods,
All the rulers and all the ruled,
    And everybody else,
These are the devils, the impious ideas;
Rebels, all cries of 'Hold – have a care!'
    Tell us where our enemies are.
Our task is to destroy them all and return
Victorious to the spirit that in us should burn,
Our sole concern, that all but all men spurn,
And that spurns all men – all men, even us;
And can make nothing of the word victorious.

Thanksgiving

O WELL may timid and grasping folk
Rejoice that once according to Holy Writ
An innocent man was tortured to death
For their benefit; and be content – now they have it!

An Unknown Quantity

WHY this flinching from happiness, this anxiety for the future,
This sense of profound disturbance as I look at you, son?
Your mother does not know what she has given birth to
And feels how incalculable is the deed she has done.

It is only the defensive dread every human organism feels
In the presence of something capable of changing it radically,
Of shaking it out of its rut, breaking its accustomed rhythm, –
How seldom, alas, a woman needs to feel this with her baby!

In the Children's Hospital

Does it matter? – losing your legs? . . .
SIEGFRIED SASSOON

Now let the legless boy show the great lady
How well he can manage his crutches.
It doesn't matter though the Sister objects,
'He's not used to them yet,' when such is
The will of the Princess. Come, Tommy,
Try a few desperate steps through the ward.
Then the hand of Royalty will pat your head
And life suddenly cease to be hard.
For a couple of legs are surely no miss
When the loss leads to such an honour as this!
One knows, when one sees how jealous the rest
Of the children are, it's been all for the best! –
But would the sound of your sticks on the floor
Thundered in her skull for evermore!

Lo! A Child is Born

I THOUGHT of a house where the stones seemed suddenly changed
And became instinct with hope, hope as solid as themselves,
And the atmosphere warm with that lovely heat,
The warmth of tenderness and longing souls, the smiling anxiety
That rules a home where a child is about to be born.
The walls were full of ears. All voices were lowered.
Only the mother had the right to groan or complain.
Then I thought of the whole world. Who cares for its travail
And seeks to encompass it in like lovingkindness and peace?
There is a monstrous din of the sterile who contribute nothing
To the great end in view, and the future fumbles,
A bad birth, not like the child in that gracious home
Heard in the quietness turning in its mother's womb,
A strategic mind already, seeking the best way
To present himself to life, and at last, resolved,
Springing into history quivering like a fish,
Dropping into the world like a ripe fruit in due time. –
But where is the Past to which Time, smiling through her tears
At her new-born son, can turn crying: 'I love you'?

Think Not That I Forget

THINK not that I forget a single pang
    Of all that folk have tholed,
Agonies and abominations beyond all telling,
    Sights to daunt the most bold.

There are buildings in every town where daily
    Unthinkable horrors take place.
I am the woman in cancer's toils,
    The man without a face.

I am all cruelty and lust and filth,
    Corruption and law-made crime –
The helpless prisoners badgered in their cells
    In every land and clime,

All 'gallant soldiers' murdering for pay
    (Plus 'little Belgium' or like affair)
And heroic airmen blithe to give
    Poor tribes Death from the air,

And all the hidden but no less hideous deeds
    Sound citizens are always privily at –
Only in the mean natures and vicious looks
    Of their children, themselves, or their underlings
        caught.

Oh, there's as much of it in Great Britain here
    As in Sing-Sing or in Cayenne –
Differently disguised, of course, and hiding
    In the most 'decent and God-fearing' men

There is no horror history's ever known
    Mob passion or greedy fear wouldn't soon
Make them do over again – slovens and cowards
    Moving pig-eyed in their daily round.

They face nothing – their whole lives depend
    On ignorance and base contempt
For all that's worth-while in the powers of Man
    From any share in it exempt.

In the midst of plenty in poverty, –
    To Art no better than apes –
Think not that I am unaware
    Of one of their loathsome shapes.

Aristocratic sentiments? – Yes! But remember
    These Yahoos belong to no single class.
You'll find far more in proportion to numbers
    In palaces and west-end clubs than in the mass.

On the Money Monopolist being like Hell

(*Adapted from Gower's* Confessio Amantis.)

THERE was no competition for riches
When God made the world and men were still few,
All was in common, with no thought of fortune
In good times or bad, until avarice grew.

The world had grown greatly in men and cattle,
When men started to use the curst trick of money,
Peace departed then. War developed on every side,
Thrusting out all love, making common goods private property.

Given the world the miser would find it too small.
He never lets go again of anything he can grasp,
But seeks more and more, as if life had no end
Or Death itself might fail to loosen his clasp.

In this he's like Hell, for as the old books say,
What comes in there, be it great or small,
Never wins out again. Thus the wealthy are poor,
And most lack that of which they have most withal.

For anyone with a decent understanding
It is impertinent to say such criminals and fools
Possess wealth. Wealth possesses *them*, –
Dehumanised and made its senseless tools!

The Covenanters

THE waves of their purposefulness go flooding through me.
This religion is simple, naked. Its values stand out
In black and white. It is the wind of God;
Like standing on a mountain top in a gale
Binding, compelling, yet gloriously freeing.
It contains nothing tawdry or trivial.
Its very ugliness is compelling,
Its bleakness uplifting.
It holds me in a fastness of security.

Another Epitaph on an Army of Mercenaries[1]

IT is a God-damned lie to say that these
Saved, or knew, anything worth any man's pride.
They were professional murderers and they took
Their blood money and impious risks and died.
In spite of all their kind some elements of worth
With difficulty persist here and there on earth.

Like Achilles and Priam

YOU speak of the terrible trials besetting mankind now.
They are nothing. Do not men still put each other to death?
Do they not fight over their different ideas, are they not
Still split into classes? They have a long way to go
Before the supreme test, when, like Achilles and Priam, –
Priam kissing the hands that slew so many of his sons –
They must all manifest too the fact that the things
That unite men are stronger than those that divide.

[1] In reply to A. E. Housman's.

In the Slaughterhouse

MUST the standards of living be forced down further
For most folk? Are we faced with another war?
Twixt us and the Age of Plenty and leisure
Are we to let a money monopoly stay as a bar?

Vain questions! The insensate nonentities who rule us
Know that all human hopes and efforts don't matter
And listen to our bleating with the confidence of butchers
That the sheep can't hear them ordering their slaughter!

A Pair of Sea-Green Eyes

KATE's eyes were sea-green. She was one of the last
    To have them that hue
    Though in the distant past
It was common enough, that's true.
    Sea-green! What's that you say?
    Impossible? A lie?
No. It's no mistake. They weren't just grey,
    But the *oculi caesii*
    Tacitus refers to,
The 'eagle hath not so green,
    So quick, so fair an eye'
Of Shakespeare – Plautus's *oculi herbei*,
And the great eyes with a green circle
    Bacon thought promised long life.
    Have you not even read Villa Real's
    Great treatise in praise of green eyes?
Then you know nothing whatever about them,
Yet you tell a man like me that he lies!
Enough! You are like the carpenter in Chaucer's tale

Who 'knew not Catoun,' or those who thought,
In Dryden's lines, they had somehow got
By intuition more about the Godhead to know
Than Aristotle found by reason, or Plato,
Or Plutarch, or Seneca, or Cicero.

The Right End of the Stick

I THINK you've all got the right end of the stick,
My Christian or pagan, extravert or introvert friend,
My dead friend, my live, my unborn – but the trouble
Is just that all your sticks have only one end.

The Salmon Leap

I SAW one shadow shoot up and over
While ten failed to make it again and again,
But most of the salmon without an effort
In the bottom of the pool all day had lain.

Suddenly, effortlessly, like a flight of birds,
Up and over I saw them all slip.
The secret, I think, was the melted snow
Coming down and flicking them like a whip.

The majority of people make no attempt
In life to explore the infinite,
But who can tell what Death's cold touch
May prompt the lazy louts to yet?

The End of Usury

THE end of international finance –
Consciously or unconsciously, it matters not –
Is universal degradation and slavery,
A foul circumscription of the human lot.

But the Puritan asceticism is gone for ever
Which made the working-masses ashamed
Of their poverty as of a crime
For which they were in some way to be blamed.

And a sense of power and set resolve
Is abroad to shatter the shackles at last
And make all usury, poverty, and needless toil
Memories of an obscene incredible past.

The Two Parents

I LOVE my little son, and yet when he was ill
I could not confine myself to his bedside.
I was impatient of his squalid little needs,
His laboured breathing and the fretful way he cried
And longed for my wide range of interests again,
Whereas his mother sank without another care
To that dread level of nothing but life itself
And stayed day and night, till he was better, there.

Women may pretend, yet they always dismiss
Everything but mere being just like this.

If There Are Bounds to Any Man

IF there are bounds to any man
    Save those himself has set
To far horizons they're postponed
    And none have reached them yet.

And if most men are close curtailed
    And keep a petty groove
'Tis their own sloth that is to blame,
    Their powers they will not prove.

Preferring ease to energy,
    Soft lives to steel-like wills,
And mole-heaps of morality
    To the eternal hills.

All Earth's high peaks are naked stone
    And so must men forego
All they can shed – and that's all else! –
    Proportionate heights to show.

Reflections in an Ironworks

WOULD you resembled the metal you work with,
Would the iron entered into your souls,
Would you became like steel on your own behalf!
You are still only putty that tyranny rolls
Between its fingers! You makers of bayonets and guns
For your own destruction! No wonder that those
Weapons you make turn on you and mangle and murder –
You fools who equip your otherwise helpless foes!

If I was not a Soldier

IF I wasn't a soldier, a soldier said,
What would I be? – I wouldn't be,
It's hardly likely it seems to me,
A money lord or armament maker,
Territorial magnate or business chief.
I'd probably be just a working man,
    The slave of a licensed thief, –
One of the criminals I'm shielding now!

If I wasn't a soldier, a soldier said,
I'd be down and out as likely as not
And suffering the horrible starving lot
Of hundreds of thousands of my kind,
And that would make me a Red as well
Till I rose with the rest and was batoned or shot
By some cowardly brute – such as I am now!

One of These Days

THE very sea will turn against you.
It will rear itself into a mighty wave
And come roaring like a thousand storms
Gathering speed across the bay
Crashing over the cliffs and over the land
Carrying your homesteads with it,
Your ricks, your boats, your cattle, your children
Engulfing them, choking them in its green belly,
Tossing them abroad like straws,
Casting their pitiful corpses
High up upon the inland moors,
Wasting its roaring power among the rocks,

Laying siege to the everlasting summits,
Then sinking back to the ocean bed
Leaving a featureless land behind,
Stript naked of every sign of human life,
Nothing but a vast mudbank
And a heavy savour of salt . . .
In the meantime it flickers below you
Like a little methylated spirits
Set alight in a bowl.

Poetry and Propaganda

IT is no doubt a natural ambition
And even perhaps a worthy one
For a poet to have his genius hailed
In seeming mounting triumphs won
Till the so-called greatest of the land
Are proud to take him by the hand.

But once he stands among them
Their peer, and more; and all
The exclusive portals gladly
Wide open to him fall
Let him in no vain pleasure reel
But only rising nausea feel.

His place is not with lords and ladies
And millionaires and learned men
Enough to prove himself among them,
And turn his back upon them then
And join the people among whom
Alone the Muse's wings have room.

Name any of the accounted great.
Who can imagine any worthy song

Addressed in compliment to such
Or allied to exploitation and social wrong? –
But any down-and-out can test and tax
The mightiest pinions – or wings of wax!

Propaganda in poetry let humbugs condemn
But slavery none can extol to-day
Nor chant in favour of charming wage-cuts
Nor sing of tyranny's bracing sway
And half our poetlings still laud in verse
Will be equally out of the question ere long.

True they do not sing of sound finance
Or praise wage-slavery openly –
But a turn in affairs and they voice
Blood-lust and theft unashamedly;
And all the sweet sentiments they fear to express
Lie hidden in their lines none the less.

A pretty tribute to the old rural scene
Can mask a base betrayal of mankind;
The mellowest religious reference conceal
The Kruschen spirit of Fascism behind,
In short, any utterance that is not pure
Propaganda is impure propaganda for sure!

The Changeful World

EARTH has gone through many great changes.
        Why should it now cease changing?
Would a world all machines be as strange as
        That in which the saurians went ranging?

I don't care although I never see again
        A bird, a beast, a flower, a tree,

Or any of the other features
  Of Earth's traditional scenery,
Nor can I understand why most folk cling
  To these so passionately,
And yet believe that they are bound
  When this brief life is done
For a land where none of these can be found
  Any more than in yonder sun.

But who from sperm to maturity
  Has come need have no fear
To leave his further course to whatever
  Arranged that incredible career!

After Two Thousand Years

THE Christians have had two thousand years
  And what have they done? –
Made the bloodiest and beastliest world ever seen
  Under the sun.

No Christian refuses to profit himself
  From his brother's misfortune.
The devil who would sup with our Christian banks
  Must sup with a hellish long spoon.

The Christian Churches are all built up
  In utter defiance of all Christ taught.
Co-religionists war at home and abroad,
  Each side supported by the self-same God.

And blandly the Bishops bestow their blessings
  On any murderer or fraud with the wit
To pay them, lip-serve the Cross, and keep
  The working-classes carrying it.

What the Eagle Said

'WHERE else would I build my nest
And have and rear my young?'
The eagle cried, 'save here,
The whole of the world o'erhung?
If men are greater than birds
Let them heed my words.'

'The children of men should arise
And take the world in their grip.
It's their natural prey,' the eagle cried
With its proud and powerful lip,
'Even as I give some poor lamb
I find without wings a free flight
And then make it one with myself
        And so put it right.'

'Alas, how ungrateful they are!
You would actually think
They have no ambition to soar
And from freedom shrink,
Preferring some patch of turf
To the infinite air –
But I pay no attention to that,
And just take them there.'

Observation by the Oldest Inhabitant

I'VE lived in this parish all my days
And I haven't much longer to live, he says,
But there's one thing puzzles me always.

There's hardly one of the people here
But's cruelled with rheumatics; and yet it's queer
Though they sleep in the open the whole round year,

I've never yet seen a bird or a beast
Fashed with this crippling curse in the least.
They never need a doctor or priest.

Joy in the Twentieth Century

LIFE isn't so bad, life isn't so bad,
No matter what the pessimists say.
Every now and again the general heart
Goes up like a lark soaring light and gay.

Life isn't so bad, life isn't so bad.
Unstop your ears and you'll hear the glad cries
Of hundreds of thousands of men and their families. –
To-day the Railwaymen get a twopenny rise!

It seems as though the very sun
Has multiplied itself. A penny had been
Great tidings; whole twopence is enough
To dazzle the entire terrestrial scene.

The Wild Duck

MOTHER Hen's in a sad state, for one of her chicks
Suddenly on the water has gone.
She stands lamenting. So unlike all her others
This had been her favourite one.

Oh, it's scrape your dunghill, but the wandering wave
That goes round the world for me!
It's stretch your bottoms for sixpence a dozen,
But here's a bird'll go free!

In the Slums of Glasgow

I HAVE caught a glimpse of the seamless garment
And am blind to all else for evermore.
The immaculate vesture, the innermost shift,
    Of high and low, of rich and poor,
The glorious raiment of bridegroom and bride,
    Whoremonger and whore,
I have caught a glimpse of the seamless garment
And have eyes for aught else no more.

Deep under the γνῶθι σεαυτόν of Thales I've seen
The Hindu Atmānam ātmanā pāsya, and far deeper still
In every man, woman, and child in Scotland even
The inseparable inherent cause, the inalienable thrill,
The subtle movement, the gleam, the hidden well-water,
All the lin-gāni of their souls, God's holy will.
As a shining light needs no other light to be seen
The soul is only known by the soul or knows anything still.

It was easier to do this in the slums, as who prefers
A white-faced lass – because the eyes show better, so.
Life is more naked there, more distinct from mind,
Material goods and all the other extraneous things that grow
Hardening over and hiding the sheer life. Behind speech, mind and will
Behind sensation, reflection, knowledge, and power – lo!
Life, to which all these are attached as the spokes of a wheel to the nave;
The immensity abiding in its own glory of which I have caught the
    glow.

The same earth produces diamonds, rock-crystal, and vermilion,
The same sun produces all sorts of plants, the same food
Is converted into hair, nails and many other forms.
These dogmas are not as I once thought true nor as afterwards false
But each the empty shadow of an intimate personal mood.
I am indifferent to shadows, possessing the substance now.
I too look on the world and behold it is good.

I am deluded by appearances no more – I have seen
The goodness, passion, and darkness from which all things spring,
Identical and abundant in the slums as everywhere else
Taking other forms – to which changing and meaningless names cling, –
But cancelling out at last, dissolving, vanishing,
    Like the stars before the rising sun.
Foam, waves, billows and bubbles are not different from the sea,
But riding the bright heavens or to the dark roots of earth sinking
Water is multiform, indivisible and one,
Not to be confused with any of the shapes it is taking.

I have not gained a single definite belief that can be put
In a scientific formula or hardened into a religious creed.
A conversion is not, as mostly thought, a turning towards a belief,
It is rather a turning round, a revolution indeed.
It has no primary reference to any external object.
It took place in me at last with lightning speed.
I suddenly walk in light, my feet are barely touching the ground,
I am free of a million words and forms I no longer need.

In becoming one with itself my spirit is one with the world.
The dull, aching tension is gone, all hostility and dread.
All opposing psychic tendencies are resolved in sweet song
My eyes discard all idle shows and dwell instead
In my intercourse with every man and woman I know
On the openings and shuttings of eyes, the motions of mind, and,
    especially, life, and are led
Beyond colour, savour, odour, tangibility, numbers, extensions,
Individuality, conjunction, disjunction, priority, posteriority –
    like an arrow sped,
And sheer through intellection, volition, desire, aversion,
Pleasure, pain, merit and demerit – to the fountain-head,
To the unproduced, unproducing, solitary, motionless soul
By which alone they can be known, by which alone we are not misled.

I have seen this abhyasa most clearly in the folk of these slums,
Even as I have known the selfless indefatigable love of a mother
Concerned only for the highest possible vitality of her children,

Leaving their lives free to them, not seeking to smother
Any jet of their spirits in her own preconceptions or wishes. –
Would such were the love of every one of us for each other!

I have seen this abhyasa most clearly in the folk of these slums
Even as I know how every one of the women there,
Irrespective of all questions of intelligence, good looks, fortune's favour,
Can give some buck-navvy or sneak-thief the joy beyond compare –
Naked, open as to destitution and death, to the unprudential
Guideless life-in-death of the ecstasy they share –
Eternity, as Boethius defined it, – though few lovers give it his terms –
'To hold and possess the whole fulness of life anywhere
In a moment; here and now, past, present and to come.' –
The bliss of God glorifying every squalid lair.

The sin against the Holy Ghost is to fetter or clog
The free impulse of life – to weaken or cloud
The glad wells of being – to apply other tests,
To say that these pure founts must be hampered, controlled,
Denied, adulterated, diluted, cowed,
The wave of omnipotence made recede, and all these lives, these lovers,
Lapse into cannon-fodder, sub-humanity, the despised slum-crowd.

I am filled forever with a glorious awareness
Of the inner radiance, the mystery of the hidden light in these dens,
I see it glimmering like a great white-sailed ship
Bearing into Scotland from Eternity's immense,
Or like a wild swan resting a moment in mid-flood.
It has the air of a winged victory, in suspense
By its own volition in its imperious way.
As if the heavens opened I gather its stupendous sense.

For here too, Philosophy has a royal and ancient seat,
And, holding an eternal citadel of light and immortality,
With Study her only comrade, sets her victorious foot
On the withering flower of the fast-ageing world. – Let all men see.

Now the babel of Glasgow dies away in our ears,
The great heart of Glasgow is sinking to rest,
Na nonanunno nunnono nana nananana nanu,
Nunno nunnonanunneno nanena nunnanunnanut.
We lie cheek to cheek in a quiet trance, the moon itself no more still.
There is no movement but your eyelashes fluttering against me,
And the fading sound of the work-a-day world,
Dadadoduddadaddadi dadadodudadidadoh,
Duddadam dadade dudde dadadadadadodadah.

The Storm-Cock's Song

My song today is the storm-cock's song.
When the cold winds blow and the driving snow
Hides the tree-tops, only his song rings out
In the lulls in the storm. So let mine go!

On the topmost twig of a leafless ash
He sits bolt upright against the sky
Surveying the white fields and the leafless woods
And distant red in the East with his buoyant eye.

Surely he has little enough cause to sing
When even the hedgerow berries are already pulped by the frost
Or eaten by other birds – yet alone and aloft
To another hungry day his greeting is tossed.

Blessed are those who have songs to sing
When others are silent; poor song though it be,
Just a message to the silence that someone is still
Alive and glad, though on a naked tree.

What if it is only a few churning notes
Flung out in a loud and artless way?
His 'Will I do it? Do it I will!' is worth a lot
When the rest have nothing at all to say.

From
SCOTTISH ECCENTRICS
(1936)

The Royal Stag

THE hornless hart carries off the harem,
Magnificent antlers are nothing in love.
Great tines are only a drawback and danger
To the noble stag that must bear them.

Crowned as with an oaktree he goes,
A sacrifice for the ruck of his race,
Knowing full well that his towering points
Single him out, a mark for his foes.

Yet no polled head's triumphs since the world began
In love and war have made a high heart thrill
Like the sight of a Royal with its Rights and Crockets,
        Its Pearls, and Beam, and Span.

From
THE ISLANDS OF SCOTLAND
(1939)

THE poem 'Perfect' was first published, as printed here, in Hugh MacDiarmid's book, *The Islands of Scotland* (1939), but the words of the poem itself, except the first line, were written as prose by Glyn Jones in a short story, 'Porth-y-Rhyd', published in a collection of his stories, *The Blue Bed* (London: Jonathan Cape, 1937). When this matter came to light in the correspondence columns of *The Times Literary Supplement* in January 1965 Hugh MacDiarmid claimed that 'any plagiarism was certainly unconscious', but immediately made the 'necessary explanations and apologies' to Glyn Jones, adding: 'The poem will of course not appear again over my name.' Through a misunderstanding, however, it was included, without comment, in MacDiarmid's *Complete Poems* (1978).

Critics are agreed that 'Perfect' is a good poem. The respective parts played by Glyn Jones and Hugh MacDiarmid in creating it are now well known, and it is with Glyn Jones's generous concurrence that the poem is included in this volume.

Perfect

On the Western Seaboard of South Uist
(*Los muertos abren los ojos a los que viven*)

I FOUND a pigeon's skull on the machair,
All the bones pure white and dry, and chalky,
But perfect,
Without a crack or a flaw anywhere.

At the back, rising out of the beak,
Were twin domes like bubbles of thin bone,
Almost transparent, where the brain had been
That fixed the tilt of the wings.

The Stone Called Saxagonus

MRS. Kennedy-Fraser's Hebridean songs – the whole
Celtic Twilight business – I abhor,
Just as in Scandinavian music I have no use
For 'the delightful taste of a pink sweet filled with snow,'[1]
The delicate pastel shades, the romantic nostalgia,
Found also in writers like Jens Jacobsen.
Ibsen's hardy intellectual virility is matched
By Sibelius but by hardly anyone else.
Give me Gaelic poets and composers again
Who will stand first and foremost as Sibelius stands,
Towering overwhelmingly over the Palmgrens and Järnefelts
(Though I do not undervalue the Finnish comic strain
– An element absent from Sibelius's scores –
Found in Palmgren's 'Humorous Dance in the Finnish style'
Though it only peeps out there, not given breadth

[1] Debussy's impression of Grieg's pieces for strings.

As in Dargomizhsky's 'Finnish Fantasia';
Comicality abounds in the Hebrides too
But our crepuscular 'creators' make nothing of it)
For harsh, positive masculinity,
The creative treatment of actuality
– And to blazes with all the sweetie-wives
And colourful confectionery.
The Orpheus Choir, Rev. Kenneth MacLeod, and all the rest!
They have bemused the geology of the islands
Till every other stone has become a Saxagonus,
Which stone 'if it be holden against the sun,
Anon it shall shape a rainbow,'
And the rest Gagates and white margery pearls.
A fit setting only for spooks![1]

In the Shetland Islands

I am no further from the 'centre of things'
In the Shetlands here than in London, New York, or Tokio,
No further from 'the great warm heart of humanity,'
Or the 'general good,' no less 'central to human destiny,'
Sitting alone here enjoying life's greatest good,
The pleasure of my own company,
Than if I were one with the crowds in the streets
In any of the great centres of population,
Or in a mile-long cinema queue, or a unit
In a two-hundred-thousand spectatorate
At Twickenham or Murrayfield or Ibrox
Or reading a selection of today's newspapers
Rather than Keller's *Probleme der englischen Sprache und Kultur,*
Or Heuser's *Die Kildare-Gedichte: die ältesten*
mittel-englischen Denkmäler in anglo-irischer Überlieferung,
Or Esposito's articles in Hermathena

[1] See the description of Ireland in the sixteenth-century Book of Howth (Cal. of Carew MSS.)

On the Latin writers of mediaeval Ireland,
Or Curtis on *The Spoken Languages*
Of Mediaeval Ireland, or Heuser on the peculiar dialect
Of English spoken less than a hundred years ago
– Direct descendant of the language of the Kildare poems –
In the baronies of Forth and Bargy in County Wexford
And often (wrongly) described as a mainly Flemish speech.

The newspaper critic was talking rubbish, as usual,
When he made the shallow gibe, the fool reproach,
That in resuming his work in the Castle of Muzot
Rilke with all his insistence on *Bejahung*
'Could only praise life when protected from it.'

If personal participation were to be demanded,
Privacy forbidden, and any abstention
From any show of 'life' – from any activity
Most people indulge in – construed
As a flight from reality, an insulation from Life,
All but the most rudimentary forms of life,
All but the 'life' of the stupidest people,
Would speedily become impossible.
Rilke at Muzot or Duino was no more
'Protected from life' than any fool
At a street corner or in the House of Commons
Or in the columns of *The Scotsman*.
To be exclusively concerned with the highest forms of life
Is not to be less alive than 'normal' people.

Island Funeral

THE procession winds like a little snake
Between the walls of irregular grey stones
Piled carelessly on one another.
Sometimes, on this winding track,
The leaders are doubled back
Quite near to us.

It is a grey world, sea and sky
Are colourless as the grey stones,
And the small fields are hidden by the walls
That fence them on every side.

Seen in perspective, the walls
Overlap each other
As far as the skyline on the hill,
Hiding every blade of grass between them,
So that all the island appears
One jumble of grey boulders.
The last grey wall outlined on the sky
Has the traceried effect
Of a hedge of thorns in winter.

The men in the stiff material
Of their homespun clothes
Look like figures cut from cardboard,
But shod in their rawhide rivelins
They walk with the springing step of mountaineers.
The woman wear black shawls,
And black or crimson skirts.

A line of tawny seaweed fringes the bay
Between high-water mark and low.
It is luminous between the grey of rocky shore
And the grey of sullen water.

We can now and then look over a wall
Into some tiny field. Many of these
Are nothing but grey slabs of limestone,
Smooth as any pavement,
With a few blades of grass
Struggling up through the fissures,
And the grey surface of that rock
Catches and holds the light
As if it was water lying there.

At last the long line halts and breaks up,
And, like a stream flowing into a loch,
The crowd pours from the narrow lane
Into the cemetery where on an unfenced sandhill
The grey memorial stones of the island
Have no distinction from the country.
The coffin lies tilted a little sideways
On the dark grey sand flung up from the grave.

A little priest arrives; he has a long body and short legs
And wears bicycle clips on his trousers.
He stands at the head of the grave
And casts a narrow purple ribbon round his neck
And begins without delay to read the Latin prayers
As if they were a string of beads.
Twice the dead woman's son hands him a bottle
And twice he sprinkles the coffin and the grave
With holy water. In all the faces gathered round
There is a strange remoteness.
They are weather-beaten people with eyes grown clear,
Like the eyes of travellers and seamen,
From always watching far horizons.
But there is another legend written on these faces,
A shadow – or a light – of spiritual vision
That will seldom find full play
On the features of country folk
Or men of strenuous action.
Among these mourners are believers and unbelievers,
And many of them steer a middle course,
Being now priest-ridden by convention
And pagan by conviction,
But not one of them betrays a sign
Of facile and self-lulling piety,
Nor can one see on any face
'A sure and certain hope
Of the Resurrection to eternal life.'
This burial is just an act of nature,

A reassertion of the islanders' inborn certainty
That 'in the midst of life we are in death.'
It is unlike the appointed funerals of the mainland
With their bitter pageantry
And the ramp of undertakers and insurance companies
That makes death seem incredible and cruel.
There are no loafing onlookers.
Everyone is immediately concerned
In what is taking place.
All through their lives death has been very close to them,
And this funeral of one who had been 'a grand woman'
Seems to be but a reminder
Of the close comradeship between living and dying.

Down in the bay there is a row of curraghs
Drawn up on the sand. They lie keel upwards,
Each one shining black and smooth
Like some great monster of the sea,
Symbols to the island folk of their age-long
Battle with the waves, a battle where in daily life
The men face death and the women widowhood.

Four men fill in the grave with dark grey sand,
Then they cover the sand
With green sods and rough-hewn boulders,
And finally an old man with a yellow beard
Helps the four young gravediggers
In levering a great slab of stone
Until it lies flat upon the grave,
And the people watch all this in silence.
Then the crowd scatters east and west
And, last, the four gravediggers,
All of them laughing now
With the merriment of clowns.

There are few and fewer people
On the island nowadays,
And there are more ruins of old cottages
Than occupied homes.

I love to go into these little houses
And see and touch the pieces of furniture.
I know all there is to know
About their traditional plenishing
And native arts and crafts,
And can speak with authority
About tongue-and-groove cleats,
The lipped drawer, and the diameters of finials.
But I know them also in their origin
Which is the Gaelic way of life
And can speak with equal authority
About a people one of whose proverbs
Is the remarkable sentence:
'Every force evolves a form.'
While this thing lasted
It was pure and very strong.
In an old island room the sense is still strong
Of being above and beyond the familiar,
The world as we know it,
In an atmosphere purified,
As it were, from the non-essentials of living
– An intangible feeling,
Difficult to describe,
But easy to recall to anyone
Who has stood in such a room
And been disturbed by the certainty
That those who once inhabited it
Were sure of every thought they had.

To enter almost any of the island rooms even today
Is to be profoundly conscious of this emanation,
At once so soothing, and so strangely agitating.
Fifty years ago a visitor wrote: 'They are there to stay,
And that fact accounts for a great deal.
It is partial explanation of the contentment
On the faces of the island women.
It is a reason for the repose and settledness
Which pervade an island village

– That indefinable something,
So altogether unlike the life of ordinary villages,
And which you feel in the air,
And are conscious of by some instinct, as men claim
To be aware of the presence of spirits.
There is no restlessness,
Or fret of business,
Or anxiety about anything.
It is as if the work was done,
And it was one eternal afternoon.'
But they have not, in fact, stayed,
Foully forced out by their inferiors –
Red-faced, merely physical people
Whose only thought looking over
These incomparable landscapes
Is what sport they will yield
– How many deer and grouse.
The old stock are few and ever fewer now.
But they expected to stay,
And they deserved to stay,
Just as they expected there would always be
Thousands of them to work incessantly and serenely
At the making of objects which said:
'There is great beauty in harmony.'
They lived as much like one another as possible,
And they kept as free as they could of the world at large.
It is not their creed as such, however,
That explains them and the beauty of their work.
It is rather the happiness with which they held it,
The light-heartedness with which they enslaved themselves
To the various rituals it demanded,
And also the circumstance that they were all
Poor people – whose notions of form
Were both ancient and basic.
They began with the barest patterns, the purest beginnings
Of design, in their minds, and then
Something converted them into artists
With an exalted lyric gift.

What that something was
No one can claim perfectly to know.
Some of them were reported as believing
In assistance from the angels.
Whatever the source, the result was some
Of the most beautiful work the world has ever seen.

And even now, in Edinburgh or Glasgow or London,
I often move my ear up close
The better to distinguish in the raucous mixture
The sound of the cornet I want to hear,
And you may see my face light up
With recognition and appreciation at various points,
And hear me comment, 'The greatest of them all.'
The term is justified – this island note,
This clear old Gaelic sound,
In the chaos of the modern world,
Is like a phrase from Beiderbecke's cornet,
As beautiful as any phrase can be.
It is, in its loveliness and perfection,
Unique, as a phrase should be;
And it is ultimately indescribable.
Panassié speaks of it as 'full and powerful,'
But also as 'so fine
As to be almost transparent,'
And there is in fact
This extraordinary delicacy in strength.
He speaks of phrases that soar;
And this, too, is in fact
A remarkable and distinguishing quality.
Otis Ferguson speaks of 'the clear line
Of that music,' of 'every phrase
As fresh and glistening as creation itself,'
And there is in fact
This radiance, and simple joyousness.
These terms tell a great deal, but there remains
Much that eludes words completely
And can only be heard.

And though one can account for the music
Up to a certain point by the quality of the person
– The 'candour, force, personal soundness, good humour' –
There have been other people – and still are, no doubt –
With candour, force, personal soundness and good humour
And one has still to explain, as always,
How these qualities translated themselves
In this instance into such musical phrases.
In the din of our modern world
The Gaelic spirit plays merely
As an unfeatured member of well-known bands
– Which means that one hears it sometimes – very rarely! –
For a full chorus, sometimes merely for a phrase,
Sometimes only in the background with the rest of the brass.
But even the phrase detaches itself from its surroundings
As something exquisite and perfect; and even playing
Along with the others in the background
It stands out from them,
Not through any aggressiveness but solely
Through the distinctive quality of its style.
'The greatest of them all' – but
There is little life left on the island now,
And soon the last funeral
Will take place there,
And in the rowdy chaos of the world
The sound of this cornet will be heard no more
– One will listen, and one's face will never
Light up with recognition and appreciation again.

Yet if the nature of the mind is determined
By that of the body, as I believe,
It follows that every type of human mind
Has existed an infinite number of times
And will do so. Materialism promises something
Hardly to be distinguished from eternal life.
Minds or souls with the properties I love
– The minds or souls of these old islanders –
Have existed during an eternal time in the past

And will exist for an eternal time in the future.
A time broken up of course
By enormous intervals of non-existence,
But an infinite time.
If one regards these personalities
As possessing some value
There is a certain satisfaction
In the thought that in eternity
They will be able to develop
In all possible environments
And to express themselves
In all the ways possible to them
– A logical deduction from thoroughgoing Materialism
And independent of the precise type
Of materialism developed.
It is quite unimportant whether we call
Our ultimate reality matter, electric charge,
Ψ-waves, mind-stuff, neural stuff, or what not,
Provided it obeys laws which can, in principle,
Be formulated mathematically.

The cornet solo of our Gaelic islands
Will sound out every now and again
Through all eternity.

I have heard it and am content for ever.

From
THE GOLDEN TREASURY OF
SCOTTISH POETRY
(1940)

The Praise of Ben Dorain[1]

Urlar

OVER mountains, pride
Of place to Ben Dorain!
I've nowhere espied
A finer to reign.
In her moorbacks wide
Hosts of shy deer bide;
While light comes pouring
Diamond-wise from her side.

Grassy glades are there
With boughs light-springing,
Where the wild herds fare
(Of these my singing!),
Like lightning flinging
Their heels on the air
Should the wind be bringing
Any hint to beware.

Swift is each spirited one
Clad in a fine fitting
Skin that shines like the sun
Of its glory unwitting.
Like a banner when they run
Of flame-red is their flitting.
A clever deed would be done
A shot in these small bellies getting.

It calls for a prime gun
In a young man's gripping
– A flint with a breach-run
And trigger hard-clipping

[1] Translated from the Gaelic of Duncan Bàn MacIntyre (1724–1812).

On the hammer with none
Of hesitation or slipping;
A sound-stocked eight-sided one
To catch a stag skipping.

Yet one born for the game,
The man to outwit them,
Who whene'er he took aim
Was certain to hit them,
Lived here, Patrick by name,
Swiftly though when he came
With his boys and dogs they might flit them.

Siubhal

Keenest of careering
Of smelling and hearing
Is the little hind rearing
Among the peaks, peering
Along the wind, fearing
Whatever is nearing,
Lightly the ground clearing
'Mid summits sky-shearing,
But never descending
Where a ball might be rending
Past mending, or ending,
The grace she is tending
Here where it's blending
With the light to which, wending,
She seems to be lending
More than the sun's sending.

She makes no complaining
Of any speed straining
The mettle obtaining
In one that's not waning
From the standard pertaining
To a breed that has lain in

These high tops each aeon in
Since Time began feigning
Eternity's reign in
A separate rule to be gaining.

I love when she stretches
Her breath and the wind fetches
A ghost of her bellowing,
But it's not for us wretches
Of men that the mellowing
Call sounds o'er the vetches
As she seeks her listening
Lover in rutting-time, glistening
With loving-kindness.
His no deafness nor blindness,
The stag of the proud head tapering,
White-flash-buttocked one, capering,
High-stepper showing his paces
With reverberant roaring.
He's always on Ben Dorain
And knows all her choice places.

It would be a masterpiece
To tell all the stags one sees
Here on Ben Dorain, and with these
Every hind going at ease,
Slim, neat, a sight to please,
With her fawns by her knees,
Or all with white tails on the breeze
Filing up through the passes.

Start yon one on the edge
Of Harper's Corrie; I'll pledge
Hardly a man in the kingdom
But would need to sing dumb
Telling truth of his trying
To follow her fast flying
That of her hoofs on the grass
Puts scarce a flick as they pass.

On a lush level straying
A fair band of them playing,
Quick-footed, cunning,
Restless, age on their running
No weight will be laying,
No sorrow essaying
To shadow their sunning;
No mental troubles are theirs,
Aching hearts or sad cares.

They owe their glossy
Coats to the cosy
Forest quiet and mossy
So broad and bossy.
– At peace there toss you
Where scarce man knows you
Nor dangers engross you,
Free heads and clean bodies
Wholesome as the sod is
To whose bounty all owed is
Your sleek flesh that no load is!

It's lush àsainn[1] that's keeping
The breast to the fawns – leaping
Speckled ones! – heaping
Them invisibly deep in
Warmth that, though sleeping
In the rude waste, can creep in
No least twinge of cramp
From the cold wind or damp.

To milk of the club-rush they're owing
What keeps their lives going
Pure as the hill-streams' flowing.
It holds their hearts glowing;
Even in nights of wild snowing
In no house they'd be stowing
But in Corrie Altrum, showing
There's still snug beds for knowing

[1] àsainn – unknown; some kind of grass.

Among the bare jutting rocks
For creatures the right food stocks;
Finding by the Fall of the Fairies
What subtle shelter there is
No one less groundwise and windwise
Than they ever descries.

Urlar

The hind as she should be
    Is in the forest
Where there's plenty free
    Of the food that's fittest.
Hill-grass bladed cleanly
    She will eat with zest;
Club-rush, heath-rush, juicy,
    Of rare virtues possessed,
Cunning with right fat to see
    Her kidneys drest;
Watercress more highly
    Than wine assessed.
She fares contentedly
    On all that is best;
Cultivated grass would be
    A plague and pest
To her so amply and meetly
    Nourished and blest
On crisp herbs of purity
    No manure has messed;
With many a tit-bit too
    Of St. John's wort, primrose,
Daisy-tops the greenswards strew,
    And orchid that grows
– Towers with flowers that as fawns do
    Have speckles in rows –
In boglands she goes to
    That no man knows.

These are the tonics true
    To which instinct goes
In trying times; they endue
    Lean frames with fat that glows
Prettily on them, without rue
    From any weight it throws.

There's no more pleasing fellowship
    Than theirs at gloaming-tide
And when through deepening shades they slip
    In safety they'll abide
Long though the night, sharp the wind's nip,
    Well sheltered by a hillside
In the place that's deemed their agile trip
    For centuries its greatest pride
– Not preferring hardship or want,
But Ben Dorain, their beloved haunt!

Siubhal

The mountain high-towered,
Well-turfed and flowered,
Stream-lit and bowered,
None other is dowered
Like her in Christendom.
I'm overpowered as I roam
Bemused by her beauty
That the maps don't acclaim
Her transcending fame
As is their bare duty
With a special sign
As the queen of her line.
All the storms that have lowered
Have found her no coward
And whatever is toward
Will find her the same.

She's exuberant in fruits
Far beyond the measure
Usually found
On like areas of ground,
And rich in rare roots
And the tenderest of shoots
And has many a treasure
Of light-woven woodlands.
Oh, hers are the good lands
For all kinds of pleasure.
The cock is high-breasted
That on her has nested
With splendid torrent invested
Of music that springs unarrested
Between him and the sun,
And other birds, many a one,
A full repertoire run.
And hers is the brisk little buck
Who could have no better luck
With such greenswards for prancing on
Without slipping or mishap,
Without failing or falling, yon
Cloven-hoofed clever chap!
Then deep corries for ranging
To the heights, or, changing,
Dallying in copsewood and bracken;
Of variety there's no lack in
Ben Dorain for all his wants.
Every winding gully he haunts,
On every crag-top balances
With audacious curtsies,
And has ample distances
To put behind him should
Aught to startle him intrude.
Every second tussock he takes
As over the moss-quakes he makes
On hoofs nonpareil thin
In his eagerness to win

To where his love will be found
Come up from the low ground
– Every second tussock, or third;
Light and easy as a bird!

As for the little growling doe
And her young fawns who bide
In a hidden glen ill to know
High up the mountain side,
The ear she has! And the eye!
And the quick deft feet to ply
Over the boggling peat-hags!
Lightning behind her lags.
Though Caoilte and Cuchullin
Sought her they'd be fooling.
The sight would not daunt her
Of them and every hunter,
With all the men and horses
Hire-bound by King George; their forces
Would include nothing to catch her
If she wished to escape; watch her,
Gallant, long-legged, swift-turning,
Incalculable, her white-flared hips burning
Like stars in the distance! No matter
How precipitous the uplands may be
Lured by no level land she'll be
Where they might win at her.
She is the incarnate spirit
Of the heights her kind inherit,
Analysing every breath of air
With instant unerring nose.
Volatile, vigilant, there
One with the horizon she goes
Where horizons horizons disclose.
Or lies like a star hidden away
By the broad light of day.
Earth has nothing to match her.

Urlar

The hind loves to wander
Among the saplings yonder.
The passes of the braes
Are her dwelling-place.
The leaflets of the trees
And fresh heather-stems – these
Are the fare she prefers,
To cattle-fodder averse.
Blithe and gentle her nature,
A glad gloomless creature,
Mercurial and thoughtless,
Going like a knotless
Thread through the landscape,
Yet bearing herself always
Circumspect and comely in shape,
With the hues of health ablaze;
Knowing precisely how far to press
Her vital force to fill out,
Without straining, her formal niceness,
At rest or in revel or rout.
In the glen of the sappiest
Green copsewood she's happiest,
Yet often goes by the Great Rock
Where bush-clumps break the shock
Of the North Wind and let
No icy jet of it get
On her slumbering there
In some favourite lair;
Or she trips up the dell
Of the hazels to the well
She loves to drink at; cold and clear,
Far better than beer.
No one could think of
Better for her to drink of.
It inspires her lithe wiles,

Her sheer grace that beguiles,
Her constant strength and speed
In every hazard of need.
The honour of the best ears
In all Europe is hers!

Siubhal

Graceful to see to me was a group
Lined up in the order of march to troop
Down by the Sron rock south through the loop
'Twixt Craobh-na-h-ainnis moor and the scoop
Of Corrie-dhaingean; no goog[1] on that herd,
And none with a staring hide covered,
That for bite and sup never begged or chaffered
Nor yet lacked though to that they'd not stoop.
That was the fine line to be watching oop
The seen parts of a path between noop and noop.
Then along Corrie Rannoch's either side
About the wing of the pass and the wide
Corrie of Ben Achalader and over
By Conn Lonn on the Laoidhre's spur,
What a host to delight a deer-lover,
Everyone in a radiant red jupe!
On to the hollow of the Feinne there
And in the Creag-sheilich beyond that
Where gather the winsome hinds that care
Nothing for grass that dunghills begat,
But whose joy it is to be strutting
On a grassy level, butting
And playing with each other or in
The rutting-bogs make a right din
Of spirited lewdness, keen, wanton,
Lusty, with no care or cant on.

No tongue could keep on thirsting
On the lower side of Meall Eanail where spring

---

[1] goog – very young meat that has no firmness (Anglo-Saxon, *geogath*, youth).

The wine-streams of Annet, honey-tasted to drink;
A flow efficacious, white, narrow,
Filtering over sand, brim to the brink,
Sweeter than cinnamon, a draught to make marrow.
This is the water to cure all thirst
That from the bottom of the earth has burst.
There's plenty of it here on the mountain top,
Free – not for sale in a shop!
This is the loveliest thing to see
In all this quarter of Europe to me,
The fresh water, mild with limpidity,
Welling so pure and harmless
From the dark roots of the watercress,
With various mosses waving about the lips
Of every ripple as it slips
From the wards of the rock and swells the pool
Uninflaming, delicious, and cool,
Coming in an eddy from the gravel,
On the shoulder of Ben Dorain,
The great demesne where you have all
The good life can set store in.

The hither side of the hill slope
Has goodliness without stint or stop;
The tumultuous tumbled moor-corrie
Opens by it – a corrie of glory.
Grouty through-other rocks, all points and pits
Shaggy and counter and ravelled – oh, it's
Easy enough for me to praise
Steep defiles such variety arrays,
For there's felicity enough on them,
All manner of fine stuff on them.
One could spend endless love on them.
Full of bells, full of buds, they are,
With everywhere the dainty clear star
Of the daisy so ruddy and fair
Twinkling in the tapestry there,
And the moorland busked in a great

Rough-figured mantle that suits her estate
What tongue can ever hope
For words with the like to cope? –
The grandest scene in all Europe!

Urlar

The lonely moorland ringed round
With glen-mouths, and hill-ends,
Corrie Fraoich, will be found
Best of all. Fawns' presence lends
It that smiling look that ground
They favour aye commends.
Its southerly setting defends
It from cold; hence they abound.
Glad is the little hind here.
Pure her body, healthy, clear,
True womanly in virtue she.
Taintless her breath would appear
To anyone who might kiss her.
It is here that, once they see
It, young men always wish to be.
Like pipes' sticks are its fanwise
Ravines through which the wind sighs.
Stags' chief meeting-ground and place
That's source of every great chase.
Rich in all that comes out with rain,
Wild berries and flowers perfume this plain.
There's heaps of fish in near-by streams
To get with a torch's gleams
And the narrow pine-shafted spear
Plied by men used to such gear.
Fine to see the trout leaping
Light flies in clusters catching
On waters so smoothly sweeping!
I've said as I stood watching,
The best things in land or sea found
All in you, Ben Dorain, abound!

Crunn-luth

Who would stalk the hind in this glen
  Needs good knowledge and cunning
To steal softly within her ken
  Without starting her running,
Carefully and cleverly inveigling
  Himself forward, her notice shunning,
Using each least thing in turn then
  To hide himself and his gun in.
Bush, rock, and hollow all in taken,
  Vastly ingenious, there's great fun in.

Details of the land all well gauged,
  Clouds' direction duly noted,
His wits are thenceforth all engaged
  In covering the space allotted,
And getting the finale staged
  Before the hind can have thought it
Enplotted – aye, all the campaign waged
  Ere hint of danger is brought it.

The hind's own instincts outplaying,
  In spite of herself she's taken
By the stalker, not without paying
  Full due to her wits wide-waken,
With tribute of stilly delaying
  And coolness never forsaken
And frame to wriggle a worm's way in
  Without affront or aching.

At last he puts the eye steadily
  To the hind on the stag still intent,
And the peg is drawn out readily
  The butt-iron's kick to relent.
A new flint's just tightened, and deadly
  The down-blow of the hammer's sent.

The spark to the packed powder flies redly
    And the hail from the barrel is sprent.

It was well loved by the quality
    To be up Ben Dorain's passes
In the hey-day of their vitality
    Where the deer troop by in masses,
While hunters of such judicality
    In the sport where nothing crass is
Stalk them with the right mentality
    That alone their wariness outclasses.

And the brisk keen dogs behind them,
    Creatures so surly and slaughtering,
Frantic at jaws' grip to find them
    With the herd like wild-fire scattering,
Till speed it seems has combined them
    – Their hair-on-end howling, shattering
The golden silence of deer-flight, entwined them
    With the foes their rabid foam's spattering.

Furious in high career that conjunction
    Of leaping dogs and fugitive deer,
And the peaks and passes echoed with unction
    The baying of the hounds exciting to hear
As they drove down their quarries without compunction
    In to the icy pools that bottomless appear
And rocked on their necks in relentless function
    While they floundered and bloodied the waters there!

. . . Though I've told a little of Ben Dorain here,
Before I could tell all it deserves I would be
In a delirium with the strange prolixity
Of the talking called for, I fear.

From
LUCKY POET
(1943)

To Nearly Everybody in Europe To-day

A WAR to save civilization, you say?
Then what have *you* to do with it, pray?
Some attempt to acquire it would show truer love
Than fighting for something you know nothing of.

Verses Written during the Second World War

AT last! Now is the time with due intensity
    To hew to what really matters – not
'Making the world safe for democracy',
    'Saving civilization', or any such rot.

But what there was about the Welsh handling, say,
    Of Arthur and Merlin (as good an example as may be got)
That conquered the imagination of Europe in a way
    Conchobar and Cuchulainn did not.

Let it at least be said of us when we die:
    'Of all the slogans to which mass-man clings
Only a Chinese could have thought more lightly than they
    – They had so much love for real things.'

Why I Choose Red

I FIGHT in red for the same reasons
That Garibaldi chose the red shirt
– Because a few men in a field wearing red

Look like many men – if there are ten you will think
There are a hundred; if a hundred
You will believe them a thousand.
And the colour of red dances in the enemy's rifle sights
And his aim will be bad – But, best reason of all,
A man in a red shirt can neither hide nor retreat.

Shetland Fisherman

WISTFUL child of whim,
Whose boating skill held scarce a mental notion,
'Twas grounded all on love and sheer emotion. . . .
His moustache settled to a careless droop,
And, when the icicles began to loop
Their bases round its fringes, he would look
Like a walrus peering from an island nook.

Krassivy, Krassivy

SCOTLAND has had few men whose names
Matter – or should matter – to intelligent people,
But of these Maclean, next to Burns, was the greatest
And it should be of him, with every Scotsman and Scotswoman
To the end of time, as it was of Lenin in Russia
When you might talk to a woman who had been
A young girl in 1917 and find
That the name of Stalin lit no fires,
But when you asked her if she had seen Lenin
Her eyes lighted up and her reply

Was the Russian word which means
Both beautiful and red.
Lenin, she said, was '*krassivy, krassivy*'.
John Maclean too was '*krassivy, krassivy*',
A description no other Scot has ever deserved.

The East

THE East
– Ah, the East!
The Watch Tower at Mandalay,
The Dragon Pagoda at Amarapura,
Sagaing!
The pottery houses at Bandigarampudur,
The Yanesh Temple at Vijayanagar,
The Rock Temple at Kondane,
The Buddhist cave at Nasik,
Champaner, Dwarka, and Yirnar! . . .

A poetry with bells ringing everywhere,
Even on the thin white ponies
In from the hill country
With loads of tsai-birds' eggs and wild oranges.

And so the poetry of a poet
Who is as much at home
In Chinese or Indian thought
As in Greek – nay, being a Gael,
Knows well how the old dark crimson rose
And the wistful tea-roses
Brought their perfume out of the East
But never exhale it so sweetly
As when washed by the rains of the West.

The Puffin

By which the whole . . . is governed and turned like fishes by the tail.
                                                    SWIFT

Old lady, studying a balloon barrage – 'They tell me there's nobody in them.
Isn't it wonderful how they manage to get them all to turn the same way!'

IN my dealings with facts I resemble
One of the puffins we see in the Shetlands here.
The puffin flies in from the sea
With as many as ten little fish
Held sideways in its beak,
And the fish are usually arranged
With heads and tails alternating.

How is it done? Even allowing for the fact
That the beak has serrations
Which slope back to the throat
It would seem a difficult task
For the bird to go to a fishmonger's shop
And pick ten dead fish off the slab
And arrange them in that fashion.

But to catch a live and presumably active fish
Under water, with nine others
Already held in the beak?
How is it done? I have the knack
Of dealing with facts as the puffin with fish,
But I cannot tell how I do it
Any more than the puffin can.

Enough human seed can be housed
In a tooth-paste cap to father
The world's 2,000,000,000 population.
In the complicated process of reproduction
48 chromosomes are released.

These minute pieces of tissue form
The physical heritage of every human's life.
Soon after fertilization each member
Of the two packs of chromosomes splits in two.
Half range on one side of the egg-cell,
Half on the other. A wall grows between,
The cell begins to divide, and soon
There are two cells in place of one.
After 48 complete divisions
There are enough cells to constitute
A fully developed baby – 26 billion.
My poems will drill the whole world of fact
Precisely like that!

Further Passages from 'The Kind of Poetry I Want'[1]

YEA, and with, and because of all this, the poetry
For which the poet at any moment may be smashed to pulp
By a gang of educated chimpanzees
Beating out the scansion with a rubber truncheon
For metronome on the small of his back
Till his kidneys burst – the poetry,
Not in Germany and certain other countries only,
But everywhere, England, Scotland, America,
The poetry of War and Civil War everywhere,
The poetry of the world-wide Night of the Long Knives
In which 99 men in every 100 are Gestapo Guards,
The poetry that entails the Family Trial
Of the poet's wife and children too,
And makes hulking Black Guards seize the Muses,
Tie their clothing tightly above their heads,
Truss, blind, shamefully humiliate them.
The Black Guards are among the helpless Muses now,

[1] The pieces which were brought together, set in their proper sequence, and published as a single poem in 1961 are reprinted on pages 1001–35.

Beating them with clubs, kicking them in the guts,
The Black Guards carry on their dastardly work
While splitting their sides with laughter,
The Black Guards – Finance, Religion, Law, Capitalist Culture.
Himmler never moves a muscle – shows no pity
When, on his departure, frightful screams from the parade-ground
Tell of the most shameful deeds of all. . . . Next day
Ladies he meets at State functions
Are charmed by his quiet courtesy.
The poetry that is scheduled as a Dangerous Occupation,
The most dangerous occupation in the world to-day.
. . . Locked in a cell with a Luger pistol
I make my poetry of World Consciousness.
But will any of it ever be smuggled out
From the Sondergericht to which all Consciousness is subject
All over the world to-day?

Long poems. The kind of poetry I want
Is poems *de longue haleine* – far too long
To be practicable for any existing medium,
For there is no editor or publisher in the world to-day
Who if he were suddenly presented with what was obviously
By far the greatest poem that had ever been written
Would give it a moment's consideration if its publication
Would take up a whole issue of his magazine
Or unbalance his publishing list,
Which, no matter how high the level taken,
Demands a certain variety, the sense
Not to put all one's eggs in the same basket,
The wise policy of having 'something for everybody'.
The sudden appearance of a stupendous masterpiece[1]
Is the last thing any of these people want.
It would shock them tremendously.
   hey would hasten to hush it up.

---

[1] John Davidson, the Scottish poet, points out that no great poet can work at all except on the assumption that the next thing he writes may out-distance all previous composition completely – so completely that all other poetry becomes negligible in comparison.

There are no means they would not take
To deny its nature and prevent its appearance.
The poetry of one sane man left in a community
All the rest of whose inhabitants are seized by epidemic insanity;
A poetry therefore that only its maker can hear,
Since all the channels of communication are blasted away,
And if the poet hopes or believes there may still
Be elements hidden away here or there
With which with a little luck he might yet get in touch
How can he do so? – The Guards are infernally cunning –
His least move would be fatal.
A poetry nevertheless that will brook no restraint,
But insist upon moving freely. . . .
The poet a Tarzan among apes all
Suddenly murderously inimical.

A poetry that hates the *à peu près*.
A poetry that sees all the pins on the floor.

A poetry that, like Mussolini, gives
Over 60,000 audiences and interests itself
In at least 1,887,112 individual 'affairs of citizens'.

A poetry taking unerring instantaneous account
Of all the angles in a complex manoeuvre
As one who in a tangled thicket
Of manzanita, cactus, chaparral, mesquite, and the like
Adjusts the sights of his Winchester,
Windage, trajectory, distance,
All taken into consideration,
And nothing forgotten.
Or again as when the butts of a man's twin Colt guns
Seem fairly to leap into his palms
As the weapons flash out
In smooth, eye-defying movements.

A poetry like a bridge player
Applying method to the plan of the hand,

Asking himself the necessary series
Of definite questions before deciding
On a piece of play after the first card has been led
And then deciding on the necessary tactics to employ
In developing the extra winners in his hand,
These tactics including the finesse, throw-in play, the squeeze,
Ducking, elimination play, and all the rest.

And, above all, a poetry
Like a billiard player
Who knows how to screw
– The gripping or clinching of the cue
At the precise moment of the contact with the ball
That prevents or lessens the chance of a miscue.
Even though the cue-tip may have been properly chalked
A miscue is almost inevitable
When the cue-tip hits the ball as low down
As is necessary for a strong screw
If the cue-hold is not tightened just then.
(Imagine a heavy piece of machinery
Fixed to the floor and at a convenient distance
From the table, and from this machinery
A piston-rod with its end
Shaped and tipped like a cue.
Made to shoot out like a horizontally-held cue
And strike a cue-ball
Exactly where it must be struck
To play a screw-back stroke,
Also that it travelled two or three inches
Beyond the point where it made contact with the ball.
Clearly this steel piston-rod
Could not be deflected
Either to the right or the left
By its contact with the ball.
Nor could its point be raised or lowered.
Its rigidity would only allow it
To move backwards or forwards
In a straight line.

When you grip your cue in screw-strokes
You are really attempting to make your cue
Resemble the imaginary steel cue
Which cannot deviate
From the line on which it travels.)
There are cuemen who will tell you
That they never grip the cue
For any kind of stroke.
These players *do* grip it
For screws and for many other strokes,
But this clinching of the cue
Is an unconscious action with them.
To-day practically all professionals
And most of our great amateurs
Hold the cue in the palm of the hand.
Watch the cue hand of any first-class player
When a screw stroke of any kind
Has to be played,
And you cannot fail to notice
This gripping of the cue.
You can see this closing of the hand
Round the cue quite easily
Even if the stroke
Is quite a gentle stroke.
– This is the kind of poetry I want.

Pinwheeling poetry.

Poetry giving a rapid premonitory perspective view
Of schemes of thought not yet articulate.

A poetry that can always turn on a dime
And leave a nickel for change.

On my muse's tea-table appear
Such delicacies as Austrian Pfeffernuss, iced honey-cakes,
Round or oblong in shape, or those other honey-cakes
From Dijon, wrapped in green and gold, very gay,

And many varieties of the German Lebkuchen,
And Oblaten, thin biscuits from Salzburg,
And delicious French pain d'épice,
While to dine with her is to know
The truffle of Perigord, the brocarra of Tulle,
Auvergnian roast ham with chestnut sauce,
The thick cabbage soup of Thiers, the poulards of Bresse,
Algerian couscous, Spanish puchero,
Polish barszcz and kromeski, Italian gnocchi,
Calves' tongues cooked with almonds from Greece,
Goulash and sherbet au Tokay from Hungary,
Bamboo sprouts from the Far East,
Watarzoie de Poulet from Belgium,
Scotch grouse, Scandinavian hors d'oeuvre,
American lemon pie, and Viennese Linzertorte.

With here, incidentally, a cultural synthesis
Of thought, action, belief, and education which covers most
Of the important gradations of thought and human learning
From Greek and Roman times, to the times, say,
Of Ignatius Loyola and the Counter-Reformation.
Religion, the eternal borderline of inarticulate science,
Led to scientific and political concepts; the Greeks
(With their philosophic contempt for things)
Began the process of anthropomorphizing
Which passed on to the Roman world.
The propulsive motivation of Christianity
Was derived from the supreme universalist, Alexander the Great.
Out of the universality of Christianity evolved
The idea of universality of education – the modern idea
That every man should be taught. Gnostic philosophy
Gave to Christianity its survival value in the West,
And the Christian teaching that passed on to the mediaeval world
Was far from being a reformed Judaism,
For in its matrix there lay embedded
All the creeds, all the orthodoxies, all the heresies.
And so, passing on to Saracenic culture, we meet,
Among the hundreds, Al-Jahiz of Basra

Admitting the debt of the ancients;
And on, past hundreds more, to Petrarch
Writing in his 'Greetings to Posterity'
Of his insignificant and obscure activities,
And on, past the German humanists, and hither
To Loyola and the Jesuits. . . .

A poetry like a lance at rest,
Motionless but vibrant with hidden power.

Poetry in a land where the hills flow down
In long, irregular curves, flattened into tables
Scored deep by canyons and ravines, shadowy, mysterious,
Where even the searching fingers of the sunshine cannot wholly
    penetrate
The sinister gorges whose gloomy, overhanging walls
Baffle all but the heavier dregs of the light
– A land where the tawny sunshine shimmers
The drooping, lily-white blossoms of the yuccas
And glints on the sky-rocket blooms
Of green-and-white mescal plants, and even
The weirdly deformed arms of the cholla cactus
Are a little de-devilled by the soft caress.
The canyon floors are littered with boulders and up-jutting fangs
Of stone, ground and scoured in the iron jaws
Of long-gone glaciers. White water brawls amid the rocks
And spatters the straggly growth with a diamond-glitter of spray,
And the giant sounding-board of the hills flings back
Its growl and grumble magnified and distorted.
But over the outer vestibule of the hills is sunshine and peace,
The rumble of the canyon water dulled to a musical whisper,
Rich tints of brown and chocolate and purple
Mottle the cliffs. Long edges of soft grey
Marbled with black and reddish-yellow
Stripe the upper slopes. Dry washes are green and gay
With gramma grass and flowering weeds.
Like a lonely ghost with fear for its pacemaker
The false dawn flees across the sky.

Follows a period of sullen darkness.
Then, so gradually as to be
Almost imperceptible, the true dawn
Drifts up over the edge of the world.
Little flecks of high clouds burn amber and gold.
The hills are formless loomings of tremulous jet.
A pale mist films the grasses with translucent grey.
All things are unreal, elusive. There is a tense silence
As yet unbroken by song of bird
Or the silvery voices of the wind.

A poetry that has developed to a high degree
An uncanny sense of direction – unerringly following
A route of general direction that, after hours of wandering
Among the buttes and gorges, leads me
To a long, twisty canyon whose far mouth
Faces almost due east, and so
As the spears of the rising sun turn the blue wind-ripples
Of the prairie grasses to long curves of bronzed gold
I ride out of the canyon on to the rangeland.

This is the land in which my poetry goes
Like two great galloping horses –
The big black goes like the shadow of a star
Before a lightning flash, but the golden horse
Is like a ripple of sunlight racing across clear water.
Ahead looms the mouth of a canyon, a narrow fissure
Slicing through a shoulder of the hills.
Straight for its blue-shadow
The two horses hurtle.

And, again, delicate as the kiss of wind-shadows
On trembling drops of dew.

The greatest poets undergo a kind of crisis in their art,
A change proportionate to their previous achievement.
Others approach it and fail to fulfil it – like Wordsworth.

Some, like Keats, the crisis helps to kill.
Rimbaud underwent a normal, not an abnormal, poetic crisis.
What was abnormal was his extreme youth, his circumstances, his
    peasant stock.
It killed Keats, but Keats was not born of French peasants.
It kept Milton practically silent for twenty years.
Rimbaud died at the end of nineteen. Yet he explored it seems
After his own manner an even more hidden way.
Claudel said that, after reading him, he felt
'L'impression vivante et presque physique de surnaturel . . .
Il n'était pas de ce monde.' The priest who confessed him
Said to his sister: 'I have rarely met a faith
Of the quality of his.' That was not to be taken
(As his sister took it) in any easy pious sense;
He remained very much *de ce monde*.
But it seems that through these years
He walked in granite within and without,
And perhaps only his poetry had not found
– And he but thirty-seven –
A method of being which was, for him,
What he desired, perdurable as the granite.
– I am forty-six; of tenacious, long-lived country folk.
Fools regret my poetic change – from my 'enchanting early lyrics' –
But I have found in Marxism all that I need –
(I on my mother's side of long-lived Scottish peasant stock
And on my father's of hardy keen-brained Border mill-workers).
It only remains to perfect myself in this new mode.
This is the poetry I want – all
I can regard now as poetry at all,
As poetry of to-day, not of the past,
A Communist poetry that bases itself
On the Resolution of the C.C. of the R.C.P.
In Spring 1925: 'The Party must vigorously oppose
Thoughtless and contemptuous treatment
Of the old cultural heritage
As well as of the literary specialists. . . .
It must likewise combat the tendency
Towards a purely hothouse proletarian literature.'

A poetry full of such tremendous insights
As when Buber cries
'Rendez-vous compte de ce que cela signifie
Quand un ouvrier perçoit dialogiquement
Son rapport avec sa machine,
Quand un typographe dit qu'il comprend
Le bourdonnement de la presse
Comme un témoignage joyeux de reconnaissance
Pour l'aide qu'il lui a apportée
A surmonter les obstacles qui arrêtaient sa marche,
L'alourdissaient, la paralysaient,
Lui donnant ainsi
La possibilité de fonctionner librement.

Buber nous parle du typographe qui,
A travers le bourdonnement de sa machine,
A perçu sa reconnaissance et sa joie,
Cela est parfaitement comprehensible pour nous
Et admissible. Mais voici une légende hasside
Du XVIII siècle; elle nous raconte
La joie qu'éprouva la fondateur de la doctrine,
Le grand saint Balshem,
Lorsqu'il vit soudain par les yeux de l'esprit que,
Dans une petite bourgade lointaine,
Dieu avait accompli une miracle uniquement
Pour qu'un pauvre relieur put dignement
Fêter le sabat, c'est-à-dire acheter
Des cierges, des pains, du vin. . . .
Cette histoire qui est parfaitement à sa place
Dans un receuil de légendes hassides
Ne pourrait se trouver ni dans *Moi et Toi*
Ni dans le *Dialogue*. Cela veut dire:
La théophanie du langage moderne
Doit essentiellement différer
Non seulement de la théophanie biblique
Mais aussi de la théophanie des hassides
Qui, dans le temps, nous sont relativement proches
Les hommes de la Bible, les hassides, et nous

Nous pouvons tous parler de l'existence quotidienne
Et des manifestations de Dieu
Dans le cours ordinaire de l'existence.

Mais à nous autres, hommes du XX siècle,
Il nous est sévèrement interdit
De penser que Dieu peut à tel point s'intéresser
A la vie de tous les jours d'un pauvre homme
Qu'il lui envoie les quelques sous dont cet homme a besoin
Pour s'acheter des cierges et du vin.
Qui ou qu'est ce qui nous l'interdit?
Il n'y a qu'une réponse à cette question:
C'est notre 'connaissance' qui nous l'interdit.
Mais n'est-ce pas 'un excès de pouvoir,
Qu'une connaissance qui sent ses responsibilités
Ne peut se permettre,'
Ainsi qui parlait Buber lui-même?
Je vais plus loin encore; est-il en général permis
A la connaissance de se mêler de ces choses?'

Martin Buber is one of the rare thinkers
Who introduce into their work that 'earnest',
That extreme intensity of which
Kierkegaard and Nietzsche have spoken.
His thought is not for him an interesting pastime,
Nor even a means of doing useful service
For culture and society. And it is the same
With his writings. He lives in his thought;
In his writings he incarnates that life.
If he 'serves' it is a case always
Of a particular kind of service.

It is not in vain
That he set himself an overwhelming task,
A task almost unrealizable for the modern man:
The translation of the Bible into German.
It was necessary to have his 'boundless (unrestrainable) passion'
('Boundless' – forcené – is the favourite expression of Dostoievsky,

'Passion', the term Kierkegaard employs;
And Kierkegaard and Dostoievsky are,
Next to Buber, the greatest spirits
Of the nineteenth century) in order to dare to recreate
At this time the researches and discoveries
Of those distant times when it was not
Men who discovered truth, but truth
Which revealed itself to men.
A task almost unrealizable;
We are, in fact, convinced that truth can be found
Only in clear and distinct judgements,
And how then can we express in our language
Which has moulded itself in accordance with this conviction
So deeply-rooted, what the men saw and heard
Who still possessed the faculty
Of entering into contact with the mystery?
'The sparks of light of the original being
Who found himself directly face to face with God,
Adam Kadmon, have fallen into the prison of *things*,
After the light has fallen from the higher spheres
Into the lower which it has burst asunder.
The Shekinah of God
Descended from one sphere to another,
Passed and repassed
From one universe to another,
From one ether to another
Till it had reached
The utmost limits of its prison,
Till it had reached us.
In our World God's destiny is accomplished.'

'Dans les autres doctrines, l'âme de Dieu
Envoyée du ciel sur la terre
Pouvait être de nouveau appelée au ciel et délivrée:
Le création et la rédemption
Ne s'effectuaient que dans une seule direction,
De haut en bas. Mais c'est inadmissible
Pour une doctrine juive qui est fondée tout entière

Sur les rapports réciproques
Entre le 'Moi' humain
Et le 'Toi' divin,
Sur la réalité de cette réciprocité,
Sur la rencontre.
Dans cette doctrine l'homme,
L'homme infirme, misérable,
Est appelé de toute éternité
A être l'aide de Dieu.
C'est pour lui que le monde a été créé,
Pour lui qui choisit, qui choisit Dieu.
L'apparence extérieure du monde
Existe pour qu'à travers elle
L'homme recherche son noyau même.
Les sphères sont écartées les unes des autres,
Afin précisément qu'il les rapproche.
La création attend l'homme.
Dieu lui-même l'attend.
Et c'est de l'homme 'd'en bas'
'Que doit venir l'appel du salut.
La grâce sera la réponse de Dieu.'
Que l'homme soit pénétré tout entier d'ardeur!
Que cette ardeur le réveille de son assoupissement,
Car la sainteté lui a été communiquée
Et il est devenu autre qu'il n'était avant.
Il est devenu digne de créer,
Et semblable lui-même au Saint,
Que son nom soit béni!
Tel qu'il était lorsqu'il créait son monde!...
Et alors, je saisis instantanément l'âme hasside.
L'antique conscience juive se réveilla en moi
Dans les ténèbres de l'exil elle s'épanouit
Pour ainsi dire en moi:
L'homme – image et ressemblance de Dieu –
Comme oeuvre, comme devenir, comme tâche.
Et cette conscience essentiellement juive,
Essentiellement humaine,
Etait le contenu de la religiosité humaine.

x

Si 'l'expérience quotidienne' ne lui avait pas montré
Que les succès et les échecs se repartissent indifféremment
Entre les bons et les méchants,
Et si les *oculi mentis*
Ne lui avaient pas suggéré
La conviction qu'il est impossible
D'échapper à cette expérience,
Il ne serait jamais arrivé à la conclusion
Que la raison et la volonté de Dieu
Diffèrent *toto caelo* de la raison
Et de la volonté de l'homme,
Qu'elles n'ont de commun avec celles-ci
Que le mot qui les désigne;
De même que l'on appelle chien
Un 'animal aboyant' et l'une des constellations du ciel.
. . . Le typographe avec lequel causa Buber
N'est pas plus près de la vérité,
Pas même d'un cheveu, que le relieur hasside.

Buber a raison de dire
Que la machine souriait
Avec reconnaissance au typographe.
Mais nous ne devons en aucune façon
Oublier le relieur hasside.
Et Buber a également raison
Quand il écrit dans *Moi et Toi* :
'Je perçois quelque chose.
Je me représente quelque chose.
Je veux quelque chose.
Je pense à quelque chose.
De toutes ces choses et d'autres semblables
On ne peut composer
Toute la vie humaine.'

Il n'eût pas été inutile
De confronter la durée bergsonienne –
Effort grandoise pour accorder le rhythme du Vorhanden

Au rhythme de l'Existence – avec la 'Zeitlichkeit' de Heidegger
Qui est une durée finie, mortelle,
Dont le temps nivelé tel que l'utilisient le sens commun et la science
N'est qu'un dérivé.
(Quoi qu'en dise Heidegger lui-même,
Sa 'Zeitlichkeit' succède à la durée de Bergson,
Ne fût-ce que pour s'opposer à elle.)
Et qu'il serait tentant d'étudier,
A la lumière de cette temporalité
Le caractère particulier de la durée musicale.
Elle se révèlerait, probablement,
Comme *l'unité extatique par excellence*
Du passé, du présent, et du futur.
Le thème musical n'est-il pas tout d'abord
Un trésor virtuel presque illimité de ressources mélodiques
Mais à mesure qu'il se déploi et se développe,
Des formales tonales ou atonales
L'engagent et le contraignent,
Des combinations harmoniques limitent sa liberté,
Des rhythmes l'asservissent.
Projetant dans le futur un univers sonore,
Il s'alourdit du passé.
Il faut qu'il cède une part,
Et non la moindre,
De ses virtualités pour que cet univers ébauché vive,
Reçoive de fermes en definitifs contours.
La melodie incarne, et en quelque sort,
La transcendance elle-même; comme celle-ci
Elle est essentiellement *'überschwingend-entziehend'*.
A chaque instant de sa durée,
Tout en s'élançant vers l'avenir
Elle est incorruptiblement son propre passé,
Les premières notes d'un thème musical, déjà,
Sont chargees du passe de silence dont elles émergent.
Parce qu'elle est connaissance, choix du possible,
La musique s'ouvre à l'extase du futur
Et parce qu'elle est expression de la 'Befindlichkeit'
Elle se fonde sur l'extase du passé.

(*Das Verstehen gründet sich primär in der Zukunft,*
Die Befindlichkeit, dagegen, zeitigt
Sich primär in der Gewesenheit.)

Comme la Zeitlichkeit de Heidegger,
La temporalité est une durée finie.
La perfection mélodique tient essentiellement
Au caractère fine de cette durée,
Aux limites que celle-ci impose à l'art musical
Et dont il faut
Qu'il triomphe en les transcendant.
Elle l'oblige à tirer d'une liberté,
Finie la liberté tout court.
Faisant violence à son intime nécessité,
A l'écoulement qui est sa loi,
La musique réussit,
Au sein du mouvement même,
A créer un équilibre sonore,
Une présence accomplie,
Où tout ce qui a été
Vibre encore et résonne,
Où tout ce qui va être
Se laisse pressentir :
Elle est l'instant parfait.
'In der . . . (mettons ici 'musique'
A la place d' '*Entschlossenheit*')
Ist die Gegenwart aus der Zerstreuung –
Nicht nur zurückgeholt,
Sondern wird in der Zukunft
Und Gewesenheit gehalten.'
C'est ce présent authentique,
A la fois tenu dans le passé,
Et dans le futur, que Heidegger nomme '*Augenblick*'.
C'est en lui que la musique atteint à l'unité
Des trois extases : 'die ekstatische Einheit'.

And above all, Chestov, my master,
Dead while I write these lines,

'Das Dasein muss wesenhaft das auch schon Entdeckte
Gegen den Schein zueignen.'
A poetry that never for a moment forgets
The crucial necessity – that Existence
Must always necessarily appropriate for itself
(In conflict with appearance) the already discovered.
To lay bare the 'existing' is to dispute it with appearance,
To wring, to ravish, its secret from it.
Truth (the discovered) must always first be wrung
From the existing. The existing is torn from the hidden.
Discovery (laying bare) is always a rape, a theft.
For this the 'courageous decision' is necessary
And that is what '*Entschlossenheit*' is.

And now I am impelled by your death
To realize afresh and far more keenly than ever
That *Entschlossenheit* is
The will-to-possess-knowledge of our nothingness:
'*Gewissen-haben-wollen*'.
This will-to-possess-knowledge of nothingness
Of Existence is, just as much
As self-comprehension, an aspect
– And not the least serious or important –
Of the *Entschlossenheit des Daseins*.
The world is not 'Nature', neither
Is it 'representation' (the perceived); it is
An ontological characteristic of Existence.
In the appearance of the world
Is manifested transcendence.
'Transcendence means surpassing'
(*Transzendenz bedeutet Übersteig*).
How are we to translate *Übersteig*?
By surpassing? That is inadequate,
Giving the idea of a precipice
To be compassed, an abyss to be bridged.
Transcendence achieves always
A *totality* which may not
Have been coherently apprehended

But which is in no wise
The sum of all that which exists.
It does not present the thing-in-itself,
It is the 'being in the world';
'*Das In-der-Welt-sein.*'
What Existence transcends is not only
The existing which distinguishes it
In every respect, it is primarily
The existing which it itself is;
In the Transcending, existence comes first
To such existing things as it itself is,
To itself as itself – with the same movement
That awakens, vivifies, and stirs a world.

Existence, transcendent, gives form to the *self*
'*Die Selbstheit*'. Creating a world ('*Weltbildend*')
And, simultaneously, creating itself ('*Selbstbildend*')
It hurls itself in advance of itself
Into the world which it permeates.

To exist means to-be-in-the-world, to be caught,
Encompassed by the existing things
Which there discover (offer) themselves,
And in that world to tie bonds,
To clear a way for oneself,
To conquer distances (*entfernen*),
To find materials (*Zeuge*)
Which one uses for a definite end.
This is what Heidegger calls
'Availability' (*Zuhandenheit*).
The existing as it is in itself is
Primarily the 'available',
That which is within my reach,
Which concerns me, which I
Interest myself in (*besorgen*).
Moreover, I must share this world with 'others'.
I must come against other existences
Similar to my own. I must adjust myself

To their rhythms, or impose my own on them.
I must lose or find myself in them.
'*Die Welt des Daseins ist Mitwelt.*'
The world of existence is a common world.
To-be-in-the-world implies
To-be-along-with-others: Co-existence (*Mitdasein*).

A poetry like the barrel of a gun
Weaving like a snake's head.

A poetry that can put all its chips on the table
And back it to the limit.

A poetry full of the crazy feeling
That everything that has ever gone into my life
Has pointed to each successive word
And I couldn't have failed to write it if I'd tried,
Since a man cannot duck away from the pattern
That life lays out for him.

Or like testing with group-reagents for every known poison
And also for ptomaine, but all the solvents
– Alcohol, benzol, naphtha, ammonia, and so forth – failing,
And testing for the alkaloids, such as
Strychnine, digitalin, and cantharidin,
And using hydrochloric acid to find
Either silver, mercury, or lead,
And also ammonia in an endeavour
To trace tin, cadmium, or arsenic
And being utterly unable to arrive
At any conclusion – though it would appear
Death was due to the virulence
Of some azotic substance, of which
There is only a secondary and most faint trace.
Briefly, like a game of roulette, wherein
We always play en plein – a game of hazard
Played by the individual against the multiform forces
To which we give the name of 'circumstance'.
With cards whose real strength is always either more or less

Than their face value, and which are 'packed' and 'forced'
With an astuteness which would baffle the wiliest sharper.
There are times in the game when the cards
Held by the mortal player have no value at all,
When what seem to us kings and queens and aces
Change to mere blanks; there are other moments
When ignoble twos or threes flush into trumps
And enable us to sweep the board.

This is the kind of poetry I want
In this world at war when I see
On the Dark Plain (la buia compagna)
'A vast multitude of spirits
Running behind a flag
In great haste and confusion,
Urged on by furious wasps and hornets.
These are the unhappy people
Who never were alive,
Never awakened to take any part
Either in good or evil'
. . . 'che non furon ribelli,
Nè fur fedeli a Dio, ma per sè foro'.
(Nor rebels nor faithful to God,
But for themselves!).

A poetry like a glacier caught between the peaks
– A landmark among the high ranges of poetry,
Not hung upon the clouds,
But steadfastly descending to the *Plain*
Where all men walk and talk and gaze and can look upward and
        forward,
Not downward and backward,
On Nature and each other.

Great art has inspired action.
Even poor Essex
Before his futile rising tried to give

Drive and tone to his endeavour
By having performed before him
And his fellow protestors *Richard II.*
When Liberty once again
Becomes a faith and enthusiasm,
When the books are opened
And tyranny's claim
That it might do any violence
Because it alone
Could be 'efficient'
Is disproved – then
It is not improbable
That we shall see the new rally
Express itself in a culmination
Of the present dance-form,
As Aeschylus in his new drama
Gave form and voice
To the Greek liberation from Persia.
This is the poetry that I want.

What Have Scotsmen to Fight For?

BUT what have Scotsmen to fight for?
All the ends they have fought for or are likely to fight for
Are greater foes than any they have ever thought they were fighting.
And the only thing worth fighting for
Is something they know nothing whatever about,
But, if they could conceive it, would regard
As the final horror, the ultimate outrage,
The inhuman unspeakable torture
Of their being forced to think!

In the most haunting single play yet written
About the last war, much of the dramatic action
Hung on the fact that two English officers
About to go over the top
Shared a fondness for 'Alice in Wonderland'.

It is not too much to say
That many Englishmen fought for Lewis Carroll
And the dear remembered things of English life,
Just as Frenchmen, loathing war,
With the intelligent distaste of that paradoxical nation,
Fought for Anatole France and the Louvre,
Germans for Bach, Beethoven, and Bierhalle,
Italians for Verdi and the Sistine Chapel.

We Scots have nothing to fight for like any of these.

The best way to keep out of war is to say,
Speaking of war, let's get busy on something else.
For it is psychologically true
That while we will never lose
Our traditions of heroism,
Of manliness and self-sacrifice,
Of all those things which were behind
The personalities which made us a nation
We can bring them down to where Santa Claus is
If we have a domestic ideal.

The Kind of Scot I Want

HE was especially full
Of this love of movement
And zeal of observation.
He manifested anew
All the leading characteristics
(The high spirits conspicuous as the valour)
Of the Scot before the Union
– Breaking anew
'An enchanting and amazing crystal fountain
From the dark rocky caverns below'.

All traceable of course
To the quick contrasts and amazing variety
Of Scotland's incomparable scenery.
Our minds should surely hold a synoptic view
Of all the stages of world culture
Like the 'geological staircase' seen on our West coast,
Or like the Tongland fish pass, the highest in the British Isles,
Of 35 pools each connected by a submerged orifice
Through which the water descends and up which the fish have to swim;
Or like a Babylonian Ziggurat, 'soul ladder',
Dante's Celestial Ladder in *Paradiso*, Canto XXI,
The Icelandic earth-mazes called Volundar-husar,
And the connexion between Daidalos and Wayland (Volundr)
And the Indian *Mahavrata*, Festival of the Revolving Sun,
Indra the Sun-god, also Nrta, 'the Dancer'.
Or like a *mc'od rten* unissant le ciel et la terre,[1]
Corroborant, nous semble-t-il, l'hypothèse
De la dérivation du *caitya* relativement
Au type ziggurat sumero-akkadien
De plusieurs millénaires antérieurs.

.   .   .   .   .

[1] *Vide* Giuseppe Tucci's Indo-Tibetica I 'Mc 'od rten' e 'Ts'a ts'a' nel Tiber indiano et occidentale. II Rin c'enbzan po e la rinascita del Buddhismo nel Tibet intorno al mille (Roma, Accademia d'Italia, 1932, 1933).

A plover requires a ploughed field to set his flight off.
It is a flight that needs a good staging.
So the Scottish spirit must be seen
In relation to Scotland.

Poetry and Science

Science is the Differential Calculus of the mind,
Art is the Integral Calculus; they may be
Beautiful apart, but are great only when combined.
                              SIR RONALD ROSS

THE rarity and value of scientific knowledge
Is little understood – even as people
Who are not botanists find it hard to believe
Special knowledge of the subject can add
Enormously to the aesthetic appreciation of flowers!
Partly because in order to identify a plant
You must study it very much more closely
Than you would otherwise have done, and in the process
Exquisite colours, proportions, and minute changes spring to light
Too small to be ordinarily noted.
And more than this – it seems the botanist's knowledge
Of the complete structure of the plant
(Like a sculptor's of bone and muscle)
– Of the configuration of its roots stretching under the earth,
The branching of stems,
Enfolding of buds by bracts,
Spreading of veins on a leaf –
Enriches and makes three-dimensional
His awareness of its complex beauty.

Wherefore I seek a poetry of facts. Even as
The profound kinship of all living substance
Is made clear by the chemical route.

Without some chemistry one is bound to remain
Forever a dumbfounded savage
In the face of vital reactions.
The beautiful relations
Shown only by biochemistry
Replace a stupefied sense of wonder
With something more wonderful
Because natural and understandable.
Nature is more wonderful
When it is at least partly understood.
Such an understanding dawns
On the lay reader when he becomes
Acquainted with the biochemistry of the glands
In their relation to diseases such as goitre
And their effects on growth, sex, and reproduction.
He will begin to comprehend a little
The subtlety and beauty of the action
Of enzymes, viruses, and bacteriophages,
These substances which are on the borderland
Between the living and the non-living.

He will understand why the biochemist
Can speculate on the possibility
Of the synthesis of life without feeling
That thereby he is shallow or blasphemous.
He will understand that, on the contrary,
He finds all the more
Because he seeks for the endless
– 'Even our deepest emotions
May be conditioned by traces
Of a derivative of phenanthrene!'

Learned Poetry

... EXCLUSION from all power be theirs
Who do not know at least
Mazumdar's Typical Selections from Oriya Literature.
Goswani's Asamiya Sahityar Chanski,[1]
Taraporewala's Selections from Classical Gujarati literature
And, traversing the great stages of Hindu literature,
The hymns of each of the Asht Chhap,
And Tulsi Das, brightest star of Indian medieval poetry,
Unapproached and unapproachable in his niche in the Temple of Fame.
The teachings of the great saints, including Swami Ramanand,
Kabir, Guru Nanak, Guru Teg Bahadur,
Guru Govind Singh, and Mira Bai,
The principal writings on the Science of Poetry,
Together with the fanciful classification of women,
Technically called the Nayika-bhed,
And the writings of Vidyapati,
Malik Mohammad Jaisi, Keswara Das,
Rahim, Raskhan, Ninbarak, Usman Senapati,
Bihari Lal, Bhupati, and Sabal Singh Chauhan.
Let them know too Krisnadasa Kaviraj,
Who begins his Shri Shri Chaityana Charitamrita
With a string of fifteen slokas on Sanskrit
And quotes freely, as I do, from all classes of books
(A poet as bookish as Silius Italicus). ...

Further Talk with Donnchadh Bàn Mac an t-Saoir

WHAT questions do I not ask
Now I have been all over Beinn Dobhrain with you
– Seeing the very small extent of the territory
Normally occupied by a particular group of deer

[1] Typical selections from Assamese literature.

Whether this observance of definite territories
Does not tend as among human tribes
To the evolution of different races?
Certainly the heads from different forests
Seem to fall into distinctive types,
As they do among the elk of Norway.
And are there not reasons for believing
The small size of the Dundonnell deer a genetic
As well as an environmental trait?
And if as I think weather conditions and insect pests
Are more important causes of movement among deer
Than the direction of the wind, does this
Hold good for all parts of Scotland? Some places
Seem to depend very largely on a suitable wind
To draw deer into them. Yet the correspondence
Between weather and movement is abundantly clear
And there can no longer be any doubt that deer
Are so sensitive to meteorological changes
As to be able to anticipate them by hours, and sometimes days.
Then, though the importance of antlers as offensive weapons
May rightly be questioned, is it not probable
Casualties would be far more numerous and severe
But for the way in which the branched points
Engage and parry one another? If so
Antlers as normally grown would have a survival value.
But is there not a closer relation between horns
And the sexual psychology than is involved
Merely in the fights of the rutting season?
Are they not an 'erotic zone'? Fascinating, too, is the thought
Of the effect of light in altering
The reproductive rhythm – a discovery
Which probably explains how the deer
Acclimatized in the Antipodes were able
Swiftly to change their rutting season from October to April.
The antlers grow again every year and clearly
The rate of growth during the year
Is far greater than that calculated
From the average size reached by the antler

Over several years. In taxonomy
The attempt is often made to distinguish
Supposed species and even genera
By the proportions of their parts.
The systematists must be warned
Percentage measurements have no value.
What *are* diagnostic are the values
Of the growth-ratio and the absolute body-sizes
At which heterogony (if not uniform)
Begins, ends, or alters. So long as the growth-mechanism persists
It must of itself result in changes of form,
And to explain these it is no longer necessary
To have recourse to some imaginary adaptation
Or to the mysterious principle called orthogenesis,
Which postulates a succession of gene
All, for no obvious reason, in the same direction.
But should the heterogony of particular organs
Come into play, this must tend –
To limit the size attained by the race,
For the animal would otherwise become overweighted
By the exaggerated organ – the great Irish deer
With its huge antlers, we must suppose
Had reached this limit of bodily growth
And only a slight change in its surroundings,
Was needed to cause its extinction.

To the Younger Scottish Writers

ART must be related to the central issues of life,
Not serve a sub-artistic purpose that could as well
Be served by the possession of a new motor-car
Or a holiday on the Continent perhaps.
What do we Scottish writers most lack, most need?
– An immediate experience of the concrete,
A rich overflowing apprehension of the definite

Day-by-day content of our people's lives,
A burningly clear understanding of the factors at work,
Of the actual correlation of the forces, in labour to-day;
A Dundee jute mill, Singer's, Beardmore's,
The ghost towns, ruined fishing villages, slave camps,
And all the derelict areas of our countryside;
The writer not first and foremost concerned with these
Lacks the centrality that alone can give
Value to his work – he is a trifler, a traitor,
To his art and to mankind alike,
A fool choosing flight and fantasy,
Not to be pitied, but despised.

It is a lying cry to say
That human nature cannot be changed.
It can be, and is being, completely.
We are long past the time when doubt of an accepted system
Liberates great minds while yet the system itself
Has not fallen into such contempt as to be
Incapable of their action within its limits.
Long past the affectation of being above the battle,
Of being socially agnostic, seeing all systems
As subject to historic change, and the will
Of great men, and accepting none.

Yet what are all our intellectuals saying?
All victimized by repetition-compulsion
They are denying these huge horizons opening out
And crying 'Fundamentally man cannot change'
And bleating 'After all there's but one kind of man.
Men's ways of thought can never become
So inconceivably different from ours!'
Can't they? They have already. Mine have
And every fit member's of the I.U.R.W.
And are speedily disposing of the bourgeois notions
That art must be 'neutral, equally indifferent
To good and evil, knowing no pity, no anger'.
And that 'neither in its high countenance

Nor looks can its secret thoughts be read',
Any more than the masked wizard-of-History's can.
We have read them all right!
The overcoming by life of its own limitations
The calling out of the major images of the future,
What and as is – and as should and will be
Reality in motion, advancing and developing
Not for us? They can keep their decrepit
Terms, which belong to a past we've sloughed off
Of realism, romanticism, classicism,
Naturalism, and all the witless rest
Of isms, flourishing in the parent mire of scholasticism.

(The primary capitalistic neurosis is narcissism.)
It is a libel to say we need these infantilisms now
And always will – lest these precious little scribblers
Prove Rip Van Winkles on the edge of by far
The greatest Kulturkampf in human history,
These fools who have already become unreadable
Not because their actual craftsmanship has degenerated,
But simply because, in the most literal sense,
They do not know what they are talking about.
So with our Scottish writers; they are forced
Either to distort the content of Scottish life
In order to make it conform
To some desperate personal wish-fulfilment
Or flee from it entirely – into the past,
Into fantasy, or some other reality-surrogate.
Outside the revolutionary movement there is no place
For any writer worth a moment's thought.
The 'culture class' for which they think they write
Has ceased to exist either as a class
Or as a repository of culture; as the strain
Of economic struggle tightens the so-called
Middle-class vanguard immediately reveals
Its essential moral weakness and above all
Its intellectual poverty thinly coated
By a veneer of artistic sophistication;

No self-respecting man can have anything to say to them.
They have no longer any real reason for existing,
And therefore literature and art can be nothing
For them except day-dreams of 'shots' in the arm,
While a few of them, the sentimental stoics,
May read such a poem as this (or bits of it)
With a wearily-approving nod of cynicism.
There is nothing whatever in contemporary biology
Either the science of heredity or of genetics,
Nothing we know of the mechanisms of inheritance,
Nothing in the nature of the genes or chromosomes
To stand in the way of the radicals' enthusiasm
For social transformation – the revolutionists'
Advocacy of profoundly-altered social systems.
On the other hand there is a vast accumulation
Of evidence from the sociological sciences,
Economy, anthropology, sociology,
Politics, the philosophy of history, to substantiate
The necessity, the sanity, and the wisdom
Of deep changes in all institutions, customs,
Habits, values – in short, civilizations.
Human nature is the last thing we need to worry about.
Let us attend to the circumstances that condition it.

We live in a world that has become
Intolerable as the subject of passive reflection.
What is our response to the unescapable reality?
Are we too like these miserable little cliques to turn
Because of theoretic inadequacy
From social causation, from the poetry of purgative action
And try to find form and significance
In pure feeling itself, transplanted and re-imagined,
Seeking the meaning of experience in the phenomena of experience,
Pure sensation becoming an ultimate value
In the neurotic and mystical attempt
To give physicality an intellectual content,
In the sensitizing of nerves already raw,
Meaningless emotion aroused automatically

Without satisfaction or education, as in melodrama?
Man can find his own dignity only in action now.

Scottish writers, the height and depth of your writings
Will be measured by the extent to which
The dialectics of our era find expression
In the artistic imagery – how widely, forcefully, clearly
(Sir Thomas Inskip permitting or not!)
The burning contemporary problems are expressed in it,
The class war, the struggles and ideals
Of the proletariat bent on changing the world,
And consequently on changing human nature.

Song of the Seraphim

POVERTY is nothing but an outlived fettering
In the depths of the material regions
– In the mechanical, dead, inanimate
Or animal life of Nature.

This life we have now outgrown.
It lays the veil of the body over the spirit
And drags everything down to the level
Of a narrow materiality.

It is nothing but meanness and ugliness,
Stench, corruption, vice, decomposition, and dumbness.
The call is to intoxicated, burning lavishness.
Nothing now can bring poverty
Creatively to the front.
Poverty merely hinders the coming
Of the new Necessity
Which leads us to the End and Aim
Of our spirit and of the world,
Will make us steep and electric

And produce by force a new race
Of mariners on new and dangerous seas.

Poverty to-day desires nothing
But a material well-being.
But the entire hopeless comfortlessness
Of a satisfied well-being
Must first be lived through,
Not merely described
Or held out to the poor
From afar.
The lower paradises
Must be outlived through satiety.
This is the call of the Seraphim.

Only he who hopes nothing more
From well-being and philistinism;
Only he who is no longer fettered
In the coarse material depths;
Only he who yearns for new needs
– The needs of the Heights,
Not the needs of the Depths,
Immense and seraphic needs –
He only perceives
The impalpable and primordial life,
The Supreme – a life
Fuller, more real, and warmer
Than the chaotic deception
Of the palpable and objective
Which is apparently only effective
For everyday lower life.

To-day we are ripe to put an end
To poverty – to make an end
Of this necessity
For richness and abundance
In this world period
Become mankind.
But there is without doubt

Also a holy poverty,
A super-richness which falls to pieces
In its own splendour,
A glowing love
That presses all fullness to itself,
Allows all small possessions to fall
More and more away from it,
All narrowness in relation
To things and to self –
Not from any ascetic discomfort,
But because of the poorness
Of these things in themselves
Such is the glory
Of holy riches
And supreme prodigality.
The purpose of the old needs, therefore,
Cannot be 'well-being'
But only a new need.
Does the mighty proletarian assault
Of the poorest today desire nothing
But 'satiety', nothing but 'well-being'
With a smattering of art and education
Built philistine-wise upon it?

Does it not want as it asserts
To overcome the bourgeoisie,
But only to establish it forever
– Bourgeoisie itself in everything,
Not a step higher?
And that disgusts the few spiritual men,
But how can it disgust
Those poorest ones?
The deliverance of the proletariat cannot be
The affair of the proletariat itself,
As demagogic teaching declares.
It is in truth more than a sectional affair,
More than a class affair.

To-day something is beginning, as if the seed
Were losing itself in the bud.
Creation wants to-day to blossom
And raise itself to its topmost heights.
And if we wish to survive and not to suffocate,
Then in this day we must mount
An entirely new step higher, a greater step
Than that from the animal world
To the world of man.

That, however, is not technique,
Science, economics, organization, learning,
Or any kind of reform or 'cleverness'.
It is a *necessity* called for
By the eternal primordial life.
The new level of life does not depend
Upon a thing, nor upon
An individual.
It is an act of the never-ending creation,
Lying far beyond all individualist action.
Nevertheless we cannot mount
On to another plane of life
Until all the old possibilities,
Unto the very last,
Have been worn out and lived through.
For the way to the Supreme
Is in no way
The quickest and shortest.
It is a way most deeply sunk
And does not pass by
The smallest possibility of life.
For every part of the way
Is of equal value
In the Supreme. Every part
Is an aim in itself,
For the Supreme knows no 'Evolution'.

'Evolution' has only an entirely
'Inner-finite' significance.
It is a barbarous adoption,
As if somewhere, quite positive,
There were a Process – if possible, quite temporal –
Which in its issue, in its *sum*, determines the
'Essence' of the real;
Is itself absolute reality,
Universalness, the Supreme.
All our ideas about such a world process
Are nothing but a human and temporal view
And entirely adapted
To a temporal standard.

Every 'World Process' that we describe
Has only a world reality,
A reality of manifestation and technique.
We comprehend in it only
That which is objective and dead,
Never its life – for all life
Is incomprehensible.
Life is greater than all that can enter
Into the comprehensible.
Though I know all the limbs,
Entrails, organs, and functions of mankind,
Still am I as far as ever
From knowing 'man'
Who is more than the sum of his organs,
Which indeed only find
Their meaning and their life
When man's action precedes them.
We do not know a mosaic
By adding up the stones.
On the contrary,
The picture comes before the stones,
Without which the picture means nothing.

Whoever regards a 'World Process'
As a final reality
Is merely pursuing the anatomy
Of the corpse of all life.
This string of pearls, which in themselves
Are single and loose,
Is not the final form.
The world reality of such a process
In Thing, Individual, and Word
Is only its lowest form.
What we call *being* is only
The functioning of our consciousness,
Not the 'final Universal of All',
But the lowest.
It is the feeling, groping, consuming spirit;
Objective, matter-bound, but not living spirit.
That higher and stronger quickening life
We seek eternally and to-day
Must discover anew
Eternally transcends the objective spirit
Because it has nothing objective,
Only life.

But we draw the supreme Source of Life
Into the kingdom of Touch and Taste and Speech
If we signify it as something
'Behind' or 'Over' or 'Near',
Conformably to some spacious picture;
Or as the 'One', the 'Without Shape',
The 'Thing in Itself'. These are all
Materialistic, mediate things,
But 'the Supreme' and 'life' are immediate.
Pleroma is immediate, and is far away
Only from the gropers who seek
To muffle the infinite
In limitations and terms.
But to the high, crushing nearness
Of my exploding primordial life

The Supreme is 'that which is quite Nigh',
That which is without distance,
Immediateness itself, love-embrace,
The paradisiacal awareness
In which all fullness immediate and unredeemed,
Since all time, is posited timelessly,
Over 'Being', blessed in 'One'.
No empty abstraction, but the Life
Which can never be grasped,
That is transcendent.
And no bridge carries us
From 'Word' to 'trans',
Even as no bridge, but a leap,
Carries us from the plane to the cube,
From shallows to the bodily likeness.

Edinburgh

Most of the denizens wheeze, sniffle, and exude a sort of snozzling whnoff whnoff,
apparently through a hydrophile sponge.

EZRA POUND

THE capital of Scotland is called Auld Reekie,
Signifying a monstrous acquiescence
In the domination of the ends
By the evidences of effort.
– Not the mastery of matter
By the spirit of man
But, at best, a damnable draw,
A division of the honours
And, far more, the dishonours!
– Dark symbol of a society
Of 'dog eat dog'.
Under which the people reveal themselves to the world
Completely naked in their own skin,
Like toads!

Yes, see, the dead snatch at the living here.
So the social corpse, the dead class,
The dead mode of life, the dead religion,
Have an after life as vampires.
They are not still in their graves
But return among us.
They rise with the fumes
From the chimney of the crematorium
And again settle down on the earth
And cover it with black filth.

To repossess ourselves of the primal power
'Let there be light' and apply it
In our new, however more complex, setting
Is all. And let us not cry
'Too difficult! Impossible!' forgetting
That the stupendous problems that obsess us to-day
Are as nothing to the problems overcome
By the miraculous achievements of men in the past
– Yes, the first problems in the very dawn of human history
Were infinitely greater, and our troubles are due
To the fact that we have largely lost
The earliest, the most essential,
The *distinctively human* power
Our early ancestors had in abundant measure
Whatever else they lacked that we possess.
Possess thanks to them! – and thanks to the primal indispensable power
They had and we have lost progressively
And affect to despise –
Fools who have lost the substance
And cling to the shadow.
Auld Reekie indeed!
Preferring darkness rather than light
Because our deeds are evil!

I see the dark face of an early mother of men
By a primitive campfire of history.
Her appearance is rendered all the more remarkable
Because of the peculiar performance of the smoke.

By some process, natural no doubt but mysterious to us,
She exercises a strange control over the smoke
As she shuffles round – with vast protruding lips
And with wide rings hanging from her ears,
Weaving her hands. And it is
As if the billows of thick white vapour
Are forced to follow her will
And make a magical dancing cloud
Behind her as she moves.
Learn again to consume your own smoke like this,
Edinburgh, to free your life from the monstrous pall,
To subdue it and be no longer subdued by it,
Like the hand of the dyer in his vat.
So all the darkness of industrialism yet
Must be relegated like a moth that pursues
The onward dance of humanity.

So the mighty impetus of creative force
That seeks liberation, that shows even through
The scum of swinish filth of bourgeois society,
The healthy creative force will break through
– Even in Edinburgh – and good, human things grow,
Protecting and justifying faith
In regeneration to a free and noble life
When labour shall be a thing
Of honour, valour, and heroism
And 'civilization' no longer like Edinburgh
On a Sabbath morning,
Stagnant and foul with the rigid peace
Of an all-tolerating frigid soul!

This is the great skill that mankind has lost,
The distinctively human power.
Lo! A poor negress teaches this rich university city
Something more important than all it knows,
More valuable than all it has!
But Edinburgh – Edinburgh – is too stupid yet
To learn how not to stand in her own light.

Dante on the Edinburgh People

IN Edinburgh – in Auld Reekie – to-day
Where 99 per cent of the people might say
In Dante's words . . . 'Tristi fummo
Nell' aer dolce che dal sol s'allegra'
        (Sullen were we,
In the sweet air that is gladdened by the sun,
Carrying lazy smoke in our hearts).

Glasgow

ONLY once in a lifetime a few of these hoodlums,
Embarrassed by some proffer of genuine affection
Or witnessing a personal friend die, may feel
Ashamed at being so poor and hard, so incapable
Of finding any place in their lives for the former, so lacking
In everything that might be of use in helping anyone to die,
And see, for an instant, that they have nothing inside them
Save things that serve the purposes of everyday life,
A life of comfort, one's own life, a damned insensibility.

They spend their lives doing anything rather
Than what if they examined their lives for a moment
Even the stupidest of them would recognize
As the chief end of man – the one thing untouched,
Their specific aboulia. They believe in everything
Except anything credible and creditable
All they need is a Blake – George Blake, not William! –
To tell them, to keep on telling them, to be forever
Telling them, their lack of culture, their horrible devitalization,
Their putrid superstitions, their terror of ideas,

Their hatred of intellectual distinction, do not matter
– Their 'replacement of intelligence by sentimentality
Is yet a lovely virtue, and a country like Scotland is happy
With so many of its people resolutely devoted to that'.

'There are to be found among them degrees of plain worth,
Of warm hospitality and unaffected decency,
Few nations of the earth can rival, and all
The understandable squeals of the young intellectuals
Of the new age against a colourless bourgeoisie
Cannot deprive that fact of its value.'
Besides, as Power says, 'Glasgow to-day
Is becoming quite a literary centre.' – Quite!

Half glow-worms and half newts!

.   .   .   .

All classes in the city are alike in this,
Running the whole gamut of life from A to B.
University, professors, lecturers, school-teachers,
Ministers, and all that awful gang of mammalia,
The high mucky-mucks. Bogged in servile and illiberal studies,
They have all the same pettifogging spirit,
So narrow it shows little but its limits,
The same incapacity for culture and creative work.
(Glasgow, *arida nutrix* of hundreds of thousands of callous Scots,
Incapable of any process of spiritual growth and conquest,
Destitute of all rich and lively experience,
Without responsibility or honour,
Completely insensible to any of the qualities
That make for a life worth having,
Pusillanimous and frigid time-servers,
Cold with a *pietrosità* deeper than the masonry accounts for
Though that would satisfy a theorist *à la Taine!*)

.   .   .   .

It's a far cry from the *Jolly Beggars* of Robert Burns
To Marc Blitzstein's *The Cradle Will Rock*,

The measure of the leeway Scottish poets must make up.
Mr. Blitzstein's unjolly proletarians are not beggars
But demanders . . . and are much more interested
In the steel strike than in warbling the delights of rolling in the hay.
Would Glasgow had a Blitzstein too! We need
His remarkable ferocity of satire, his raffishly amusing lyrics,
And his savagely cumulative absurdity even in the smallest matters
    of life,
For above all we need artists who live
Somewhere near the human centre and know
Innumerable truths that cannot be taught,
And thus can be good-natured without being sentimental,
Ridiculous without being fatuous,
And with whom, as with any first-rate artist, we feel
We are in good hands . . . artists
We can trust with our hearts and our wits.
Scotland has scarcely had a hair of one since Burns.

The British Empire

THE English play the waiting game the longest,
The best, and win most often. In this angry world
They will be the last to relinquish
Their hereditary and imperial property rights.
They have an experienced technique for elastic decisions
Which may end in eventual war and dismemberment,
But not until every humanly conceivable policy
Or possibility of avoiding the latter
Has been consciously employed and exploited.
Their modest and resilient stupidity,
Inexorable acquisitiveness and stubborn ownership
Are their God-given armour; and we have cause
To know how fierce a God they get their gifts from.
The tragedy of Lord Dufferin's declining days,
His involvement in just the sort
Of hideous and criminal scandal which would most

Hurt and destroy such a charming man,
Was not mitigated by his innocence
Or by his almost accidental connexion with the fraud.
Dufferin's tragedy is in miniature
The present drama of the British Empire.

So Here I Hail All the Fellow-Artists I Know

So here I hail all the fellow-artists I know
And all the singers and narrators everywhere,
*'A rum lot they are, as the Devil said when he looked over the ten
    Commandments.'*

Ashugi, akyni, zhirshi, bakhshi, and other folk singers,
Minstrels, histriones, jongleurs, juglares,
Skomorokhi, guslari, forsangere, recitadoras,
Kaleki, ciegos, Sidney's 'blind crowder',
And all the descendants to this day everywhere
Of Teiresias and blind Maeonides
(Filí, ollamhs, cáintí, vates, and ἱεροποιοί
And the 'poluphloisboisterous' music
Of every anruth, clí, cano, and all the rest
From the rí-bhárd down to the bó-bhárd and the bárd loirge,
And shanachie after shanachie
Down to the shanachie of the chimney-corner,
Wandering scholars, clerics of the Marbhán type,
And all the Cliar Sheanachain,[1]
The children of Manannán, *lá binn, lá searbh,*[2]
'... the patron saint
Of merry rogues and fiddlers, trick o' the loop men,
Thimblemen and balladmen that gild the fair.'
Ah, fain would I follow if I could
The *Imtheacht na Tromdháimhe*[3]

[1] Strolling satirists.
[2] One day sweet, another sour.
[3] The Proceedings of the Great Bardic Assembly.

Of the whole round world!)
Ashugi, akyni, zhirshi, bakhshi, and other folk singers,
Creators of the new heroic epodes of to-day.
The Turkic poems of Hussein Bozalgonly of Tauz,
Uzbek and Darginian songs,
The songs of Suleiman Stalsky,[1] the singer of the Daghestan people,
The blind old *kobzar,* Ostap Vyeryesai,
And Timofei Ivanitch, the old *skazitel',*
Who knew all the songs of all Russia.
The songs of the *akyn* Kenen of Kazakhstan
(Kazakhstan in renaissance, strengthened by its new 'iron roads');
Tajiks from a *kishlak* in Obi-Garma
Singing of the flaming Stalin;
The lyrics of the Mordovian minstrel Krivosbeyeva;[2]
The Armenian legend *Lenin-Pasha;*
The song of Jambul . . .
 'Run as a herald through our Kazakh auls,
 Make the whole steppe attend
 You, song of *Akyn* Jambul.
 Listen, Kaskelen, Karakol, Kastek,
 Glorious is the great Soviet Law,
 It enacts joy to the peoples;
 It waters the steppe and brings fruit;
 It lifts up our hearts to sing;
 It commands all Nature to live
 In service and praise of the people;
 The song of the old Kazakh *Akyn* Jambul
 To Hassem Lakhuti, the Persian Communist poet.
 The ripened song swells in our hearts.
 Let us strike up together, *Akyn* Lakhuti . . .
 The centuries will reverberate with our song,
 And all the world's tongues will repeat it.'
See . . . on the steppe, barren and waste,
A huge thousand-handed man moves in great circles

---

[1] Died 23 November 1937.
[2] I have elsewhere written my appreciations of such poets as the Kirghiz poet Toktogul Satylganov (born 1871); Ivan Franko (1856–1916), the Western Ukrainian poet; the Bashkir poet, Mazhit Gafur (born 1880); and many others.

Ever wider girthing the earth,
And in his path the dead steppe comes to life,
Quivering, juicy grass shoots forth,
And everywhere towns and villages emerge;
And he strides ever on,
Further towards the edge,
Sowing what is live and human.
Then one feels towards people
A new tenderness and respect;
Feels in them an unquenchable vitality
That can vanquish death,
That eternally transforms what is dead into life,
Moving towards immortality by mortal roads.
– Death overshadows people,
But it cannot engulf them.

Scotland

IT requires great love of it deeply to read
The configuration of a land,
Gradually grow conscious of fine shadings,
Of great meanings in slight symbols,
Hear at last the great voice that speaks softly,
See the swell and fall upon the flank
Of a statue carved out in a whole country's marble,
Be like Spring, like a hand in a window
Moving New and Old things carefully to and fro,
Moving a fraction of flower here,
Placing an inch of air there,
And without breaking anything.

So I have gathered unto myself
All the loose ends of Scotland,
And by naming them and accepting them,
Loving them and identifying myself with them,
Attempt to express the whole.

I Am with the New Writers

I AM with the New Writers who waste no words
On manifestoes but are getting down
To the grim business of documentation,
Not seeking a short cut to the universal
But with all their energies concentrated
On gaining access to the particular.
I rejoice in André Chamson's description
Of the upsurge of his native *langue d'oc*
Against the pressure to 'talk French'.
This renewed impetus
Towards the local and the vernacular
Implies a changing conception of culture,
No longer a hothouse growth but rooted.
If all the world went native
There would be a confusion of tongues,
A multiplication of regionalisms.
Partikularismus, however,
Is hostile to nationalism
And friendly to internationalism.

I remember how Thoreau wrote:
'I have a commonplace book for facts
And another for poetry,
But I find it difficult always
To preserve the vague distinctions
I had in mind – for the most interesting and beautiful facts
Are so much the more poetry,
And that is their success.
– I see that if my facts
Were sufficiently vital and significant,
Perhaps transmuted more
Into the substance of the human mind,
I should need but one book of poetry
To contain them all!'

We Do Not Belong to the Family

WE do not belong to the family – that is our trouble –
This is the analogy perhaps that comes as near as
Any, the family a group of sense-data actual and obtainable,
Consisting of a standard solid and infinite number of distortion series.
That he had in full and these he ranged at ease
With the genuine simplicity of immediate awareness while we
Had only the pseudo-simplicity of perceptual acceptance at best,
And little if any power of coping with obstacularity,
But if awareness of new existents is, *pro tanto*, a boon,
Many quarters condemned him too wholly and too soon.

In My Early Teens

I CAN'T remember anything before I was six.
Aren't I backward? – But, later, in my early teens
I had a friend who taught me to remember everything.
(I mean everything about Scotland, of course.
Thanks largely to him I have lived my life
Fully and happily – finding fact
Not only delightful but sufficient
And needing no escapes into fantasy.)
Many a happy day I spent with him
Discussing the natural determinants of routes
In Lower Nithsdale; white quartz pebbles
And their archaeological significance;
Cumberland, Scottish, and Norwegian words;
Logan of Restalrig as a letter-writer;
Yevering, the place and the name;
The Scalacronica of Gray of Heton;

The Great Storm of 1785;
A Banffshire leader of Zouaves;
Icelandic sagas and their bearing
On the population of the Moray Firth;
Ptolemy's geography of Albion;
The crannogs in Carlingwark Lock;
Relics of the Norse language in Lewis speech;
Oriental elements in Scottish mythology;
Gaelic elements in South-west Lowland Scots English;
Vernacular Gaelic in the Book of the Dean of Lismore;
The story of Scottish dictionary-making;
The dialect of upper Teviotdale;
Gipsy loan-words in the Roxburghshire vernacular;
Kossuth in the Borderland;
The status of the Gaelic bard;
The speech of Stirling in the sixteenth and seventeenth centuries;
Points of resemblance between *Beowulf* and the Grettla or *Grettis Saga*;
William Herbert and his Scandinavian poetry;
Weather words in the Orkney dialect.
– Beetle-heads from a little owl's nest,
Which contained 705 of them
By the time I was fifteen.
And now, of course, I agree with H. G. Wells
That all the facts which are known should be collated
And available for immediate practical use,
Knowing that, about a great number of things,
Upon which men differ, there is exact knowledge,
So that they should not differ on these things.
That is true not merely about small matters in dispute
But about vitally important things,
Our business, our money, our political outlook,
Our health, the general conduct of our lives.
We are guessing when we might know.

The Nature of Will

IT is hard to rid ourselves of the phantasy
That will is an independent compartment of our nature.
We have trained ourselves so long to think of it
As a reservoir of magical fluid – as a force
That can be increased or diminished – shall I say at will?
But will is merely the interior side of our actions.
It is as strong and constant whatever we do.
For it is nothing but the deed considered in its origin.
What we do, we will. The *doing* is the will.
The *deed* once accomplished is the exact definition of the will.
There is no will which does not issue in a deed.
– If you flog yourselves to will harder,
To make stronger efforts, you will turn everything to phantasy;
Nothing is needed but clarity of feeling and objectivity of thought.

Manual Labour

ABOVE all – though primarily a poet myself –
I know I need as large an area of brain
To control my hands as my vocal organs
And I am fully alive to the danger
Of only grasping so much of the scientific outlook
As is expressed in words or symbols
Rather than actions
– The common mistake of regarding
The skilful manipulation of symbols
As an activity altogether more respectable
Than the skilful manipulation
Of material objects.
I am organically welded with the manual workers
As with no other class in the social system,
Though superficially my interests may seem to be rather
With the so-called educated classes.

Advice to Younger Writers

SOME of our younger writers ask me to give them a maxim.
I reply, the most useful perchance
Is 'Remember, the best snow for ski-ing on
Is also the most likely to avalanche.'

Or, again, 'A writer is a universe whose moments
Cannot be measured by equations, whose forces will ever give the slip
To the quadrants of science. Only the earth can be spelled by its seasons.
Watertight compartments are useful only to a sinking ship.'

Or, again, 'Remember how, detached from the forest,
Trees are apt to become deciduous
That would otherwise have remained evergreen.'
Such facts are pointers to us.

The Future of Poetry

Is poetry done for? Wars, the Robot Age, the collapse of civilization,
These things are distracting and annoying, it is true
– But merely as to an angler a moorhen's splashing flight
That only puts down a rising fish for a minute or two!

The Gaelic Muse

AT last, at last, I see her again
        In our long-lifeless glen,
Eidolon of our fallen race,
Shining in full renascent grace,

> She whose hair is plaited
> Like the generations of men,
> And for whom my heart has waited
> Time out of ken.

Hark! hark! the *fead chruinn chruaidh Chaoilte*,
Hark! hark! 'tis the true, the joyful sound,
Caoilte's shrill round whistle over the brae,
The freeing once more of the winter-locked ground,
The new springing of flowers, another rig turned over,
Dearg-lasrach bho'n talamh dubh na h-Alba,
Another voice, and another, stirring, rippling, throbbing with life,
    Scotland's long-starved ears have found.

Deirdre, Audh[1] – she has many names,
But only one function. Phaneromene,[2]
Hodegetria,[3] Chryseleusa,[4]
Chrysopantanasa – Golden-universal Queen –
Pantiglykofilusa,[5] Zoodotospygi,[6]
Like the sun once more in these verses seen
The light *angelicae summaeque sanctae Brigidae*,[7]
Goddess of poets, of whom Ultan[8] sang;
The golden, delightful flame; the branch with blossoms,
The actual Air-Maiden once more we see,
Incorporated tangibility and reality,
Whose electric glance has thrilled the Gaels
Since time beyond memory.
Twelve centuries ago Scotland with her praises rang.
Mary of the Gael! Brigit born at sunrise!
Her breath revives the dead.
Your songs, my friends, are songs of dawn, of renaissance too.

---

[1] Audh – the Deep-Minded.   [2] Phaneromene – made manifest.
[3] Hodegetria – leading on the way.   [4] Chryseleusa – golden-pitiful.
[5] Pantiglykofilusa – all-tenderly-embracing.
[6] Zoodotospygi – the life-giving fountain.
[7] 'Of the most angel-like and most saintly Brigit' (see *Leabhar Imuinn*, Dublin 1855–69).
[8] Ultan of Ard Breccain, died in A.D. 656. Composed a great 'Hymn in praise of Brigit.'

Twigs of the tree, of which it is said
Primo avulso non deficit alter
Aureus.[1] Worthy heirs and successors you
Of *Céile Dé,*[2] of Ultan, of Broccan Cloen.[3]
  Let your voices ring
  And be unafraid.

Múscail do mhisneach a Alba![4]
Set up your *Cúirt na h-Éigse*[5]
With a resounding Barrántas,[6] my friends!

Ah, Scotland, her footsteps, her voice, her eyes,
Agniotisa here, entire in our skies!

Too long the Bible-black gloom has spread
     Now let your red
Radiance and melody wed
Over all Scotland be shed
Till the Giants in the cave awake
And with a snap of their fingers break
Forever dull England's chains of lead
And every Scot turns from Britannia of the sugar-bowl jaws
To our own long-lost Queen of Queens instead.
  You have sounded the rallying cry.
  It cannot be long
  Till the hosts of our people hie
  On the heels of your song,
And we all make a colour to your red[7]

---

[1] From Virgil, *Aen.* VI, of the Golden Bough: 'Though one be torn away, there fails not another, golden.'

[2] *Céile Dé*, Gaelic bard of 'the time of Aengus,' whose poem (sometimes ascribed to Brigit herself) is preserved in the Burgundian Library.

[3] Broccan Cloen, flourished about A.D. 500, author of chief poetic tribute to Brigit's name.

[4] *Múscail*, etc.: 'Waken thy courage, O Scotland!' (after Pádraigín Haicéad's (?1600–1656) similar cry to Banba, i.e. Eire).

[5] *Cúirt na h-Éigse* – Court of Poetry.

[6] Barrántas – poetic summons.

[7] 'Make a colour to your red,' Gaelic idiom, meaning 'match you in colour'.

And flush redly to your Muse's fair bright cheek.
    Ho ro[1] *togaibh an aird* !
'*Mi eadar an talamh 's an t-athar a' seòladh*
Air iteig le h-aighear, misg-chath', agus shòlais,
A's caismeachd phìob-mòra bras-shròiceadh am puirt.'[2]

She is our Scottish *Gile na Gile*[3] – the strange pulchritude
That is the secret Scotland of the Gael,
The personification of Alba as the discrowned,
Wandering heart of beauty, our Sheila ní Gadhra,
Our Cathleen ní Houlihán, our *Druimfhionn Donn*,
Our *pé'n Éirinn í*, 'whoe'er she be,'[4]
Seán Ó Tuama's[5] Móirín ní Cullenán,
– And she leads us all over Scotland and the Isles
As the faery queen in Eire led Seán Clárach[6]
To view the faery strongholds – Cruachain, Brugh na Bóinne,
Creeveroe, Tara, Knockfeerin, and the rest
– The knot of white ribbon on the hair
Of the image of fine-tressed Gaelic womanhood !

Here only is there no makeshift
Of seeking intimacy with other human beings
And never finding it.
– Ah, my Queen, slender and supple
In a delightful posture
As free from self-conscious art
As the snowcap on a mountain !
– An absorbing attachment of the spirit,

[1] *Ho ro*, make ready to go.
[2] Alexander MacDonald's lines beginning 'Mi eadar . . .' mean 'Between earth and heaven in the air I am sailing, on the wings of exultance, battle drunken, enraptured, while the notes of the great pipes shrilly sound out their tunes.'
[3] *Gile na Gile*, brightness of brightness, the best of the Irish *aislingí*, or vision poems, telling of encounters with fair phantoms. By Aodhagán Ó Rathaille, 1670–1726.
[4] Uilliam Dall O'Heffernan's *Pé'n Éirinn í*, 'Whoe'er She Be,' is 'a song of rare finish . . . the poet communicates the thrill that startled him on Fionn's Hill, where he had gone to seek despairing solitude, when she, that lovelier than Deirdre, came to him – whoe'er she be. The wonder of that secret love lives across two centuries.'
[5] Seán Ó Tuama, 1708–75.   [6] Seán Clárach MacDomhnaill, 1691–1754.

Not a sexual relationship as that is generally understood,
But an all-controlling emotion
That has no physical basis,
Love resolved into the largest terms
Of which such emotions are capable,
The power of the spirit beneath that exquisite tremulous envelope
Possessing moral courage to a rare degree
Which can keep her steadfast in the gravest peril,
And a dignity so natural and certain
That it deserves the name of stateliness.
Death cannot intimidate her.
Poverty and exile, the fury of her own family
And the calumnies of the world
Are unable to bend her will
Towards courses she feels to be wrong
– Imparting with every movement, every look,
Some idea of what the process of literature could be,
Something far more closely related
To the whole life of mankind
Than the science of stringing words together
In desirable sequences.

(What is the love of one human being
For another compared to this?
– Yet I do not underestimate
What such love can be!
On vit plus ou moins à travers des mots
As a rule, but sometimes these moments do come
When words and thoughts are one,
And one with the receptive understanding;
And in such moments
The individual reality of two lives
– For reality is subjective, personal
To each one of us, held in
By the crystal walls of our experience –
Can be fully understood;
The crystals are broken down for a space,

And two realities mingle and become one.
There is little better.
The physical falls away,
Almost irrelevant,
When naked spirits meet in kindness.)

Alas! The thought of ninety-nine per cent of our people
Is still ruled by Plato and Aristotle
Read in an historical vacuum by the few
From whom the masses receive
A minimum of it but along with that
A maximum incapacity for anything else.
The Greek, being a Southerner, was (and still is)
By temperament excitable and easily roused
To excessive display of feeling. Greek troops, we know – unlike Scots –
Were peculiarly liable to sudden panic,
And the keen intelligence of the race
Was no more rapid in its working
Than was their susceptibility to passion.
Wisely, therefore, the Greek moralists preached restraint;
Wisely they gave their impressionable countrymen advice
The very opposite of that
The more steady Northerner requires,
And we in modern Scotland most of all!

To Make One Thing[1]

I

OUT of this cloud, O see: so wildly hiding
The star which just has been – (and out of me),
Out of yon mountain country which has now
For long had night, nightwinds – (and out of me),
Out of the river in the valley-basin, river catching
The glitter of the torn sky-glade – (and out of me);

[1] From the German of Rainer Maria Rilke.

Out of me and all these things to make a single
Thing, O Lord: out of me, me and the feeling
With which the herd, pent up within the pen,
And breathing out, takes in the mighty darkened
No-more-being of the earth – out of me
And every light within the darkness of
The many houses, Lord, to make one thing;
Out of strangers, for I know not one, O Lord,
And out of me and me to make one thing;
Out of sleepers, out of strange unknown old men
In hospices who cough importantly within
The beds, and out of sleep-dazed children on
So strange a breast, and out of many unprecise
Vague people, always out of me and out
Of naught but me and things unknown to me
To make one thing, O Lord, Lord, Lord, the thing
Which cosmic-earthly like a meteor
Assembles in its heaviness naught but
The sum of flight: naught knowing but the arrival.

II

Why, why must one go and take thus on oneself
Strange things, just as, perhaps, the carrier
From stall to stall lifts up the market-basket
More and more filled full by strangers, and
Thus loaded follows on and cannot say:
Lord, wherefore the banquet?

Why, why must one stand there like a shepherd
So exposed to all excess of influence
And so assigned to spaces full of swift
Event, that, leaning up against a landscape-tree,
He would possess his fate with no more action,
Yet has not in the much too great beholding
The quiet solace of the herd. Has naught
But world, has world in every looking-up,
In every bending downward, world. What fain
Belongs to others blindly penetrates

Into his blood, as hostilely as music,
Changing on its way.
There rises he at night and has the call
Of birds outside already in his being and
Feels bold, because he takes with difficulty all
The stars into his vision – not, O not as one
Who now prepares the night for the beloved
And indulges her with all the felt heavens.

Our Gaelic Background

TO-DAY the spiritual values of Gaelic civilization have not dissolved.
They have, however, shifted. They no longer form one
With the flesh of human substance. We can still
Attain to every one of the subtlest goods in Gaelic culture,
But only mentally, analytically, or rationally. We must return
To the ancient classical Gaelic poets. For in them
The inestimable treasure is wholly in contact
With the immense surface of the unconscious. That is how
They can be of service to us now – that is how
They were never more important than they are to-day.

Our Gaelic forbears possessed their great literature
As nothing is possessed by peoples to-day,
And in Scotland and Ireland and Wales
There was a popular understanding and delight
In literary allusions, technical niceties, and dexterities of expression
Of which the English even in Elizabethan times
Had only the poorest counterpart,
And have since had none whatever
And have destroyed it in the Gaelic countries too.

Le moment semble venu d'une resurrection de l'humain.

The counterpoint of incompatible societies
A characteristic and actual phenomenon of Scottish life.

Bagpipe Music

LET me play to you tunes without measure or end,
Tunes that are born to die without a herald,
As a flight of storks rises from a marsh, circles,
And alights on the spot from which it rose.

Flowers. A flower-bed like hearing the bagpipes.
The fine black earth has clotted into sharp masses
As if the frost and not the sun had come.
It holds many lines of flowers.
First faint rose peonies, then peonies blushing,
Then again red peonies, and behind them,
Massive, apoplectic peonies, some of which are so red
And so violent as to seem almost black; behind these
Stands a low hedge of larkspur, whose tender apologetic blossoms
Appear by contrast pale, though some, vivid as the sky above them,
Stand out from their fellows, iridescent and slaty as a pigeon's breast.
The bagpipes – they are screaming and they are sorrowful.
There is a wail in their merriment, and cruelty in their triumph.
They rise and they fall like a weight swung in the air at the end of a
    string.
They are like the red blood of those peonies.
And like the melancholy of those blue flowers.
They are like a human voice – no! for the human voice lies!
They are like human life that flows under the words.
That flower-bed is like the true life that wants to express itself
And does . . . while we human beings lie cramped and fearful.

A Language Not To Be Betrayed

I SHOULD use . . .
A language not to be betrayed;
And what was hid should still be hid
Excepting from those like me made
Who answer when such whispers bid.

The Young Audb[1]

UPON that morning following the night
Which anxiously had passed with calls, unrest
And tumult, all the sea broke up once more
And cried. And when the crying slowly closed
Again and from the pallid day and heaven's
Beginning fell within the chasm of mute fish:
The sea brought forth.

And with the earliest sun the hairfoam
Of the waves' broad vulva shimmered, on whose rim
The girl stood upright, white, confused, and wet.
Just as a young green leaf bestirs itself
And stretches forth and slow unfurls its inrolled
Whorlings, so her body's form unfolded into coolness,
And into the untouched early wind.
As moons the knees rose upwards clear and dived
Within the cloudy outlines of the thighs.
The narrow shadow of the legs retreated
And the feet grew tightened and became as light
As silence and the joints lived like the throats
Of drinking ones.

And in the hollow of the hip's deep bowl
The belly lay and seemed a fresh young fruit
Within a child's hand. In its navel's narrow
Cup was all the darkness of this brilliant life.
A little wave below it lightly raised
Itself and ever sped across towards the loins,
Whereon from time to time a silent rippling was.
But all translumined and already without shadow,
Like a copse of silver birches pale in April,
Warm and empty and unhidden lay the sex.

[1] From the German of Rainer Maria Rilke.

Now stood the shoulders' poised and mobile scales
In perfect balance on the upright body,
Which from the bowl of hips arose as though
It were a fountain, downward falling,
Hesitating in the long and slender arms,
And faster in the fullest fall of hair.

Then went the face quite slowly past;
From out the deep foreshortened darkness of
Its inclination into clear and horizontal
High-upliftedness. And 'neath it was the chin closed steeply
And when the throat was now forthstretched and seemed
A water-ray or flowerstem in which sap rose,
The arms stretched also forth like necks of swans
Who seek the shore.

Then came into this body's darkened earliness
Like morning wind the first indrawal of breath.
Within the tender branching of the veintrees
There arose a whispering and the blood began
To purl and murmur o'er its deepest places.
And this wind increased: it threw itself
With every breath into the newborn breasts
And filled them full and pressed far into them –
So that like sails, full of the distances,
They urged the windlight maiden t'wards the shore.

So landed the goddess.

Behind her,
Quickly stepping through the young green shores,
The flowers and flower-stalks raised themselves
All morning long, confused and warm, as though
From deep embraces. And she went, and ran.

But at the noon of day, all in the heaviest hour,
The ocean once more roused itself and threw
Upon the self-same spot a dolphin.
Dead, red and open.

Shipshape

EVERY inch of canvas must catch and pull,
Every line, brace, and clew hold,
The running rigging render
And the standing rigging stand.

Burak

WHEN I see a possible poem, I work
With the utmost economy of effort.
The old scarred Visalia kak is stripped
To fundamentals – the skirts trimmed down
Till they barely cover the tree – the stirrups
Cut off close to the rosettes. No stirrup fenders,
And the doubled stirrup straps wrapped
With rawhide to keep the stirrups in position.
A lass-rope and hackamore
Complete my equipment
– And you can bet your boots I'm going to take
A good whirl at breaking it!

And ever and again it shall be with me
As when on the night called *lailat ul mi'raj*
Muhammad ascended to Heaven from Jerusalem
On the fabulous mule named Burak.

From
SPEAKING FOR SCOTLAND
(1946)

Two Memories

RELIGION? Huh! Whenever I hear the word
It brings two memories back to my mind.
Choose between them, and tell me which
You think the better model for mankind.

Fresh blood scares sleeping cows worse than anything on earth.
An unseen rider leans far out from his horse with a freshly-skinned
Weaner's hide in his hands, turning and twisting the hairy slimy thing
And throwing the blood abroad on the wind.

A brilliant flash of lightning crashes into the heavens.
It reveals the earth in a strange yellow-green light,
Alluring yet repelling, that distorts the immediate foreground
And makes the gray and remote distance odious to the sight.

And a great mass of wraithlike objects on the bed ground
Seems to upheave, to move, to rise, to fold and undulate
In a wavelike mobility that extends to an alarming distance.
The cows have ceased to rest; they are getting to their feet.

Another flash of lightning shows a fantastic and fearsome vision.
Like the branches of some enormous grotesque sprawling plant
A forest of long horns waves, and countless faces
Turn into the air, unspeakably weird and gaunt.

The stroke of white fire from the sky is reflected back
To the heavens from thousands of bulging eyeballs,
And into the heart of any man who sees
This diabolical mirroring of the lightning numbing fear falls.

Is such a stampede your ideal for the human race?
Haven't we milled in it long enough? My second memory
Is of a flight of wild swans. Glorious white birds in the blue October
 heights
Over the surly unrest of the ocean! Their passing is more than music
 to me
And from their wings descends, and in my heart triumphantly peals,
The old loveliness of Earth that both affirms and heals.

POEMS OF THE EAST–WEST SYNTHESIS
(1946)

I. *The Fingers of Baal*[1] *Contract in the Communist Salute*

The name of *Sgeind*, applied to the *Indus*, constitutes another valuable link in the long chain of marks of authenticity. The Hindu designation has always been, and is still, *Sind* and not Ind, and the province through which the river flows, before it empties itself into the Ocean, has always been known by the same name since time immemorial. An average forger of the eighteenth century would have first of all more probably invented the direct western route from Turkestan via the Caspian Sea; having once chosen the descent to the valley of the Indus, he would have used the generally known Latin name. The assumption that *Cier-Rige* spied out the original Hindu name of the river, which he turned into *Sgeind*, requires too great a stretch of imagination. After all we know of the general state of knowledge at about 1800, and of the character of the patriotic Irish resuscitator of the Chronicles in particular, we refuse to believe in such a Mount Everest of dissimulation. . . . *Sgeind* is explained by the Irish author as meaning a 'current of an uneven course, now slow, now rapid'. The appellation might also be derived from *sgeim*, in Irish: foam (Swedish: scum, German: Schaum). The Gaelic origin is in either case beyond doubt. The fact that nearly all the geographical names in Central Asia and Mesopotamia can be explained by the Irish tongue, as demonstrated in the writings of Eolus, is extremely significant. This phenomenon cannot be attributed to the linguistic juggleries and fancies of a counterfeiter; it proves, on the contrary, that the very ancient connection between the Gaelic stock and the cradle of civilisation really existed!

L. ALBERT

---

[1] The original character of Druidism was essentially Oriental, and corresponded in many important particulars with Persian theosophy. But side by side with Oriental theism appeared in process of time an element-worship, which identified the objects of nature with the memory of deceased heroes and worshipped the sun and stars, the thunder and storm, as the visible representatives of superior beings. Hence, the Roman Commander thought he could discern a likeness between the objects of Celtic worship and the host of Olympus (Caesar, *Bell. Gall.* VI, 17). Thus in Teutates he recognised Mercurius; in Belenus (compare the old name Apello, Apellen, which was also the Spartan name for the sun) he saw a likeness to Apollo; he identified Taranis ('Taran' is Celtic for thunder) with the thundering Jupiter; while the god whom he calls Mars was probably Esus or Hesus (the name is supposed to linger in *Hesary Tor* in Devonshire). As the Minerva he mentions was not a Grecian but an Etruscan and Roman goddess, her worship among the Celts may have been of the same character as in those countries, and she has been identified with a goddess, Belisana, whose name has been found on an inscription (*vide* Martin's *Religion des Gaulois*, I, 504).

Gael-ag (at present Gallice or Galicia), the name which the newcomers, according to Eolus, gave to the occupied regions of north-western Spain, is another of those precious linguistic revelations which we owe exclusively to the great Iberian sage and by which the genuineness and accuracy of his writings is proved more conclusively than by heaps of dusty parchments. The literal meaning of 'Gael-ag' in Irish is 'with the Gaels'! It is a notable speciality of Irish grammar that it lacks entirely a verb expressing possession like the English 'to have'. For this the queer sentence 'it is with me' (or you, him, her, etc.) is substituted. Such peculiar methods of expressing the idea of ownership are met in so-called 'agglutinative' languages only, called thus because articles, pronouns, adverbs and prepositions are 'glued on' to the noun, that is, appended. The Magyars (Hungarians) also classed among the 'agglutinarian' races, and therefore unjustly called Mongols (from Irish: *Mion-gal* – Crown of the Gael) say, for instance, not unlike the Irishmen, 'it is to me' instead of 'I have'. From the above the following inferences may be drawn: (1) that the Gaels, regarded at present as Indo–Europeans, were formerly members of the legendary mighty race of 'agglutinarians'; (2) that the bold assertion of our mysterious 'forger', implying that the Gael-Scots, though apparently pure Indo–Europeans, were closely related to the agglutinative races of Iberians, Basques and Georgians, is borne out by linguistic testimony and well-founded.

L. Albert

> And even as I write our hearts are thrilled
> By the appalling events in Spain,
> And chords most ancient and august
> Are struck in us again.
>
> Alarodian accents stir anew
> Our nature's deepest roots,
> Georgian and Basque – and six millenia's diaspora
> To dear blood–brotherhood again commutes.
>
> Basque mystery? There is no mystery,
> Save to those most blind who will not see.
> Basque origin to Borrow was Mongolic,
> The speech of Tartar, not Sanskrit, family.
>
> Infernal fantasies contrived to hide
> The simple unacceptable truth!
> – Read Hommel's History of Babylonia,
> And Fink's Die Sprachstamme des Erdkreises, sooth.
>
> A branch of *Finnish* to Lucien Bonaparte,
> To others of Semitic origin,
> Sib to Punic and Carthaginian – time indeed
> To *finish* this rubbish and let daylight in.

The ancestors of the Basques were Gaal-Sciot of Georgia,
The name Basque is Irish, 'Buais-ce'[1] 'land of cattle.'
Aspiration eliminates the 'b'; the Basques still
Call themselves not Basques, but *euscaldunae*,
Their language *euskara*, their country *euskaleria*
– Three terms with the same first syllable in common,
Eusk or *Esk*, with the primordial *Buais-ce* or *uais-ce*.

This is a Cornish song; think of the words
Casan-tir-eider (Cornwall) – did the astute
Forger thus manipulate the Greek *Cassiterides*
His incredibly far-reaching fraud to suit?

Or have we not here the true account
Of the separation from the mainland of the Scilly Isles?
O most fortunate forger to find to his hand
The word *Scaoilead* (pron. squilly) to serve his wiles!

The Atlantis fable is but a colossal exaggeration
Of the natural catastrophe of 1031 B.C.
Which broke in upon Cornwall – fantastically embellished
To hide the simple report of the Scilly Islands tragedy.

The original Irish form of Devon is *Dun-mianac*,
The mining enclosure; *mian* – mine, pronounced *veen*.
Dun-veen to Devon: here again
The infallible truth of Eolus is seen.

As countless of his other details are amply borne out
In Jasti's 'Meder und Skythen'; by Reshid Eddin;[2]
Abdulla Bahadur Khan,[3] Mar Abas Catina,[4]
Moses of Khorene, and Ben Jaldin.[5]

Let us recall, too, the Gael-Aquitanian chief
Who proudly protested to Caesar, 'Scoti sumus, non Galli.'
Let this be lifted up as a banner again
To which all our far-flung kin can rally

[1] Let us always keep in mind that the Irish 'c' is pronounced 'k'.
[2] Persian historian, died 1318 A.D. [3] Died 1663.
[4] Armenian historiographer. [5] Arab writer.

And form a Gaelic Front that none can assail
Built on the manifest truth of the 'Chronicles of the Gael.'

The deliberate drowners of the true history of the Gaels
Are responsible for all the preposterous tales
– Tales even due sense of the glorious role
Of Galician genius in Spain must set aside;
Triumphs in all the arts, to the Gaelic place
In British intellectual development clearly allied.

Cier-Rige,[1] whom the English denounce as a forger,
Alone tells the truth in a tremendous record
Of all-round and unfailing verification
Pivoted again and again on an unforgeable word.

Where did *Cier-Rige* find *Cruimtear*, for example?
What a prodigious forgery this would have been
– A word nowhere else but in the *Edda*,
In the *Voluspa* there, as *Hrimthur*, seen!

Indeed a super-divine, a super-divinatory
Omniscient master-crook is pre-supposed
If we are to credit the vast falsification
With which English 'scholarship' these perspectives has closed!

And *Sgadan* – for Sidon of Phoenicia –
Where did *Cier-Rige* find this most ancient word,
And *Aoi-Mag* (for Phoenicia or Syria)?
Long after his death there was disinterred

---

[1] Cier-Rige, 'chief of the prostrated people of Eri,' Roger O'Connor (1762–1834), the immortal preserver of the oldest and only truthful history of the Gaelic race, *The Chronicles of Eri*, which he published in 1822. The most recent edition including the writings of Eolus is *Six Thousand Years of Gaelic Grandeur Unearthed*, Vol. I, 5357 to 1004 B.C., edited by L. Albert, with a preface containing the history of the discovery, and a long and very able dissertation presenting numerous proofs of the authenticity of these incomparable records (Berlin, 1936). It should be read in conjunction with L. A. Waddell's *The British Edda*, the reports on the excavations at Maiden Castle, and Dr. T. F. G. Dexter's *Civilisation in Britain 2000 B.C.* (New Knowledge Press, Treberran, Perranporth, Cornwall) which ends: 'Perchance before the next century is far advanced, the history of Britain will be commenced not at 55 B.C., the date of the Invasion of Julius Caesar, but at about 2000 B.C., the approximate date of the erection of Avebury.'

The Tell-el-Amarna correspondence in the ruins
Of the palace of Amenophis IV and here
As in the old Sumerian cities of the Euphratic Plain
The vindicators of the honour, complete and clear,
Of the calumniated Irishman rise
From the depth of the soil to all honest eyes.

Do not the Slavonic designation 'niemetz'
And the corresponding Hungarian (Magyar) 'nemet'
Lead us right back to the 'Land of Noah' and the ancient name
– Nomades[1] – preserved by our Gaelic annalist yet?

Pivotal words – aye, pivotal letters too!
For the Irish alphabet (not shaped after the Latin characters)
Is limited to the primordial sixteen letters
Of the Phoenicians still – the additional eight letters
Invented by the Greeks many centuries after Eolus's death
And adopted by the Latins were never taken up by the scholars of Eri;
Irish never had a y, an x, a v, or a k.

The authenticity of Eolus admitted
English Ascendancy at once falls dead.

The Bible is shown as a faked and falsified story
Of what, truly told, is our great Gaelic glory.

'Stalin the Georgian,' I have said. We are Georgians all.
We Gaels.
The name *Karthweli* by which the Georgians themselves call
Their race and their country is none other
Than our Scottish Argyll – the Georgian equivalent
Of 'Ard-Gael' (the high place of the Gael).

'Og pierced,' we read, 'towards the fingers of Baal
Even unto Gabacasan. Now let the fingers clench back
To come to rest in the palm of the sun's hand again,
The reconcentrated power of the human race.'
So let the first conceivers and builders of civilisation give now
(Since the others have poisoned the wells and perverted

[1] i.e. *Naoi-maid-eis.*

The noble impulse that originated with our fathers)
The sign of the Clenched Fist – the Communist salute,
For the Gaelic refluence, and the re-emergence
Of the Gaelic spirit at the Future's strongest and deepest root!

II. *Ceol Mor*

. . . the subtler music, the clear light where time burns back about th' eternal embers.
                                                          EZRA POUND

Our *Ceol Mor*, like the Sumerian music
. . . The hymn on the creation of man
On the tablet of Asshur . . .
Is timeless.
The words settle the time
As with plainsong.
For the Sumerians by that time . . . 800 B.C. . . .
Had an alphabet of initials,
Their cuneiform writing was developed
From the first letter of a word
Which named a thing,
And the letter was known
Only by knowing the word.
The meaning of the thing-word
Depended on the context, and the context
Depends on nice scholarship.
They had a harp with twenty-one strings,
They had a diatonic scale,
And they applied twenty-one letters of their alphabet
To the three octaves of this.
And nothing was known at the time of accompaniment
But the Greek 'magadising' (filling in with the octave)
Except possibly the licence (in China) of a few passing fourths.
And the whole thing depended on some allowance
(Mentally) for grace-notes.
Anacreon speaks of a magadis of twenty strings.
But the magadis I speak of here

Calls for recognition of the fact
That the descendants of these Sumerians
First conceived the thought of the music of the spheres
Which we have even now not quite forgotten
And even as Yeats, following Morris, has gone
Via early saga literature to the Upanishads,
I, poet of Scotland and of Cornwall,
(I whose Empire is not the Bulpington of Blup's Varangian vision
Of Canute's Empire . . . all the north of the world . . .
Reaching from Massachusetts to Moscow, but that vast Celtic Empire
Which about the fourth century B.C.
Claimed as its frontiers the Dneister in Russia
. . . Where the city of Carrodunum was constructed . . .
Ah, greatly I love still to tread the frontiers of Nordalbingia,
In the wake of the shining figures of Vicelin and Gerold
Before Henry the Lion spread his peace of solitude and destruction
Over the land of the Abodrites . . . and weigh again
Every detail of the chronicles of Helmold, priest of Bosau,
Regarding the frontier struggles of Saxon and Slav ! . . .
In the East, to the shores of Portugal in the West;
From the ocean off Scotland in the North
To the central part of Italy in the South,
And even extended through the Balkans to Asia Minor,
To the Galatians of whom St. Paul so often spoke)
Speak of the Sumerians and realise the need
To refresh the Gaelic genius at its oldest sources.[1]

[1] Of the fourth sub-race, the Celts, were the Ancient Greeks and Romans, and to it belong their descendants the Greeks, Italians, French, Spaniards, Irish, Welsh, Scots, Manx, and the Bretons. As to their origin and the path they travelled to the present, Schwarz states, 'That the Manu selected the most refined people for the nucleus of this fourth Sub-race, striving to awaken imagination and artistic sensibility, to encourage poetry, music, and painting. About 20000 B.C. this nucleus proceeded along the northern frontier of the Persian Kingdom to win for themselves a home among the mountains of the Caucasus. They established themselves in the district of Erivan on the shores of Lake Sevanga, but in course of time the whole of Georgia and Mingrelia was in their hands. In two thousand years they occupied Armenia and Kurdistan and later Phrygia. They looked on the Caucasus as their home and it was really a second centre from which the Sub-race went forth. By 10000 B.C. they began to resume their western march, travelling as tribes, not as a nation, so that they arrived in Europe in comparatively small waves. The first section to cross into Europe were the ancient Greeks, sometimes called Pelasgians . . . These emigrations into Europe were almost continuous. The second sub-

Remembering how the 'Norse' epics of Thor (Icelandic)
Were compiled in the British Isles
And were known to the Ancient Britons,
Whose traditional hero, Arthur,
Is the Icelandic 'Her Thor'
Ultimately identifiable by his exploits
With the Sumerian King, Dur.
Remembering how much the ancient languages
Used by the semitic peoples
... Assyrian, Chaldean, Hebrew and the rest ...
Owed to inheritance from the non-semitic Sumerians;
Remembering how these early Aryan inhabitants of Asia Minor
Were the originators of the Cretan (Minoan),
Achaian, Tyrrhene, Indo-Aryan, Norse and Gothic cultures
... Remembering the Hittite origin of the brachicephalic type
Appearing in Europe in the mesolithic period
And carrying elements of civilisation to Europe
Which otherwise would have remained at the palaeolithic stage
Without any knowledge
Either of animal domestication or of agriculture
... And remembering how urgently civilisation to-day
Needs, like its quintessential element (the stone
The builders have neglected) the Gaelic genius,
To renew itself at its original springs!

Lift every voice!

---

division were the Albanians, the third the Italian race, then came the Keltic as the fourth wave of astonishing vitality. This slowly became the dominant race over the north of Italy, the whole of France and Belgium, the British Isles, the western part of Switzerland, and Germany west of the Rhine ... The fifth wave of the Keltic migration practically lost itself in the north of Africa. Traces of it are left among the Berbers, the Moors, the Kabyles, and the Guanches of the Canary Isles. This wave encountered the fourth and intermingled with it in the Spanish Peninsula, and about 2000 years ago it contributed the last of the many elements which go to make up the population of Ireland; for to it belonged the Milesian invaders who bound Ireland under curious forms of magic. But a far more splendid element of the Irish population had come into it before from the sixth wave, which had left Asia Minor in a totally different direction, pushing north-west as far as Scandinavia, where they intermingled to some extent with the fifth sub-race, the Teutonic, and descended into Ireland from the north. They are celebrated in its history as the Tuatha-de-Danaan.'

PAPE: *The Christ of the Aryan Road* (1927).

III. *Tristan and Iseult*

Aн, Cornwall ! Le roman de *Vis et Ramin*
N'est autre chose que l'histoire de *Tristan et Iseult*.
Le parallélisme est absolu. Et pas plus dans un cas
Que dans l'autre, les détails fondamentaux
Des caractères, des moeurs, des habitations,
Détails identiques dans la version persane
Et dans la version occidentale,
Ne correspondent à ce qu'étaient la Perse,
La Géorgie, ou l'Occident des onzième et douzième siècles.
Les palais des rois ressemblent à des huttes.
L'arme préférée de Tristan n'est point
Comme à l'époque de ces transcriptions
Pour les guerriers nobles, la lance ou l'épée,
Mais simplement l'arc,
Fait à remarquer l'arc est aussi
L'arme préférée de Apollon-Phoibos,
'Le dieu archer,' 'l'archer céleste,' dont les Grecs
Avaient fait un dieu de la lumière
– Également chasseur, marin, et musicien
Comme Tristan.

La linguistique japhétique nous apprend que Isolde
Est une forme géorgienne,
I, préfixe, *sol*, base, et *de*, signe du pluriel,
Révélant l'origine très ancienne du nom,
En provenance d'époques oû les noms propres
Désignaient à la fois les divinités-totems des tribus
Et ces tribus elles-mêmes. On retrouve de la sorte
En Géorgie ancienne la déesse-totem Sar-Mat
Qui a donné son nom à la tribu qui la vénérait
La tribu des Sarmates, *t* étant ici
Le signe dental du pluriel dont les diverses formes
Sont *d* et *t*, devenant *de*, *te*, *den*, *ten*, *dan* et *tan*.
Et la racine *sol*, qu'on retrouve sous les formes

Sal, *sar*, et même *dal*, signifiait, jadis, à la fois *mer*, *eau*, et *femme*.
En étudiant suivant les mêmes règles
Le nom de Tristan, on y trouve, aprés le préfixe *T*,
La base japhétique *r*'s et la terminaison plurale *tan*.
(Variations : *Drostan*, *Drost*, *Drust*, etc.)
Cette base *r*'s (*ros*, *ris*, *res*, etc.) signifiait
Soleil et cheval, divinité-totem Etrusques.
D'autrepart, d'attentives recherches dans le domaine
Des noms de lieux ou de peuples confirment
Les liens singuliers existant
Entre la Bretagne et le Caucase géorgien.
On sait que Pline, parlant de la sorcellerie ou l'art des mages
Déclarait que la Bretagne cultivait merveilleusement cet art
Et que tout donnait à croire que c'étaient les Bretons
Qui avaient enseigné La Magic aux Perses.
Nous pouvons maintenant comprendre cette affirmation de Pline.
Les Perses ont occupé en Iran et jusqu'au Caucase
Des territoires soumis, avant leur venue,
Aux influences caucasiennes, Breton est un mot
D'origine géorgienne ; *M-reh* ou *Res-tan*, abrégé :
Mret ou Bret – comme *Et-rus-k*
(*Et* étant une déformation fréquente de *te*) –
Et s'applique à de tribus ayant originairement vécu
Au Caucase et en Iran. La légende de Tristan et Iseult
Est originaire du Caucase. Cette légende a été emportée
Si l'on peut dire, par les tribus qui, du Caucase,
Ont essaimé sur les rives de la Méditerranée,
Pélasges et Etrusques, puis sur les rives de l'océan,
Basques, Bretons, et Pictes. Qui sait si on ne la retrouverait pas
Dans le tribu japhétique de Verchik, ou Bourichask,
Qui subsiste encore sur le versant du Pamir,
Ou chez certaines populations chinoises ou coréennes
Dont l'origine caucasienne ne fait plus doute aujourd'hui ?

A KIST OF WHISTLES
(1947)

Of Two Bulgarian Poets[1]

To Dafinka L. Doganova

TODOROFF exile-pent in Switzerland
And Slaveikoff in Italy
Untimely died: but left their poesy,
Rare winds of love whereby forever fanned
Bulgarian hearts will glow and understand
Th' incomparable joy of purity,
And from the pinnacles of faith foresee
The glory that the poet, Truth, has planned.

When peace returned a faithful nation brought
Their bodies to Sofia's holy spot.
Their bodies! – for the singer of 'Cis Moll'
Immortal lives in our mortality,
Even as Beethoven, and Todoroff's soul,
Receiving naught, gives light eternally.

Soneto del Soneto

VOITURE and Desmarets in French essayed
The sonnet on the sonnet with success,
Marini in Italian. (Ah, yes!
My first four lines are very easily made!)
Hurtado de Mendoza, it is said,
First thus displayed his ready cleverness
Although Lope de Vega's, more or less,
Has kept all other efforts in the shade.

[1] Pentcho R. Slaveikoff and Petko Jordan Todoroff.

But little trouble has my octave given!
I need not name my predecessors who
In English have tried variants of the trick.
Already, as you see, I have not striven
In vain this pleasing exercise to do
With verbal skill and just arithmetic!

In the Golden Island[1]

On reading the Antologia de Poetes Cataláns Moderns

N o w let us pass through Carner's[2] fairy wood,
Where flowers their blue eyes ope'd so very wide,
Whiles pines told ancient tales of kingly pride
To hours and birds spelled into quietude;
Or see the peasant's door that open stood
Handlike inviting all to step inside;[3]
Or the old olives that so subtly hide
Dead men's desires in many a flying mood.

In Chopin's monastery[4] by candle-light
Shakespeare, Tagore or Machado we'll read,
Or walking back from Palma through the night
Know how for every guest[5] the roses still
Blush out, and deem us Daríos[6] indeed
For whom the singing fountains gravelier spill.[7]

---

[1] Mallorca.   [2] Josep Carner.
[3] Na Maria Antonia Salva's 'Casa Pegesa.'   [4] At Valldemosa.
[5] Joan Alcover's 'L'Hoste.'   [6] Rubén Darío.
[7] Rubén Darío says, 'The olives have made the groves of the Golden Island a Gethsemane where tortured passivity is eternal. . . . They guard the secret desires of the dead with the wills, the gestures, the attitudes of living men,' Josep Carner, of Barcelona, found a fairy wood where the pines told stories 'De Reys i de Donzelles,' and the flowers opened their blue eyes very wide. In his noble poem 'L'Hoste' (the guest, i.e. Rubén Darío in Mallorca) Joan Alcover sang, 'Roses are redder where he passes, and the fountain sings with more solemnity.' Na Maria Antonia Salva, who learned her craft in translating Mistral, found the real stuff of poetry in her pictures of country life.

On Reading Professor Ifor Williams's
'Canu Aneurin'[1] in Difficult Days

Only barbarism, villiany, and ignorance do not respect the past, cringing before the present alone.

PUSHKIN

STAY me with mosses, comfort me with lichens.

Opening the Gododdin again and renewing
My conscious connection with the gwyr y gogledd[2]
I who never fail to detect every now and again,
In the Hebridean and Shetland and Cornish waters I most frequent,
By subtile signs Myrddin's ship of glass[3]
Which has floated invisibly around the seas
Ever since Arfderydd a millennium and half ago,
(Since Arfderydd – a few miles from where I was born!)[4]
I am as one who sees again in a stark winter wood
(And the forest of Celyddon[5] is indeed in death's grip to-day)

The lichens and mosses, earth's first mercies, shine forth
– The dusk of Lincoln green warming the ragged tree-bole,
Dark flaked liverwort on dank cliff,
Rich velvet mosses making a base
For the old stone dykes – all glowing
In a lustrous jewel-like beauty for the enjoyment of which
One might well endure the rigours of winter!
Contrary to common belief, the lichens and mosses
Love the winter sunlight as wise human beings do.
(Thus, of two retaining walls of a sunk lane,

[1] Published by the University of South Wales Press Board, Cardiff, 1939.
[2] Men of the North.
[3] After the battle of Arfderydd, Myrddin, sometimes called Myrddin Wyllt or Merlinus Sylvestris, the Merlin of the Arthurian romance, fled to the Caledonian forest and finally escaped with his paramour, Chwimleian (Vivien), in a ship of glass.
[4] Arthuret, near Carlisle (A.D. 575). The author was born twenty miles away, just over the Scottish border.
[5] The forest of Celyddon, the Caledonian forest.

The lichens and mosses are most abundant and vigorous
On the side that receives the largest volume of sunlight,
And a warm stretch of dykefoot facing the low-set
Southern winter sun is the most resplendent
In fairy velvet of any exposure known to me.)

Even so, at the feet of the great grim vertical problems
Of contemporary life I am sustained and cheered
By the perennial shining of a few
Little personal relationships,
Surely in these days of Massenmensch
A singularly blessed example
Of the transcendent function[1] emerging
From an enantiodromic movement.

Even so in these sterile and melancholy days
The ghastly desolation of my spirit is relieved
As a winter wood by glowing moss or lichen,
And the sunk lane of my heart is vivified,
And the hidden springs of my life revealed
Still patiently potent and humbly creative
When I spy again the ancestral ties between Scotland and Wales,
And, weary of the senseless cacophony of modern literature,
Recur to Aneirin's Gododdin, one of the oldest poems
In any European vernacular – far older indeed
Than anything ever produced on the Continent
Outside Greek and Latin; and not only
Note how (great topical lesson for us to-day)
It is not the glory, but the pity and waste, of war
That inspires its highest passages, but realise
That the profoundest cause in these Islands to-day,
The Invisible War upon which Earth's greatest issues depend,
Is still the same war the Britons fought in at Catraeth[2]
And Aneirin sings. The Britons were massacred then. Only one
Escaped alive. His blood flows in my veins to-day
Stronger than ever, inspires me with his unchanged purpose,
And moves me alike in Poetry and Politics.

---

[1] C. G. Jung's term.   [2] Catterick in Yorkshire.

Between two European journeys of Neville Chamberlain's
And two important speeches of Herr Hitler's
I return to the Taliesin and Llywarch Hen poems,
Full of hiraeth, of angry revolt
Against the tyranny of fact, even as Malesherbes
Spent the time lesser men would have devoted
To preparing their case against the forty-three accusations
Contained in the Acte énonciatif
Of December 11, 1792,
In reading Hume's History of the House of Stuart.

So I am delivered from the microcosmic human chaos
And given the perspective of a writer who can draw
The wild disorder of a ship in a gale
Against the vaster natural order of sea and sky.
If man does not bulk too big in his rendering
He does not lose the larger half of dignity either.

Aneirin stays me with mosses
And comforts me with lichens
In the winter-bound wood of the world to-day
Where the gaunt branches rattle like gallows bones.

It is like one of the commonest and at the same time
One of the most indeterminate factors in the life of men
– An experience so intensly private
And so jealously guarded and protected
It scarcely reaches the level of articulation.
It is felt to be precious and indispensable.

It belongs to the very foundations
Of temperament and character,
Yet it seldom rises to the clear-cut stage
Of positive affirmation.
It lies somewhere between wistfulness and perception,
In the borderland between longing and knowing.
It is like music from some far-off shore
Or a light that never was on land or sea.

Hostings of Heroes

There are two days, two sights, I covet most
Of all in the depths of our history lost.

First, Clontarf,[1] where, says the Irish annalist,
Earl Sigurd in person led into battle
The wild men from the Orc Islands and the Cat Islands,
From Manann and Sci and Leodus,
From Ceinn-Tire and from Airir-gaidhel,
And 'an immense army' from the Innis-Gall.

Next, that glorious scene when Dundee
Sent out the Fiery Cross, and the Chiefs
Met him in their war array,
Like the muster of the war-chiefs in the Iliad
As James Philip portrays it in his epic (in Latin)[2] –
The divers branches of Clan Donald, all with tufts
Of heather tied to their spear-heads, and each
Under its own chieftains
– Black Alasdair of Glengarry, young Clanranald,
Glencoe huge as a giant, with his twisted beard
Curled backward, and his wild eyes rolling,
And Keppoch in gilded armour,
The two Macleans, Duart and Otter,
Macleod of Raasay, in the old Highland dress
Of saffron shirt, belted plaid, and rawhide shoes,
Raasay who could outstrip the deer
And take the wild bull by the horns and master him,
Young Stuart of Appin, MacNaughton of Dundarave,
Grant of Glenmoriston, MacAlaster of Loup, and a host of others,
And above all, Lochiel, the old Ulysses
– A helmet covers his head

[1] Battle of Clontarf, 1014.
[2] The epic, *The Grameid*, has been published, with a translation, by the Scottish History Society.

A double-edged brand is girt to his side.
Blood-red plumes float on his crest,
A cuirass of leather, harder than adamant,
Girds his breast – on his left arm hangs his shield,
His tartan hose are gartered round his calf,
Mail covers his shoulders
And a brazen plate his back.
His very look, so fierce,
Might fright the boldest foe,
His savage glance, the swarthy hue
Of his Spanish countenance, his flashing eyes,
His beard and moustache
Curled like the moon's horns.

But in the place of all this
What have we to-day?
Dingy parades of vermin!
Details of the English army
In clothes the colour of excrement;
Or processions like that in Edinburgh
In honour of Sir Walter Scott's centenary,
A funeral trickle of Baillies and Lawyers,
Members of the Leith Water Board,
And, sole representative of the Republic of Letters,
Hugh Walpole!

God! What a crawl of cockroaches!

They Know Not What They Do

BURNS in Elysium once every year
Ceases from intercourse and turns aside
Shorn for a day of all his rightful pride,
Wounded by those whom yet he holds most dear.
Chaucer he leaves, and Marlowe, and Shakespeare,
Milton and Wordsworth – and he turns to hide
His privy shame that will not be denied,
And pay his annual penalty of fear.

But Christ comes to him there and takes his arm.
'My followers too,' He says, 'are false as thine,
True to themselves, and ignorant of Me,
Grieve not thy fame seems so compact of harm;
Star of the Sot, Staff of the Philistine
– Truth goes from Calvary to Calvary!'

The Kulturkampf

To WILLIAM POWER

I sing the mighty kulturkampf,
The way he dramatised our Scotland for us,
His stupendous dialogue between
Anglo-Scotland and Gaelic Scotland,
The greater potentiality so long
Buried alive beneath grey Englishry –
The nation that took the wrong turning!

To him as a true artist
Scotland became significant because of her artists
And her artists significant because of Scotland.
These men and women – whose very names
Were unknown to ninety-nine per cent of Scots,
Whose works were in languages unknown to them
And on levels of the spirit inaccessible
To all but a handful of folk –
Were shown at last as aspects of our country,
As certain aspects of our country which had reached
A tangible and visible maturity.

He traced them one by one from their very birth
In the past and the soul of our country
Slowly, and with marvellous security,
Through thoughts that are sometimes intricate

But always limpid – thoughts that have sometimes
The lovely intricacy of arabesque and sometimes
The sonorous simplicity of songs;
These artists in Gaelic and Latin and Scots,
Artists shown as aspects of their own land,
In Scotland – Scotland! – where artists were
Considered as people out of the scheme of things
And belonging nowhere. A great deed!
A deed bespeaking the birth
Of Scottish artistic consciousness.
Scotland for the first time for five hundred years
Became aware of her place in the culture of the world.
The whole monstrous Anglo–Scottish mythology
Was roundly battered at last.

No longer could the voice of the truth
Be silenced in the time-honoured way;
'They detect the falsehood of the preaching
But when they say so all good citizens
Cry "Hush, do not weaken the State,
Do not take off the strait jacket
From the dangerous persons. Every honest fellow
Must keep up the hoax the best he can;
Must patronise providence and piety,
And whenever he sees anything that will keep men amused,
Royalty, Parliament, the Empire, Progress,
Schools, churches, novels, picture-galleries or what not.
He must cry Hist-a-boy!
And urge the game on." '

But the game was up at last; the hoax
Could be sustained no longer.
His vigorous profession of faith,
His valiant attempt to complete
The vacuous features of modern Scottish life
With an expression, was irresistible.
All who journeyed with him through this Scotland
Found themselves aligned with revolt:

Revolt, not expressing itself
In clamorous contending cries of stump orators,
Disorderly gestures, resolutions of public meetings,
But in passionate and unwavering affirmation
Of the dignity and needs of man,
In the unqualified rejection of the whole network
Of powers incapable of satisfying these needs
And whose weight crushes this dignity
– Showing us as the associates of individuals
Who offer us not their goods
But the daily bread of their souls
– People who know another hunger
Than that of the belly
– A greater music than the clinking of coins
– Comrades of Art!

It is the essential quality of the dramatist
That he can never accept simpleness of utterance.
For him there are always two voices
From whose interchange comes the silent revelation
Of the mysterious beauty of truth;
And it is his task to relate
The truth of his subject with universal truth.

No man can state the truth of Scotland,
But he can establish some sort of relation
Between his truth and the absolute,
And that, in the theatre of the intellect, he did.
That was precisely his process.
And the principal protagonists in this great drama
Were the two civilisations that have been face to face
Through modern Scottish history, or, rather,
Roman civilisation face to face
With our ancient Gaelic civilisation;
And his style was like the country he described,
Flowing like the great moors and fertile straths,
And often strong and staccato
Like the Highland hills.

The effect was magnificent.
Artists cannot be taken out of their own times and places
To be shown around – just as the beauty of a tree
Cannot be made visible by uprooting the tree;
Here, they were shown together with their country.

The vitality of his conception was shown by the fact
That it provided a concrete touchstone
For most of the problems of our contemporary civilisation.
All the movements that were working themselves out
In Scotland referred back to just these 'unwelcome men,'
These forgotten figures in Scottish arts and affairs,
In whom almost alone lay the promise
Of a richer and more rounded Scotland-to-be.
It was as the opponents of the Union had predicted
Two centuries earlier – it had led
To an appalling deficiency of human preferences.
Half the ineffectualness of our Scottish reformers
Had sprung from the fact that they had never
Visualised in the concrete the human demands
They were striving to fulfil. Here was his value.
Even as Russia, without her novelists,
Might have become conscious of the vacuity of her life,
But it was the novelists nevertheless
Made her actively conscious of it,
Conscious enough to seek values and create them.

For Scotland was simply Russia turned inside out;
Russia was the richest of nations in spiritual energy,
We were the poorest; Russia the poorest
In social machinery, we among the richest.
The problem of the Scots therefore
Was not to find an external career
Or the incentive that makes an external career
Seem desirable; the real trouble was not
That out material instincts were unable to find any scope
But that our spiritual instincts were unable to develop
Sufficient intensity to give them a survival value,

Even under the best conditions, while the conditions themselves
Far from being the best were almost the worst
The world had known. It was this
That was creating a vast army of young men
Whose minds were filled, if not with thoughts of war and suicide,
At least with a sense of the futility of living.
The primitive, material, national job
Had so largely been done that they were thrown out
Of the only employment they were bred for
Into a world that had not been interpreted
And made ready for them. Up to now the Scots
Had demanded so little of life they could not understand
Why any ordinary person should even desire
To develop and express more than one or two
Strands of his nature. But all these young Scots
Were simply boys and girls all the sides of whose nature
Had unfolded themselves tentatively to the sunlight
        – And the sunlight wasn't there.
And everywhere cynicism, blindness, helplessness,
The inner poverty of the vast majority of adult Scots,
Were so many ever-present negations
Of the significance of life
– A significance all our national 'leaders'
(Saving the mark!) were totally unable to grasp
If only because they were the offshoots
Of a stock that had immemorially denied it.

His aim and achievement was to create
A concept of Scotland founded
On realities, not lies – to lift
Scotland into self-knowledge
That should be luminous so that she would shine,
Vibrant so that she would be articulate.
It was an inspired psychological history
Of Scottish civilisation – and it created
A vivid definite contagious concept of Scotland.
He showed how the puritan-industrial-Anglicised rhythm
Had perverted all the genius and talents of Scotland,

Devitalised church and university, buried Gaelic culture,
Spawned a limited philosophy of utility,
Produced Glasgow, the city without a voice,
Discarded the inner life of man.
He showed the dominant rhythm of Scottish life
As doing just that – and reasserted against it
The values of life; and out of the past
He brought to life again all those
Who had lived through that developing history
And yet asserted life – George Buchanan, Arthur Johnstone,
Thomas Muir (*Thomas* Muir – not *Edwin* Muir),
William Livingston, John Murdoch, John Maclean – and showed how
    these
Create for us a tradition, inspire us with faith,
Help us to find new gods
To replace the old we cannot worship.

'There,' cried a commentator in the early days.
'You have a temperament coming forward,
Outlining its shape, suggesting its weight,
Revealing its wings.
And of the equipment of this temperament,
Its youth, its daring,
Its gifts for social and psychological dissection,
Its capacity for aesthetic criticism,
Its verbal command, are obvious.
If there be an artist in control of this temperament
Whatever aesthetic he works out successfully
Must be in accordance with it.
Whatever form he sets up
With the aid of his equipment
Must liberate his temperament.
If there be no artist there
Or if the aesthetic and the temperament do not match
We shall have only another
Rich and potential personality
Choked up by friction
And unable to channel itself

In its unique and most effective manner.'

But the general reception
Was in terms like this –
'Swift, rhythmical, dynamic;
Passionate, optimistic, singing;
Economical, imagistic, energetic;
Intelligent, documented, and, above all, controlled;
Its diverse materials absorbed
Into a forward-moving logic
Which rises into thrilling prophecy.
It points. It functions freely.
It synthesises all the available researches
And gives them an irresistible drive.
The extraordinary thing is it is unanswerable.
Bitterly hated as it is by conservative minds
It has drawn from them only epithets and innuendoes.
Never, never has a conservative
Met it squarely, point by point,
Issue by issue, and by honest means
Demolished it. Its strength
Is the strength of a brilliant new science.'
– And all this against the many-sided activity,
The busy idleness of the average Scot,
Enterprising and yet totally futile,
Unable to become anything or grasp anything,
Living in a region of eternal dampness,
Moral and physical vapour, mental and bodily fog.

In this grey Scotland of the general mind
He saw himself like Sluchevsky's *Snow Whirl* –
Which sweeps along, here unnoticed, there more openly,
Twists and twines round rocks and tree-trunks,
It has passed over the moor.
Now it breaks its way through the wood,
The senseless creature wrestles with the mighty space,
Into the mountains it penetrates,
Into the dark solitudes, into the clefts it pierces.

It creeps out of the dead, rotting marsh
To the bright pinnacles of solid eminences.
It leaps without bridges or slopes.
It at times leads you such a dance
That the wanderer's heart stiffens,
Then it runs somewhere saucily up,
Remains hanging in the air as if in sport,
And darts down again, and merges secretly
In God's wilderness, the sleep–encircled. . . .

All this in passionate oratory – with such a commingling
Of resistance and surrender until, as in Mahler's Symphony No. 2, in
    C Minor,
The very quakes and belchings of the earth seemed implicated in his
    assertions,
Though here, as in Mahler, there were lovely lulls in the symphonic
    struggle
– Like the dawn of 'primaeval light' so pleadingly heralded
By the contralto in the fourth movement.

He seemed to be undeniably of his time, and yet out of it.
His problems, his language, the options he set for choice,
All pointed to the pervasive social and philosophical tradition
Within which he developed and against which he revolted.
But the vigour of his thought, the wrestling – at once intense and
    subtle –
With ideas, the colour, daring, and imaginative sweep
Of his own choices were qualities transcending social context.
All the problems of philosophy lived in him; he rediscovered them
By reflection upon his own cosmic fears, hopes, and consciousness of
    activity.
What a progress that was – the unfolding of his thought,
The brilliant and incalculable profusion with which he threw new ideas
    off,
Suggests nothing so much as a psychic analogue
Of the mutant-bearing *Oenothera Lamarckiana*
Or, at times even, the sudden simultaneous appearance
Of one specimen of each of the different varieties

Of *Drosophyllum melanogaster*, for which, as we know,
There is not enough matter in all the known heavenly bodies
And probably not in the universe.

Or like that synthesis of all the possible organic molecules
Of a molecular weight less than 10,000
For which as we know even if humanity lasts
For a million million years and devotes itself entirely
To science and mathematics there will yet
Not have been time or space enough.

But there was one virtue the meanest allotment-holders have
Which he conspicuously lacked – they *weed* their plots
While he left to time and chance
And the near-sighted pecking of critics
The necessary paring and cutting.
A towering abundant figure, far more remarkable
As a personality than as a systematic thinker,
His service was a tremendous series of fructifying insights
Which illumined problems and suggested solutions

But which could never be presented as consistent doctrines.
He opposed life to abstract consistency,
Not because he had any hankering
For the obscurantisms which taught that since the truth is dark
There are no degrees of clarity,

But because the norms of consistency were drawn
From fixed patterns of logical discourse
Which taught everything
But the temporal, the developing, and the particular.

A single and separate person
Indubitably alive during a particular stretch of time,
He contrived to weave a singularly brilliant
Unbroken thread of evidence that this *was* so.

Losing himself in thousands of friends he found himself;
Living completely in the present he stumbled upon the long view;

Surrendering and dispersing his identity
He yet made the world feel him at last
As something tough, something singular, something leathery with life.

The world – the Scotland – which he could not do without
And had to set down patiently lest it be lost
Was not his own world merely; it was everybody's.
He was not introspective. Yet he was in it too.
He was by no means an insentient recording-device.
It was his in the same way that it is ours.
Which is why he could be both friendly and intelligent,
Both wise and witty, both tolerant and intransigeant.

All his works provide the clue
To that kind of consistency in himself
Which he looked for in others.
They show that for him
The most authentic qualities of experience
Were its unpredictability,
Its uniqueness, its individual centres
– Precisely those elements imperfectly recognised
If not denied outright
By the reigning monisms
Of absolute idealism
And mechanical materialism.
Almost every one of his important utterances
Reflects his great twist in the direction of the immediate,
Modifying the principle that the meaning of an object
Is its conceived effects, he stressed the importance
Of particular consequences in individual experience.
He sought to fit consistency to the 'each form of reality'.
Nor could he of course on his own philosophy deny
Whatever traits of constancy, order, and regularity
Experience is discovered to possess.
The type of consistency which characterises
The 'each form of reality', known as a man's philosophy,
Is to be found in the set of qualities
Which distinguishes his personality from others.

Philosophies then become a series of visions which must be understood
In terms of the imaginative hunger and concrete decisions of
    philosophers
Before the evidence marshalled in their support
Can be intelligently examined
Or even declared relevant.
His theory made all the temporal, spatial, and logical relations
Which tie things together
Matters of direct particular experience.
To safeguard the qualities of experience
Which concepts must disregard
In order to get their work done
He converted the immediate awareness of qualities
Into a kind of knowledge.
His philosophy was a protest
Against the ontological imperialisms
Of the traditional systems,
With their categories
Of eternity, totality, and invariance.
He was an inveterate foe
Of bigness, jingoism, and regimentation. . . .

    The 'he' of this poem is of course the ideal figure of whom Mr. Power, the author himself, and all the others associated in the new Scottish Literary Movement, form parts.

Cornish Heroic Song for Valda Trevlyn

COME, let us drink, beloved. You have brimmed my glass
With a supernaculum of a cherry bounce
(More *chia*, as the Chinese say, than Chian is,
 Or Chianti, and beyond reckoning finer far
Than even the Coan wine my friend Sturge Moore has sung[1]
In one of the first longish poems my boyhood knew).

    [1] *Vide* 'Sent from Egypt with a Fair Robe of Tissue to a Sicilian Vinedresser' by Thomas Sturge Moore.

– No red Hermitage for me as long's there's this about,
Nor yet *fìon geal as maith tuar* (white wine fine of hue)!
I pour you now the *odhaerir* you desire.
I have a *slàinte chùramach*[1] to give.

Witch, you foreknew my mood to-night. I see you wear
The golden lunula I had copied for you
From the finest of the four found in Cornwall yet,
Linking the Early Bronze Age and the Twentieth Century,
This crescentic collar or gorget of thin gold,
Linking Scotland and Cornwall too,
For was not the lunula a Scots creation?
Linking the fogous and our 'aonach'[2] here, with its trick drive-way
No one we do not want can ever find,
Cunningly contrived as the prehistoric communications
Between our peoples were – between
North Scotland, Ireland, and Cornwall,
The Cornwall from Chun Castle to the Stripple Stones,
The coastwise movement, from the south-west, of the Castle complex.
Presupposed in the bronze industry of Jarlshof
And illustrated by the souterrains and fogous,
Identical with the coulisses, the nervous system,
Of all my politics and my poetry now,
Strange as the catalysis by which we found each other,
Cuireideach[3] as the difference of one man's blood and another's;
As any Plotinus's 'transition into another field';
As that secret of great men which lies in the relationship they find
Between things whose laws of continuity escape all lesser men,
So that their supreme achievements which astonish the world
Are, for them, quite simple affairs – like comparing two lengths;
And subtle as the style of jewellery to-day in which
(Subtle as your sacral dimples and lozenge of Michaelis)
A bracelet keeps its platinum to itself as though
The precious substance were a Huguenot, and stones are cut slender,

---

[1] A very important toast.
[2] Means (1) a solitary place, a mountain top, a hill; (2) a place of union. Cf. Latin, *unicus*, single; *unire*, to unite; both from *unus*, one.
[3] Full of turns and twists; tricky.

A single sliver to hold all the fires that were expected
Of a brilliant with its fifty-eight facets or of the eighteenth-century
Pearshaped stone with its whole surface faceted.
– A trend, with which we are in sympathy
In all connections, to achieve something like a balance
Between Earth's own efforts and her children's work!

I sing of Cornwall.

Chip of Atlantis, that clings to England still,
Alien in its traditions, utterly different,
This granite-bound corner, storm-washed,
With the smell of seaspray in its fields,
This boon to man, with its gentle air,
Its entrancing colours – Cornwall!
– Cha! I am no good at *natures-mortes!*

Cornwall, epic *intime!*

Cornwall and England, David and Goliath!

Not the ideal but the actual Cornwall
Full of the wandering abscess of the English influence!

It is only the initial force, *id est* temperament,
That can carry one to the goal one is seeking,
Effect the seposition of the Cornish yet
From the indiscriminate English who make
A bolus of the whole world.
Cornwall, that little world apart, whose essence,
– Not whose existence – is to establish men
As different from those of any other land
As Chinaman from Dutchman!

Despite a branch of the League of Nations Union at Tintagel
And the whole Duchy poxed with British Legion Clubs,
Boy Scouts and Girl Guides and branches of the Junior Imperial League,
Despite – nay, because, and in the teeth of these.

Easy to cry: 'And shall Trelawny die?'
Impossible to ask: 'And shall Cornwall die?'
And count on forty Cornishmen to know the reason why.
Yet the form abides, the function never dies
And perhaps we are not alone in again
(Though little resipiscence can yet be seen
In this xenomorphic and stasimorphic land,
Caught in England's sarmentous toils, every strand of which
Is hairier than the sarothrum on the leg of a bee,
Reptant strands more numerous than the thalline hyphae
And deadlier far, making an accursed raphe
Between these two unrabbetable lands,
A poor rough réseau with no lace work on it,
A monstrous irregular retitelarian web,
The Anglo-Cornish border, rempli
With khaki instead of with sericon,
A hideous symphysia, a foul cinenchyma,
All Cornish life there like deadhead in a sprue.
Sprue? Rhabdite! England's ovipositor!)
In relation to the genius of Cornwall
Entertaining something of the great Aristotelian insight
Into the metaphysical basis
Of the concepts of Formal and Final Cause,
While, alive as we are to the entire multitudinous world,
(Northern Europeans are at their best by day;
Latins, nocturnal, only come to life
By artificial light; being Celts
We are at home with either)
Our stand for Cornwall involves not 'criticism',
It is just 'selection', the root motive of κριτικ- that informs us,
Rather than 'condemnation', or even 'judgment'
– Phacoids of Cornwall as the new world shapes!

I sing of Cornwall, not of Lyonesse,
(Though I too cherish that pre-Arthurian Celtic flicker of being
Which has seemingly disappeared so entirely
Of bare, dark, and elemental Tristan's land – old
Celtic, pre-Christian – Tristan and his boat and his horn,

– If that is only in my life like the quotation
From *Tristan und Isolde* in Berg's *Lyric Suite*,
Which nevertheless does not seem out of place,
And I know King Arthur – *pace* Layamon,
Chaucer, Malory, Spenser, Dryden, Wordsworth,
Tennyson, and all the rest of the romancing bards –
Is none other than Thor, Her-Thor, Ar-Thur,
Thor Eindri of the Edda, the Indian Indra,
And realise the full relation of this
To 'Poesy's unfailing river
Which through Albion winds forever')
Of Cornwall (that land without imagination, being poetless),
And of art as the knowledge of the noumenal world,
Of Cornwall, and of that old *scat bal*,[1] her speech,
– Scat *bell* rather! Buried in its fallen *cleghty*[2] from the reach
Of all the braced farcers of the Arthurian Congress! –
(I fear no sudden sound of it behind me
– If I have nerves, they are like veins in rock! –
When I survey with full content my infinite world,
No ringing, hellish wounding like a treacherous shot,
No envious noise declaring my possessions impure.
Since we have passed all that has been, is, and will be
Through the Athanor of our love.
Nay, now, if I am vulnerable to any attack it is
But slowly as Cornwall's bastions to the sea,
And from forces as different from anything human
As salt-water is from basalt.)
Her speech, her condition, her *Ur*-motives, her all, complete and clear,
> A necklace for my love appear
> Moniliform in my verses here,
My little lusty broad-browed strong-necked love;
And down the shining stream awakens every here and there,
Among the other lights and hues, the ancient dark-red flame,
(The Celtic genius – Cornwall, Scotland, Ireland, Wales –
Is to the English Ascendancy, the hideous khaki Empire,
As the white whale is to the killer whale,

---

[1] Disused mine.   [2] Belfry

The white whale displaying in its buccal cavity
The heavy oily blood-rich tongue which is the killer's especial delight.
The killer slips his head into the behemoth's mouth
And rives away part after part of the tongue until
Nothing remains in the white whale's mouth but a cicatrised stump.
Yet to-day we laugh gaily and show our healthy red tongues,
Red rags to John Bull – the Celtic colour flaunting again
In a world where the ravening sub-fusc more and more
Prevails. We young Celts arise with quick tongues intact
Though our elders lie tongueless under the ocean of history.
We show ourselves as ever and again through great grey volumes of
    smoke
Red blasts of the fire come quivering – yea, we dare
To shoot out our tongues under the very noses of the English.
The fate of our forefathers has not made us afraid
To open our mouths and show our red glory of health,
Nay, we sail again, laughing, on the crown of the sea,
'Not so much bound to any haven ahead
As rushing from all havens astern,'
The deepest blood-being of the white race crying to England
'Consummatum est ! Your Imperial *Pequod* is sunk.'
We young Celts disport ourselves fearlessly
Knowing that we are the units
Of a far greater cycle than Melville's great Northern cycle
And that in us it completes its round.)
The Aldebaran light as in the hollows of your stroked hair's curves,
Stroked till the unsufflaminate dye comes up like suffioni,
'Like little lamb-toe bunches springs
In red-tinged and begolden dye
Forever,'
Gleaming from honey-colour to tangerine
('Gold for goodness and copper for cleverness')
Like the *caoir* of the very *clanna-speura* in your *clannfhalt*[1]
– Or like the witch of Atlas's crimson well of refuge
Whence came constant impulsion to the beautiful
To new intensities, to priests to renounce their idols,

---

[1] *caoir*, blaze, stream of sparks; *clanna-speura*, heavenly hosts; *clannfhalt*, clustering hair.

Kings their regalia, soldiers their armament,
Gaolers to set their prisoners free, lovers to defy convention.
The weight of your tresses, as Damodaragupta says,
Like the cloud of smoke ascending from the furnace of Love,
Your Meliboean tresses, for the hair of thine head is purple
As the Song of Songs which is Solomon's says,
Dense pillars of dusk through which every now and again
Glows a deeper undershade of crimson as though
Some trapped genius almost thrusts itself out
Of the moving prism that holds it, colour of *fìon na Spàine*,
Or like Fate's message to me in the sympathetic ink
Of a solution of gold in hydrochloric acid
That turns purple with tin in the same acid.
Your hair, for an omen, is the very colour of the Phoenix's wings,
Or like Typhoean breathing winning free through all its overburden
Than which no vastier deep, no heavier handicap,
Occludes the Cornish genius and holds it from its triumph,
Coming out slowly, slowly, buldering and heavily,
The lazy cordial colour, the appeased blood and full-content,
Or out, moliminous, banner of red moccado and locram,
The arcane colour of Cornwall's number
And basic shibboleth glory-hue of true Cornish things!

No poet worth his salt, amid the press
Of Earth's accabling problems, has time, far less
Desire, to waste on skiascoped mythologies
The prepotent, rare, and priceless energies
Filially, and protoparentally, true History's
Whose issues, in proseuchae such as these
– Else Cornish religion, *ionraic* religion, is to seek; the common
Religiosity is all a horrible departure from the idiom
Of Cornish genius, as UnEnglish even as UnChristian too,
Irreconcilable with sovereign life, mongrel, base, awry –
Can be my prayers' only addressees,
Maugre voices off, 'Rex quondam, rexque futurus.'
                                        Fables! Faiblesse!

Though such multivious falsity's the strongest power one sees
In the world to-day; even as 'fairy rings' kill trees

So collapsed Cornwall's veridical qualities
In Wesleyans and myxoedematous sectaries like these
Felled by the abundant centrifugally-spreading hyphae
(Terrible as an army without banners, appalling
As summer visitors, or as 'for dullness, the creeping Saxons,'
Or as, to Occidentals, the reeling ant-heap East's nimieties.
– Thicker, my darling, than your head of hair
The inexorable threads fare,
Kill the grass here, then, beyond the ring
                              Stimulate it there
Even as where chalcopyrite is changed to chalcocite,
At greater depths, beyond the reach of concentrating waters,
The original chalcopyrite may remain, or in opposite wise
To those curious Hollywood types who are pretty and can act
But who, mysteriously enough, seem paralysed
So far as all other mental development is concerned
– On the screen charming, even convincing artists,
Off it, collapsing into nothingness)
Of the responsible fungi. Toadstools! Toad's tales!

How Cornwall has suffered from this disintegrity!
The wine gone and nothing but the bagasse left!

Horrible fog-cowls of fungi everywhere, umbrella-like phallic symbols,
Or in crescent thick ears or in hoof-like shapes,
As with the Birch Polypore – *Polyporus betulinus* –
Whose powder-like spores gain entry to trees
Through wounds and kill them – fungus bodies in themselves
Of little use, save, trimmed, to sharpen razor blades,
Or serve as substitutes for cork, or, cut in strips,
Do insect-collectors to pin their captures on!

Our love is free of all such mushroom growths,
Local morals, fashions of feeling, and blind-spot science
And of all fear of fungus-wrought overthrows.

His attitude towards woman is the basic point
A man must have thought out to know
Where he honestly stands.

Since praise is well, and compliment is well,
But affection – that is the last and final
And most precious reward any man can win.

I remember when you were like that shrub
Which is smothered with carillons of little brick-red bells
Finely striped with yellow lines;
That, when the sun shines through them,
Glow like hot blown glass.
But ah! now, beloved, it is as when on the Carmine Cherry,
A hundred feet high and with a spread
Coinciding with the circumference of the earth,
The ruby-red flowerbuds open, and the whole tree
Bursts into carmine flame, a mass of blossom, stark crimson.
To see the sun through its branches
When the tree is in full bloom
Is a thing that can never be forgotten.
Nor the sight of your eyes now, Valda,
Through the toppling wave of love.
Love's scarlet banner is over us.
We conquer Chaos, a new Creation.

The Divided Bird

AH! Peirce[1] was right. His 'minuter logic
Could only avail towards what he sought
As the scrawl on an infant's slate
To a cartoon of Raphael.

The alethetropic barrenness of a Formal Logic,
The characteristic vice of mathematicians,
Of taking any hypothesis that seems amusing
And deducing its consequences, can do no more
Than pluck our bird and scatter its feathers.

[1] Charles Sanders Peirce, the American philosopher.

Silly as the peacock's feather Lord Kames[1] declared
Not specified so would leave us at a loss to form
An accurate image of the fanciful feat
Described in Henry V[2] to exemplify what
A poor and private displeasure can do against a king:
'You may as well go about to turn the sun to ice
With fanning in his face with a peacock's feather'
. . . 'Plume yourself upon it as much as you like,
But what will that do to the king?'

Let us rather
Be with the bird as we are with the full-blown
Yellow rose of Space and Time whose petals we've counted
But will not pluck for our answer
Since it would work out 'No!'

Tyun, tyun, tyun, tyun
    Spi tui zqua
Tyo, tyo tyo, tyo, tyo, tyo, tyo, tyo, tix;
      Qutio, qutio, qutio, qutio,
      Zquo, zquo, zquo, zquo.
Tzy, tzy, tzy, tzy, tzy, tzy, tzy, tzy, tzy, tzy,
Quorrox tui zqua pipiquisi.[3]

Ah, song! – I think of the stupendous gulf between
This bird's song (so-called) and Webern's Das dunkle Reich
Carrying the notation of Pierrot Lunaire to farther limits,
And how it must be sung accurately, not recited,
While substituting for the counterpoint of Pierrot Lunaire
A roving, tenuous pianoforte accompaniment,
And how I once heard Erika Storm
Cope with its fantastic intervals
As most of us might hope to do

[1] Lord Kames (1696–1782), Scottish judge and author, wrote *Elements of Criticism* (1762), and other legal, historical, philosophical and aesthetic works.
[2] Act IV, Scene I. See discussion of this, and of Kames' contention, in Professor I. A. Richards' *The Philosophy of Rhetoric*.
[3] Song of the northern nightingale. The 'tyo' is a long-drawn and plaintive note.

With those of the Italienisches Liederbuch,
– And she followed that with the square massive phrases
And intelligible design of H. E. Apostel's
Gross trägt der Berg des Himmels stürmische Brandung!

What speculative grammar, what pot-hooks of thought,
What three and three-quarter millions of words,
Like Sigwart's, are these in my mind as I look
At one turn of the flight and think of the bird's
Automatism of feathers altering their angles
Closing and opening the airspaces between them
As wind and weather require? The whole point
Of my crusade against 'German' tendencies
Is carried . . . by a mind none the less out of joint!

A wing-beat ends ontological pragmatism;

The Boole-Schroeder algebra, too, ceases to serve
Though its application to terms in intension
As well as in extension I clearly observe:
The conception of consistency between propositions
And the mathematical conception may be harmonised
In vain. . . . In vain as many non-Aristotelian logics
As there are non-Euclidean geometries devised.

I am like one who listens to a song
That might enter his blood and being, heard
In terms of the instrument it was written for,
But here to another colour medium transferred
. . . All the instrumentation of a modern mind . . .
Where the original conception, it seems, was so unified,
So infallibly realised in every detail,
It loses more than it gains to my learning allied.

As in Der Einsame I first cast away
All thought of the bird an inspiration to seize
But immediately after I too make my form
'Give' to the bird; and the difference of these

Consecutive thoughts is that the lack of the bird
... Though its source ... from the first can no longer impair
The mental music; but the justification and meaning
Of the second require the bird visibly there.

The first has been the usual source of my art.
Now the second – the departure from that – must be
– Craftsmanship not for its own sake now,
But as blood, bones, nerves of an organic idea,
Wolf not Schubert ... the bird to my thought
As the words to his songs; a method that cannot be taught
Or learned; being too infinitely varied,
Too organic to the conception. So the bird may be 'caught'.

I shall look no more at special poses then
Like the work of some great Eastern artist.
The methods perfectly opposed, the results the same
(And yet I don't know – the bird may have wit
And employ its power of striking effects
As I remember a cock-bullfinch did,
At mating-time frequenting the alder roots by a stream
Where its gem-like colouring best with the drabness contrasted!)

O thou who every darkling storm that we obey
Revealest, every sombre surge dost find
Turning our obscure night to sleepless day
With celestial showing, wherefore, O mind,
Findest thou inexpressible this natural sense
Both of a structure and its internal rhythms, till
This bird seems, like that Chinese idea of art,
As valuable to me as alien to Western skill?

Am I left, as with my sense of the antinomy between
The ideal of conscientious action and the actual
Aberrancy of the Unglückselige Bewusstsein,
To return from vain fancies to the baffling factual,
Or, like a subjectivist, always forced at last
To consequences paradoxical to common sense
Where linked to an ultimate human impulse
An idealist might establish coherence?

But what idealist can sing this song?
Resolve my desperate imbroglio with this bird?
Only that study of structure it seems will serve
To which I have already glancingly referred.
Else we have a mass of disconnected facts
Which cannot be traced to a common source.
Yet the bird is no more most itself
In fleeting moments we seize than a man is, of course.

If all men were as passionately devoted
To Science, Philosophy, and Art as I
The vain thoughts that make some of these verses halt
Would be impossible to any man. But you cry
'Men can never be that but only a few.'
You are wrong. All men are ripe for the highest any man knows.
That is a present fact, as the mind of any man stript
Of all its accretions and pushed back to its foundations shows.

For lack, alone, of the good will to live
Nay, for lack of love, Mankind is debarred
From the individual economic independence
Of every man, and all our science is marred
And turned to misery, madness, and murder to-day
Instead of abundant life. . . . I can get
Far nearer to this bird simply by longing to fly
To all men's ears and hearts with this message yet.

What prevents me from getting close to the bird is the same
As what – mobile as my thoughts are – frustrates this song
And as that which has destroyed the oneness of man
In all men, defeating all science and breeding all wrong;
For a poet – so must brother-men – lives by results,
Not premises, acts of creation, not decrees,
Postcepts, not precepts; and all true love,
And a bird's flight and song, are made of these.

The movement to seek values is impulsive in character
Like the flair of an artist who feels impelled

To realise in his work the value of beauty
He has discerned; only so the ideas we have held
Of freedom and brotherly love can be realised,
Not deliberately willed as a duty is willed,
Not pursued as the result of a pure act of choice,
. . . All our efforts are vain save with true love filled.

The normal outlets of the push of the impulse
Towards all values are almost all shut to-day
Just as I fail to express my sense of this bird,
Just as I find it ever harder to slip away
Into that clear and silent zone, where the intention
That led me to enter it solidifies;
Where the opposites command – light, shade; faith, unfaith . . .
Giving the perspective in which song like a bird flies.

All else is spiritual death – the lie in the soul,
Whence ethics usurps the throne of ontology,
And science subverts philosophy's rights.
. . . In the long history of humanity
I can find none righteous; and the condition of the world,
. . . With Plans everywhere; no healing in these! . . .
The essentially hellish character of politics,
Shows to-day the worst ravages of the foul disease.

We have been like the Chinese painter who
Dare not paint the eyes in his dragons, lest they should fly away.
I too am a slave in body with a soul that soars
Worshipping the Heart of Man and the Unknown to-day,
Dreaming again how to bring to mankind, divided
And blinded by hate, the blue freedom of the birds
And make them all one family under the sky.
– I dream no longer. These are my words:

'How the swift flight shines and the shadows fall!
I did not know the hidden stream in my mind could hold
So much darkness as that – it has crowded in
Shadow by soft shadow like sheep to a fold.

So light and smooth is the flight of the bird
Its pure elusive essence has entered into me
Like the genius of Spain . . . that spirit unchanging, so close in its fibre,
No foreigner can enter . . . that can express itself once and once only.'

I am filled with shadows now as with snow
– The shadowy snow of the woes of all mankind;
Blinded with the laurels of lead that the wings
Of the years that are useless to them round me bind.
The shadows are borne into my inmost being
On the dark swift stream that is mightier far
Than that other stream confused with the lights
Of things as mere reason says that they are.

Why will you not come to me save darkly thus,
Bird of the Heavens? The solitude
Of its habitat makes no creature wild
Save men have pursued it. Have I pursued?
Birds' fears are all based on bitter experience.
Fear you men's reason? Then you have cause!
Who know your worth, and want and care for it,
You meet more than half-way. These are Nature's laws.

If a bird is a solitary it is never
Because it cares for solitude for solitude's sake.
That is true of the Joy and Peace men seek.
Let them search their hearts to find the mistake
That keeps these unfound and always will.
The bird thought most shy turns out to be
The most confiding at last; and love
Will bring the genius of 'God' to humanity.

Into the innermost core of my life
Flock the quick shadows; and now I know
Wings are spread over the world to-day
Only conceived in the depths of darkness so.
From the stream of intuition rises a truth
That reason, since it lacks it, denies the name;

More august than reason, more enduring, outsoaring it
With Earth's loveliest song, and amplest pinions aflame.

And here in the shadows in my thalamus[1] now
The bird has disclosed all its secrets to me;
I know the destiny of man, the call
Of the Seraphim to the life that's to be,
That still, like the pure birdliness I now hold,
Only in the darkest depths of intuition lies;
In poverty and peace and selfless love
. . . From these alone can humanity rise.

Tell me no more that proud ambition,
Material means, the lusts of the eye,
All we can see and feel and take apart,
Are the stays of mankind, or the power to fly
Of birds is born of their feathers and shape.
I know that nothing like these in myself at all,
No erudition or effort, will enable me to sing
. . . Or men to make a better world withal.

The world in which nothing will evade us
Having cause to mistrust the limitations of our love,
We who, since Elijah, should no more halt
Between two opinions than that bird above!
The obscure sense of value does not discriminate
The principle . . . Justice, sympathy, are of no avail;
All divisions disappear before love alone
. . . It means we have too little love if in aught we fail.

I am as one who is still pursuing
The bird behind all I can think of it
And see and hear and feel . . . as one
Who faithfully quests the Holy Grail yet,
Priesthood within priesthood, mass behind mass,
Without sodality, or institution, or order,

[1] The poet here expresses his agreement with those brain physiologists who find
intuition – as distinct from cortical understanding, which is what he calls 'mere
reason' – localised in the thalamus.

Heard only in the heart's silence . . . .Now the bird stoops;
With its eyes filling mine, I tremble on the border

With its eyes filling mine . . . O would I could go
To Everyman with the power of the Age of Plenty so!
The bird is in them all if they'll liberate it
From the cage of vain reason that holds it yet.
That is, reason better; for true reason knows
The abyss it rests on, and distinguishes with fairness
Between the pseudo-simplicity of perceptual acceptance
And the genuine simplicity of immediate awareness.

Ballad of Aun, King of Sweden

Surely Hell burns a deeper blue
With each noble boast of men like you.

With each noble boast of men like you
– Such men as all but all men it's true.

See what I'm doing for England, you cry,
Or for Christendom, civilisation, or some other lie.

And no one remembers the story of Aun,
The Swedish king, who sent son after son

To death, buying with each another span
Of life for himself, the identical plan

All governments, all patriots, self-righteously pursue.
How many sons have *you* given, and *you*, and *you*?

Nine sons in succession was the grim
Record of Aun, till the people rose and slew *him*.

But when will the people rise and slay
The ubiquitous Aun of State Murder to-day?

Realising murder is foulest murder no matter
What individual or body for what end does the slaughter!

A Golden Wine in the Gaidhealtachd

To W. D. MacColl and our hosts and hostesses in
Arisaig, Eigg, South Uist, Raasay, Skye, Barra, and Mull

In Scotland in the Gaidhealtachd there's a golden wine
Still to be found in a few houses here and there
Where the secret of its making has been kept for centuries
– Nor would it avail to steal the secret, since it cannot be made
    elsewhere.

In Scotland in the Gaidhealtachd there's a golden wine.
Carelessly and irreligiously quaffed it might be taken
For a very fine champagne. But it is not an effervescing wine
Although its delicate piquancy produces a somewhat similar effect
    upon the palate.

In Scotland in the Gaidhealtachd there's a golden wine,
A wine that demands so deliberate a pause,
In order to detect its hidden peculiarities
And subtle exquisiteness of its flavour, that to drink it
Is really more a moral than a physical delight.
There is a deliciousness in it that eludes analysis
And like whatever else is superlatively good
Is better appreciated by the memory
Than by present consciousness.

In Scotland in the Gaidhealtachd there's a golden wine.
One of its most ethereal charms lies

In the transitory life of its richest qualities,
For while it requires a certain leisure and delay
Yet if you linger too long upon the draught it becomes
Disenchanted both of its fragrance and its flavour.

In Scotland in the Gaidhealtachd there's a golden wine.
The lustre should not be forgotten among the other
Admirable embodiments of this rare wine; for, as it stands in a glass
A little circle of light glows round about it,
The finest Orvieto or that famous wine,
The Est Est Est of Montefiascone,
Is vulgar in comparison. This is surely
The wine of the Golden Age such as Bacchus himself
First taught mankind to press from the choicest of his grapes.

In Scotland in the Gaidhealtachd there's a golden wine.
There is a tradition that if any of it were sent to market
This wine would lose all its wonderful qualities.
Not a drop of it therefore has ever been sold,
Or ever will be. Indeed the wine is so fond
Of its native home that a transportation
Of even a few miles turns it quite sour.
Yet the custom of those who have it has always been and still is
To let it flow freely whenever those
Whom they love and honour sit at the board
But it cannot be drunk in all the world
Save under these particular roofs in Arisaig and Eigg,
In Tobermory, South Uist, Barra, Raasay and Skye,
Nor can they see or smell or taste it who are not
Competent receivers – nor could they bestow
Who lack the sense of operative form – this consecrated juice
Symbolising the holy virtues of hospitality and social kindness.

Through what else can Scotland recover its poise
Save, as Very Hope believes, this golden wine yet?

Off the Coast of Fiedeland

SHETLAND (WEST SIDE) HERRING FISHING, JUNE 1936
Written during a week aboard the sailing ship Valkyrie

TO SKIPPER JOHN IRVINE, OF SALTNESS, WHALSAY

TWENTY miles out to the main deep
Due west o' the Ramna Stacks
And sou-west o' the Flugga Light
I ha'e a' that my pleasure lacks.

Gannet, haud wide. Seek the bush-raip alang
Till aiblins at last you may sight
A single white cork amang a' the broon
On which you may like to alight.

But awa' doon here on the inshore grunds
Twenty miles sou-west o' the Flugga Light
I row at ease on a broon mysel'
And ha'e nae need to seek for a white.

For shootin' oor nets parallel to the Ramna Stacks
I think o' the sixareens[1] o' the auld Fiedeland fleet
And their hardy fishermen a' langsyne in the mools,
And life ony auld gait is fell sweet.

Rinnin' oor nets oot in line wi' the Stacks
Wi' oor ain broon sails clashed doon at oor feet
There's nae white to be seen save yon toom face o' a mune
Till we haul up syne, when oor shot[2] may compete.

Gannet, haud wide. Swing awa' roon' the buoys.
It's my watch to-night while we lie to the nets,
And I'm blithe to be whaur the hert o' darkness
Wins back sae muckle day aye needs forgets.

[1] Sixareens – the old square-sail boats.
[2] Shot – haul of herring.

My een compete wi' the Aeschiness Light,
There's little else to be seen wi' the ootward eye,
But it's no' the ootward eye that contents my mind,
Nor yet that difference, gannet, 'twixt you and me.

And I ken the morn we'll pit in at North Roe[1]
And I'll see wi' the lassies in the guttin' ranks there
The wee Whalsay lassie I lo'e best o' a'
Wi' a wreath o' white gulls roond her bonnie broon hair
– Aye, when her skinklan' tresses she combs
She's bonnier than ocht on the Floo'ery Holms.

Fillin' oor cran-baskets and swingin' them up
And alang on the trollies, a look and a smile,
A word in the bygaein', and, if I'm lucky, a touch,
'll haud me gaein' again for anither while.

Praise be, it's only a plain Shetland lad
At whom ony sweet Shetland lass e'er keeks.
God or the King or Heaven kens wha
If they tried to butt in 'ud be deemed juist freaks.
Ony fisher lad 'ud hae them beat to the wide
If they cam' here ettlin' to find a bride.

Syne we'll bear awa' yont the Stacks aince mair
Till I'll feel like a 'reincandescent' again,
But whaur the white light that glows in me's frae
Only mysel', and the lassie at North Roe, ken.

Oh, awa' yont the Ramna Stacks again
For anither night on the edge o' the Main Deep there!
– Lassie, I doot I never saw afore
Hoo bright the gowd glints in your bonnie broon hair.

Furth frae your breists and oot through the ocean
Pearl-white stream ne'er confused in the maelstrom o' waters.
As the needle to the Pole my hert to you,
Fairest 'mang the haill o' Hialtland's daughters!

---

[1] Roe – pronounced Rew.

Seaward again yont the Erne's Crag
And the horns o' the neeps o' Greevlan',
And I praise the Lord that your love for me
In the weavin' waters needs nae unreevlin'!

Looks, there's a tystie fleein' wi' his boat full![1]
But I've dipped a raip owre and sprinkled oor deck
Wi' the sparklin' saut draps for luck's sake again
Or the tystie's gobbled the fish doon his neck.

Ho, there Jimmy! Jimmy Williamson, ho!
Sing to the herrin' as you used to do.
I'll join in the chorus, but there's twa bright herrin'
Loupin' in my chest'll no answer to you!

Sing: *'Come on, peerie[2] fish. Fill the hungry hold.*
I see a straggle. I see white in the lum.
I see faither awa' there at the back o' the bed.
Here's a better bit strollie. Let her come. Let her come.
The seals are snuffin' a' alang the tow-heid,
Hannah[3] abune is squealin' wi' greed.
Come on in. You're safer wi' us indeed,
Bonxie[4] and maulies[5] are seekin' their feed.
There she's again. I see her. I see her.
Toddle up, toddle up. You're far better here.'

I hear the tirricks[6] roarin' astern.
'I'll sing to the herrin' in the mornin', lad.
I'll tell her to shiver her noses then
When she's taen the best cravat ever she's had.'

The fish Christ Jesus and my ain bonnie lass
Flash sidewise in my blood-pool a' the time.
There's twa fish loupin' in my bosom, Jimmy,
Wi' an ever-mair-glorious skyme after skyme.

---

[1] Tystie (Black Guillemot) – with his boat full – with a fish in his mouth. (The following three lines refer to an old fisherman's superstition.)
[2] Peerie – little. [3] The herring gull (the little black-backed gull).
[4] The great skua. [5] The Fulmar petrel. [6] Arctic terns.

Flickerin' birds fade into the grim rocks where they nest
As the starry hosts in the sunrise fade.
My body may swing on the fishin' grunds here
But my spirit in the light o' her love is stayed.

Let the night darken. They'll brighten the mair,
My een and the Aeschiness Light and them.
And *them*, I say – but in the howe o' the night
Guid kens they shine like a single flame.

Borin' its way through the hert o' the dark
And bearin' me wi't – till we come aince mair,
Tackin' up the Soond to the Biorgs again
And I see her standin' in the guttin' ranks there
Wi' a wreath o' gulls like wavin' white lilies
Plaited aboot her bonnie broon hair
– Sae I'll see her again in the first o' the day
Till she and I blend in yae flame tae,
Fairer than yon that's erst seemed sae fair !

Certes if she[1] rises to soom the night
There'll be something to meet her afore her face !
Mair than sixty vessels shootin' their nets
In the light o' the sunset a' roond oor place.
Yet aiblins the morn I'll hae white in my net
Purer than ony the ocean's gien yet.

White as driven snaw and warmin' as wine
And mine, my sweethert, mine – mine !
Witch that I burn in my hert ilka night,[2]
The *Valkyrie*'s luck and my pride and delight !

Nae lass in the crews[3] at the Shetland stations
Can gut herrin' mair deftly and quickly than you.
But, certes, you've put the guts *into* me,
And I'd sail for you into Hell's reid mou'.

[1] 'She' here – also 'her' in stanzas 17 and 18 – refers, of course, to the herring.
[2] Refers to another old fisherman's superstition.
[3] Three girls constitute a gutting crew.

It's a fine clear trusty sky the night,
The fires o' the sunset are playin' reid yet
Roond the Blue Mull, Valleyfield and the Pobie astern
– Like the fires o' my hert roond you, my pet.

An' I'll sail Earth's seas as lang as I maun
Mixin' my blood wi' the bitterest brine
If that is the only airt I can win
At last to mixin' my blood wi' thine.

For a workin' lad and a workin' lass
Can lo'e each ither juist at least as weel
As Royalty or the wealthiest folk
Or onybody trained in a public skeel.

It's a perfect miracle, lassie, hoo near
You can seem to me whiles even awa' oot here
On the edge o' the main deep. It was ill to ken
It was only a dream I had o' you then.

When the kaim o' Foula lifts on the Smew
My peerie lass I'm aye thinkin' o' you,
And aye I'd leifer see yours instead
O' even the finest dry weather heid,
And when there's nocht else in the warld in sight
You're aye in view.

O Love that pours oot through the welterin' sea
In a constant inviolable muckle moonpath to me
Frae my lass at North Roe, I'se warrant that current
'll find a' life's troubles, and Death itsel', nae deterrent!

Grain o' wind now, boys, and the auld boat
In through its blasts like a greyh'und coorses
Doon the tricky tideways o' Yell Soond, fu'
O' sunshine noo – on white horses!

Three reefs and nae comfort up or doon
Where I'm still thinkin', my love, o' you
While we play Lant[1] in an air smoke, steam,
And sweaty socks mak' like an Irish stew.

The Wreck of the Swan

EVEN SO – as a man at the end tries no more
To escape but deliberately turns and plunges
Into the press of his foes and perishes there –
I remember the lesson of the wreck of the *Swan*,
Within her own home harbour and under the lights
Of her crew's native city, swept to doom on Christmas Eve.

The lights were warm on happy family parties
In hundreds of homes. – One wonders
If a man or woman here and there did not part
The curtains to look out and think how black
Was the night, and foul for men at sea.

Few could know that quite near at hand, just beyond
The bald fisher-rows of Footdee, the crew
In the lifeboat *Emma Constance* were fighting to save
Five men in the wheelhouse of that trawler, the *Swan*,
That wallowed in broken seas.

It was not what a seaman would call rough in the channel
But there was a heavy run of broken water
Along the inside wall of the North Pier
And for some reason unknown the *Swan* grounded
Two hundred yards within the pier-head,
Swung round, held fast, and took to labouring
In a welter of breakers and spray.

[1] An old and complicated card game much favoured by Shetland fishermen.

Less than ten minutes later a gun
Fired a rocket from the Pier and a line
For the breeches-buoy was across the *Swan*.
Had it been accepted that would have ended the tale.
But the men of the *Swan* – who knows why? –
Refused that line of safety.

Meanwhile, with the celerity of firemen, the lifeboat crew,
Had assembled and tumbled into their powerful sixty-foot boat,
And she was off, and, in a few minutes, alongside the *Swan*,
Between that helpless ship and the pier.
Again the door of safety was wide open to the men of the *Swan*
And again they refused to pass through it.

The coxswain of the lifeboat roared at them,
Through his megaphone, to jump; but the five men
Of the *Swan* turned away and took refuge
In their doomed ship's wheelhouse instead.
There is a dark fascination in trying to appreciate
The spiritual inwardness of that strange situation.
Five men, for their own good reasons, refusing
To leave the shelter of their wheelhouse, while the lifeboat laboured
In the seas and the darkness, its crew dedicated to rescue,
Shouting to them in vain to come out and be saved.

A great wave hissing angrily came down on the lifeboat
And broke her adrift from the wreck.
Wielding the force of many tons it threw her
Against the foundations of the pier.
Along the length of 100 feet of solid masonry
She was flung like a piece of stick.

But the coxswain got her out again – a feat of seamanship
To hold the imagination in itself! –
And back alongside the *Swan* the *Emma Constance* went,
And again the lines were thrown,
But none of the men in the wheelhouse
Would come out to make them fast.

This time they had refused their last chance,
A sea of enormous weight broke over the wreck.
It carried away the upper part of the wheelhouse.
It swept the *Emma Constance* once more
Against the adamant wall of the pier.

This is the story of the men who wouldn't come out.
They were never seen alive again – and the coxswain and crew of the
       lifeboat
Carry the dark knowledge that up against
Something more formidable, more mysterious even,
Than wind and wave they battled largely in vain.

Four times they had gone back to that tragic wreck,
Manoeuvred with high skill in the cauldron 'twixt ship and pier,
Played the searchlight continuously on the battered bridge,
Cruised about for an hour,
But the men of the *Swan* refused to come out!

No dreamers these but hard-bitten men
Used to all the tortures of Old Feathery Legs
– The black villain who rides every crested wave
North of 65 degrees – he and his accursed legions,
The fog, the blizzard, the black-squall and the hurricane.

Up to their waists in water on the foredeck,
Gutting fish in the pounds, a black-squall
Screaming around, and the temperature 40 degrees below,
Working like automatons, 30 . . . 40 . . . .50 hours,
Grafting like fiends, with never a break or blink of sleep between.

A wave as high as the mast-heads crashing on deck
And sweeping all hands in a heap in the lee-scuppers,
Their arms and hands clawing up through the boiling surf
Still grasping wriggling fish and gutting knives.

And every now and then a message like this
Throbbing out of the black box.

'VALKYRIE calling all trawlers!... He's got us.... Old Feathery's
got us at last.... We can see the rocks now ... just astern.... Another
minute, I reckon!... We're on!... Good-bye, pals.... Say good-bye
to my wife ... to my kiddies!... Good-bye, Buckie.... Good-bye,
Scotland!'

In 31 years at sea, he'd spent less
Than four years ashore, mostly in spells
On an average of 36 hours
Between trips – that's the price
His wife and kids had to pay for fish.

Time the public knew what these men have to face.

Nearly 100,000 of them at sea.
Nor are they the only men concerned.
Shipbuilders, rope, net and box manufacturers,
Fish-friers, buyers, retailers, salesmen,
Railways and road transport,
Coal, salt, and ice industries,
– About 3,000,000 folk would have to look elsewhere
For their bread and butter
If there were no trawlermen – or fish.

'Stand by all hands!' Down below
The lads along the starboard scuppers,
Backs bent, hands clawing the net,
Long as the ship, wide as a street,
Keyed to high-tension point,
Every muscle tense and taut.
'Shooto!' Over she goes.

Off the South-East coast of Iceland,
The East Horns, a famous landmark,
About five miles off the port-quarter.
All along the coast the great, barren, sullen mountains,
Eternally snow-crested, and shaped

Like monstrous crouching animals,
Sweep down to the water line,
And many a brave ship lies
Under the lowering evil shadows
Of the terrible rocks.

The successful skippers read the 'fish sign'
In a thousand different ways.
The gulls, the wind, currents, tides,
The depth of water, the nature of the bottom,
The type of fish caught in certain patches,
The nature of the food in their stomachs
Exposed by the gutting knife,
These factors and a thousand others
Supply information to be had or read
Only after years of battle and bitter experience.

Trawling along the lip of a marine mountain,
Covered by 200 fathoms of water,
On what is veritably a narrow mountain pass,
Scooping up hard 'sprags' (cod)
And 'ducks' (haddocks),
Each net sweeping up fish in hundreds of thousands,
Towing for miles over an area wide as a town.

The skipper has been on the bridge
For nearly 60 hours on end,
Down below, in the fish-pounds for'ard,
The lads are reeling like drunken men,
The decks awash, swirling high
As their arm-pits, and icy-cold.

These men are no dreamers.

Rex est qui metuit nihil.

A true man chooses death as he can in no part lie to a girl
But will put himself conscientiously into the worst possible light.

Töten ist eine Gestalt unseres wandernden Trauerns. . . .
Rein ist im heiteren Geist,
Was an uns selber geschieht.[1]

(Killing is only a form of the sorrow we wander in here . . .
The serener spirit finds pure
All that can happen to us.)

'Death is ugly.
Tomato is crashing to.'[2]

The Gaels never die! They either 'change' or 'travel'.

'Happy the folk upon whom the Bear looks down, happy in this error,
whom of fears the greatest moves not, the dread of death. Hence their
warrior's heart hurls them against the steel, hence their ready welcome
of death.'[3]

   'It was possibly the inculcation of these doctrines that moved the
Celtic warriors to hurl their bodies against cold steel – a characteristic
the world is only too familiar with in the conduct of our Highland
regiments. They can still listen to the battle-songs of a thousand ages,
with a susceptible mood nowise estranged amid the crumbling
foundations of a former sovereignty. A German military authority –
Clausewitz, I think – said that the Highlander is the only soldier in
Europe who, without training, can unflinchingly face the bayonet.'

For now I see Life and Death as who gets
The first magical glimpse of Popocatepetl,
Its white cone floating in the rare winter air,
Incredibly near, . . . incredibly unreal,
And its sister peak which the Indians call
'The sleeping woman,' like a great prone goddess,
Above her circlet of clouds,
Or like Mount Elbruz's mile-apart twin breasts of snow!

I don't look the kind of guy, do I,
Who aches to get away from the high truth

---

[1] Rainer Maria Rilke.   [2] Tio Nakamura.   [3] Lucan, *Pharsalia*.

Of the passing mountains into the close heat
Of the Pullman again, and the company of his pals
– Into a small enclosed space where I can feel
Confident and important again?
I am accustomed to the *altura*, believe me.
I am what the guides call *schwindelfrei*.

This is not the poetry of a man with such a grudge against life
That a very little of it goes a long way with him.
No great barbaric country will undermine and ruin me,
Slowly corroding my simple unimaginative qualities,
Rob me of my conventions, of my simple direct standards,
Who have no undefeatable inner integrity to take their place.
I love this country passionately, expanding
To its wild immensity as a flower opens in the sunshine,
I am the last man in all the world to hate these great places
And depend for my only comfort on the theatres and cafés,
The wide, well-lit *avenidas*, the scandal and gossip of the cabarets,
The emotion and danger of the bull-ring.
I would not rather be sitting in the closed comfort of the Pullman,
A drink before me, surrounded by people I know,
And things I can understand.

I feel with Life
As a man might towards a little child,
But towards Death, as towards one of my own contemporaries
Whom I have known as long
As I have known myself.

MORE ABOUT PENGUINS, PELICANS
AND PUFFINS

For further information about books available from Penguins please write to Dept EP, Penguin Books Ltd, Harmondsworth, Middlesex UB7 ODA.

In the U.S.A.: For a complete list of books available from Penguins in the United States write to Dept DG, Penguin Books, 299 Murray Hill Parkway, East Rutherford, New Jersey 07073.

In Canada: For a complete list of books available from Penguins in Canada write to Penguin Books Canada Ltd, 2801 John Street, Markham, Ontario L3R 1B4.

In Australia: For a complete list of books available from Penguins in Australia write to the Marketing Department, Penguin Books Australia Ltd, P.O. Box 257, Ringwood, Victoria 3134.

In New Zealand: For a complete list of books available from Penguins in New Zealand write to the Marketing Department, Penguin Books (N.Z.) Ltd, Private Bag, Takapuna, Auckland 9.

In India: For a complete list of books available from Penguins in India write to Penguin Overseas Ltd, 706 Eros Apartments, 56 Nehru Place, New Delhi 110019.

BURNS

A selection by William Beattie and Henry W. Meikle

Robert Burns' verse reflects the work of a man very consciously aware of his contemporary, local world.

Burns was not, however, as he is sometimes portrayed, an unlettered peasant. He was familiar with the Bible, Shakespeare and the *Spectator*. Nevertheless, for copiousness and fertility of phrase and image the nearest parallels to Burns's Scots language are colloquial Chaucerian and Elizabethan English. It was through this very personal manipulation of the language that he used his verse to reveal the complexity of life, and to display his shrewd insight into human nature and his comic–satiric appreciation of the Scottish community. Rooted in the local and particular, Burns' poety rises above the parochial to present his unique vision – and criticism – of human life.

Penguin Poetry Library

DRYDEN

A selection by Douglas Grant

'They say my talent is satire . . .' wrote Dryden in 1692, towards the end of his life.

Dryden's genius for satire extends from the most light and delicious comedy to that facility in assured insult which lead T. S. Eliot to describe him as 'the great master of contempt'. In their conversational ease, vivacity and wit, and in the cut and thrust of their character sketches, Dryden's great satires – particularly *Absalom and Achitophel* – can be enjoyed as much now (without having to be revived by explanatory footnotes) as they were in Restoration England.

As well as selections from Dryden's satires, songs, odes and familiar verses, this Penguin edition includes his heroic tragedy *Aureng-Zebe*, and his two most celebrated critical essays: *An Essay of Dramatic Poesy* and *Preface to Fables Ancient and Modern*.

Penguin Poetry Library

POPE

A selection by Douglas Grant

'After Shakespeare, the greatest genius and the most impossible model of all, Pope is probably the funniest, the most sinuous and all-including, and morally the strongest English poet' – Peter Levi.

Although the Age of Reason might seem particularly remote today, Pope's verse, written from the fringes of aristocratic London society, has dated no more than that of Chaucer or Shakespeare. He is the great poet of worldly and human experience, and out of the sting, erudition, passion and contradictions of his poetry he emerges, not simply as the Poet of his Age, but as one of our irreplaceable investigative geniuses.

As well as selections from Pope's shorter poems and epistles, this Penguin edition includes the full texts of *An Essay on Criticism*, *The Rape of the Lock*, and *Eloisa to Abelard*; and excerpts from *The Dunciad*, *An Essay on Man* and his translations of the *Iliad* and the *Odyssey*.

KEATS

A selection by J. E. Morpurgo

'I would sooner fail than not be among the greatest.'

Thus wrote Keats in 1818. His first volume, *Poems*, was published in 1817; four years later he died of consumption at the tragically early age of twenty-five. Yet, despite his short creative life, he has, in the words of one eminent critic, 'become a symbolic figure, the type of poetic genius, a hero and martyr of poetry'. This volume contains almost everything of his mature achievement, together with much of his early work and extensive selections from his longer poems.

During his lifetime Keats met with much criticism and with 'some good success among literary people'. Through his worship of beauty he is often thought of as the supreme practitioner of 'art for art's sake'. But the richness, warmth and sensuous vitality of his verse reveal his joy in art and his irresistible delight in life itself.

Penguin Poetry Library

COLERIDGE

A selection by Katherine Raine

'His genius . . .' wrote William Hazlitt, 'had angelic wings and fed on manna. He talked on for ever; and you wished him to talk on for ever . . .'

Like no other poet Coleridge was, in five short years, 'visited by the Muse'. The great flowering of his poetry happened in the single year from the summer of 1797 when he first became friends with Dorothy and William Wordsworth. That was the year in which he wrote *The Ancient Mariner*, the first part of *Christabel Kubla Khan*, and other poems that were, as Kathleen Raine writes, 'the works not of his talent but of his genius'.

As well as Coleridge's finest poems, this Penguin edition contains selections from his letters and his main critical writings, including extracts from *Biographia Literaria* and several of his revolutionary essays on Shakespeare.

BROWNING

A selection by W. E. Williams

Browning was considered 'difficult' in his time, with Henry James observing that his ideas appeared 'like an unruly horse backing out of his stall, and stamping and plunging'. More recently, he has come to be recognized as a remarkable stylistic innovator, and with Shakespeare, the great illuminator of character in verse.

Many of Browning's best poems included here are dramatic monologues, spoken by the poet disguised as an alchemist, an Italian Renaissance painter, a musician or a horseman riding with his lover for the last time. They prove Browning to be an enthralling conversationalist, passionately interested in the way people reveal themselves through their ambitions, failures, loves and hatreds.

BLAKE

A selection by Jacob Bronowski

No English poetry is more rewarding or difficult to plumb, more surprising or inspiring to read than that of William Blake. In his own lifetime (1757–1827) his art – the poetry, engraving and painting that he believed to be the expression of a single genius – went virtually unrecognized. Although Wordsworth declared that 'there is something in the madness of this man which interests me more than the sanity of Lord Byron and Walter Scott'; and later T. S. Eliot described how 'because he was not distracted, or frightened, or occupied in anything but exact statements, he understood. He was naked, and saw man naked, and from the centre of his own crystal . . . There was nothing of the superior person about him. This makes him terrifying'.

This edition contains selections from Blake's early lyrics, including *Songs of Innocence* and *Songs of Experience*, passages from the prophetic books, and some of Blake's annotations and letters that give a flavour of the man and of the circumstances in which he worked. Jacob Bronowski's succinct and illuminating introduction provides the essential background to Blake's rebellious philosophy and life.

PENGUIN POETRY

☐ *The Penguin Book of American Verse*
   Ed. Geoffrey Moore   £5.95

'A representative anthology which will give pleasure to the general
reader and at the same time presents a full range of American poetry
of all periods' – *The Times Literary Supplement*

☐ *Selected Poems* **Pasternak**   £2.50

Translated from the Russian by Jon Stallworthy and Peter France.
'These translations from *My Sister Life* and the other famous collec-
tions are the best we have, faithful to the originals, and true poems in
their own right' – *The Times*

☐ *The Penguin Book of Bird Poetry*
   Ed. Peggy Munsterberg   £3.95

'Beautifully produced and intelligently compiled. Peggy Munster-
berg has done a fine job. Her anthology will please lovers of birds
and of poetry alike' – *The Times Literary Supplement*

☐ *The Complete Poems* **Jonathan Swift**   £9.95

A new, authoritative edition of the poems of this great satirist,
pamphleteer and author of *Gulliver's Travels*. With an introduction,
notes and a biographical dictionary of Swift's contemporaries by the
editor, Pat Smith.

☐ *London in Verse* **Ed. Christopher Logue**   £2.95

Nursery-rhymes, street cries, Shakespeare and Spike Milligan trace
a route through the streets, sights and characters of London in this
lively anthology, which has a linking commentary and illustrations
chosen by Christopher Logue. 'A rare and delightful book' – *Country
Life*

☐ *The Penguin Book of Spanish Civil War Verse*
   Ed. Valentine Cunningham   £4.50

Poetry and prose making up 'an outstanding piece of historical
reconstruction . . . a human document of absorbing interest' – *The
Times Literary Supplement*

PENGUIN POETRY

☐ *The Penguin Book of Women Poets*
Ed. Cosman, Keefe and Weaver   £3.95

From Sappho and Li Ching-chao to Emily Dickinson and Anna
Akhmatova, this acclaimed anthology spans 3,500 years and forty
literary traditions; it also includes a biographical/textual note on
each poet.

☐ *Selected Poems* **William Carlos Williams**   £2.95

Poems extracted by Williams from small-town American life, 'as a
physician works upon a patient, upon the thing before him, in the
particular to discover the universal'. Edited and introduced by
Charles Tomlinson.

☐ *The Memory of War* and *Children in Exile*
James Fenton   £2.25

Including 'A German Requiem' and several pieces on the Vietnam
War, this collection of Fenton's poems 1968–83 is a major literary
event. 'He is a magician-materialist . . . the most talented poet of his
generation' – Peter Porter in the *Observer*

☐ *Poems of Science*
Ed. John Heath-Stubbs and Phillips Salman   £4.95

This unusual anthology traces our changing perceptions of the
universe through the eyes of the poets, from Spenser and
Shakespeare to Dannie Abse and John Updike.

☐ *East Anglia in Verse* **Ed. Angus Wilson**   £2.95

The sea, flat wheat fields and remote villages of East Anglia have
inspired poets as diverse as John Betjeman, Thomas Hood, Edward
Lear and Horace Walpole. Containing theirs and many other poems,
this is a collection 'full of small marvels' – *Guardian*

☐ *Selected Poems* **Lorca**   £2.50

With music, drama, the gypsy mythology, and the Andalusian folk-
songs of his childhood, Lorca rediscovered and infused new life into
the Spanish poetic traditions. This volume contains poems, plus
excerpts from his plays, chosen and translated by J. L. Gili.

PENGUIN POETRY

☐ *Contemporary American Poetry* **Ed. Donald Hall**   £2.50

Robert Lowell, Richard Wilbur, Denise Levertov, Frank O'Hara, Dudley Randall, Sylvia Plath and Anne Sexton are among the thirty-nine poets represented in this virtuoso collection.

☐ *New Volume*
Adrian Henri, Roger McGough and Brian Patten   £1.50

A new anthology from three of the most popular poets writing today. This Penguin also contains some poems originally published in their bestselling volume: *The Mersey Sound*.

☐ *Paterson* **William Carlos Williams**   £2.95

Part autobiography, part the story of the New Jersey city near which Williams lived, *Paterson* is among the greatest long poems in modern American literature.

These books should be available at all good bookshops or newsagents, but if you live in the UK or the Republic of Ireland and have difficulty in getting to a bookshop, they can be ordered by post. Please indicate the titles required and fill in the form below.

NAME _____ BLOCK CAPITALS

ADDRESS _____

_____

_____

Enclose a cheque or postal order payable to The Penguin Bookshop to cover the total price of books ordered, plus 50p for postage. Readers in the Republic of Ireland should send £IR equivalent to the sterling prices, plus 67p for postage. Send to: The Penguin Bookshop, 54/56 Bridlesmith Gate, Nottingham, NG1 2GP.

You can also order by phoning (0602) 599295, and quoting your Barclaycard or Access number.

Every effort is made to ensure the accuracy of the price and availability of books at the time of going to press, but it is sometimes necessary to increase prices and in these circumstances retail prices may be shown on the covers of books which may differ from the prices shown in this list or elsewhere. This list is not an offer to supply any book.

This order service is only available to residents in the UK and the Republic of Ireland.